BELVA PLAIN

THREE COMPLETE NOVELS

~

Blessings

~

Whispers

~

Homecoming

WINGS BOOKS
NEW YORK

This 2003 edition is published by Wings Books®, an imprint of
Random House Value Publishing, a division of Random House, Inc.,
New York, by arrangement with Bantam Dell Publishing Group,
a division of Random House, Inc.

Wings Books® and colophon are trademarks of Random House, Inc.

Random House
New York • Toronto • London • Sydney • Auckland
www.randomhouse.com

Printed and bound in the United States of America.

A catalog record for this title is available from the
Library of Congress.

ISBN 0-517-22247-7

10 9 8 7 6 5 4 3 2 1

CONTENTS

BLESSINGS

The human heart has hidden treasures,
In secret kept, in silence sealed;—

—CHARLOTTE BRONTË

CHAPTER

1

The day on which the sky cracked open over Jennie's head had begun as gladly as any other day in that wonderful year. It had been the best year of her life until then.

At noon she had been standing with Jay on the lip of the hill that overlooked the wild land called, by the town to which it belonged, the Green Marsh. It was one of those Indian summer intervals, when, after two weeks of rain and premature gray cold, everything suddenly burns again; the distant air burns blue and the near oaks flare red; in the marsh, cattails and spreading juniper glisten darkly after the night's rain. Canada geese come streaming, honking their long way to the south; and ducks, with a great flapping racket, splash into the pond.

"You see, it's not all marsh," Jay explained. "There's meadow and forest at the other end. Over a thousand acres, all wild. Been here for Lord knows how many thousands of years, just as you see it, untouched. We're trying to get the state to take it over as part of the wilderness system. That way it'll be safe forever. But we've got to hurry before the New York builders put their bid through."

"Do you suppose they'll be able to?"

"God, I hope not. Imagine ruining all this!"

They stood for a little while listening to the silence. Totally at ease, accustomed as they were to quiet hours with each other, they felt no need for a continuous flow of speech.

A small sudden wind blew a dry shower of leaves, and at the bottom of the hill Jay's children came into sight, running with the wind. They made themselves fall, the two girls rolling their little brother in the leaves. They shrieked; the dog barked; and the wind, carrying the sounds back up the hill, shattered the Sunday peace.

"Darling," Jay said.

Turning to him, Jennie knew that he had been watching her while she watched his children.

"I'm happier than anyone has a right to be," she murmured.

He searched her face with such intensity, such love, that she felt an ache in her throat.

"Oh, Jennie, I can't tell you . . . You give me . . ." He threw out his arms to encompass the whole bright scene in one characteristic, generous gesture. "I never thought . . ." Not finishing, he put his arms around her shoulders and drew her close.

Into the curve of his arm she settled, feeling a perfect happiness. Memory ran backward to the beginning of this miracle. A year and a half before, when they had first met, Jay had been a widower for two years, his young wife having died most terribly of cancer. He had been left with two small girls and an infant son, a rather grand

Upper East Side apartment, and a partnership in one of New York's most prestigious law firms, a position not inherited as sometimes happens, but earned through merit and hard effort. One of the first things Jennie had observed about Jay had been a strained expression that might signify anxiety, overwork, loneliness, or all of these. Certainly if loneliness was a problem, the city had enough desirable young women to fill a man's vacant hours, especially those of a tall young man with vivid eyes and a charming cleft in his chin. When she knew him better, she understood that he had been very, very careful about involvements because of his children. Some of his friends had asked her whether she didn't find his devotion to the children a bore or a hindrance; on the contrary, she admired it, was glad of it, and would have thought less of him if he had not felt a loving, deep responsibility toward them.

She turned her face up now to see his. Yes, the look of strain was definitely gone, along with that nervous habit of pulling a strand of hair at his temple, and along with smoking too much and sleeping too little. Indeed, this last month he had stopped smoking altogether. Smiles came easily now, and certainly he looked much younger than thirty-eight.

"What are you staring at, woman?"

"I like you in plaid shirts and jeans."

"Better than in my Brooks Brothers vest?"

"I like you best in nothing at all, since you ask."

"Same to you. Listen, I was thinking just now, would you like to have a little summer place up around here? We could build something at the far end of my parents' property, or somewhere else, or not at all. You choose."

"I can't think. I've never had so many choices in my life!"

"It's time you had some, then."

She had never been one who craved choices. In her

mind she stripped things bare to the core, and the core now was just her pure need to be with Jay always and forever; houses, plans, *things*—all were unimportant beside that need.

"Have you decided where you want the wedding? Mother and Dad would be glad to have it at their apartment. Mother said she's already told you."

A woman was supposed to be married from her own house. But when the home consisted of two cramped rooms in a renovated walk-up tenement, even the simplest ceremony presented a problem. Obviously Jay's mother understood that, although with kindest tact she had not referred to it.

"Yes. It was a lovely offer." But in Jay's apartment, Jennie thought, it would seem a little bit like her own home. "I'd like your place. Would that be all right? Since that's where I'm going to be living?"

"I'd love it, darling. I was hoping you'd want to. So, now that's settled. One thing more and we'll be all settled. What about your office? Do you want to stay where you are or come to my firm's building? There's going to be some available space on the fifteenth floor."

"Stay where I am, Jay. My clients would be intimidated, scared to death on Madison Avenue. All my poor, broken-down women with their miserable problems and their shabby clothes . . . It would be cruel. Besides, I couldn't afford a move like that, anyway."

Jay grinned and ruffled her hair. "Independent cuss, aren't you?"

"When it comes to my law practice, yes," she answered seriously.

She supposed that his practice must mean as much to him as hers did to her. After all, why else would he have chosen it and stayed in it? But she couldn't imagine anyone, certainly not herself, caring as deeply about wills and trusts and litigation over money as about people—the battered wives, abused children, dispossessed families, and all the other pitiable souls who came asking for help. Yet no one could be more kind and caring than Jay. And money, after all, did grease the world's wheels, didn't it? Obviously, then, somebody had to take care of it.

At the foot of the hill they could see the setter's tail waving above dead weeds. The children were now stooped over.

"What on earth are they doing?" Jay asked.

"Collecting leaves. I bought scrapbooks for Sue and Emily to take to science class."

"You think of everything! They're going to love you, Jennie. They do already." He looked at his watch. "Hey, we'd better call them. My mother's having an early lunch, so we can get back to the city by their bedtime."

The two-lane blacktop road passed dairy farms and apple growers' wide, level spreads: little old houses with battered swings on front porches stood close to big red barns; horses in their shabby winter coats drooped their heads over wire fences; here and there a glossy white-painted house at the end of a gravel drive bordered with rhododendrons and azaleas proclaimed ownership by some local banker or, more likely still, by some city family who enjoyed its two or three summer months of rural peace.

"I can't believe my noisy little rooms in New York are only hours away," Jennie said.

When the winter-brown fields gave way to the town, they entered the main street. Here chain stores, gas stations, a bowling alley, a pizza parlor, a redbrick consolidated high school, a Ford dealership, a dingy movie theater, and three or four new, low office buildings reflected modern times, while a saddlery, a volunteer fire department, and a feed store with a sign above the front entry—FOUNDED 1868—spoke of a life that had been and was now changing.

"As I remember it, the town was half this size when Dad bought our place," Jay remarked.

"Do you think of this as your true home?"

"Not yet. Maybe someday when I'm my parents' age. You know, I wouldn't be surprised if they were to give up their New York apartment and stay here all year, now that Dad's selling the factory and retiring."

Mrs. Wolfe was spreading compost over a rose bed at the side of the house when they drove up. She straightened, took off her gardening gloves, and spread her arms to the little boy, who ran into them.

"Did you have a good ride, Donny? Did you see the horses?"

The girls interrupted. "We went to the academy, but Donny didn't want to get on the pony."

"Daddy promised us chocolate bars, but the stores were all closed."

"A good thing, too, or you wouldn't eat any lunch. And we've a beautiful chocolate cake for dessert." The grandmother smiled at Jennie. "I hope we haven't tired you out this weekend."

"No, Mrs. Wolfe, I could walk ten miles a day through these hills."

"Well, I'm sure Jay will take you up on that sometime. Let's go in, shall we?"

Jennie stepped aside to let the other woman precede her into the house. She must be careful to remember every little nicety. . . .

It was only natural to feel unease in the presence of one's future husband's parents, wasn't it? Especially when this was her first visit after only two previous meetings, and those in the impersonal setting of a restaurant. Enid Wolfe, for all her welcoming manner, possessed an elegance that easily could be daunting. Even

in her gingham shirt and denim skirt, she had it without
trying.

The whole house had it. Its very simplicity told the
story of people who were above any effort to impress.
Through a white-paneled door one entered into a low-
ceilinged hall; people were shorter two hundred years
ago, so Jay had explained, when this farmhouse was built.
Now worn old Oriental scatter rugs lay on the wood-
pegged floors. Mixed fragrances of pine logs, furniture
wax, and flowers hung in the air. On the coffee table in
the living room lay a mound of splendid, blood-red roses
—the last of the year, someone said. A pair of chintz-
covered sofas faced each other in front of the fireplace.
The cabinets looked antique, and there was a handsome
baby grand piano at the far end of the long room. Two
small paintings of blurry skies above a river stood on the
pine mantel. They looked like the Turners Jennie had
seen in the museum, but knowing so little about art and
fearful of making a foolish mistake, she refrained from
saying so. Really, she must make an effort to learn more
about these things, for Jay knew and cared about them.

She suspected that the taste here was faultless, and
undoubtedly expensive. Yet the room, the whole house,
said: "I don't pretend, I am who I am." Fat, homemade
needlepoint pillows lay about. Books stood in piles on
tables, with a tumbling stack on the floor. Photographs
cluttered another large round table: there was a 1920s
bride in a short skirt and a long train; there were children and a graduation picture and one of a pug dog.
Tennis rackets were propped against a wall in a corner.
A tortoise cat had wrapped itself in an afghan on one of
the easy chairs, and now the setter came bounding in to
flop in front of the fire.

Jay's father got up from the wing chair in which he
had been sitting with a drink in hand. He was craggy,

with a beaky, aristocratic nose, and taller than his tall wife. Jay would look like him someday.

"Come on in. Daisy is just about to put things on the table. Where've you people been all this time?" he inquired as they went to the dining room.

"Oh, around," Jay said. "I wanted to show Jennie the neighborhood. We finished at the Green Marsh. What's new with the situation since I talked to you?"

Arthur Wolfe gave the table a startling thump. "They've been up from New York, thick as thieves all over town these past weeks. Made a big offer, four and a half million." He made a grim mouth. "It'll tear the town apart, I predict, before we're through."

"What's happening with the state? The park negotiations?"

"Oh, politicians! Red tape! Who knows when they'll get around to it in the legislature? In the meantime the developers are on the move, and fast. I'm disgusted."

Jay frowned. "So what are you doing about it?"

"Well, we've got a committee together, Horace Ferguson and I. He's doing most of the work. I'm too old to do much—"

"Arthur Wolfe, you are not old!" his wife protested.

"Okay, let's say I'm doing enough. I've been talking to the people who'll be sure to see it the right way, especially on the planning board." The old man took a spoonful of soup, then laid the spoon down and exploded again. "Good God, the whole nation will be paved over before you know it, with nothing green left alive!"

"Hmm," Jay reflected, "that marsh is an aquifer. They'll wreck the water table if they start to tinker with it. It'll affect every town in the area, and all the farms. Don't they know that?"

"Don't who know it? Developers? What do they care? Come up from the city, pollute the place, make a bundle, and leave."

"Arthur, eat your dinner," his wife said gently. "The soup's getting cold. We're all very conservation-minded in our family," she explained, turning to Jennie. "But you've probably noticed."

"I agree with you all," Jennie answered. "It's high time we cleaned things up—the water, the air, the strip mines, everything. Otherwise there'll be nothing left for people like Emily and Sue and Donny."

"Jennie's an outdoor girl," Jay said. "Last summer in Maine we took a thirty-mile canoe trip with portage a good part of the way, and she held up as well as I did. Better, maybe."

The old man was interested. "Where'd you grow up, Jennie? You never said."

"Not where you might think. In the city, the heart of Baltimore. I guess maybe I was a farmer's daughter in another incarnation."

Now, as the meal progressed, the conversation was diverted. Donny's meat had to be cut up for him. Sue had complaints about her piano teacher. Emily spilled milk on her skirt and had to be dried off. Enid Wolfe inquired about tickets for a new play. They were having dessert when Arthur returned to the subject of the Green Marsh, making explanations for Jennie's benefit.

"It's almost fourteen hundred acres, including the lake. The town owns it. Was willed to it . . . oh, it must be close to eighty years ago. Let's see, we've been summering here since our first son, Philip, was born, and he's going on fifty. At first we rented, and then after I inherited a little money from my grandmother I bought the place for a song. Well, so the town has the land and it's understood that it would be kept as is. It's full of wildlife, you know, beaver and fox. And, of course, it's a sanctuary for birds. Some of the oaks are two hundred years old. Local kids all swim in the lake. Then there's fishing and nature trails for the schools, everything. It's a treasure, a common treasure for everybody, and we can't let it go. We're not going to." He balled his napkin and thrust it from him. "Our group—concerned citizens we can call ourselves, I guess—is pooling our money to hire counsel and fight this thing hard."

"You really expect a hard fight?" Jay asked.

"I told you I do. I hate to be a cynic—good liberals aren't supposed to be cynical—but money will talk to a lot of folks around here. They won't care about natural beauty, not even about the water table, poor fools. There'll be promises of jobs, increased business, the usual shortsighted arguments. So we'd better be prepared."

"I see." Jay was thoughtful for a moment. "Hiring counsel, you said. Somebody in town?"

"No. The lawyers around here aren't on our side. They all hope to get business from the developers."

"Got anyone in mind, then?" asked Jay.

"Well, your firm's diversified, isn't it? Would somebody take it on? Of course, there won't be much of a fee. It'll depend on what Horace and I and a handful more can raise among us." As Jay hesitated, the sharp old eyes twinkled. "Okay, I know your fees. I'm only teasing."

"That's not it at all! You know I'd do it myself for nothing if you asked me to. The fact is, I was thinking of Jennie."

"Me!" she cried.

"Why not? You can do it beautifully." And Jay said to his parents, "I never told you that the first time we met, Jennie had just won an environment case. I had happened to read an article about it in the *Times* that morning, and so when somebody at this party pointed her out, I asked to be introduced."

"How did you come to do that, Jennie?" Arthur Wolfe wanted to know. "It's not what you generally do, is it?"

"Oh, no, I almost always take women's cases, family

problems. It happened that I defended a woman with four children against a landlord who wanted to evict them. Well, she was very grateful, and later she asked me to help some relatives on Long Island who had a land-use problem. I had never done anything like it before, but it appealed to me—the justice of it, I mean—so I wanted to try it." She stopped. "That's it. I don't want to bore you with the details."

"You won't bore us. I want the details."

"Well." Suddenly aware that she was using too many *wells,* she stopped and began again. "It was a working-class neighborhood. Blue-collar, without money or influence. At the end of the street on the cross avenue there was a vacant tract that was zoned for business and bought by some people who wanted to build a small chemical plant. There would have been noxious odors and, quite probably, carcinogenic emissions. It would have blighted the neighborhood. We had a very tough fight because there were political connections—the usual thing."

"But you won," Jay said proudly. "And you haven't mentioned that it was a test case and set a precedent."

His father was studying Jennie. "Do you think you'd be interested in our case?"

"I'd need to know more about it. What do they want to do with the land?"

"They want to build what they call a recreational sub-division. Vacation homes. Corporate retreats. It would be high-density condominiums one on top of the other. You see, the new highway makes it accessible, there's skiing only half an hour away, and after they dredge the lake they'll double its size and—" He stopped.

Enid interjected, "And incidentally, if we should have a wet season, flood all the fields south of town. Oh, it makes me sick! This is one of the most beautiful areas in the state—in the East, for that matter. I see it as a symbol. If this falls victim to greed, then anything can. Do you see what I mean, Jennie?"

"Oh, greed," Jennie said. "I deal with it every day. It's the ultimate poison, whether it's rat-infested tenements or polluted oceans or mangled jungles—" Again she stopped, feeling still the slight unease of being there under observation, and was conscious of her voice, which tended to rise in her enthusiasm, and of her hands, which she had been training herself to keep in her lap. "It will destroy us all in the end," she finished more quietly.

Jay smiled. He approved of her enthusiasm. "Not while there are people like you to fight."

"I take it that you accept," said Arthur Wolfe.

She thought, So I shall be defending the rights of a piece of land to exist! A curious change for an urban person who'd never owned a foot of land. And yet, ever since she had been a child, taken for an occasional Sunday ride in the country, she had felt a pull toward the land, as if the trees had spoken to her. Later, reading Rachel Carson's book, or the Club of Rome's, and watching the *National Geographic* programs on television, she had felt a stronger pull, with greater understanding.

"Yes, I'll do it," she said, and felt a warm surge of pleasurable excitement.

"Great! If Jay says you're good, you're good." Arthur got up from the table and stood over Jennie. "We've already had the first reading of the proposal before the town council, and the matter's on the way to the planning board. They'll be hearing it in two or three weeks, so you'll be coming back up here pretty soon. Jay can fill you in on the town government. I won't take up your time now, but it's the usual thing, nine elected council members, one of whom is the mayor." He shook Jennie's hand, pumping it. "Before you leave now, I've a mile-high stack of papers for you to take back, reports from engineers and water experts, a survey, the petition to the legislature, and of course the developer's lousy proposal." He pumped her hand again. "We're on the way, I think."

"It's a challenge," Jennie told him. "I'll do my best."

Jay looked at his watch. "Time to get started. Let's get our bags, Jennie, and go."

Jennie was in the guest room collecting her coat and overnight bag when Mrs. Wolfe knocked.

"May I come in? I wanted one private minute with you." She was carrying a flat maroon leather box. "I wanted to give you this. Quietly, upstairs here, with just the two of us. Open it, Jennie."

On a velvet cushion, curved into a double circle, lay a long strand of pearls, large, uniform, and very faintly, shyly, pink. For a second Jennie went blank. She knew really nothing about pearls, having owned only a short string bought at a costume-jewelry counter, so as to seem less strictly tailored in the courtroom. The instant's blankness was followed by an instant's confusion.

"They were my mother-in-law's. I've been keeping them for the next bride in the family," Enid Wolfe said, adding after a second's hesitation, "I'd already given away my own mother's necklace."

Jennie's eyes went from the pearls to the other woman's face, which was subdued into a kind of reverence. She understood that the gift had deep meanings.

"Oh . . . lovely," she faltered.

"Yes, aren't they? Here. Try them on." And as Jennie leaned forward, she dropped the necklace over her head. "Now look at yourself."

From the mirror above the chest of drawers a round, young face, much younger than its thirty-six years, looked back out of a pair of unusually sharp green eyes. "Cat's eyes," Jay teased. At this moment they were rather startled. The cheeks, which were naturally ruddy so that they had never needed to be rouged, were flushed up to the prominent cheekbones.

"Pearls always do something for a woman, don't they?" Enid said. "Even with just that sweater and skirt."

"Oh, lovely," Jennie repeated.

"Yes, you don't see many like them anymore."

"I'm . . . I'm speechless, Mrs. Wolfe. That's not like me, either."

"Would you like to call me Enid? Mrs. Wolfe is too formal for someone who's going to be in the family." Enid's austere face brightened suddenly. "Believe me, I don't say lightly what I'm going to say now. One doesn't watch one's son give himself and his precious children over to the care of another woman without thinking very, very carefully about her. But you've been so good for Jay. We've seen it, and we want you to know . . ." She laid a hand on Jennie's shoulder. "I want you to know that Arthur and I are most happy about you. We admire you, Jennie."

"Sometimes I think I'm in a dream," Jennie said softly. She stroked the pearls. "Jay and I and the children . . . and now you. All of you being so wonderful to me."

"Why shouldn't we be? And as for Jay, I surely don't have to tell you how loving he is. You'll have a good life with him. Oh," said Enid, smiling with a mother's indulgence, "he has his faults, of course. He can't stand to be kept waiting. He likes his hot food burning and his cold food icy. Things like that." Perched now on the bed, she was confiding, intimate. "But he's a good man, a good human being. The word *good* covers so much, doesn't it? Total honesty, for one thing. Jay says what he means and means what he says. He's entirely open, easy to read. And I see the same in you. Of course, Jay's told us so much about you that we felt, before we even met you, that we already knew you." She stood up. "My goodness,

I'm talking my head off. Come, they're waiting for you. You've got a good three-hour drive ahead."

On the way home Jay remarked, "I haven't seen my father so worked up about anything since the days when he used to fight in the city for public housing and better schools for the poor."

They were talking in low voices while the children dozed in the backseat.

"I hope I can handle the case. And I guess I won't be able to think of anything else until I've done it."

"Are you that nervous about it already? I don't want you to take it if you're going to be. I want my bride to be relaxed. No worry lines around the eyes."

"I have to do it now. I said I would."

"Come on. Don't let Dad foist it on you if you feel any hesitance. I'll get one of the young guys in the office to do it, that's all."

She answered with mock indignation, "What? Turn it over to a man, as if a woman couldn't handle it? No, it's just that—it's your father, your family. I so want them to think well of me."

"For Pete's sake, they already do. You know that. Do you need more proof than having my grandmother's pearls in your lap? My mother would as soon part with her teeth as see those in the wrong hands. Seriously, though, for such a feisty lady, you shouldn't be so unsure of yourself around my family."

"Am I? Is that the impression I give?"

"A little. Don't worry about it." Jay reached over and squeezed her hand. "More seriously, hang on to that box until I can get it insured in the new name tomorrow."

It was dark when they drew up in front of the apartment house. Two handsome brass coach lamps gleamed at the entrance under the green awning. Down Park Avenue, a double row of parallel streetlights shone on the white limestone and the brick and granite fronts of the fine solid structures that stretched all the way to the low facade of Grand Central Terminal, with the Pan Am Building behind it, at the base of the avenue. It was one of the most famous views in the world, as typical of the city as London's Trafalgar Square or Paris's Place de la Concorde. Jennie stood a moment to take it all in while Jay helped the children out of the backseat. Her life seldom brought her to this part of the city; in fact, she had never even been inside a building like this before knowing Jay.

"Is the nanny back yet?" she asked now.

"No, she comes early Monday morning in time to get them ready for school."

"Then I'll go up and help you put them to bed."

"No need to. I can manage. You've got a big day tomorrow, you said."

"You've got a big day too. Besides, I want to."

Upstairs, while Jay undressed his little son and settled him in bed among a mound of assorted teddy bears and pandas, Jennie supervised the girls.

"It's late and you had a shower this morning, so I think we'll skip baths tonight," she said.

Sue clamored, "A story? Do we get a story?"

Jennie looked at the clock on the table between the two ivory-enameled beds. "It's too late for stories. I'll read you some poems instead." Becoming more and more accustomed to and accepted by the children, she felt competent, equipped to mother them. "How about A. A. Milne? Good? All right, into the bathroom with you."

They brushed their teeth and washed their hands and faces. They dropped their soiled clothes into the hamper and put on their pink cotton nightgowns. Lastly Jennie unwound their braids and brushed their long, straight tan hair. Jay and his family were dark-haired. Probably the girls were like their mother.

Emily touched Jennie's hair. "I wish I had black curls like yours."

"And I wish I had hair like yours. Mine gets all frizzy when it rains. It's a nuisance."

"No, it's beautiful," Sue said. "Daddy thinks so too. I asked him."

Jennie hugged her. They were so sweet, these children, with their fragrant skin and moist, sloppy kisses! Oh, they could have nasty tantrums now and then—she had seen a few—but that was natural. She felt a surge of something that, if not love—how easily one tosses the word *love* around!—was very close to it. Back in the bedroom, she got out the beloved book and read about Christopher Robin.

"They're changing guard at Buckingham Palace;
    Christopher Robin went down with Alice."

She read about water-lilies.

"Where the water-lilies go
    To and fro,
    Rocking in the ripples of the water—"

She closed the book—"Now, bedtime"—and drew the embroidered curtains against the night.

In the rosy, lamplit room, all was orderly and clean. This peace did something to Jennie's heart. So much did she see of life's other side, of the abuse and hurt and ugliness that human beings inflict on one another! Taking a last look at the two little girls, she felt waves of thankfulness that they, at least, had been spared. Complicated feelings these were, almost prayerful.

She turned off the light. "Good night, darlings. Pleasant dreams. That's what my mother used to say to me. Pleasant dreams."

Jay was standing at the door of the master bedroom. "I know you said you don't want to change anything in the apartment," he began.

"It would be awfully extravagant when everything's in perfect condition."

The thought of redecorating all these rooms was distressing. She wasn't prepared with the right knowledge to do it, and moreover, she wasn't really interested. She looked down the corridor now into the long living room, over a sea of moss-green carpeting on which stood islands of mahogany and chintz in pleasing, quiet taste, and then across into the dining room, where she surprised herself by recognizing that the table was Duncan Phyfe, and the chairs, with seats of ruby-flowered silk, were Chippendale.

"But the bedroom, at least," Jay said. "We'll want a new bedroom."

Yes, she would concede that. She didn't want the canopied bed in which he had slept with another woman. Also, she would replace the armoire and chests in which Phyllis had kept her clothes. She would take time next week and attend to that.

On a tall chest, which she supposed was Jay's, stood a silver-framed photograph of a young woman wearing a spreading ball gown and the other grandmother's pearls. Her eyes were large, with traces of amusement in them; her face was round, with prominent cheekbones. Why, Jennie thought, except for the straight, light hair, she looks like me! She wondered whether Jay was conscious of the resemblance. Probably he wasn't. It was said that people unconsciously made the same choice over and over. She paused, examining the face and comparing.

Somewhat anxiously Jay said, "That won't stay, of course. I should have put it someplace else."

"Why shouldn't it stay? You wouldn't be much of a man if you were to forget her."

Poor soul, dead of cancer at thirty-two, leaving all this life, these beloved people behind!

"There's nobody like you, Jennie." Jay's voice was rough with emotion. "Not one woman in fifty would say that and mean it, as I know you do."

And she did mean it. Strange it was that, alone with Jay, she felt no insecurity, not the least dread of invidious comparisons with anyone else. Alone with him, she was absolutely certain of her own worth. It was only the family, the parents, the setting that caused a wavering, a dread of not belonging in spite of all their welcome. But she would get over that. . . .

He put his arms around her and laid her head on his shoulder. "I'm in such a damn hurry to get this wedding business over. Couldn't sleep together this weekend at my parents' house, can't sleep together here because of the children and the nanny. It's hell."

"My place again any night this week," she murmured, then raised her head to look into his face. She ran her finger down his nose. "Have I ever told you that you remind me of Lincoln? If you had a beard, you'd be a dead ringer for him."

Jay burst out laughing. "Any man who's tall and thin and has a narrow face and a long nose is supposed to look like Lincoln. For a hardheaded young lawyer, you're a romantic," he said.

"Hardheaded I may be, but softhearted too."

"Darling, I know that well. Now listen, you need your sleep. I'm going to put you in a taxi. And phone me when you get home."

"I can put myself in a taxi, Jay. I've never been so pampered! You don't think the taxi driver's going to kidnap me, do you?"

"No, but phone me, anyway, when you get back."

———

The flat in the renovated walk-up near the East River was a different world. Here lived the singles and the live-together couples, young people from the theater, the arts, and business, either on the way up or hoping to start on the way up soon. Their homes ranged from empty—futon on the floor and a standing lamp—to half furnished—raw wood painted over in brave black enamel or scarlet, with Victorian wicker rocking chairs from the secondhand stores—to the furnished, complete with rugs, books, records, and plants. Jennie's was furnished.

The moment she turned the key in the lock, the door across the hall was opened.

"Hi! How was it?" Shirley Weinberg, in a chenille bathrobe with a wet head wrapped in a towel, wanted to know. "I was just drying my hair when I heard you. How was it?" she repeated. "All right if I come in?"

"Sure, come on."

They had been neighbors for five years and hadn't much more than neighborliness in common, that and friendly goodwill. Shirley, secretary to a theatrical producer, thought in terms of Broadway and what she saw as glamour, certainly not in terms of battered wives and dingy courtrooms. She sat down on Jennie's sofa.

"Was it gorgeous, their place?"

Shirley's vision, no doubt, was of marble floors and gilded wood.

"Not really. It's a farmhouse, a hundred fifty years old or more. I liked it, but you wouldn't."

"They're terribly rich, though, aren't they?"

Questions like this were offensive, yet one should take them from where they came. Shirley was blunt and kind. But why did so many people ask such questions? From somewhere a memory stirred, a voice asking, "Who? When?" The memory dissolved. . . .

"I don't suppose they are 'terribly rich.' But they're

not poor, either," Jennie replied patiently. "Somehow one doesn't think of them that way."

"*You* may not. But you're a funny duck," Shirley said affectionately. "What's in the box?"

"A necklace. I'll show you."

"My God, will you look at that!"

"You scared me. What are you shrieking about?"

"These, you idiot. You've got ten thousand dollars' worth of pearls here, don't you know that? No, what am I saying? More than that. Pearls have gone way up again."

"That's not possible," Jennie said.

"I'm telling you what I know. I used to work on Madison Avenue at a jeweler's, didn't I? They're nine-millimeter. Do you know what that means? No, of course you don't. Put them on."

"Now I'm afraid to touch them. I'm afraid they'll break."

"They won't break. Put them on."

"I feel silly if they're really worth that. Where will I wear them?"

"Lots of places. They're gorgeous. Look."

"I never knew about things like these," Jennie said wonderingly. "I mean, why would anybody want to hang all that money around her neck?"

"You *are* a funny duck," the other repeated. "They really don't matter to you at all?"

"Well, in one way they do. They're very beautiful, of course, but what matters to me is what they stand for, that I'm wanted in their family, and I'm very, very happy about that. I just never craved things like this. And a good thing I didn't, because I never could have afforded them."

"Well, it looks as if you'll be able to afford them now. You're really mad about him, aren't you?"

Jennie raised her eyes to the other's face, on which a

certain tenderness was mingled with curiosity. "Yes," she said simply. "That's about it. I am."

"I've never seen you like this about anyone before."

"I haven't felt like this about anyone before, that's why."

"You're lucky. Do you know how darn lucky you are?"

"Yes, I know."

"To be in love with a man who wants to make it forever. God, I'm sick of guys who don't want to promise you anything except that they'll never interfere with your freedom. I'd like to give up a little freedom—not all of it, just some of it—to have a home and a kid. Two kids. The men you meet these days are all kids themselves," Shirley finished, grumbling.

Jennie, hanging up her coat, had no answer. She remembered how, not much more than a year ago, Shirley, like most of her contemporaries, including Jennie herself, had gloated over total independence, being able to experience the adventure that had once belonged only to men. And then the biological clock, as they called it these days, had begun to tick very loudly.

"The biological clock," she said now.

"Yeah. Well, I'm glad for you, anyway." Shirley stood up and kissed Jennie's cheek. "Couldn't happen to a nicer gal. Listen. Be sure to get a piece of flannel and wipe those every time you wear them. And have them restrung every couple of years. I'd go to Tiffany for that, if I were you."

When she went out, Jennie stood for a few moments with the pearls draped over her arm. Thoughts flooded her mind. She looked around the little room. You certainly wouldn't call it a handsome room, but it was comfortable and pretty, with its prints, Picasso's doves and Mondrian's vivid geometrics. Sometimes she thought what fun it would be if Jay could just move in here with her, instead of the other way around. She had painted the yellow walls herself, bought the homemade patchwork quilt from Tennessee mountain craftspeople, and nurtured the tall palm that stood in the brass container at the window. The books, which were her extravagance, and the first-rate stereo equipment all were the fruits of her own labor, and that was a good feeling; probably there was no better satisfaction.

Indeed she had come far. Now, having confronted the world and proven that she could survive in it alone, she was ready, willing, and glad to relinquish some of her independence to Jay.

They had met at one of those big, fancy gatherings of disparate people in a fancy, renovated loft filled with abstract sculpture, stainless-steel mobiles, sushi, white wine, and buzzing talk. Somebody had made a remark about Jennie's Long Island environment case, and somebody else had casually and hastily introduced Jay. Almost at once they had drifted away by themselves.

"You're a lawyer too?" she asked.

"Yes. With DePuyster, Fillmore, Johnston, Brown, Rosenbaum and Levy."

"Very different from me."

"Very different." He smiled. His eyes held a twinkle of amusement. "Are you thinking that I'm a wicked defender of wicked corporations?"

"I'm not stupid enough to think that corporations are all wicked."

"Good. Because I'd like you to approve of me."

"It's just something I could never imagine myself doing."

"Fair enough. But I do pro bono work also, you know."

"That's good too." She smiled back.

"You're not enjoying this," he said. "All the pop sociology and psychology. You know what it boils down to? 'Look at me, I'm here, listen to me.' When it's all over, you've nothing but a headache to show for the whole evening. Let's leave."

In a quiet bar downtown they sat half the night telling each other all about themselves: their politics, their families; their taste in music, food, books, and movies; their interest in tennis. They liked Zubin Mehta, Woody Allen, Updike, and Dickens. They hated golf, buttery sauces, zoos, and cruises. Something clicked. Afterward they both agreed that they had known it right then, that very night.

The next day he sent flowers. She was touched by the old-fashioned gesture, and expectant as she had never been before. Suddenly it was clear to her that she had never known the possibilities of loving, never known what lay at the core of things. She had only thought she knew.

So it had begun.

She had come a long, long way since the row house in Baltimore and Pop's delicatessen. A long way from the University of Pennsylvania and its tuition, so painfully eked out. About the time she had graduated from the university, her father became ill with a degenerative kidney disease. When he died, she was already twenty-five. Her mother sold the store and with the small proceeds of the sale, plus Pop's small insurance, went to live with her sister in Miami, where the climate was benign and living was cheaper. Then, having saved enough for law school, Jennie went back to Philadelphia and enrolled again at the university.

She had no time to waste, for she had lost four years. She was all purpose, working hard and seldom playing. At twenty-nine, she graduated with an outstanding record, enough to provide her with a prized clerkship for the following year. The clerkship would have led to a position in an esteemed Philadelphia law firm, if she had wanted it to. But during the intervening hard years, a

distinctive character had been formed and a point of
view had been taken. The times were ripe for what she
wanted to do, and the logical place to do it was, in her
mind, New York.

In a modest neighborhood downtown near Second
Avenue, she established an office, two rooms sublet in
space belonging to a striving partnership of three young
men who were just barely out of law school themselves
and eager to get a footing in criminal law. Having no
interest in family cases or the particular problems of
women, they were glad to refer all such to Jennie. So she
began and gradually was able to build a reputation as a
dedicated, caring, tough defender of women's rights,
especially those of the poor.

And the years went by then in the style of the times
and the place. She went to consciousness-raising groups,
learned something from them, and left them behind.
Like Shirley, she had her share of men, who were bright
and fun but wanted no permanence. She fell briefly in
love—or thought she did—with a nice young man who
finally, half in tears, confessed that he had tried hard, but
he really preferred nice young men, after all. She was
pursued by one or two decent men who would have
married her and whom she would have married if only
she could have loved them. She met a charming man
who adored her but had no intention of divorcing his
wife. Somehow nothing worked out. So she was thankful
to have her work and all the good things that the city
afforded, the ballet and opera at Lincoln Center, the
first-run foreign movies, jogging on Sundays in the park,
Fifth Avenue bookstores, Italian trattorias in the Village,
and courses at the New School.

A busy life it had been, a productive and useful one,
but it had led nowhere in particular, and when all was
said and done, there had been a coolness at its heart.

Until Jay had come into it. Almost two years it was now, and here they were.

Her reflections ended, Jennie wiped the pearls as she had been advised to do, laid them carefully on their velvet cushion, and hid the box under her nightgowns. Undressed, she regarded herself in the full-length mirror on the bathroom door. Not bad. She had never had much trouble keeping her weight down, which was a blessing because she loved food, good rich pastas and lots of bread. No flab, either, thanks to tennis and running. Humming to herself, she whirled and did a little dance in front of the mirror. Happy, happy—

The telephone rang.

"Is this Janine Rakowsky?" Janine. Nobody except her mother called her that anymore.

"Yes," she answered cautiously.

"My name is James Riley." The voice was courteous and refined. "I know that what I'm going to say will startle you, but—"

Mom. An accident in Florida. Mom's hurt. In the flash of a second, brakes yelp. Rain glitters on the highway. Sirens. Police converge. An ambulance comes racing. Red lights revolve.

"What is it? What's happened?"

"No, no," the man said quickly. "Nothing bad. I'm sorry I frightened you. It's just this. I represent a service for adoptees. We're called Birth Search. You've probably heard about us."

"I don't believe so." She was puzzled. "Are you in need of an attorney?"

"Oh, no. This isn't a legal matter. It's this way—"

She seemed to see the man settled back for a lengthy explanation, and so she interrupted quietly. "I'm an attorney, so since it's not a legal matter, I really don't have time to talk. I'm sorry—"

Now it was he who, with equal quietness, interrupted.

"If you'll just give me a minute or two, I'll explain. You're aware, I'm sure, of the numbers of adoptees who are now seeking their natural parents. So many organizations have sprung up to help, of which ours is just one, and we—"

A long sigh quivered in Jennie's chest. "I give as much to charity as I can afford. If you'll send me a brochure describing your work, I'll read it," she said.

The man wasn't about to let go. "This isn't a call for charity, Miss Rakowsky." There was a long pause. When he spoke again, it was almost in a whisper. "You gave birth to a girl nineteen years ago."

Seconds passed. The second hand jerked and ticked on the desk clock. Small crackling sounds came over the wire, or maybe they were the sounds of blood rushing in the arteries.

"She's been searching for more than a year. She wants to see you."

I'm going to be sick, Jennie thought. I'm going to faint. She sat down.

"I called you at home rather than at your office, since this is so personal."

She couldn't speak.

"Are you there? Miss Rakowsky?"

"No!" A terrible sound tore out of Jennie's throat, as if she had been cut without anesthesia. "No! It's impossible! I can't!"

"I understand. Yes. Of course this is a shock to you. That's why your daughter wanted us—me—to call first." A pause. "Her name is Victoria Miller. She's called Jill. She's here in the city, a sophomore at Barnard."

Cold fingers ran on Jennie's spine. Her leaping, crazy heart accelerated.

"It's impossible. . . . For God's sake, don't you see it's impossible? We don't know each other."

"That's the point, isn't it? That you ought to know each other?"

"It's not the point! I put her in good hands. Do you think I would have let them give her away to just anybody? Do you?"

Now Jennie's voice squealed and ended with a sobbing breath.

"No, I certainly don't think you would, but—"

"Why? Is there something wrong with her? Has something happened to her?"

"Not a thing. She's quite happy and well adjusted."

"There! You see? I told you! So she has a family, they're taking care of her. What does she want with me? I never even saw her face. I—" Clutching the phone, Jennie sank to the floor and leaned against the desk for support.

"Yes, she has a family, a very good one. But she wants to know you. Isn't it natural for her to want to know who you are?" The voice was quiet and reasonable.

"No! No! It's over, it's ancient history. Everything was settled. When things are settled, leave them alone. I couldn't have taken care of her then! You don't know what it was like! I had to give her away. I—"

"No one is saying a word about that, Miss Rakowsky, it's well understood. We're all professionals here, psychologists and social workers, and we do understand. I understand you. Believe me, I do."

Sweat poured on Jennie's palms and all over her body. The sweat, the racing heart, and the weakness in her legs were terrifying in themselves. She had to pull herself together, had to; she couldn't collapse here, have a heart attack alone—

"Jill is a delightful young woman, very intelligent," the voice coaxed. "You would—"

"No, I said! There's no sense in it! We can't just—just start up after nineteen years. Oh, please!" Now she wept. "Please tell her it's impossible. Tell her to be happy and to leave me alone. Forget this. It's better for her the way it is. I know it's better. Please. For God's sake, go away and leave me alone! Oh, please!"

"Miss Rakowsky, I won't bother you anymore now. Take a few days to think it over. I believe, if you try, you'll understand it's not such a bad thing, not a tragedy. I'll talk to you again."

"No! I don't want to talk to you again. I—"

The connection was broken.

She laid her head back against the desk, holding the dead phone in her lap. Her heart still hammered so fiercely that she could hear it in her ears.

"Oh, my God!" she said aloud. "Oh, my God!" She closed her eyes and put her head down between her knees.

"I'm going to vomit, I'm going to faint. . . ."

When she opened her eyes, the pattern on the big chair was spinning. Brown, white, and black circles, squares, dots, and stars flickered and flashed. She closed her eyes again, squeezing the lids against the eyeballs.

All these years. I didn't want to remember her. I had to forget her, didn't I? And sometimes I did forget her. But other times? I don't dare think of the other times . . .

"Don't you see?" she cried out into the silent room, cried out to no one, to everyone, to the world, the fates. "Don't you see?

"Oh, my God . . ." she sobbed. With her hands over her face, she rocked and sobbed.

After a long while then, her mind began to click. She summoned it now, the little machine in her head, to take control lest she fly apart and scatter in broken pieces.

Think, Jennie. You can't afford to panic. There's an intelligent way of handling everything, isn't there? You always tell other people so. Now tell yourself. Think.

The phone rang again. Muffled in the folds of her bath-robe, it sounded far away.

"You didn't call me," Jay said.

She went blank. "Call?"

"Your line was busy."

"Yes, it was a client."

"Must they bother you on Sunday too?"

"Well, it happens sometimes." She began to babble. "The landlord's been harassing the woman. It's awful. And Shirley was here, so I couldn't use the phone, any-way. She just left this minute. I couldn't get rid of her."

Jay laughed. "She'll miss you, that one. Oh, wasn't this a perfect day? I'm just sitting here thinking about it."

"A perfect weekend. Yes, it was."

"We still haven't gotten your ring. Can I pin you down one afternoon this week?"

How can I just suddenly produce a child? If I had told him the first day—

He spoke again, interrupting her thoughts. "We'll go to Cartier's. It won't take long."

"Jay, I don't need such an expensive ring. Really I don't."

"Jennie, don't be a nuisance, will you? Don't argue with me. Go to sleep. I'm half asleep already. Good night, darling."

She hung up and cried out loud into the room. "My God, what am I going to do?"

Walk into the family all of a sudden with a nineteen-year-old daughter, dropped down from nowhere . . . Jay's babies . . . the wedding just a couple of months away . . . the Wolfes, that decorous, trusting, honor-able pair. Liberal. Decent. But never fool yourself, the code behind the pleasant surface is a rigid one. And Jay . . . I've lied. . . . Concealment like this, all this time, is a lie and nothing but. Yes . . . yes.

An intelligent girl, the man had said. Jill, they call her.

Why should she want me? I'm the one who gave her away. Poor baby. Given away. She came out of me, out of the very core of me. I heard the newborn squall of protest, and that was all, one pitiable, helpless cry, and then they carried her out, a small wrapped bundle carried out of the room, out of my life. Does she look at all like me? Would I feel any recognition if I were to meet her someplace, not knowing who she is? But I did right. You know you did right, Jennie. And she can't come back into your life now. She can't. It won't work. Think, I told you. But I can't think. I haven't got the strength. I'm drained.

After a while she got up from the floor, turned off the lights, and, still huddled in the bathrobe, lay down on the bed. She had begun to shiver. For a long time she lay with the quilt drawn over her head. Absolutely alone . . .

Alone, just as she had been on that bus heading back east from Nebraska. It felt the same. She could smell the exhaust again and swallow the threat of nausea as the bus swung, lurching too fast through all the monotonous small towns, passing the supermarkets, used-car lots, and malls, going back to pick up a life. Going back . . .

CHAPTER

2

It begins in the Baltimore row house, in the kitchen over a cup of tea after the supper dishes have been washed and put away. Sometimes, rarely, perhaps on the Sabbath, the tea is drunk in the cluttered front room where dust gathers on the paper flowers. The sofa and chairs are covered with plastic sheets except when there's company, and the blinds are darkly drawn to keep the meager north light from fading the carpet. "Blue is the most perishable color," Mom says.

Actually, the story begins even farther back than Baltimore, for is not each of us only the latest link in a long, binding chain? It begins in Lithuania, in a town with an unpronounceable name, near Vilna, the city of great scholars. Mom's parents, who were not scholars, peddled horseradish for a living. "If you can call it a living," Mom says. It is a simple story that she tells, and yet with each repetition she has something with which to embellish it, some comical or pathetic anecdote. The part when the family leaves for France is dramatic, with the pathos of departure and the adventure of novelty. There is new scenery, another language, and for the little girl, Masha, a new name: Marlene. She goes to school wearing a pinafore, like any little French girl. It does not take her long to feel French, to lose all but the vaguest graying memory of the muddy road to Vilna. Then the Germans come, and the girl learns that she is, after all, not French. Her parents are taken away back east again, to be consumed in the fires. And she, in some miraculous fashion, is swept up into a group of fleeing refugees and brought to America.

"We came across the Pyrenees. You wouldn't believe —I can't believe it myself—how we did it, Janine."

Janine, the name she has given to her daughter in memory of Jacob, her father, is the last, wistful, prideful memento of her short-lived Frenchness.

"There were German patrols and observation planes. We had to hide among the trees, we had to climb above the treeline, climb through the rocks in the terrible cold. A man had a heart attack and died there. . . .

"Well, I got here, anyway. I was sixteen. I had no money at all, and not nearly enough education to do much. But then I got lucky. I met Sam."

Sam, too, has a story to tell. Unlike his wife, though, he refuses to tell it. It is through her mother that Jennie learns how Pop survived the concentration camp: An expert tailor, he was put to use making uniforms for the Germans. He has unspeakable memories, and now he will not touch a needle, except that once in a long while he will copy a suit or coat from *Vogue* for his wife or daughter. He is more or less cheerful in his delicatessen, making sandwiches and ladling salads, while Mom takes the cash.

Jennie is an only child. Her parents' labor is for her alone. Their savings, the things they do not buy for themselves, and the vacations they do not take are all for her. They never say so, but she knows it. She is aware that they are giving her "good values": work, family, respectability, and education. Their daughter must have the education they missed. The world's evil must not touch her. They keep her safe.

Pop is the more religious parent. Orthodox, he closes the store on Saturdays, even though it could be the busiest day of the week. He is clean-mouthed; she has never once even heard him swear. She thinks she will remember him best at the table on Friday nights, washing his hands before prayers, while her mother holds the basin and the little white towel, and the flames waver in the brass candlesticks.

Jennie doesn't share all their beliefs, but she respects their beliefs and them. They are gentle parents, overworked, grateful for what they have, disappointed over what they missed, and sometimes remote; lost, she understands, in their remembered experiences. And while, even when she was still in high school, she knew she would leave their world, she also knows that in spirit at least she will always be part of it.

"So he lives in Atlanta?" Mom says. Her hair is in curlers. She looks chubby, even in her enveloping housedress. Now she frowns a little, trying to decipher the letter's smart-looking backhand script. It is a woman's writing on thick gray paper. The envelope is lined and the paper is engraved in navy blue. Mom runs a finger over the raised letters. "Nice that the mother writes to invite you."

"Mom, it's proper. She's supposed to."

"Atlanta—it's far?"

"Only a couple of hours by plane." Jennie feels delightful excitement. "They live in the suburbs. They'll meet us at the airport."

"They're rich people, I suppose."

Now, for some reason, Jennie feels embarrassment and irritation. "Mom, I never asked."

"Who said 'asked'? Of course you didn't. But a person can tell."

"I don't care. That doesn't interest me."

"Doesn't interest her, she says!" Mom leans on her elbows and holds the teacup between both hands. Her eyes, glinting green-brown over the cup's rim, are reflecting and amused. "What do you know? You've never been without money, thank God. Do you know what it is to wake up at night where you're hiding in your bed, and you look at the clock and in a few hours you have to face the landlord and the butcher—they want their money and you haven't got it? No, you don't. So it doesn't interest you. Tell me, what will you wear?" And without waiting for an answer, she says, "Listen, your father will make you a spring suit, a traveling suit."

"Don't bother Pop. He's tired. I can find something."

"One suit won't hurt him. A few nights and he'll finish it. What color do you want? I'll tell you, it should be gray. Gray goes with everything. A nice suit so you'll look like somebody when you get off the plane. He's a nice boy, Peter. Why do they call him Shorty?"

"Because he's six-feet-three."

"He's a nice boy."

And Mom, wearing her familiar, warm little smile, pours another cup of tea.

It had begun even earlier than that, soon after the start of Jennie's first year of college. Having skipped lunch to study for a test, she had stopped for a sandwich in the middle of the afternoon at a luncheonette off campus.

"Do you mind if I sit with you?"

She looked up at the tallest boy she had ever seen, with a head of the reddest hair she had ever seen.

"No, of course not." In a new school and a new city, one needed to keep meeting people. And she moved her books aside on the table.

"I've been wanting to talk to you. I watched you here every day at lunch last week."

A fast talker. A wise guy? She answered, revealing neither surprise nor pleasure, "Why didn't you, then?"

"You were with a crowd. There wasn't any good way to begin."

She waited. She wasn't going to help him without knowing more about him. He had friendly eyes, but he'd begun too fast and had made her wary.

"I like the way you look. And your voice was something else I noticed. You don't have a shrieking soprano."

"I'm noticing your voice too." His accent was full of soft vowels. "You from the South?"

"Atlanta. My name's Peter Mendes."

"Jennie Rakowsky. From Baltimore."

He put out his hand. People didn't do that on campus. Maybe it was a southern custom. Southerners were supposed to be more mannerly, more formal.

"I'd like to know you better, Jennie."

She'd heard that before. Drinks and then bed, taken for granted, without having known each other more than a couple of hours. Well, he'd have a surprise in store for him if he was counting on that.

"Would you have dinner with me tonight? Do you like Italian food?"

"Everybody likes Italian food."

"Okay, then. I know a great place. It's not fancy, but it's all home cooking. What time can I pick you up, and where?"

"I didn't say I'd go. I said I liked Italian food."

"Oh."

She saw a flush almost as bright as his hair rise on his cheeks and was instantly sorry. He wasn't a wise guy. He was straight and simple.

"Please." She reached out to touch his hand. "I was only teasing. I'll go with you, and thanks. I'm in the new dorm, and six would be fine if it's all right with you."

There was a tenderness about his mouth as it widened into a smile. In that instant she knew that she liked him, and all the way back to the library she hummed to herself.

What did they talk about over the ubiquitous checked tablecloth, the candle, and the tomato stains? On the college campuses of 1969, one didn't hold a ten-minute conversation without reaching the subject of Vietnam. Jennie said she'd wanted so much to get to the convention in Chicago the year before, but she still had been in high school and her parents had been adamant. Peter's experience was the same.

"It's not that they don't think it's all horrible, what's happening in Vietnam," Jennie said. "But, well, they think kids shouldn't go out in the streets. It doesn't accomplish anything. They think Chicago was just a wild scene. You know how it is."

Peter nodded. "Everything's a mess. Sometimes I think the whole world's going to rack and ruin. Sometimes I have so much angry energy, I think I'll really be able to change things when I get out into the world." Earnestly he drew his brows together, and as suddenly relaxed into a laugh. "The funny thing is, here I am ranting about fixing things in the future, and do you know what I'm going to study? Archaeology! Crazy, wouldn't you say?"

"Not if that's what you like. Why do you?"

"It started one summer in New Mexico when I saw the Indian reservations and read about the Anasazi, the Ancient Ones. They have a wonderful philosophy, all about their place in nature, about how things are joined, all things with one another—trees, animals, and people— and we have to live in harmony."

Oh, she liked his face, his generous thoughts, his long, clean hands, his freckled neck and arms, and his clean white shirt! She liked the fact that his middle name was Algernon and that he could laugh about it.

"They say, 'My mother the earth, my father the sky.' Have you ever heard that?"

"No. It's a beautiful idea," she acknowledged, but what she was seeing was the head of thick russet hair, the eyes like opals: gray shot through with lavender light.

"So that's what got me started. Now what about you?"

"I want to go to law school if I can afford to. I'm on a partial scholarship here, so I have to keep my grades up."

Their talk bounded then from topic to topic. Music. Disco. Tennis. He was a seeded player. They had a tennis court in their yard, he said, so he'd always had lots of practice time. She had never known anyone who owned his own tennis court.

Had she ever ridden out to the Amish country? he asked. No, she hadn't, although she'd read about them. So had he; he hadn't spent much time in the North until now, and one of the places he'd wanted to see was the Amish country. Would she like to go there with him some Sunday? They could rent a car and take turns driving, if she liked to drive.

"I haven't got a license. I'm only seventeen," she told him.

"I'm eighteen. You're young to be here."

"I skipped a year in junior high."

"I'm impressed."

She flirted now, looking downward, then sideways, then upward, in a movement she had practiced before the mirror years ago. It revealed her thick black lashes and a curve of black curl across her temple. She thought of it as her piquant look.

"You needn't be. I'm really not all that smart. I just work hard, for the reasons I told you."

"You have amazing eyelashes," he said.

"Really? I never noticed."

"Well, they are. Gee, I'm glad I saw you this afternoon. I'd been thinking, this place is so big, maybe I wouldn't ever see you again—or not for months, anyway."

"I'm glad you did too."

"I thought at first you didn't like me."

"I was only being careful."

"So how about what I was saying, renting a car next Sunday?"

"I'd love to."

They walked back across the campus, gone dark and almost vacant in the chill of early fall. Peter left her at the door.

"It's been great, Jennie. Let's start early Sunday and have the whole day. Good night."

"Good night."

He didn't even make an attempt to kiss her. Ordinarily she would have felt this to be an insult, a rejection, even by someone whose kiss she didn't want. Now she felt only that there was something serious in the quiet "Good night." Odd, she thought, and hard to explain, even to herself.

They took their ride to Lancaster County, the first of many rides together. At an inn they ate seven sweets and seven sours, shoofly pie, and cider. They drove and walked past rich, rolling farms, fields of winter rye, and herds of dairy cattle in thick winter coats.

"No electricity, no machines," Peter said. "They milk by hand."

"You mean you can milk cows by machine?"

"Of course. That's how it's done these days."

"How do you know so much about farms and animals?"

"Oh, we have a place in the country. I spend a lot of
time there."

"I thought you lived in the city."

"We do, but we have this other place too."

As fall turned to winter they began to see each other
every day in their free time. They went to the zoo, the
airport, and the waterfront. They sat on a bench in Rit-
tenhouse Square and talked for hours. They took the
train to New York and saw a French movie in Greenwich
Village, where he bought her a silver bracelet.

"It's too expensive," she protested. "You spend too
much, Peter."

He laughed. "You know what? Let's go back to the
store."

"What for?"

"To get the necklace that matches. Don't look so
shocked. It's okay, I said."

She looked up into his face while he fastened the silver
chain around her neck. Happiness showed in his smile,
in the fit of his fine lips, curved and upturned at the ends.

She loved his cheerfulness. It was contagious, in the
same way that Mom's worrying was contagious. At home
she felt an underlying anxiety, even when conversation
was pleasant enough; she felt a vague fear that things—
what things?—might at any minute crumble, that there
were no supports. It felt good to be with a person who
was happy. Happiness made you strong.

Toward the middle of their second month together
Peter kissed her. Afterward she remembered her first
thought: *This* kiss, unlike any other, means something. It
was late one afternoon and raining, so that there were
hardly any people out to see them. She was holding an
umbrella when he took her in his arms; letting the um-

brella drop, she reached around his neck, and they stood like that for a long time in the soft rain.

For another week or two there were more such fervent, innocent embraces, becoming each time more and more disturbing, as they pressed against each other with the heat of their bodies flaming through all the layers of heavy cloth. When he let her go, her nerves were alive. When she trudged upstairs to her room, she felt as if part of her had been torn away. Not enough, she thought. It's not enough.

"It's not good like this," Peter said one day. "We have to do something about ourselves." And as she did not answer, he said, "We need each other, Jennie. Really need. Do you understand?"

"I know. I understand."

"Then will you leave it to me to plan everything?"

"I leave it all to you. I always will."

"Oh, darling Jennie."

All that week before the great change was to come, she could think of nothing else. She had always slept in pajamas, but now she went out and bought a pink nightgown trimmed with ruffled lace. Her moods fluctuated. Sometimes she felt the excitement catching in her throat; then she read poetry or turned the radio to splendid music, something that soared in triumph, like Beethoven's Ninth. She felt like crying. Then she felt like laughing. As the weekend came closer, a thin strain of fear crept into her spirit, and she was afraid of the fear, afraid that it would be there to spoil the joy.

But he was very gentle, and she need not have been afraid. When the door to the motel room closed, he turned toward her with an expression so reassuring, so loving and protective, that all fear vanished. Tactfully he dimmed the strong glare of the overhead light, leaving only a lamp in the corner. With none of the haste or roughness that others had described, or about which Jennie had read, he took off her clothes.

"I'll never hurt you," he whispered. "Never in any way."

And she knew it was true. He would never willfully hurt anyone. The beating heart under the hard male chest was soft. So she came to him willingly and gladly.

She never got to wear the fancy nightgown. In the morning they laughed about that. They took a last look around the drab room and laughed about that too. It had been warm and clean, and that was enough. They would be back.

How exquisite was the world! The way a sparrow left its tiny arrow-shaped prints on the snow. Pyramids of apples, sleek as red silk. The smile of a stranger holding a door for her to pass through. All were beautiful.

Yet sometimes—rarely, it is true—before falling asleep or while dreaming over a textbook, Jennie wondered whether these marvelous feelings could last through four more years. Four years! It was forever. And a little chill would shake her.

"Don't leave me, Peter," she said aloud into the darkness.

He told her gravely one day, "This is forever, you know."

"We're very young to know our own minds," she answered, testing, waiting for his denial.

And it came: "Only a couple of generations ago people married at sixteen. They still do, in some places. We'll just postpone it, that's all. Get there a little later, when we graduate."

"That's true."

Best not to think about it too hard. If you don't think about a good thing, it will happen.

"I have to visit some people in Owings Mills next weekend," Peter said one day. "That's near you, isn't it?"

"Not far. We never go there."

"They're old friends of my parents. Mr. Frank went to the U of P with my dad, and he's been sick, had some sort of awful operation on his neck. They've invited me, and Dad wants me to go."

"Well, as long as you're not going to be here, I'll go home this weekend. Mom's been at me to come. Do you want to have dinner at my house before you go out to your friends?"

"Sure. I'll take the train to Baltimore."

"You'll have to take a taxi to my house. On Saturday my father doesn't drive."

"That's okay."

She wanted to make sure that everything would be really nice. Sometimes, when Mom had been working in the store all day, things were a little hurried and careless. Today, however, because it was Saturday, Mom was setting the table in the dining room.

"Oh, darling, I've one little job for you. Take the silver from the drawer and give it a good wash, will you, while I finish the stuffed cabbage? I hope he likes it."

"He's not a fussy eater. You needn't go to so much trouble."

"You must be serious about him, Janine. You never invited a boy to have supper here before."

She wished her mother would stop saying "boy." Peter was a man. But she answered quietly, "Please don't jump to conclusions, Mom. You'll embarrass me."

Perhaps it had been a mistake to invite him. Yet it would have been more embarrassing not to invite him, when he was going to be right in the area.

"Don't worry, I understand. Play it cool, isn't that what you young people call it? Go, give the silver a wash, will you?" Her mother picked up and weighed a fork. "It's good silver plate, the best. Wears as long as sterling. Put a towel in the sink so you won't scratch it."

From the window over the sink one looked directly into the Danielis' kitchen, across the concrete strip that divided the yards. In the summer when it was too hot to eat indoors, everybody moved card tables to the back porches. You could smell the pungent gravy that was always simmering on the back of the Danielis' stove.

"Yes, they all chipped in where I worked and gave me that set when I got married. So generous. I remember I cried . . ."

Pop, curious about the preparations, came into the kitchen. "Why does he call you Jennie?"

"At school everybody does."

Mom, who was energetically chopping onions, joined in. "Why do you let them change it? Your name is Janine, such a beautiful name."

"It doesn't go with Rakowsky."

"Sam, do you hear? So it's Rakowsky she doesn't like. A good thing your grandfather—may he rest in peace—can't hear. He was proud of the name. He was a hero. That time there was a fire, you remember—"

"Mom, I know about Grandpa." Jennie spoke with affection. "How many times have I heard it?"

"Well, so you'll change the name," Mom said cheerfully. "You'll pick out a man with a beautiful name."

Jennie moved toward the dining room, where the best plates lay on the best cloth and the plastic covers had been removed from the chair seats. Her father's voice followed her.

"Mendes. What kind of a name is that? Mendel, I know, it's common, but Mendes—"

"It's Spanish or Portuguese."

"Spanish! Well, Jews are everywhere. Even in China, I read someplace. Yes, even in China."

Everything went well, so Jennie needn't have worried. Peter brought a bunch of daffodils and she arranged them in a low bowl on the table. It was surprising what a few flowers could do for a room. Mom's dinner was delicious. She was her usual talkative self but made no remark more personal than when, bringing the ketchup bottle to the table, she patted her husband's head and declared that Sam would soon be putting ketchup on ice cream too.

Pop did more talking than he usually did. Peter and he were both enthusiastic about baseball. It surprised Jennie to know that her father knew so much or cared so much about the Orioles. Probably, living in a house with two women, he hadn't felt the need to talk baseball.

She could see that he liked Peter. "Janine tells me they call you Shorty."

"She doesn't, but a lot of people do."

"If you were any taller, you wouldn't get through our front door," Pop said. "Have you heard the one about the dwarf and his brother?" And he went on to tell a joke in Yiddish.

When Peter obviously didn't understand, Jennie explained it as best she could. Pop was astonished.

"You don't understand Yiddish?"

"I'm sorry, I never learned it," Peter apologized.

"Learned it! It's something you don't learn, you just know it. Your people come from the other side, don't they?"

"From Europe, yes, but a while ago."

"Your grandfather came?"

"No, before that."

"How long?" Pop persisted.

Jennie hoped Peter would understand that he wasn't being rude but merely interested and curious.

"Well," Peter said, "they came to Savannah from South America sometime in the 1700s. Before that, they'd been in Holland."

"Two hundred years in this country?" Pop shook his

head in wonderment. Probably he thought that Peter didn't know what he was talking about.

When jokes—in English now—were exhausted, they came inevitably to politics. They were all concerned and angry over the Vietnam war and the American role in it, which they believed to be senseless and wrong. While the talk went on, Mom filled Peter's plate again. Then came warm apple pie, merging the smell of cinnamon with the sweetness that came from the narcissi. Peter ate and argued and was, Jennie saw, at home. She had good feelings.

Of course, if they had any idea about Peter and herself, that would be something else. . . . But these were other times. Mom and Pop weren't out in the world enough to know, except from reading the papers and being shocked by what they thought of as exceptional behavior, how different these times really were.

So the evening wore on, until Peter said someone would be coming at nine to take him out to Owings Mills.

"Too bad you can't stay here overnight," Mom said. "We can put a cot in the front room. It's a very comfortable cot."

"Thank you, I'd like that, but they're expecting me."

The man who came for Peter drove a station wagon. When the front door was opened, they could hear barking and see three terrier heads in the back of the car. Peter peered out and signaled that he was coming.

"Tell your friend to come in and have a cup of coffee with us," Pop urged. "And there's plenty of pie left too."

"I don't think he can, on account of the dogs. He won't leave them in the car even for a minute. They're show dogs, very rare, Tibetan terriers. They've a wall hung with blue ribbons in their house," Peter explained.

Then he thanked the Rakowskys, was careful to be casual with Jennie, and went down the steps.

Pop and Mom watched the station wagon drive away.

"Blue ribbons," Pop muttered. "What was he talking about? But he's a nice fellow, all the same. Very nice, Janine, even if he does call you Jennie."

Peter said, "I liked your parents. They're good people."

"I'm glad. They liked you."

"I hope you'll like my family too. Will you come for a few days over next spring vacation? I'll have my mother write next week if you want to."

He had never said much about his people, except that he had one sister, age fourteen. His father was in some sort of investment business, which, Jennie supposed, you would call "banking." She imagined a fair-sized house with a tennis court, the sort of prosperous white house that one saw on Sunday drives through the suburbs.

"He wants his parents to meet you, and if they like you —why shouldn't they?—" Mom fancied, "then he will ask your father if he can marry you."

"Mom! This is 1969. People don't ask fathers anymore. Besides, for Pete's sake, neither of us is ready for marriage. We're too young."

"So you'll wait a year or two. I was nineteen," Mom said positively.

A long dark blue car driven by a black man in a dark blue uniform met them at the airport in Atlanta. Jennie assumed it was a hired limousine, and, never having ridden in one before, was impressed.

Then the black man said, "Good to have you home, Mr. Peter. Seems like a long time between visits."

"How's everybody, Spencer? Mother? Father? Aunt Lee?"

"Your folks are all right, and your Aunt Lee, she's still the same salt of the earth. Isn't that what you call her?"

"That's what she is, the salt of the earth."

This was their own car and chauffeur! Jennie smoothed her skirt. She smoothed and smoothed the good gray wool that Pop had made.

"Hand-stitched," Mom had marveled. "You know what this would sell for in the stores? Golden hands, your father has. Now you need a yellow blouse, black patent-leather pumps, and you can go anyplace."

Peter put his hand over hers. "You're nervous."

He saw everything and felt everything, as if his nerves were connected to hers.

"Yes. Do I look all right?"

"You look beautiful."

She couldn't say "It's this car that's done something to me. Riding in this car. I'm scared."

Somebody had left an umbrella on the floor, a Burberry plaid. A girl at college had one, with the raincoat to match. "Cost a fortune," Mom would say.

They turned off the highway into city streets and then onto a wide road bordered with old trees, now in full leaf. Then there were lawns, hedges and fences, and houses set back at the end of long driveways. Soft air, much milder than it was at home, poured in at the window, cooling Jennie's hot cheeks.

"Jennie, my parents won't eat you. They aren't ogres."

Peter's parents. It's absolutely stupid to feel like this. So what if they have their own car and chauffeur? So what?

The car slowed down, swung into a long drive, and moved up a slight slope under a ceiling of pink blooms.

"Dogwood. Atlanta's famous for dogwood," Peter said.

At the top of the rise the car turned around an enormous circular bed of scarlet tulips and came to a stop. It flashed through Jennie's mind that they must be stopping to call for somebody at a country club or a private school. Two-storied columns blazed white against red brick; a short double staircase curved and joined the veranda under the columns. She had a second's vision of *Gone with the Wind*, or perhaps the Parthenon. When she saw people standing in the white doorway, she understood in a second flash that this was the home, Peter's home.

She had to say something. Trivial words came from her mouth. "Oh, all those tulips!"

He was already out of the car and running up the steps. The driver helped Jennie and took her suitcase. She went up the stairs to where, with a welcoming gesture, Peter had already turned to her.

"Mom, Dad, this is my friend, Jennie Rakowsky."

Jennie put her hand out to a blur of a woman, a symmetrical, pale blur with elderly pale skin and keen, quick eyes.

"How do you do, Jennie? We're always glad when Peter brings another of his friends," said Peter's mother.

The father was a large man, white-haired and powerful, like someone you see on the television news, a senator or a general. She felt small beside these tall people, under these tall columns.

Inside there was a lofty, two-storied hall with a crystal chandelier on a long golden rope, and more curving double stairs that united with a landing halfway up and under a bright window.

"Here's Sally June," Peter said.

A young girl was coming down the stairs, wearing a short white tennis dress and swinging a racket. She had her brother's red hair and freckles.

"Hi," she said, not smiling, and went on past them out the front door.

You don't even hug your brother? And you're supposed to smile when you greet someone, Jennie thought, with her own smile unacknowledged. The girl had made her feel foolish.

"Let me show you to your room," Mrs. Mendes said.

Jennie followed her up the stairs. It was pleasant to climb on such wide treads and low risers. But the straight, narrow back ahead of her looked in some way forbidding. There had been a vice principal in high school, a formidable, correct woman with dark, gray-streaked hair in a French twist, who had walked like that.

They entered a room at the end of a wide corridor. "Dinner's in half an hour," Mrs. Mendes said. "You needn't bother to change, after all that traveling. Just make yourself comfortable and join us downstairs whenever you're ready. There'll be drinks in the library. Oh, yes—if there's anything you need, just ring. Press the button next to the light switch."

I shall be careful not to press it by mistake, Jennie thought, and said, "Thank you. Thank you very much, Mrs. Mendes."

Mrs. Mendes closed the door. It clicked neatly, letting silence fill the room. Jennie stood at its center, circling it with her eyes. A mahogany four-poster bed was covered with a print of miniature lemons and green leaves on a dove-gray background. Full draperies of the same print were looped back from the windows. The carpet was a gray sea on which stood plump yellow-and-white chairs; a pair of dark, gleaming wooden chests; and a round table that bore a bouquet of the red tulips she had seen outside.

Change. You needn't bother to change. Change into what? I'd have thought my suit would do for supper . . . dinner. Then my dark blue silk in case we go to the movies or someplace tomorrow— The thought broke off and she went to the window. Automatically she always went to a window to see where she was.

The room overlooked the front of the house. Over to the left was a corner of lawn, very green. There was no other house in sight, nothing but grass and thick trees. The late afternoon lay in deep quiet.

Here, indoors, it was also completely quiet. At home one always heard things: a flushed toilet, voices from the yard next door, trucks passing, or footsteps going up the stairs on which there was no carpet. "It wears out too fast on stairs," Mom said.

Now she opened her door and looked down the corridor into the face of a grandfather clock. No, you were supposed to call it a "tall clock," she remembered, having read that someplace, maybe in *House and Garden,* which she sometimes picked up at the beauty parlor when she went for her occasional haircut. Another piece of random information, she thought, that I seem to collect without trying to or wanting to. The clock struck: Bong! Bong! Come downstairs whenever you're ready. She'd better wash her hands and go.

Her room had its private bath, all pale yellow tiles. The towels were thick and white with yellow monograms, the same monogram that had been on Mrs. Mendes's notepaper: a large *M,* flanked by a small *c* and a small *d. C* for Caroline, *M* for Mendes, of course, and the *d* must be for her maiden name. That's the way you did a monogram. Another piece of useless information that sticks on me like flies on flypaper, she thought, beginning to laugh. She felt silly. Shall it be when—if—we are married, shall it be Janine Rakowsky Mendes? Monograms! Mom buys our towels at Sears when they wear out, and they're good enough.

She ran a comb through her hair, her good, strong, curly hair, so easy to maintain, which meant one less worry and expense. A fresh comb had been provided on the dressing table. On the bedside table were a carafe of ice water and some magazines, *Town and Country* and *Vogue.* If the guest were a man, the magazines would probably be *Time* and *Newsweek.*

Peter, I never imagined you lived like this. You never said. But why should you have said? How could you have?

Jennie, we're very rich, we live in a mansion.

Idiot! she thought. My cheeks are so hot, they'll think I have a fever.

She went out, closing the door without a sound. Across the hall, through an open door, she saw another bedroom, this one decorated in a vivid ink-blue. There were at least eight bedrooms on the floor. All the doors were open, so you were supposed to keep them open. She went back to open hers, then went downstairs to find the library. First there was a large room with a bow window at one end, and great cabinets filled with books to the ceiling. She wondered whether the presence of these books meant that this was the library, but there was nobody there.

"This way, miss," someone said.

It was the same black man who had driven the car. Now he wore a white jacket and carried a silver tray. Through several rooms she followed him, treading on almond-green velvet carpet and Oriental rugs and once on a carpet flowered in pale peach and cream. At the other end of the house people were gathered in a long, wood-paneled room lined with bookshelves. There were leather chairs, some models of sailing ships, and over the mantel a portrait in oil of a man wearing a gray uniform. All this she saw through peripheral vision as she walked in.

The men stood up and introductions were made. There were Peter, his father, a grandfather, and an uncle. Mrs. Mendes and an aunt made room for Jennie on the sofa before which, on a low table, the man had set a silver tray holding bottles and glasses. Peter offered Jennie the glass.

"You haven't asked your guest what she wants," his mother said.

"I always know what Jennie wants. She drinks ginger ale."

Jennie sipped while the men went on with whatever they had been talking about. She remembered to keep her ankles neatly crossed. "With a straight skirt," Mom said, "you have to be careful. It rides up when you cross your knees." Mom knew about things like that. Jennie smiled inwardly. Sometimes, but not always, it paid to listen to Mom.

"I suppose," said Mrs. Mendes, "your garden can't be as advanced as ours? They tell me you're at least a month behind us up north."

Your garden. Jennie was careful not to look at Peter.

"Oh, no, it's still pretty cold at home."

"How nice to have a house full of young people," the aunt remarked. She could have been a clone of Peter's mother, even to her silk shirtwaist dress and ivory button earrings. "I understand Sally June has a guest for the weekend too."

"Yes, Annie Ruth Marsh from Savannah."

"Oh, the Marshes! How nice! So the girls are friends?"

"Yes, we got them together last summer at the beach, didn't you know?"

"I didn't know. How lovely. So many generations of friendships."

Meanwhile Jennie was examining her surroundings, and recalling a fascinating book for Sociology 101, with a chapter about house styles and ethnic backgrounds. Some Anglo-Saxons were supposed to like old things even if they weren't inherited, because they like to make believe they were inherited; they want to proclaim that they're not new immigrant stock. Some Jews go in for modern to proclaim that they *are* new immigrant stock, and see how far they've come! These people were Jews who were as "old-family" as any Anglo-Saxon. And all of it so foolish . . . But it was none of her business. The room was handsome, with so many wonderful books.

"You're looking at the portrait, I see," said Mrs. Mendes, suddenly addressing Jennie.

She had not been looking at it, but now saw that the gray uniform was indeed a Confederate one. The man had side-whiskers and held a sword.

"That's Peter's great-great-grandfather on his father's side. He was a major, wounded at Antietam. But"—this spoken with a little laugh—"he recovered to marry and father a family or we all wouldn't be here."

The grandfather echoed a little laugh. "Well, let's drink to him." He stood, flourishing his glass, and bowed to the painting. "Salutations, Major. He was my grandfather, you know, and I can remember him. I'm the only one left who can. I'll tell you, I was five when he died, and all I remember, to be honest about it, is that he kept bees. Hello, here's our Sally June."

A second girl in a white tennis dress came in with her.

"Annie Ruth Marsh, Jennie Rakowsky. Thank you so much for the cake, dear," Mrs. Mendes said. "Annie Ruth remembered how we all adored that Low-Country fruitcake their cook makes."

"Mother thought they'd be a nice house gift for this time of year," said Annie Ruth, "because you can keep adding brandy all summer and they'll be perfect for the holidays."

House gift. Then you were supposed to bring a present? Why hadn't Peter told her? He should have told her. But how could he have said, "Listen, you're supposed to bring something, Jennie."

It was cold here, cold and foreign. She was relieved when dinner was announced. Eating would take up the time. There wouldn't be a need for conversation.

The table was polished like black glass. On each linen mat stood a glittering group of objects: blue porcelain, silver, and crystal. For a moment Jennie had a recollection of her mother bringing the ketchup bottle . . . Dinner was served by the same black man, Spencer, in the white jacket. Talk was easy, chiefly carried on by the men, who spoke about the local elections, golf, and family gossip. The food was delicately flavored and included a soup that Jennie learned from someone's casual comment was black turtle, roast lamb fragrant with rosemary, and beets cut into rosebuds. She ate slowly, seeing herself as a spectator, observing herself as she observed and listened.

Suddenly came the inevitable subject of Vietnam, with a report of yesterday's battle and body count. The grandfather spoke up.

"What we need is to stop pussyfooting, once and for all. We need to go in there and bomb the hell out of Hanoi."

Peter's father added, "We're the laughingstock of the world. A power like this country allowing itself to be tossed around like"—he glanced indignantly around the table—"like, I don't know what. These young people marching, this rabble protesting! If any son of mine did that . . . Believe me, if this war is still on—and I hope it won't be, that we'll have trounced them by then—but if it should still be on when Peter's through with college, I'll expect him to put on a uniform like a man and do his duty. Right, Peter?"

Peter swallowed a mouthful. He looked past Jennie to where his father sat behind the wine decanter.

"Right," he echoed.

She was aware that her astonishment was showing on her face, and she wiped the expression away, thinking, But you told me, whenever we spoke about it, you told me that you would never go, never; that it was an immoral, useless war. All the things you said, Peter!

"And most of your friends, what's their attitude, Peter?" the grandfather inquired.

"Oh, we don't talk about it that much."

Not talk about it that much! That's what everybody talked about most—in class, after class, in the cafeterias and half the night. You might even say that's all we talk about!

The grandfather persisted. "But they must have some opinion."

Peter's face was reddening. "Well, naturally some think one way, some another."

"Well, I hope you speak up like a man, unlike these whining cowards, and defend your President. You just can't let them get away with defeatist talk. That's what weakens a country. I certainly hope you don't sit silently and let them get away with it, Peter."

"No, sir," Peter said.

Mrs. Mendes interrupted. "Oh, enough politics! Let's talk about happier things, like Cindy's birthday party tomorrow." She explained to Jennie, "Cindy's a cousin, actually a second cousin, who's turning twenty-one, and they're having a small formal dance for her at home. I do hope it doesn't rain. They're planning to dance outdoors. It should be lovely."

A small formal dance . . . He didn't tell me that, either. Maybe he didn't know. But I have no dress . . . Jennie thought. Never had she felt so much a stranger.

The talk continued. "Have you heard what Aunt Lee gave her?"

"No, what?" asked the uncle.

"A horse!" said Mrs. Mendes. "A colt, to be accurate. You've met our Aunt Lee," she reminded Annie Ruth, "the one who has the horse farm."

"She's such a queer! A regular skeleton in the closet," said Sally June.

"Sally June, what a dreadful thing to say!"

"Well, it's true, isn't it?"

"I don't know what you mean," Mrs. Mendes answered stiffly.

Sally June giggled. "Mother! You do know."

"My sister has always been a tomboy," Mr. Mendes said, probably for the benefit of Jennie, the stranger in the room.

"A tomboy!" the girl persisted. "She's over fifty. Everybody knows she's a—"

"That will do," Mr. Mendes said, and repeated sharply, "That will do, I said!"

In the silence one heard the clink of silver on china. Sally June hung her head, while a fearful flush spread up her neck. She looked frightened.

Peter broke the silence. "Speaking of horses, it reminds me that when I was at Owings Mills that weekend, I saw Ralph out riding. We passed him in the car. I didn't know he's at Georgetown now."

How gracefully Peter drew the new subject out of the old! Of course, he had felt the tension in the room. He continued, "He may be going into the diplomatic service like his brother."

"And get killed like his brother," the aunt said, explaining politely to Jennie, "These are old friends of our family's. Their son was killed during a riot in Pakistan."

"Fifteen years it must be," said Mrs. Mendes. "And his mother still mourning. It's ridiculous." She spoke briskly, addressing the table. "I have no patience with people who can't face facts."

"It was a terrible death," Peter reminded her gently.

"All the same, she ought to shape up," his mother said. "People can, and they do." Unexpectedly she turned to

Jennie. "Peter tells us that your father was in a concentration camp in Europe."

So he had talked about her here at home. "Yes," she
answered. "He was very young and strong, one of the
rare survivors."

"What does he do now?"

Peter hadn't told them that. "He has a store. A delicatessen."

For an instant the other woman's eyes flared and flickered. "Oh. Well, he got through it all right. He picked
himself up and survived."

"Yes," Jennie said. *Survived. His nightmares. His silent
spells.* And for the second time that day she found herself staring at the cuff that was finished with the skill that
had kept her father alive, the skill he couldn't bear to
remember.

She glanced back at Mrs. Mendes, who had begun on
another subject. You have no heart, she thought.

The servant was placing before her a plate on which
lay a doily and a bowl of ice cream; on either side of the
bowl were a spoon and an implement that she had never
seen before. It seemed to be a cross between a fork and a
spoon. Having no idea what to use, she was hesitating
when, without changing his expression, the man placed
his forefinger almost surreptitiously on the handle of the
curious implement. All at once she remembered having
heard about such a thing as an ice-cream fork and knew
that was what it must be. She wished she could thank the
man and decided to do so if ever there should be an
opportunity. He had seen her bewilderment. She
thought, He knows more about me than does anyone
else in this room except Peter. I do not like it here. It's
colder than the ice cream.

But the ice cream was different from any she had ever
had, with possibly a trace of honey in it, and some sort of

tart liqueur. She ate it slowly, finding an odd comfort in its smoothness, as if she were a child with a lollipop.

After dinner Peter showed her the grounds. Beyond the tennis court lay an oversize pool shaped like an amoeba and seeming as natural as a pond. A pretty, rustic poolhouse faced it. Groups of pink wrought-iron chairs and tables under flowered umbrellas stood about on the perfect grass. Peter turned on some lights so that the pool shone turquoise out of the dusk. Jennie stood quite still, looking into the gleam, past it to the shadowy shrubs, beyond them to the distant black trees, and heard the silence.

"I didn't know you lived like this," she said at last. "I don't know what to feel, what to think."

"Think nothing. Does it matter how I live? Does it?"

"I suppose not."

"Is it important?"

He was standing so near that she could feel, or imagine that she felt, the warmth of his beloved body. Of course it wasn't important. What mattered was Peter, not what he owned or didn't own. Yet there was something . . .

"You agreed with them about Vietnam."

"I didn't, really. I just didn't disagree."

"It's the same thing."

"No. Think about it."

"I'm thinking."

"Well, it's to keep the peace, and I hate arguments. What would have been the point in starting a long one that would only end as it began? We'd all keep our opinions. And you saw how it was in there."

She considered that. Yes, it was true. At home there were subjects better left alone. No quarreling with Pop, for instance, about the old-fashioned custom of separating women from men in the synagogue. Pop knew it was right because it had been ordained, and nobody was going to change his mind, so there was no point in trying.

Yes, Peter was right. He had peaceable ways, as when he had turned the subject away from Aunt Lee when his father was so angry. It was one of the things she loved about him.

"I wish we could sleep together," he said. "The poolhouse would be so great. There's a sofa."

"Peter! We can't. I wouldn't dare."

"I know. Oh, well, we'll be back home soon."

It pleased her that he spoke of school, the place where they were together, as "home." Then she thought of something else.

"You didn't tell me there was going to be a dance. I would have brought a dress."

"I didn't know. I have this ridiculous cousin. . . . For God's sake, who gives formal dances these days?"

"Apparently people still do."

"I hate them."

"But what'll I do? I've nothing to wear."

Peter looked at her doubtfully. "Nothing?"

"Only this suit, my good dark blue silk that I always wear, and some skirts and shirts. I don't even want to go. Do we have to? I suppose we do." Her voice trailed away.

"We'll ask my mother. She might have something to lend you."

"I can't do that."

"I'll ask her. Come inside. Come on in now."

"Oh, dear," said Mrs. Mendes, "you're sure you haven't brought a thing?"

Jennie shook her head. As if there were some secret compartment in her suitcase from which, if she looked hard enough, she could turn up a formal gown and slippers!

"I hate to be such a bother," she said.

"No bother at all. Let me go upstairs and see what

Sally June has in her closet. Of course, you're taller than she is, but still— Oh, dear," she repeated.

Sally June and her friend were sprawled on the twin beds. Mrs. Mendes opened the closet where hung a long row of clothing and racks of shoes. "We'll have to borrow one of your dresses, Sally June. Jennie hasn't brought one."

"Not the blue eyelet. I'm wearing that."

"Of course not."

Mrs. Mendes regarded Jennie with a measuring eye and took a dress from the closet. "This is floor-length on Sally June. It will probably be ankle-length on you. Try it and let's see."

She felt naked, with the three others watching her in silence as she got out of her suit and into the dress. It was white cotton, soft as a handkerchief, with a deep ruffle off the shoulders and another one at the hem. The short puffed sleeves were laced with ribbons and bows. It was a little girl's party dress, just barely passable for a girl of fourteen. On Jennie it was ridiculous. Dismayed, she regarded herself in the full-length mirror.

"A charming dress," said Mrs. Mendes. "We had it made for Sally June's birthday. But she's been gaining weight." She wagged a finger at her daughter. "It fits you perfectly, though," she said to Jennie. "Pretty, isn't it?"

"Very," Jennie said, and thought, Mom would laugh her head off if she could see me in this.

"Your bra straps show, but you can pin them back. And shoes. What size do you wear?"

"Seven and a half." What will she bring out, Mary Janes?

"Oh, dear, Sally June wears six." The shoes, white kid slippers with low curved heels, were acceptable, except that they were a size and a half too small and set up an instantaneous shock of pain.

"Do they hurt?" asked Mrs. Mendes.

"Yes, some. Yes, they do."

"Well, my feet are even smaller, so I guess you'll just have to manage." At the door she remembered something else. "I have a bag I can lend you. Fortunately it's unseasonably warm, so you won't need a wrap."

Jennie, emerging from under the ruffle, caught sight of the girls lying on the twin beds and silently giggling. Sally June's eyes slid away as soon as she met Jennie's. Strange that the same beautiful eyes, which were so kind and mild in her brother's face, could be so cold and mocking in hers!

She put her suit back on and folded the dress over her arm. "Thank you," she said quietly. "I'm sorry to have bothered you with this."

"I don't mind at all," Sally June told her.

They despise me. I don't look queer, I have manners as good as theirs, and a hell of a lot more heart, Jennie thought. But they despise me all the same.

The cousin's home out in the country had ample land around it, fields, and a brook with a bridge, but the house was very like the Mendeses', even to the portrait of the same ancestor over the mantel.

Mrs. Mendes, standing next to Jennie, whispered, "You recognize the portrait? He's their great-grandfather, too, but this is a copy. Ours is the original. Somebody allowed them to have a copy made, which I thought a mistake. However . . ." She shrugged and moved on.

Jennie, barely hobbling on her tortured foot, was on her way to the powder room. They were three hours into the party; if her feet hadn't pained so much and she hadn't felt so conspicuous in the foolish dress, she would have enjoyed the spectacle. To her it was just that: a spectacle. The enormous house, the servants, the lanterns on the terrace, the flowers in stone jardinieres, the orchestra, the girls in their beautiful dresses were all theater.

For someone who hated these affairs, Peter was having a surprisingly good time. He had introduced her all around and danced with her so often that she had told him he must pay attention to someone else, certainly to the cousin whose birthday was being celebrated. She had had many partners herself, neat young men with neat faces and neat haircuts, very different from the men she knew at home. Their conversation was different, too, mostly courteous banality. Over their shoulders, as she whirled and turned, she kept glimpsing Peter's laughter and high spirits. But why not? These were his people, and he hadn't seen them since Christmas. So she kept whirling and turning until her feet could tolerate no more and she had to excuse herself.

The powder room was really a little sitting room with mirrors, a couch, and two soft chairs. In one of the chairs an elderly woman sat reading a magazine. Jennie took the shoes off and groaned, rubbing her feet.

"Your heel's blistered," the woman observed. "It's bleeding."

"Oh, God. Blood on Sally June's shoe. That's all I need."

"You seem pretty miserable."

"I am. To add to it, this pin's gotten loose and my strap shows." She wriggled, trying to reach her back.

"Come here, I'll fix it for you."

They stood before the mirror. Jennie saw a stocky woman with graying hair cut like a man's, and a large, egg-shaped face with drooping cheeks. She wore a plain black dress of expensive silk.

"There. The pin's fixed. What're you going to do about your feet?"

"Relieve them a little and then suffer through the rest of the night, I guess. There's nothing else I can do."

"Are you the girl who's visiting Peter?"

"Yes, how did you guess?"

"The accent. Everyone else is from around here. Besides, I heard you were coming. And the dress I remembered from Sally June's party. I thought it was a namby-pamby dress even on her."

Jennie burst out laughing. The words were so apt, and she liked this woman's bluntness, the bright, shrewd eyes that redeemed the homely face.

"It was nice of them to lend it to me, though. I really have no right to complain."

"That's true, you haven't. By the way, I'm Aunt Lee Mendes, the one who gave Cindy a colt for her birthday. I suppose you heard about that." She chuckled.

"Well, yes, it was mentioned."

"I'm sure it was. They all love me in their way, my family, but they feel I'm an odd one, and I daresay I am. However, the colt's a beauty. If your feet weren't killing you and it wasn't so dark, I'd take you out to the stables now and show him to you. To tell you the truth, at the last minute I hated to part with him. I'm crazy about animals. Are you?"

"I would be if I had any room for them. Where I live, there's not even decent space for a dog."

"A fancy apartment in New York, I suppose?"

"No. A row house in Baltimore." Jennie looked squarely at Aunt Lee. And from her mouth came words that she hadn't intended to speak, that were perhaps entirely out of place. For some reason, nevertheless, once she had spoken them, she felt good. "My family's poor."

The woman nodded. "Then I suppose you've never been at a party like this before."

"Frankly, no."

"Feel out of place, do you?"

"A little." She added quickly, "At college we all get

together a lot, and I'm really very friendly—" She stopped, wondering why she was spilling out such personal revelations.

"I see you are. And very determined. Peter isn't, though. You've probably noticed."

They certainly were right about this woman's oddness. Yet maybe one only thought she was odd because most people covered up all the time, and she simply said what she was thinking. It puzzled Jennie.

"No, Peter isn't," Aunt Lee repeated, "but he's the salt of the earth."

"That's what he said about you."

"I'm pleased he did. We're very fond of each other. I remember all our summers at the farm, where he'd spend weeks at a time. I taught him things, real things, taught him to ride a horse, to drive a tractor, to plant and harvest and love the earth. Yes, he's a good boy. Too good for his own good, I sometimes think. Too—obliging. That's the word. Obliging."

Jennie had begun to feel restless. She didn't want to discuss Peter with this strange woman. Wincing, she put on the shoes and said, "I'd better be getting back."

"Yes, you'd better. I'm staying here a little longer. The din from all those talking heads gives me a headache."

Peter came over to her. "Where've you been?" he asked. "I've been looking for you."

"I had to take off my shoes. I met your famous Aunt Lee."

"What did you think of her?"

"Well, she's certainly different. But I liked her, in a way. Do you mind if we don't dance anymore? I really can't."

"Oh, I'm sorry. Your poor feet."

They sat down at a small lace-covered table near the French doors that opened onto the terrace. Music floated in. A waiter brought drinks.

"It's not such a bad night, after all," Peter said.

"You said you couldn't stand formal dances."

"I can't. But one has to make adjustments, do what's expected. . . . Poor baby, you're unhappy about the dress," he said softly.

"I didn't tell you I was."

"There are lots of things about you that you don't have to tell me."

Immediately she was contrite. "I'm sorry. I shouldn't spoil things. The dress really isn't that important."

He took her hand under the table. "You've been uncomfortable with my family. They're not easy to know. They can seem distant. But when you get to know them, you'll see. You'll feel easy with them. I'm sure you will."

He was right. Like a child, she had been fretting inwardly, but nevertheless it had showed.

"We'll have tomorrow to ourselves," he said. "They're all going to a play after dinner, but I told Mother to return our tickets because we already saw the play and it was awful."

"What play?"

"I don't know. I never heard of it."

They laughed, and Jennie's spirits rose as fast as they had fallen.

It was like an evening in full summer. Birds swooped down across the lawn and up again to the topmost branches, catching gnats in midair, calling and twittering, darting and sailing until the fall of night. At last they were still.

"How beautiful it is," Jennie murmured. From the dim house a few lamps glimmered in the downstairs rooms, left on until the family should return. Only the maids' rooms on the third floor were bright. Unlit, the pool lay black as silk, puddled with silver wherever a moonbeam fell. And the two who had been silently gazing into the silver recognized the moment, stood up, and, still without speaking, entered the poolhouse together and closed the door.

She was to look back upon this visit with mixed memories. Love in the poolhouse had been a different experience from love in a motel on a highway with the sound of trucks shifting gears at the intersection. To rise from each other's arms and walk out into the still, sweet night . . . But then there was Mrs. Mendes's farewell to remember.

"So nice to have had you with us," she had said, but her lips had closed on the words with faint dismissal. Or was that just more of Jennie's nervous nonsense? Well, whatever it was, it was a learning experience, she told herself, amused at the schoolteacherish phrase. Now they were both back to their own world on the campus, to work and friends and weekend love. She was seventeen, and life was good.

C H A P T E R

3

One afternoon while working on her term paper for Sociology 101, she happened to glance up from the desk to the calendar. The date jumped up off the page; something crossed her mind. Afterward she could not have said why it should have done so at just that moment, but it did. She looked again at the date, counted back, frowned, and counted again. Her periods often were irregular, so lateness never worried her. Besides, Peter had been very careful, he said. Nevertheless, her heart made a rapid leap before it subsided into a steady hammering.

I'll wait a week, she thought. It's nothing.

She did not mention it to Peter, and she waited more than a week, trying to put it out of her mind. It had always been her way of coping with problems, to admonish herself: Pull yourself together; use your head, not your emotions. Calm, calm. Things have a way of straightening out if you just keep calm.

But one day toward the end of the second week, on her way to buy a pair of sneakers, she passed a doctor's office and on the spur of the moment walked in.

The doctor was a middle-aged, tired-looking man who, with kind consideration, did not look into her face as she spoke. Nor did he ask any personal questions, for which she was grateful. If he had probed, she would have begun to cry in spite of her determination, and probably he understood that. She left a urine specimen, and he promised to call her with the results of the rabbit test.

She paid the woman at the reception desk; then, out on the street, she suddenly began to shake and tremble as reality, as actual possibilities, swept over her. The businesslike exchange of money and the impersonal mask of the receptionist's face had somehow made things seem official. Having no heart to go shopping for sneakers, she went back to study, reading words without knowing what they meant. That night she slept fitfully, bothered by dreams, in one of which a pitiable rabbit came to her with tears in its eyes.

A few days later the telephone brought news of the positive result.

"Would you like to make an appointment now to see the doctor? It's important to start prenatal care at the very beginning, even though you seem to be a healthy young woman."

"Well, not just now. I'll call back."

Carefully she replaced the receiver and sat for a while in a sort of trance. Through the open window came the familiar sounds of life, which was continuing quite without regard to what was happening to Jennie Rakowsky. A voice called, "Bobbee-e-e-e." Somebody dropped a pile of books with a thunderous slam on the stairs outside the door and swore. From the floor above came the tremolo of a harmonica.

She sprang up. Peter would be in the library this afternoon. At once she felt lighter. The weight of fear shifted within her. What was she thinking of? She wasn't alone, for heaven's sake! Peter would know what to do. He'd think of something.

He was at his usual table, with elbows propped and chin in hands, concentrating over a bulky book. She had a glimpse of a diagram embedded in a rectangle of thick text before he looked up in surprise and closed the book.

She smiled. "Hi. You almost through?"

"I can be. What's wrong?"

"Does something have to be wrong for me to stop by?" She was satisfied that her voice had no tremor.

"You don't fool me."

His concern almost broke her resolve. She steadied herself. Be brave and controlled. "Why? Do I look funny or something?" Light. Keep it light. It's not a disaster.

"It's your eyes. Something's happened." He stood up to gather his books and papers. "Come on outside."

They went out into a bright late afternoon. Friends stopped them; they stood under the thick trees along the walk, unable to break away. More people came and walked along, talking of unimportant things, and Jennie's heart began its hammering again. She sensed that Peter was trying to get away from the group, but they were accompanied across the street. Two girls from Jennie's hall passed; they had taken off their sweaters and tied them around their waists; they were eagerly talking; she had been like them only a little while ago.

When finally they were alone, they circled back and sat down on some steps. He put his hand under her chin and turned her face up to his.

"So? Tell me."

Fear flooded back, even under his steady gaze. "You can't guess?"

"I don't think I can."

"I went to the doctor a few days ago." She met his eyes. "Now you can guess."

"Oh. Oh."

She sighed. "Yes. Peter, what are we going to do?" This time her brave voice ended in a kind of wail, and tears sprang, blurring the trees, the grass, and the bricks.

He looked down at his hands, turning them palms up. And she, following his gaze, saw what an intimate thing a hand is. She knew his so well: the long fingers, the narrow white rims on the oval nails, the fine reddish hair on the wrist.

And she waited. A breeze abruptly shook the leaves, sending a shiver of cold down her back. He looked up from his hands.

"It may not even be true."

"It's true."

Her own hands had suddenly come together in a piteous gesture and lay twisted in her lap. Peter reached over and separated them, taking one between his own hands.

"Well, then, we'll just have to do something about it, won't we, if that's so?"

And he smiled. The smile went straight to her heart.

"Like what?" she asked.

"Give me time to think."

Neither of them spoke for a while. The wind came up more strongly, and Jennie clasped her cold arms. She wondered what he might be thinking of. Then he looked at his watch.

"It's six already. Come on, let's go to our spaghetti place. We can think better on a full stomach."

There was no one they knew in the restaurant, and

they got a booth in the rear where they would be unseen.

"I'm not hungry," she said, the familiar menu in hand.

"You have to eat."

A ridiculous expression came into her head: *Eating for two*. She felt like gagging. "I can't, I really can't."

"Just some soup. I'll have the same. I'm not hungry, either."

For a few minutes they sat again without speaking. Jennie managed a few mouthfuls and laid down the spoon.

"God, Jennie, I'm sorry. I feel like a clumsy, ignorant fool. I thought I was being so careful. I was being careful. Dammit, I don't understand."

"Nothing's a hundred percent." It hurt her to see him like this. Only yesterday he had been so carefree, had bought a new guitar and some music. "It's my fault too," she acknowledged. "I mean, I should have kept track. I was careless; I am careless. It's pretty far gone already."

He looked up quickly. "Too far to do anything about it?"

"You mean an abortion?"

"Well, yes. Of course, I would find the best place where it would be safe. My God, I wouldn't let anything happen to you! You must know that."

She sighed again. All afternoon such deep sighs had been rising, as if her lungs needed to be filled. "I couldn't . . . I don't want . . . Regardless of the time, I couldn't, anyway."

Very gently he asked, "Why not? Why couldn't you?"

"I'm not sure." Pop's Orthodoxy? Rooted, after all, in her agnostic head and in spite of her indifference to it?

"So if you're not sure, that means you could. Think about it. It's done all the time."

"I know."

A girl in high school had had an abortion during senior

year. Everybody knew it. She'd gone on to graduate with the class, had gone on with her life as if nothing had changed. And yet Jennie shuddered. Involuntarily her hands went to her hard, flat stomach.

She had no feeling for what was growing in her, no vision of its possibilities. It was an interloper, feared and unwelcome, and yet she couldn't kill it.

Peter saw her gesture. "There's nothing much there, Jennie. An inch or two—maybe less."

But it's life, clinging and fastened. To rip it out and throw it away, a bloody mess . . . Her thoughts trailed off and she raised her eyes to Peter's, which were questioning and troubled.

"You have to believe me, Peter. It's all right for some —I don't judge anybody else—but I just know I can't."

Silence again, while he spooned the soup. Then he raised his head, struck the table lightly with his fist, and made a firm, cheerful mouth.

"What the hell! What's the fuss about? Then we'll be married. That's that!"

A tremendous joy made a huge lump in her throat and almost choked her. A second later it receded in doubt.

"Peter, I wouldn't want to be married to a man who 'had to' marry me and would resent me afterward." At the same time she knew that she was hoping for and counting on a denial.

"Jennie, darling, how could you even have a thought like that, when we're the way we are? It's true this is all the wrong time for it, but we were going to get married eventually, so we'll have to find a way to manage it now. Come on, don't be afraid. I'm here with you." He summoned the waiter. "Bring us dinner, after all. We're hungrier than we thought we were."

And while Jennie listened, letting the words pour comfort like a warm shower, he kept on talking. "Forgive me for what I'm going to say. It sounds like crap, I know, but the fact is—oh, hell, you saw, so why be coy about it? My parents are well off, really well off. Money doesn't mean a thing. I never thought I'd give a damn about that. You know me well enough to know that actually I've sort of been in a mild rebellion against their style of life and some of their ideas, but in a pinch like this"—he grinned—"in a pinch like this it comes in handy."

His confident grin gave wonderful relief. Quickly, calmly, he had accepted her position and adjusted to it. She, who was given not to calmness but to mercurial changes and large gestures, felt the strength in his quiet posture.

"They'll see us through, no doubt of it. Oh, it won't be the most pleasant thing to have to explain, but once all the stiff lectures are over, they'll come through. Listen, we're not the first guys this has happened to, and we won't be the last. Buck up, Jennie, and eat the spaghetti."

A vision took shape in her head, a vision so clear that she could see it in color. There'd be a small apartment, two rooms—maybe even one—off campus; they could go to classes and take turns with the baby. They'd go on to graduate school; she'd pay them back herself once she was a lawyer, pay them back with her own earnings, not Peter's, because she'd want to show them who she was and earn their respect. Yes, she would earn their respect in spite of it all. And when they saw how happy she made their son, they would come to love her.

"I'll get a part-time job in the labs or someplace, work nights and weekends so we won't have to depend on my parents for everything," Peter said.

Visions, then, were already taking shape in his head too. He added, "You'll be going home to tell your parents this weekend, while I fly home." It was partly a statement and partly a question.

Jennie shook her head. "I'll probably go home, but I'm not sure I can tell them before we're married."

How could one hurt them, remembering their past? She had read all the books about children of the Holocaust survivors and heard about the groups that met to advise and learn from one another, although she had never gone to one. It was true, you really did have a different feeling about your parents when you saw pictures of the European terror and knew that the father and mother who sat across the table from you every night talking about household bills and homework had been through all that. They weren't like other people's parents. How could you put their strength again to the test, the strength that surely must be so fragile?

"You're really not going to tell them?" Peter asked, raising his eyebrows.

"Maybe I will. I'm not sure. They're very loving." And she said simply, "You would have to know them to understand."

He asked no more. "Well, I'll talk to my folks. I know they seemed formidable to you." He gave a small, rueful laugh. "My mother's favorite saying is 'Shape up,' and frankly, it's an expression that makes me sick, it's so military. But two things they both respect are frankness and courage. So I'll be frank and they'll be fair. I have to hand it to them—they're absolutely fair, Jennie, they really are." He reached across the table and kissed her fingers. "There isn't a thing in the world to worry about."

He looked so earnest. She hoped they wouldn't put him through too much at home before they got over their first anger.

"Trust me, Jennie."

"I trust you. I always will."

———

"How's Peter?" Mom asked.

"He flew home this weekend."

"So that's why we have the pleasure of your company?" Mom laughed. "Sit down. I just came in from the store. Have a cup of tea before I start dinner."

Beyond the kitchen the dining room was visible, with two plates set and the candlesticks in place, ready for the blessing. On Friday night they ate in the dining room, just the two of them, observing the ritual exactly as if they were surrounded by children and relatives, as Jennie knew they longed to be. She sat down across from her mother at the kitchen table.

"I got beautiful geraniums this year, double pink ones, something new. Look," Mom said.

On the porch railing stood a row of geraniums in pots. A few feet beyond them stood Mrs. Danieli's pots, but her geraniums were the common red. Mom followed Jennie's gaze.

"No comparison, is there?" she asked.

"No, Mom." The question touched her. Almost anything these last few days since the scene in the restaurant with Peter could have brought her to foolish tears: a Dylan Thomas poem read in English class, or an old wife helping her old husband onto the train in Philadelphia. Now it was the geraniums, the meager flowers stretching toward the sun. She felt a swelling in her throat. Foolish. Mom expected conversation. Unlike Pop, she needed to fill every silence. Besides, there was something Jennie wanted to know.

"So how's everybody on the block? The Danielis? The Dieters?"

"Oh, the Danielis are fine, happy about the baby. Not like the Dieters down the street," Mom said darkly.

Jennie wanted to talk about the Dieters. Gloria Dieter had "gotten in trouble" last year and was back home with her unwanted baby.

"Are they treating her any better than they did?"

Mom shrugged. "I don't know. People hardly ever see them. They hide in the house. Gloria puts the carriage on the porch and runs inside."

With a shaking voice Jennie spoke softly. "It's not as if she'd robbed a bank or killed somebody."

And she waited for an answer. . . .

"True, true. But these are crazy times. I don't know." Mom took up the folded newspaper. "Look at the stuff you read! It makes you sick. What has the Vietnam war got to do with the way these kids behave, I ask you? It's a bad war, but what has free sex got to do with it, I ask you? A disgrace. Look, look at this!" It was an article about a well-known activist who was pregnant. "Look at her! Not married, having a baby, and proud of it! Proud of it, mind you. A college girl with all that education, but when you come down to it, behind all the fancy talk, what is she?"

Jennie was silent.

"Oh, but I pity the parents! You work with all your heart to make a good life for your children, and this is what you get for it?" Mom shook her head, commiserating with the unknown parents. Then, sighing deeply, she allowed her face to brighten. "Thank God your father and I don't have such worries about you. You're a good girl, Jennie, and always have been. Do you know, you've never given us one minute's trouble since you were born, God bless you?"

Jennie said, very low, "But things can happen to what you call 'good girls' too. What should a mother do—I mean, I'm just being curious—what would you do, for instance, if I came home like that girl and told you I was—" Her own little cracked laugh brought her to a stop.

"My God, I can't even think of such a thing, so how can I answer? A girl like you, to wreck her own life?"

If I could tell you, put my head on your shoulder and tell you, what a relief it would be—

"You'd throw me out, I guess. Out the door." And she forced a laugh, a convincing one this time, meaning, Of course, all this is ridiculous.

"Throw you out the door? Who throws a daughter out the door? But I'd rather die myself, I'll tell you that." Mom took off her glasses, revealing the soft, remote expression that came upon her plain face whenever she spoke of her murdered parents, of her wedding day, or of the day when Jennie was born. "It would mean that everything we ever taught you went past your ears. Deaf ears, it would mean; wasted words. All the years, the way we live, thrown out like garbage. Oh, come on, what kind of sad, crazy talk is this? Have a dish of ice cream with me. I've got a sudden yen for coffee chip."

So it's quite clear what I can expect, Jennie thought. The ice cream slid down her throat, giving no pleasure. She had a recollection of herself at the Mendeses' table eating ice cream; there, too, there had been a feeling of detachment from the others in the room. Here, though, the reason was hardly the same. She could almost feel how it was to stand in Masha-Marlene's shoes, to be of her generation, with her past and her memories in her head. One had to understand.

On Monday, back at school waiting for Peter's return, she had reassuring thoughts. When we're married, even though the baby will be arriving early, it will be different. Mom and Pop will be happy for me. What parents wouldn't be pleased to see their daughter married to someone like Peter? It will be fine, then, when we're properly married.

He was not there for Monday's classes, nor for Tuesday's. Was that a good sign or a bad one? A good sign. Naturally there would be arrangements to make.

Late Wednesday afternoon the telephone rang at the end of the hall, and Jennie was summoned.

"I'm back," Peter said.

Her heart sprang high. "And what happened?"

"I'll tell you when I see you." His voice was flat, without answering joy.

Her heart sank. It was an organ that might as well have gone floating around her body for all the stability it had; sometimes it even went down into her feet.

"I've rented a car. I'll pick you up in ten minutes."

"Rented a car! Where are we going?"

"Just to have a place to talk. There's never any private place around here where some jerk won't interrupt."

"That's silly—" she began.

"Ten minutes." He hung up.

A drenching rain blew in the wind. She got her raincoat and was waiting at the door when Peter drove up. She got into the car and saw his solemn face. When he moved to kiss her, she turned her lips so that his met her cheek.

She knew, she knew.

"Give me the bad news," she said.

"It isn't necessarily bad news. Why do you say that?"

"Because I can tell. Don't play with me, Peter. Give me the whole story straight out."

He started the car. "Let me find a quiet street to park on, and we can talk."

On a side street, in front of a row of quiet homes, he stopped the car. In the now torrential rain, the street was deserted. When the motor was shut off, there was no sound except the rain clattering on the car roof, spattering the windows. It was a desolate sound.

"Well, Peter?"

"They don't want us to get married now." He looked not at her but straight ahead through the windshield.

Her mouth went dry. "No? What do they want, then?"

"They think, they say, we're too young."

"That's true. We are." She spoke steadily. "But what about . . . shall we call it our little complication? Or isn't that important?"

He turned to her now. In the gray half-light she could see a pleading expression. "Jennie, don't be sarcastic. Please, I've had a hell of a time."

She was instantly tender, responding to his need. "I'm sorry. But what about it? What are we to do?"

"They think you should . . . get rid of it. I explained how you feel about that, but you know—you know, it does make sense, Jennie. I've thought it over. They convinced me. It really does make sense."

"They convinced you," she repeated. *"They* think it makes sense. While I am the one at the center of it all. What do they, or you, have to do with my body, with *me?"*

"Jennie, darling, listen. You can't imagine what it was like. Such anger. It took me two days to get us all to stop ranting and to talk. My mother was in tears. I never saw her like that except when her own mother died." And he repeated, "You can't imagine."

"Oh, yes, I can imagine, but what difference does it make? They're telling me what to do with my own body." She began to cry. "Peter, I told you I can't bring myself to do that. I don't want a baby, I don't love it, but I told you—and I'm telling you again—I can't kill it."

"But think! In a few years we'll be married and have as many babies as you like. You want to finish college and go to law school, don't you? Where's the money to come from if we get married now?"

"You said they were rich and they'd help. You said so."

"Well, I thought so. But I can't squeeze something out of them that they won't give, can I?" For a second he put his head down on the rim of the steering wheel. "Oh, Christ!" he groaned. He turned back to her. "My father's willing to give whatever you need to take care of it. And more. Anything you want, he said. Take a trip to Europe. Rome. Paris. Buy things. Rest yourself and get over it. As much as you want, he'll give you."

Then Jennie was shaken by a rage such as she had never known. It was a killing rage; she could have killed. And she pounded the dashboard.

"What does he think I am? A slut to be paid off? Europe? Do you know what you're saying? He offers me a vacation . . . what do I want with a vacation when I'm asking for love, for help, to be accepted—"

"Jennie! You have love! I love you, you know I do. How can you talk like this?"

"How can *you*, unless they've convinced you too? Am I a slut to you too?"

"Don't use that word. It's nasty. It stinks."

"Don't tell me what words to use! I'll use whatever words I want. I'll tell you right now what happened there. I can hear it and I can see it as clearly as if I'd been hiding behind the door. Your mother, that icicle . . . You think I don't know what she wants? A girl like that snippy kid—what was her name? Annie Ruth or Ruth Annie or something? 'We've been friends for generations, you know. And isn't it just lovely that the young people are engaged? A secret romance—we never guessed.' Yes, it would be a different story if I were Miss Old Family instead of Miss Nobody. There'd be no talk of abortion, just a quick wedding under the trees in your garden. No, pardon me, in Miss Old Family's garden. I'm sure they'd have one. And the baby would be a seven-month, such a darling—" Her voice had risen in outrage.

"God, Jennie, don't! It's not like that at all!"

"Of course it is! Any idiot can see it. I knew it the moment I walked in the door. And you—you let yourself be brainwashed. You, the big, brave man who was going to take care of me. 'Don't worry, darling, I'll take care of everything.' "

Peter turned the ignition key, and the windshield wipers began to clack.

"There's no sense going on like this if you're only going to scream at me, Jennie. We have a problem, and screaming won't help."

Her nerves snapped. "Shut those damn wipers off, will you? I can't hear myself think."

When he obeyed, she sat for a moment, bringing herself under control. Then she remembered something.

"Did you by any chance see your Aunt Lee?"

"Yes, I went to her."

"Ah! And she said?"

"I'll tell you. She said we should get married. She liked you. She said she'd lend us some money."

"She did?" Jennie's eyes filled. "Why, that's absolutely wonderful of her!"

"Well, she's like that. Romantic under the crust. Funny for a Lesbian, when you think about it."

"That's a cruel thing to say."

"I didn't mean it to be cruel. It's just the way it strikes me."

"Will she lend us enough to get by?"

"Jennie . . . I can't take anything from her, no matter how little or how much. My parents would be furious. They were furious when I told them."

"Why? If they don't want to help, I should think they'd be glad to have somebody else do it for them."

"It's a long story. She has a tendency to interfere. I shouldn't even have said anything about it."

"To them or to me?"

He sighed. "To either, I guess."

But he had told her, had been honest enough to tell her, and she softened.

"Oh, Peter, what are we going to do?"

The windshield wipers echoed, *To do, to do, to do.* He turned the key again and the wipers stopped.

"What are we going to do?" she repeated.

"I don't know." He was staring out at the rain.

Gloom seeped into the car. Her swift, furious outburst had left her tired. If I could just go to sleep, she thought, just sleep and wake up with all of this gone away. And she, too, stared out onto the black, wet street. The walls of the houses that faced one another on either side made a tunnel out of the street, a long, dark tunnel with no light at the end.

Peter spoke into the silence. "If you would have the abortion, it would solve everything."

She had that picture again, the red picture, the color of blood, the sharp, steely flash, the destruction. She gasped.

"Is it that you're afraid?" he asked, gently now.

"Afraid of pain? You know it's not that."

A few years ago she'd had a compound fracture of the arm and had borne the pain bravely, they told her. She knew she had. Besides, giving birth was hardly painless.

"What, then? Can you really tell me?"

"I have told you as best I can."

"It's done all the time. Quite safely. Even though it's illegal. There are safe places. Competent doctors."

Wearily she repeated, "Maybe it's the way I was brought up. I can't do it. My parents are Orthodox—"

Now Peter interrupted. It was his turn to be angry. "Your parents! You can't even talk to them about it! You're afraid to talk to them. At least I was able to talk to mine."

"I've told you that too."

Mom in the kitchen, scooping the ice cream: "Everything we taught you, all thrown out like garbage."

Jennie's anger rose again. "You don't want to understand. I can't talk about it to my parents. Why don't we get married, Peter? We could manage somehow. Your father would have to help. He couldn't let us starve. My parents would do something, too, some little something—"

"My father would tell me to quit college and go to work."

"He wouldn't!"

"Wouldn't he? You don't know. He has principles."

"Principles! How can they possibly justify themselves?"

"I'll tell you. They'll say that if a man is old enough to father a child, he's old enough to support it."

"That's what they did say, isn't it? And you believed them."

"You have to admit it makes sense."

"Sense, yes, but no heart. There's no heart. Cold, cold moneybags," she said, clenching her teeth. "Yes, if my father didn't own a delicatessen . . . You think I didn't see your mother's face when I told her? A face like a shark."

"Jennie, that's far enough. Leave my mother out, please."

Loyalty, after all this. Loyalty to his mother. She felt choked.

"How can I leave her out when she's in control of my life?"

"No, we were in control of our own lives, Jennie."

"How can you talk like that? What have they done, how did they brainwash you? Well, maybe they've managed to make you feel like dirt, but I don't feel like dirt, I can tell you. I don't, I won't, and they can't make me. Neither can you."

"This is a stupid conversation." He started the engine. "You're all wrought up, and we're getting no place fast."

"Stupid is right. Take me back to the dorm."

She wanted to hit him. Was this Peter? Where were

the strength and the smiling confidence? She had relied on him, but the soft, appealing opal eyes with which she had fallen in love were, perhaps, too soft. "Too obliging," the old lady had said. He was only a scared boy. . . . And she was lost.

Neither spoke until they drew up before the dorm. Then he laid his hand on her shoulder.

"Jennie, take it easy. We're both beside ourselves. That's why we're quarreling. I'm going to phone my father tonight and talk to him again."

She pulled away and opened the door. "Good luck," she said bitterly.

"Don't be bitter. We'll work out something. Please. Believe in me."

She mustered a small smile. "Okay, I'll try."

"I'll call you after I've talked to him tonight, okay?"

"No, wait till the morning. I'm exhausted. I want to sleep and not have to think about anything for a few hours."

"All right. First thing tomorrow, then. And, Jennie, remember that we love each other."

Maybe I'm being unfair, after all, she thought as she trudged upstairs. It's awful for him too. She was so tired, just so tired.

All the next week she cried silently at night and woke heavy-headed, forcing herself to go to class and study. It was like waiting for a train or a plane so long delayed that one begins to think it may not be coming at all. Peter was in the same condition. Every day he consulted his father, who needed to consult with others.

"His lawyer, probably," Peter said. "He never moves a step without lawyers."

Every day he met Jennie briefly, always in a public place where they were never able to touch each other. Neither of them was in the mood for it, anyway. But the mute appeal in each one's face was reflected in the other's.

"Are you feeling all right?" he kept inquiring.

She was perfectly well. There was no hint of any change in her body. She would probably go close to the end of term without showing.

By the second week Peter had news. His father had arranged for a place in Nebraska, a respectable, church-run home for unwed mothers. It sounded like something out of the nineteenth century; Jennie hadn't known that such places still existed. But apparently they did, and a girl would be anonymous there, cared for until she gave birth, at which time, if she wished, the baby would be given up for adoption.

"How does that sound?" Peter asked.

They were in a car again, parked this time outside of the zoo. A woman, passing by, was trying to comfort a squalling baby in a carriage while a toddler pulled at her skirt. This image fled across Jennie's eyes and printed itself in her head after the woman had turned the corner and gone from sight. The image was soft and blurred, all curves in the flicker of light under new leaves. The mother, her long hair drooping like a loosened scarf, bent over the infant; the child's round, strong head butted against the mother's red skirt; it was an image of unity.

And she knew that this was one of the rare random pictures that she would keep, as she had kept the face of the most beautiful woman she had ever seen, while riding on a streetcar at least five years before. Or the morning when, through the silence of a street thick-muffled in snow, there had come the sudden clamor of church bells, and she had stood until the last vibration ceased.

Peter asked again, "How does that sound?"

She could barely open her lips, so great was the tiredness that lay on her.

"I'm thinking."

The same thoughts ran over the same track. The little flat could be furnished so cheaply; the bedroom things could even be brought from her room at home; they'd need, then, only a table and two chairs for meals; a desk and lamps for studying; the baby furniture; and some yellow paint, a sunshine color for the corner where the baby would sleep; it would take so little. . . .

But he didn't want to. I suppose I could force him, she thought. It's been done often enough, God knows. Yet to live like that, begrudged . . . To bring up a child like that . . . Surely the child would come to feel it.

"Have you thought?" He took her hand. "Your hand's so cold. Poor Jennie. Oh, poor Jennie."

She began to cry. All this time she had been able to keep her tears for the privacy of her bed, but now suddenly they came in a gush, an explosion of tears.

He put her head on his shoulder. "Darling, darling," he whispered, kissing her hair. "I'm so sorry. What a stupid bastard I am to put you through all this. Jennie, we'll have babies, I keep telling you. You'll be a lawyer and we'll have a home. We'll have everything we want. It'll be better for the baby, darling, don't you see that? To be in a wonderful family—so many couples can't have children and want them so much, older couples, ready to take proper care of a child. We just aren't ready yet, don't you see that?"

He held her close, repeating himself as if to reinforce what he had already told her a dozen times or more.

A wonderful family, she thought. Ready to take proper care. That's not like killing, is it? That's life. Giving life. It seemed now that she could feel the life moving in the pit of her body, although that was, of course, absurd, since it would be months before she would feel anything. Yet it was *there*.

After a long while her weeping subsided with a long, deep, final sigh.

"I suppose it will have to do. Yes. Adoption," she murmured.

"We'll handle it this way," Peter said at once. "You're due around the first of November, you say. You can go out there whenever you think best. I don't know what excuse you'll make at home or how to explain that you won't be coming back here for the start of the semester, but you'll think of something."

"Yes, I'll think of something," she said wanly.

"Maybe you could say you're taking a special course out there or have some sort of scholarship in French or something. I don't know. I don't suppose—I mean, would your parents know about special courses or anything like that?"

"You know they wouldn't."

"Then you could get away with it?"

"Yes. Yes."

"And, Jennie—you'll be back here for the second half of the year. We'll be together again."

So they spoke. And so, out of necessity, there was a mending. Amid the rush of final examinations, at brief intervals they clung to each other, reassuring themselves that all was as it had been, all was well. Then came separation: Peter home to Georgia and Jennie home to Baltimore. He was to come back before the start of the new semester to see her off to Nebraska.

By late summer when Jennie's time for departure came, she had gained a little weight, which pleased her mother.

"See how beautiful you look with a little weight on? Now don't start to diet again, will you?" And she said, "I hope you're doing the right thing, making this transfer. I don't know anything about college credits, but I do know about men. I mean, when you've got a boyfriend like Peter, it does seem crazy to leave him. I know it's only for a few months, but still," she said, while pressing Jennie's miniskirt, which was already too tight at the waist.

Pop looked up from the newspaper. "Jennie will have ten boyfriends in love with her before she's married, don't worry."

In Pop's eyes she was a miracle of beauty and brains. She was perfection.

And she said gently, "Yes, Pop, Mom, don't worry about me. I'm fine."

Her mother looked up. Hairline creases bunched on her forehead between her eyebrows.

"I worry. Who can help worrying about a child? You'll find out when you have one." She looked old. "I love you, Daughter."

There was such a sore, hard lump in Jennie's throat that she had to turn away and bend over the suitcase.

"I love you, too, Mom. I love you both."

Peter and Jennie met in Philadelphia the day before the plane was to leave. He rented another car, and they drove out in late afternoon beyond City Line Avenue, onto the highway, and to the motel where they had first made love. In a dismal fast-food restaurant across the road, they ate a rather silent supper. He held a hamburger between shaking hands, then put it down half-eaten, as if he were unable to swallow.

"You all right, Jennie?"

"I'm fine. Just fine."

"Maybe I'd better give you the tickets and all the papers now, before I drop them or something. Here, put them in your bag. Everything's there, the bankbook and the cash. There should be plenty. The place—the home —has been all paid for, so you don't need to lay out a thing. This is just for you."

She glanced at the bankbook. Five thousand dollars had been deposited.

"This is ridiculous," she said. "It's much more than I'll need. I want a couple of maternity skirts and that's it. I can wear my own blouses without fastening the bottom button."

He was staring at the wall behind her. She had embarrassed him. Maternity clothes were too intimate for him, who knew every part of her body.

How awfully young he is! she thought, feeling tall and taut, mature and proud.

"There's more if you need it," he said, ignoring her objection. "That's one thing about my father. He's generous, and always has been."

Generous. Without a visit, a letter, even a telephone call in acknowledgment of the situation, or of her very existence as a human being.

"You have the address at home, of course. You're to get in touch if you need anything. Anything at all."

"I told you, I won't need anything."

"You never know. I wish you would take more, but you said it was insulting."

"And so it would be." She sat up straighter. "Will you get me another glass of milk? I haven't had my quota today."

He flushed. "Of course."

So the prenatal diet was an embarrassment to him too. Strange. Well, not strange when you think about it, she realized as her hand clasped the tumbler. She, after all, was the one who had to feed this—this *person*. Just then the person moved within her, rippling, stretching its arms or legs, making itself more comfortable. She smiled.

He caught the smile. "What is it?"

"It moved."

"Oh. I didn't know."

"Yes, they move. It's what's called 'feeling life.' "

He bent his head, feeling miserable.

"You don't show anything yet," he observed after a minute.

"I'm carrying small, the doctor said."

"Is that good?"

"Yes, it's good."

"I'm glad."

"I need some dessert."

"Of course."

"Just fruit. A baked apple, if they have one."

He sat there watching her eat the apple. She was thinking that she would remember this moment, this hour, the way the chill seeped into the room with the sound of thunder and approaching storm, the way the light speckled the dirt on the windows as the daylight faded. . . . A man stood up and got a bun from under a glass dome on the counter. Philadelphia sticky buns, they were called. He put his feet up on the heavy sales-man's case next to his chair. She heard his sigh. He looked a little like Pop.

"It's going to storm in a minute," Peter said. "We'd better make a run for the room before lightning strikes."

There stood the bed, wide enough for three, with a hideous pea-green spread on it. The television faced the bed. Its huge blank eye stared into the dingy room. It hadn't seemed dingy like this the first time. Yet it must have been.

But all we saw then, all we felt, Jennie thought, was the burning and the haste. It didn't matter where we were. He unbuttoned my dress, my red wool, bought new for the occasion. He took off my shoes and un-hooked my bra in that order. I remember everything, how the clothes fell and how I stood there feeling proud because of the look on his face. I remember everything.

"Shall I turn on the TV? Anything you want to see?" he asked now.

"Not especially. Just if you want to."

"Well, it's too early to go to sleep."

"I'll take a hot shower. I'm suddenly freezing."

"Summer's just about over, I guess."

It was strange that such simple, declarative sentences were all it seemed either of them could summon to express the feeling that should have been boiling in them.

They'd lost what they had. At least *she'd* lost it. Where had it gone, the love? Frozen. Did that mean it would thaw again?

Huddled on the bed in her bathrobe, Jenny watched a play on public television. It was one of those fine English productions with marvelous actors and exquisite scenery, all lanes, fields, old stone houses with portraits, fires under great carved mantels, and big black retrievers stretched out in front of the fires. Secure and solid. Did people ever feel lost and lonely in such places?

Half of her mind watched it, and half of it watched Peter. The bright light of the television screen gleamed in the darkened room and glinted on his face. She thought again, He's so young. Too young to have faced his family down. I'm older inside than he is. Why? Is a woman always the older one? So many questions without answers! What difference does it make? It is the way it is. We are what we are. He's under his family's thumb. But then, so am I, although for other reasons. It's 1969, and people like us are doing things that were scarcely heard of ten years ago. Maybe those people who do whatever they want to do without fear, without shame, all come from what they call "liberal" families who've trained them that way. I don't know. At any rate, there are more like us than like them. They're only the ones who get written about.

The play was over.

"Beautiful," Peter said. "The English know how to do it, don't they?" And he said, "Someday we'll go to England. You'll love it all, the Cotswolds, the Lake District, the moors."

In bed, he put his arms around her, and she knew he was waiting for a response. She laid her head against his chest. A few cold tears ran down over her temples and stopped. Not only grief, but also desire, had ended within her, and only a numbness remained. Stress did that. Pregnant women, she had read, felt desire as much as ever. In normal circumstances they would. Looking forward together, being together, staying together.

She was shivering again. He stroked her hair. "Jennie, Jennie, it will be fine. You'll come back and everything will be the same."

He had already said that so many times! And she had believed, had wanted to believe. Now, suddenly, she knew it would never be the same. She couldn't have said how she knew that everything was all over and finished. Did he really believe they would see England or anything else together? She supposed that he did because he wanted to believe it.

But when something is dying, one shouldn't prolong the pain. Fear wounded what we had. Now let it die in peace.

He held her. They held each other. And after a while they fell asleep.

In the morning he took her to the plane. Going down the ramp after the final embrace, she turned to look. His lips moved to say: *I'll write*. His hand went up with a little wave, meant to encourage and cheer.

She knew she would never see him again.

The house, once a rich man's fine Georgian home, was spacious, with spreading wings. Jennie's room was one of the best, a single room overlooking a sea of autumn trees, oaks and maples, red and gold. One window faced a side driveway so that she was able to watch the arrival and departure of the girls—and some of them were really girls, no older than fourteen—who like herself had come here to hide. She noted the Lincolns, Cadillacs, and Mercedeses, the well-dressed parents, the expensive luggage. This place must cost a fortune. But then, Peter's parents were generous, weren't they?

On the first night she was so overcome with loneliness that she had to pull her hand back from the telephone. She had begun to dial the number at home. In her mind's ear she heard herself crying, "Mom! Pop! Help me, I want to tell you the truth." And thought then of Pop's blood pressure, his kidneys, money, the rent at the store, how they would manage if he became too sick to work. . . . And thought, I must get through this alone.

But strong resolve did not suffice. She woke that first day to find herself encompassed by a thick, gray, muffling cloud that muted the sunlight. She wanted only to stay in bed with the covers pulled over her head, and had to force herself to get up. Where was the courage that, up until now, had stiffened her? She was cold with nonspecific, nameless fears. The future was void. After the child was born, who would Jennie be? What kind of a person, with what purpose?

The chilly web of gloom still clinging, she went through the expected motions. It was a good place and people were kind. No one asked questions. Some of the young women, waiting, wanted to chat with her about themselves, while others kept their silence. As she looked around in the dining room Jennie thought, Everyone here has essentially the same story, and still it is different each time. Variations on a theme.

Peter wrote to her. The letters were filled with assurances and admonitions to take care of herself; they were marked with Xs; they might as well have said nothing.

She answered with banalities: "The place is nice, the food is good, I am well." And these words also added up to nothing. When the fourth or fifth letter came, it seemed too much of an effort to answer it.

During the second week she was sent to a counselor. Mrs. Burt was a purposeful young woman with an array of diplomas behind her desk. After the first visit, which was taken up with practical concerns—the doctor, the birth, and the proposed adoption—Jennie ventured to confess.

"Is it terrible of me not to answer his letters? It seems so useless." And she said, "I don't understand what's happened. Where has love gone? I wanted to spend the rest of my life with him. I would have died for him. And now . . ." She put her face in her hands.

"It's all right to cry," said Mrs. Burt.

But Jennie's eyes were dry. "I don't cry anymore. I've done all that. This is worse. I feel as if nothing matters at all. I've even stopped thinking about the baby, and I'd been so careful to eat well and make it healthy. Now I don't feel hungry, and I don't even try to eat."

"Maybe nothing else matters to you just now, but *you* matter." The voice was both gentle and positive. *"You* are really all you have, do you know that, Jennie? The *me* —that's all anyone of us has. Because if that falls apart, then there's nothing left for us to give to anybody else. Now, if you don't want to write or talk to anyone, the decision is yours, and you're entitled to it without guilt."

Jennie looked up. Maybe if Mom had been like this, she could have told her the truth. But then, this little American lady surely hadn't had Mom's wounds, hadn't lost her parents in the gas ovens or fled across the Pyrenees with strangers. So leave Mom out.

She said only, "Thank you."

"You're a mass of guilt about everything, Jennie— about why you're here in the first place. And about your parents, your interrupted education, the whole bit. And anger—you're seething with it, though you don't want to admit it. But recognize that you've a right to be angry! It's why you're depressed."

"You can tell I'm depressed?"

"Of course, my dear. I've surely seen enough depression in this place. Depression is anger turned inward. Did you know that, Jennie?"

"I didn't."

"Well, it is. Now, if yours doesn't lift very soon, we'll get some help for you. But I have a hunch it will. You're tough. You'll make it."

And in time it did lift. One morning when Jennie awoke, the cloud was gone. Whether it would return was open to question, but for now it was gone. She raised the window and looked out with pleasure at early winter, at snow-covered hemlock and spruce, at juncos fluttering on the bird feeder. She felt an appetite for breakfast and for a walk in the cold, brisk air. Many of the girls at the home, including Jennie, avoided the shopping center because they feared being stared at by people who would guess where they came from. This morning she didn't mind.

"This is a time to be used, not wasted," Mrs. Burt had advised. "Why don't you get some books and read ahead on the subjects you'll be taking when you go back to school in February?"

So she made her first withdrawal from the fund that the Mendeses had put in a local bank. With it she went to browse in a bookstore and came back to put Sandburg's *Lincoln* and Tennessee Williams's plays, along with a fat new novel, on her dresser, there to be gazed at and cherished because they didn't have to be returned to a library. Then she sat down with a box, not a bar, of chocolates and began to read.

Peter wrote again with the news that he was transfer-

ring to Emory University in Atlanta in February. He
didn't understand why she hadn't written in so long. She
must please let him know whether anything was wrong.

Transferred. To keep him away from her, from further
contamination. So his family could keep an eye on him.
She tried to imagine their conversations. At the shining
table in the dining room? No, Spencer, the servant,
would be there, and they wouldn't talk in front of him.
Perhaps in front of the fireplace, under the ancestor's
portrait. Or in the room with the flowered carpet, talking sense into their son. Poor boy. She felt contempt for
them all.

Could he really believe, as he had said, that they
would be back together someday and go on after this as
though nothing had happened to change them? Yes,
maybe he really could believe; it was much more comforting that way.

Now Jennie's time drew nearer. As she thought less
and less about the baby's father, she began to think more
about the baby and about all the babies in this house who
were waiting to be born and given away. All was accident! From their very conception to the moment they
were turned over to strangers, whose pasts they would
inherit and whose benefits would shape them, all was
chance. But then, didn't chance also govern those who
were not given away?

One morning she was summoned to Mrs. Burt and
greeted by a smile of unusual pleasure.

"We have a couple who want to take your baby, Jennie. We think they're wonderful people, really perfect.
Do you want to hear about them?"

Jennie folded her arms on her little, pointed belly,
which looked like the narrow end of a watermelon.
Something moved under her palms, thumped lightly,
and rippled away. A warning, a reminder, a plea?

Mrs. Burt must have read her silent lips, crying, *No, I*

can't . . . can't part from you. God, tell me how I can, for her look was keen.

"Are you sure you want to talk about this right now? We don't have to if you don't feel like it."

But you have to feel like it, don't you? There can't be any going back. Back where? Oh, you don't want to do it, Jennie, but you know it's best; you've gone over it a thousand times.

She raised her head, straightened her slumped shoulders, and spoke clearly. "Please go ahead. Tell me."

"He's a doctor. She's a librarian and plans to retire for a few years until the child is of school age. They're not yet thirty, but they've been married for seven years without a pregnancy. They have a loving relationship. They travel and ski and hike in the mountains." Mrs. Burt paused.

"Go on," said Jennie. A librarian. There will be books in the house.

"We try to match the child to the home, as you know, with the same intellectual background and physical appearance if we can. These people both have your dark hair. Hers is curly like yours. They're of medium height and healthy, of course. They're both Jewish. Do you want to hear more?"

"Please."

"They live in the Far West. The home is very fine, not a rich one, but the child will want for nothing. There's a large yard, a good school, and a warm extended family of grandparents, aunts, uncles, and cousins. We've checked everything most carefully."

"I suppose they wanted to know about me and about . . . the father."

"Of course. And they're very eager to have your child."

Jennie shook her head. Strange. They'll take him . . .

her . . . away, and our nine months together will vanish as if they had never been.

"You'll have plenty of time to change your mind after the baby is born, if you wish."

"No. This is the way it has to be. You know that."

"Nothing *has* to be. But I think we both seem to have agreed that this is a good solution all around."

"I think—" Jennie swallowed. Unexpectedly a lump had come into her throat. "I think—tell the doctor I don't want to see the baby at all."

Mrs. Burt's eyes were very kind. She spoke softly. "That's probably best. In these circumstances we often advise it."

"Yes. So you'll be sure to tell the doctor?"

"Yes, Jennie, I'll tell him."

Several times at the shopping center, Jennie found herself looking intently into carriages and stopping to make comments to young mothers, in order to have a chance to look at the infants. She stood staring down into the pink or red face of an eight-pound human being, either wiggling or asleep under its covers. And always her feelings fluctuated between resolve, so painfully achieved, and that so terrible sorrow at having to part with what was still as tightly attached as her arms and legs.

One day on her way to the bookstore she passed a shop and went in to buy a yellow bunting with a carriage cover to match.

"For a friend of mine," she said, and was struck in the instant by this shocking denial of her own situation. "I want her to have it before the baby comes. Yellow will do no matter what she has, won't it? And I'd like that cap, too, the embroidered one."

The saleswoman looked at Jennie's old coat, which now barely closed in front. "That one's expensive. It's hand-embroidered."

"That's all right."

A bitter thought crossed her mind. The most expensive one—why not?—for the Mendeses' grandchild. She stifled the thought. Nasty, Jennie, and not worthy of you.

In her room that night she examined her face in the mirror for a long time. Would there be anything of her in the child's face? It might be round like hers, or square like her mother's; opal-eyed like Peter's; or—God forbid —long and sharp like his mother's.

After a while she got up and began to write a note.

Dear Child,

I'm hoping that the parents who bring you up will give you this when you grow old enough to understand it. The mother who will give you birth and the—

She'd started to write *man* but instead changed it to *boy*.

—who fathered you are good people but foolish, as I hope you won't be. We were too young to fit you into our lives. Maybe we were selfish, too, wanting to go on with our plans undisturbed. Some people wanted me to do away with you—to abort you—but I couldn't do that. You were already growing, and I had to let you grow to fulfillment. I had to let you have your own life. I hope with all my heart that it will be a wonderful one. I will give you away only to wonderful people who want you, and who will do more for you than I can. I hope you will understand that I am doing this out of love for you, although it may not seem much like love. But it is, believe me, my daughter or my son. It is.

Then, without signing the note, she laid it on the embroidered bonnet, closed the box, and retied the taffeta bow.

———

They took her in the middle of the night. The birth was quick. Shortly before dawn, after no more than four hours of a pain that grew sharper and sharper, so that the last ones were agonizing and inhuman, so that she bit her lips and pulled with desperate, sweating hands at the side of the bed, she felt one last awful lunge. Then abruptly there was relief and ease. Lying there in that merciful first relief, she heard a cry like a lament, and then high over her head, it seemed, a distant voice saying, "It's a girl, a fine girl, Jennie. Seven pounds, three ounces."

Raising herself on one elbow and tired now, so very tired, she saw a vague, dizzy blur: A nurse or a doctor, someone in white, was carrying something wrapped in a blanket and walking away with it.

"Has she got everything she's supposed to have?" Jennie whispered.

"Everything she's supposed to have. Ten fingers, ten toes, and good lungs. You heard her cry."

"Nothing wrong?"

"Nothing at all. She's perfect. You've done a good job, Jennie."

She went home. She withdrew the Mendeses' money from the bank, over four thousand dollars, having spent only five hundred. For a moment she had thought of returning the balance with a courteous, cold letter to express her independence and contempt, and then she thought better of it. Be practical! Mom had taught her that, and some of the teaching had rubbed off. The money would go part of the way toward law school. Next summer and every summer she would go to work and put every possible penny away. Then, with whatever little Pop might be able to give her, she would somehow get through. She had to get through. This she wanted now—more than anything in the world.

Because it was the cheapest way to go, she took the bus back home. Now, in November, she rode for two days through continuous cold, traveling through the back streets of run-down cities and out again onto the highway. The tires sang in the wetness; past bare, twiggy trees, roadside litter, and rusty junkyards.

Suddenly, in a vacant lot beside a ramshackle dwelling, she had a glimpse of two horses nodding over a fence. And one threw up his wonderful bronze satin head to snort and began to run, with the other following, and the two went racing with pure joy around that derelict, bare lot.

I'll remember that, she thought. It's one of the odd, small things that stick in one's mind. Perhaps it's an omen.

At home things were as they had always been. Her story was well rehearsed and was accepted.

"It's good to have you closer to home again," Pop said.

"Not that we see you all that much, but it's nice to know you're only a couple of hours away," Mom amended.

Pop remarked that Jennie had lost weight, and Mom said that was too bad, but what can you do with these girls? They all want to be thin as a board.

"Our college daughter, God bless her. Only one thing bothers me. You broke off with Peter, didn't you? You found somebody else?"

"Yes to the first and no to the second. I've plenty of time, Mom. Don't rush me." Jennie gave them a smile. It was supposed to say: See how young and carefree I am?

"Who's rushing? I was only being nosy."

"Well, I just don't like him anymore. If he ever telephones, tell him I'm out. Tell him I went to Mexico or Afghanistan."

Peter didn't telephone, but he wrote again, asking why she hadn't answered his last letter. She read that letter again. What was the matter? he asked. Had she cast him out? He was concerned about her health. He loved her. And he was sorry about not returning to Penn, although he hoped he could manage to come north during Christmas week. But he made no mention of any future beyond that.

So much for the golden months and the golden promises! Childish and strengthless it must all have been, to have ended this way. And in her bed she pressed her face into the hard mattress, forcing the tears back into her head because she didn't dare show wept-out eyes in the morning.

Very, very slowly, as the agonies began to lighten, she felt a dull anger creeping to replace them. He had never even asked about the baby, only about her *health,* as though she had merely gone through sickness or surgery. No, the Mendeses didn't want to hear about the baby, that was clear. And they had brainwashed their son, crushed him into subjection. Poor, weak Peter. And poor baby . . .

But the baby wasn't poor, she reminded herself. She was cared for and loved, sheltered somewhere in the unknown West. Jennie glanced at the globe that had stood on the desk in her room since grammar-school days. The West was vast. San Diego had palm trees and ocean. Mountains and snow encircled Salt Lake City. Portland? They called it the Rose City. It would be nice to think of the child growing up in a place with such a pretty name.

One day, piece by piece, she tore all Peter's letters into shreds, gave away everything he had ever given her, and sat down at her desk. Writing a final letter to him, she surprised herself by being able to dismiss him without recrimination. She said nothing about the child;

since he had apparently been afraid to ask, he didn't deserve to know.

With the letter sealed and stamped, she felt proud, decisive, and mature. The past was past. The way now was forward. There was no Peter and there was no baby. It never happened.

It happened.

What can I do? I'm about to be married and my life is organized; it has direction. Why must this happen *now?* Why must it happen at all? Please. Oh, God, please don't let this happen. . . .

Then she put her face in her hands and sobbed aloud.

After a while she got up, pulled on a pair of slacks and a jacket, and went out onto the street. The wind was blowing icy cold from the East River, or maybe all the way across from the Hudson. She drew the jacket closer and began to walk, then to run. She had no idea where she was going, but she had to move. When you're exhausted, Jennie, you may go home.

The streets were quiet. Occasionally a car went by with a swish of tires and a flare of light, two menacing lights approaching and two sparks of red glare receding as it sped away. Lights were few in the apartment houses, dark fortresses in which sleepers lay stacked thirty stories high. It was long past the middle of the night.

Only the great hospital, dark bulk under the moving, cloudy sky, was awake. From a distance of two blocks, as she ran, the sight of lighted windows scattered up and down the building's height and breadth distracted her from her terror. Always, coming home at night, should she pass that way, she would feel a sharp awareness of what might be happening behind any one of those windows.

Now, approaching the emergency entrance, she was

halted in her run. Police cars, ambulances, and a cluster of onlookers—from where assembled at this hour?—blocked the sidewalk. A few feet from where she stood, a stretcher was lifted; there was a small commotion of white coats; there were the lights of another ambulance whining to a stop; then another stretcher, and she had a glimpse of long black hair and a frightful, bloody mask where a face ought to be.

Jennie's breath went hot in her throat, and the salty taste of blood was in her mouth as she looked away, and then, against her will, looked back.

"Move on," a policeman ordered, dispersing the group on the walk.

Among them, a woman wept with her hand over her eyes. A man walked away, damning the legal system.

"He was out on parole. Ten days out, broke into the house and slit their throats. Raped her first. The husband's dead, they said—"

Wanting to hear no more, Jennie resumed her run. The bloody face . . . She sped out into the middle of the street, away from doorways and alleys, running as if she were being pursued.

When she had raced up the stairs and locked her door, she was exhausted. But the terror at the hospital had put things back into proportion. The macabre night scene, the cries, the bloody face . . . This other trouble, this phone call, was nothing in comparison.

Reason reasserted itself. Victoria Jill Miller had lived nineteen years without her and could surely go on living without her. She would be better off not knowing Jennie. She might think she wanted to see her natural mother, but that would only lead to an emotional crisis in the end. These adoption committees were a lot of busybodies. What could a committee understand about that long-ago agony and despair? It was no business of theirs, anyway. What right had they to come now, to encourage this intrusion?

I have so much to do, Jennie thought, tense with the pressure. This case is so terribly important. Jay feels responsible for me, he's told them all how competent I am, and now I have to prove myself. It won't be easy. The builders are a big outfit, Jay says. They'll fight hard. I have to prepare so thoroughly, I can't waste a minute. I have to get started tomorrow morning. Call experts, water engineers, make traffic studies, roads, access, assessments. Get moving. Can't let anything else clog my mind. Can't.

Her thoughts were on a seesaw: Now that I've refused to see the girl, she'll think better of it and let it drop. They'll probably not call again. And if they should, I'll just repeat my position until they get discouraged. But surely they won't call again.

Will they?

4

Two weeks later Jennie went back upstairs for the meeting of the planning board. Although she felt sufficiently prepared by now, having put all other business aside, she clung to Jay.

"I wish you could go. Are you sure you can't?"

"Sure. I've got to be in court all week. But you'll do fine without me. Dad's got the group together for supper before the meeting, so you can be introduced to everybody and have time to talk over any new angles. You'll charm them, Jennie girl."

"Charm isn't exactly what they need. They're looking for results."

"Do as well as you did in the Long Island case and you'll give them results. Come on! You'll knock them dead."

The New York Times reported temperatures of five to

ten degrees above zero upstate. Her warmest coat was two years old but still good-looking, although the edges of the cuffs were slightly worn. She stood at the closet door, holding a sleeve, arguing with herself, and then, abruptly thrusting the coat away, went out to buy a new one. She was feeling something she seldom felt: a need for indulgence. So she set off toward Fifth Avenue, where it took very little time to find an extravagantly beautiful russet woolen coat lined with fur, and a skirt to match. With them went a cream-colored cashmere sweater and, for a change, a cream-colored blouse of heavy silk. On the way home she made a long detour to an ice-cream shop, one of the fern-hung copies of a turn-of-the-century ice-cream parlor that were so popular again, and bought her second extravagance, an enormous tower of chocolate and whipped cream, a sweet, sweet comfort.

If anybody ever needed comfort, she told herself, I'm the one. For two weeks she had been walking around with her thoughts still on a seesaw. Will they phone again? Won't they? And she called to mind those terror-filled minutes before examination papers are handed out: Will I make it? Won't I? She finished the chocolate sundae and went home to pack.

Shirley, watching, gave approval. "That's a stunning outfit. Now put on the pearls."

"Pearls? I'm going to a business meeting in a country town."

"So take them off for the meeting. But they look perfect with both the blouse and the sweater. Don't you think it would be nice to show your mother-in-law—"

"She's not my mother-in-law."

"Don't quibble. She will be in another couple of months, and it would be nice to show her how much you appreciate her present."

"Okay, maybe I will."

Yet Jennie knew she wouldn't. Why not? Because something was there, the knowledge of being under false pretenses, and a sense of not being deserving of the pearls. That was why.

Jay's father met her at the railroad station and drove her the rest of the way. A glossy, white film spread over the fields and laid long, drooping fingers on the hilltops.

"Snow's early this year," the old man remarked. "Quite a sudden change from when you were here." And glancing down at Jennie, "You look very lovely today."

"Thank you." Demurely she accepted the compliment. It hadn't been conventional flattery; there had been approval in it.

False pretenses. I am not what I appear to be. An outsider is what I am. It was the same in Georgia nineteen years ago.

For nineteen years she had wiped away all memories of Peter, expunged them as with an ink eradicator. Only once, when a stranger had left open on a library table a directory of American scholars, driven by a momentary curiosity, not caring at all, not giving a damn as she had put it to herself, she had looked under *M*, and there she had found him, Peter Algernon Mendes, with a list of his degrees and writings. He had made a name in archaeology as he had wanted to do and was now—or had been, three or four years ago—teaching in Chicago. So each of us, she had reflected then, and did again now, each of us has gotten what we set out to get, with nothing kept of that year's starry infatuation—or had it perhaps and truly been love? If we could have stayed together then, might we still be together now? And then this girl, this Victoria Jill—queer name—would be living with us instead of searching all over the country.

"Enid's got a good crowd coming," Arthur Wolfe was saying. "The committee's grown so, it's surprised even me—how this thing has gotten people all fired up. There's been so much publicity since you were last here, it's amazing. Both sides have plastered the town with posters. Of course, the newspapers are in the fight too. There's a chain that has half a dozen papers throughout the county, and it's liberal, all for keeping the land in wilderness, but the local paper wants the development. There's a lot of nastiness coming into it all, I'm sorry to say. It seems it's all people talk about—more than Russia and disarmament, or the election."

Evening had fallen when they arrived. Cars were lined up in the driveway and parked far down the road. Light streamed out of every window of the house, so that it stood snug and bright among the dark, tossing trees.

Safe haven, a house like this—if you belonged here, Jennie thought.

The pleasant buzz of conversation was audible even before Enid opened the door, crying out in welcome, "Why, here you are, Jennie! Everybody's dying to meet you. Come in."

Forty or fifty people moved through the rooms. Probably, Jennie thought, they were the cream of the town: two doctors, the consolidated school's principal, some teachers, the owner of the variety store, a nurseryman, a Christmas-tree farmer, and some dairy farmers. Altogether, an assortment of people who were decently united on one thing: the importance of preserving some part of the natural earth for the future.

Jennie was given hot buttered rum, led around and introduced, and taken to the dining room, where a fire snapped and a long buffet table had been set.

"No lawyers, you noticed," Jay's father remarked as they filled their plates with turkey, corn pudding, and salad. "As I told you, they're steering clear of our side. No money in it."

Jennie smiled. "So you've had to come far afield, all the way to New York, to get me."

"Yes, and we're glad we did. Jay says you've been working overtime on this, rounding up expert witnesses."

"It wasn't too difficult. Fortunately the same engineers who did the studies on my Long Island case have been prompt and cooperative. They'll be here tonight."

The old man's admiration was plain in his face. "I'm going to compliment my son. He always did know how to judge people. Come, I'd like you to spend a few minutes with our best friend on the town council. I introduced you when you came in, remember? George Cromwell, over there with the woman in the plaid skirt? He's a dentist. He's got the energy I used to have."

Cromwell was dressed, like everyone else, in country fashion—woolens, sweaters, and heavy shoes. His thick white hair contrasted with a plump, unlined face, young for his age.

"I think you two ought to get together and talk strategy," said Arthur Wolfe. "Why don't you take your plates out to the sun parlor? I'll see that you're not interrupted."

"May I call you Jennie? I'm George to you," Cromwell began.

"Of course."

"I understand congratulations are in order. They tell me it's not official, not till you get your ring, but I'm an old friend, so they've let me in on the secret. You know, they're wonderful people, the Wolfes. They don't seem like summer people. Not that we have many summer people up here—we're too far away to attract them. They fitted right into the town, have been so generous to the police and the volunteer fire department. Why, Arthur was a volunteer himself when he was younger."

Jennie glanced at her watch, and George caught her glance.

"Well, down to business," he said. "Is there anything you want to ask me?"

"Just about some of the people I might need to persuade especially."

"Well, there's the mayor, of course. We'd certainly like to have him on our side. He controls most of the rest of them."

Jennie nodded. "Because he controls the goodies, appoints the police chief, et cetera."

"So you're familiar with all that. But you ought to know that our mayor—well, I'm not very fond of him, I can tell you. I never liked him. Chuck Anderson's his name, owns a couple of gas stations here and over at the lake. Looks like his name. I don't know why the name Chuck always suggests somebody beefy and tough. But I could be all wrong. Gosh, your name suggests a little brown wren, and you are definitely no wren, young lady."

Jennie controlled her impatience. "Tell me who's on the planning board."

"You've met them all here tonight. The planning board is a mix—some of them top-notch and some of them Chuck's people. He never bothered too much about the planning board, though, because they serve without pay. Let's see, there's a librarian, Albert Buzard; then there's Jack Fuller, who owns the biggest dairy farm, five miles north of town. They'll be on our side."

"What about the rest of them?"

"Well, frankly, it depends on whether you can sway them, fire them up. I understand you've done that before. They'll be surprised to see a woman, though. We've never had a woman lawyer in town."

Oh, my, Jennie thought, stifling amusement.

"The council can override the planning board, you

know. So even if you win out tonight, you'll still have the
council to reckon with. They'll all be there tonight too."

Arthur Wolfe opened the door and peered in. "Time
to start. There's an overflow crowd, I hear, so they've
had to move the meeting to the school auditorium."

"Wow!" George shook his head. "It's a pretty big
school building, too, a consolidated school. You've got
your work cut out for you, Jennie."

The parking lot was almost filled, and a large crowd in
boots and woolen caps was already streaming up the
steps of a typical redbrick, white-trimmed, small-town
American school.

Arthur Wolfe chuckled. "Will you look at that!" Just in
front, a battered old car splashed with muddy snow was
plastered with signs: I DON'T GIVE A DAMN ABOUT
DUCKS; VOTE FOR PEOPLE, TO HELL WITH RACCOONS;
KISS MY AX.

Enid was worried. "It's getting so nasty. I was told that
the developers have brought people to this meeting who
don't even live in the township."

"Nasty, it's true. But you can see the other side too. It's
hard to explain to a man who sees the possibility of a few
years' worth of jobs that we have to think of the larger
community and of future generations. Put yourself in his
shoes if you can," Arthur Wolfe said.

Jennie sighed. "I can. I work every day with people
who don't have enough of anything. There could be
conflict in my mind, too, over this issue, except that I've
told myself, and I really know, that we're right in the
long run. But as you say, that's hard to explain to people
who need things right now."

And Arthur, helping the two women as they slid across
the icy pavement, repeated Cromwell's friendly warning: "You've got your work cut out for you, Jennie."

———

With the aid of a large map and pointer at the front of the auditorium, the proposal was outlined for all to understand: five hundred attached condominiums, seventy-five single-family structures, dam, lake, golf course, tennis courts, swimming pools, and ski run.

The board members sat in a row, slightly elevated, on the platform from which the principal, flanked by the Stars and Stripes on one side and the school flag on the other, ordinarily conducted school assemblies. They wore the same air of authority. Occasionally Jennie intercepted a glance from one of them; male and middle-aged, they were probably thinking that she ought to be at home right now preparing the next day's lunch boxes for her children.

The meeting was now about to enter its third hour. After the customary give-and-take among experts; technical reports from environmental engineers, consulting engineers, surveyors, and sundry planners; after keen, persistent questioning by Jennie and by the attorney for Barker Developers—the audience, some of whom had had to stand, was restive. People wanted to be heard. They wanted action.

"We have a procedure now," said the chairman, "that we have to follow. I believe we have some letters to be read into the record. If you will, Mr. McVee."

"Just one. We have a letter from David and Rebecca Pyle, dated September fourth."

Dear Sir,
We write to tell you of our concern about the proposed development in the Green Marsh. Our adjacent farm lies lower than the northern end of the property in question, and it is our fear that the water supply, on which our dairy herd depends, will be curtailed and contaminated if the marsh is drained and the lake enlarged. We

now have a clear, pristine lake, and it must not be destroyed to become instead a breeder of disease.

If the developer really believes that this will not be the case, then we think he should be made to guarantee in writing that the development will bring no harm, and be prepared to meet the cost of any damages if it should.

We rely on this board to make the right decision and to protect our interests.

> Sincerely,
> David and Roberta Pyle

A letter with a legal tone, Jennie said to herself. They've already had advice.

A question came from the dais. "Do you have any comment about that, Mr. Schultz?"

The attorney for Barker, quick on his feet, was standing before the question had been half spoken. He was a young man, about Jennie's age, wearing skillfully chosen country clothes, slightly worn but not too much so, with a sweater visible under his jacket. His manner was engaging.

"As to written guarantees, Mr. Chairman?"

"Yes, if you care to."

Mr. Schultz smiled, raising his eyebrows in mild surprise. "Well, sir, as we all know, that's unheard-of. We stand on our record, which should be sufficient. Barker Development has built condominiums in Pennsylvania, New Jersey, throughout New England, and in Florida. The quality of their work is what has built their reputation."

Jennie responded. "May I speak, Mr. Chairman? This is not an answer to the very reasonable request in this letter. We have a serious problem here, one that I have certainly tried to bring out this evening. We need to know specifically about things like backup flooding, water elevation, and so forth and so on, if they build as they have outlined. I have noted that Mr. Schultz has not brought a water expert to testify."

"Mr. Chairman, Mr. Bailey spoke at some length. He is a qualified engineer."

Jennie persisted. "But not a water specialist."

Schultz gave a slight shrug, as if to say, Why quibble? "Specialist enough, I think it's reasonable to say. We had no idea we would meet up with . . . may I call them rather finicky objections? We expected to be welcomed with enthusiasm, and I believe we shall be, because we are going to improve this town, and most of its citizens understand that."

Jennie, still facing the chairman, shook her head. "But there are some citizens who do not see things that way. They're not unsophisticated people who can have the wool pulled over their eyes. There have been other doubts and objections besides the one we just heard: letters to the newspapers—"

A harsh voice interrupted, loudly enough to startle the whole assembly. "They don't speak for me, and neither do you!"

All heads turned. In the third row a man stood boldly, as if he had just thrown a fastball and was waiting to see who would catch it. About forty-five years old, he had a strong, rather good-looking face with thick black hair and several days growth of dark beard. He wore a motorcycle thug's black leather jacket; opened, it revealed a soiled shirt and a powerful chest.

The astonished chairman reprimanded him. "Address the chair please, and no one else."

"Fine. I'll tell you just what I think. They and their preservation committee! And a bunch of foreigners come up here from New York. They don't want anybody to make a dollar, do they? Sure, they've got all they want, so who cares? Who gives a damn!"

Voices broke out all over the hall.

"Foreigners? Since when is New York City a foreign country?"

"Quiet here!"

"He knows what he's talking about!"

"Damn right, he does!"

"Should be thrown out, the fool!"

"Good boy, Bruce!"

"Oh, shut up!"

"Quiet here! Have some respect!"

"You're out of order, Mr. Fisher. Please moderate your language or sit down."

The gavel was pounded fiercely. Order was restored and questions were resumed. Someone asked about recreation facilities, to which Mr. Schultz replied that there was to be a clubhouse, a baseball field, and water sports on the enlarged lake.

"All for the use of the purchasers?" inquired Jennie.

"Well, yes, it will be a club community. A clubhouse with the usual features."

"But at present," she said softly, "the land is available to everyone, to all citizens, for recreation. Your development will take it away from them, and that should be noted, I think."

The harsh voice rang out again. Fisher stood up and scoffed. "For everyone! For a handful of nature nuts, that's who. Bunch of Communists from the city come up here and talk about nature. Wouldn't know an owl from a polecat if they fell over one. Communists, that's all. Against progress, against private property. People want to invest. They've a right to invest their money. The country was built by people like this Barker outfit."

Young Mr. Schultz put on a benign expression in acknowledgment of the praise. Crazier and crazier, Jennie thought.

The chairman raised his voice. "I'm telling you again, Mr. Fisher, sit down."

Fisher ignored him. "You're nothing but a hired gun, Miss Beluski, or whatever your name is. I can't pronounce it. I'm not a rich man like the folks who hired you."

There were cries of "Shame!" and also some applause.

"Out of order," shouted the chairman, his mild face now flushed, his expression baffled.

"I represent a group of concerned citizens, and I'm no more a hired gun than Mr. Schultz is." Taking care to observe protocol, Jennie replied not to Fisher but to the chair.

"A hired gun!" repeated Fisher in defiance.

The chairman rose from his seat. "Mr. Fisher! We shall have you removed from this hall if you don't sit down and keep quiet."

Fisher sat down. Out of the corner of her eye Jennie watched him. What she saw was concentrated hatred. But why? That voice . . . He looked about seven feet tall. And the black leather jacket seemed a symbol of violence. She controlled a shiver. Silly . . . He was only a common tough, some sort of mental case. It was all in a day's work.

"It's late," the chairman said. "There's time for a brief summation if either of the attorneys wishes to make one. After that this board will study the matter and will report by the end of the month. Mr. Schultz?"

Schultz spoke briefly. "Actually I have nothing to add. Barker Development rests on its reputation and its willingness to invest substantial sums in this town, thus showing confidence in the town's future as it enters—as we all make ready to enter—a new century. We hope that no overemphasis on conservation will be an obstacle to the welfare of human beings. It is a sentimental, elitist attitude, revealing a preference for wildlife—for deer or migrating birds—over human beings. I thank the board for its courtesy," he said agreeably, "and leave with confidence that you will vote on the side of progress."

Jennie had intended to be brief and factual. But the easy smugness of her opponent, coming after the hostile disruption, shook her intensely, and when she stood to speak, her voice quivered.

"Mr. Chairman, this is an historic moment for your town. I do believe that everybody here will have reason to remember how you decide the question that has been brought before you this evening.

"I'm well aware of the conflicting thoughts some of you must have. You want jobs, and these people are offering to create them. But I remind you that the jobs will be short-lived. They don't really solve your problems. These builders will flock in and be gone in a couple of years.

"I'm aware, too, that if the Green Marsh is destroyed, it won't be the end of the world. But it will be the end of a part of your particular, familiar world."

The auditorium was quite still. People were listening. The members of the board were leaning forward, watching Jennie.

"Even if it should be true—and I don't believe it—that this project wouldn't affect the water table, there are too many other things to be reckoned with. Think! All that gorgeous land and the creatures who have lived on it for thousands of years would be gone forever. All the space and the peace that have served you and your children . . ." She felt impassioned, which surprised her. She saw herself as she'd stood with Jay that morning at the top of the rise overlooking the marsh, the lake, the dripping trees; the immensity of foggy green had stretched as far as one could see, to the northern line where the silent hills began.

Her mind wandered. She had been so free that morning, as if she'd had wings. There'd been no weight, no looming threat of disaster, no hovering cloud. Now the cloud closed in again, the weight clamped down on her throat, and she faltered. And then in panic remembered where she was. They were waiting. . . .

Mercifully her mind picked up the thread of her thoughts, and she was able to go on.

"It is not fair to vote all that away, to give it away in exchange for short-lived dollars. Let us at least give the state a chance to incorporate this land within the wild and scenic system, so that others, years from now, may walk there and fish and swim and watch the birds and the changing seasons. I ask you, gentlemen, I plead with you to deny this application."

For several seconds after Jennie stopped speaking, there was a marked, unusual stillness, without a cough, a rustling of paper, or shuffling of shoes. Every face in the row on the dais was turned to her, and she had a flashing thought: Why, they all look surprised!

The chairman said as he rose, "Thank you very much. Thank you all. The meeting is now adjourned."

Slowly Jennie made her way through the crowd as it pressed toward the exit. As they moved forward, some people offered congratulations. "I teach sixth grade, and I'm trying to give my pupils some understanding of what you said." And, "You spoke to the point," and, "I couldn't agree more." But other faces were stony, staring at her with disapproval as they passed, and deliberately turned away.

Far ahead, at the foot of the short flight of steps that led to the outer lobby, she saw the Wolfes waiting for her. Suddenly she was weary, unsure of her accomplishment. It was just then, as she started down the steps, that she was roughly shoved in the small of the back. She staggered, tripped, and was saved from falling only by stumbling against, and being caught by, the man in front of her. Shocked and furious, she cried out, and turning, she found her face only inches away from the laughing mouth—wet, red lips; decayed brown teeth—of the man in the black leather jacket.

"Why, you . . ." she began. "What do you think you're doing?"

Still laughing, he gave her a jab in the side with his elbow as he slipped through an opening in the throng and ran out the front door.

Jennie's heart was still pounding when she reached the Wolfes. They were flushed with excitement, and for some reason unexplainable even to herself, she hid her distress.

"Jennie! You were marvelous!" Enid cried. "You really were. Wait till we tell Jay!"

It had begun to snow. Sticky, wet flakes fell slowly through the still, windless air and must have been falling during the hours when they had been indoors, for the icy pavement was hidden now under soft fluff, as was the car. Jennie and Enid got in while Arthur scraped the windows.

"I really think you moved the board people. I kept watching their faces. Some of them I'm sure of," Enid said. "The chairman, certainly."

"He was probably on my side, anyway, before I said a word," Jennie reminded her.

"Well, all right, but there are others who were on the fence before. I know. Mr. Sands kept nodding at some things you said."

Arthur started the car, and they joined the slow line leading out of the parking lot.

"Yes, you gave them something to think about," he agreed. "You did well, coming up against Schultz. Talk of smooth! He knows his business and knows how to persuade."

Through the veil of snow Jennie thought she recognized the battered car with the signs, and her enemy

driving it. The huge head; the huge, round shoulders
. . . but perhaps not . . .

"Who was the man in the windbreaker who made all
the noise?" she asked.

Arthur Wolfe sighed. "A bad sort. Name's Bruce
Fisher. He's a cousin of our mayor. He lives in a shack on
a couple of acres just this side of the Green Marsh. The
way I figure—and it's pretty obvious, since his land gives
level access to the lake on that end, where otherwise the
road would have to go up a steep grade—he's had a good
offer and he doesn't want anything to get in the way of
it."

Anything or anybody, Jennie thought. He actually
tried to trip me on the stairs! But that's crazy! Of course
it is. Yet don't people shove people in front of subway
trains? So why not this?

"He's been in trouble with the law half a dozen
times," Arthur continued. "Served a few years in jail too.
I think Chuck got the sentence reduced. Funny, they're
not close—outwardly, anyway. Chuck wouldn't exactly
invite Bruce to a dinner party, and yet they stick together. Once he aimed a shotgun at some kids who took
a shortcut across his land on the way to the lake. Chuck
got that squashed. He lived with a woman until he beat
her up one time too often, so now he lives alone. Or, I
should say, lives with a pair of pitbulls he's trained to kill.
In short, he's not a nice guy."

"Was I too emotional in my summing up?" Jennie
asked now, needing to change the subject. "I'm sort of
hearing myself all over again. Was I?"

"Goodness, no," Enid said. "It was just right."

"But don't be too encouraged," Arthur reminded her.
"Even if you should win over the planning board, the
town council has the final vote. They'll be the tough
ones. Don't underestimate our mayor. Chuck loves
money."

"Most people do," Jennie said.

"Yes, but I have the feeling he loves it more than most of us do. He's not above selling his vote, nor are some of his cronies I could name but won't."

Jennie thought aloud. "The Barker people have a good reputation. I wonder whether they'd risk it to bribe a small-town mayor. They've got much bigger projects than this one."

"It wouldn't have to be a bribe. Just a big offer to the mayor's cousin, as I said. Ten times what the land's worth, for instance. A perfectly legitimate offer."

"I should have figured that one out myself."

Arthur stopped the car at the front door of the house, where the potted evergreens in their wooden tubs formed two white pyramids.

"I'll put the car away, and maybe you'll make us some hot buttered rum, Enid? It's the right kind of night for it."

"Yes," he said as they sat in the kitchen, warming their hands around pewter mugs. "Yes, you might want to go on and make a name for yourself in this field of law, Jennie. You've got the feeling for it, and goodness knows these are tense issues, and we're going to see more and more litigation over them as the planet gets more crowded." He reflected, "It's not easy to pit immediate gains against the long-range view. Most people don't want to imagine what the world may be like after they're not in it anymore."

"Don't keep her up, Arthur," Enid said. "Her eyes are closing. Go on up to bed, Jennie."

But her eyes were not quite ready to close. Lying in bed in the plain, snug room with its one dormer window and sloped ceiling, she listened to the last noises of the night, the dog being let out to bark at whatever he might have seen or heard in the profound country quiet, then the dog being let back in, the door thudding, and finally the footsteps on the stairs. Family sounds, routine and comforting. This was the first time Jennie had been with Jay's parents without his presence. And unlike the gift of pearls, unlike any formal words, the simple fact of being there not as a guest but as a family member who sat with them in the kitchen and slept under their roof meant full acceptance.

And just as suddenly, in the lovely warmth of this awareness, the hovering cloud of fear descended again, falling over her to chill and cling.

She's in New York. . . . She wants to see you. . . .

CHAPTER

5

Whenever the phone had rung at home in the evening, Jennie had run to it in hopes that it would be Jay calling, and it usually was. But these days it was different, because she knew it was foolish to go on hoping that there wouldn't be another call from Mr. Riley.

That night, however, it was Jay.

"Just got off the phone with Dad. Then he put George Cromwell on. They're all delighted with the way you handled things. They're delighted and I'm proud."

"I'm so glad, Jay."

"Now listen, I've decided that tomorrow's the day. We're going for the ring. I want you to meet me downstairs in front of my office at three. And I won't take no for an answer. We can walk over to Cartier's."

When he had hung up, she sat for a moment at the telephone, assessing her own feelings. Cartier's. A ring, to make official the bond that was so strong and tight between them. She ought to be feeling unadulterated bliss. She was the luckiest of women! It was wrong and absurd to let fear, to let anything, spoil—

The telephone rang again.

A woman said, "Miss Rakowsky?"

A woman this time, yet Jennie knew before another word was spoken. She knew.

"My name is Emma Dunn. Mr. Riley talked to you a while ago. He's turned the case over to me."

The case. I'm a case in a social worker's file.

"There's no case," Jennie said.

"Well, we needn't call it that. But there is a problem, although there shouldn't be. Have you thought about it any more?"

Act sure of yourself. Don't let her feel that you're wavering or intimidated.

"Yes, I have. I gave Mr. Riley my answer, and I haven't changed my mind."

"We were hoping so much that you would change it after you'd had time to think it over."

"I thought I made myself very clear." Jennie spoke sternly. "This . . . this matter was settled years ago. It was supposed to be a confidential arrangement, and a permanent one. That's how I want it to stay."

"She's such a delightful girl. If you could see her—"

"Look, do you know what you're doing? You're opening an old wound, and it's cruel of you. Don't you realize that?" She ought to hang up. Just slam down the receiver on this intruding stranger. And yet it would do no good. They'd only keep calling. Maybe she'd even find them at her door one night when she came home. Maybe Jay would be with her. Jennie shuddered. Now her voice was shaking.

"I was eighteen years old. I was all alone. His family didn't want me. I wasn't good enough. And he was a helpless baby, no good to me at all. My parents, poor souls . . . Listen to me, I had to fight my way through my trouble then without any real help from anybody! And I'll fight now if I have to. So will you please just leave me alone? Will you just do that?"

The voice became conciliatory. "Nobody wants to fight, Miss Rakowsky. Quite the contrary. Your daughter wants to come to you with love. She feels that need."

"Mr. Riley said she didn't need anything. I have no money, anyway, you know," Jennie said, and felt instant regret. It had sounded so coarse, and she hadn't meant it to.

"Money is not what Jill wants."

She didn't want to know; she wanted only to be rid of the whole business, yet something compelled her to ask, "Isn't she happy with her family?"

"Oh, it's nothing like that at all. In fact, the family is quite understanding about her wish to see her parents."

"Understanding! What about my wishes, my needs? This was a closed chapter in my life—" Jennie's voice caught in her throat.

The woman must have heard the catch, because she responded sympathetically. "Why don't you come to our office to talk? Telephone talks aren't any good. Face-to-face, we'll understand each other. Come in for counseling. We want to help you."

"I don't want help!" Now Jennie was openly weeping. "I haven't asked for any, have I? I'm getting along fine the way I am—or was getting along, until you opened this Pandora's box that was meant, according to law, to stay shut."

"The law is changing. People want to know where they came from. They have a right to know—"

"I have rights too! This is my private life you're talking about. I don't want to hear about the laws changing. I'm a lawyer, and I understand—"

"We know you're a lawyer, Miss Rakowsky. So surely you, of all people, know that the law often changes with the mores, with the times."

Jennie was exhausted. It was too much of an effort to hold the telephone.

"Look, I don't want to talk anymore. I've said it all. I just want you to go away. I'm going to hang up. I just want you to leave me alone."

"I'm afraid that isn't possible," the mild voice replied.

Jennie hung up. Her tears were not tears of sorrow but of anger and fear. Even while they were falling, cold and slippery as glycerin, she knew that. Behind shut lids, between eye and brain, dark anger and bitter resentment were taking shape, billowing like smoke, coal-black and furnace-red, swirling in the image of a rising genie. How dare they track her down like detectives, as if she had committed a crime?

And yet . . . Poor girl. Perhaps she's desperate. No, she isn't, she's at Barnard, and they said she's fine. Except that she thinks she needs me. How could she possibly be desperate, though? No, it's me. I'm the one who's desperate.

The room, with only one lamp lit in the corner, was dim. The armchairs took on the shapes of seated men, a tribunal sitting in judgment upon Jennie. The tall curtains were men standing, frowning, waiting to seize and take her away. Then the light, as it struck the round copper pot that held the fern, printed a jeering face upon its bulging surface, and as Jennie moved, changing the angle of vision, the face moved, too, and opened an ugly, mournful mouth to weep.

Am I to go crazy here in this room?

"Looking for her parents," the woman had said. Yes, she had said that, hadn't she? Could they then possibly have found Peter too? She searched her memory. Had she given his name to those people at the home? But of course there was a record; his father had paid the bill, so there had to be a record.

Well, if the agency had traced him to the Mendeses—tall people beside tall columns in the blossoming Georgia afternoon—she'll get no welcome, that's for sure. God knows, Peter may have six children by now. God knows. You'd do well to stay away from those folks, Victoria Jill.

And now came an ache. It caught her like a stitch in the side after a breathless run uphill. It hurt so sharply that for an instant she could not breathe for the pain. Victoria Jill. "They call her Jill." I wonder whom she looks like? She must be a little bit like me—a little bit, at least.

Dry-eyed now, Jennie put her head down on the desk beside the telephone. If only there were someone to talk to! But there was no one, not even Shirley, her neighbor, who would only give quick comfort and end by telling her not to take everything so seriously. Long minutes passed before she could raise her head and go to bed.

There was a cold wind on the avenue, and Jennie went into the lobby to wait for Jay. The filigreed bronze entrance of a brokerage office faced the identical entrance to a bank on the opposite wall. Farther from the street, close to the elevators, was a florist's shop, its windows filled with pastel, out-of-season blooms, bringing an incongruous gaiety to the serious environment of business and finance. But then, maybe it wasn't incongruous at all. People walked briskly in this neighborhood and looked pleased with life; they were just the people who would celebrate life with flowers. She chided herself: Don't be bitter. People may look carefree, but that doesn't mean they are, any more than you. Anyone seeing you in this coat—for a visit to Cartier's she had thought it proper to wear the new coat, along with

Enid's pearls—would think you hadn't a care, either. Nobody rides free, Jennie.

Nothing escaped Jay. He hurried over, kissed her, and drew back with a little frown of concern.

"You look so tired! Done in. What's wrong?"

"I didn't sleep well, that's all."

"Anything bothering you?"

"No, it just happens sometimes."

They walked west toward St. Patrick's Cathedral. Across Fifth Avenue stood a succession of airline offices. Even at this distance one could see the splashed color of the posters in their windows. Jay, glancing in their direction, said, "I've been thinking—those two weeks at Caneel Bay won't be long enough for a honeymoon. Next summer, when school's out, my parents can take the children up to the country and you and I will have a month in Europe. We'll get a car and drive around with the top down. We'll stay at châteaux, drink wine, and eat foie gras. That'll be our real honeymoon." He tightened his hold on her arm as they crossed the side street. "However, I must say I'm looking forward to the two weeks all the same."

She didn't answer. Traffic lights turned red at the intersection; brake lights were red; bloody red blinked everywhere. She wasn't prepared for a vacation in the West Indies. The Isles of June, some explorer had once called them, and she had been looking at pictures of palms and beach grapes, unmarked sand on crescent beaches, gulls and pelicans, sails and parasols. But with things grown shadowy and uncertain, she didn't feel like simply packing up and departing for pleasure, leaving behind a looming, unsolved threat that would have to be faced when she got home. It would be less risky to hang on at her desk in the office and be here to cope with trouble when it came, as assuredly as it would. Yes, yes, it would.

"Here we are," said Jay.

Even the outside of Cartier's was a jewel, a Renaissance palace of cut stone. Walking in ahead of Jay, Jennie felt that people must know this was her first time inside.

He went straight to the rear, where a rather elegant gentleman, who had been seated at a desk, stood up.

"Mr. Wolfe? Good to see you again. I've put some very nice rings aside for you, I think."

Jay made an introduction, adding, "Whenever I see you, it's a happy occasion."

"Yes, your father's golden wedding present to your mother was the last. About a year ago, wasn't it? Well, now, since you didn't specify anything, I've got some pear-shaped, some marquise, and some emerald-cut stones to show you."

On a velvet tray, half a dozen brilliant diamonds shimmered under the chandelier's light. All was sparkle and velvet. The exquisite shop was a velvet box, hushed and hidden from the roar of the city.

There was a minute of silence, during which Jennie was supposed to be considering the rings. Instead she was thinking again, with hands joined and sweating in her lap. If only I had told him at the start! But now, going into the second year, when he thinks he knows me . . . I've told him all about my family, my childhood, what I want out of life. I've opened myself, I've told him everything. Everything except . . . And he has opened himself to me. I know, because of the most secret, intimate things he has disclosed, that he has hidden nothing; if he had wanted to hide, he could have hidden them too. He has been honest with me. . . .

Jay looked curiously at her, thinking perhaps that she was overawed and unsure of what was expected of her.

"Look carefully, Jen," he said. "I want you to fall in love with one of them before you say yes."

"They're all so beautiful. I just don't know."

"You have long fingers," the salesman observed. "You would wear an emerald-cut well. Not every woman can."

Jay held up one of the rings. "Blue-white?"

The man nodded. "Very, very fine, Mr. Wolfe."

Jay knew about diamonds. He must have bought them for his first wife, Phyllis. A girl with no secret past. A wife for a man like him.

"Try this one on, Jennie."

She reprimanded herself: Show some excitement, for heaven's sake.

"Oh, it's gorgeous, Jay. Yes, gorgeous."

The ring slid easily onto her finger.

"Hold your hand up to the light," said the salesman.

Every color of the rainbow met there, and yet the fire on her hand was white, as sunlight glittering on sky reflected in blue water turns all to white, to silver and white.

"Well, what do you think?" asked Jay.

It was so obviously expensive! If it were less so, maybe she would feel less like cringing.

"Don't you think . . . something smaller would be better?" she asked.

"Why? You're thinking it's ostentatious?"

"I wasn't. No."

"You were. I know you. But you know me too. I wouldn't want you to wear anything ostentatious. This size is right for you. Now try the other shapes."

She submitted, holding her hand out to one ring after the other. What a pity not to be thrilled at a moment like this!

Now Jay, perceiving her shyness, took charge. "The pear-shaped one is less becoming," he said, and the salesman agreed.

The two men considered. A yellow diamond was brought out and rejected, as was a round one. Her choice narrowed down to a marquise, the original emerald-cut, and a second emerald-cut. The salesman kept taking them off and putting them on. The two pairs of eyes questioned Jennie.

"I'm confused," she murmured.

"Do you want to leave it to me?" asked Jay.

She mustered an easy smile. "You pick it. You're the one who's going to be looking at it across the table."

So the first emerald-cut ring was chosen. Then a wedding band of diamond baguettes, narrow enough to be worn on the same finger, was put away to be sized, after which Jay wrote a check, which Jennie didn't see, and they went out to the street.

"Painless, after all, wasn't it, Jennie? Are you happy, darling?"

"You know I am."

"You were so quiet."

"I was embarrassed. My fingers are ink-stained. Didn't you notice?"

"So what? Sign of honest labor, that's all." He laughed. "I didn't tell you, I'm not going home tonight. The kids are staying with Phyllis's parents. It's their grandfather's birthday. So you'll be having an overnight guest. Hope you don't mind."

She felt a quick rise of desire. There were never enough nights when they could be together. She didn't answer, just looked up at him, and the look spoke enough.

"My Jennie," he said.

They walked quickly downtown, then east. The cold increased as dusk fell, with a damp prediction of snow in the air and a wind that took one's breath, making speech difficult. Jay spoke first. "The usual place?"

"Why not?"

"The usual place" meant a restaurant two blocks from her apartment. Small and plain, it served superb Italian food. Lutèce, La Côte Basque, and others like them were for weekends after a day of leisure—or relative leisure, to be more exact, since Jay always had some weekend work.

"Everybody loves Italian food," he observed, unfolding his napkin.

Years ago in Philadelphia there had been another "little Italian place," a cheap one with red-checked tablecloths. All day these startling images, so long forgotten, had come flickering back.

This table had a fresh white cloth and a handful of carnations in a glass container. And she urged herself silently, It's 1988. I'm in New York. Here. Now.

Facing the table hung a garish picture in thick, oily blues, ultramarine and cobalt, framed with hideous gilt.

"Awful, isn't it? It doesn't half do justice to the Bay of Naples. We'll go there, too, Jen."

"Oh, I want to."

"We ought to be hearing soon from the planning board about your case," he said.

The cloud clung, gray and damp. She wanted to dispel it; she wanted comforting, the way a troubled child, wanting to be comforted, pretends to have a pain. So because she was unable to tell him of the real pain, she found a secondary one.

"I had such a nasty experience, Jay, really nasty." And she told him about the man who had shoved her on the stairs.

"My God!" Jay cried. "Did you tell my father?"

"I didn't want to. I don't know why, I just didn't want to."

"You should have."

"What could he have done about it? Nothing. I couldn't prove it, could I?"

"Well, true enough. But the next time you come before the town council, I'm going to be there. Not that I expect any open attack or anything," he said quickly. "The man's a low-life, a sneak. A psychopathic personality."

"Your father's guess is that he's had a big offer for his land, which he'll split with the mayor."

"It makes sense. There's no telling how many others on the council are in on the deal too. Those few acres, because of where they lie, are worth plenty. You know, Jen, in a way I'm almost sorry I got you into this fight. You take your work so much to heart! I'm afraid you'll be awfully upset if you lose."

"You're thinking I will, aren't you?"

"There's a chance. The mayor only needs five votes on the council to win. So I just don't want you to be too encouraged, that's all."

"So much skullduggery in such a little town!"

"You've no idea. City people, when they're fed up, like to imagine a life that could be more innocent and decent if they moved out of the city, but let me tell you"—Jay grinned—"Chuck Anderson was elected as a man with a clean record. Chuck the Challenger, Honest Chuck. There'd be no more graft in road repair, no kickbacks on building permits—the usual stuff. Then, six or seven years back, an ugly business was dragged out into the light, something about Bruce Fisher—your friend— who'd been involved in a gang rape out near the lake. A rotten thing; the girl was fourteen. Well, it's a tangled story, and I don't remember all the details, but what does stand out in my mind is that Chuck had known all along about Fisher being involved in it and had at the time lied to protect him. So with the next election coming up, what does he do but come out in public with a full admission and apology? A heartfelt, teary repentance, beating his breast: 'I did wrong, I should have told you all long ago, I can only ask your forgiveness.' Et cetera. And so everyone admires his courage and they reelect him."

"Well," Jennie said. "it did take courage. He didn't have to admit it, did he?"

"Yes, but you see, when a person has waited that long to come out with a truth, you wonder what else he hasn't admitted about himself and what's going to come out next. I can't feel the same ever again about anyone who does that, no matter what else is good about him. I simply lose my trust."

Jennie was silent. Pasta and veal lay on her plate in a heap that suddenly was repulsive.

"And you see," Jay said, "he's straying from the straight and narrow again right now, isn't he, in spite of the past few years of good government? We all really know he is, even if we can't prove it. At least not yet."

Jennie took a forkful of meat. It was like rubber in her mouth, although she knew it had been well prepared. Jay was eating his with obvious enjoyment.

"Yes," he resumed thoughtfully, "it's sometimes too late to make a clean breast of things."

"Too late?" echoed Jennie.

"Too late for anyone to have confidence."

"Yes." She nodded.

"You're not eating," he remonstrated. "Don't you feel well, honey?"

"It's just that I'm tired. I told you."

"Maybe I shouldn't stay tonight."

"Oh, please! I want you to. I'm not *that* tired!"

Flash your bright eyes, show him that you want him, because you do want him so terribly, though at this moment, not with desire but for reassurance.

Jay, Jay, don't leave me. I can't lose you.

"Has my mother called you about next week?" he asked.

"No. What about it?"

"Well, she will. They're coming in next week, or maybe the week after, and she thought you might like to do some Saturday-afternoon shopping with her and the girls. She's been buying Sue's and Emily's things ever since they lost their mother, and she thought you'd like to start taking over the job."

"Of course. Of course I would."

"Family obligations descending on you already." He smiled, teasing.

"I don't mind obligations."

The words sounded flat to her ears, unlike the thoughts that now ran in a frenzy around and around in her head: If only he didn't have a family, parents, children, and heaven knew what other relatives, to sit in judgment of her! If only they weren't who they were, if only Jay were a nobody with no home, no job, no name, no ties, and they could go to some faraway place where no one could find them and start fresh in a whole new life without a past!

Fantasy, absurd fantasy. And she remembered the night, so short a time ago, when she had put his little girls to bed and been so filled with thankfulness and confidence and love.

They walked back through the wind again, now risen to a blast, so that they had to push against it, running with heads down. Back in the apartment, they rubbed icy hands together.

"Hot showers next," Jay said.

"Hot coffee first or afterward?"

"Neither. Just a shower and bed. We'll be warm enough in bed."

Together they stood under the prickle and sting of rushing water, soaped and brushed each other's backs, then, in the steaming little box that was Jennie's bathroom, toweled each other dry.

He held his palms against her breasts, curving his fingers.

"Look, they fit exactly."

And the familiar softness ran, dissolving like some sweet, thick liquid in her throat, and her knees unlocked so that her legs could hardly hold her straight. There was such force in him, but not like the force in other men, which could sometimes be frightening, so that one had to hold back or meet it with one's own strength, to defend oneself both physically and emotionally against domination. With Jay, there was only giving, total giving, so gentle was his power.

Yet at the same time she knew her own power over him too. He needed her. She felt the miracle of his need, saw it in his eyes, widened now with anticipation and a kind of joyful mischief.

He picked her up, carried her to the bed, and turned the lamp off. And the night closed over them.

In the morning she made an early breakfast: freshly squeezed orange juice, pancakes, and coffee.

"I hate rushing in the morning," she informed him. "I always like to get up an hour earlier and take my time."

"That's funny, I do too. Jennie, isn't it marvelous that we keep on finding new things about ourselves that are just alike!"

"Don't think I eat pancakes every morning, though. This is only in honor of last night, I want you to know."

"They're good. You make a helluva pancake."

A narrow band of sunshine fell over the little table. In another half hour the sun would have moved around the corner of the building and the kitchenette would require electric light, but at this moment its glow was a celebration, and she loved it, loved the fragrance of roasted coffee, the flaming gloxinia on the windowsill, the black-and-yellow striped tie against Jay's white shirt-front, the quiet closeness of being just two together instead of encircled by children or relatives or strangers in a restaurant.

"Well, the date's coming closer," Jay said, "and I've even bought a new suit."

"Me too. Very bridelike. You'll be surprised."

"Let me guess. Pink?"

"I'm not telling. But you'll like it. Shirley helped me pick it out."

"Oops!" Jay made a funny face.

"Don't worry, she knows what's what, and then I only have to tone it down a little."

"Jennie, darling, whatever you wear will be—"

The telephone rang. She went to the living room and picked it up.

"Good morning," said Emma Dunn. "I'm sorry to call you this early, but I tried the last few nights and you were out."

In those few seconds Jennie's palms went slippery with sweat.

"I can't talk to you. I'm on my way to work," she said, keeping her tone calm.

"I understand. I'll take just a moment. Tell me when you can come in to see me. At your convenience. You name the time."

"Quite impossible. I'll have to hang up now."

"This isn't going to go away, Miss Rakowsky. Jill isn't going to go away, I have to warn you. So you'd do better to face—"

Jennie hung up, wiped her hands on a handkerchief, and composed her hot, stinging face.

"Trouble?" asked Jay.

"No, why?"

"You look bothered."

"Well, I am. This client . . . poor thing, she has such a sad life, it's awful."

He said kindly, "You can't mix emotions with law. They'll grind you down if you do. Maybe you should have an unlisted number at home. Although, come to think of it, you won't be at this number much longer."

He stood up and reached for his briefcase. A fit of trembling seized her when he bent down to kiss her. Tears, in spite of all the resolve, lay in her eyes, not falling.

Jay looked astonished. "What is it? You're crying!"

"No, no. I . . . it's just . . . I'm thinking about us, and it just got to me. I felt . . . I'm so happy."

"Good grief! Women!" He laughed, mocking his own stereotypical male reaction. "Can a man ever understand them? Hey, I'd better run, and you too. I'll call you this afternoon."

Jill won't go away. Persistent, isn't she? Tenacious. Like you, Jennie? she asked herself.

She washed the few dishes, dabbed on eye shadow and lipstick, and, still shaken, went to work. It was a relief to know that the whole day was to be spent in the office rather than in court. Like an animal in its den, she thought, I take shelter in my small space, with its desk, books, two chairs, window high above the street, and closed door. The typist answers the telephone and will say I'm not here if I instruct her to. I haven't done that yet; I'm not entirely beaten down yet.

Jill won't go away.

Today, of all days, clients came in with children and babies. Poor women, rootless in the indifferent city, they had no place to leave them.

"This is my Ramon. He was two last week. Say hello to the lady."

Ramon stared out of ink-black eyes, then ducked, hiding his dirty nose in his mother's skirt.

"He's a big boy for two," Jennie said, having no idea how big two-year-olds are supposed to be.

"Yes, and strong. This is Celia. She's eight months."

The baby, held in the bend of the woman's elbow, was

extraordinarily beautiful, with delicate features that bore no resemblance either to her mother's or her brother's. She gave Jennie a jubilant smile and reached a pink hand out to her, as if in recognition of some shared, joyful secret. Jennie took the hand, and the small fingers clung to it.

"She's lovely," Jennie said.

The woman nodded. "They're my diamonds, my jewels, these two."

The words rang in Jennie's memory of ancient history, taken for two semesters at college: Roman Cornelia displayed her children: *These are my jewels.*

And this woman, too, was tired and dispossessed. She looked curious now, wondering perhaps why Jennie was still holding the baby's hand. Jennie dropped the hand.

"Well, now, let's see what we can work out for you, Mrs. Fernandez."

Late that afternoon, when Jay made his regular telephone call, he had news.

"Good or bad?"

"Both. The good is that the planning board turned down Barker's proposition. And the credit goes to you."

Pleased, Jennie nevertheless had to examine things candidly. "They were a good group to start with. As I told your parents, they had probably had their minds pretty much made up before I opened my mouth."

"That's only partly true. Some of them were impressed with what you said when they met you beforehand at the house, and some only changed their minds when they heard you at the meeting. They thought you really bested the other side. The vote was close, with two dissents."

"What's the bad news?"

"It's not so much bad as merely disagreeable. My father and a couple of others on the preservation committee have been getting a series of scurrilous, anonymous letters, mailed from ten or fifteen miles out of town. Dad read one to me over the phone. It was pretty disgusting."

"Threats?" She thought of the vicious shove at the top of the stairs.

"In a way, but not precisely. Cleverly done, just not enough to pin down legally. But very abusive, all the same. You were mentioned, too, in some of them."

"I'm that important? I'm flattered."

"Apparently they feel you are. Obviously whoever's behind all this is worried about the town council's vote next month, and they're afraid you might persuade them. George Cromwell—who's on the council, you remember—says that Barker has sent in rafts of papers, more of those detailed water reports you spoke about, from a specialist this time, as well as a lot of other things. They're really worried, he says."

"But they couldn't be the people behind those letters, could they?"

"They *could*, but somehow I don't think they are. It seems too crude for them to do. And yet, who knows? That's some rough gang in the town. Fisher's a prime example, as you found out. And our mayor might well be using him for his own purposes. Don't forget there's big money at stake. Big money. Anyway, I don't want you walking around town alone when you have to return. I'm going to stay with you." Jay changed the subject. "How about a movie tonight? There's a great one right around the corner from your place."

Ordinarily, Jennie thought when she had hung up, this business of the Green Marsh wouldn't be so disturbing. She would have called it a tempest in a teapot, a bunch of disgruntled locals writing nasty letters—that was all. But she was so tense these days, and it wasn't like her.

A glass of milk might help soothe her. When she took

the carton out of the refrigerator, she dropped it, and a white river slid across the floor. On her knees, wiping it up, she thought, A feather's touch will snap these nerves of mine.

And this news of Jay's was more than a feather's touch, on top of everything else. For even though there had been no further calls from Emma Dunn, the expectation of another one was ever-present, so that every ring of the telephone sounded alarm.

This anxious, expectant waiting was like a fear of falling. Once, a long time ago, she had seen a movie in which a train, having become detached from its engine, began to hurtle down from an alpine pass. Rattling and clacking down the track, slamming around curves, it sped and quickened as it descended, while the passengers, helpless, frozen, incredulous in their seats, too horrified even to scream, stared out at flying pines, angled cliffs, snowfields, tilted arcs of sky, and whirling mountains; stared down to where, thousands of feet below, doom waited. It was strange that she had no memory of how the movie ended, only of the awful helplessness.

Saturday: a difficult, disjointed day whose events had no logical relationship to one another.

In the morning there had been the trying on of the wedding outfit, which Jennie had ordered at Saks. It was only her second experience with what Shirley called "courtier" clothes, the winter coat having been her first. Facing the mirror in the fitting room, she almost did not know herself.

Ruby velvet brought a pink cast to her face, which glowed against her bright black hair. Pleated ecru lace framed her neck and circled her wrists. The skirt lay smoothly on her narrow hips and swayed at the hem.

"It couldn't be better," the saleswoman said with satisfaction.

No, it couldn't.

"I would suggest black sandals, very thin straps, almost no shoe at all except for heels. Very high ones, unless your man isn't . . ." The woman hesitated.

Jennie smiled. "He's very tall."

"Well, then. And a tiny black bag. Velvet, preferably. Or a very fine suede would do nicely."

"You've been such a help," Jennie said. "I want to thank you."

"Oh, you're easy to work with. It's been a pleasure. So many women don't know what they want."

What I want. A clear mind. And she stared back at the mirror. You there in red velvet, dressed for your wedding, you're an impostor, you know that, don't you? You have misrepresented yourself, concealed the truth about yourself, you of all people, you who've sworn to uphold the law. You've lied, to put it plainly. Impostor!

Under a brilliant sky in motion, with a winter breeze shaking the flags all up and down Fifth Avenue, and the air just cold enough to be charged with energy, she walked toward Bergdorf Goodman, where the girls were to buy dresses for birthday parties and dancing school. Enid would have to show her how to care for these children. All of a sudden the responsibility she was to undertake loomed very large.

They were waiting for her on the ground floor: the imposing woman dressed quietly in gray with two small girls beside her. Sue and Emily stood on tiptoe to be kissed.

"Hi, Jennie."

"Oh," said Enid, "is that what they call you?"

"Why, yes," Jennie said, surprised. "What else?"

"Aunt Jennie, I should have thought."

"Well, either way I don't mind."

Why did the trivial comment start up such a troubling train of thought? In the elevator; upstairs in the children's department, where they'd bought dresses in navy-blue taffeta, in white lawn and flowered challis; later, as they crossed the street and entered the Palm Court for lunch—Jennie saw darting images, like sparks, of Atlanta again, and then the same chilly reaction: *Outsider! You don't belong.* Why? For there was really no resemblance between those people and these, between that woman and this. These people had welcomed her! Yet there was something. . . . They had standards, rigid standards. Their liberalism was for the less fortunate, people from whom less was expected "because they haven't had our advantages."

And sitting now over chicken salad, while the little girls' big eyes were already fixed on the desserts, Jennie was aware once more of that quality of elegant, superior assurance that had been her very first impression of the Wolfes, most particularly of Enid.

No, decent as they were, they would be shocked; they would find it hard to forgive her for starting her life with their son in deceit, with a lie.

The conversation around the little table was light and pleasant. Enid made only brief mention of the Green Marsh affair, just to say that it had grown even more ugly than expected and that it seemed to be the only thing anybody talked about in town. Otherwise the talk was dominated by the children, whose day it was intended to be.

After lunch they crossed the avenue to F.A.O. Schwarz, where Emily and Sue chose a birthday present for Donny, a life-size toy raccoon, an accurate replica complete with tail rings.

"Girls, I should say you've had a wonderful day," said Enid. "And I should say it was time to take you home. You must have plans for the rest of the afternoon, Jennie. With your tight schedule you don't have time to spare, I'm sure."

"That's true. I can always find plenty to do."

"Well, then, we'll be leaving you here." Enid kissed Jennie's cheek. "Say good-bye to your Aunt Jennie, girls."

The response was obedient. "Good-bye, Aunt Jennie."

Jennie watched them walk toward a taxi and thought, They have aunts, but I'm not one of them. Funny, Enid got her way. I don't mind. What difference does it make whether they call me "aunt" or not?

I said I always had plenty to do, and I have, but I don't feel like doing it. I just feel like sitting down and doing nothing.

She crossed back over the avenue and sat down on a bench, warmed enough by the full sun to be comfortable. And drawing her coat about her, her hands thrust into the pockets, she sat for a while thinking of nothing special, just watching the traffic pass, halt, and start up again.

She couldn't have said how, or from what buried cells in her convoluted brain an impulse came, but suddenly it was there—uninvited by any conscious process; not even welcome; startling; perhaps even somewhat crazy. After only the smallest hesitation she got up and began to walk westward toward the subway. Never before having been where she was going, she had to ask for directions. At 116th Street and Broadway, she left the subway and climbed to the street. Barnard was only a short walk away. Surely no one would see any reason to question a young woman who sat on one of the campus benches, ostensibly waiting for somebody.

Nevertheless, having sat down, she felt the absurdity of being there. All right, it's foolish, foolish curiosity. I wouldn't know her if she were to stand in front of me. How could I? Maybe she's that one in the Norwegian ski cap, walking slowly while she reads. Maybe she's one of that group, gossiping by the door. Yet perhaps I would know her through some resemblance—not to her father, God forbid. If I did see her and was sure that it was she, the curiosity would be satisfied and I'd just walk away. Isn't she the one person in the world I don't want to know?

For an hour Jennie waited. Nothing happened. There were neither hints nor clues. Girls, graceful, clumsy, sloppy, chic, dull or vivid, occasionally beautiful and occasionally ugly, passed before her. One thing they possessed in common: youth. You could only wonder what each was going to do with the years that lay ahead, or what the years would do to each, for the world in the eighties, and woman's place in it, were more complex and difficult than ever. And Jennie's chest filled with pity and nostalgia, sorrowful and tender.

As the sky went gray, the short winter afternoon turned colder. It had been a mistake to come, an aberration, and it was a good thing she hadn't recognized the girl. She ought to have known better. And shivering, she stood up and walked back to the subway. There would just be time to shower and dress before going out to dinner with Jay.

How sad it was now to feel unnatural in his presence! Bitterly she remembered how, such a little while ago, she had watched the clock's hands creep and had counted the minutes until he should ring the doorbell.

That afternoon he telephoned. "Jennie, I've got to beg off. I've got a fever, a rotten cold coming on. I'm home in bed."

"Oh, darling, I'm sorry. I wish I could take care of you."

"Well, you'll have that privilege soon. I hear you had fun with Sue and Emily. They really love you, Jennie. I'm so glad."

"I am too."

"Jennie?"

"Yes, dear?"

"I want one of our own, yours and mine. Is that okay with you?"

"I've dreamed of it so much, Jay, with a cleft in its chin, and your eyes . . ."

"But, darling, if it should turn out that you couldn't have any, it wouldn't matter, you know that too. We'd be together and that's everything. . . . What'll you do with the evening now that I've stood you up?"

"Oh, read. I've brought some files home from the office. And go to sleep early."

"Good. Build yourself up for Caneel. Have you got your new racquet yet?"

"Next week. I've been putting everything together. Don't worry."

"I won't. Hey, I'm sneezing my head off. I'm going to hang up."

Actually she had not been putting everything together but had been postponing her lists and errands. These last weeks, during which she ought to have been making ready, had been too stressful to think of lists and errands. But time was growing short and tonight would be a good night to start.

With pencil and paper she began to check off. Bathing suits. Three, the good blue from last year, plus two new ones. Beach robes—to wear at lunch, Jay said. A beach bag, that flowered one she'd seen in a window; it would go with everything. A white cardigan in case of a cool night. A new folding umbrella. The old one was a wreck. Shoes for the traveling suit, navy-blue. Shoes for—

The doorbell rang. That was strange. She never had unexpected visitors. People always called first.

Cautiously she approached the door and looked through the peephole. The hall was very dim, so that she could barely distinguish the figure that stood, miniaturized and distorted, in the tiny, round glass: a woman with full, shoulder-length hair. Jennie strained and blinked.

"Yes? Who is it?"

There was a second's pause before the voice, nervous and young, replied.

"Jill. It's Jill. Will you let me in?"

"Oh, no," Jennie whispered. Her spine froze.

Yet, like those helpless people on the mountain train, she had known what was to come.

CHAPTER

6

Home was more than two thousand miles away from the astonishing city that rumbled beyond the dormitory. Gladly and bravely, Jill had left it for this place; yet there were unexpected moments when, coming upon her own face in the mirror beside the bed, the memory of home flared so vividly that she could hear again the voices calling in the yard behind the house, or smell the dinner's meat broiling on the kitchen grill, or feel on her bare feet the slippery coolness of the floor in the upstairs hall. Curiously the room that Jill remembered best was not so much her own small, rose-colored bedroom—in which stuffed animals and, later, books stood on the shelves, where at bedtime the single window framed the rising stars—but rather the large room at the end of the hall where her parents slept.

There in a top drawer was kept the bedtime box of

chocolates from which, after her bath and before her teeth were brushed, the treat was given. There before the bay window stood two soft, wide chairs. The one on the left was Dad's; on Sundays, if he didn't have to see any patients in the hospital, he sat and read, scattering the paper around his feet. The opposite chair was the "story chair," wide enough for Jill and Mom to sit together while Mom read aloud.

At the foot of the enormous bed, whenever there was a new baby in the family, stood the bassinet. Refurbished each time with fresh ribbons and netting, it remained until the baby was old enough to be comfortable in a regular crib in a room of its own.

"Very tiny babies like tiny spaces," Mom explained, "because they've just come out of a tiny, warm place, you see."

That must have been the second time, when Lucille was born. Jill was four, and she remembered how her mother had grown fat and suddenly been thin again as soon as Lucille came out of her tummy. When Jerry had been born, Jill had been a baby herself, not even two years old, so she didn't remember him. But Lucille's arrival was clear in her mind.

A tiny, warm place. That was puzzling because the baby looked too big to have been inside anybody.

"Was I inside of you too?" Jill asked.

"No," her mother said. "You were inside another lady's tummy."

Well, that was all right. It wasn't important. For a long time she thought no more about it, although it was odd that later, when she did begin to think about it, that scene could revive itself and be so sharply drawn: Lucille wrapped tight in a flannel cocoon, Jill at the head of the bassinet, and her mother dressed in something long, with black shapes on white.

Years later she asked, "Mom, did you ever have a bathrobe or a housecoat that was black-and-white, plaid or flowered, maybe?"

"Why, yes. I had a Japanese kimono that Dad bought on our trip to Japan before we had you. It was beautiful, black peonies on white silk. I wore it till it fell apart. What makes you ask?"

"I don't know. It just suddenly came into my mind."

But that was much later. Her childhood was crowded, the days were full, and the neighborhood was filled with children. Relatives came and went in the afternoons. She supposed, when she was older and learned about sibling rivalry and jealousy, that the reason she hadn't suffered them as much as she might have was that there were so many laps for a little girl to sit on, so many arms to hug her. If her parents were momentarily too busy with a younger child to play a game with Jill or take her somewhere, there were always Aunt Fay, two sets of grandparents, and three sets of cousins.

People smiled at her and praised her red hair. When she started school, every morning Mom tied it back with ribbons to match her sweaters and skirts. Once, as she left the living room where Mom was having coffee with a friend, she heard the friend say, "Such a lovely child, Irene. And what luck she brought you! To think you had three of your own after you adopted her!"

"Yes," Mom said, "she brought us luck."

But weren't there "four of your own"? If you were adopted, were you not really Dad's and Mom's "own"? By then, of course, Jill knew the meaning of the word *adopted*. And that night when Mom came to tuck her into bed, Jill drew her down on the bed.

"Stay here," she said.

Mom took her hand. "Is it a story you want, Jill? A short one then, a chapter in *Winnie-the-Pooh*, because this is a school night."

"No." The question she wanted to ask seemed babyish

for a girl in third grade, a girl in the advanced reading group.

"What, then?"

Jill, clinging to the hand, shook her head.

"Please. If anything's troubling you, you'll feel better if you tell me."

The question burst out of her mouth. "Do I belong to you? Like Jerry and Lucille and the baby?"

"Oh," Mom said. "Oh." She pulled Jill from under the blanket and rocked her. "What makes you ask that? Did anybody say . . . ?" And without waiting for an answer, she rushed on. "Belong to us! You are our dearest, beautiful, big girl, our very own. . . . Why, everybody loves you, Grandma and Grandpa, and Aunt Fay . . . and Dad and I most of all. Why, of course you belong to us. Why, whom else would you belong to?"

She pressed her cheek into Mom's neck and whispered, "I thought maybe to the lady who grew me."

"Oh," Mom said very softly. And she waited such a long time before answering that Jill drew back to look into her face. It was very serious, the way it had been when they had that talk about taking things out of the medicine chest.

"No, darling. You don't belong to her anymore."

"What was her name?"

"I don't know, Jill."

"Was she nice?"

"She was very nice, I'm sure, because she had you."

"But why did she give me to you?"

"Well . . . well, it's a little hard to explain. You see, sometimes things happen to people, like not having any money, for instance, not having a nice house with room for a little girl. So you see, since she loved you and wanted you to have all that, and since we wanted a little girl very, very much, so . . . well, that's how it happened. Do you understand?"

Jill supposed it made sense enough. "But is there any more?"

"Any more to tell? Oh, yes! We were so happy, Dad and I. We ran out right away and bought the bassinet. You were the first baby to sleep in it. You were one day old when we brought you home, younger than Jerry or Lucille or Sharon. Remember how small Sharon was a year ago? Well, you were even smaller."

"And I had red hair."

Mom laughed. "Not right away. You were bald, like all my babies."

All my babies. Mom's voice had a warm, good feeling, a sleepy feeling. After a while Mom laid her back down in the bed and drew the blanket up. She pulled the blinds down, kissed Jill's cheek, came back to kiss her again, and closed the door.

My babies. We wanted a little girl so much. Then it was a good thing to be adopted. It meant that you were really wanted. People wouldn't go to such trouble to get you, buying houses and high chairs and carriages and all that stuff, if they didn't want you.

No one in the neighborhood ever asked Jill about being adopted, because most people knew it, anyway; but she wouldn't have minded if they had asked. It could, in a way, be a distinction, like bringing home an excellent report card, or knowing how to get the dinners ready that whole week after Mom had broken a bone in her foot. Being adopted was only another aspect of her *self,* like having freckles on her arm or being sure on skis—all things taken for granted and therefore seldom thought about.

One day the sixth-grade teacher gave an assignment. They had been talking in class about how America was made up of people who had come from many different places, bringing their differing customs and experiences.

Now they were to find out all they could about their own ancestors and draw a family tree.

"See how far back you can go," the teacher said.

One boy in the class had an Indian great-grandfather and was very proud of being a "Native American." Another boy knew his great-great-grandmother, who was ninety-seven and could tell about coming to New Mexico when it was still a wilderness.

"It's really fun," the teacher said. "In learning about your ancestors, you'll be surprised what you learn about yourselves. So ask plenty of questions!"

After supper that evening, Jill walked over to her grandparents' house. Mom's parents had both died a few years before, but Dad's were healthy and lively; they were immediately interested in Jill's project.

"You would have enjoyed my father," Grandpa said. "He was a great dancer. When he was an old man, he could still do the peasant dances he'd learned when he grew up in Hungary. You should have seen him! He had a strong heart and a lot of good humor."

Gran wrote down the names of her parents and even remembered the maiden names of her grandmothers. She added anecdotes. Jill saw that Grandpa and Gran were both enjoying themselves. Reluctant to let her go, they made her sit down at the table for lemonade and cake. A sudden stream of sea-green light from the spring evening outside fell on the table across from Jill, lay on the man's graying head, touched the woman's manicured nails, and traveled up to her tanned, plump, animated face. It was at this moment that Jill had a profound sensation of separateness.

All of this has nothing to do with me, she thought. It is not my history.

At the proper time, careful not to hurt their feelings by making an abrupt departure, she thanked them and walked home. Boys from the high school were playing baseball in the field. At the corner house, the father was tending his carefully irrigated lawn; it would be dead and brown by June, no matter what he did. From the house opposite Jill's, piano music tinkled. Everything was cheerfully familiar, yet she felt distant from it, faintly sad.

At home they were all on the back patio. From the front hall she could see their dark heads clustered, bent over something on a table—a newspaper or a map. She went quickly upstairs to her room and stood before the full-length mirror to study herself. Her face was long and narrow, not like any of theirs. Already she was taller than Mom. Jerry and Sharon looked like Mom, while Lucille looked like Dad's father. She brought her hair forward over her shoulders. Bronze glinted in the copper ends; the sun had laid gold streaks from temple to crown. Who had given her this hair? Or these teeth that were being straightened, when everyone else in the house had even teeth?

On her desk lay a sample family tree. She sat down and began to draw a copy, filling in the spaces: Mother, Irene Miller; Father, Jonas Miller. She put the pen aside, and sat gazing out at the blank sky. Night fell abruptly, as if a shade had been lowered. There were noises downstairs as the cat was called in and doors were shut. The brother and the sisters came up arguing over first use of the shower. Because Jill's room was dark, no one came looking for her, and she sat alone, not exactly close to tears but very still inside, troubled by the strange new sadness.

Her light flashed on. "Jill!" Mom cried. "We wondered what took you so long. Dad called Gran just now and she said you'd left an hour ago. You scared us." From over Jill's shoulder she looked at the blank paper. "Tell me, what's wrong?"

Jill swiveled on the chair. "This. I can't do it." And now

her eyes grew wet. "If I put down all I know, it'll be a lie."

"I don't think that's the kind of lie, if you want to call it one, that matters. Just write down everything you know about our family. You're part of it." Staunchly Mom added, "Write it as if you were Jerry or Lucille or Sharon. Or the baby."

Jill whispered. "But I'm not any of them. I'm me."

Mom closed the door. "Sit in a comfortable chair," she commanded. "We need to talk, you and I."

Now that the moment for some sort of revelation was apparently here, Jill was afraid. It was like opening a box received from strange hands; you didn't know what might jump out, a bomb or snakes.

Trembling, she asked, "What about?"

"About what's obviously on your mind. I promise I'll tell you as much as I know."

"What did she look like?" Jill whispered.

"I was told," Mom said evenly, "that she had dark, curly hair like mine. They try to make a close match. So maybe she was much like me."

"I see. And my father?"

"They never told us."

"I wish I knew their names."

"That can't be, darling."

"I suppose they weren't married."

"No."

"It's all right, Mom. I'm twelve. I know about things like that. She got pregnant and he wouldn't marry her."

"I don't know whether it happened as you're putting it, that he wouldn't. Maybe he couldn't. They were both so young, not halfway through college. It must have been very perplexing, very hard for each of them."

"They should have thought of that before they . . . did things," Jill said, feeling unexpected anger.

"People don't always think, Jill."

"You always say—a girl, especially—you tell me it's wrong to let boys do things."

"I know I do. And yes, it is wrong. But still, when people do wrong things, we try to understand them and forgive, don't we?"

An image formed itself: In tall grass a girl lay looking up into the eyes of the boy who bent over her. The image was alluring and at the same time repellent; at the movies one waited to see what would come next, and yet one didn't know whether one wanted to see it. And if the boy and the girl were one's father and mother . . .

Mom was watching Jill. The corners of her mouth turned up into a fraction of a smile, but her eyes were anxious. It was the expression she wore when a child hurt himself and had to be comforted, an expression grown familiar over the years, as were the parallel creases on her forehead, or the small gold studs that she wore every day in her ears.

"Don't we, Jill?" she repeated, and continued, "You shouldn't blame her. She didn't do anything bad. She made a mistake, that's all."

"May I come in?" Dad knocked. "Or is this a private conversation?"

"No, come in. Jill and I are having a talk about her birth."

"Oh, are you?" Dad sat down and frowned a little, as though he were prepared to listen hard.

"I think Jill's bothered because her birth mother wasn't married," Mom said. "I think she feels that makes her different from other children, from her friends. Am I right, Jill?"

Dad took his glasses off and put them back on. Somehow the gesture made him seem serious and wise. It's the way he must look when he talks to patients in his office, Jill thought.

"Listen, Ladybug," he said. "I'm going to say a very

selfish thing. If that poor young girl hadn't had so much trouble, we'd never have had you. And you're one of the best things that ever happened to your mother and me. Don't you know that? Don't you?"

She nodded.

"And I think—I hope—we've been best for you."

"I know." Close to crying, now that they were giving her all their earnest attention, she forced herself not to. "But what I need to know is . . . Oh, you've told me she had no way to care for me, and I guess I understand that, but still, how could she have done it? Could you give Mark away?"

The parents glanced at each other. They were thinking, probably, of Mark in his crib right now. He slept with a teddy bear on either side, which made three heads on his pillow. When you went to see him asleep, you smelled talcum powder.

It was Mom who spoke first. "Yes. If we had no home and couldn't give him what he needs, we love him so much that we would."

"Think of how she must have loved you to do what she did," Dad said. "Think of that. And then try not to think of it anymore, if you can. You have a whole, good, wonderful life ahead, with so much to do." He laid his hand on Jill's knee; the hand made firm pressure, as if he *owned* her, and that felt good. She wanted them to *own* her. When she put her hand over Dad's, the lump of tears melted away out of her throat.

"Anything else you want to say, Ladybug?"

"Well, I have to finish the family tree."

"Let's see." Dad examined the paper. "You have two choices. You can tell the teacher why you don't want to do it, or—"

Mom interrupted. "I can write a note of explanation instead."

"Yes. Or you can fill in the spaces with the information you have. Either way will be all right."

They were both standing over her, smiling, but their raised eyebrows were questioning. She felt that she was expected to smile in return, and actually now, seeing them there so united and solid together, she began to feel more like doing so.

"It's late," Mom said. "So finish your homework." Her no-nonsense voice was comforting too. "Skip the shower tonight, for once. You need your sleep more."

Alone again, Jill took up the pen. Two choices, there were. She thought hard and in less than a minute had made one. One path led nowhere, just trailed off into darkness, as in those closed canyons that they sometimes saw when hiking in the Jerez Mountains. The other was a straight road to be traveled on a clear day.

So she took up the pen and started to fill in the spaces. Father: Jonas Miller, born 1918, in Phoenix. Mother: Irene Stone, born 1920, in Albuquerque. Grandfather: Otto J. Miller, born 1888 . . .

To say that as she grew toward, and finally into, adolescence, Jill was afflicted by heavy doubts about her birth would be untrue. She was too active, too successful, and too secure within her family for that. Yet it would be equally untrue to say that she never doubted again.

In certain circumstances the subject was jolted abruptly back into her consciousness, there to lie and trouble her until with effort she was able to argue it away. As she grew older it became more difficult to argue it away.

On a weekend camping trip with friends near Taos, the sun deceived her on a windy day, burning hot enough through the clouds to raise painful blisters.

"People with your complexion have to be wary of the sun," the strange doctor admonished kindly. "If you've got brothers and sisters, tell them to guard against skin cancer. It's the price red-haired families pay for their beauty."

Her hair was such a marker! Sometimes she almost wished she didn't have it. For if her hair had been brown like the rest of the family's, would she have thought so much about herself? Now, whenever she saw a tall, red-headed woman in her thirties, she thought: Could she be the one? Briefly her heart would thump and then subside as she remembered what Mom had told her about dark, curly hair. Was it the father, then?

The bad thing was that such questioning made her feel not only that vague, recurring, quiet sadness but guilt besides. Why was she not able to accept her good life as it was?

In the summer before her senior year in high school, Gran, who had taught French, took Jill and Lucille to France. It was adventure and delight; the three were to speak no English if they could help it, even to one another. They traveled on local trains and buses to villages off the tourist track. They walked on country roads and ate basket lunches in the shade of the plane trees. Gran was young enough to keep up with the girls' pace, while the girls were old enough to care about the museums and cathedrals that Gran knew so well.

They spent the last few days in luxury, resting at the sea at Eze-sur-Mer. The hotel was filled with Germans, British, and Americans. One evening after Lucille and Gran had gone up to their rooms, Jill became acquainted with a girl of her own age who had, like herself, been observing in the center of the garden an enormous, room-size cage, filled with exotic, tropical birds. They ordered ice cream and sat talking on the terrace.

The girl, Harriet, was friendly and blunt. "Are you here with your family?"

"My grandmother and my sister."

"Oh, is she your sister? You don't look at all like her, do you?"

Jill could not have said why she replied as she did. "I'm adopted," she said.

"Really? So am I."

For a moment neither girl spoke. Then Jill said, "You're the only person I've ever met who's like me."

"You've probably met plenty but didn't know it. People don't talk about it. I know I don't."

"That's true. I never said it till now."

"I think it's really nobody's business, is it?"

"That's true, too, but I don't believe that's the reason."

"No? Then what is?"

"I think it's because we—I, at least—don't want to think about it."

Harriet drew her chair closer, and Jill understood that this stranger was feeling the same emotion that had just swept her: a sense of close understanding never felt before with anyone else.

"I said I don't want to, but I do think about it," Jill said.

"I don't. Not anymore."

"You don't want to know who your mother was, at least?" Jill asked softly.

"I know who she was—is. I've seen her."

Jill was aghast. "How did that happen? Tell me," she begged.

"I was born in Connecticut. It's one of only four states that don't keep sealed records."

"Is Nebraska one of them?"

"No. And let me tell you, when records are sealed, they're sealed. You'll get nowhere, so best forget it."

"I can't forget it. The older I get, the more I seem to need—" Jill's voice cracked and she stopped.

The other girl waited for a considerable time, until Jill was ready to speak again.

"Tell me. What was it like when you saw her?"

Harriet looked away at the squawking birds and the sea beyond the rocks. "She was drunk," she said. She looked down squarely at Jill. "I've never told anyone except my father and mother, but I'll tell you because I'll never see you again and because . . . well, I see you need to know. So this is it. She was awful. She was tragic and terrible. She's married—he looked as if he liked his liquor too. They had two boys, my half brothers. They were fighting when I got there. The house was filthy. I don't know where my original father is, and I doubt that she knows, either. She clung to me and cried and begged me to come back again. Yet in a way I don't think she really wanted me to. I think she was ashamed. We had nothing to say to each other." Harriet paused. "It was another world."

The brutal images darkened Jill's spirit. "Have you ever seen her again?" she asked.

"That happened three years ago, and I've gone once every year since, during Christmas vacations. I live in Washington, and I'm glad I'm no nearer. We write to each other, although there's not much to write about. They're—she's—kind, and I feel—I don't exactly know what I feel about her, except that I'm awfully sorry for her and awfully glad I have the parents I have. As I said, it was another world."

"I suppose you wish you'd never found her."

"No, to tell the truth, I don't. It's much better this way. I don't have to worry and dream anymore. Now I know."

Gran was reading in the next room when Jill went upstairs. "I saw you from the windows, so I knew you were all right. You had a long talk with that girl. Is she nice?"

"Very. She's adopted. We were talking about it."

Gran was silent.

"She met her mother. Her birth mother."

Gran looked over the top of her reading glasses at Jill; the look was long and touched with pity.

"I don't think that's a good thing at all, Jill," she said.

Now Jill was the silent one. And her grandmother asked, "Was it a good experience for her, did she say?"

Jill was not going to betray a confidence, so she answered only, "I don't know."

"It could destroy another family, you know. What if the woman was married now and hadn't told her husband about the child? What about any other children she might have? Or her own parents, for that matter? The damage could be fearful."

"One could be very careful about all that."

When Gran took her glasses off, Jill saw that her eyes were very troubled.

"You could be—if it's you we're talking about, and I assume it is—you could be totally rejected. We don't want you to be hurt that way, Jill."

"I think I'd like to take that chance," Jill said, very low.

Gran sighed. "There's something more. Have you thought how you might hurt your parents?"

"I would ask them first. I would explain how I love them and that this has nothing to do with my love for them." Jill crossed the room and put her hand on her grandmother's shoulder. "Are you annoyed with me, Gran?"

"No. But I'm unhappy because you are. Will you think this over more carefully, Jill? Think further and then, if you must, talk to your father and mother about it when we get home."

So she thought some more but still held back from bringing up the subject when she got home. Arguing with herself, she could see conflicting possibilities. Suppose the woman who had given birth to her turned out to be a tragic disappointment like Harriet's drunken mother? On the other hand, the girl had said, in spite of it all, she was relieved at last to know. . . . And then, of course, that first mother might well be the loveliest woman on earth, kind, wise, beautiful. . . . Somewhere she breathed and lived—oh, she was too young to have died!—but where?

On a dim, rainy, Saturday afternoon, Jill and Mom, alone in the house, were cooking together, baking bread and pies for the next day's dinner with guests. It was a pleasant custom. Mom had taken a course with a pastry chef and was now teaching her daughters.

But today Mom, humming while she peeled apples, was distracted and unlike herself. Wondering, Jill glanced at her from across the floured board and caught a glance in return.

"You've had something on your mind for a while, haven't you?" Mom asked.

Jill evaded the question. "I don't know what you mean."

"Gran told us about your talk when you were away. We waited for you to say something, but you didn't. I suppose we should have spoken first. I suppose we hoped you'd forget, but I see you haven't."

"I've tried," Jill murmured.

Her mother went to the stove, moved a pot that needed no moving, and came back.

"There's something Dad and I intended to give you when you were eighteen. But last night we decided to let you have it now. I'll go upstairs and get it."

In a moment she returned and handed Jill a letter, saying, "Let's sit on the sofa in the den."

The handwriting was feminine but firm. Curious and apprehensive because of Mom's solemnity, Jill began to read. There was only a single sheet, and she scanned it in moments.

Dear Child,

I'm hoping that the parents who bring you up will give you this when you grow old enough to understand it. The mother who will give you birth and the boy who fathered you are good people but foolish, as I hope you won't be. We were too young to fit you into our lives. Maybe we were selfish, too, wanting to go on with our plans undisturbed. Some people wanted me to do away with you—to abort you—but I couldn't do that. You were already growing, and I had to let you grow to fulfillment. I had to let you have your own life. I hope with all my heart that it will be a wonderful one. I will give you away only to wonderful people who want you, and who will do more for you than I can. I hope you will understand that I am doing this out of love for you, although it may not seem much like love. But it is, believe me, my daughter or my son. It is.

"Oh, my God!" Jill cried. "Oh, my God." She put her hands over her face and rocked and cried.

"I know, I know," Mom whispered, and, taking hold, laid Jill's head on her shoulder. So they sat close, holding each other.

After a long time Jill sat up, wiping her eyes. "I've gotten your shoulder all wet."

"It's nothing, nothing. Are you all right?"

"It's a beautiful letter. . . . I can't believe I'm holding it in my hand. Such a beautiful letter."

"Yes, I cried, too, when I first read it."

"If only she'd signed her name!"

"Darling, you're missing the point. That's the last thing she would have done. She wanted confidentiality above all things. She was scared. She felt threatened."

For a while Jill considered, imagining herself in a situation like that, but she wasn't able to make it ring true.

"Maybe," she said, "since so much time has passed, she's changed her mind and wishes she could see me."

"It's possible. But even so, I don't know what either she or you could do about it. That's the law."

"I think it's wrong, and I'm not the only one who thinks so. I've read that there are lots of people and active organizations who are trying to change it. Don't you agree they should?"

"I'm not sure I do. There's much to be said about keeping a child secure in one family, with one loyalty and no conflicts."

"A child, yes," Jill countered. She was beginning to feel a renewed impulse toward action. "But not an adult. Mom—in a few more months I'll be eighteen."

"I know that." The mother's voice was touched with sadness.

And Jill, at once aware of the sadness, put her arms around her. "Mom, you'll always be my mother. You've done everything for me, you've been—"

"Oh, when I think of what we went through to get you!" Now the sadness merged into laughter. "References and investigations, a thousand questions. We were so afraid we wouldn't be as perfect as the agency seemed to think we ought to be. And when finally we came to get you, that raw November day, it was sleeting and we had you wrapped like an Eskimo . . ."

So they sat and talked all the rest of the afternoon, while the rain splashed from the eaves and sluiced the windows and the dinner went uncooked.

It was decided: Dad would go to Nebraska with Jill and find out what they could.

"It looks the same," he said as they drove up in the car they had rented at the airport. "I wonder whether Mrs. Burt is still here."

Down the long corridor between the mansion's library

and solarium, Jill followed him. She thought, My mother walked here. Right here.

"You all right, Ladybug?" Dad asked.

"Fine. I'm fine."

Dad went into the office. "I want to pave the way, show my credentials as a doctor—it might carry a little weight, who knows? And make clear that you've come with your parents' blessing."

Jill sat down in the anteroom, a beige, neat place with comfortable chairs and magazines. It was the waiting room of a doctor or lawyer in any prosperous community. Hearts beat faster in these waiting rooms, she thought.

After a long time Dad came out to her. He whispered, "Mrs. Burt retired two years ago. This one's not the most lovable person in the world, but come on in, anyway, and do your best."

The young woman behind the desk was attractive, but she didn't smile when Jill was introduced. She was a businesslike type.

"Your father has told me what you want," she began, addressing Jill. "Surely you must know you can't have it."

"I suppose I hoped," Jill murmured.

"The records are sealed. The original birth certificate, not the new one issued after your adoption became legal, is in the hands of the state, in the Bureau of Vital Statistics. And sealed," she repeated. It was as if she were slamming the door.

Nevertheless Jill persevered. "But your records here? I thought—oh, I want so much to know, only to know!" And realizing that she had clasped her hands in supplication, she unclasped them and continued in a reasonable tone, "I hoped you would understand and help me."

"But you knew better, Doctor," the woman said to

Jill's father. Her manner was respectful, yet it contained a reprimand.

"Yes, I knew. But there is here a psychological need that can't just be ignored."

"It is curiosity, Doctor."

"I differ with you. It is more than that."

"If we were to satisfy all these requests, then the promises that were made to the original mothers would be worthless, wouldn't they?"

During this exchange Jill's eyes rested on the desk. A Lucite nameplate stood facing away from her. She had a quick knack of reading either backward or upside down: Amanda Karch, it read. Behind it lay a large legal-size file. Clearly it must be the agency's private record of her birth. She felt a surge of ferocious anger. Here lay the truth only a few feet away, and this woman, knowing the truth and seeing as she must Jill's awful need for it, refused it. By what right? This insignificant bureaucrat, this self-important—

And suppressing her anger, she asked quietly, "Are there ever any circumstances in which records are unsealed?"

"Very rarely. You have to convince the courts that you have good cause; for example, a serious illness that is difficult to diagnose and which might be genetic, or a severe illness of a psychiatric nature that might be a threat to sanity. Rare situations."

"I see."

"None applies to you."

Jill did not answer. Her eyes returned to the file and stayed there.

"I would advise you to dismiss this from your mind. You have, so your father told me, no other problems. Then you're a lucky young woman, aren't you?"

"Yes," Jill said.

Dad took her hand as he spoke. "Needless to say, Miss . . ."

"Karch."

"Miss Karch. Needless to say, we are terribly disappointed."

The woman half rose, dismissing them. "I understand, Dr. Miller. But I can only tell you again, for your own good, put this out of your mind. Don't let this useless question become a neurotic obsession. Don't disrupt your lives."

"Thank you very much," Dad said.

They were driving back to the airport when Dad suddenly drew over to the side of the road.

"What do you think, Jill? Shall we go home? Have you got any other ideas?"

Miserable in her defeat, she answered with a question. "What idea could I have?"

"Taking it to court."

"You heard what she said about that."

"Cold fish," Dad muttered. "Though I suppose she must know what she's talking about."

"It would cost so much to get lawyers, Dad."

"Don't worry about that." He started the car. "As soon as we get home, I'll make some inquiries. Now let's have a bite to eat. Dinner on the plane won't amount to much."

It was late evening when the plane began its descent over New Mexico. The mesas threw dark blue shadows over the brick-red earth. To those who knew nothing about this land, the cliffs were no more than immense walls of rock. But to those who knew it well, they were the home of an ancient people. Down there the mesquite grew, the piñon pine shook in the wind, and the river ran. Jill stretched and craned to see whether she could identify any familiar places.

"Remember the time we started on a Sunday and

Jerry forgot the water bottles?" Dad asked. "Which reminds me, I think we're going to win the battle for the farmers over those water rights. It's a hell of a thing, diverting water from farms to supply a resort hotel for dudes."

Jill understood his attempt to take her mind off her problem. It saddened her to see her father look so troubled, and she said quickly, "Dad, you don't have to humor me. I've lost today, but I'm not down-and-out, and I'm not giving up."

A month or so later Dad reported the results of his investigation. There was indeed no chance at all of winning in court. Attorneys here at home, as in Nebraska, were positive about it. The court required good cause, and Jill had no good cause.

She took the news stoically. By that time she had been admitted to Barnard College in New York and had her game plan in place. Once there, she would seek out one of the adoptee organizations about which she had read. Others in her situation had been successful, so there was hope for her.

With some bitterness she remembered the warnings of that chilly woman at the home for unwed mothers. She had called Jill's search an obsession. Well, it was as good a word as any, she supposed.

So she packed her new clothes with many differing emotions: sorrow at leaving home, excitement about her new life in New York, pride in her achievement—and the obsession.

The organization's office was in a wing of a simple, private home in a small town not far from the city. There were two little rooms, in each a desk and a row of green metal filing cabinets.

"We're a small group," said Emma Dunn. "I'm a retired social worker, and this has become my full-time project. I'm adopted myself, you see. Mr. Riley is the sole other staff member and the rest are volunteers, a few of them teachers, psychologists, a couple of lawyers, and the others just plain good people. Now sit down and tell me about yourself."

When Jill's brief story was finished, she nodded. "It's the usual beginning. Do you have your birth certificate? I mean, it goes without saying, the certificate that was given out after you were adopted."

"It's at home."

"We'll need it, unless you know the names of the hospital and the doctor."

"I do, but he wouldn't tell anything, I'm sure."

"You said your father's a doctor. Could he get in touch with this doctor? Sometimes doctors do things for each other."

Foolish, Jill thought. It wouldn't work. But she conceded that it would be worth a try.

When she phoned home that night, Dad agreed to try, as she had known he would. A few days later he called back. His voice had a downbeat.

"It didn't work, Jill. He's an old man, still in practice, and very sympathetic. But he can't break the law. He made that clear, and I understood. I was even a little embarrassed about having asked him to."

"Thank you, Dad. Thank you, anyway."

"Is everything else all right, Jill? Working hard? Having fun?"

"Yes to both. New York's wonderful. I've made friends and I love it, but I'm thinking of Christmas vacation and coming home too."

"So are we, dear. We miss you terribly."

"Christmas vacation" put a thought in her head. How would it be to take a detour on the way home with a stopover in Nebraska? Suppose she were to see the doctor herself? Maybe a nurse or secretary could be approached. The thought turned into a resolution and stayed with her through the term.

Accordingly, on a day of bitter cold, with snow high on the western plains, she found herself sitting before still another desk opposite a white-haired, partially deaf old man. The lighted windows from the building across the narrow street enlivened the dark afternoon. When he had finished, very kindly and clearly repeating to Jill what he had already told her father, the doctor remarked, "You're looking at the hospital where you were born."

Quite dispirited by now, Jill only nodded.

"I only wish I could help you, young lady. I really wish it. But if I were to speak those words to you, they would haunt me. I've never stepped outside of the law, and I'm too old to start now."

"Words? What words?"

"Your record. When your father called and gave me the date of your birth, I went back to my dusty files. I only delivered one baby that day, a girl."

Jill's eyes filled. So close, so close again . . . right there on the desk.

The old man coughed and bent down to open a drawer. "Darn those pills. I never know where they are."

And Jill leaned forward. On a typed sheet she had time to recognize only one name upside down: Peter . . . Alger something . . . Mendes. She drew back just as the old man's head came up.

"I'm really sorry I can't help you, my dear."

She had to get out of the office fast, to write down the name. Her heart was hammering. Had she imagined a twinkle in the doctor's eye? He'd given her a bit of a chance without breaking the law. Whoever this Mendes was, it was a clue, at least. Perhaps he was a relative or a friend of her mother's. Or perhaps he was her own father?

At home late that night, trembling, she told her parents.

"Peter Alger," Mom said.

"Not Alger. There were more letters."

Mom reflected. "What else could it be but Algernon?"

"It's an odd name," Dad said. "Why does it ring a bell in my head?"

"You've heard it?" Jill cried.

"It seems to me I've seen it. Seems to me that I read it in some periodical. Maybe he's a doctor who wrote something in one of the medical journals. Well, I'll have one of the girls in the office go through the medical directory on Monday. There are lists of all the physicians in the United States, you know."

"No, not a doctor," Dad reported on Monday evening. "Still, that name bothers me. It's the Algernon that sticks in my mind. Maybe I'm imagining the whole thing, yet I seem to see it on a page and see myself reading in the office, the way I do when I eat my sandwich for lunch. Doesn't seem to be too long ago, either."

"Well, what do you generally read, then, besides medical journals?" asked Mom.

"A lot of things. All the magazines for the waiting room, *National Geographic, The Smithsonian,* besides all the popular stuff. And then my special-interest pamphlets and brochures, Bureau of Indian Affairs, the Sierra Club—whatever's lying around."

"You'll never find it," Jill said.

"Don't say that. The more I think about it, the more sure I am that I saw that name within the past year. And we generally keep things on the shelves for a year or so. They fill up the space and look nice."

It's a wild-goose chase, Jill thought. And yet one never knows.

The winter passed, the summer came and went, and the sophomore year began. She had gone back to Emma Dunn and given her the name for whatever use the committee might be able to make of it. And then one evening Dad telephoned.

"You're not going to believe this! I've found Mendes. It was in an article on Indian archaeology that came today. He's a professor of archaeology in Chicago. Wait, here it is. Write this down. . . . What are you going to do, write to him?"

"I think I'll telephone right now," Jill said. "I wouldn't be able to sleep tonight if I didn't."

"Okay, good girl! Call us back. Let us know what happens."

How to begin? "Hello, my name is Jill Miller. I read about you, and are you a relative of mine"? No, that was stupid. He wouldn't know Jill Miller from a hole in the wall. Just tell him the truth.

She was weak in the knees, but she obtained the number from Information and dialed it. A brisk voice answered. When she had given her name and identified herself as a student at Barnard, she began:

"I have a strange request. I was adopted at birth, and I'm looking for my parents. Somehow, by accident, I came across your name, and I wondered whether you know anything about . . . about who I am."

There was a pause before a reply came. "Where was it that you found my name? In what state?"

"In Nebraska. That's where I was born, in a home for unwed mothers. But I'm speaking from New York now. Are you perhaps a relative of my mother's?"

"Tell me"—and now the man's voice was no longer brisk—"tell me how old you are."

"Nineteen."

There was a long, long pause. Jill thought he had left the telephone.

"Mr. Mendes? Are you still there?"

"Oh, God, yes, I'm here."

"Mr. Mendes? Do you know my mother?"

"I knew her."

She thought the man might be crying, and she was suddenly afraid. There was a beating, a wild throb in her head. Her voice came in a whisper.

"Her name? What was her name?"

And the man's voice trembled back. "Janine. She was called Jennie . . ."

Jennie. Dark curly hair. That's all I know. But this man, at the other end of the wire, knows the rest.

She gripped the phone. "You do understand that you have to tell me everything, don't you? It's not right to let people suffer—"

"She was Jennie Rakowsky. We were at college together. She's a year younger than I, and we—" He stopped.

Jill had to lean against the wall. "Then you—you must be—are you?"

"Yes. Oh, yes! My God, I don't believe this. Out of nowhere. I want to see you. Can I see you? When can I?"

"Oh, you can . . . you can. But where is my mother?"

"I don't know. I haven't seen her since, nor heard."

Jill wept. "It's so terrible! And still . . . I looked so long. I tried. How can I find her?"

"I'll give you the address where she lived in Baltimore. And my address. I want to see you. Jill, what do you look like?"

"I'm tall; I have red hair. Long red hair."

"I have red hair. Jill, give me your address and your telephone number. Let me call you back, this is an expensive call."

"It doesn't matter."

"How did you find me?"

"I'll write and tell you. My father saw your name. He reads about Indians, we live in New Mexico—"

"Out of nowhere. My God, out of nowhere you came."

She hardly slept. She called home with her astonishing news and on Saturday took the train to Baltimore, where she went to the address that Peter Mendes had given. It was a row house on a poor street. A black woman answered the door. No, she had never heard the name. The people behind her, they were named Danieli, they had been here for years, and maybe they knew. Oh, yes, they remembered the Rakowskys, but they had moved away years ago, after the father died. Jennie Rakowsky had been a sweet girl, pretty, and so smart. No, they had no idea where to look for her.

On Sunday she telephoned Peter Mendes to report.

"I thought of something yesterday, Jill." He was excited. "I phoned you but you had already left. It's this. Jennie always wanted to be a lawyer. There's a national directory of lawyers. I was stupid not to have thought of it before. It's Sunday, so I can't search, but tomorrow I will, and I'll let you know."

Again she hardly slept. "Sweet, pretty, and so smart," they'd said. He was tall and had red hair. Even over the telephone you could tell he was sensitive and good. Peter and Jennie. Jennie and Peter. All day she walked around with the awareness of their existence overlying every thought.

Late in the afternoon, Peter telephoned. "Jill, imagine, she's in New York! She's an attorney; she got her wish. I have the address for you."

Jennie in New York. And all last year we were both here and didn't know it. When I tell Dad and Mom— I've got to tell them tonight.

"Jill, I think you should go easy. She wanted, insisted, on secrecy. You mustn't call her the way you called me. It's too much of a shock."

"I wouldn't have done it to you the way I did if I had known who you were."

"It didn't harm me. But it might harm her. She may have a family, probably does. Be careful, that's all I'm saying."

"I will be. Oh, I will be! I've been working with an adoption organization, and I'll ask them what to do."

"Good idea. And I'll keep in touch with you. I can't wait to see you. Send me a picture in the meantime, and I'll send one to you. Jill, is this real? I keep asking myself . . ."

Emma Dunn brought Mr. Riley to hear Jill's story, which she poured out in a rush, her words tumbling and falling, her face flushed and her hands waving in emphasis. She saw that they were both moved.

"I have to see them! I'm going to Chicago to see Peter, but first Jennie. Imagine! So close. I could probably walk to where she is."

"Well, don't do that, Jill. Let us do it for you. We've seen too many of these meetings end in great pain. That's not to say that this one will," Emma Dunn said quickly. "Let's do it right so that it won't end that way."

But the suspense and the joy were overwhelming. Things had gone so well after the long year of failed attempts that now Jill felt free to assume there would be no more obstacles. So it was that her light, exultant heart fell all the more heavily when Mr. Riley called to tell her that Jennie Rakowsky wanted only to be left alone.

"She says what was done nineteen years ago can't be undone now."

"She said that?" Jill asked.

"Yes, but it doesn't mean she won't change her mind. Let's give her some time to think it over."

"Is it because she has other children, do you think?"

"I don't know. We'll find out."

"How will you?"

"We have ways. I'll let you know. And, Jill, I wasn't surprised, so don't you be. It happens all the time, as I warned you."

When she told them at home, Dad said the same thing, and Mom added, "We were afraid this might happen. I hope it all works out for you, but, Jill, if it doesn't, you have to accept it. You can't let it crush you. Be satisfied with Peter in Chicago."

When Peter called, he gave comfort. "It will all straighten out," he said cheerfully. "Just be patient." She saw him at the other end of the wire, youthful, perhaps too cheerful in the face of her distress, not fatherly like Dad, but still so welcoming. And she was grateful.

Days went by, and a week, then more weeks. The next time it was Emma Dunn who called to say that she had made another unsuccessful try to talk to Jennie.

"Don't give up. It's only two times, Jill. I'll call again. She has neither husband nor children. I have a feeling she'll finally say yes."

Now, though, Jill was beset with a sense of urgency. It was as if she had done all but half a mile of a marathon; the goal was there, but her legs were so tired and her breath was so short; yet she must make that great, final push; she mustn't lose now. Never mind all the cautionary advice. Never mind her parents or Peter, or the Rileys and the Dunns. Just go for it.

So one night after dinner she went to her room, showered, and changed her clothes, to present herself at her best. She called a taxi. I will be calm, she told herself, and in the telling, she believed she felt her heart slow down. She entered a house and climbed some stairs and rang a bell.

A woman's voice answered: "Who is it?"

"It's Jill," she said. "Will you let me in?"

CHAPTER

7

With arms and legs gone rubbery, bracing herself with her left hand on the wall, Jennie unlatched the door. Light from the living room's lamps fanned out upon a tall young girl. Hair, Jennie saw first. Masses of splendid, undulating, russet, shining hair. Copper. Red. Red hair.

She slumped against the wall. Stared. Put her hand flat on her chest where her heart knocked, and knocked, and might suddenly stop altogether.

"I'm sorry," the girl said softly. "I'm sorry. . . . Are you going to faint?"

Jennie straightened up. For a fraction of an instant, outside of herself, she saw herself having a dream, a nightmare from which she would awaken in gratitude for daylight and reality. And then in the next instant, wrenched back into herself, she saw that this *was* reality:

that the girl was alive and real and poised to come through the doorway. She moved aside, her rubbery legs hardly holding her up.

"Come in," she whispered.

They stood in the center of the room facing each other, six or seven feet apart. There was no feeling in Jennie, suddenly no feeling except a frightful awareness that she was numb. Shreds of thought blew like leaves across vacant ground: What am I supposed to do, to feel? I'm numb, I'm not able to do or feel, don't you see? And, anyway, this may be a mistake. Yes, of course it's a mistake. Yes.

But then there's the hair. How many people have hair like that? Now look into her face. Look into the stranger's face.

"You're thinking you're not sure who I am. But I'm in the right place. I'm Jill. Victoria Jill. They've told you about me."

"Yes," Jennie said, her voice making no sound, so that she had to repeat, "Yes, they have."

They were still standing apart, at almost half the distance of the little room.

"You need to sit down," the girl said. "You're shaking."

They moved to the chairs that flanked the sofa. Now they were only four feet apart.

She stares at me, Jennie thought. Her gaze moves from my stocking feet to my face and stops there. She wants to meet my eyes, but I have seen a glisten start in hers, and I cannot cope with, I am not ready for, tears, and I have to turn away.

Still, we have not touched each other, not even grazed hands. If this were a movie, we would be hugging and crying, but I am still empty. She looks away toward the window, which is black except for a slender oblong of light where a curtain across the street has fallen open. She looks toward the light. Her white silk shirt is low at the neck, so that I see the muscles of her throat contract as she swallows hard. Her face is narrow, thin, and lightly, delicately freckled over the nose, which is small but beaky, not like mine, nor like his. Her eyes are dark with heavy lashes, and the whites are so clear as to be almost blue. Piece by piece, still only half believing, I pick her apart.

The girl turned suddenly around. "This is terrible for you. I'm sorry."

And Jennie, the strong one, who so proudly coped with crises, was unable to answer.

"Do you need anything? Water? Brandy?"

"No. Thank you, no. I'll be all right."

"You're sure?"

"I'm all right. Really."

Jennie listened to the silence, and to the clamor of her thoughts. A fire engine shrieked alarm in the street below; when it went, the silence was deeper. Without sound she was speaking to herself: My head has begun to hurt; hammers smash it from forehead to nape. I put my hand to my forehead, as if a hand could halt pain. I have just realized that if Jay weren't sick, he would have been here a minute ago when the doorbell rang and would be here with us now. The scene is absolutely unimaginable. . . . And I look again at the girl—daughter—in my chair. Now she is concerned, as if afraid I may be sick, and she won't know what to do with me. She doesn't understand—how could she?—that she is a bomb tossed into the middle of my life.

The girl spoke. "Aren't you going to say anything? You're not just going to sit there looking at me, are you?"

The faint rebuke was tempered by a small, coaxing, rather rueful smile, along with an anxious puckering of the forehead, or what could be seen of the forehead under the bangs.

Jennie's answer slipped out of itself. "Do you mind my looking?"

"No, of course not." Jill leaned toward her with chin in hand. "Well, what do you think of me?"

Jennie's eyes stung, stretched wide to let no tears form. She answered, "You're pretty. . . ."

"You're pretty too. . . . Oh, do you have a feeling that this can't be happening? Can you believe we were in this same city all last year and didn't know it? I had no idea. I always thought you must be someplace in the Midwest, since I was born in Nebraska."

How calmly she speaks! Such poise! One would think we were a pair of acquaintances who, after many years, had just met somewhere by accident. She must be quivering inside just as I am, but she is handling her tremors and this astounding situation so much better than I am. My hands are still shaking while hers lie still on the arms of the chair.

"I was born and grew up in Baltimore."

Be prepared now for hundreds of questions. Answers are what she came for. Her mind, going back and back, must be a tangle of questions.

And now Jennie began to feel the girl's pain along with her own. Imagine what it must be not to know who made you! All my life I shall remember Pop: his mustache; his kind, hairy hands; his voice, so gravelly even when he laughed. And Mom, round, cheerful, warning, talking, eternally talking.

"We live in Albuquerque."

"I knew you were somewhere in the West. I wondered where."

"It's beautiful, but New York is marvelous for me. I've been to the opera and the Museum of Modern Art, everywhere. It's marvelous."

The poise was waning. Not quite ready yet for knife-sharp truth, she wants to touch neutral things first, to chatter, to come very gradually to the heart of the matter. For me, too, Jennie thought, it is the only possible way.

"So college gave you your chance to see New York."

"I'd been here once before. My grandmother took me to Europe for my high-school graduation present, and we stayed here for a few days."

"That was a wonderful present." How banal, how ordinary my remark, while my heart still races!

"I know. This was my other present, this bag. She bought it for me in Paris."

A large Vuitton bag stood on the floor at the girl's feet. "I know it's nice, but I didn't really want it."

Paris. Vuitton. The girl—she must stop saying, even mentally, "the girl"—wore a good bracelet watch and tiny diamond studs in her ears, things that Jennie had never had for herself and never could have given.

But some comment was expected. "It's a good size. You can even carry a couple of books in it."

"Oh, I use it, even on campus sometimes. We have a nice campus for a college in the city. You should see it. Have you ever?"

"No," Jennie said. I was there this afternoon, hoping to see you. Hoping not to see you.

"Well, you should sometime."

We circle, spiraling idiotically through trivia, coming fearfully closer and closer to the center where the knife lies.

Jill opened her mouth and closed it, then opened it again. "Just a while before I graduated from high school, that's when Mother gave me your letter."

"My letter?"

"The one you wrote before I was born, that was in the box of baby clothes."

"That one. Oh, yes."

Actually she had forgotten. It was true, then, that you

could really block out anything you wanted to, anything that hurt too much to be remembered.

"We were alone in the house one afternoon. She sat with me and waited while I read it. We both cried."

"I can't remember what I wrote."

"Do you want me to tell you? I know it by heart."

Jennie put up her hand. "Oh, no! Please, no."

I will not let myself be torn to pieces. Now that she has told me this much, I will have to keep seeing them, her and the woman who is her mother. . . . On a porch, she said. Bare mountains. Red mesas. Is Albuquerque on a mesa? Wind chimes tinkle. Cactus grows on the lawn. There's a swing on the porch, with the two of them in it, and the woman's arms around the girl's shoulders; I see she has a thoughtful face, the face of an intellectual, with a gray streak in her dark hair. I don't know why I see her like that.

"That was the day I first knew I absolutely had to find you," Jill said.

"Not before then?"

"Not really. But once the idea came, it stayed with me all the time. I knew I had to know where I came from."

"And your . . . parents?"

"Whether they minded? Not at all. They understood." Jill paused. "My red hair . . . I looked so conspicuous among the others in my family. If you know what I mean."

That glorious hair. Poor soul, wondering where it came from.

"You have your father's hair," Jennie said. And she, too, paused. "It ran in that family. Maybe you look a little like them. . . . I didn't know them well." Then she blurted out, "It's painful for me to talk about them."

"You don't need to. Just tell me about yourself."

"Tell about myself?" Jennie repeated, feeling a bitterness. "A lifetime in an evening?"

"There'll be other evenings, Jennie. Do you mind if I call you that? I wouldn't feel right calling two people Mother."

"I don't mind."

To tell the truth, it seems absurd to call me Mother. I haven't been a mother. And "other evenings," she says. It's only to be expected. Once having taken the first step, others must follow; one doesn't just stop in place. So the road extends, with no imaginable end, except possibly a stone wall for me. She waits now for my history. Her ankles are crossed, the posture seemingly demure, yet already I know that this girl—Jill—is not demure. But then, neither am I.

"You came from Baltimore, you said."

"My parents were poor Jews from Europe, survivors of the death camps. We had very little, but it was a good home. My father's dead, my mother lives in Florida, I have no brothers or sisters—" She choked and stopped.

Crazy, this is, we two here, having this conversation, all of it surreal like Dali's melting clocks and dream vistas, distant houses, lost time. And I, reluctant, as if on a doctor's couch, awakening blurred memories, long ago put away to sleep.

"Excuse me," Jennie said, wiping tears. "I don't usually cry."

"Why don't you? There's nothing wrong with crying."

"Once I start, I'm afraid I won't be able to stop."

She's strong, this girl, sensible, in charge. She leads tonight, and I follow. I'm not used to that.

Jennie made a lump out of the wet handkerchief and straightened herself again in the chair, saying almost timidly, "I'm not sure how to go on."

The response was a quiet one but prompt. "I suppose —I wish—you could tell me why you haven't wanted to see me, why you've resisted for all these weeks. I didn't want to force you by coming here like this, but there wasn't any other way."

"It was—" Jennie said, stumbling. "I mean, it's impossible to face, to be reminded—"

She backs me into a corner. In a courtroom I can thrust and parry; I haven't been trapped there yet. But this girl is not going to let me go. And now she's in my mind to stay, so that I'll never forget her. I'll see her face forever and hear her voice. She speaks well, good diction is so important, young people all seem to slur these days, they speak so badly. . . . And she sits with grace, tall in the chair. She'd fit into Peter's family. . . . And isn't *that* ironic? Oh, the pain in my head won't stop.

At that moment Jill said, "I wanted so much to fit into your life, to be a part of it."

Jennie gasped. "How can that be? It's so late. Too late for us. You don't—I mean, we don't fit into each other's lives."

"No, you were right the first time. You could fit into mine. You just don't want me in yours. You said so to the people who called you."

"I didn't say it like that."

How cruel, how stupid of them to have told her that way! And yet I did say it, didn't I? I said they should leave me alone. Look at her. . . . Her skin is like milk, and the blue veins at the temples, where the hair falls away, are so thin, her lifeblood flows in them. . . . Now she's grieving, she's hurt. . . . I was right from the beginning. It was better for neither of us to know the other, ever.

And Jennie spoke very softly. "I only meant, it's hard —yes, I said impossible—to have any relationship after nineteen years. That's all I meant."

"We could try. We can try right now to communicate." Jill looked at her watch. "It's only nine. You could tell me a lot in the next hour or two. If you wanted to," she finished.

Jennie sighed. "I'll do better. I'll sketch a family tree and send it to you. I'll write some anecdotes, all that I know about my side. As to the other—his—I can't tell you much. I knew nothing except the very little he told me, that they were Southerners—you might call them Jewish aristocrats, I suppose. I don't know any more."

"It doesn't matter. I've already talked with Peter, and he's told me."

Jennie stared. "You . . . you *what?*"

Jill stared back. "I found him, the same as I found you. We've had long conversations by telephone these last few weeks. He's in Chicago, and he's asked me to fly out there next weekend. *He* was so excited when the committee people called him! *He* wanted to get in touch with me that same day."

Dumbfounded, Jennie could only let the words pour over her like ice water.

"We have a lot in common." The girl's voice, rising, held triumph. "He's an archaeologist. You didn't know that, did you? He's a professor. And I went on a dig once in Israel, so we had a lot to talk about. He sounds like a wonderful person. I can't wait to see him."

After shock, thoughts flowed, and Jennie began to see more clearly the young person who sat opposite. An extraordinarily determined young person, she was, and clever, too, keeping back the business about Peter until she had heard first what Jennie had to tell her.

And she said carefully, "I'm glad for you, Jill. And for him, too, if this is what you want. I hope good comes of it."

"Why shouldn't good come of it?"

"I don't know, exactly, because I don't know anything about him. I only know that a life can have many complications—"

"Like your life?" Jill's eyes, demanding, met Jennie's and held.

This time Jennie's held too. "Yes. Like mine."

"But you won't tell me what yours are."

"No. My complications are my own."

The momentary, following silence threatened Jennie, and she opened her lips to break it. But Jill spoke first.

"He wants to see you."

Jennie started. "Who? Peter? Wants to see me?"

"Yes, he says now that I've made the move, it would be a good thing for us all. He's coming to New York during the semester break."

"Oh, no! Oh, no! You're not going to do this to me, either of you."

"I don't know how you're going to prevent it. He wants to, he told me so."

"I won't have it, do you hear?" Jennie cried out furiously. "I simply won't have this outrage!"

Netted and caught. Peter again, summoned back from the dead. In the next room the clothes for a honeymoon are spread on the bed. The impostor's honeymoon . . . Jay . . . oh, my dear, my dear, am I going to lose you? Oh, I'm determined not to, and yet I know I will. I see the writing on the wall. I see it.

"What are you people trying to do to me?" she screamed.

Jill picked the Vuitton bag from the floor and stood up. Her eyes were filled with tears, but she spoke coldly.

"You're not at all what I hoped for. I never thought you would be like this."

Jennie stood too. "What did you think I would be like?"

"I don't know, but not like this."

Tense, taut, trembling, the two confronted each other.

"Yes," Jill said bitterly, "I do know. I thought at least—at least you would kiss me."

And Jennie wept. Grief burst open in her throat.
"Oh," she said incoherently, "you come here like this
. . . so that I can't even believe what I'm seeing . . .
nineteen years. I open the door. And now he too . . . I
can't think straight. . . . Of course I'll kiss you."

Jill drew back. "No. Not that way. Not if I have to ask
for it."

The tears ran over and, unwiped, slid down her
cheeks. She opened the door and ran out into the hall.

"Wait!" Jennie called. "You mustn't go like that! Oh,
please—"

But the girl was gone. Her quick steps clattered on the
stairs; the outer door thumped shut and echoed through
the house. For a long minute Jennie stood hearing the
echo, then turned back into the apartment and sat down
with her hands over her face.

The first immediate sense of unreality returned. This
couldn't have happened. Yet the girl's lipstick was there
on the floor as proof of her presence. It had rolled out of
her purse most probably, when at the start of tears she
had reached for a tissue. Jennie picked it up: Marcella
Borghese, Rimini Rose Frost. She let it lie on her palm. It
grew warm, lying there so long, while she thought of the
girl's smile, her angry, beautiful eyes, and her tears.

"I read the letter that came with the baby
clothes . . ."

A child looking for her mother. Poor child.

But she has a mother, has always had a good one. Why
me, now?

You know why. Don't ask.

Poor child.

But they will ruin everything, she and Peter. Peter
coming back from the dead.

How can I ever keep the two of them separate from
Jay? How dare he, how dare the two of them do this to
me?

After a long time Jennie got up, turned the lamp off, and took a Valium from the medicine cabinet. Only once in her life, under stress of root-canal surgery and an infection, had she taken a tranquilizer. Tonight, though, she would have swallowed anything that could dull the confusion and despair.

In the morning her mind felt clearer. "The important thing always," she reminded herself aloud as she sat in the little kitchen having coffee, "is to keep one's head."

But Jill had gone crying, and gone like that across the city in the dark. Surely amends must be made! I don't remember exactly what I said, Jennie thought. I only know I was beside myself. Something had to be done, though. A sensible, quiet talk. We could go someplace for lunch and I could explain things better. We'd both be less emotional a second time, I think.

She was reaching for the telephone book when the telephone rang.

"Good morning," Jay said. Amazing man, he was one of those people who are cheerful and vigorous when they wake up. "A miracle! My fever's gone, I feel fine, and how would you like to have a Sunday jog in the park? The kids are with the grandparents all day."

She thought quickly. "Oh, darling, I thought you were sick and I made other plans."

"Oh, hell, what other plans?"

"I . . . there's some friend of my mother's in town from Miami. I have to take her to a museum or something. We're supposed to have lunch."

"Well, I could put up with that. I'll take you both to lunch."

"She's an old lady, Jay, you'd hate it."

"What makes you think I hate old ladies? Listen, you'll be an old lady someday, and I don't expect to hate you."

"Honestly, it would be awful for you. As a matter of

fact, there are two of them, and one of them has a husband. They're nice, but they're really very boring people."

"You meet plenty of boring people when you practice law. I'm used to them."

"Yes, but why should you suffer on a Sunday? Besides, you had a fever last night and you're supposed to stay indoors for a day afterward at least."

"I'm actually being rejected," he complained in mock sorrow.

"Yes, for today you are. Go on back and relax with the paper. I'll call you later."

She hung up. Lies and subterfuge already. I hate myself for it. That's what comes of lies. They beget more lies.

Nevertheless she dialed the Barnard number. Now, waiting for Jill to come to the phone, she had a recollection of dormitory smells—sweet talcum powder and the sharp odor of cleaning fluid—of dormitory noises, rock music, ringing phones, and high heels rapping; she saw Jill hurrying down the corridor, the hair lifting from her shoulders as she ran, anticipating a call from some young man, or perhaps from home.

"Jill," she said, "this is Jennie."

"Yes?" The tone was cool.

Say it boldly. "I was concerned about last night, about whether you got back all right."

"I got back all right."

"I'm sorry that my being upset was so hard on you. I thought maybe you and I could have a talk and clarify things a little. Would you do that?"

"Well . . ." Now the tone was cautious. "When?"

"Today. Lunch, I thought. Around one o'clock." She decided quickly; best to make it downtown on the West Side, someplace where none of Jay's friends, most of whom lived on the Upper East Side, would be apt to go strolling on a Sunday. "The Hilton on Sixth Avenue at Fifty-third Street. It's nice there, they don't rush you. Shall I meet you at the registration desk?"

"I'll be there."

"And, Jill . . . it'll be easier for us both this time."

"I hope so." A hesitation. "I'm glad you called, Jennie."

We'll talk things over calmly and work them out, Jennie said to herself. She's old enough, and surely she's smart enough to understand that people have differing circumstances, that you have to make allowances for one another.

Jennie's spirits were still sanguine as she waited in the lobby of the great hotel. She had always been a people watcher, and today her observations of the passing scene were especially sharp.

Here was a handsome, petulant woman with a tired husband, there a middle-aged man pushing a young girl in a wheelchair, here a young couple with shining faces and cheap new honeymoon luggage, there two businessmen arguing, and an embarrassed mother struggling with a kicking child. Ebb and flow, and survive.

She saw Jill before the girl saw her. She hadn't realized last night how tall Jill was. The height, like the hair, came from him. She had good carriage, a long, free stride in her pleated plaid skirt and camel-hair jacket. For a moment the men with the attaché cases stopped arguing and turned to look after her.

Something leapt in Jennie. "Surprised by joy." Who had written that? I'm surprised by joy. This person coming toward me now belongs to me! She put out her arms, and this time Jill came into them.

They stood then, laughing a little and crying a little, until Jennie spoke. A surge of energy and hope came running through her, and she grasped Jill's hands.

"Didn't I say it would be better today? I knew it would! Come on, let's eat, let's talk!"

But in the dining room they suddenly became silent.

"It's funny, I don't know how to start," Jill said. "That's what you said yesterday, isn't it?"

"Just let it come as it wants."

"It's not coming."

"All right, I've an idea. Tell me about your first time in New York."

"Well, we stayed at the Plaza. I'd read all the Eloise books when I was a child, so I wanted to see it. We ate in the Oak Room, where Eloise must have had dinner some nights. And once we went out to a French restaurant— Lutèce, I think—and had duck with orange sauce and two desserts."

She seems younger than she did last night, Jennie thought. I mustn't stare like this, she told herself, and buttered a roll instead.

"I love everything French. Of course, I'm glad I'm American, but if I couldn't be American, I'd want to be French. My grandmother taught French before she retired."

"Did she? My mother speaks French—not very well. She lived in France before the Nazis came, but she's forgotten a lot. If you don't use it, you know . . ."

"I'd like you to tell me more about her."

"Well, I will. But it's a long story."

Mom would be stunned by all this; then she would weep.

"We had the best time together in France," Jill resumed. "The best. She knew just where to go."

"She sounds like fun."

"We always had fun in our family. Would you like to see some family pictures? I've brought an envelope full." Jill leaned across the table. "Here's one with all of us, taken last summer on Dad's birthday."

Eight or ten people stood and sat on some steps below a door with flowering shrubs on either side. In a corner of the foreground was the edge of a barbecue kettle. An American family scene, Grant Wood, but contemporary. Jennie startled herself with a touch of jealousy and stifled it at once.

"All those children . . ." she began.

"Isn't it amazing? Mom had four of her own with no trouble at all after they got me. But I understand that often happens. This is Jerry next to me, he's a year and a half younger. This is Lucille, she's fifteen, this is Sharon, she's twelve, and here's Mark, the baby. He's seven."

"And this is your mother?"

"No, that's Aunt Fay. This is Mom here in front of Dad."

Here they were, this very average-looking man and woman in T-shirts and shorts, smiling for the camera and squinting into the light. These were the parents who had held and cherished the hand that now brushed Jennie's as they passed the pictures back and forth.

Some comment had to be made. "They look young."

Jill considered. "Yes, younger than they are. And they act young. They're happy people. . . . You know, I feel sorry for people with messed-up families! Half the people I meet seem to come from homes where nobody laughs. Or where they hate each other, you know?"

"I know."

"Were you ever married, Jennie?" The tone and the look were childishly blunt; in an older person they would be thought of as rude.

"No," Jennie said, feeling discomfort, which she covered with enthusiasm. "Have you got more pictures?"

"Well, let's see. Here's one. We go skiing a lot. We only have to drive an hour."

Behind the group and around it lay mountains, folded and ridged like newspapers that someone had crumpled and flung to the ground, dark and dry, the color of cinders next to the snow.

"Once I imagined you were in California," Jennie said. "I kept seeing the Pacific."

"New Mexico's just as beautiful, in a different way. Our sky's so large, so blue all day, and the sunset's rose-colored, so bright that it burns."

Jennie smiled. "You speak like a poet."

"I write poetry. Very bad, I'm sure."

This girl, like most people, was multifaceted, a cluster of contradictions. The previous night she had been, among other things, cool and controlling. Today she was ever so charmingly naïve.

"You really ought to see New Mexico. Do you ski?"

Jennie shook her head. "It's an expensive sport."

"Oh. Have you got problems? Are you poor?"

The question amused Jennie. "Some people might call me poor." The top-floor walk-up, the simple furnishings. "I'm satisfied with what I have, so I don't feel poor."

"You must be happy with your work, then."

"I am. I'm a defender of women—poor women, mostly. And now I seem to be taking on another interest, too, something I didn't know I cared about that much." She was aware that pride had crept into her tone, born of a surprising impulse to show who she was and what she had achieved. "I'm in the middle of a tremendously important fight right now."

"I'd like to hear about it," Jill said, laying down her fork.

So Jennie, divulging neither name nor location, related the story of the Green Marsh. The story grew vivid in the telling; this was the first time she had spoken of the issue to anyone not involved in it, and as she talked, she could feel the strength of her own convictions coming through.

"There's a movement something like that at home,"

Jill said when Jennie had finished, "to save the Jerez Mountains from developers. Dad's active in it. He's on every conservation committee you can think of. We've each got our thing. Mine's Indians, their social structure, ancient and modern." She regarded Jennie over the rim of the coffee cup. "Peter's done work on the southwestern Indians too. That's an odd coincidence, don't you think?" And when no comment came, she asked, "Do you mind that I even mention him at all?"

Jennie's reply was quiet. "Jill, I do mind some. I don't want to think about him. Please understand that."

"If you hated him so, why didn't you have an abortion?"

"Oh, my God, the questions you ask! It wasn't a matter of hatred. I didn't hate him then, and I don't now." She put out her hand and laid it over the girl's free hand. "I never even considered an abortion." She could have said, "They wanted me to," but she refrained. "Never."

Jill looked over Jennie's head across the room. Jennie thought, I'm learning her ways already. She looks beyond you, or down at the floor as she did last night, when she is considering her next words.

The next words came. "I'm surprised you never married. Didn't you ever want to be?"

An honest answer was expected. But Jennie could only be halfway honest about this.

"Once."

"To my father?"

"It didn't work out."

"How awful for you!"

"For the moment, yes, it was."

"Only for the moment? But didn't you love him?"

"If you can call it love. I thought it was, anyway."

Jill, not answering that, looked down again. And Jennie, relieved for the moment of face-to-face contact, examined her once more. How much might she already know of love? Men would find her appealing; to be sure, she didn't have classic beauty, the symmetry that once had been essential in our culture, but standards had changed. That hair alone was enough, then the assurance, the intelligence—"A delightful girl," Mr. Riley had said, or maybe it had been Emma Dunn.

"So whether or not it was love, you had me."

Jennie said steadily, "Yes, I went away by myself and had you. I was alone. My parents never knew."

"Why didn't they?"

"It would have hurt them too much. It's hard to explain. You would have to know them to understand why."

"I can't imagine having a baby at my age."

"I was younger than you are now."

"How frightened you must have been. No, I can't imagine it," Jill murmured in a tender voice.

"I couldn't imagine it, either."

That cloud again, that heavy gray blanket, oppressed Jennie. A dull sadness fell into the iridescent room. People were pleasantly chattering away; so many were in family groups of all ages. Festive and at ease with one another . . .

Jill cried out, "How brave you were!"

"Where there's no choice, one had better be."

"How terribly hard for you to give your baby away!"

"If I had known you or even held you, it would have been impossible, and I knew that. So I never once looked at you when you were born."

"Did you think about me often afterward?"

Where am I finding the strength for this torture? Jennie asked herself.

"I tried not to. But sometimes I imagined where you lived and what your name might be."

"It's a silly name, isn't it? A silly combination. Victoria

is for Mother's sister, who died. Jill is the name they call me by."

Jill smiled, showing teeth of the immaculate evenness that is usually the work of an orthodontist. Yes, she had had the best care.

"I couldn't allow myself to think about you. It was done, finished. You were in good hands, and I had to go on. You can see that, can't you?" And Jennie heard the plea in her own question.

"You picked yourself up and went to law school. You made something out of your life. Yes, I can see."

It was a simple observation to which Jennie could think of no reply, so she made none. The even dialogue —statement given, statement returned—seemed to have reached a stopping place.

Jill spoke next. "But after all, you haven't told me very much about yourself, have you?"

"I don't know what else there is to tell you. I've given the facts. There aren't very many."

Abruptly a new expression passed across Jill's face: a puzzlement in the eyes; a tightening, almost a severity, about the mouth. Subtly but unmistakably, another *atmosphere* had come between the two women. But it was understandable, wasn't it? With such floods of feeling, two sets of experiences, two lives so wide apart in age, in place . . . and everything . . .

Cheerfully, to dispel this atmosphere, Jennie suggested dessert. A waiter came, fussed with the plates, and recommended pastries from the cart.

"I really don't want one," Jill said. "I only took it to make the lunch last longer."

The admission touched Jennie. "We'll find a place to sit and talk some more in one of the lounges. No need to hurry," she coaxed brightly.

"I thought perhaps you might be in a hurry. Then why don't we go to your place?"

Jennie shrank. They had been an hour and a half over this lunch, and still she hadn't made the point she'd intended to make. Jill must understand there could be no more visits to the apartment. She must. What if, for instance, Jay were to take it into his head to drop in this very afternoon? Or any other time?

"Jill, I have to tell you, I'm sorry, but we can't go to my place."

The clear eyes opened wide, alert on the instant, probing as they had done last night.

"Why not?"

What trust can you have in a person who hides her true self for years, and then suddenly decides to reveal herself? Jennie thought. You can only wonder what else is hidden. . . .

Her nervous hands, palms upturned, made a small protest.

"It's terribly difficult to say this, to explain. But there are things—deep personal things, reasons—" Helpless before that probing gaze, she stopped.

Jill waited, saying nothing, which forced her to begin again.

"You see . . . I tried to say it yesterday, but I did it very badly, I know, and gave you the wrong idea, that I didn't care about you. But the way things are with me . . . There are reasons." The nervous hands were in her lap now, clasping each other. "What I'm trying to say is, you mustn't get in touch with me. You mustn't ever come to my house or even telephone. You have to promise me that. I'll be the one to get in touch with you."

"I don't understand," Jill said. Her cheeks were flushed.

The aura that had begun to warm them when they embraced in the lobby and talked across the table, the intimate sadness, the tenderness, the animation, all now vanished under the new atmosphere.

"I don't like it, Jennie. First you give and next you take back. Why?"

"I know it's hard to understand. If you could just trust me—"

"You don't seem to trust me!"

"How can you say that? I do trust you. Of course I do."

"No, you're hiding something."

How stern she was! And a fighter too. She'd fight for principles and stand up for rights, her own and others'. In the space of an instant, Jennie saw who Jill was.

Jill's eyes were wet and shining. "Is it me?" she persisted. "Are you ashamed of me?"

The word *ashamed,* containing as it did an element of partial truth (not ashamed of you as a person but of your emerging from my denial of the truth), along with this attack, yes, this furious attack from someone whom Jennie had never harmed, for whom God alone knew she had done the very best she could, made anger rise again. And she knew that she was angry at herself for having to inflict this hurt, for causing these tears.

She had to defend herself. "Shame has nothing to do with it, believe me, Jill. Can't you try to accept what I offer? I want my independent life." Need pushed her; she spoke rapidly, urgently. "You have yours. Peter has his. I never bothered him for anything. Isn't it fair for me to have my independent life?"

Now Jill's tears ran hard. She spoke through them scornfully. "Independent life! Am I stopping you by sitting in your living room?"

"Of course you don't mean to, but all the same, it would be—"

Jill interrupted her. "This lunch was a deception. You came here to tell me in the nicest possible way to stay out of your way. That's all you came for." And she pushed her chair back as if to rise.

"Sit down, Jill. Sit down. Let's be reasonable. I beg you. Eat your dessert."

"Jennie . . . I'm not a baby to be pacified with sweets."

"You're not being fair to me! I said I'd call you, didn't I? Whenever I can, I will. I only said you shouldn't be the one to—"

"I won't call you, don't worry. You needn't have any fears about me. But I'll tell you something. I can't answer for Peter. He was pretty well shocked by what you said to the search committee. He'll be more shocked next week when I tell him about today."

Jill rose abruptly, upsetting her chair. A waiter rushed to retrieve it, heads turned toward the small commotion, and Jennie reached for Jill's arm.

"Don't go like this," she pleaded, keeping her voice low. "Don't run away again. Let me pay the check and we'll sit someplace and talk."

Jill gathered bag, gloves, and scarf. "There's nothing to talk about unless you tell me we can behave normally to each other. That I can ring your phone like anybody else and . . . can you tell me that?"

The waiter stood holding the check, and a woman at the next table was staring in open curiosity. Appalled and shaken, Jennie sought new words, a fresh approach.

"Can you?" Jill repeated.

"No, not exactly. But listen, hear me out—"

"I've heard you, and I don't want to hear any more. Thank you for lunch."

Jennie watched her go. Without strength to follow and aware that it would be of no use, anyway, to do so, she sat gazing at Jill's plate, on which the ice cream was already melting over the pie. Strawberry, it was. A pink puddle. So that's the end of my daughter, come and gone in the space of a day. Raging eyes, a retreating back, and a puddle of ice cream in a dish.

The waiter coughed, a reminder of his presence. She took the check, paid, and went out to the street. Taxis stood at the curb before the hotel's entrance, but she had no wish to get home so soon, there to sit bewildered and alone. So she turned north instead and began to walk.

In the park, brown with winter, the twiggy treetops, still wet after rain, were washed with a metallic sheen. The cold sky raced. Sunday afternoon was a bleak time, no matter what the weather, unless you were with someone you loved.

Yet she was in no condition just now to be with Jay. She was in no condition to be with herself, either. And, giving up, with no place to go but home, she hurried eastward. Nearing home, she began to run down the last street, up the stairs and into the apartment, where she bolted the door and sat down, out of breath with effort and weariness.

Voices rang: Jill's, Jay's, Mr. Riley's, her own father's, her own mother's, and Jay's mother's making a plaintive clamor, each for his own reason. Jennie, Jennie, what's happening to you?

When she turned the television on, the voices were stilled, only to be replaced by that of an enthusiastic young woman chuckling with delight over a new detergent. She switched the television off and lay down on the sofa.

I'm tired. So tired. Sick at heart, as they say. I thought we could iron things out, that I could find some compromise. I really believed I could, and look what happened! Such a quick temper the girl has! She hardly gave me a chance. Still, from her point of view, I suppose my secrecy is baffling, like a door slammed in her face. But I was willing to go partway, and I said so, didn't I? I had in my mind that I would call her sometimes; I really would. I couldn't just go on for the rest of my life as though I'd never seen her. How could I?

And yet my offer would be no real relationship at all, would it? She knew that. And it wouldn't work, anyway. No, married to Jay, in his house, with his children, I would be a juggler with a dozen balls in the air; eventually I'd be bound to miss one, and then they all would tumble. . . .

She fell into an exhausted doze and was awakened, in a room grown dark, by the ring of the telephone.

"Hello," Jay said. "How was your day?"

"My day?" she repeated, and then remembered her mother's friends, the museum and lunch. "Oh, not too bad. A little too long. I was asleep just now."

"Well, I had a miserable Sunday. Being alone in this apartment is like being alone in a stadium. It echoes. I couldn't stand it. I took the dog for such a long walk that he's knocked out."

"I'm sorry I abandoned you. I won't do it again."

"Don't forget tomorrow night."

A client of Jay's was the sponsor of a modern-dance recital which, being a lover of ballet, Jennie did not especially enjoy. But feeling the need to keep up her courage, she made herself sound bright.

"Of course not. I'm looking forward to it."

She slept restlessly, waking often to hear traffic dwindle as the night deepened and to hear it start again as black turned to gray, to white, and finally to a row of yellow bars between the slats of the venetian blinds.

There was just so much that makeup could do. Trouble left its wretched mark even on a young face, even after the most careful application of eye shadow, eyeliner, lipstick, and blush. Tie on a red-and-white scarf, walk briskly, and smile; it made little difference because the mark was there.

Dinah, the typist, inquired whether Jennie felt all right. Her first client advised her to take it easy because there was a lot of flu going around. By mid-afternoon she was starting to wonder whether she really might be ill. Her eyes wandered, unseeing, over the records on the desk, and then out toward the building across the street where lights were coming on as the afternoon darkened. For an instant she saw a picture of Jill, also at a desk, and also, perhaps, unable to focus her thoughts. Then she was almost overwhelmed by pity, until returning anger surged. Unfair, unfair to be held this way, "between a rock and a hard place," as Mom used to say.

Dinah appeared at the door to inform Jennie that a Dr. Cromwell wanted to see her.

Cromwell. What on earth could he be wanting? Jennie's mind was a million miles away from the Green Marsh.

The old man wore, along with a polka-dotted bow tie, the affable expression that she remembered. Natty and spruce, he looked exactly like what he was, a small-town gentleman visiting the big city.

"Gosh," he said, "I was expecting to see one of those offices with a mile of corridors, carpets, and oil paintings. I was in one of those places one time, made me feel small. Even New York dentists' places are—" Aware of his unintentional disparagement, he corrected himself. "This is nice, though. Comfortable place to work in. Well, how are you? Busy getting ready for the wedding?"

"Oh, it will be very quiet," she said.

"Even so, I hate to come to you with another problem. It's about a phone call." His bland face took on a timid, worried expression. "First we had all those anonymous letters, but you know about those."

Jennie nodded. "Anonymous, but no secret that Bruce Fisher probably wrote them."

"Probably. No secret that he's half crazy, either."

The more recent events in Jennie's life had pushed some others to the back of her mind, but now they leapt

up in full, vivid force: the vicious thrust on the stairs and
the cunning grin as the man fled past.

"But what I want to tell you is— Oh, I don't know
whether he had anything to do with it, maybe not, but
you never know. Why, I remember that case, it was
twelve or fifteen years back, more likely fifteen, when he
and a crowd of—"

Jennie, concealing impatience, said kindly, "You were
going to tell me about a telephone call."

"Yes, of course. Well, I've had two, actually. They may
not mean anything, but then again they may. And Arthur Wolfe says I must talk to you about them. He can be
a worrier, Arthur can. Still, in the circumstances—"

"Who called you? Do you think it was Fisher?"

"It didn't sound like Fisher at all. I'd know his voice.
Besides, this man gave his name. John Jones."

Jennie made a wry face. "John Jones!"

"Yes, it sounds phony, doesn't it? But he was very
polite, even friendly. He said he was interested in the
Barker proposition—"

"What does that mean, 'interested in it'? Is he a partner, or what?"

"Well, he wasn't clear about that. I got the impression
he just worked for them or something."

"What did he want with you?"

"Well, he knew I was on the town council, and he
realized I had the town's interest at heart, and he
thought it would be a good idea for us to get together
and talk. He thought we'd find out we weren't so far
apart, after all."

"And what did you say?"

"Well, I said I didn't think we could, but that if he had
anything new to say, it should come up at the town
council's next meeting."

Jennie gave approval. "Just the right answer, George."

"But he said no, that most ideas were developed in

executive discussions beforehand. He said he'd heard about me and had a lot of respect for the intelligent work I'd been doing on the council, and he'd been wanting to meet me. I can't figure out how he knew so much about me." The old man blushed.

"Why? What else did he know about you?" she asked, feeling as though she were leading a child through cross-examination.

"Well, it really surprised me that he knew about Martha's cancer. My wife, Martha, you know. It's been in remission for three years, but now they say she needs another operation. As a matter of fact, she's with me in the city. We're seeing somebody new at Sloan-Kettering tomorrow."

And Jennie, observing the old, wrinkled throat above the natty bow tie, the old throat that she hadn't noticed before, felt soft pity.

"I wonder how he knew. Surely you don't have friends in common."

"Oh, no. He comes from New York."

Unless he's made inquiries in town, she thought, and asked, "Exactly what did he say about your wife?"

"Just that he'd heard about her illness and that I must have a lot on my mind. That I must have big expenses."

"Oh?"

"Of course, they are awfully big. That's the God's truth. Not that I wouldn't spend my last cent for Martha. Still, I'm only a small-town dentist. . . . Say, are you thinking this could have something to do with a bribe? Are you? Because Arthur Wolfe said—"

"Do you think so?" Jennie queried. Poor old man. Poor child.

"Well, I did wonder. And Arthur Wolfe—"

"Don't wonder anymore. Of course that's what he's leading up to."

"Oh, my," George said. He reflected a moment. "I

suppose he's trying everybody on the council, one at a time."

"No, George. That's not the way it's done. And certainly not in this case. I'll tell you why not. The way it is now on the council, the vote stands four to four. You've got the mayor and three cronies on one side. The mayor says he hasn't decided yet, but we all know he has. And on the other side, you've got four who probably aren't going to budge, two summer people who probably don't want a development near their rural retreats; Henry Pope the lawyer, who's got a rich wife; and the Presbyterian minister. So that leaves you. Speaking plainly, you're the only one they think they can easily buy off, and you cast the ninth vote, the deciding vote."

"You've got it all figured out." Cromwell gave a long, tired sigh.

"It's my job to figure it out."

Neither said anything for a moment until Cromwell exclaimed, "So all I have to do is refuse to see him! Then what am I worried about? Nothing!"

"I wouldn't say that. I said there were four who probably wouldn't budge. Probably. Okay, the minister won't be bought, but while I don't think the others would be, either, still . . . they might be. Henry Pope, for instance. The Wolfes tell me his law practice isn't all that great. Who knows what he might do if the offer were big enough?"

Cromwell looked dismayed. "Oh, I don't believe Henry would ever—"

Jennie interrupted. "You don't believe, but you don't know, either, do you? So if this Jones person fails with you and then tries Pope or someone else, he could get his fifth vote, couldn't he?"

"I suppose so. What are you getting at?"

"What I'm getting at is that he mustn't fail with you. We have to get the bribe offer on record."

"How do we do that?"

"I'm not exactly sure. I want to think about it."

"Now, you mean?"

"Stay awhile. I want to look something up."

Row on row of brown-bound volumes stood on shelves across the room. Searching, Jennie found what she wanted and set it on the desk with a thump. She read, took some notes, and called Dinah.

"Bring me the file on the Fillipo case, will you, please?"

One of her clients had been released from a wretched affair with a drug dealer when he had been sentenced to prison. There was something in the record, she recalled, although the case had been finished at least four years earlier, about the defendant's having been trapped by a taped conversation.

George watched her nervously while she turned pages; his foot, which was in her line of vision whenever she raised her eyes for a moment, kept tapping the floor in rapid rhythm.

At last she put the papers aside. "Would you consider wearing a wire, George? Go to lunch with Jones and tape him?"

George started. His answer came with a quaver. "That's—I mean, that's awfully dangerous, isn't it? If he should find out—"

"There's always a chance. I can't tell you otherwise," Jennie replied seriously. "But it's also highly unlikely. Very. This sort of thing is done all the time in crime investigations, you know."

"How's it done?" The foot was tapping harder now.

"I honestly don't know the exact mechanisms. We'll find out when we see the district attorney."

There was a long wait, during which the old man seemed to be searching Jennie's face. She met his eyes frankly.

"All right. I trust you, Jennie. I'll do it. If I didn't trust you, I wouldn't do it."

She was touched. "Thank you for the trust, George."

He hesitated. "It's a matter of principle," he said. "Being a good citizen. I suppose that sounds corny these days."

"Not to me, it doesn't."

"Well, then, let's go. What's my next step?"

"Just this. When he calls again, which he will, you'll set up an appointment. Meanwhile I'll see the district attorney. If he okays this, then you'll go to be wired, and that's it. That's the whole thing."

She saw that George, in spite of his apprehension, was beginning to expand with pride.

"Wired," he repeated. "It's like something in the movies."

"Like the movies and like life."

George looked at his watch and stood up. "Gosh, I've got to get Martha at four, in ten minutes."

Jennie rose, too, and held out her hand. "Don't worry too much if you can help it," she said kindly.

"I'll try not to. It's just having too many problems at one time, that's the hard part."

"Yes," she said to herself when the door had closed behind the old man. "I know. Well do I know. Too many problems at one time."

"I have a strong hunch that it's our good mayor who put 'Jones' on to George Cromwell," Jay said. "Obviously somebody with a motive told him about George's problem."

After the dance recital they had stopped at a delicatessen for corned-beef sandwiches and coffee. The privacy of a back booth, high-walled, was a relief after the recital, which had given Jennie more of a headache than she had already. The pounding music, the jerky, piston thrust of the dancers, all angular jutting knees and elbows, were supposed, she knew, to represent the fragmentation of modern life. But she herself was too fragmented to care.

"Yes," Jay said, "the more I think of it, the surer I am. It's Honest Chuck the mayor who's behind this."

"There's so much I'll never understand. A firm like Barker—would it make so much difference if they lost this one job when they've made, and are making, millions elsewhere?"

"So much difference? Seven or eight million difference, I'd estimate. But there's more to it than money alone, Jennie. It's a question of not wanting to lose. It's a power game. They don't want to be beaten by a handful of jackass nature lovers, which is how they see people like us. These people hang tough."

"I suppose that's why they are where they are, isn't it?"

"That's why a lot of very gentle, decent people are where they are, too, because their ancestors hung tough."

Sadness, like a chill, swept over Jennie. For a moment she seemed to see the world as on a map, a maze of intersecting paths, an elaborate board game in which all the players were competing to cut one another off, so that no matter what anyone wanted to accomplish, even the most simple thing, which was just to be let alone, was not possible without fighting for it.

Jay continued thoughtfully. "There's another angle we could take, you know, through the Environmental Protection Agency. Half the tract is wetlands."

Called back to the subject, she agreed. "It's another approach."

"But it all takes time. Meanwhile we've got to stop them in their tracks. Or rather, old George will have to stop them. I'm surprised he's willing to go ahead with it."

"He's scared to death, poor guy. But he feels committed. He said it's a matter of principle. He's such a fine old guy."

"When are you going to see the DA?"

"I'll call tomorrow and hope to see him in the afternoon."

"You ought to have my dad along, don't you think?"

"Of course. George can go later. He's going to stay here for a day or two while Martha has tests at the hospital."

Jay shoved the plate away. "I'm not as hungry as I thought I was."

"You're tired," Jennie said tenderly.

"To tell you the truth, I am. A bad thing happened today. One of our young men sort of fell apart in my office. His wife walked out on him yesterday, and he had to go to somebody to cry, I suppose, and he picked me."

"What made her leave?"

"He says she told him she just got tired of being married, wanted an open marriage, all that stuff. But who knows? I wasn't there, I didn't live with them. But I'll tell you, his tears got to me." Jay reached across the table and grasped both her hands. "Oh, Jennie, what a blessed thing it is to believe in someone absolutely and completely, to know another human being as well as you know yourself! I want to be married to you so badly, I can't wait."

What wouldn't Shirley give, she and all the others, for a man who would say this!

"You don't answer me," he said. Two small lines appeared between his eyebrows.

"Do I have to? Darling, you shouldn't even need an answer. You ought to know."

"I do, I do. Shall we go back to your place?"

She felt a flood of longing, and of sorrow also, because the longing for him was now diluted, and because his familiar hands, the nails with half-moons, and the cleft in his chin, and the single dark wave that kept falling over the temple were all not perfectly her own anymore. She had such queer feelings sometimes, as though they were about to disappear while she was looking at them.

And Jill, young Jill, was the sole reason for these queer feelings. When her eyes filled yesterday, the tears made a path down her cheeks and rolled inside her collar. Will I dream about her tears tonight? Will I ever see her again? Can I bear never seeing her again? But I don't think she wants to see me—not on my terms, anyway. And I can't see her on hers. How can I?

Jay was waiting. "But you said you were so tired," she told him.

"All right, then. No love tonight."

They went out to the street. Under a lamp he tilted her face up to his. "So sweet you are. I don't mind tonight. I can wait. In a few more weeks I'll never have to wait again, will I?"

CHAPTER

8

It was Arthur Wolfe's authority and name that had impressed young Martin, the district attorney, with the importance of their story. There had, after all, been no actual offer, in so many words, of a bribe, Jennie reflected. And Martin had remarked as much at the beginning.

"Not yet," Arthur had told him. "But there will be one, make no mistake. I know what I'm talking about. I've seen our mayor and his friends in action here. I've been active in township affairs for a good many years, you know."

The young man had nodded. "And county affairs, Mr. Wolfe." He had smiled. "I'm remembering that article a while back where they called you 'the watchdog.'"

Arthur had laughed. "And now we have two dogs," he had said, indicating Jennie, who had added somewhat grimly that the way things looked, they'd be needing a pack before they were finished.

Now Martin was questioning her. Wary and keen, he kept his eyes on hers as his questions and her answers flowed.

"So you really believe there's a relationship between the man who shouted at the meeting and shoved you on the stairs and the one who telephoned Cromwell?"

"Yes, I do. To begin with, there's his reputation. And you have only to look at him to feel the anger in him. But there have to be others too. A person or persons in Barker Developers, making connections. I know it's all still vague, hard to tell where the connections begin or where they may end. But there are connections, I'm positive."

She looked out of the window, where a worn-out, dark green shade, stopped at the halfway mark, revealed through the lower part of the pane a network of thin black branches and a complex webbing of twigs. A web without beginning or end. The waning wintry light was ominous, and she understood the primary cause of her dark mood.

Martin got up and switched on a fluorescent light that hung above the massive desk so that it could glare upon the stained blotter, scarred chairs, heaped papers, green metal file cabinets, and tan walls. No brightness could cheer this government-issue room. Nevertheless Martin's tone was brisk.

"And you think this man Cromwell can handle it?"

Arthur looked uncertain. "He's not a quick thinker, by any means, my old friend. But he's brave, he's willing to try, and we have no other choice."

"You people really care," Martin said rather gently.

"Somebody has to," Jennie answered.

Martin tipped back in his chair. He made a steeple with his fingertips and reflected.

"Can he switch lunch places? What I mean is, at a lunch wagon on a country road there's no way any man I send could make himself invisible. There mightn't be more than two cars in the parking lot. Can't Cromwell find a busier place in the center of town?"

Arthur shook his head. "The arrangement's already made. George can't ask to change it without arousing suspicion."

"Well, then he'll have to chance it all on his own. Without protection."

"Are you thinking he'll need any?" Arthur was troubled.

"Hardly likely. Our being there is more moral support than anything else. So he'll just have to do without it."

"George will manage," Jennie said. She had a momentary picture of the old man's proud stance and his proud words: "It's a matter of principle. Being a good citizen."

Martin stood up. "I want you to meet Jerry Brian. I put him on the case when you called." He pressed a button in his desk, and a moment later another young man, almost a double of Martin himself, entered the room.

Martin made introductions, explaining, "Jerry's the man who'll get Cromwell ready."

Arthur was interested in the mechanics of the procedure.

"Simple," Brian explained. "There's a microphone under your shirt, a recorder, some wires not much thicker than a hair, and that's it. Simple."

"Jerry will prepare your man early that morning. Have him here and ready by nine at the latest," Martin directed.

"Tell him there's nothing to worry about," Brian added. "Nothing to worry about."

The two of them are the same type, a reassuring one, Jennie thought. It's the height, the physical strength, and the calmness. In a strange way, although they were so different from him, they reminded her of Jay. . . .

Outside in the parking lot, Arthur gave a sigh of relief.

"Well, step number one is finished. I was afraid they might think we were making a mountain out of a molehill."

"No, Martin understood. I think he was impressed that we're doing all this when there's nothing in it for us."

"Just the shape of the country's future. That's all that's in it for us."

"Of course. Nothing personal, is what I meant."

White hills loomed over the town. The afternoon was still, with the moist feel of snow in the air. Arthur paused.

"Listen to the silence. I love this north country. I hope you'll come to love it too."

Jennie just smiled.

"I believe you're learning to, the way you're fighting to save it." They got into the car. "But you do look tired, Jennie. Are you working too hard?"

"Work has a way of piling up. I guess I've been doing too much."

"Well, try to level off if you can. Take time to smell the roses."

The cliché, which ordinarily in someone else's mouth could have been irritating, now rang with kindness. It was—the word leapt into Jennie's mind—*fatherly*. And a cold-water chill ran through her. He was fatherly to her, and she was lying to him.

"At least," the old man continued, "you'll have a break over Thanksgiving weekend, with nothing to do but sleep and eat. Enid's getting in enough food for an army."

It was, fortunately, not more than a ten-mile ride to the station where she was to take the train back to the city. All the way Arthur kept talking, so that she had to

respond appropriately to his remarks about Barker Developers, the mayor, and George—or to his comments
about Jay and Jay's children—while through it all her
internal voice was crying: Jill . . . what about Jill . . . ?
I'm so afraid . . . afraid.

CHAPTER

9

It was five degrees above zero when Jennie and Jay and the children arrived in the country for the long Thanksgiving weekend, but the air was dry, the sun dazzled the icicles that hung like stalactites from the eaves, and one didn't feel how cold it was. Indoors, the house was pleasantly crowded, for Jay's brother and his grown children had arrived, along with various aunts, uncles, and cousins. Every fire was lit; every room had an arrangement of gold and bronze chrysanthemums; every little table bore a dish of grapes or nuts, of popcorn or chocolate or ginger cookies. Jennie was surrounded and bathed in the warmth of talk and the fragrances of wood smoke, food, and flowers. This was her first real introduction to the extended family, and she understood their natural curiosity. She had taken great pains to look good, and saw, as a result, their frank approval of her new white knit on which Enid's pearls gleamed so softly.

Mom, after learning of Enid's gift, had sent a pair of pearl bracelets from Florida. Playing with the bracelets at her cuff, she thought of Mom. A woman needs another woman to confide in. . . . At this moment Mom was probably boasting a little about her daughter to a circle of widows in the courtyard of the apartment house. Dusty palmettoes, heat and clatter . . . At this moment, too, in Chicago, Jill and Peter were meeting. Where? How? Jennie's head spun.

"Well, thank goodness George got through safely yesterday." Arthur Wolfe spoke into her right ear. "You've heard from him, of course."

"Only that it was definitely an offer of payment, which we expected. He didn't read the tape on the phone, so Jay and I will go over to his place and listen, if you'll excuse us."

"Poor fellow. I admit it was a case of better him than me. It took a bit of courage to sit all wired up in a diner. I'd be thinking the wire might fall down around my ankles, or that something else might go wrong."

"It took more than a bit of courage," Jennie replied, and thought again of Bruce Fisher, who might or might not have had anything to do with the business. More likely might. It was a shivery thought.

George Cromwell's office was in a wing of a simple frame house, on a street of similar houses a few blocks from the center of town. The house, which needed paint, was obviously not the home of an affluent man. This impression was fortified by the interior. In the sitting room, into which George led them, the upholstery was shabby, the old oak pieces dark and dowdy. The house and its furnishings had passed intact from Martha's grandmother on George's wedding day, along with Martha, who was now resting upstairs.

George placed his little machine on the table and held up a tape with an expression both proud and a little sheepish.

"You won't believe your ears. It's all here."

"What does he look like, this John Jones?" Jay asked.

George grinned. "He gave me his right name. Said you couldn't be too careful on the phone. His name's Harry Corrin. Fellow about forty-five, but then—it's hard to tell. Enormous yellow, crooked teeth. Bad bite. Being a dentist, that's what I always notice first, the teeth."

Jennie saw a twitch of amusement on Jay's lips. "I suppose he was very friendly, George?"

"Oh, friendly, yes. But here, let me start the tape. I'll give you the second one, where he really gets down to business. The first time we just talked about the town and the kind of buildings the Barkers put up, and how I really ought to see some of them and then maybe I'd understand better that they didn't come here to ruin the town. That sort of thing. It took up the whole tape. Sort of getting acquainted, you might say."

"Did you give any opinions?" Jennie wanted to know.

"Oh, just enough to let him think I was interested. I wanted to lure him along." The tape whirred. "Ah. Here it comes."

Interspersed among the background sounds of passing voices, the screech of chairs on a bare floor, the clink of dishes, and the occasional ping of a cash register came the two voices: George's elderly quaver; the other one young and with a coaxing quality.

"So, do you see things a little differently than you did before we talked yesterday, George? If you don't mind my calling you George?"

"Not at all, Harry."

"Well, do you get my meaning? That we're not going to mess up your town?"

"Well, in a way I do, although I'm not certain. I'd have to do a lot more thinking."

"Sure. Sure. You're a very intelligent man. Shrewd too. You like to make dead certain before you give your opinion."

A silence followed, during which one could imagine George nodding rather gravely and the other man observing him, during which dishes rattled again and somewhere outside an engine backfired.

Then Harry's voice resumed, lower this time, more sympathetic. "You've got a lot to think about these days, anyway. I know. I mean, your wife's being so sick. It must cost you a bundle."

"Yep. Big bills." One heard George's sigh.

"I hear it's terrible what hospitals and doctors charge these days. Can eat up a man's life's savings."

"True," George said. "Very true."

"And more, I hear. Some people even have to go in debt."

"I hope I won't have to do that. But it may happen yet, who knows?"

"Is it that bad, George? That's terrible. A man your age stands on his feet all his life filling teeth, and now he's come to where he has to borrow to keep his head above water." Silence again. "Yes," said Harry mournfully, "I get a laugh when I hear somebody say 'Money isn't everything,' when I know—and you must know it, too, right now—that it sure as hell is. What a difference it would make to your peace of mind if you had a nice little bundle put away!" The voice went low, so that Jay and Jennie had to strain to hear it. "Say, if you had fifty thousand in the bank, in cash in a safe-deposit box, you could sleep nights. Right, George?"

"Well, fifty would help. But as you say, the bills are something to see."

"All right, seventy-five. If you had that, you'd sleep even better, wouldn't you?"

"Hah! And where the dickens could I ever hope to find that kind of money?"

"Hey, George! There are ways, you know it. And when you have friends, nothing's impossible. Listen, George, I like you. You're smart and you're a man of your word, I can tell. And I'm a man of my word too. Good faith, that's what it's all about in this life. Right, George?"

"Sure. Always."

"Okay. So one hand washes the other, as they say. I snap my fingers, and in my hands I can have seventy-five thousand green whenever I want it, just like that. Whenever."

"Whenever what?"

"Whenever Barker gets the go-ahead to build. Simple as that."

"You don't mean—"

"I mean."

Silence followed. One imagined George pretending to be absorbing the fact. Presently he said, "Oh. And the seventy-five—would it be for me only?"

"The way we figure it, you're the one, aren't you? Your vote does the trick."

Once more there was a silence, into which Harry broke rather anxiously. "It's even possible—don't hold me to it—but I have an idea that could even be raised to a hundred."

"A hundred! I'd be in the money!"

"Yep. All green. Nice and tidy in the safe-deposit box. How about it, George? You like that all right?"

"Oh, boy, I guess I do."

"You'd better believe you do. Listen. I'm going back to the city tonight to get the go-ahead on the numbers. I'll be back here Sunday."

"Same time, same place?"

"Right. And listen, I'm pretty sure it'll be okay for you to count on twenty-five now and the rest when it passes. If it doesn't pass, you return the twenty-five." There was the sound of chairs being scraped back, and then Harry's voice, friendly and upbeat. "But it'll pass. Okay, George? It's up to you."

"Sure. Okay. Sounds good to me."

"See you."

George switched the tape off, exclaiming as if he had just thought of it, "Didn't he take a chance, though, being seen with me?"

"Not really," Jennie said. "Neither a chance for him nor for you. Nobody around here knows him."

"Ah, yes, of course. I see."

"You'll need to set aside some time so we can give the tape to the district attorney," Jennie said.

"Do I have to go along?"

"Of course you do. You're the star witness."

"Ah, yes, I see. I suppose he'll be bringing the twenty-five thousand tomorrow. What do I do with it?"

"Nothing except hold on to it."

George sighed, and Jennie said gently, "Buck up, George. Everything's working out just right, and you've nothing to fear. We're starting back to the city at about four tomorrow, so will you give us a call right after your meeting?"

Jennie kissed the old man's cheek. "George, you've been perfect. Just perfect."

Sunday was a mild day. In the direct sunshine icicles began to shed slow drops, and the tip of a breeze blew powder from the surface of the snow. In the morning the children went sledding, after which Jay and Jennie took them to the drugstore in the village to buy candy bars for the long drive home.

While Jay went into the store, she waited in the car,

stifling as always the same tormenting thoughts. Suddenly she had one of those odd, almost uncanny sensations that come with an awareness of being watched. Turning then, she looked directly into an unforgettable face. Bruce Fisher was leaning against a lamppost a few doors down from where the car had stopped. For an instant only, they made eye contact, but even after Jennie looked away, the feeling persisted that he was still staring at her. When Jay came out of the store, she told him.

"Don't look now, but Fisher's standing over there."

"I know. I saw him when I went in."

"He makes me shiver."

"Understandably. Still, we mustn't let ourselves be paranoid about him. After all, he does have a right to stand on the street in his own town."

Yet afterward they were to wonder. . . .

The rest of the morning followed a quiet Sunday pattern: the newspapers and a long game of Monopoly, which included everyone except Donny, who watched cartoons on the VCR. Then came midday dinner, followed by Donny's nap and packing their suitcases.

It was almost four o'clock. Jay was just saying "If George doesn't call, we'll reach him tomorrow" when the telephone rang.

"You take it, Jennie, it's your case."

George's booming voice came over the wire with such intensity that Jay and his parents looked up in surprise.

"George! You're all out of breath!"

"Oh, I've had a terrible time! Terrible! It's no wonder I'm out of breath. You won't believe what happened. Harry came in, I was sitting in the booth waiting, having a cup of coffee, and the minute he walked in the door I saw he was mad, but mad as you can't imagine. You never saw such a face, it was black. I swear the blood was black, it was so dark and—"

Jennie interrupted. "Please. Just tell me what happened."

"Well, people have been watching my house! They must have been! He knew you and Jay were there yesterday. Who could have told him? Oh, you can't believe . . . He called me every kind of filthy name. I don't mind that, but he was in such a rage! He said I had double-crossed him and I was dead wrong if I thought I could get away with it; nobody ever did that to him and got away with it." George was almost sobbing. "And then he reached across the table—there was nobody in the place except the counterman, and he'd gone back into the kitchen—and he grabbed me by my necktie and said he'd bash my face in. And then—I hate to tell you this—but I lost my head and I told him to go on and try to do it, just try, because I have everything on tape and he was in big, big trouble and he'd better know he was."

"You didn't! You couldn't have!"

George said mournfully, contritely, "Yes, I did."

Jennie turned from the phone. "They had an argument, and George told him about the tape."

Arthur, in disgust, threw up his hands.

"I'm awfully sorry," George was saying. "Awfully sorry. I know it was careless of me, I know—"

"Careless!" Jennie cried. "Is that what you call it?"

"Oh, I'm so sorry. I just lost my head when he grabbed me, just lost my head."

She sighed. "What happened then?"

"He threatened me."

"Tell me how. Specifically."

"Well, not specifically. Just . . . just threatened, I don't know. Said I'd pay for it unless I handed over the tape. The one from before and the one I had on me. And I told him I didn't have one on, and that the other was in safe hands where he couldn't get it. Of course, it's home, hidden in my house."

"Of course," Jennie said.

Safe hands. It wouldn't be hard for anyone to figure out who else besides George might have it.

"I hope you people won't be too furious with me."

She sighed again. "Being furious won't help. Where are you now, home?"

"No, I'm at a pay phone on the highway. I just left the diner."

"Well, go on home and rest. You've had a bad time."

"Yes, I'll be on my way. I left Martha alone."

Jennie hung up. "Well, here we are."

"Naturally I always knew," Arthur said, "that George had, shall we say, limitations? But of all the simpletons!"

Jay considered the situation. "Wait a moment. This really may not be the very worst scenario. Now that they know they've been taped, the prudent thing would be for them to disappear from the scene, withdraw their offer, and hope against hope that the tapes won't be submitted to the authorities. Or"—and here Jay looked very sober—"or else, if anyone should decide to get hold of the tape, it could be a bad scenario, an extremely bad scenario."

All were silent while obvious, rather nasty, possibilities were considered. After a moment Jay looked at his watch.

"Well, it's Sunday and there's nothing we can do now, so I suggest we just start back home."

Enid laid her hand on her son's arm. "You will be careful? I'm thinking of some awful person storming into your office or into Jennie's. Whatever would you do?"

"We'd manage."

"You would, I guess, but what if they think Jennie's got the tapes?"

"Jennie's tough." Jay grinned. "You don't know her yet. She'll keep her eyes open."

"Well, I hope. Do take care of yourselves."

By tacit agreement nothing more was said on the subject during the ride. The children opened bags of M&M's and counted red cars on the road. On the way out of town they passed the lane that led from the highway to the Green Marsh. And Jennie, recognizing the turnoff, had a poignant recall of the morning, not six weeks past, when she had stood there with Jay and life had seemed so bright, so hopeful and easy. And only a few hours later the telephone had rung.

Her mind went back now to Peter and Jill. Right this minute, very likely, Jill was flying back to New York after seeing Peter.

"What's wrong?" Jay asked.

"Nothing. Why?"

"I thought I saw out of the corner of my eye that you were frowning."

She made light of the remark. "Hey! You're supposed to keep your eyes on the road. Yes, I guess maybe I was frowning, thinking about George and the whole business. We're getting more than we bargained for."

"Talk about it tomorrow. Let's have music for now. Want the tail end of the Philharmonic?"

"Fine."

The Eroica swept into the car. And Jay's hand, for a minute or two, covered Jennie's, which lay on the seat. The pressure, the possessive gesture, the living warmth of that hand, the majestic music—all caught at her heart.

Oh, my God, please. Please . . . Jennie begged silently.

She closed her eyes, and he, thinking she wanted to sleep, withdrew his hand. Indeed, the music and the hum of the engine would soon put her to sleep if she allowed them to. She knew she was one of those rare people who, instead of being sleepless when they are beset, are overwhelmed by sleep. It's only a form of escape, she thought, remembering her course in elementary psychology. Laying her head back on the seat, she allowed the escape.

Traffic was light on this winter Sunday, and they reached the apartment sooner than expected. Jennie went upstairs to expedite the children's going to bed. Jay took charge of Donnie, and Jennie, as usual, supervised the girls.

While they brushed their teeth she drew the curtains, pulled the blue-sprigged coverlets off the bed, hung up their country pants and jackets, and put out their school clothes for the morning, plaid kilts and red sweaters. Racks of clothing hung in the twin closets: down coats for weekdays, velvet-collared English coats for parties, yellow straw hats with daisies and ribbon streamers for the coming spring. On impulse she picked up a hat; the streamers dropped long, these innocent ribbons worn in places to which little girls went all dressed up—to the circus, maybe, or to visit relatives on holidays. And she wondered whether Jill had ever worn a hat with ribbons when she was eight years old.

Squeals of hilarity came now from the bathroom. Emily, who had recently discovered what she thought of as dirty jokes, was regaling her sister with them from the superiority of two more years. In another mood Jennie would have been amused by their mirth. But in this mood she could only question: Had Jill worn a bow in her hair when she was eight? Or six? And had she worn plaid kilts and told wicked jokes and stolen candy to hide under her pillow and been quick at checkers or Monopoly?

The ribbon was still in her hand when the girls came back to the bedroom. Sue looked surprised.

"I was admiring the hat," Jennie explained.

And again guilt chilled her. It was as if even her thoughts had had no right to intrude on this place. And with only a part of her mind, she finished the bedtime ritual: the hair combing, the brief story, and the good-night kisses.

She had just turned out the light and gone into the hall when Jay summoned her.

"Did you hear the telephone ring?"

"No, why?"

"Come in here." She followed him into the living room. "Sit down and prepare for a shock." Jay was pacing, excited and at the same time grim. "That was my father on the phone. You're not going to believe this. George Cromwell's dead."

"My God!"

"His car turned over on the back road going home." Jennie shuddered. "Killed outright?"

"Yes, they're positive. No pain, thank God." Jay was still pacing up and down the room. "The police suspect foul play. He had not been speeding. He was hardly the type for it, anyway. There were car tracks only inches behind his, but unfortunately they can't be identified. There were snow flurries, which started right after we left, Dad said, and everything's blurred. The way it looks, he was deliberately cut off at an elbow bend and forced off the road. There's an outcropping of rocks at that point, and he smashed into them." Jay clenched his fists. "They killed him. Or caused his death. It's the same thing."

"Do you suppose he was followed from the diner or from the pay phone where he was talking to me?"

"I'm almost positive, Jennie." Jay hesitated. "It's so rotten, I hate to tell you, but whoever did it— They found his pockets turned inside out. But nothing was taken, and his wallet was intact."

"So they were looking for a tape."

"Yes, but of course he had none on him this time."

"It's—it's unreal. Only a couple of hours ago I was talking to him."

"My dad's just broken up. George and he were friends for almost fifty years."

"Old George . . . I'm so sorry we ever got him into this business! Such a good soul! An innocent. Never really grew up."

"Honey, he wanted to be in it. And how could we have expected a thing like this?"

"Now I'm thinking about Martha. To walk into a dying woman with news like that! The world's such a rotten place, sometimes I can't stand it, Jay."

He came over to sit next to her and put his arms around her.

"I don't suppose," he said, "it'll ever be different. I almost have to believe that evil is inborn. Original sin, or something like that. To be so greedy that you kill. If they're the ones who did it," he added after a moment. "We can't be sure."

"That's the lawyer in you speaking. The rest of you is sure, isn't it? You sounded as if it were."

"I guess it is. Yes. It is."

There was for a little while nothing more to be said. The room was so still that Jennie could clearly hear the hurried ticking of Jay's wristwatch. Suddenly her eyes filled with tears and her choked cry broke the hush. Jay's arm tightened and his free hand grasped hers. She felt small, shrunken with shame because he was surely thinking how soft she was, how compassionate, to cry so for George. And she was crying for George, truly, but for so much more: for Jill; for herself; for lives that should, if only one were decent and kind, be lived so easily, so simply under the sun—and were not.

Presently Jay said, "First thing in the morning, I don't have to tell you, Dad and you will have to get in touch with the DA and tell him what you know about the lunch. Unfortunately there's hardly a clue, except that the man had big teeth. There are an awful lot of people with big teeth," he finished wryly.

Jennie closed her eyes. "The mind doesn't take it in. All this hatred because of a piece of land. I keep seeing the cattails around the pond. And wasn't there an enormous weeping willow at the bottom of the hill, or do I imagine it?"

"No, it's there. A very old one, which is unusual. They seldom get that old."

"They want it all so badly, those people."

"Many, many dollars, Jennie."

Both fell so still again that the silence tingled in the room. This sheltered space—where long draperies spilled over onto Persian rugs and lamps held pearl-pink lights aloft on crystal arms—was a safe cocoon ten floors above Park Avenue, a million miles away from a lonely road where no one watched while a man crashed headlong into death.

Jay said gravely, "Keep your door locked."

"Who doesn't do that in New York?" she answered in a light tone to reassure him. Nevertheless, she understood his meaning.

"If they think you have the tape, it's the same as if you actually had it."

"They can't very well run me off the road here in the city."

"You're right, but still I worry. You know me, I'm a worrier. I don't like where you live. There's no security. I'll feel satisfied when you're living behind these doors with me. And you won't wear your ring when you go to court, will you? Or in your office?"

"Of course not."

He could not know how uncomfortable, quite apart from any fear of being robbed of it, that ring made her feel. Over this past weekend, when naturally she had had to wear it, to stretch forth her hand so that it might be seen and admired, she had had such a queer feeling, as though she were wearing something that was not hers. She had not shown it to any of her friends but kept it hidden in a box of cereal on the kitchen shelf.

"Well," Jay said, "I'll call downstairs to the doorman and have them get a taxi for you."

They parted somberly. The old man's death had laid a heavy hand upon them.

10

For Jennie there were now two heavy hands, one on each shoulder bearing her down, but the weightier hand belonged to Jill. If only they could have made some agreement! For those few moments when they had had their arms around each other, she had been moved beyond words. This resilient, hard young body, this thick, sweet-smelling hair, had come from her, from Jennie Rakowsky. But the girl was hot-tempered and unreasonable, she thought again with sharp resentment. She at least could have tried, couldn't she? She didn't even listen or try to see that I must have some reason on my side.

She felt helpless. And there was so much else to be done this morning: neglected mail, telephone calls to clients. And, immediately urgent, a call to the district attorney.

"I've already talked to Mr. Wolfe," Martin said. "Understandably, he was pretty upset, and I didn't get much information from him. Anyway, you're the last person who talked to Cromwell. What can you give me?"

"No leads, I'm afraid. George was practically incoherent. To tell the truth, I was pretty upset myself, too, and—"

"Of course. Just take your time. You'll be surprised how much you'll recall."

So speaks the surgeon before the operation, with calm encouragement. Jennie took a deep breath as she tried to retrieve disjointed scraps of that fateful conversation.

"I do remember the name. Harry Corrin. Naturally he wasn't John Jones. I suppose he isn't really Harry Corrin, either. I think George said he was in his forties. He had huge yellow teeth. George noticed teeth." Foolishly, hysterically, Jennie giggled. Then, recovering quickly, she went on. "It was an angry scene. Furious, George said. It seems that somebody saw me and Jay—Arthur Wolfe's son, Jay—going to George's house. So he, this Corrin, figured that George was double-crossing him, and he threatened to, I think, 'bash his face in.' And then George lost his head and told him he had something on tape, and he, Corrin, was in trouble."

"Good Lord," Martin said.

"It's so, so awful! I'm sure he's the man, aren't you?"

"We're never sure of anything until we're sure. Incidentally, who's got that tape? You?"

"No, no. It's got to be in George's house."

"Okay, we'll let it lie till after the funeral. It's safe there, and we can't bother the poor woman today."

"When is the funeral?"

"Day after tomorrow."

"What time, do you know?"

"Afternoon. But it's private, in case you were planning to come up."

"Of course I was."

"Well, it's strictly private because of Mrs. Cromwell's illness. If the weather's bad, she won't even get to the cemetery."

"Awful," Jennie said again.

It was a relief, though, not having to go. Funerals always made one think too much, but this one would be harrowing. She could see it and smell it: sweet, musky flowers blowing on the heavy coffin; sleet whitening the turned earth next to the grave.

She came back to the present. "If I can help, Mr. Martin, you have my number."

"Fine. I'll keep you informed as we go along."

When she had hung up, she sat for a few minutes, looked with unfocused eyes at nothing, and was acutely aware of feeling weak. At the same time she was seeing herself as her clients would be seeing her today, and the contrast was strange indeed. For them, Miss R. was the problem solver, capable and sharp-witted, the modern professional whose oxford-gray skirts stood for serious purpose, whose apricot silk shirt and silver earrings stood for womanly warmth, and whose large, paper-laden desk, textbooks, and computer were her impressive tools. All morning people came and went, bringing their questions, puzzles, complaints, and tears. All morning she listened, took notes, and gave answers, while in the back of her mind her own hard questions ran their rounds.

She thought about Jill's weekend in Chicago with Peter. It was infuriating to think of them together. Where had he been when Jill was born? He had no right, no damn right to play the father now! "He wants to see me," Jill had said so proudly. "He's not like you." It was absurd. No, worse, it was obscene.

Peter had had nothing to do with the girl, nothing at all beyond those few minutes of sexual delight on a spring evening in a garden, while she, Jennie, had grown a human being, fed her with her own blood, felt the birth pain and the pain of relinquishment. He hadn't even asked about the baby then! And now he welcomed her. Now he claimed her!

Oh, but when Jill walked with him, wherever they had walked in Chicago, strangers must have seen, without pausing to think, that here was a father and his daughter! That height and that hair alone were unmistakable bonds. There was no sense trying to deny it. What a shock of recognition must he have felt at first sight of that splendid girl! And Jennie trembled with outrage and the unfairness of it.

Meanwhile, in the midst of this turmoil, and with another part of her mind, she was still thinking about yesterday's tragedy. Jay would be keeping in touch with developments through his father. She looked at the desk clock. It was time for Jay's call, which always came toward the end of the afternoon. So when the telephone rang, she picked it up without waiting for Dinah to answer first.

"Hello, Jennie? This is Peter."

She almost dropped the receiver. She could have ripped it from the wall. Damn phone, I hate it! Like a snake, it whips out of the innocent grass as you stroll down the hill.

"Is that you, Jennie?" The voice lifted, youthful and jaunty.

"It's Jennie, all right."

"Of course you're shocked to hear from me."

"Not really. Jill said you threatened to call."

"Oh! She couldn't really have said 'threatened,' could she?" The question was touched ever so lightly with humor.

"To me it was a threat."

Peter ignored that and went on. "She's so lovely, Jennie. Just so lovely. This weekend, the whole thing—I can't believe it's real."

"It's real enough." She heard her own voice, its dry tone, the dismissal of it. Remarkably, a cold calm had settled over her.

Why am I even listening to this person? I ought to hang up. So damn mannerly I am.

"A lot of water's gone over the dam."

"Nineteen years. What do you expect?"

"Well, I certainly didn't expect what's happened."

"Nor did I, I assure you."

"You sound so angry, Jennie."

"Should I be throbbing with joy?"

"There really could be some joy in all this, you know."

"Hooray for you if you've found some."

"I'd like to help you find some. That's why I've come here."

"Come where?"

"To New York. I flew in with Jill last night. She had to go back to her classes, but I'm rather a free agent, so I decided to take a little time off to see whether I can get you and Jill together."

"You've turned out to be an altruist, haven't you?"

"Jennie, hate me. Go on. You've every right. But don't take it out on the girl. She's so unhappy that you don't want to know her."

"That's not true!" The cool, calm surface cracked. "I never said I didn't. I tried to explain, but she didn't give me a proper chance, just stood up and ran out in a temper."

"I can imagine. She's impulsive, or just plain young. Don't you remember being young?"

"All too well!"

There was a moment's pause before Peter spoke again. "Jill said you looked wonderful."

"That's nice. That should make me very happy, I'm sure."

"Jennie, please. Give her a chance."

"I thought I gave her a chance."

"You did, and it didn't work. Okay. But will you try once more? Really, you should."

This man, resurrected out of a buried nightmare, has the nerve to tell me what I should do! she thought angrily.

"I'm staying at the Waldorf."

The Waldorf. Yes, only the best. Staying with his wife, maybe? God only knows.

". . . dinner tonight," he was saying. "The three of us. I'd like to make peace between the two of you."

It wasn't in her, after all, to ignore sincerity. And she replied quietly, "I've thought about this—I've thought of very little else these past weeks. It would have been so much better if she'd never found us. Found me, anyway. I don't know about you."

"As for me, I have to say I'm glad she did. I never dreamed it would happen, but now that it has, I'm glad. I've had my share of shame over the years, Jennie. I don't think there are words enough in the language to express my sorrow over what I did."

Against her will, she was moved. The phrase *over the years* made a falling cadence, an echo remote, nostalgic, sorrowful, and lost. She saw him standing at the airport gate with arm upraised in farewell, a bewildered, anxious, frightened, useless boy.

"So, will you?" he pleaded. "Tonight at seven? It's not for my sake. I have no right to expect anything from you. It's for her. She tried so hard to find us and looked so long."

"I don't want to," Jennie said very low, but thought, And yet, in another way, I do.

"I didn't hear you."

"I don't want to," she repeated, and cried out suddenly. "There's too much pain here! Too much pain!"

"I know."

"You don't know. You didn't give birth to her."

"Mine's a different kind of hurt. It concerns you; what I did, and didn't do, to you."

"Peter, this talk serves no purpose. You're tearing open a wound that healed a long time ago. Don't do it, please."

"All right, I won't. But will you come tonight, however hard it is? Please?"

How could she refuse? "I suppose I'll have to."

"I'll wait for you in the lobby on the Park Avenue side. Will I know you? I mean, you haven't dyed your hair or anything?"

"I look the same."

"At seven, then."

"At seven."

She looked up to face a blur of rain on the greasy window glass. Vague impulses stirred and mingled: reluctance and a trembling dread, along with an unfamiliar sense of fatefulness. As rational and practical as Jennie was, she scorned the idea that anything could be "ordained." Yet it seemed as though this happening today were inevitable, as if everything in the past had been treacherously, secretly moving toward it.

Now, although it was not easy to admit, she felt a touch of curiosity to know whether or how in nineteen years Peter had changed. And there was something more: Really, she wanted him to see how well she had survived, how successful she was, and how desirable still. It embarrassed her to have such a foolish wish, but there it was.

She was to meet Jay for dinner tonight. Now, what excuse to give? Biting her lips, she frowned and thought, then thought some more. He wouldn't be pleased with any reason, that was sure. And Mom always said she wasn't a good liar, that anyone could see through her excuses. But she had to find something plausible. Finally she concluded: a client. That would do. A poor woman who works late and has to be seen in the evening. That was something he would understand and condone.

She picked up the telephone. Lie upon lie, the edifice was building higher.

CHAPTER

11

He came striding from the bank of elevators down through the carpeted, gilded splendor of the lobby. Tourists clustered, bearing cameras; women in glittering formal dress on their way to grand events moved past; but the tall man with the red-crowned head stood out in the diverse crowd. For an instant he stood scanning the scene; then, finding Jennie, he came swiftly toward her with both hands outstretched.

"Hello, Jennie."

"Hello, Peter."

They shook hands. The gesture was curiously formal. She wasn't sure what she had expected him to do—or expected herself to do, for that matter.

"Gosh, Jennie, you're right," he said. "You really are just the same."

"And so are you."

The bright opal eyes still smiled. The voice still had the old ring that could bring enthusiasm to the most simple remark.

Then simultaneously they remembered Jill, who, standing slightly in back of Peter, was regarding them both with open curiosity. Peter put his arm around Jill, pulling her close.

"This is an historic moment, and it calls for champagne. I don't know what the drinking age is in New York, but whatever it is, you're going to have champagne tonight, Jill."

Jill didn't answer. Perhaps she didn't want to acknowledge Jennie, or perhaps she was only waiting for Jennie to speak first.

"Hello, Jill," Jennie said. "We meet again, don't we?" Conciliatory, pleading.

"Hello." The tone was flat.

"Well," Peter said, obviously choosing to ignore the awkwardness, "it's past time, and we've a table waiting."

Jennie fell deliberately behind and followed them. They shine together, she was thinking. They have the same walk, with long, springing, almost loping steps. Without knowing it, Jill was a Mendes. Suddenly Jennie felt too small, despised herself for the feeling, and did not understand it.

At Peacock Alley they turned left, entered the restaurant, and were led to a table on which stood an arrangement of pink roses. Peter had made a celebration. Another pink rose lay across Jennie's plate and Jill's. Beside each of the two plates was a little blue Tiffany box tied with white ribbon.

"Open them," he commanded. His face sparkled when two identical silver bangle bracelets emerged from their tissue-paper nests. "They did me a special favor with the engraving, a rush job."

Jennie's bore, in a swirl of old-fashioned script, the

words "From Jill to Jennie with love" and the date. Obviously Jill's must say the reverse. What a childish gesture, in spite of being kind and well meant! As if this conjunction of three human beings who, in their various ways, were suffering through these moments, were a festival!

"I want you to remember this day," Peter told them.

As if it were a day one could forget.

Jill spoke first. "It's lovely. It goes with my necklace." She had taken off her beaver jacket, revealing a silver chain worn over a gray wool dress.

Jennie followed. "Yes, lovely. Thank you, Peter."

"Let's order, shall we? Then we can talk. We've a lot to talk about." He kept smiling. He was working hard to stimulate them. "How about shrimp for an appetizer? Or else soup? It always goes well on a cold night. I got the hot-soup habit from living in Chicago. That wind off Lake Michigan took some getting used to after living in Georgia most of my life, let me tell you. I think I'll try the lobster bisque myself. But take your time, you two, no hurry." He went through the menu. "Veal. Swordfish. Let's see, filet mignon sounds good, doesn't it? Can't make up my mind."

Jennie urged silently, Do stop trying so hard, will you? It's foolish, it's crazy, being here like this. If all the elegant people in this room could know who we are, they'd have something else to talk about. "Fantastic," they'd say. . . . Why did I come here? Oh, I know very well why I came. . . .

But it wasn't going to work, because Jill obviously intended to ignore her. She, too, probably had been coaxed to this meeting against her will. Nevertheless she was eating heartily, while carrying on a dialogue with Peter. It seemed almost as if they were in league against Jennie. No, that was absurd; Peter wasn't a man to be in league with anyone or against anyone. That much she remembered. He simply wasn't aware of Jennie's exclusion, or of the charged atmosphere.

When the champagne was poured, Peter raised his glass. "To health and happiness and peace among us."

Jennie's swallow, on a churning stomach, sickened her. When she put down the goblet, he looked anxious.

"Don't you like it? It's Dom Pérignon."

"It's excellent, but I'm usually a Perrier woman."

"I remember when you were a ginger-ale woman."

She could have corrected him: I wasn't a woman. I was a girl, a child who turned into a woman too soon. But the reminder would have been brutal and would have served no purpose, anyway.

The dialogue, like a volleyball, passed over her bent head while she tried to eat.

"There's no landscape like it," Jill was saying. "All those miles of yellow and cedar and piñon. And the sweet air. Nothing like that anywhere, either."

"And quivering aspen along the river," added Peter, and said to Jennie, "Jill says you talked about New Mexico together. She knows a lot about the Anasazi, the Ancient Ones, probably more than I do. I only spent a couple of weeks two summers ago, mostly studying the kivas. Religious meeting places, council houses. Below ground. Very interesting. But you probably know about them."

"No, not a thing," Jennie said, refusing to help him.

For a moment he looked pleading and hurt, then, once more mustering cheer, he returned to the land of mesquite and staghorn cactus.

As for me, I'm done with pleading, Jennie thought. I can't even as much as catch Jill's glance, although I know that when she thinks I can't see her, she is examining me slyly. Perhaps she's trying to imagine the primal scene—don't we all at some time or other? At least they say we do. Yes, it was a warm, silent evening, the gravel on the driveway smelled of dust, and we had to hurry before they all came home. That's how it was. That's how you come to be sitting at the Waldorf Astoria, Jill, in your fine dress and your dignity, with your poor heart pounding, as it must be.

"I feel sort of melancholy when I've wasted a day," Jill was saying, "because it can't be retrieved. There's one less day to live. It's not that I need to have accomplished anything much. It's more that I need to have been aware and really alive."

"I know exactly what you mean." Peter was eager again. "I'm the same way myself. I suppose we'll be finding more and more ways in which we're alike."

Jennie laid the fork on the plate. The food simply would not go down. This Situation—years ago she had capitalized it in her mind, and did so now—was intolerable. Like an octopus, Jennie's anger reached out now, stretching its tentacles toward the two across the table, and then sucked back into itself, disgusted. How quickly she had changed! In a few short weeks her cherished confidence in herself had vanished. And they just went on talking, those two, their glib words pouring, unhampered by whatever inner turmoil they might be undergoing. Yet they were in control.

She reached into her purse for her lipstick, which she did not need. In the little mirror her wounded eyes were darkly circled.

"Jennie, you've not said a word. Come talk to us," Peter urged.

It was as if he were delicately reprimanding a sulky or a bashful child. What could he be thinking of? Surely he must see that Jill wasn't speaking to her.

"It's pretty obvious why I'm not talking," she replied.

Peter put down his fork. "All right. All right. Time to get down to brass tacks, I see. You two have to get together, you know you do. You have to reach some understanding."

"Nobody *has* to do anything," Jennie said. "This is a false situation to begin with."

"I don't see anything false in a girl's wanting to know her parents."

"Maybe not. If it worked out smoothly for everyone, it would be wonderful. But this hasn't worked smoothly, and you can't force it to, Peter. Nor can I."

"But it happens that I'm certain you can, Jennie. Why don't you want to accept our daughter completely, with no secrecy? What are you hiding from?"

The words *our daughter* and *hiding* enraged her. "You may not question me!" she cried. "You just may not, do you hear? Who do you think you are, you of all people, to question me?"

Hurt and reproachful, Peter said, "Well, if you're going to be so hostile—" when Jill interrupted.

"The first time I see the two of you together—the first time, mind you, a thing I dreamed about—you fight! It's unbelievable! You actually *fight!* I used to imagine—" She stopped. "I'm all choked up. Oh, why didn't you marry each other and keep me? Keep your own child? Why? Oh, I don't even know what I'm saying. But look at this mess you've made! Look at it!"

Jennie turned to Peter. His flush was as painful as newly grown skin after a burn. Under lowered lids his eyes glistened. She saw that he was stricken, unable to reply, and in a flash she understood his memories: the windshield wipers clicking in the rain on the dark street and his own words, "Jennie, Jennie, don't worry, I'll take care of everything." In that second, pity for him, and for them all, obliterated anger.

Jill's tears spilled and she moved aside in the chair, showing to Jennie only her profile, humiliated as a woman is by public tears. The silence that fell upon the flower-decked table and its pathetic gaiety was accentuated by a burst of laughter that rose somewhere above the moderate buzzing in the room. Dismayed by Jill's pain, neither Jennie nor Peter could meet each other's glance.

Presently Jill dabbed at her eyes and took a sip of water. Jennie waited with resignation. Peter's flush had still not died down, but he began to speak cautiously, as if addressing the air.

"This is too much for us all. I should have known it would be. It was stupid of me to expect it to go smoothly." No one refuted him. His fingers made nervous taps on the tablecloth, as if he were considering something. Then, abandoning the empty air, he addressed Jennie. "A restaurant is no place to talk our hearts out," he continued. "I know you and Jill broke up at your lunch because she wanted to go back to your apartment and you wouldn't. I thought that was such a strange issue! Maybe, if you'd make it clearer, it would help us."

Jill answered, this time including Jennie in her remarks by giving her an intense, almost a challenging look. "It wasn't only that. It wasn't especially that I wanted to *be* there, only that I wanted to know why I *couldn't* be there. Why I must never get in touch with you but wait for you to call me. You've built a wall. It felt like—it feels like—the Berlin Wall."

Yes, Jennie thought. And I, like a Berliner, am trapped behind it. Caught. Locked in. And once more, moderately, with obstinate patience, she tried to present herself as a person with rights.

"Sometimes I think that privacy's becoming a lost privilege. Why shouldn't it be enough to say that I have my own reasons?"

"In the circumstances it's not nearly enough," Jill said sternly. "You wouldn't say it was exactly a loving welcome that you're giving me, would you? I know the committee people—Mr. Riley and Emma Dunn—told me it wouldn't be easy. They said I should be patient and —and I think I have been, but I never expected anything like this."

For an instant Jennie dropped her forehead into her hands, which were cold on her aching eyeballs.

"Ah, you won't see. . . . Is it impossible for you to take me as I am?"

Very softly Peter asked, "Let me ask you something frankly, Jennie. Are you perhaps married? With children? Is that it?"

She raised her head. "No. No to both."

"Then you're free, like me."

The room was hot, and although not crowded, it still gave Jennie the sense of too many people crowding in. She felt dizzy; perhaps in her agitated state the half glass of wine was doing it.

"Then you're entirely free," Peter said again, this time in a rising tone, a question.

Jennie was sick. It must have shown in her face, because Peter broke off to stare at her. I can't take any more of this, she thought. They're people who can't be trusted. I never could tell them the truth. They would harry and harass me until Jay found out.

They will do it, anyway.

Overcome, she now had to flee from them, had to get out, to shut a door behind her. She stood up, seizing the suit jacket that hung on the back of her chair.

"I can't stay," she said brusquely. "I can't. Don't you see I'm sick?" And repeating, "Sorry, sorry, I can't stay," she left, almost running, racing through startled strollers in the vast lobbies, just as her daughter had run from her that other day.

On Park Avenue there was snow in the air. Low clouds above the skyscrapers were stained rust-brown where the city flung up its lights. I'd like to get on a plane and fly beyond those clouds, she whispered to herself; I'd mount and soar and fly to any place at all. Instead she got into the first taxi that drew to the curb, opened the windows to inhale the sharp wind, gave the driver a bill, and, without waiting for change, raced up the stairs to her refuge.

The bedroom was untypically neglected. She had dressed in such haste, in order not to be late, that her workday clothes were not put away and now lay where they had been dropped: a skirt on a chair, a blouse on another chair, shoes in the center of the floor along with the overturned contents of her briefcase, which had fallen off the bed. Scattered papers trailed on the bed and the floor. She scuffed through them without picking them up, pulled off the bedspread, flung her outer clothes away, and, in bra and petticoat, threw herself down on the bed.

The room was a prison, yet there was no place else to go. She turned and turned on the mattress. Demons, winged and black, plucked and clawed: the old, simple man lay dead on the frozen road among dark trees; Peter and Jill nagged and probed and wouldn't let her go; Enid Wolfe appraised her with level, steady, analytical gaze. . . . The demon wings, bat wings, fluttered, and the hands were alligator claws.

She leapt from the bed. If nothing else could drive them off, maybe whiskey could. It wouldn't take much to get the ginger-ale woman drunk. She had never in all her life been drunk.

Filling a fruit-juice glass, as if she had a July thirst, with the Chivas Regal that was kept on the shelf for Jay, she swallowed it and shuddered. Awful stuff! Burning rubber! It singed her mouth, ran to her head, and flamed its way down to her feet. It was like being struck by lightning, or hit by a truck.

Barely able to walk, she clung to the walls all the way back to the bedroom, where she managed to turn off the phone and the lamp before falling again across the bed.

Something was ringing. It sounded far away, as if some pests on the street were making merriment with a damn-fool bell.

"Oh, God Almighty, will you stop that?" she mumbled. Her lips felt thick, her mouth dry, and it was too much trouble to open it.

Suddenly she understood that the ring was close; it was in the apartment, her own doorbell.

"I'm sick of this," she said aloud. The room swayed when she sat up and spun as she stumbled toward the light that burned in the little foyer.

"Who are you? What the devil do you want?" she cried, pulling so hard at the door that it slammed against the wall.

"Peter. It's Peter."

She blinked, not sure she understood. "Wha-what are you doing here? Peter? You?"

He stepped in, closed the door, and locked it.

"You scared the hell out of me! I didn't know what was happening to you. But I had to pay the bill before I could rush after you." He was out of breath. "And you'd just disappeared! So I put Jill in a taxi, had to scrounge around for a taxi for myself, and—and here I am. How are you? Are you all right?"

"So . . . you see how I am. Fine. I'm just fine. Just."

He came nearer, to stare at her in astonishment.

"Jennie, for God's sake, you're drunk!"

"I don't know. Maybe." She began to laugh. "I can't stand up. I guess I'll have to sit on the floor."

"No, no." He caught her just as her legs gave way; her bones were melting. "Come on. You're going to bed."

"I was *in* bed. Damn you for getting me up! Now I'll have to cry again."

He shook his head. "What have you been drinking?"

"I don't know. Lemonade. Mouthwash." She giggled and wept. "Oh, I'm sad, so sad. You can't know how sad I am. Nobody knows."

He was holding her. Strong hands under her arms held her upright. He spoke gently, "I'm sorry, Jennie. But let's get you to bed. You're not used to drinking, are you? Still the ginger-ale girl, are you?" Half carried, half pushed, she was being led toward the bed.

"Ginger-ale girl. Sure. That's me. All the time."

"This crazy bed . . . Papers and pocketbooks and shoes all mixed up in it . . . How can you lie in a bed like this?"

"None of your business. Mind your own business. Keep out of my pocketbook."

"I'm not in your pocketbook. Look, I'm putting everything on the chair. Look."

But propped up against the headboard, she was looking directly at the mirror over the dresser. Her eyes wavered over a watery shape, gaped at puffed cheeks and smudged mascara, at a transparent half-slip and at one round breast that had escaped from the lace brassiere.

"I'm a mess. Oh, Lord. Oh, Lord, I'm a mess."

"You won't be a mess in the morning, after you've slept." He pulled the blanket over her naked breast. "Seriously, Jennie, I have to tell you, you shouldn't open the door without knowing who's there. Don't you know that? Don't you know what could happen?"

"I don't care. I don't care, don't care, don't care, don't—"

"All right, that's enough. Here, let me straighten the pillows. Now lie back and sleep. I'm going to go stretch out on your sofa."

"No you're not! You can't stay here. Get out!"

"I am definitely not going to leave you in this condition. In the morning you'll feel a whole lot better, you won't believe me when I tell you about this, and you'll even laugh at yourself. Then we'll talk about things, and after that I'll get out."

"I don't want to talk about things with you. I want you to leave me alone, you hear me? Go away. Stay away."

"I'm going away, as far as the other room for now. Okay, I'm turning your light off."

"Leave it! I have to get up, go to the office. I'm a working woman."

"Jennie, it's Monday night, a quarter to ten, and you're going to sleep this off the rest of the night."

Darkness dropped down again. It was warm, warm darkness, like tropical air. You don't know anything about tropical air, Jennie. You don't know anything, don't want to know anything. Peter's here, and isn't that funny? I'm laughing, it's so funny. I'm crying. Oh, let me sleep, all of you, everybody. Get out of my life.

She woke. Again she had no idea how long she had been sleeping, but this time, although terrible knives and hammers were savaging her head, consciousness was a little clearer. She knew what had happened and what was happening. Peter was on the couch in the next room, and beyond him, someone was at the door ringing and pounding.

She sat up. The light went on in the living room. Stocking feet slid over the bare floor where the rug stopped, moving cautiously over the creaking board toward the door. She had a subtle awareness of relief at not being alone. Those men . . . looking for the tapes . . . Nonsense . . . not nonsense.

Peter called out, "What do you want?"

"Take that chain off the door and let me in or I'll have the police here in three minutes," Jay shouted.

Jennie's heart stopped.

"Who the hell are you? I can have the police here in three minutes myself."

"What have you done to Jennie? Damn you, take that chain off, I said!"

"Damn yourself! I haven't done anything to Jennie. She's asleep in bed."

And Jennie was whimpering into the dark: Take hold of yourself. The moment's come, it's here, not even in the way you feared, but worse, so much worse. She turned on the lamp. Her brassiere had come loose and fallen off; the half-slip was wrinkled over her thighs. In her dizzy haste she looked for a robe and couldn't find one; throwing on the suit jacket that lay on the chair and holding the skirt in front of her, she ran to the living room.

Peter, in undershirt and trousers with belt unbuckled for comfort, was still at the front door, through which, in the gap where the chain had been loosened, there appeared the frantic face of Jay.

Jennie's voice was broken. "It's all right, Peter. Open the door."

Jay entered. He stared first at Jennie, who was holding the skirt like a screen, then at the disheveled man and back at Jennie.

"Who is this? Jesus Christ, what's happening? Has he hurt you?"

"No, no. He's a friend. It's all right."

"All right? A friend?"

"Yes, I mean, it was unexpected, he just came. I didn't know he was coming, and so—"

A wave of vertigo unsteadied her, and with knees buckling, she crouched against the wall. Jay pulled her up. Holding her by the shoulders, he examined her intently.

"You've been drinking, or someone's given you something." He whirled around at Peter. "What's going on? Who the hell are you? What have you done to her?"

Bewildered, with his customary flush mounting, Peter fumbled. "Peter Mendes is the name. And it's true, I'm just a friend, Jennie's friend from Chicago."

In her weakness, hysteria took hold of Jennie. Peter looked so funny, with his hair all mussed and no shoes; while Jay stood in his dark suit, white shirt, and foulard tie. She made a sound like a giggle, terror and tears in a giggle.

Jay shook her gently. "Jennie, for God's sake, talk to me! I've been wild with worry all evening. There was no answer on the phone. I called your office and a woman in the next office said you hadn't been there since half past five. With muggers on the streets and what's happened to George—" He stopped, looking puzzled. "You knew we had to talk tonight, and you broke the date. It's the second time you broke one—" He stopped again. "I'm thinking, I'm thinking I've gone crazy here. I think I'm not seeing what I'm seeing. You're naked!"

Through the open door, the bed loomed like a sultan's pleasure couch; tumbled in quilts, with both pillows crushed, it dominated the cramped little room. The three pairs of eyes, as if directed by the same thought, now focused on that bed.

Jay's face was as bleached as the other man's was reddened.

"You," he said queerly, "is it you I'm seeing, Jennie?"

"Please, just let me tell you—"

"Yes, tell me why you lied to me about having a client. Tell me what's happening here in the middle of the night." His voice was rough, close to tears. He panted and trembled. "On the other hand, maybe you shouldn't bother to tell me."

She ran to him and, raising her arms to plead, forgot the skirt, which fell to the floor. When she bent to pick it up, the jacket parted, revealing her breasts. Jay pushed her arms away and turned from her.

The most tragic situation could be partly ridiculous. Wasn't that strange? And stranger still that in this most awful despair a person can stand apart and see herself, beaten and ridiculous.

"Jay, hear me." Her words tumbled askew from her mouth, and she began to weep. When her hands flew to her face, the skirt dropped again, revealing her in the transparent petticoat.

"Is this you?" Jay repeated thickly, as if he had been stunned.

"You have to excuse her," Peter said. "She never drank before. She was upset. She's not herself, not the real Jennie."

Jay looked at him. "And I take it you know who the real Jennie is?"

"I knew her a long time ago. We had some things to talk about."

"Ah, yes. So you did. I see you did. Plenty to talk about."

With arms straight at his side, like a soldier at rigid attention, Jay stood. Only his hands moved, clenching into fists, loosening and clenching again.

"If someone told me my father had set fire to our house or my mother had robbed a bank, would I have believed it?" He spoke to himself, as if he were alone. "Oh, my God, when white is black and black is white, then anything can happen. Anything at all."

"Jay . . ." She wanted to speak, but horror grasped her throat and no words came. She was aware that she wasn't functioning as one ought to function, and yet her mind seemed to be working right; the contradiction was bizarre.

Jay moved to the door, which was still open to the public hall, and looked back across the room. Jennie had a swift perception: He had the expression of one who is leaving his home for the last time, printing it on his memory, or—could it be so?—of one who, with contempt, is casting away all that he had ever known of a place. There was a stillness without speech, a very brief stillness, only enough for the chiming brass carriage clock on the desk to strike the half hour and then to encompass the tinkling vibration it left in the air. In the brevity of those few moments an image, not even a thought, rather a shred or a fragment, flashed in Jennie's mind and dissolved: the coach, the white horses, the glass slipper, and all the brightness dissolved.

"I'll never believe in anything or anyone again," Jay said.

And he walked away. The door swung on its weight behind him and clicked shut.

Jennie stood with her back and the palms of her hands flattened against the wall. Peter went to the bedroom closet, came back with a robe, and put it over her. In silence she begged, Don't ask me anything. Please, no questions.

And he did not. As if he had understood, he took one of her hands and held it between his to warm it, saying only, "You're cold."

"I can't," she began, meaning, "I can't talk."

That, too, he understood. "You needn't talk. I'm not going to ask you anything. But you have to go back to bed while I make some tea."

The tea was hot and milky. He held the cup and wiped the spill that came from her dry, quivering lips.

"The hot milk will put you to sleep," he whispered.

When she had drunk, she lay back on the pillow. The lamp in the corner, distant and dim, threw a rosette on the ceiling. He stroked her forehead; firm fingers moved in rhythm. And she let herself sink and sink. Die . . .

——

When she woke in the morning, Peter was sitting in a straight chair near the bed. It occurred to her that he might have been sitting there all night.

"I've made breakfast," he said. "First, though, go shower and do your hair."

But now she was completely clear, and everything that had been foggy the night before sprang out like a headline in the *Times*. Jay's face had been blurred, doubly blurred, by his anguish and her own. Yet she was distinctly seeing his eyes; they must have registered in her subconscious. Now they were fixed upon her in a fierce glare of pain. Once, while still a young girl living in the row house, she had seen a man in the yard at the end of the street whipping a dog and had never forgotten the poor dog's eyes. . . .

She turned her face into the pillow and cried, excruciating sobs that shook her body. So people weep when someone dies. I remember Mama when Papa died. I thought the crying would kill her too.

After a while, when the sobbing ceased, Peter came back to the room. He waited, not speaking, only shaking his head a little, smiling a little as one pities and gently reproaches a child: *Ah, don't cry.* . . .

"There was nothing," she said. "We did nothing."

"No, but it certainly looked as though we had done something."

"We were going to be married."

"Who is he?"

"A lawyer."

"You don't trust me?"

"No."

He smiled again and shrugged.

"Are you angry because I won't tell you his name?"

"It doesn't matter."

"You've been very nice to me, Peter."

"Of course. Wouldn't you have done the same?"

"I suppose so."

"You would. You of all people would." He had sat down on the straight chair in the corner and now gave her a straight, piteous look of appeal. "I'm feeling horribly guilty. I don't know your story, but it's not hard to figure it out—some of it, anyway—and I see that my being here has made terrible trouble for you again." When she didn't answer, his forehead wrinkled. "It's the second time I've come into your life. What can I say? Can I do anything at all?"

"Nothing. What is there to do?" It took too much strength to talk, but he looked so wretched that she had to say something more. "You didn't do this on purpose. You meant well, staying here with me."

"You scared the life out of me when you left the table like that. Jill was scared too. You looked—well, frantic. Yes, frantic. That's why I had to come."

"I've been frantic for quite a while."

"Because of him? You didn't want him to find out about Jill?"

A leftover sob caught in her throat. "That wasn't—that wasn't thinkable."

He asked no more, and for a minute or two neither spoke. She felt unkempt, unclean, and miserable because of it. Making a great effort, she forced herself to sit up and asked him to leave the room. Modestly wrapping herself in her Turkish bathrobe, she went to the shower.

Under the lulling patter of warm water, she stood, mechanically soaping herself. In a kind of lethargy she stood too long, wasting water, taking refuge in the curtain of gentle heat. Then she got out, brushed her teeth and flossed them, and brushed her hair; its dark waves fell into place. But the face in the mirror was devastated, with red eyes sunken to half their normal size under fattened, glossy lids. Ugly. It didn't matter. Nothing did. One tidied one's hair and flossed one's teeth. What sense did it make? What difference, if one's teeth should rot?

"You look better," Peter said.

"I look like hell. Look at me." Perversely she wanted him to acknowledge the devastation.

"Well," he said, changing the subject, "how about having coffee in bed?"

"Bed? I have to go to work, Peter. It's eight o'clock."

"You're in no condition for work today, and you know it, Jennie. Go on back to bed for now. You can get up later."

He had made toast and a boiled egg, which she didn't touch. It had been days since she had had any appetite, anyway. For a while he watched her sipping the coffee, hugging the cup between her palms, and then said, "I'll call your office for you, unless you want to do it, and say you're sick."

"You can do it. Just ask for Dinah." All energy, all ambition had seeped away, yet she had to show fortitude in the face of devastation. "Say I'll definitely be in tomorrow."

"I'm not sure you will be. You're entitled to time off."

"I'm not 'entitled' to anything."

"Why are you so hard on yourself? You've had a shock. You were in a state of shock, as if there'd been a death."

That was a strange way to describe it, yet it did feel like a death. I'm not certain I know how to go on from here, she thought. It makes no sense, that everything can end this way. All over in two or three minutes.

"He said something when he was standing at the door," she began. "I can't seem to remember exactly what it was. Can you?"

As Peter looked puzzled, she prompted, "Last night when he was leaving. I'll call him Joe because that's not his name. I'm trying to think. Was it something about not believing?"

"Oh. Do you really want to know? Do you have to go back over it?"

"Yes, I want to know."

"He said, 'I will never believe in anything or anybody again.' "

The words, even secondhand, had an elegiac ring, a terrible finality. For a time she listened to them inside her head, then asked Peter whether he thought "Joe" could have meant them.

"Never is a long time, Jennie."

"You're right. It was a stupid question."

So then, sometime or other, there would be another woman. And shutting her eyes, she let herself imagine in every fleshly detail the women to whom he would turn in bed and open his arms. What words would he speak? The words they had said to each other in their special language?

Oh, they can fill a thousand pages with pop psychology, and write off jealousy as something immature and degrading, but it's true nevertheless that jealousy is torture, and people kill because of it, and kill themselves too. It's loss, final loss, and worse.

So now you know, Jennie, you know as if you were in Jay's skin, how he felt when he saw you here last night.

The doorbell rang so abruptly that Peter started.

"It's Shirley from across the hall. She generally rings to ask whether I want to walk to work with her."

"Okay. I'll say you've got the flu."

When he returned, he looked amused. "If you ever saw amazement on a face! Her eyebrows went up to her hairline."

Jennie said bitterly, "I can imagine. You don't look at all like the man she's used to seeing here in the mornings."

"She wanted to come in, but I said I was taking care of you, that I'm an old friend and a doctor too."

"Thank you. I didn't want her to see me like this." It was odd that she wasn't ashamed to have Peter see her. "Shirley's a good soul, but she talks too much. She knows everything about everybody."

"You must have other friends. I think you should talk to a friend today."

"I don't want anyone."

He countered gently, "But you need some help until you can straighten things out."

"They may never be 'straightened out,' don't you see? I'll probably have to manage by myself, so I might as well get used to doing it now."

They were brave, commonsense words; still, Jennie only half believed them. Surely Jay would come back and want some explanation. . . . Then she reminded herself: Even so, the question of Jill would still be there, and she would only be back where she had been in the first place.

"Excuse me. May I ask you why you say 'never'?"

"It's a long story."

"Maybe you can make it shorter."

"Well, I lied to him. And he has never lied to me. Oh, you don't understand! You would have to know him, and everything that's gone before."

Peter looked doubtful but asked no more. And Jennie, stepping outside of herself for an instant as was her habit, saw herself sitting up in bed facing this longtime stranger who was subtly beginning to become familiar again. A faint red stubble had grown on his cheeks overnight; she could remember the time he had talked about growing a beard. She could remember . . .

And she made a comparison: He wasn't much younger than Jay, although he looked much younger, lighter somehow, as if life were easier for him. Maybe it had been. She realized that she knew nothing about him except that he was a professor. For a second she had a vision of him in a professional pose, perched on a desk with one leg swinging; he would wear polished loafers and a cashmere pullover in an argyle pattern. She wasn't sure whether he would smoke a pipe and decided that he probably wouldn't; it would be too much of a cliché. The girls would be arch with him. The boys would respect his height and powerful frame. But she really knew nothing about him.

"Are you married?" she asked.

"Me? What made you ask?"

"I don't know. Just wondered."

"Not married."

"I read about you once. It was in a directory of American scholars. I was glad to know you were a success. That you'd arrived where you wanted to be."

"You were glad?" He was surprised. "After everything that happened between us, you could be glad for me?"

"The one thing has nothing to do with the other," she said simply.

He shook his head. "What makes you so kind? But then, you always were."

She smiled slightly. Indeed she had been kind to him. And she said, "It's not just that. I admire a good mind that hasn't been allowed to go to waste."

"Well, I'm certainly no Schliemann in the ruins of Troy, but I have written about some interesting discoveries in our southwestern deserts, and I do like teaching, so all in all, I'm fairly satisfied with my life. But tell me about yourself, about the law business."

He was almost jocular, and she saw that this was an awkward effort to divert her thoughts and change her mood. But everything went abruptly queer and bleak again. The winter light, thin and blue as skimmed milk, was unkind to the little room that could be so cozy at night: the chest of drawers was scarred; the white curtains were yellowed and flimsy. Failure dwelled here.

Since she had not replied, Peter spoke once more, this time more seriously. "I don't like to leave you alone this way. I wish I didn't have to go."

"Back to Chicago now?"

"No, I've planned on a week here in the city. I'm to meet a few people in the Archaeology Department at Columbia. There's a conference this afternoon and a couple of dinners. Then next week I'll have to fly back to Atlanta."

She made no comment.

"It's my parents' fortieth anniversary. A milestone."

Still she was silent.

"I know you don't want to hear about them."

She could have countered with a question: Since you know it, why talk about them? But that wasn't her way, so she answered only, "It really doesn't matter to me at all, you know."

He flushed. "Well, I only wanted to say that I have to go to Atlanta. Otherwise I'd stay and try to help out. Help Jill and you. . . . Oh, you know what I'm trying to say, Jennie. Mostly help you, although I don't know how."

"I don't, either. So you'll do just as well by going to the celebration in Atlanta," she said coolly enough.

He seemed to have a need to pursue the subject. "It'll be only a small celebration. The family's shrunk. A lot of the relatives have died off since you— I mean, there won't be so many of us there. Sally June has no children—"

Jennie could see them all at the dark-grained, candle-lit table, each of them seated behind a neat pool of white linen. In winter the view from the tall windows would be subdued: dark evergreens and sere lawns. The sister has no children, so they have no grandchildren. That would be a hurt, especially for people like them, with all their pride in lineage and continuity.

And she couldn't resist a question. "Have they never asked, never mentioned . . . ?"

"No." She saw that he was unable to meet her eyes. Yet he added, "I often wonder whether they think about it or ever mention it between themselves."

"Are you going to tell them, now that you know?"

"I'm not sure. I can't think what's best. Can you?"

"Me? I can't think at all," Jennie said with bitterness.

They were both silent until Peter said, "I hate to leave you here alone with trouble like this, but I have to."

"Of course you do. Please go. Don't be late because of me."

"I'll telephone you. Or maybe I'll stop by again."

"You don't need to."

"I know I don't, but I will. There's a pitcher of water on the table. Lock the door when I leave."

Another wave of despair swept over her when he had gone. It was as if all the radiance of life, the hope, the sunlight, and all the wild, sweet joy had been swept away. And never, never had she been so tired.

She prayed for sleep. For a long time it would not come. But after a while the separate noises of horns and engines began to merge into a single monotonous, oceanic roar, and sleep was ready to engulf her. Even while she knew she was making only a temporary escape, the escape was blessed.

Off and on, Jennie slept through the day and the night. On the second morning her physical strength had returned enough for her to get up quickly, dress, eat a little something, and take stock. Another day away from the office would not bring disaster, she decided. Hope, which she doubted even as she felt it rise, encouraged her nevertheless. Perhaps it would be wise to wait at home. Jay might come. . . . He would telephone the office, learn that she was sick, and then—

She was considering this when the doorbell rang. She went to answer it.

Shirley's glance swept over Jennie. "All better, are you?"

"Pretty much. A twenty-four-hour bug, I guess. Or just a touch of flu or something."

"Good. Lucky for you your friend was here. He said you almost fainted."

"It hit me hard."

"Tough. Well, I'm taking the afternoon off. I'll probably come home early, so if there's anything you want, you'll know where to find me."

"Thanks so much, Shirley. But I'm all right. I really am."

When Shirley left, Jennie poured a second cup of coffee and sat down again. Things in the tiny kitchen had been put back in the wrong places. The black-lacquer tray was on the top shelf instead of the bottom. It looked better on the top shelf next to the black-lacquer jar of Chinese tea. Peter had done that; he noticed such things. He was meticulous and perfection was important to him; he was, after all, the son of the house with the tall white pillars. The house where Jennie had been unwanted. And she had borne a grandchild for them! Her head dropped into her hands, and although she had been shivering a few minutes ago, she was overcome with the heat of her pounding blood.

Yet Peter had just been so good to her! And Shirley too. They'd wanted to help, and she must be grateful. She was. But the only one who could really help was Jay.

And the morning drifted past.

Early in the afternoon she became shockingly aware that, lost within herself, she had given no thought to George Cromwell. Under the frozen earth, the guileless, kind old man lay in his new grave. Guilt brought a hot flush to her cheeks. She must at least send some flowers to his widow and drive up to see her soon. In her despair she had almost forgotten that other woman, and she frowned now, weighing that woman's pain against her own. But they were too different to be weighed; they were at the opposite ends of life.

I'll go now about the flowers, she thought. It'll only take a few minutes, and if Jay comes and finds I'm not here, he will wait.

He will not come.

When she opened the door to the street, she saw with dismay that Peter was approaching the house. This was too much!

She had no need of him, and no wish for any heart-to-heart talks about themselves or Jill.

"So you're going out!" he exclaimed. "Well, you look better than you did yesterday, anyway. How are you feeling?"

"I'm fine, as you see."

He peered down at her. "I don't know about 'fine.' But certainly improved. Going anywhere special?"

"Only to the florist on the avenue."

"Mind if I walk with you?"

"No." And she told him, "I know I said I'm fine, but I'm very tired. So please excuse me if I don't say much."

He made no answer. Few people were out on this raw afternoon, so that the nervous, rapid clack of Jennie's heels was loud, and Peter's silence, in consequence, was heavier and mournful. She felt oppressed by a strange sensation of distance, as if she had been away for a long time. At a drugstore on the avenue, next to the florist, she stopped as if to collect herself, and stood watching a boy arrange a little pyramid of perfume bottles, Nuit de Noël, Calèche, Shalimar—all the lilting names. Shalimar was sweet, like roses, sugar, and vanilla. Sweet candy, Jay always said, kissing her neck. And turning from the window, she was so blinded by her tears that she would have bumped into a man going past if Peter had not caught her arm.

In the flower shop she gave her order for roses to be telegraphed to Martha Cromwell, and went out again into a day grown blustery and heartless.

Peter broke the silence. "May I ask you just one thing? I won't burden you, Jennie, but have you talked to him?"

"No."

He winced. "Oh, God, it's my fault."

"It would have ended, anyway, in the circumstances."

"Jill, you mean. It's because of her, you're saying."

"Oh, Peter, I'm not saying anything. For God's sake, don't make me think anymore! I want to be empty forever."

"Funny, that's what Jill said about herself yesterday."

"You've seen her again?"

"Yes, I had to be at Columbia, I told you. So we had lunch. I told her about you, told her everything. Do you mind that I did?"

"If I do, it's too late, isn't it? But no, I guess I don't mind."

"She cried, Jennie. She thinks she treated you harshly. She wouldn't have been so insistent if she'd known how things were with you."

"She didn't mean to be harsh. Tell her I understand that. I don't want her to feel guilty because of me."

"It would be better if you would tell her all that yourself, Jennie."

Jennie threw up her hands. "Don't you know we'd only go over the same ground? It wouldn't come to anything."

"You can't be sure of that. Isn't it worth trying?"

Apologies, explanations, and probably more tears, she thought, and repeated, "It wouldn't come to anything."

"I'm not trying to force anything on you. But she is so young. Her childhood was yesterday. Please think about it."

Jennie sighed. "All right. I'm thinking, and this is what I think."

"Think about it some more, please."

His voice was soothing. He was coaxing her, and she knew it. And he was probably right. No, he was surely right. Jill's childhood . . . what do I know about it? But I know how it hurts not to be understood. As Jay to me, so I to Jill. All related, intertwined like a knot.

But I can't unravel it now. I can't.

And lowering her head against the wind, she hurried homeward. Halfway there, she stopped and held out her hand.

"Peter, I want to say good-bye here."

"You don't want me to go back to the house? That's okay, Jennie. It makes sense. But will you do one thing? Will you really think about talking to Jill?"

"I'll do my best, Peter."

She was turning the key in the lock when Shirley's door opened.

"Hey, where've you been, anyway? I thought you'd never get back."

"What do you mean? I wasn't out more than half an hour. Forty-five minutes, maybe."

"Jay was here."

Jennie's heart shook. "And? Did you talk to him?"

"He rang my bell when you didn't answer. I told him I'd seen you go down the street—I was just coming home then—with your friend, that doctor from Chicago."

"You told him that?"

"Of course. Shouldn't I have?"

How amazing that one's heart can faint while one's voice stays steady!

"What did he say?"

"Nothing. Just thanked me and left. He's such a gentleman! Oh, I did tell him you were feeling better this morning, and that your doctor friend must have said it was all right to go out for a while."

With a hopeless gaze Jennie's eyes rested on her friend. Sophistication could be a surface quality, a flair for dress and a collection of worldly mannerisms; beneath all these, Shirley was only a good-hearted, thoughtless, garrulous child. Her chattering tongue, unknowing, had just now put the final seal on Jennie's fate. With this second event, the return of her "Chicago friend," there was no way at all Jay could trust her again.

"I think I'll lie down awhile," she said faintly.

"You shouldn't have been out in this weather. You look positively white. I don't care what anybody says, it doesn't make sense to risk pneumonia—"

But Jennie had already gone in and closed the door.

Now she was numb. She sank onto a hard chair in the hall and stared at the floor. The little rug was marked in squares, four from side to side, seven up and down. Seven fours are twenty-eight. . . . Time bent, and her wandering mind began to spin, so that Peter, the young one and the present one, began to spin, merged with Jay, so that light merged with dark and fear overlaid them all. What should she do next with her life? What *could* she do next? And abruptly, as on a cold morning after long postponements one suddenly jumps out of bed, she went to the telephone and dialed Jay's office number.

The secretary's familiar voice was ever so slightly unsure, or embarrassed, or cool; whichever it was, Jennie knew at once that the response was untrue. No, Mr. Wolfe had not come in. As a matter of fact, he probably was not coming in at all today. No, she really didn't know when he would be back or where he was. This from the friendly gray-haired woman who had always had a few words for Jennie and had even been promised an invitation to the wedding!

It was three o'clock. Three was a reminder: The children had come from school. Of course, she thought, this is what I must do. Emily and Sue will tell me if he's at home. Her hand was poised above the telephone. If he was there, what would she say? How to begin? Oh, my dear, my dearest, hear me. Hear what? Yet her fingers dialed the number.

"Is this you, Sue?"

"No, it's Emily."

"How are you, darling? This is Jennie."

"I know," the child said.

"Tell me, is Daddy there?"

"I don't know."

"Darling, what do you mean, you 'don't know'?"

The child murmured unintelligibly.

"I can't hear you, Emily. What did you say?"

"I said Nanny doesn't want me to talk on the telephone now."

"Does Nanny know you're talking to me?"

"I think so. Yes."

So Jennie knew well what had happened. Never, never would Jay have told his children anything ugly about her; certainly he never would tell them to be rude to her. He must simply have told Nanny that he didn't want to speak to her, and Nanny had said something about it to the children.

And she saw Jay in the library, where he most often used the telephone. It stood on the desk, next to the statue of Lincoln on the chair in the memorial. The wing chair was dark green leather with brass nail heads. He might even be sitting there now, alone with his disillusionment.

She saw Emily answering the telephone in the hall. Emily always liked to run to the phone, which made Nanny angry. The woman was so rigid, and Jennie had been thinking how, after they were married, very tactfully she would convince Jay to find someone else.

"I've missed you, darling," she said now.

"I've missed you, too, but Nanny say I'm not to talk anymore."

"Good-bye, Emily," Jennie answered quietly, replacing the receiver.

Suddenly she heard herself wail; a most terrible cry it was, an outburst of anguish and despair. When a knife cuts or a child dies, such cries are heard. She clamped her hand over her mouth to choke her sobs, which shook her body so that she was bent over in pain.

After a while, a long, long while, the sobs died away into a deep, exhausted sigh. She stood up. She reached into the cupboard and drew from the cereal box the Cartier's box with the ring. Then she went to the bedroom and took the velvet box with the pearls from under a pile of sweaters. The ring had never belonged on her finger. Its cold diamond eye was aloof. The pearls, opulent as silk, slid through her hands; let them go back to be worn on the kind of neck to which they were accustomed. In the kitchen she packed both boxes into a small carton, wrapped it with heavy twine, and sealed it with heavy tape. All the time her teeth were clenched; she became aware of that when she had to telephone the post office for the ZIP code.

Writing, with a hand that had to be steadied, the name J. Wolfe, she thought, This is the last time I shall need to write his name.

At the post office it took all of her money, all she had had in the secret emergency cache at home, to pay for insurance on the package. It seemed to her as she handed it over to the man at the counter that this must be the feeling one had after surgery, pain and relief that it was over.

The way now lay ahead, she thought resolutely. Yet there came a flicker of doubt, a question: When have I said that before? And the answer came: You said that after your daughter was born. Don't you remember?

Maybe I ought to move, she thought on the way home. This neighborhood, although it isn't his, is too full of him. That store where we watched the angora kittens and almost bought one, our Italian dinners, the record shop where we stocked up on compact discs— Shall I remember every time I walk past?

The day was darkening toward night, and the wind was cutting. Discarded papers scooted along the dirty gutters of the iron-gray city. I must take hold of myself, she said silently. A mood like this mustn't be allowed to last. It was too easy to slide into depression. She remembered those grim weeks before Jill's birth, when she had sat staring out of a window into afternoons like this one, dirty, windy, and frozen.

At the front door of her building she passed a man hurrying down the steps. She thought his glance lasted a few seconds too long, as though he was taking notice of her. She thought perhaps she knew him and then thought he was the man with whom, earlier in the day, she had collided at the drugstore window. Yes, surely it was he. Nonsense. In her present state of mind she was apt to imagine anything. But maybe it *was* he. The tape, she thought. Oh, surely not!

Back upstairs, she found that she had left her door unlocked. "Nerves," she said aloud and sternly. "You never did that before. You're just not thinking." She began to shiver. The temperature must have dropped very low. No, it wasn't that. It was nerves again. She scolded herself. "Make some hot tea and eat. You've not had a mouthful since breakfast."

Warming her hands around the cup, she sat staring out at the cold sky. Thin clouds scudded over the pale, sinking sun. The kitchen clock's loud tick emphasized the silence and the emptiness. When she had drunk the tea, she stood up and began to walk up and down the living room. Her mind traveled through the day just past. There was something—wasn't there something?—she was supposed to think about.

Yes. She was supposed to think about Jill. "She's so young," Peter had said. "Her childhood was only yesterday."

That's true. And now she grieves because of me. Why should she grieve so young? Time enough for that later when she's older. Plenty of time . . . There's no longer any reason why she can't come here now. No reason at all.

Very subtly Jennie began to feel that an exchange was in the making: a lover, a husband lost and a daughter found. Plans erased and substituted by some gigantic finger in the sky, as if one's own will didn't count for anything. Well, it hasn't counted, has it, Jennie? All the hope wasted, and all the energy gone down the drain! One has an image of another person, like mine of Jay, but how true is it? For that matter, can one's image of one's own self be true?

After a while a decision made itself. She went to the telephone and called Peter's hotel.

"I've been thinking, as you asked me to," she told him. "Tell Jill to feel better and to come for supper—you call it dinner—tomorrow."

"Oh!" Peter said. "Not at your place?"

"Yes, here, not in a restaurant. The three of us, at six."

"Jennie, is it all over, then—with him?"

Firmly, quietly, she answered. "It is, and I don't want to talk about it."

"I feel for you, Jennie. I feel for you; believe that I do.

But I can't help feeling a little gladness too. For Jill. And she'll be so happy when I tell her." He was genuinely, almost tearfully grateful. Jennie imagined the smile that opened upward to his eyes and crinkled there. "God bless you, Jennie. I had a hunch we could count on you in the end."

She put the receiver down on the desk, where a heap of files from the office lay neglected.

You'd better see to them, she said to herself. Go back to work. Get used to the way things are. You have no other choice.

But the ache lay like a stone.

CHAPTER

12

Through Peter's efforts the little supper, which had begun so warily, turned lively in the end. He added a bottle of wine to Jennie's simple menu of salad, chicken, and fruit. He flourished a tight bouquet in a lace paper collar. The expansive gesture, so typical of him, made her feel slightly irritable; he acted and always had, she remembered, as if flowers were a cure for every mood, quick cheer and a kind of balm. Nevertheless they did grace the plain table.

Jill brought one of those expensive cakes made of nuts and bitter chocolate that came from European bakeries on the Upper East Side. In contrast to Peter's jovial manner, she seemed chastened, with the anxious look of someone bringing a little gift to a house of mourning, offering it with a half-apologetic murmur. Peter must have drawn a portrait of disaster, of Jennie in collapse.

It was he at first who led the conversation, carefully steering it away from the personal. He apparently had decided that food was a safe topic, and began to entertain them with anecdotes about a clambake in Maine, snake meat in Hong Kong, and Sacher torte at the Hotel Sacher in Vienna. The last, he said, was overrated.

"Much too dry, I thought."

Jill had spoken very little, so little that Jennie had begun to think, in spite of what Peter had reported, that she was still filled with resentment. Or perhaps only with apprehension? Now, suddenly, she spoke.

"Mine's not dry at all. I have a better recipe for it. And, anyway, I always take a cake out of the oven five or six minutes before you're supposed to."

Somehow this fashionable young woman with her short black skirt, high black boots, and long scarlet fingernails didn't fit the picture of one who always took cakes out of the oven.

"Then you can cook?" Jennie inquired curiously.

This time Jill looked straight back. "I'm a good cook. Mom and I take courses together."

"I think that's wonderful. It wouldn't hurt me to do something like that. I'm not much good in the kitchen," Jennie said, thinking, She *unfolds*. It's like turning new pages in a book, a whole shelf of books.

The reply was polite, conventional, a guest-to-hostess reply. "But you can't be in the courtroom and the kitchen at the same time, after all."

And Jennie, understanding that the implied compliment was a peace offering, smiled. "No excuse. I could find time if I tried hard enough."

Peter, seeing that the conversation was beginning to warm up for flight, and obviously wanting to keep it flying, added eagerly, "I see all those files on the desk there. You haven't told me anything about your practice. Is it general law or do you specialize?"

"Jennie's an advocate for women, didn't you know? Poor women, battered women, working women," Jill said quickly.

It seemed to Jennie that there was admiration in Jill's tone, and this excited her, and remembering suddenly Jill's remarks at their ill-fated lunch about conservation in New Mexico, she responded as quickly. "That's certainly most of what I do, but I've also done some environmental work. In fact, I'm in the middle of a hot fight right now."

Then fear came, a pang of alarm; if she was in the middle of it, she ought to be attending to it. Four days had passed since George's death. Assuredly Martin had secured the tape by now and perhaps even had gotten hold of some clues to the death. Why had she not heard from him? She thought in dismay that she should be talking to Arthur Wolfe or with whoever had taken George's place, and yet how, in the circumstances, could she?

And she said in a bleak voice, the words escaping involuntarily, "George was buried yesterday."

Puzzled, Peter inquired who George was.

"No, I haven't lost my wits," she said. "I was only thinking aloud."

Now it was natural for her to explain about George. So it was that, without divulging names of either people or places, Jennie began to tell the story of the Green Marsh.

The other two were fascinated. And to Jennie's ears it seemed that a fervor had crept into her telling, as if she had been recounting or pleading the case of a child or woman who had been treated without justice or care. Wordlessly Jill and Peter finished the meal, helped to clear the little table, and took their coffee into the living room with Jennie talking all the while.

"I'm very torn. I'm seeing this work of conserving nature as important, as important as my work with women's rights. If we don't stop devouring our lakes and hills for profit, there won't be any rights left for women—or for men, either—will there? Oh, if I were rich, I'd just buy land and buy land and give it away to the state to keep! That place is so beautiful, it makes your heart ache to think of what they want to do with it."

"I know what you mean," Jill said indignantly. "The papers at home are always filled with the same kind of news, a lot of angry litigation over zoning and water rights. And what do you think of them cutting redwoods in California? Trees that have been growing for a thousand years! It makes my blood boil."

Peter made a gesture of discovery, as if a new idea had surprised him. "I'm sitting here thinking: Wouldn't it be great if we could meet out West some summer, up in the California redwood country, or even down in Santa Fe, maybe, and rent a jeep to go exploring?" He glanced at the other two. "Maybe it's impossible . . . I don't know. I just thought . . ." he finished somewhat wistfully.

And Jennie thought, You're moving much too fast. It was typical of Peter, but the motive was praiseworthy, and it was wonderful that they were all really able to talk to one another by now, instead of at one another.

This was no surface chatter, it had substance; and Jennie began to feel her muscles shedding tension. Her shoulders relaxed, and she leaned back on the couch. Jill's hand lay near hers; the narrow, pretty fingers and bright nails were somehow touching in their contrast to the girl's sober words.

"And can you believe somebody actually wants to build a shopping mall on a Civil War battlefield? They're messing up the Arizona desert, there'll be nothing left. . . . Listen, Jennie, you've got to stay in this fight. You've got to." Jill's eyes flashed boldly.

Something stirred in Jennie, a quickening of pride and self-respect. The events of the past few days, her behav-

ior, her failure—all had diminished her; it had been so
painful to be inadequate and small, rejected, in contrast
to these two. Now she had spoken to them with authority, and they had listened.

"I surely want to stay in the fight," she replied, then
had to add, "Though it may not be possible to stay in this
particular one. But there'll be others."

"Why not this one?" Peter asked.

"There are reasons too complicated to go into."

"Just answer this much: Would there be any danger in
it for you if you did go on with it?"

"Oh, I don't think so."

"It's so awful, what happened to that man in the car.
Do be careful," Jill warned.

The girl really likes me, Jennie thought. There's a note
in her voice that isn't fake. She means it.

"I'll be careful." She smiled at Jill, thinking, A few days
ago I wanted to die. Now I don't. Mom lost everyone
during the Hitler years, yet she lived, didn't she?

Jill smiled back. Peter had a peaceful, satisfied expression. For just a second it occurred to Jennie that the
three of them looked like a family settled back for a quiet
evening at home after a good dinner.

Such queer twists and turns! She'd felt so much righ-
teous rage, and now she was thinking how kind Peter
was, how warm Jill was.

Jill looked at her watch. "I've a history quiz tomorrow
and I'm behind in the reading. I really should do some
work tonight."

Jennie stood at once. "Of course. Peter, you'll get a
taxi for her."

"I'll do better than that. I'll ride back with her." He
put his hands on Jennie's shoulders, turning her toward
himself. "I want you to know this was wonderful tonight.
Wonderful." He shook a little with emotion. "We'll never
forget it, any of us."

"No," Jill said. She hesitated a moment before saying quietly, "I'm sorry you've had so much trouble, Jennie. And I know it's because of me."

It was a piteous appeal. The proud young face seemed to recede into what it must have been in the childhood Jennie had not known, wistful and moody, with darkly circled eyes and mobile lips ready on the instant to quiver into anger, grief, or laughter. Who among her ancestors had bequeathed this volatile nature?

"Oh," replied Jennie, purposely vague, "causes go way back. There's never any one cause."

"But I've ruined everything for you. I know I have. I told Peter so."

"I've had my part in the ruination too," he added glumly.

There was no possible answer except assent, yet nothing was to be gained by adding blame. All were at fault, each in his or her own way. So Jennie made a small gesture of dismissal and, needing to say something, said only, "Let's look ahead if we can, not back."

Jill spoke. "I wish I didn't have to leave when there's still so much more to be said."

"Maybe you two can get together some afternoon soon," suggested Peter.

Jill said quickly, "I could do it tomorrow. My last class is at one." She was eager. She wanted to cement the new relationship in a hurry. "We could go anywhere. The museum, the Metropolitan. We could look around a while and have tea."

Jennie had planned to go back to the office. She had hidden at home, licking her wounds, long enough. Dinah had been calling with messages. She ought, furthermore, to be checking with the district attorney. It puzzled her that she had heard nothing about the case.

But in the face of Jill's appeal, what difference could one more day make?

"All right. We'll meet at the front steps, just inside the door if the weather's bad."

She heard them walk downstairs, and on impulse ran to the window to see them emerge from the building and walk away to the avenue. And again there came that odd sense: We are linked, joined, we belong. The feeling darted, pricked a little hole in her head, and fled. Yet she still watched, craning her neck until they were out of sight.

The dark blue night sky raced above the city; wind-blown clouds billowed, hiding the stars. Mesmerized by the moving sky, she reflected, We should look up more often. It chastens and puts things in proportion. At least while you're looking at it, she thought wryly, and was about to pull the blinds down when something caught her attention. A man was standing in the light of the streetlamp, peering up at the house. Was it absurd to imagine that he was watching her window? Of course it was. He had only paused to turn up his coat collar. Then he went, walking toward the river.

My God, my nerves again. They're shot, Jennie thought, whether I want to admit it or not.

She wanted to keep her mind on Jill, but it kept wandering. They looked at an Egyptian statuette, four thousand years old; man and wife stood together, she with her arm around his waist and he with his arm around her shoulder. Timeless, endless human love! And a terrible resentment flared in Jennie, driving the blood into her cheeks and throbbing in her temples, so that she had to force herself to speak normally.

"Well, have we had enough? I could use a chair and some tea."

"You're tired? Have I made you walk too much?" The girl was anxious; this was genuine concern, just as on that first night when she had thought Jennie was about to faint.

"No, no, of course not. I'm not an invalid." Then, as if she had sounded impatient, Jennie added quickly, "You're such a kind person, Jill."

"And so are you."

"I try to be," Jennie said seriously.

"Well, you are. I know that, now that I understand more. I truly do, and I want you to know that I do," Jill replied with equal seriousness.

Jennie ordered tea and sat for a while gazing over the surrounding tables and heads. If there were a window, Jill would be looking out of it, Jennie thought. I am really learning her ways; she likes long necklaces to play with; today she's wearing two strands of burnt-orange enameled beads, probably Burmese or Indian, smooth to fiddle with and click together.

All at once Jill said, startling Jennie, "I'm glad you like Peter again."

"What makes you say I do?"

"You're not angry at him anymore, and you were terribly angry when he first called you."

"There's a big difference between just not being angry and actually liking someone."

"But you do like him, I could tell last night."

"It was just that we were having such a nice time."

"More than nice. It was beautiful. Didn't you think it was beautiful?" Jill insisted.

The girl's ardor disturbed Jennie. Slowly she stirred her milky tea and considered a moderate reply.

Finally she said, "It's good that we did it."

"But wasn't it astounding? I mean, think about it! We were like a family. We *were* a family."

When last evening the same thought had sped through Jennie's mind, she had dismissed it as an exaggeration. Now the thought alarmed her.

"You already have a family, Jill," she said firmly, as if to sound a warning.

"I know that I've been very lucky. I had a wonderful childhood, and I still feel all the warmth of it. I didn't have to become an adult overnight the way you did, and I'm very, very thankful for that."

"And I," Jennie said, "am very, very thankful to your parents for giving you that wonderful childhood."

Now she hesitated between her native instinct to express herself, letting the waters flow, and her learned control, protecting her privacy, damming the waters.

And she said, frowning a little, feeling a tension in her forehead, "I want to say things that I've made myself forget. I worried so! I wondered whether you were still alive. Perhaps some childhood disease . . . or an accident? And I thought, What would become of you if *they* died? It could happen. Your birthday was such a bad day for me. I never looked at the calendar when November came." She glanced at Jill, who turned her eyes away as one turns from the sight of pain.

"Jennie—don't. There was never anything like that."

"You're told you will forget, once the child has been given away," Jennie murmured. "But it's not true. You don't."

"That's what Peter says. You don't forget."

Peter. What had *he* to forget, for heaven's sake? But of course he had plenty, and of course, being the person he was, he must have lived through sadly troubled hours. I'm in such a strange mood today, Jennie thought. I seem to feel a kind of pity for the world, even for all these chatting strangers, sitting here at lunch in this beautiful place. How can anyone know what any one of them has endured or will have to endure?

Yes. Peter.

"I've been thinking—" Jill began, and stopped. "You won't be angry if I tell you something?"

Jennie had to smile. "I won't be angry."

"All right, then. What I've been thinking is, is there maybe a chance that you and Peter could ever—I mean, you both got along so happily last night. Not right away, of course. But maybe sometime?"

"Jill, don't fantasize. Please."

"Oh, but is it really fantasizing? I don't think so! I have a feeling that Peter would—"

Jennie interrupted. "Why? What has he said?"

"He hasn't actually said anything. I just have a feeling." Jill laughed, moving her hands so that her scarlet nails sparkled. "Full circle. It would be so tidy! I'm a very tidy person. Compulsive, almost."

"I'm not," Jennie said rather dryly, looking down at her own unvarnished nails.

There was a silence until Jill spoke, flushing as brightly as Peter could. "Oh, I've said the wrong thing! I only meant, now that the man you were going to marry—" She stopped. "Oh, worse and worse! I've really put my foot in my mouth, haven't I? People always tell me I should think before I open it. I'm awfully sorry, Jennie."

She seemed for the moment so extremely young and so contrite that Jennie could say only, "It's okay. Really, okay. Just a difference of opinion."

Jill said more happily, "Well, that's what makes horse racing, as Grandpa always says."

"Yes, my mother always says it too."

"Shall I ever see your mother?"

Oh, Mom had so wanted a grandchild! She never would have moved away to Florida if there had been one.

"I don't know, Jill. I don't know whether it would be the best thing for her if I were to tell her about you now. I'd have to think hard about it."

Jill nodded. "I understand. I do understand a lot better than I did last week, you know."

Jennie touched Jill's hand. "You've told me, and I'm thankful for that. How about a piece of cake to wash down another cup of tea?"

"My weight. I've got to watch it."

"Oh, have a piece. You don't do this every day. Besides, you're skinny."

"Men like skinny girls."

"Not all men."

"My boyfriends do."

"Did I hear plural or singular?"

"Plural. I did have a special one all last year, but I decided it was dumb to be tied down to one person, especially when I wasn't in love with him. He was very smart, a physics major, and nice-looking, but that's not reason enough to give all my time to him. Don't you agree?"

"I definitely agree."

"Someday," Jill said earnestly, "I want to love somebody so much that I can't imagine living without him. And I want to be loved like that in return. Is that too romantic, too unrealistic for the 1980s, do you think?"

"No." Jennie spoke very softly. "I should say it's the only way."

"So in the meantime I've been selective. Right now I've got three who like me a lot. One's a musician and gets tickets for everything, even when they're sold out. We go to the opera on Saturday afternoons. I learned to like it in Santa Fe. You've heard about our opera there, I'm sure."

Eating cake, drinking tea, Jill rattled on about men, friends, grades, and books.

"Then there's this group I go with. There're about eight of us and we're open to everything, rock and disco —I love to dance—and now a few of us are wading through Proust in French for our seminar. It's a challenge, let me tell you."

All this energetic cheer was, Jennie knew, partly for her benefit, to create an optimistic atmosphere, but also it was because Jill was feeling comfortable with her. And Jennie, listening not so much to words as to tone and mood, said to herself again, How young she is! How innocent and wise, how trusting and wary, how very dear! No real wounds yet except for the one I gave, and I think that's healing. I'm healing it for her now—thanks to Peter, who made me do it. Maybe she'll get through her years with no wound more terrible than this. I hope so. Some people do.

When they parted, they kissed each other.

"I wish for you," Jill murmured, "whatever you wish for yourself."

What I wish for myself, Jennie thought as she walked away. At this point and after everything that's happened, I just don't know. I'm only drifting.

"In bed already?" Peter asked when she answered the phone.

"Yes, I want to get up very early and get down to the office."

"Are you sure you're ready to go back into the rat race?"

"As ready as I'll ever be."

"You haven't heard anything? Do you mind my asking?"

She dodged purposely. "Heard what?"

"You know. From . . . him."

"It's over, Peter," she said somewhat sharply. "I've already told you that."

"God, what a shame! I don't understand people."

"Peter, I don't want to talk about it."

"Okay, okay. I just want you to know you have me."

She didn't answer.

"You're not alone in the world."

The phone clicked.

"Jennie? Are you there?"

"I'm here."

The phone clicked again.

"That noise. I thought you'd hung up on me."

"You know I wouldn't do that."

"I was thinking. You know I mentioned something about next summer. Do you think you'd like that? Just a week or so out on the Indian reservation, you and Jill and I?"

In spite of herself, she was touched. And she answered softly, "Peter, I can't think that far ahead."

"All right. Another time, then. I really called just to find out how it went today."

"Oh, it was good! We saw some wonderful things. She wanted to see some eighteenth-century portraits for her art history class, and then we went to the Egyptian wing. She's very well read, very bright."

"She's a treasure, Jennie. We produced a treasure, you and I. Sometimes when I think of her I have to chuckle, she's so much like you."

"Like me? Why, she's a carbon copy of you."

"She looks like me, but I mean her attitudes, that high indignation over injustice. And a temper. What a temper!"

"You think I have a temper?"

"Can you ask? You've got a fierce one! And stubborn! Once you've made your mind up—when you made it up to get rid of me before Jill was born." He fell silent and then said sadly, "I've worn a hair shirt ever since. Believe me, Jennie."

"Don't, don't," she whispered. "This is no time to talk about it."

"I suppose it isn't. Well, take it easy, will you? Don't overwork yourself tomorrow."

When she hung up, she thrust aside the document she

had been reviewing. From somewhere in the old building came the sound of music, someone's record player turned on too loud. But it was pleasing, a piano concerto, melodious and nostalgic. Wine and roses, she thought, and put her head back, closing her eyes. The bed was soft and the quilt so beautifully warm, making sleep seem possible this time . . .

Peter, in a white summer suit, danced under paper lanterns. She was troubled because she knew so little about him. They really had spoken only of Jill. Now Jay came, his dark, mournful face framed in a doorway. Then someone who was neither Jay nor Peter, but both of them, was standing over her in a painful light. And she was terribly sad because she didn't know who it was.

Waking, she saw that the lamp was glaring into her eyes. Now, switching it off, she was wide-awake again. For a long time she would have to lie staring into darkness.

CHAPTER

13

The peach-colored silk blouse rustled, her mother's gold bracelets clicked on her wrist, and her feet slid into the black lizard pumps that she had been saving for "afterward." Since there was to be no afterward, she might as well wear them now, might as well put her best foot forward. But she was jelly inside.

On her way to the bus she analyzed herself. You're dreading the return to the old life, the one you liked because it was so stimulating, so full of color while you were living it. But now you dread going back, because now you know it was empty jingle and jangle, for all the important talk, the plays and galleries and bright young men. The bus lurched. With every stop and start, it carried her farther downtown and farther back in time. She stared straight ahead. Desolation chilled her and she hugged her coat closer.

A woman got on and sat beside her. Moving to make room on the seat, Jennie was repelled. The woman had a hostile face; hard and jutting, it looked as if it had been cut out with a can opener. Jennie moved nearer to the window and pulled her coat tighter.

Suddenly the woman spoke. "Excuse me, but I do admire your shoes. I wish I could wear shoes like those, but I have such trouble with my feet." She smiled and the eyes that had seemed so harsh shone mildly.

"Thank you," Jennie said, adding, since it seemed only right to say something friendly, "They're very comfortable." And as intensely as the quick aversion had come, Jennie felt a rush of gratitude toward the stranger. To think that one could be comforted, that one could find human warmth in a trivial remark about a pair of shoes! And she arrived at her office oddly quieted.

"The flu really knocked you out, didn't it?" Dinah observed. "You've lost weight."

"A little, I guess. I didn't expect you in on Saturday."

"I'll stay half a day. I've postponed all but the most important appointments so you can get your strength back." She followed Jennie to the inner office. "Look at these. They came a few minutes ago."

On Jennie's desk in a tall, thin vase stood a spray of ruby-red roses, their heavy perfume sweetening the stale air. For a second she thought they might be from Jay. Stupid! She touched a lush, curved petal. There was no need to read the card, but she read it anyway, surprised that she could still remember the unusual script, partly cursive and partly printed.

"Good luck on your first day back. Love, Peter," it said. And then, squeezed below, came an afterthought. "And Jill."

Peter and his flowers! She fingered them thoughtfully.

"A dozen. I counted. Aren't they gorgeous?" Dinah was impressed and curious. And as Jennie didn't answer at once, she added, "There's a pile of mail. I've sorted it and put the important stuff on your desk. There was a special-delivery certified letter that I opened. I thought you'd want me to."

"Of course. What is it?"

"From those people up in the country. The land case."

It was a short, typewritten note on Arthur Wolfe's letterhead, written in his capacity as the new head of the Preservation Committee. She was informed that "other arrangements" had been made for legal counsel and was requested to send the bill for her services. And that was all.

She stood still, holding in her hand what was in essence a repudiation of her total self. A flush of shame prickled down her back, as if her body were burning. She had been stripped. How could they have done this to her? All her work, so dearly wrought, had gone for nothing. And yet, given the circumstances, how could they have done otherwise? And, anyway, would she want to continue working with Arthur Wolfe? No, it would be impossible, and Arthur Wolfe had seen that it was.

Yet her heart broke.

"Write an answer, Dinah," she directed. "Say I acknowledge receipt of the letter and that I am not sending a bill for services. What I did, I did because I believed in it, and I never expected to be paid in the first place. Say that. And do it now, please, Dinah. I want it to go in the mail this afternoon."

She kept standing there holding Arthur's letter. Then suddenly something occurred to her that should have occurred before. She had every right not to be excluded from knowledge of events that she herself had set in motion! She had every right to know at least what was happening to Martha Cromwell. What if that man or those men had gone to the house looking for George's tape? It would only be logical to try there, where the sick old woman was now alone, wouldn't it? Cold fear shocked Jennie's veins at the picture: the frame house hidden behind gloomy hemlocks at the end of the street, its front door darkened by overgrown vines on the porch. A man could slip in and slip out again, unseen and unheard. . . . She had to know.

Without another thought she picked up the telephone and dialed.

"This is Jennie Rakowsky. I'm a friend of Martha's, and I'm calling to ask about her," she said.

A young woman's voice sounded against a background of buzzing talk. "Oh, I know who you are! You're the lawyer who spoke so beautifully at the meeting that time."

The words brought a little glow to Jennie, a glow that she needed just then, and she thanked the woman.

"How is Martha? I hear so many voices, and I'm glad she's not alone in the house. I was afraid she might be."

"Alone? Goodness, no. The neighbors are taking turns to be with her. There are never fewer than two of us with her, day or night. Right now the place is jam-packed, and we intend to stay."

"Oh, that's wonderful! I was so worried."

"You can speak to her yourself. She's in bed, of course, poor soul, but there's a phone upstairs."

"I'm doing fine," Martha told Jennie weakly. "I'm holding up better than I ever thought I could."

"You're like George. You've got guts. Tell me, Martha, has anybody been looking for the tape? Have you got it safely hidden till the case comes up?"

Martha sighed, began to speak, then sighed again. "Jennie, I don't know how to begin to tell you. This business has been a fiasco from the start."

"What do you mean?"

"Well, on the day of the funeral my niece came to tidy up the bedroom. George had put the tape, disguised in a paper grocery bag, under the bed. I didn't think about it —naturally I wasn't thinking very well that day—and she threw the bag out in the trash. It's incinerated, Jennie. Gone."

Jennie felt a surge of crazy laughter. A grocery bag under the bed! How typical of George!

"I'm so sorry, Jennie. The chief weapon's gone now, isn't it?"

"I'm afraid so. Well, the Preservation Committee is back where it started, that's all."

"I hear you're not the lawyer anymore. What happened?"

"It's a long story. Too long."

"Without you they're going to lose."

"Oh, you give me too much credit. I have no influence on the board. They'll vote the way they want to vote."

"No, there's a couple of swing votes that can go either way, easily as not. And you're a spellbinder, Jennie."

"Well, thank you for the kind words, but I'm out of it now. Take care, Martha. I'll keep in touch."

Out of my hands, she thought. So Barker Development will win, the land will be destroyed, and Martha and I and the rest of us will be safe. A mixed bag, after all the effort, the fuss and fury. Talk about irony!

Her work had piled up to the sky in less than a week. Papers and appointments filled the morning. As always, almost every woman who came in either brought a child along, had left one with a neighbor, or was ripely pregnant with one. So many of these women had no dependable, permanent man, having either been deserted by one or having never had one. Hard lives, these were, and still Jennie could not help but think, with some bitterness, that they had a certain freedom, too; there was no secrecy about the way they lived, and no explanations were needed.

All morning they came and went. She had lunch at her

desk, a bad sandwich, mostly mayonnaise, and a soft drink, there being no time to go out for anything better. The telephone rang. The mail came and another pile accumulated. By one o'clock when Dinah left, Jennie was working away.

"You must be awfully tired," Dinah said with concern. "Why don't you go home?"

"I'm fine. I'll just stay on another hour or so."

She wanted to be tired. It would be such comfort to go home exhausted, there to eat some simple cheese and fruit, go to sleep and not think about Arthur Wolfe—or anybody.

Someone was knocking at the outer door. Her first impulse was to ignore it and let whoever it was go away. The knocking became insistent. It occurred to her that it might be the terrorized girl who had come in a few days ago with blue-green bruises all over her neck and arms. Her lover may have come back in another temper. She got up and opened the door.

A well-dressed man of early middle age, wearing a gray overcoat, stood before her.

"My name's Robinson. I know it's late, but I saw the light. May I come in?"

He was already in, following Jennie into her room, where the debris of the busy day, papers finished and papers not finished, littered every surface.

He laid his attaché case—pin seal and brass buckles—on the floor beside a chair, removed a small sheaf of Jennie's papers from the chair, and handed them to her.

"Mind if I sit down?"

She took her papers from his hand, thinking, He's cool, mighty cool. Who is he?

"You've got a nice place here," he said, looking around at the mess. "And the flowers. I raise roses myself. It's a hobby of mine."

"What can I do for you?" Jennie asked, wary now.

"Somebody's got to think a whole lot of you to send those. They cost, those long stems. They cost a bundle."

Who was he? The hairs on Jennie's forearms rose. An animal besieged in its den recognizes danger. But where is safety? Where can one hide?

"I asked you," she said, keeping a level tone, "what I can do for you. What is your business?"

"Well, this and that." When he smiled, his gums, which were knobby, white, and slick, were revealed above extraordinary, oversize, yellowed teeth.

"Big teeth," George had said. "The biggest teeth you ever saw."

But the name hadn't been Robinson, she was sure, although at the onset of panic, alone here with everyone gone home from next door and silence in the outer hall, she couldn't think of the name. It made no difference, anyway. She tried to steady her thoughts.

"Yes, this and that," the man said. Manicured fingers played with the hand-tailored cuff on the other arm.

" 'This and that' tells me nothing. Do you have a legal problem? I'm a lawyer."

"Well, I know that, don't I? And also that you've had experience with adoption law. I know that too."

Startled, Jennie looked into a pair of narrow black eyes, the eyes of a rodent watching from a hidden corner.

"Adoption?" she said. "Not particularly."

"No? I heard you had."

"Not at all."

"Oh, come, I know better. You're surprised." He smiled again, and the teeth glistened. "People hear things. Crossed wires. There are ways."

The click on the phone, the man on the steps and under the streetlight. The day she forgot to lock the door . . .

It all came clear. They had stopped at nothing in their

search for that tape. They couldn't go to George's house because of the crowd; moreover, hadn't George led them to believe that "someone else" had it? Logically that someone would be Arthur Wolfe or Jay or herself. All this flashed through her mind in a few seconds under the scrutiny of those cold, basilisk eyes.

A short pain shot through her chest. One could have a heart attack; even as young as she was, it was possible. Still, she kept silence.

"Yes, yes. There are certain people, a certain person, who would be interested to know what it is that you know about adoptions. Even one that happened a long time ago."

How strange, Jennie was thinking. The twisted strands come together. Peter and Jill and the Green Marsh meet and twist together at Jay's feet. Or they would, if Jay's feet were still standing where they stood before.

"You'd just as soon he wouldn't know, I'm sure. No more good life, no more riding around the country in his cute two-seater Mercedes."

This was the man, then. The car belonged to the Wolfes and was kept in the country. She'd been out in it with Jay.

"What do you want?" she asked, forcing herself to speak.

"You know what I want."

"If I knew, I wouldn't ask," she retorted, astonished that she was not only able to talk but also to show a bit of defiance.

"Look, we've each got something on the other. So if you're smart, you won't play games with me. I want the tape." And when she didn't answer at once, he leaned forward in the chair as if he were about to leap out of it. "And don't say 'What tape'? This isn't the time to play dumb." At the same time his voice was low and controlled.

Her palms were wet with the sweat of terror. "I haven't got any tape." The black eyes looked at her now without expression. And she said, "That's the truth. I never had any."

He swiveled around in the chair and looked toward the window. Across the street the office building had gone mostly dark, except that here and there lights were being turned back on as the cleaning crews began their rounds. She tried to remember what time they started work here on this floor but couldn't remember, couldn't think of anything except fear. She should have had more sense than to stay alone in a deserted building.

"Too bad about the old man, wasn't it?" he said, still with his back to her.

"What old man?" she said, parrying.

He whipped about, leapt from the chair, and stood over her so that she drew back, instinctively protecting her face from a blow.

"Jennie, Jennie, you're wasting my time." He was smiling at his effect upon her. "I'd just as soon not knock your teeth out. Now, you're a smart gal, a lawyer, so you don't need me to draw pictures for you. Here it is, final offer: Hand over the tapes and I keep my mouth shut about the kid and the other guy. What could be sweeter?"

"As to the kid," Jennie said, "you can tell the world, for all it matters. And as to the tapes, I tell you I know nothing about them. I haven't anything to do with the entire affair anymore."

"What the hell do you mean by that?"

"What I said. I'm not the lawyer. I've been fired."

"I don't believe you."

"If you'll let me get up from this chair, I'll find the letter."

She was beginning to think again. The animal in its lair fights for its life.

"I'm not stopping you," he said, and showed his feral grin.

"You're standing too close to me. I want to protect my teeth."

He laughed slightly and stepped back. "You've got nerve. I like that in a woman."

With shaking hands she rummaged through the stacks of papers on the desk while he stood waiting, so close to her that she could hear his breathing. In a desperate hurry she whipped around and overturned the stacks.

"I guess you haven't got it. I guess you've been feeding me a lot of bull."

"You guess wrong. It's here. It has to be." Unless I threw it out. Did I? If I did, God help me.

"I thought he was going to smash my teeth in," George had said. But he had done worse than that.

"I don't know. Give me a minute."

"I'm not going to stand here all night, you know."

She could hear the silence in the stone corridor beyond the door. Silence roars, one says. Like the sound of waves when you hold a shell to your ear. Like the rush of blood to the head.

She bent down. The wastebasket hadn't been emptied yet. That's where it would be. Oh, it had to be!

He grabbed her arm, the strong fingers pinching painfully. "Hey! What do you think you're doing?"

She tipped the overflowing basket onto the floor, knelt down, and feverishly separated scraps, crumpled advertisements, torn envelopes, the morning paper. Please, please, let me find it. . . .

"Here it is!" The letter had been partially ripped across the top but was clearly legible. She held it up to him.

"You see, I told you. I've been fired."

He studied the letter first, then studied Jennie, who

had risen and sat down again because her knees were buckling.

"So," he said, "so you don't really give a damn what happens now, do you?"

She thought, He will go to the Wolfes next. But there is nothing I can do about that, and nothing that they can't cope with better than I can.

"No," she said, "that's right. I don't give a damn."

"And you don't give a damn, either, whether he finds out about your kid."

He was standing so close now that his knees brushed hers. "So you're playing the field again."

"I don't know what you're talking about."

"Sure you do. The kid's father." He seemed amused. "Old home week, hey?"

Her teeth began to chatter. She'd read about chattering teeth but had never experienced them. It was strange, the way they rattled and wouldn't be still.

He reached out and touched her breast. "You're a good-looking woman."

Her hands flew to her breasts. He pulled them away.

She looked up at him, trying sternness and reason. "Why do you want to do this? It's not worth the trouble you'll have."

"I'll give you six guesses why. You thought you'd out-smart me, didn't you? Putting a wire on the old fool." He had a tight hold on her hands. "I wonder how you'd look with a broken nose. Or maybe a few cuts on your pretty face?"

"I'll scream—"

"Go on, scream. Who'll hear you?"

His fist, on which there gleamed a gold ring, solid and domed like a rock, flashed toward her face. Quickly she dodged and fell, striking her head on the edge of the desk. Pain shot through her stomach; vomit rose in her throat. He bent down, seized the front of her shirt, and raised her. The tearing silk screeched. His huge, slick teeth loomed, his face was distorted with fury, his tobacco breath was hot, the fist came up again. . . .

Then from the far end of the corridor sounded the noisy clash of the elevator door and a babble of voices, a clatter of heavy shoes and clinking pails. "The cleaning crew! They're coming in!" she cried out, sobbing.

In an instant he was up on his feet. "Shit!" Grabbing his attaché case and overcoat, he was out the door before Jennie was up off the floor.

Faint and swaying, she held on to the back of a chair. She was still standing there, pulling the ripped blouse together, when the door opened and a boy came in, trundling the paraphernalia of pails, mops, rags, and brooms. He stopped and stared at her.

"That man!" she gasped. "Look in the hall! Has he gone?"

The boy shook his head. "No English."

She wanted to thank him over and over, to get down on her knees before him. He would have thought she was crazy. Perhaps he thought so, anyway.

Trembling, hoping her knees would hold her up, she put on her jacket; gathered her coat, bag, and gloves; and then, afraid to go downstairs, sat down again. What if he was waiting for her on the sidewalk? But no, she must try to think logically; of course he wouldn't be out on the street where she could cry for help. But would he try again at home?

The telephone was at her hand, but she was shaking so badly that she couldn't hold it. She said aloud again: "I have to think. Call the police? To look somewhere for a man in a dark overcoat among the thousands of men in dark overcoats on the streets of New York? Absurd! Call Martin upstate?" Her face ached, she was weak, she needed someone to tell her what to do. How alone she was without Jay! Then sudden terror struck her. What if that—that *creature* were to go to Jay's house? The stupid, snobbish nanny would admit him simply because he wore an expensive coat and looked like a gentleman, wouldn't she? She and the children might be there alone. Or even if Jay were there by himself and the creature had a knife—

Now Jennie's quivering hands behaved as she dialed the number. This was only a call of warning, for nothing else, for no plea or intrusion where she was no longer wanted. A call of warning. She would make that clear.

There was no answer at the apartment. When she tried the office, the answering service reported that the office was closed until Monday morning. Did she wish to leave a message? No. One could hardly leave a warning to watch out for a man with protruding yellow teeth.

She called Martin next, tracked him down at his home, and cried out her story. "I'm sure it was George's man," she concluded. "George was right, the teeth are the giveaway."

"If he's not the killer, he obviously knows who the killer is."

"Well, he practically said as much. I wonder whether Fisher did the actual job on George."

"I don't know. We're watching him very closely. And there are other developments out of town, which I can't talk about on the phone. Incidentally, be careful on your phone until we get rid of the bug. I'll see that it's taken care of on Monday." There was a pause. "I understand you're not on the case anymore."

"That's true. I was dismissed." A kind of defensive pride rose in her. "Not for any professional reason. It was entirely personal."

"I had an idea it must have been. And I'm sorry. You're a credit to the profession."

She felt a renewed surge of tears at the praise and thanked him.

"Well, good thing you weren't hurt. That's the most important thing. But you've had a close call, and my advice is to go home, have a shot of Scotch, and rest."

When the telephone contact was broken off, fear flowed back into the room. I need someone, anyone, she thought. Not friends, who knew nothing of all these troubles. Not Jill. One didn't lean on a young girl, nor did one scare her to death.

But there was Peter . . . And she telephoned the Waldorf-Astoria.

He sounded surprised and pleased. "You just caught me. I was on my way to dinner with some people who flew in today from Chicago."

"Oh." These words, finally, defeated her. "Oh," she said, sighing.

"What's the matter? Are you crying?"

"No. Yes." And again she sobbed out her story.

"My God! Did you call the police?"

"No. He didn't actually *do* anything to me. What can I prove?"

"That's ridiculous. What are police for? Call right now."

"You don't understand! I deal every day with these things! They must get a thousand calls a minute in this city. You don't know. They're not going to bother about something that almost happened but didn't. And the man's . . . vanished, anyway." She faltered. "Besides, I'm exhausted."

"I'm coming right over," he said promptly. "Lock the office door until I come up. I'll keep the cab waiting and take you home."

"You have a dinner appointment."

"The hell with it! Wait there for me."

"My phone was bugged. Can you imagine? He knew about Jill." She had taken off not only the torn blouse but also the jacket and skirt, everything she had been wearing, as if they were defiled; she would never wear them again. Now she sat enclosed by the wings of the chair, huddled and trembling, cold even in her thick quilted housecoat.

"My God, if I hadn't found that letter! He was in such a rage, a queer, quiet rage. He never raised his voice. It was eerie. Thank heaven I found it, and thank heaven he believed it." She hadn't stopped talking since Peter had brought her home. Her words poured out in a high, nervous voice. "I can't get it through my head. The land is so innocent, Peter, it's lain there forever just growing trees, so quiet, with little wild things and geese coming in from Canada. So innocent!" she cried. "And then come the two-legged beasts to fight over it, tearing one another to shreds or killing for it. Yes, beasts! I've seen plenty, you know. In my work one doesn't exactly deal with sweetness and light, but still, until you go through it yourself, you can't believe what people will do for money. The violence you read about is nothing until you become a victim, an object. . . . Oh, I can still smell him; can you understand that, Peter? He had a cologne or shaving cream I would recognize again; it had a sweetish smell—like cinnamon, almost. If those cleaners hadn't come—oh, God, do you think . . . do you think maybe he would have killed me afterward? Or maybe just slashed my face? He said something about cutting it. There was a case like that, remember? Oh, I can't believe this happened to me! It's something you only read about in the newspaper."

With her hands around her knees she rocked, making herself small in the chair. A gust of wind-driven rain rattled the windows and startled them so that they both looked around.

"It's nothing," Peter said. "Only a miserable winter night, and we're facing north." He looked large and calm. "No one can get in, Jennie. The door's locked. I slid the bolt."

She had to smile. "Thank you for reading my thoughts." With him there she felt safe. It was the second time. "You're being very good to me," she said.

His brows were ruefully drawn together. "I never thought I'd live to hear you say I was good to you."

"I didn't mean *then*. I'm talking about *now*. These last few days and this minute. You're helping me get through this minute."

"I'm staying all night. I'm not going to leave you."

She raised her eyes to meet a painful, troubled frown. He seemed about to speak, then closed his lips, looked away, and finally did speak.

"I haven't told you enough about the guilt I've felt."

"Yes, you have, Peter. Don't beat your breast anymore. It's not necessary."

But he persisted, "I should have gone after you when she was born whether you wanted me to or not."

When she raised her hand in protest, he resisted. "Don't stop me. Yes, I should have. I want you to know that. And I did think about the child. But you made it so clear that you wanted nothing more to do with me—"

She interjected, wanting to hear no more, "It's true. I did. So what use is it now to—"

"Only to unburden myself. That's the use. Maybe this is selfish of me, I don't know, but it's been bottled up, stored away in an effort to forget it or to deny it, and I want—I need, Jennie—I need to say it all."

Things stored away, to forget or to deny. And she said, very low, "I suppose, after all, that I hurt you too."

He turned his hand out, palm up, in a gesture of rueful dismissal. "A scratch compared with a sledgehammer blow. It's not enough of an excuse, the one I've made to myself, that I was very young. Not enough."

The lamplight fell on his bent head and clasped hands,

emphasizing sadness and penitence. There was something familiar to her in the posture. It took a few minutes
for her to recall when she had seen him like that before.
Among all the fleeting, faded images, now one returned
with sudden, shocking clarity: On the last night before
she had taken the plane to Nebraska, he had been sitting
just like that at the end of the bed in the dingy motel,
watching television.

"Jennie? It doesn't seem like nineteen years, does it? I
mean, I don't feel the strangeness that I imagined I
would feel. Do you?"

She turned away from the searching question, answering, "I guess not."

"We did well together while it lasted, didn't we?"
There was something hopeful in his voice, wanting confirmation.

"That's true."

She felt a wave of sadness at this reminder of loss. Was
that what life was, a series of adjustments to loss? The
optimist in Jennie refuted that; there had to be more to
life. There *was* more. Nevertheless the sadness settled.

"Do you want a sleeping pill?" Peter asked.

"I never take them." The words sounded brave.

"I thought maybe after today you'd need a little help."

"No. But I think I want to go to bed now. Are you sure
you want to stay here?"

"Sure."

The decision satisfied her. On the surface she could
maintain bravery, but still, it was good not to be alone. It
wasn't natural to sleep alone; even a dog liked to be near
somebody, to feel a presence at night.

"I'll get some blankets. I'm sorry there's only the sofa."

"It's fine." When he curled on his side to demonstrate,
his knees were brought up almost to his chest.

"Shorty," she said, looking down at him, and giggled.
"Pop asked me why you were called Shorty, and I told

him because you were six feet three. You'll be miserable on that thing. You'd better go back to the hotel."

"I'm not going back. Not after what you went through a couple of hours ago."

She considered something. Her bed, which she had brought from her parents' spare bedroom in Baltimore, was king-size. Three strangers could sleep in it without even touching one another. And she made a hesitant offer.

"You can have the far end of my bed if you want. It does seem ridiculous for you to be cramped on the sofa. You won't be able to sleep."

"If you really mean it, I'll accept the offer." He sat up and grimaced. "This is really pretty painful."

"Then it's settled. I'll turn out the light and you can just crawl in whenever you're ready."

"No problem."

For a long time she stayed awake, fighting the memory of that creature's contempt and violent hands, trying to wipe out the hideous memory of what had been, what had almost been, and what would have happened next if . . . if . . .

The night sky above the city poured its glow through the blinds, so that she could just see the outline of Peter's motionless back as he lay on his side. Wryly she thought, I was accused of being in bed with him when I hadn't been, and now I really am in bed with him. The very last time was at the motel all those years ago. We lay apart then, too, but for a different reason. He was afraid to touch me, scared because I was pregnant, I suppose, or perhaps even repelled by what was in my belly. The bitterness of that night!

But once we used to consume each other, counted the hours of longing from weekend to weekend. From one Friday night to the next was one hundred sixty-eight hours. When, during the week, we met in passing, our

eyes used to speak what they remembered and anticipated.

How lovely their beginning had been! Fresh as spring
all that year through, and warm with its light. There had
been so much wild, young laughter between them. And
she wondered now whether, if their marriage had not
been blocked by other people, they would have lasted
together, after all; lasted with all that tenderness and
laughter.

There would have been no Jay, then. Queer thought.
She would never have known his tenderness, his subtle
wisdom, or his special grace. Neither would she have
known nor lost him. Queer.

The sheets rustled now as Peter turned.

"Stretch out your arm."

Across the wide bed their fingers barely managed to
touch.

"I only wanted to say good night. Have easy dreams,
Jennie. Try not to think about today, if you can."

The voice and the brief touch were consolation. The
sound of his breathing soothed. You're safe, she argued
with herself. You're not alone. Traffic on the avenue was
a distant rushing, like surf. She felt herself drift. . . .

And she dreamed. She dreamed she was enfolded,
that arms enclosed her, loving, tender arms; at the same
time she was saying, "Yes, you are having this healthy
dream so you won't think of how sex can be a terrifying
weapon. So go on, dream, don't wake up, don't stop, it's
delicious, it's wonderful."

She was half awake. Someone was kissing her, and she
had been responding.

"Darling," Jay said.

And "Yes, yes, don't stop me," she heard, and started,
fully awake now.

"Peter, for God's sake, what are you doing?" she cried,
appalled, and sat up to slide out of the bed.

"I've been holding you for the last ten minutes. You wanted me to," he said simply.

"I was dreaming! You don't understand," she said, hiding her face in her hands.

"I know. And I was too. I dreamed that you wanted to be loved."

Her lips quivered. "This was a stupid idea. It's I who should have thought of sleeping on the sofa. It's long enough for me."

She turned on the bedside lamp. Peter's eyes, the prominent opals with the lavender tint, were frightened and ashamed.

"Dream or not, you did want to be loved, though."

"Yes," she said miserably.

"But not by me."

She couldn't answer, and he said, persisting, "By him, still?"

"You ask too many questions. I can't answer. I don't know."

Yet she did know. In her dream it was with Jay that she had lain, it was his face she had seen and his name she had spoken. And she knew, abruptly and sharply, that she was not ready for anyone else. Would she ever be?

The light fanned out over the carpet, over the rumpled blanket, over Peter's crestfallen, heated face.

"Only one more question," he urged. "Are you furious with me?"

She was painfully confused. He'd had no right to think that she would. . . . And yet, asleep or half asleep, she had lain in his arms, in the warm, tight cave. And she understood that he felt his manhood had been rejected, and she was sorry.

"You're still one of the most attractive men I've ever known," she said gently.

"Thank you, but you don't have to say that. You're saying it because you think you've hurt me."

"That doesn't make it any less true. You still are one of the most attractive men." She clutched her throat and her mouth twisted. A sudden, tearful awareness of the absurdity of the situation, the scene, the picture they made, had overwhelmed her.

Peter said at once, "I'm going to the sofa. You get back to bed."

"I'm wide-awake. I can't go back to sleep."

She followed him into the other room. It had grown colder because the heat was lowered at night. The wind was still rattling the windows. Now he, wrapped in a blanket, and she in the quilted robe, sat down to face each other again. After a minute Peter broke the bleak silence with another question.

"It was he who got you into the land case, wasn't it?"

"He?"

"Tom, if you like. It's as good a name as any."

"That's why you were relieved of your job."

"Yes. Why bring that up?"

"Just wondering. Anyway, it's as well you're out of it. The party's gotten rough and dangerous."

"But I wanted to win that case. My heart was in it."

"There'll be other cases. Other people too," Peter added after a pause.

"I don't know."

"But you've had others all these years."

"Other cases or other people?"

"Other people, I meant. Men."

"Yes, but this time it was different."

"Don't people always think that?"

She smiled slightly. "But sometimes when they think so, it really is. One person dies or—or goes away, and the other one is changed forever."

Peter gave her a serious look, which she returned; their eyes touched. And he said slowly, "Yes, I believe

you're one woman who can be like that if anybody can."
And he sighed.

She sensed things waiting to be spoken. Perhaps he
had really hoped that he and she might come full circle;
hadn't Jill said it would be so "tidy"? That she had a
"feeling"?

And at that moment he said, "I might as well tell you
I've been having some unexpected thoughts these past
few days. I should have known they were unrealistic.
May I tell you what they were?"

"Of course."

"Well, then. Naturally I didn't expect an immediate
miracle, but I did think that maybe there was some sort
of fate, something that would in time, plenty of time,
bring us together again. I'm not superstitious, you must
know that, but I really did think I saw some sort of
pattern in the way things have turned out with Jill, and
the way you and I have come together without anger.
But you don't want it." His sigh was wistful.

"Peter . . . I'm sort of dead inside, don't you see?"

"No, you're not. You're alive and in very much pain.
And you don't deserve it."

She didn't answer. For a moment he waited, then
asked quite softly, almost in a whisper, "Won't you talk
about him?"

"No. I've had my message. What's finished is finished."

"It just struck me . . . how odd that both times in
your life it was Jill who caused the breakup! First with
me and now with him."

"In very different ways, Peter."

"True. But you ought to be married," he said abruptly.
"It's time."

She smiled at his vehemence. "You think so? What
about yourself?"

"I have been married. Three times." He turned away,

as if he was making an effort to conquer embarrassment. "That startles you, doesn't it?"

"A little."

"It doesn't make for an impressive résumé. Not anything to be proud of or easy to talk about."

"Don't talk about it, then," she said, pitying him for his confession.

"I never do. But for some reason I want you to know." He drew a deep breath. "The first one was my sister's friend, the one who was visiting that weekend."

The brat who sat on the bed while I tried on that ridiculous dress, she remembered.

"We married the day after my college commencement. She was seventeen and a half. We never had anything to talk about. I bored her when I went on to graduate school."

"Why on earth did you marry her?"

"She grew up to be a beauty. And the families . . . I don't know. We were always thrown together."

"I see." The hovering families—nudges, winks, hints, little suppers, and picnics artfully arranged. "I see."

"We lasted not quite two years."

"No children?"

"Good God, no. The next was a studious girl from Alabama, a country girl with a scholarship at Emory. She and my mother didn't get along. She hated my family and didn't try to hide it. And my mother wasn't exactly pleased with her, I admit."

I can imagine, Jennie thought. A chill came over her, as though again she were sitting in that vast room under the regal portraits on the wall.

"So it made things tough all around."

She could imagine that too: Peter caught between wife and mother, when all he wanted, generous boy that he had been, was peace.

"It couldn't last. I still have a strong sense of loyalty to

my family, you know, even when I don't always agree
with them."

Jennie knew. Why take a stand about Vietnam? Go
along and pretend to agree. It's orderly, it's pleasant that
way.

"She wouldn't live in Atlanta after her graduation, and
I wanted to. So that ended it. The funny thing is, I left for
Chicago a few months afterward, anyway. Well, that was
number two." Peter stopped. "Are you shocked? Disgusted?"

"Neither."

She was moved by this tale of defeat, as well as by his
candor. He still had his frank naïveté. In contrast and in a
flickering instant, it brought to her mind Jay's reflective
manner and, no matter how intent his feelings, his habit
of prudence.

"What happened with number three?"

As a sudden wind shuts with one blow a door that had
been wide open, Peter's face closed. She had to wait a
few moments for his answer.

"Alice," he said. "She died." And then, as if the door
had blown open again, he almost cried out. "She was
wonderful, Jennie, really wonderful. She had a little boy.
We had fun together, the three of us. Her parents took
him after—after she was gone. I miss him, miss her—
Well, you get over things, don't you? Or try to, anyway."

She could say only, "I'm so sorry, Peter."

He gave her a quizzical look, a strange look, sad, hurt,
yet with the faintest touch of humor.

"I'll tell you something. She was very much like you.
Full of ideals and energy. She even looked a little bit like
you."

Again Jennie found few words, just, "Thank you, Peter."

She was immensely moved by his tribute and saddened by his story. Would not Alice probably have been

the one who lasted? On the other hand, after two fail-
ures, and if he was still his mother's boy, she might not
have been. They were so complicated, the ways in which
people connected with one another; one needed more
knowledge than Jennie possessed to puzzle it all out. She
knew only two things surely now: that Peter was a good
man and that he was not for her, in spite of what Jill or he
himself might think.

"You look sorrowful," he said anxiously. "I shouldn't
have dumped my troubles on you."

"Please!" she protested. "After all that's been dumped
on you this week? I'm thinking, I'm hoping that something very good will happen to you."

"Oh, plenty of good things already have! You mustn't
think I'm mourning over my life. I like where I live, I've
had plenty of friends, and I'm doing the work I always
wanted to do. Besides, although I guess it sounds too
boastful, I have to admit that I've made a rather big
name for myself."

"I know. Jill told me you're pretty famous. Her father's an amateur archaeologist, and he's been looking
you up ever since she told him about you."

"They sound like very decent people."

"They are. You have only to look at Jill to know that
they must be."

Peter laughed. "Don't you and I get any credit for
her? Let's not be so modest."

"Yes, yes, of course we do."

Jennie was suddenly exhausted. This incredible day,
which had begun with bitter disappointment, continued
with shocking violence, and ended with a confusion of
dreams had overwhelmed her.

She stood up. "It's late. This time you'll take the bed
and I'll sleep here. The sofa fits me."

"Afraid to try me again, are you? Don't trust me?"

"It's not that. I just think it's better this way." She kissed his cheek. "Good night."

In the morning she woke up late to find him gone and the big bed made. He had left a note: "Be careful at the office from now on. Check the door at home too. I'll call you before I go back to Chicago."

After a while, bestirring herself, she went ahead with the morning's routine, cleaned the kitchen, and washed her hair. Then came files to study, a whole day's worth of them.

Toward noon Shirley called through the door.

"Hey! You in there?"

In her new coat, with flamboyant, multistriped hoops in her ears, Shirley was dressed for a day of leisure, Jennie saw. She also caught Shirley's quick investigative glance around the apartment.

"You feeling up to lunch and an afternoon movie? I'm meeting some of the girls."

"Thanks, but I can't. I've that whole pile of work to make up."

Shirley, perched on the edge of a chair, complained, "You've been behaving so mysteriously. Frankly I've been worried about you."

"I haven't meant to be mysterious." Jennie, shuffling papers, wished Shirley would just go away.

"Good Lord, what happened to your face?"

The bruise on her cheek was turning livid.

"I had to get up last night, and I bumped into the bathroom door."

The other raised skeptical eyebrows, then waited a few moments, as if deciding whether or not to plunge.

"Jennie—what's happened between you and Jay? I suppose I'm prying, but after all, we've known each other for more than a few years, and I can't help but care. I *am* prying. I see I am."

For into Jennie's eyes, in spite of the determination

that had been restraining her, the tears had sprung. She bent her head over the papers without answering.

"Oh," Shirley said. "Oh, I'm sorry. I didn't mean—"

"Just don't be kind. And don't feel sorry for me. It makes it worse."

At once Shirley stood up. "I know. I won't. But please just remember that whenever you want to talk about it, if you ever do, I'm here."

"I'll tell you sometime. But I have to learn to live with it first."

For long minutes after the door closed, Jennie sat with her head down on the desk. How do you cope with such pain? You clamp down on it, that's what you do. So with clenched teeth and clenched fists, she conquered it, at least for the moment, and returned to her papers. Steadily, one by one, she dealt with them, compiling notes; breaking off briefly to make a supper of toast and eggs, she went back to them and was still at work when, shortly after nine o'clock, the telephone rang.

"How are you?" Jill asked.

The faintest thrill of pleasure passed through Jennie. "Fine. And you? What are you doing phoning me on a Sunday night? You're supposed to be out having fun."

"My boyfriend's father was taken to the hospital this afternoon. So I'm here in the dorm." Jill lowered her voice. "Peter called and told me what happened to you yesterday. So savage, so horrible! They ought to kill men like that."

"Unfortunately it's not the way the law works. But I wasn't hurt. I was lucky."

"Do you feel well enough to talk about something?"

"Oh, sure. What is it?"

"Well, I got tomorrow's paper ahead of time, and there's an article in it about an environment case, a tract upstate called the Green Marsh. That's your case, isn't it? I thought I recognized it."

There was no longer a reason for elaborate secrecy; Jennie answered directly, "It *was,* you mean. I've been fired."

"Peter told me. That must hurt awfully, when you've done so much work on it."

"What hurts most awfully is that I'm afraid the builders will get their way."

"Isn't there anything you can do?"

"Nothing. I'm not a resident, and I don't pay taxes in that town."

"I don't agree. You're an American citizen, aren't you? This kind of protest is going on all over the country. You can go anywhere you want and talk up. There's no reason why you can't go to that meeting and speak your mind."

Jill was talking in her most emphatic manner, so that Jennie could visualize the wide gesture with which she tossed her hair back from her cheek, could imagine the two vertical lines of frowning concentration and her vivid glance. All this contrasted to her own weariness.

"I've lost my energy," she said.

"Are you afraid because of yesterday? But you'd be safe in a public meeting."

The implication of fear offended Jennie's pride, or her false pride, she thought, and she answered promptly, "That's not the reason. I just don't have the heart for it."

"You have to have the heart," Jill insisted. "You've come this far. Do you want to lose now?"

"It's not my fight anymore."

"It is your fight, I told you! It's everybody's. My parents travel all over the Southwest, they go to every meeting, write to their senators, never give up."

Jennie remembered Martha Cromwell's words: "You're a spellbinder, Jennie."

Her appeal, the one that as an attorney she had already outlined, would have been striking. It would have gone straight to the heart and conscience of anyone who possessed a heart and a conscience.

"I'll go with you if you'll do it," Jill was saying.

It took a moment or two for this astonishing offer to register.

"You'll go with me?"

"I'd surely like to. I can afford to cut a couple of classes."

You're a spellbinder, Jennie.

It was a wild idea. On the other hand, maybe it wasn't so wild. As a private citizen, she could be even more outspoken than counsel could be. She began to feel the stirring of excitement. There was dramatic intrigue in the undertaking.

"Jennie? Are you thinking about it?"

She conceded slowly, "It might be interesting."

"I should say it would be! Then you will?"

There came another pleasurable thought: This would be a chance to display her talents to her daughter. For the first time the word came unselfconsciously and naturally: daughter.

"Well, it's worth considering. Let's see, I could rent a car. We'd have to leave by three at the latest. Can you do that?"

"Earlier, if you want."

"Three will be okay."

Suddenly Jennie was charged with a spirit of adventure. Part of her mind, observing the rest of it as was her habit, told her that she needed something like this. It would propel her forward, to the land of the living.

Then defiance flashed a little spurt of fire: Listen, there was life before Jay and there'll be life after him. There has to be. To hell with him.

"Yes. Okay. I'll pick you up at the main gate on Broadway."

CHAPTER

14

On Sunday she polished and refined her brief remarks. As a mere private citizen, no longer the legal adviser, she would have to talk fast before someone cut her off. She would have to make her points clearly without sacrificing eloquence. She was working away when Peter called to say good-bye.

"I was glad to hear about your expedition with Jill."

"It was her idea. She encouraged me."

"I guess you two are going to be pretty solid together now."

"I hope so. I think so."

"Then something good *has* come out of it, after all, hasn't it? I hope it'll help a little to make up for the rest, Jennie." And when, not knowing what to answer, she was silent, he added more brightly, "I'll be coming back. You'll not get rid of me so easily."

She said, meaning it, "I'm not trying to get rid of you."

———

They passed through a corridor that smelled of cleaning fluid and was flanked by doors labeled Health Department, Dog Licenses, Police Department, Traffic Violations, Tax Collector. They entered the courtroom where the town council sat on its dais with the American flag on a stand at its side.

A man who was standing against the rear wall touched Jennie's arm, and she recognized Jerry Brian, who had "wired" George. He was in plainclothes. "Are you still interested?"

"That's why I'm here," she responded.

"I thought you might be. Okay." And drawing her away from bystanders, including Jill, he whispered, "You won't believe it, but we've already got a lead."

"So fast?"

"The boss has been working day and night. This fancy-looking company's got a bad reputation. Mob connections."

"Barker Development, you mean?"

"I mean. The top honcho's built in California under another name, got in trouble, got out of it, then came East and started to look respectable." Jennie let out a faint, low whistle. "What kind of trouble?"

"A bomb in somebody's car. Something to do with a site they wanted to buy and the owner wouldn't sell. Something like that. Martin says they weren't able to prove it, but everybody knew it, anyway."

"So can they prove this? About George?"

"Martin thinks so. Mind you, I'm not in on the whole picture. I'm only here tonight to keep my eyes open, see who's here. Not that we're expecting Mr. Teeth to show up." Even in the dim corner Jennie could see the young man's grin. "I hear you got off lucky with him."

"That I did." She thought of something. "And Fisher, that creep? Where does he fit in?"

"He doesn't. A creep is all he is. Small fry who happens to have a piece of land he wants to sell and gets mad at the opposition."

"I could have sworn he was in it," Jennie said. "I guess I'm not so smart, after all."

"You're smart enough. Look, it's filling up. You'd better get a seat."

A large crowd had already taken most of them. From the rear Jennie searched the room for a pair of vacancies. Her moving eyes recognized a few faces on the dais, then flickered back up the sides of the room and caught the silver-gray heads of Enid and Arthur Wolfe. They were alone, which was to be expected, for Jay hardly would have given up a day in the office or a federal courtroom to be up here tonight. Their heads turned for only a fraction of a moment, yet Jennie was certain they had seen her. With Jill beside her, she walked in full view to the third row down front, where there were two places. If they want to acknowledge me, she thought defiantly, now is their chance. And if they should wonder about this beautiful young woman who is with me, why, I shall simply tell them who she is. I came to that point just a minute ago. I don't know how I reached it but I did, and here I am.

The Wolfes, however, made no move. What must Jay not have told them! She imagined their widened eyes, their horrified astonishment. And, vividly, she saw them in their kitchen—blue-and-white gingham curtains, African violets in red porcelain cups, the dog at their feet— having their evening tea and cake. They'd have shaken their heads, commiserating with each other and marveling: "But she was so sincere, so frank and open!"

As quickly as confidence had risen, so quickly did it ebb. She shouldn't have come back here, abrading her wounds. The sensible thing would be to turn around and go home right now. Let someone else fight for the Green Marsh and win it or lose it. But that would be humiliation in front of Jill. Hadn't she come here in part to show off a bit before Jill?

So, waiting her turn, Jennie sat through the routine procedures, the pledge of allegiance, the minutes of the previous meeting and all the technical reports. Again the lawyers argued. Barker's young man gave a repetition of his arguments, persuading his listeners of the benefits that Barker Developers was prepared to bring to the town. She wondered whether this engaging, respectable-looking gentleman with the open, confiding manner could possibly be acquainted with Robinson, also known as Harry Corrin, and decided that he probably was not, because in organizations of Barker's size and nature, it would be prudent and necessary to keep the right hand from knowing what the left was doing.

The tired, middle-aged lawyer who had replaced Jennie was a poor match for the other man. Droning statistics, he was beginning to lose the councilmen's attention; the mayor was yawning contemptuously.

Discussion eventually was thrown open to the public. Jennie waited until half a dozen citizens had expressed their opinions. They were fairly evenly divided. The council, too, she supposed was probably still evenly divided, as it had been a few months ago. So the vote would be close. She raised her hand, was acknowledged, and stood up to speak.

"My name is Jennie Rakowsky," she began firmly. "Some of you may remember that I've spoken here before. This time I'm here just as a citizen. I want to talk to you about Barker Developers. Like all developers, they come with a fine speech, luring you with talk of jobs, tax abatements, and all the wonderful improvements they're going to bring to your town. Don't you believe a

word of it," she cried, and raised a warning finger.
"They've come to make money, that's all they've come
for. They don't give a damn about anything but the
bottom line. There's nothing new about these people,
either. They were around back in 1890, trying to cut
Yosemite National Park in half right at the start. If good
citizens hadn't fought them then, we'd have no Yosemite
or Grand Canyon or any other wilderness park today."

Somebody clapped and was immediately hushed. The
Wolfes were staring over Jennie's head toward the dais,
or perhaps toward the ceiling, for all she knew, but
someone else had applauded; it spurred her on, and Jennie began to gallop.

"We can go a lot farther back than that, to Isaiah more
than two thousand years ago, or to the ancient Greeks.
Plato knew that when you cut forests down, you don't
hold rain, and the earth washes away to the sea."

She had notes in her hand yet didn't need them. "And
part of your land here is wetland, a sponge to slow water
that could flood your lands. It's home to wildlife, it's
beauty and recreation. It's an ecosystem that took thousands of years to build. If it's destroyed, it can't be rebuilt. You know that, and these people know it as well as
you do, but they don't care. That's the difference."

Heads turned to Jennie. There wasn't a sound in the
room.

"We can always save 'farther out,' people say. But
what about when there is no more 'farther out' to save?
This planet's not elastic. And right now it's the only
planet we have."

She talked on. It already had been six minutes and she
kept expecting to be stopped, but no one on the dais
stopped her. She was aware of upturned faces, of Jill's
rapt attention and the flow of her own energy.

"It's not as if this were a question of housing the homeless here. There's no real need for this construction, for condominiums and golf courses. It's frivolity—that and greed." She paused a second. "We all know greed when we see it. The world's full of it. People even kill because of it, don't they?"

That's for you, Robinson, she thought, and in that very instant she caught sight of Fisher. He was sitting diagonally across the aisle in the row ahead. She hadn't noticed him before, but there he was, wearing the same black jacket with the same black, malevolent sneer on his face. Well, you fooled me, she thought. You certainly did. You didn't kill George. You're only a street-corner tough. You're not smart enough to be in on a scheme like this one. Still, you're not the type I'd care to meet on a dark night!

She recovered her train of thought; having spoken well, it was time now to stop. And she quickly concluded, addressing the rows of heads on the dais.

"We need a new way of seeing our world. I hope you've begun to see it and will agree that this application has to be refused."

Her heart was still hammering when she sat down.

"You were perfect. Eloquent," Jill whispered. Her eyes shone with admiration.

A surge of joy passed through Jennie. At the same time she would have liked to know what the Wolfes were saying.

The mayor then asked whether there were any more comments from the floor, and since there were none, the discussion was closed.

Now it was the council's turn to deliberate and vote. Discussion was short and offered no surprises; as at the first meeting, there were angry remarks about do-gooders who cared more for skunks and weasels than for people, remarks that brought laughter from some in the audience and applause from others. Fisher got conspicuously to his feet to show approval. The librarian spoke for preservation. The thin man who seconded him was Jack Fuller, the dairy farmer. "You've got a fantastic memory for names," Jay had said.

Then came the vote. One for. One against. Two against. Three in favor. Jennie leaned forward in her seat.

A heavy man wearing cataract glasses got to his feet. "I have to say that I was, at the start of the evening, still wavering. I could see merit in voting either way. But after listening to the young woman who spoke last, I made my decision. Yes, we do have an obligation to future generations. She's certainly right. And so I vote no to the proposal. Leave the Green Marsh alone."

"Four to four," Jennie murmured. Jill squeezed her hand. The mayor was flushed and furious as he polled the man at the end of the table.

"Mr. Garrison?"

The one with money troubles. A decent sort, Jennie recalled. But they said he could be swayed.

Now he cleared his throat, as if about to give a speech, and took on a solemn expression. Obviously he was feeling his own importance.

"I, too, was of two minds," he began. "There's always something to be said on behalf of conservation. But there's also much to be said for creating jobs, and certainly we can use ratables to ease the tax burden."

Jennie groaned silently.

"It's a question of weighing the two. On the one hand—"

Oh, for Pete's sake, she cried silently, will you get to the point?

"On the other hand—"

After two minutes' worth of weighing hands, he did get to the point. "So I vote to turn down the application. Let the state take over the land as a wilderness park."

Jennie laughed. Her eyes filled with tears. Jill kissed her cheek.

"You did it! You did it!"

The crowd moved slowly toward the night and the dimly lit parking lot. Behind and around her in the crush, Jennie heard comments.

"If it hadn't been for that young lady lawyer, it's my opinion they'd have voted the other way."

"Maybe so. She helped, that's for sure."

"She swayed them. I watched their faces."

"You could almost feel Garrison making up his mind."

"There's a lot of anger here, though. You don't see money like that go sliding through your fingers without getting pretty mad."

"You must feel wonderful," Jill repeated as they drove away. "You did it all."

"No, I didn't do it all. I did some, and I'm happy about that," Jennie replied.

Jay would have applauded that speech. It had been concise, it had been damn good. All my pride and all my heart were in it, she thought.

They passed through the town and were soon out on the highway. Jennie looked at the clock on the dashboard. "Nine-thirty and no traffic. We'll be back in the city by midnight."

Fields, divided by the road's black thread, were a black-and-white patchwork where snow had melted and refrozen. The sky was white and calm.

"I never realized there was so much empty space in the East," Jill remarked.

"Well, you've only been in New York. Look over there, that's the little road that leads to the Green Marsh. The lake's just half a mile in. It's one of the prettiest places you could hope to see, even in New Mexico."

"All right, let me see it."

"Now? At night?"

"Why not? See how light it is out? And it's only half a mile, you said."

Jennie was moved by the girl's eagerness. "Okay. Then we'll just get home fifteen minutes later."

The little car bumped and slid on the ruts and stopped where the lane became too narrow. A short walk over crunching snow brought them to the crest of the hill above the lake. It, like the land, was a patchwork of black and white. Where the ice was broken, the water glistened like black marble. A deep quiet lay on the hemlock-covered hills and on stark birches, unmoving in the windless night.

Here under the benign sun she had come upon this place and stood in the bright air, perhaps on this very spot, with his arms around her and their life lying ahead of them, as warm and gold as the sun and the air.

"Oh, look, Jennie, an owl!"

From a low branch, it stared out of round, amber eyes; then, raising its great wings, it sailed downhill above their heads, crossed the lake, and disappeared in shadow among the trees.

"How beautiful it is here! I know what you mean and why you fought for it," Jill whispered.

And Jennie understood that she was being considerate of the silence. She had gotten the feel of the place. Her hands clasped before her, she stood and gazed at the sleeping wilderness while Jennie just gazed at her.

Then they got into the car and started back to the city. For a while they rode in silence, the whir of the tires and the thrum of the engine making the only sounds. It was Jill who spoke first.

"I told Mom and Dad everything."

"Everything?"

"Yes, about you and the reason you didn't want to see me. Mom said I shouldn't have insisted."

"Just tell Mom it's turned out all right."

"Really?"

If only it were so simple, so clear a division between black and white!

"Yes. Really!"

"I just want to say one thing. Your secret—about me— would have been safe. I never would have told."

A lump rose in Jennie's throat. "I couldn't have lived with a lie. Gotten up every day and faced him, knowing something he didn't know."

"It's been done."

"But not by me."

For the second time that night Jill placed her hand on Jennie's; the two hands rested lightly on the wheel.

What do I feel? Jennie asked herself. A flow of love, a mingling of gratitude and grief. Then she thought, silently chiding herself, Oh, we are all too self-absorbed these days! Stop all this analysis! Just take things as they come. Stop asking yourself what you are feeling or why. It does no good.

And she said practically, "You must be starved after that hurried little supper. Let's stop somewhere for a bite."

"I'd rather not. I didn't realize it would take so long to get back."

"Okay, it is pretty late. Too late to go back to the dorm. You'd better stay at my place overnight. Why don't you put your head back and sleep? You've had a long day." Looking over at Jill, she thought, I sound like a mother.

"You sound like Mom," Jill said.

"Do I? That's nice."

The girl slept. Rolling toward the city, the car passed landmarks that Jennie would not be seeing again: a bridge; a roadside stand where Jay always bought apples to take home. And here I am, she thought, with my child of chance, unexpected and unwanted, beside me. Her beautiful hair is a collar around her pure, sleeping face. The two of us are riding through the night.

It was shortly before one o'clock when Jennie stopped the car. The street was dark, but the windows in her apartment were all lit.

What now? Who now? She felt an urge to flee, to get back in the car and keep going.

"What's wrong?" Jill asked.

"The lights are on in my apartment. I don't think we should go in."

"Why not?"

"After what happened at my office, can you ask?"

"Give me the outside key. We'll go up, and if anything's wrong, we'll scream, that's all, and wake the house."

"You're making me feel like a coward. All right, I'll go, but I want you to stay down here."

"I'll stay a few steps behind you."

"Not a few steps! Downstairs, I said."

"You're sounding like Mom again."

Jennie started up. On the third landing she stopped to listen. There wasn't a sound in the house. See, she reasoned, it's just another burglary. They've somehow gotten in, taken the stereo, the television, and some clothes because there's nothing else in there to take. It's not the worst thing in the world. In this city it happens every day.

The door was ajar, and she hesitated, gathering courage. Jill reached in front of her and pushed the door open.

"Go on in, Jennie. Go on."

At the far end of the living room two men stood up. Peter was laughing, and Jay, with reaching arms, was running toward Jennie.

"Oh, Jennie!" he cried.

Unable to absorb the reality of what she was seeing, she stammered. "W-what is it? What are you doing?"

"Oh, Jennie," cried Jay again. He put his arms around her. "You ought to hit me! Beat me! Throw me down the stairs! What I've done to you! What I've done!"

Through starting tears she said again, "What are you doing? I don't understand."

"Peter came to my office this afternoon and told me everything. Why . . . oh, for God's sake, why didn't you tell me yourself?"

She hid against his shoulder.

"You could have told me," he protested when she did not answer.

"No, she couldn't have," Peter said.

Jay raised Jennie's head so that she was forced to look at him.

"Why didn't you?" he repeated.

Still she was unable to answer, and could only put her hand on her heart as if to cover its fierce beat.

And Peter, in whom the first laughter had died, so that his eyes were stern, said, "I've explained the way I see it, the way it is. . . . She was too afraid."

"Afraid of *me?*" Jay was bewildered. "Not of *me?* I can't believe it."

"Please," she whispered.

"Darling Jennie, you should have told me at the very beginning when you first found out."

Somehow now, Peter was taking charge. "I'll answer for her. She was afraid of losing you. And," he said in a roughened voice, "as I also told you, it goes back to me. Me and my family. I've done a lot of thinking these last few days. . . . We marked her. After that she never thought she was good enough. This was just a repeat situation."

"Is that the way you felt about it, Jennie?" Jay said sorrowfully.

"I guess so. Something like that," she whispered.

"We would have lost everything if Peter hadn't come to me. The way it looked, I thought . . . I *had* to think . . . I went a little bit crazy, the way you'd feel if you suddenly found out that your mother was a spy for the enemy—" He broke off. "And this is your girl?"

For Jill had been waiting, observing the scene with curiosity and tenderness.

At last Jennie found coherent speech. Proudly she said, "Yes, this is Jill. Victoria Jill."

"So you're the cause of it all!" Jay took hold of Jill's shoulders and kissed her on both cheeks. He looked from her to Jennie and back again. "If this is what you can produce, Jennie, you ought to have a dozen."

There was a swirling in Jennie's head, a weakness in her knees, and she had to sit down.

"Such a week," she murmured, wiping her eyes.

"The worst," Jay said. "The worst. But what am I talking about? I've just heard what happened to you at the office. I went crazy all over again when Peter told me."

Jennie closed her eyes to shut out the dizziness, while Jay, sitting next to her, laid her head on his shoulder and stroked her hair.

"I feel as if I'd lived a lifetime since this afternoon," he began slowly. "When Peter walked into my office, I couldn't believe what I was seeing."

Peter chuckled. "He recognized me by my hair. It's very hard to disappear in a crowd when you've got hair this color."

"He came in and started to lecture me. He attacked me and told me I had no right to be treating you like that, that it was brutal and—"

"I must have seemed a lot braver than I felt. I really expected to be thrown out of the office. But I had to do it. I couldn't get on the plane back to Chicago and leave Jennie like that when it was my fault."

"Not really your fault," Jennie objected.

"Well, however you want to look at it. Anyway, I remembered your neighbor, Shirley. You'd said she knew everybody's business, so I came over here and asked her some questions—as your friend the doctor, of course. That's how I got Jay's name. It was easy." Peter was pleased with himself.

Now Jay laughed. "It's never hard to get Shirley talking, bless her. The trick is to stop her."

"I knew all the time what Peter was planning," Jill said now. "And when we drove up and I saw the lights on, I knew it had worked out all right. I was on pins and needles all day thinking about it."

"No wonder you were in a hurry to get back and wouldn't stop to eat," Jennie said.

"Oh!" Jay exclaimed. "I forgot all about today. I've been in such a condition that I didn't give a damn anymore about the Green Marsh or anything else. But Jennie didn't forget. Jennie, you went—"

"It was Jill who made me go."

"Yes, and aren't you glad you did? She won," Jill told the men. "She gave the most marvelous speech, and that's what turned the vote. She fought and won."

"Yes, my Jennie's a fighter."

Then came Peter's voice. "For good causes, yes. For other people."

No one said anything for a moment. Then Jay asked somewhat uncertainly whether his parents had been at the meeting.

"They were there. But we didn't speak." There was something she had to know. "What did you tell them about me?"

"Only that I thought, I had reason to know, that you'd found somebody else. I was vague. I couldn't have said anymore, and they didn't ask anymore."

"They're such good people," Jennie murmured.

"Well. They liked you so much. But of course, when they believed you'd hurt their son, you can understand why Dad got another attorney. I asked him not to, but he wouldn't listen, he was just so hurt himself."

"I'll make it up to them, Jay."

"You don't have to make up to anybody for anything! And listen, the first thing in the morning, we're going for the marriage license. Forget the fancy wedding arrangements. I don't want to wait any longer than three days." He reached out and took Jill's hands. "I want you there too. You're Jennie's daughter, and you're going to be mine." And very softly, so softly that Jennie barely heard him, he finished. "I love your mother so much, Jill. And I almost lost her. Through my own fault."

"When you come down to it, it started with me. My fault," Jill said. "I can't bear to think I almost ruined everything."

"I think it's time now to stop all the talk about fault and being sorry," Peter objected. "Let's look to the future." He yawned and stretched. "It's late and I'm catching an early plane, so I'm going to say good night." He took his coat. "Will I be seeing you sometime in Chicago, Jill?"

"Sure. I could change planes on the way home for Christmas vacation and have lunch with you. I'm in a hurry to get home, though, to see Dad and Mom and the kids."

Jay was looking at her intently.

"You look puzzled," Jill remarked with a smile.

"Not exactly. It's just that I don't know anything about you, and I want to."

"You will. I'll visit a lot whenever you ask me. I'd love to."

"Just 'visit'?"

"Oh, were you thinking I would move in with Jennie? I never wanted that! I've got a wonderful family of my own! What I wanted," Jill said earnestly as Jennie watched the now familiar flash of eyes and toss of hair, "what I wanted was only to know who I am. And now that I know who I am, and love who I am," she added, touching Jennie's arm, "I'm at peace. Yes, I'm very peaceful."

"Well, you can have two families," Jay said.

Peter corrected him. "Three. I am a family of one."

"Can't you stay for the wedding?" Jay asked as Peter put on his overcoat. "Only three days more?"

Peter shook his head. "Thanks, but I'm off. A rolling stone, that's me." He shook hands, kissed Jill, and was about to shake Jennie's hand when she got up and kissed him.

She laughed. "You don't mind, Jay?"

"No—I could kiss him myself."

"Please don't," Peter said, and they all laughed, breaking the strain.

As if by common agreement, the three went to the window when he had gone. They watched him cross the street under the lamps and move toward the avenue in loping, boyish strides.

Jay said abruptly, "I liked him."

"I thought I hated him," Jennie answered.

"But now you don't," Jill said.

"How could I? He gave you both back to me." She took Jill's hand and with her other held Jay's, which was warm and firm.

"It's been a long time, a long way," she said.

A softness flowed in her, sweet rest, as on seeing home again after a journey. This plain little room contained a world, a full, bright, new world.

Then she thought of something.

"Hey, Jill! Aren't you the person who said she would keep the secret, who would never tell?"

"Well, I lied," Jill said cheerfully.

WHISPERS

PART ONE
◇
Spring 1985

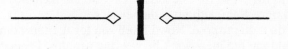

IN dodging Robert's hand, the furious hand aimed at her face, she fell and struck the edge of the closet's open door instead. Now on the floor, stunned by a rush of pain, she leaned against the wall, touched her cheek, and, in a kind of astonishment, stared at the blood on her hand.

Robert's eyes and his mouth had become three dark, round holes in his face.

"Oh, good God!" He knelt beside her. "Let me look. No, let me, Lynn! Thank goodness it's nothing. Just a break in the skin. An accident . . . I'll get a washcloth and ice cubes. Here, let me pull you up."

"Don't touch me, damn you!" Thrusting his hand away, she pulled herself up and sat down on the bed between the suitcases. Her face burned, while her cold fingers felt for the rising lump on her cheekbone. Another lump, thick with outrage and tears, rose in her throat.

Robert bustled between the bedroom and the bathroom. "Damn, where's the ice bucket? In a first-class hotel like this you'd think they'd put—oh, here it is. Now just lie back. I'll fix the pillows. Hold this to your face. Does it hurt much?"

His expressions of anxiety were sickening. She closed her eyes. If she could have closed her ears, she would have done so. His voice, so rich, so beautifully modulated, was trying to soothe her.

"You tripped. I know I raised my hand but you tripped. I'm sorry, but you were so angry, you were almost hysterical, Lynn, and I had to stop you somehow."

She opened her eyes. "I? *I* was so angry? *I* was almost hysterical? Think again and tell the truth if you can."

"Well, I did lose my temper a little. I'll admit that. But can you blame me? Can you? When I depended on you to do the packing and you know how important this convention is, you know this could be my chance for promotion to the New York headquarters, the main chance of a lifetime maybe, and here I am without a dinner jacket."

"I didn't do it on purpose. Now I'll tell you for the third time that Kitty Lombard told me the men won't be wearing tuxedos. I specifically asked about it."

"Kitty Lombard! She steered you wrong on purpose and you're too stupid to know it. How often have I told you that people like nothing better than to see somebody else look like a fool? Especially in the business world. They all want to sabotage you. When will you learn to stop trusting every Tom, Dick, and Harry you come across? Never, I suppose." Striding across the room, in his powerful indignation, Robert looked about ten feet tall. "And by the way, may I remind you again that it's not called a 'tuxedo'? It's a 'dinner jacket.' "

"All right, all right. I'm a hick, a small-town hick, remember? My dad ran a hardware store. I never saw a dinner jacket except in pictures until I met you. But I never saw a man raise his hand to a woman either."

"Oh, let's stop this, Lynn! There's no sense going over it all night. It's almost six, and the dinner's at seven. Your ice is melting. Let me have a look again."

"I'll take care of myself, thanks. Let me alone."

In the bathroom she closed the door. The full-length mirror reflected a small, freckled woman, still girlish at thirty-six, with bangs and a curving cap of smooth sandy hair worn as she had in high school. The face, pleasing yet unremarkable except for a pair of rather lovely light eyes, was disfigured now by the bruise, much larger than she had imagined and already more hideously, brightly blue and green than one would have thought possible. She was horrified.

Robert opened the door. "Jesus! How can you possibly go downstairs looking like that! Unless—" He frowned over his thoughts.

"Unless what, if you please?"

"Well—I don't know. I could say the airline lost the bag with my clothes, and that you have a stomach virus, one of those twenty-four-hour things. Make yourself comfortable, take a hot bath, keep the ice on your face, get in bed, and read. Call room service and have a good dinner. Relax. It'll do you good. A nice quiet dinner without kids."

Lynn stared at him. "Mr. Efficiency. You have it figured out, as always."

Everything was ruined, this happily anticipated weekend away, the new dress, spring-green silk with crystal buttons, the new bottle of perfume, the manicure, all the joy gone. Sordid ruination. And he could stand there, confident, handsome, and secure, ready to cope, to go forward again.

"I hate you," she said.

"Oh, Lynn, cut it out. I am not, I repeat, not going to go over this business ad infinitum. Just pull yourself together. I have to pull myself together for both our sakes, make an appearance and make the best of this opportunity. All the top brass will be here, and I can't afford to be rattled. I have to think clearly. Now I'm going to get dressed. Thank God my other suit is pressed."

"I know. I pressed it."

"Well, you got one thing straight, at least."

"I keep *your* whole life straight every day of *my* life."

"Will you lower your voice? People can hear you in the hall. Do you want to disgrace us both?"

Suddenly, as water is sucked down a drain, her strength rushed out. Her arms, her legs, even her voice refused to work and she dropped facedown onto the wide bed between the open suitcases. Her lips moved silently.

"Peace, peace," they said.

Robert moved about, jingling keys as he dressed. When he was ready to go he came to the bed.

"Well, Lynn? Are you going to stay there like that all rumpled up in your street clothes?"

Her lips moved, but silently, again. "Go away. Just go away," they said.

The door clicked shut. And at that moment the tension broke. All the outrage at injustice, the humiliation of helpless defeat, flowed out in torrential tears, tears that she could never have shed while anyone was watching.

"You were always a proud, spunky little thing," Dad used to say. Oh, such a proud, spunky little thing! she thought as she collapsed into long, heaving, retching sobs.

Much later, as abruptly as the torrent had started, it ceased. She was emptied, calmed, relieved. Cold and stiff from having lain so long uncovered, she got up and, for lack of any other purpose, went to the window. Forty floors below lights moved through the streets; lights dotted the silhouettes of Chicago's towers; light from the silver evening sky sprayed across Lake Michigan. Small, dark, fragmented clouds ran through the silver light and dissolved themselves within it. The whole scene was in motion, while the invisible wind rattled at the window glass.

Behind her the room was too still. Hotel rooms, when you were alone, were as desolate as a house emptied out after death. And Lynn, shuddering, ran to her carry-on bag, took out the photo of her children, and put it on the dresser, saying aloud, "There!" They had created an instant's presence.

And she stood looking, wanting most terribly these two girls whom she had left home in St. Louis only that morning and whom, like any other mother, she had been glad to leave behind for a while. Now, if she possibly could, she would repack her bag and fly back to them. Her beautiful Emily, the replica of Robert, would be at the sophomore dance tonight. Annie would just about now be going back to Aunt Helen's house from a third-grade birthday party. Smart Annie, funny, secretive, sensitive, difficult Annie. Yes, she would fly home to them right now if she could. But Robert had the tickets and the money. She never did have any cash beyond the weekly allowance for the household. And anyway, she thought, remembering, how could I just walk in with this face and without their father?

The silence began to buzz in Lynn's ears. A sensation of fear as of some desperate, unexplainable menace came flooding. The walls closed in.

"I have to get out of here," she said aloud.

Putting on her travel coat, she drew the collar up and wrapped a scarf around her head, drawing it like a peasant's babushka over her cheeks as far as it would go, which was not far enough. Luckily there were only two other people in the elevator during its long descent, a very young couple dressed for some gala event, and so tenderly engrossed with each other that they truly did not give a glance to Lynn's face. In the marble lobby people were either hurrying from cocktails to dinner or else lingering at the vitrines with their displays of glittering splendors, their jewels, leathers, satins, and furs.

Outdoors, cold spring air stung the burning bruise. At a drugstore she stopped to get something for it, a gauze bandage or some ointment, anything.

"I bumped into a door. Isn't that stupid?" she said. Then, shocked at the sight of her swollen eye in the mirror behind the man's head, she added clumsily, "And on top of that, I have this miserable allergy. My eyes—"

The man's own eyes, when he handed her a little package of allergy pills and a soothing ointment, reflected his disbelief and his pity. Overcome with shame at her own naïveté, she rushed away into the anonymity of the street.

Then, walking in the direction of the lake, she remembered vaguely from a previous visit to the city that there would be a green space there with walks and benches. It was really too cold to sit still, but nevertheless she sat down, tightened the coat around her, and gazed out to where the water met the sky. Couples strolled, walking their dogs and talking peaceably. It hurt so much to watch them that she could have wept, if she had not already been wept out.

The day had begun so well. The flight from home was a short one, so there had been time enough for a walk on Michigan Avenue before going back to the room to dress. Robert was a window-shopper. He loved dark, burnished wood in fine libraries, eighteenth-century English paintings of fields and farms, classic sculpture, and antique rugs, all quiet, dignified, expensive things. Often he stopped to admire a beautiful dress, too, like the one they had seen this afternoon, a peach silk ballgown scattered with seed-pearl buds.

"That would be perfect on you," he had observed.

"Shall I wear it to the movies on Saturday night?" she had teased back.

"When I am a chief executive officer, there will be occasions for a dress like that," he had replied, and added then, "It suits you. Airy and delicate and soft, like you."

It had begun so well. . . . Their life together had begun so well. . . .

"Why do they call you 'Midge'?" he had asked her. He had never noticed her before that day. But then, he was the head of the department, while she only sat at a typist's desk. "Why? On the list it says your name is Lynn Riemer."

"I was always called that. Even at home. It's short for 'midget.' I guess it was because my sister's tall."

"You're nowhere near being a midget." He looked her up and down quite seriously. "Five foot two, I'd estimate."

It was his eyes that held her, the brilliant blue, darkening or lightening according to mood, that held every woman in the office, for that matter, and possibly, in a different way, the men too. The men had to have serious respect for authority; authority could praise and promote; authority could also discharge a man to creep home in defeat to his family. But the women's fear of Robert Ferguson was diluted with a tremulous, daring, sexual fervor. This fervor had to be secret. Each would have been embarrassed to admit to another, for fear of seeming ridiculous: Robert Ferguson was totally beyond their reach, and they all knew it, worlds apart from the men with whom they had grown up and whom they dated.

It was not only that with those vivacious eyes and his long, patrician bones he was extraordinarily handsome. It was an aura about him. He was absolutely confident. His diction was perfect, his clothes were perfect, and he demanded perfection of everyone around him. Lateness was not tolerated. Papers put on his desk for his signature had to be flawless. His initials had to be accurate: V.W. Robert Victor William Ferguson. His car must be kept in a quickly accessible place in a parking lot. Yet, for all of this, he was considerate and kind. When he was pleased, he was generous with a compliment. He remembered birthdays, making happy occasions in the office. When anyone was sick, he became earnestly involved. It was known that he volunteered at the men's ward at the hospital.

"He's an enigma," Lynn had once remarked when Robert was being discussed, and he often was discussed.

"I'm going to call you 'Lynn' from now on," he said that day, "and tell everyone here to do the same."

She had no idea why he should have paid enough attention to her to remark upon her name. It was silly. Yet she was sufficiently flustered by the happening to tell her sister Helen that she would not answer to "Midge" anymore.

"Why? What's wrong with it?"

"I have a perfectly good name, and I'm not a midget. Even my boss says it's ridiculous."

Helen had given her a look of amusement that she remembered clearly long afterward. Ever since her marriage and the birth of two babies, Helen had assumed a superior air of motherly protectiveness.

"Your boss? It seems to me you talk about him a good deal."

"I do not."

"Oh, yes, you do. You may not realize it, but you do. 'My boss has a stereo in his office. My boss treated us all to pizza for lunch. My boss got a big raise from the main office—' "

It was true that he was more and more in Lynn's thoughts, that she watched without seeming to do so for his every arrival and departure.

She had begun to have passionate fantasies. So Helen was probably right. . . .

Then one day Robert asked her to go to dinner with him.

"You look as if you were floating on air," Helen said.

"Well, I am. I thought, I still am thinking, Why me?"

"Why not you? You have more life and more energy than any six people put together. Why do you think boys all—"

"You don't understand. This man is different. He's distinguished. His face looks like the ones you see on statues or on those old coins in Dad's collection."

"By the way, how old is he?"

"Twenty-seven."

"And you're twenty. Twenty, going on fourteen. Filled with dreams."

Lynn still kept the dress she had worn that night. Sentimental almost to a fault, she held on to everything, from her wedding dress and her children's christening gowns to the pressed flowers from the bouquet that Robert had sent after that first dinner, a splendid sheaf of white roses tied with pink ribbon.

"Tell me about yourself," he had begun when they sat down with the candlelight between them.

She had responded lightly, "There isn't much to tell."

"There always is, in every life. Start from the beginning. Were you born here in the city?"

"No, in Iowa. In a farming town south of Des Moines. My mother died, and my father still lives there. My sister moved here when she was married, and I guess that's why, after graduation from high school, I came here too. There were no jobs at home anyway. This is my first one, and I hope I'm doing well."

"I'm sure you are."

"I wanted to see the city, to see things, and it's been fun. Having the apartment, going to the concerts—"

He nodded. "A world-class orchestra. As fine as anything in New York."

"I've never been there."

"When I was at the Wharton School, I went often to the theater. It's only a short train ride from Philadelphia."

Her tongue was loosening. The wine might be helping. "I'd like to see the east. I'd like to see Europe, England, France, Rome."

His eyes were shining and smiling at her. "The places that you read about in *Portrait of a Lady* last week?"

She was astonished. "How did you know?"

"Simple. I saw the book on your desk. Don't they call me 'Hawkeye' in the office?"

She laughed and blushed. "How on earth can you know that? Nobody ever says—"

"I've also got sharp ears."

She struck out boldly. "Is that why you invited me tonight? Is that what gave you the idea, that I read Henry James?"

"That had a little to do with it. I was curious. You must admit that the rest of them on the staff don't go much beyond movie magazines, do they?"

"They're my friends. I don't pay attention to things like that," she said loyally. "They're not important."

"Don't think I'm a snob. I don't judge people by their knowledge of what's in books either. But you have to admit that it's pleasant to be with people who like the same things you like. Besides, you're beautiful. That must have had something to do with it, don't you think?"

"Thank you."

"You don't believe you are beautiful, do you? Your eyes say that you're doubtful. I'll tell you. You're a porcelain doll. Your skin is white as milk."

She parried, "Is it good to look like a porcelain doll?"

"I think so. I meant it as a compliment."

This dialogue was certainly different from any she had ever had before, with Bill or anyone else. And she was not sure what she ought to say next.

"Well, go on with your story about yourself. You've only just begun."

"There isn't much more. Dad couldn't afford college, so I went to a very good secretarial school that had courses in English lit. I'd always loved to read, and it's there that I learned what to read. So I read and I cook. That's my second hobby. Maybe it's boasting, but the fact is, I'm a very good cook. And that's all, I guess. Now it's your turn."

"Okay. Born and grew up in Pittsburgh. No brothers or sisters, which made for a bit of lonesomeness. I had a good home, though. My parents were especially loving. They spoiled me a little, I think. In their way they were unusual people. My mother played the piano and taught me to play. I'm not all that good, but I play because it makes me think of her. My father was a learned man and very quiet and kindly, with an old-fashioned sort of dignity. His business took him around the world. Every summer they went to Salzburg for the music festival." He paused. "They were killed in an auto accident the summer I was graduated from college."

She felt a stab of horror. "How awful for you! It's bad enough when someone has a heart attack, as my mother did. But a car accident's so—so unnecessary, so wrong!"

"Yes. Well, life goes on." His face sank into sadness, the mouth and eyes gone still.

At the back of the room, just then the pianist was singing, "A tale told by a stranger, by a new love, on a dark blue evening in a rose-white May."

The poignant words of the forties, so long ago, coming at this moment of Robert's revelations, filled her chest with a longing almost painful, a confusion of sadness and thrilling joy. Tears came to her eyes.

When he saw them, he touched her hand. "Gentle girl . . . But enough of this. Come, we'll be late for the movie."

She went home and lay awake half the night. I want to live with him for the rest of my life, she thought. He is the one. But I'm an idiot. We had an evening together, that's all. He won't seriously want me. How can he? I'm not nearly good enough for him. He won't want me.

He had wanted her, though, wanted her badly. In the office they hid their intense emotion; passing each other, their eyes turned away. Joyously, she kept their secret. She alone came to know the other side of this man whom others found imperious, the part of him that was so very tender. She alone knew about the high tragedy of his parents' deaths, and about his lesser sorrows too.

He confided. "I've been married."

She felt a rush of disappointment, a pang of jealousy.

"We met at college and were married in commencement week. Looking back, I wonder how it ever happened. She was very beautiful and very rich, but spoiled and irresponsible, too, so we were completely unsuited to each other. Querida—her mother was Spanish—was 'artistic.' She did watercolors. I don't mean to disparage her, but she was just a dabbler. She took a job in a small gallery and on her day off was a volunteer docent at the museum. Anything to get out of the house. She hated the house. The place was a mess, no meals, the laundry not even sent out half the time, nothing done. I could never bring anybody home from the office, never solidify the contacts one needs to make it in the business world." He shrugged. "What can I say except that hers was an entirely different way of life from what I was used to? We grated on each other's nerves, and so of course we argued almost daily. She disliked my friends, and I wasn't fond of hers, I can tell you that." He smiled ruefully. "We would have parted even sooner if it hadn't been for the child. Jeremy. He's six now."

"What happened to him?"

"I haven't seen him since he was a year old. But I support him, although he wouldn't be in want if I didn't. Querida went back to live with her parents, so he's growing up in a mansion. She didn't want joint custody, said it was too confusing for a child, and I didn't want to fight her decision."

"Still, how awful for you not to see him! Or for him not to know you."

Robert sighed. "Yes. Yes, it is. But he can't remember me, so for him at his age I suppose it's as if I had died. I hope so much, though, that he'll want to see me when he's old enough to understand." And he sighed again.

"I'm sure he will," Lynn said, in her pity.

"Well, he'll know how to find me. His money goes into the bank every month. So that's the end of my little story."

"It's a sad story."

"Yes, but it could be worse, Lynn. It seems like something that happened a lifetime ago," he said earnestly. "I've never talked about it to anyone before this. It's too private. And I'm a very private person, as you know by now."

Inevitably, the affair of Robert and Lynn had to come to notice. In the second month she took him to Helen's house. Helen's husband, Darwin, was a good-natured man, round featured with an extra chin. Beside him Robert sparkled with his white collar glistening above his dark blue blazer. Darwin looked rumpled, as if he had been napping in his clothes. In a nice way—or perhaps not such a nice way?—Lynn was proud to let Helen see the contrast between the two, proud and a little ashamed of being proud.

The next day Helen said, "Of course you want to know what I thought of your new man. I'm going to tell you right out flat: I didn't like him much."

Lynn screamed into the telephone. "What?"

"I'm always honest with you, Lynn. I know I can be too blunt—but he's not your type. He can be sarcastic, I notice, and I have a hunch he's a snob. He thinks he's better than other people."

Lynn was furious. "Have you anything else nice to say about a man you don't even know? Any more hunches?"

"He has a critical, sharp tongue."

"I've never noticed it."

"I thought it was in poor taste, even cruel of him, to talk about that girl in the office and her long nails. 'Filthy long nails. Can you imagine the bacteria snuggled under them?' It was belittling to name her, and Darwin thought so too."

"Oh, dear! I am so sorry you and Darwin don't approve. Really sorry."

"Don't be angry at me, Lynn. Who wishes you more joy in life than I do? Dad and I. I just don't want you to make a mistake. I see that you're infatuated. It's written all over you."

"I'm not infatuated."

"I feel in my bones that he's not right for you."

"Does it possibly occur to your bones that I might not be right for him? Robert's brilliant. He's head of computer marketing for the whole region. I hear the salesmen talking—" Indignation made Lynn almost breathless. "An international company—"

"Is it that that impresses you? Listen, Lynn. You never know about big corporations. You're on top today and out tomorrow. It's better to be your own boss, even in a small way, instead of at other people's mercy."

Helen's husband had a little plumbing business with five employees.

"Are you accusing me of being ambitious? Me? You think that's what I see in Robert?"

"No, no, I didn't mean that at all. You're one of the least materialistic people. I didn't express myself well. I meant that perhaps you felt—a kind of admiration, hero worship, just because he is so successful and—I only meant, don't get too serious so fast."

"Do you know what I think? I think you're an idiot," Lynn said before she hung up.

But it was not in her nature to hold a grudge very long. Helen was transparent. She was undoubtedly not even aware of it, and would deny it, but her motive was envy, even though she lived happily with Darwin. Pure and simple envy. And Lynn forgave her.

Almost three months passed before they went to bed together; Lynn had to wait for her roommates to go out of town.

On the weekend this finally happened, the two women had scarcely reached the airport before she had a lavish dinner prepared, and he arrived with flowers, record albums, and champagne. In the first moment they stood staring at each other as if this sudden marvelous freedom had transfixed them; in the next moment everything happened, everything moved. The flowers in their green tissue paper were flung onto the table,

Robert's overcoat was flung over a kitchen chair, and Lynn was lifted into his arms.

Quickly, deftly, in the dim light of the wintry day, he removed her clothes, the sweater and the white blouse with the lace collar, the plaid skirt and the underthings. Her heart was speeding. She could hear its beat.

"I never—this is the first time, Robert."

"I'll be very gentle," he murmured.

And he was. Persistent, warm, and gentle, he spoke soft, endearing words while he held her.

"So sweet . . . So beautiful . . . I love you so."

Whatever little fear there had been now dissolved, and she gave herself into total passionate trust.

Much later when they released each other, Lynn began to laugh. "I was just thinking, it's a good thing I hadn't yet turned the oven on when you arrived. We'd be having cinders for dinner."

Over her expert ratatouille and *tarte normande* they talked about themselves.

"Twenty-year-old virgins are becoming very rare these days," said Robert.

"I'm glad I waited." She was still too shy to say: It makes me belong all the more to you. Because, would this last? She trusted, and yet there were no guarantees. Nothing had been said. But I shall die if he leaves me, she thought.

They went back to bed. This time there was no need to be as gentle. She worshiped his strength. For a man so slender he was exceedingly strong. And, surprisingly, she found herself responding with a strength and a desire equal to his. They slept, until long before dawn she felt him return to her and, with willing arms, received him. Sleeping again past dawn, they awoke to see that a heavy snowfall was darkening the world.

"Let's stay indoors the whole day," he whispered. "Indoors, in bed."

All through Saturday and Sunday they knew no surfeit.

"I'm obsessed with you," Robert said. "You are the most erotic woman —I've never known anything like you. And you look so innocent in your sweaters and skirts. A man would never guess."

On Sunday evening Lynn looked at the clock. "Robert, their plane gets in at ten. I'm afraid you have to leave in a hurry."

He groaned. "When can we do this again?"

"I don't know," she said mournfully.

"This is no way to live!" he almost shouted. "I hate a hole-and-corner business, skulking in highway motels. And I don't want 'living together' either. We need to be permanent. Lynn, you're going to marry me."

They set the wedding for June, taking advantage of Robert's vacation to have a honeymoon in Mexico.

"Of course, you'll have to quit your job," he told her. "We can't be in the same office."

"I'll find another one easily."

"Not yet. You'll need time to furnish an apartment. It should be done carefully. Buy things of quality that will last."

Helen generously offered their house for the reception. "You can't very well have it at Dad's, since he's only got three rooms now," she said. "With luck, if the weather's right, we can have the whole thing in our yard. Darwin has plans for a perennial border, and you know his green thumb. It should be beautiful."

To give her fullest credit Helen did not speak one disparaging word from the moment the engagement was announced. She kissed Lynn, admired the ring, which was a handsome one, and wished the couple every happiness.

"Every happiness," she said now as a chill blew in over Lake Michigan, loudly enough, apparently, for the couple with the poodles, who had circled back, to turn and stare. An eccentric woman, huddled there talking to herself, that's what she was. An object to be stared at. Ah, well, there was no stopping memory once it got started back and back. . . .

Robert endeared himself to everyone during that expectant enchanted spring before the wedding. Helen's little boys adored him; he bought small bats, taught them to pitch, took them to ball games, and showed them how to wrestle. While the ice held, they all went skating, and when the days warmed, had picnics in the country.

In Helen's kitchen Lynn cooked superb little dinners, quiches, cassoulets, and soufflés out of Julia Child's new book.

"You put me to shame," Helen said.

After dinner Robert would sit at the old upright piano and play whatever was called out to him: jazz, show tunes, or a Chopin waltz.

At his suggestion the two couples went to hear the St. Louis symphony. Darwin had never gone before and was surprised to find that he liked it.

"Once you acquire the taste, you'll never be without music," Robert told him. "For me it's another kind of food. We've got to get season tickets next year, Lynn."

Naively, kindly, Darwin praised Robert. "It beats me, Lynn, how he *knows* so much. I can just about make it through the daily paper. And he sure knows how to get fun out of life, too, and knows how to fit in with people."

Her father approved. "I like him," he said after Lynn and Robert's weekend visit. "It'll be good to have a new son. And good for him to have a family. Hard on a young fellow to lose his parents like that. What kind of people were they? Do you know anything about them?"

"What is there to find out? They're dead," Lynn answered, feeling impatient.

"That's all he has, the old aunt back in Pittsburgh?"

"And an uncle in Vancouver."

"Practically alone in the world," Dad said with sympathy.

In the hardware store, being introduced as customers came in, most of them from the farms, Robert knew how to meet their jovial simplicity in kind. She saw that they approved of him, as did her father.

"I like him, Midge," Dad kept saying. "You've got yourself a man, not like the kids who used to hang around you. No offense meant. They were all good boys, but wet behind the ears. This one's a man. What I like is, he hasn't let the education or the job go to his head. I'll be glad to dance at your wedding."

A woman remembers every detail of her wedding day. She remembered the long ride, the organ singing, and the faces turned to watch her marching toward the altar.

Her hand had trembled on her father's arm. *Easy now,* he said, feeling the trembling hand. *There's Robert waiting for you. There's nothing to fear.* And then it was Robert who took her hand, while they stood together listening to the gentle, serious admonitions: *Be patient and loving with each other.*

The rest of that day was jollity, music, dancing, kissing, teasing, and ribald, friendly jokes. The office crowd came, of course, and friends from the hometown came. Darwin's and Helen's friends were all there and Robert had invited the friends he had made in St. Louis; he had been away from Pittsburgh too long to expect people he scarcely knew anymore to come to his wedding.

One relative came, Aunt Jean from Pittsburgh, the uncle in Vancouver not being well enough to travel. It was curious, Lynn reflected now, that such a pleasant, rather self-effacing little woman, with graying curls and a conventional print dress, should have been the cause of one out of the two false notes in the wedding.

It was not her fault. It was Robert's. They were at the family table after the ceremony when Aunt Jean remarked, "Someday I'll have to get at my pile of photographs, label them, and bring them when I come to visit you. There are some of Robert that you just must have, Lynn. You'd never believe it, but his hair—"

"For once, Aunt Jean," Robert interrupted, "will you spare us a description of the blond curls I had when I was a year old? Really, nobody cares."

Chastised, she said nothing more, so that Lynn, with a gentle look of reproach in Robert's direction, said gaily, "I care, Aunt Jean. I want to hear anything you can tell me about Robert and all the family, father, mother, grandparents, cousins—"

"It's a small family," Jean said. "We don't have any cousins at all, on either side."

Then Dad, who had heard only this last remark, cried out, "No cousins? Heck, we'll be glad to lend you some. I've got a dozen on my side alone, in Iowa, Missouri, even two in California." And in his friendly way he inquired whether Jean was related to Robert's mother or his father.

"His mother was my sister."

"He got his music from her, didn't he?" Lynn said. "And his father must have been remarkable, from what Robert tells me."

"Indeed."

"It was such a tragedy, the way they died."

"Yes. Yes, it was."

Dad remarked, "It must have been lonesome when Robert was a kid. Christmas with just his parents and you."

"Well, we did our best," said Jean, "and he grew up, and here he is." She gave Robert a fond smile.

"Yes, here we all are, and let's look forward. Reminiscences are for the old," Robert responded, after which he patted his aunt's hand.

He was making amends for having been sharp toward her. But the mild old woman annoyed him. And there seemed to be no reason why she should.

On a day like this, at a moment of lonely desperation, Lynn thought now, you remember these false notes.

There had been dancing on the deck that Darwin had built with his own hands. In the yard his perennial border was rich with pinks and reds;

peonies and phlox, tiger lilies and oriental poppies, fired the blue dusk. Robert was at the railing, looking down at them.

"Isn't it just lovely what Darwin's done with this house?" Lynn asked.

He smiled—she remembered the smile—and said, "It's all right, I guess, but it's really a dump. I'll give you so much better. You'll see."

He meant it well, but just as it had hurt to hear him reprimand his aunt, it hurt to hear him scoff at Darwin's garden, at Helen's little house. Small things to have remembered for so long. . . .

Each night as they traveled through Mexico, when the door closed on their room, Robert said again, "Isn't it wonderful? Not having to scrounge around for a place to go? Here we are, forever and ever."

Yes, it was wonderful, all of it. The sunny days when, in sneakers and broad straw hats, they climbed Mayan ruins in the Yucatán, when they drank tequilas on the beach, or drove through stony mountain villages, or dined most elegantly in Mexico City.

And there were fourteen nights of passion and love. "Happy?" Robert would inquire in the morning.

"Oh, darling! How can you even ask?"

"You know," he told her one day, "your father's a fine old soul. Guess what he said to me when we were leaving for the airport? 'Be good to my girl,' he said."

She laughed. "That's a sweet, old-fashioned thing to say."

"It's all right. I knew what he meant. And I will be good to you."

"We'll be good to each other. We're on top of the world, you and I."

On the very last day they went shopping in Acapulco. Robert saw something in the window of a men's shop, while at the same time Lynn saw something in the window of another shop just down the street.

"You do your errand while I do mine, and I'll meet you down there," he said.

So they separated. Since she was quickly finished, she walked back up the street to meet him. When some minutes had passed and he had not appeared, she went into the men's shop and learned that he had left a while ago. Puzzled, she walked back. By now a rush of tourists just discharged from a cruise ship filled the sidewalks and spilled out into the traffic on the street. It was impossible to see through the jostling mass. She began to feel the start of alarm. But that was absurd, and fighting it down, she reasoned: He has to be here. Perhaps on the other side of the street. Or down that alley, out of the crowd. Right now he's looking for me. Or maybe, not finding what he wanted, he had gone to the next block.

Alarm returned. When an hour had passed, she decided that her search was making no sense. What made sense, she reasoned, was to go back to the hotel where he had probably also gone and where he would be waiting for her.

When her taxi drew up to the entrance, he was indeed waiting. And she laughed with relief.

"Isn't this the silliest thing? I looked all over for you."

"Silly?" he replied very coldly. "I would hardly call it that. Come upstairs. I want to talk to you."

His unexpected anger dismayed her. And wanting to soothe, she replied lightly, "We must have been walking in circles, looking for each other. A couple of idiots, we are."

"Speak for yourself." He slammed the door of their room. "I was about to go to the front desk and have them call the police when you arrived."

"Police! Whatever for? I'm glad you didn't."

"I told you to wait for me in front of that store, and you didn't do it."

Now, resenting his tone, she countered, "I walked up to meet you. What's wrong with that?"

"I should think the result would tell you what's wrong with it. Disorderly habits, and this is the result. Saying one thing and doing something else."

She said angrily, "Don't lecture me, Robert. Don't make such a big deal out of this."

He was staring at her. And at that moment she realized he was furious. Not angry, but furious.

"I don't believe it!" she cried when he seized her. His hands dug into the flesh of her upper arms and ground it against the bones. In his fury he shook her.

"Let go!" she screamed. "You're hurting me! Let go of my arms!"

His hands pressed deeper; the pain was shocking. Then he flung her onto the bed, where she lay sobbing.

"You hurt me. . . . You hurt me."

As quickly as it had come, his anger went. He picked her up and held her.

"I'm sorry. Oh, I'm sorry. I didn't mean to. But I was terrified, Lynn. You could have been kidnapped—yes, in broad daylight—dragged down an alley, whisked into a car, raped, God knows what. This country is full

of thugs." He kissed her tears. "I was beside myself. Don't you understand?"

He kept kissing her cheeks, her forehead, her hands, and when at last
she turned to him, her lips.

"If anything were to happen to you, I wouldn't want to live. I was so
frightened. I love you so."

She put her arms around his neck. "All right. All right, darling. Robert, forget it, it's over. We misunderstood each other. It's nothing. Nothing."

And all was as it had been, as glorious as ever except for the ugly dark
blue blotches on her arms.

Two days later they were home, visiting her father. It was hot, and forgetting her raw bruises, she put on a sundress.

"What the dickens are those marks?" Dad asked at once. They were
alone in the house.

"Oh, those? I don't know. I don't remember how I got them."

Dad removed his glasses and came closer. "Identical, symmetrical
bruises on both arms. Somebody did that to you with strong, angry hands.
Who was it, Lynn?"

She did not answer.

"Was it Robert? Tell me, Lynn, or I'll ask him myself."

"No. No. Oh, please! It's nothing. He didn't mean it, it's just that he
was so scared." The story spilled out. "It was my fault, really it was. He
was terrified that something had happened to me. He had told me to wait
on the street, and I wandered around the corner and lost my way. My
sense of direction—"

"Has nothing to do with these marks. Don't you think I was ever upset
with your mother from time to time? You can't be married without getting mad at each other. But I never laid a hand on her. It isn't civilized.
No, damn it, it's not. I want to have a little talk with Robert—nothing
nasty, just a sensible little talk."

"No, Dad. You can't. Don't do this to me. Robert is my husband, and I
love him. We love each other. Don't make a big thing out of this."

"It is a big thing to me."

"It's not, and you can't come between us. You mustn't."

Her father sighed. "It was easier when people married somebody from
the same town. You could have a pretty fair idea of what you were
getting."

"Dad, we can't go back to George Washington."

He sighed again. "I feel," he said, "I don't feel—the same about things."

"Meaning that you don't feel the same about Robert."

Now it was he who did not answer. And that exasperated her. The thing was being carried much too far. She saw a crisis looming, one that might change, might color, all their future. So she made herself speak patiently and quietly.

"Dad, this is foolish. Don't worry about me. You're making a big deal out of something that happened once. All right, it shouldn't have, but it did. I want you to put it completely out of your mind, because I have. Okay?" She put her hand on his shoulder. "Okay? Promise?"

He turned, giving her his familiar, reassuring smile. "Well, well, since you want me to, I'll promise. We'll just leave it at that. Since you want me to, Midge."

It was never mentioned again. But neither Helen nor Dad ever had reason to raise any questions about the marriage of Robert and Lynn. They were to any beholder a successful, beautiful pair.

Emily was born eleven months after the wedding. They had scarcely equipped an apartment before Robert bought a house, a ranch house not far from Helen's but twice the size.

"We'll have more children, so we might as well do it now as later," he said.

They went together to furnish the house. Whatever he liked, he bought, and Lynn had only to admire a chair or a lamp, and before she had even glanced at the price, he bought it. In the beginning she worried that money was flowing out too fast. But she saw Robert was earning bonuses as business expanded. And besides, he kept telling her not to worry. Finances were his concern. She never had cash. She charged things and he paid the bills without complaint.

"I wouldn't like that," Helen said once.

"Why should I mind?" Lynn responded, glancing around the pretty nursery where the pretty baby was waking up from a nap. "I have everything. This most of all." And she picked up her daughter, the daughter who already had Robert's bones and black silk hair and dark blue eyes.

Because Robert had been so aware of names, she had chosen the child's name with subtle care. "Names have colors," she told him. " 'Emily' is blue. When I say it with my eyes closed, I see a very high October sky without a cloud."

Caroline was eighteen months later. "Caroline" was a gold so light that it was almost silver.

And memory, a reel of pictures in reverse, sped on. . . .

"What a fabulous house!" Lynn exclaimed.

The house belonged to her neighbor's parents, who were giving the birthday party for their granddaughter, aged five. The terrace was bordered by a lawn, the lawn extended to a distant meadow, and the meadow attached to a pond, which was barely visible at the foot of the slope.

"What a wonderful day for a party!" she exclaimed again.

And it was a wonderful summer day, a cool one, with everything in bloom and a breeze rustling through the oaks. Under these oaks the tables were set for lunch, the children's table dressed in crepe paper with a balloon tied to every chair. It looked, she thought, like a scene in one of those British films where women, wearing silk or white linen, moved against a background of ivy-covered walls. She, whose daily garb was either shorts or jeans, wore yellow silk, and her girls wore pink sister dresses and white Mary Janes.

"They look almost like twins," one of the women remarked. "Caroline's tall for her age, isn't she?"

"We sometimes think she's three going on ten. She's strong and fast and into everything," Lynn said comfortably.

There was probably nothing more satisfying to a parent than knowing that her children were admired. No book, no symphony, no work of art, she was certain, could rival the joy, the pride, and, she reminded herself, the gratitude that came from these creations, these two bright, sweet, healthy little girls.

Gratitude grew when she thought of two friends who were unable to have a child. And all through the lunch and the pleasant gossip she was aware, deep inside, of thankfulness. Life was good.

After lunch a clown arrived to entertain the children, who sat in a circle on the grass. For a little while the mothers watched him, but since the children were absorbed and fascinated, they went back to their tables in the shade.

"Talk about attention span," someone said. "He's kept them amused for more than half an hour."

It was just about time for the party to break up. Emily came trotting to Lynn with a bag full of favors and a balloon.

"Where's Caroline?" asked Lynn.

"I don't know," said Emily.

"But you were sitting together."

"I know," said Emily.

"Well, where can she be?" asked Lynn, feeling a faint rise of alarm and in the same instant driving it down, because of course there could be no reason for alarm here in this place.

"She must have gone to the bathroom."

So they looked in the downstairs bathroom and all through the house; they searched the bushes where possibly she might be hiding, to tease them. Alarm turned to panic. Kidnappers? But how could anybody have come among all these people without being seen? They searched the fields, treading through the long grass. Then they thought, although no one wanted to voice the thought, that perhaps, being an adventurous little girl, Caroline had gone as far as the pond.

And there she lay facedown, in her ruffled pink dress. Quite near the shore she lay in water so shallow that she could have stood up and waded back.

One of the women there was a Red Cross lifesaver. Laying Caroline on the grass, she went to work while Lynn knelt, staring at her child, not believing . . . no, no it was not possible!

People drew the children away from the sight. Someone had called for an ambulance; someone else had called the doctor in the next house. There was a bustle and hurry and yet it was silent; you could almost hear the hush and a following long, collective sigh.

Men came, two young ones wearing white coats. Lynn staggered to her feet, grasped a white sleeve, and begged, "Tell me! Tell me!"

For answer he put a gentle arm around her shoulders. And so she knew. Hearing the women cry, she knew. And yet, "It isn't possible," she said. "No. I don't believe it. No."

She looked around at all the faces, all of them shocked and pitying. And she screamed, screamed at the fair sky, the waving grass, the summer world. Screamed and screamed. Then people took her home.

She was wild with despair and denial. She *knew*, and yet she would not let herself know. They had to hold her down and sedate her.

When she woke up, she was in her living room. The house was crowded. It seemed as if a thousand voices were speaking; doors were opening and closing; the telephone kept ringing and being answered, only to ring again.

Helen said, "Leave her alone, Robert. She's not even awake."

Robert said, "How can she have been so stupid, so careless? She will never forgive herself for this."

She could not decide whether or not to wake up. In one way the dream was unbearable, so perhaps it would be better to open her eyes and be rid of it; but on the other hand perhaps it was not a dream, in which case it would be better to sink into a sleep so deep that she would know nothing.

Still she heard Robert's sobs, repeating, "She will never forgive herself."

There came another voice, belonging to someone who was holding her wrist: "Quiet, please. I'm taking her pulse," it said sharply, and she recognized Bill White, their family doctor.

"You'd better stop this talk about forgiveness," said Bill White. "First of all it's hogwash. This could have happened just as easily if you had been there, Robert. Secondly, you'd better stop it if you don't want to have a very sick woman here for the rest of her life. Don't you think she will torture herself enough as it is?"

And so she had, and so she did still, here on this bench beside Lake Michigan. The images were imprinted on her brain. Caroline laughing at the clown, Caroline—how many minutes later—dead in the water. Emily's little face puckered in tears and terror. She herself surrounded by kind arms and soft words at the heartbreaking funeral.

"I don't know why my aunt had to come," Robert complained. "Who sent for her, anyway?"

"Helen got her number out of my book. She's your family, she's all you have, and she belongs here."

It was strange that he never wanted Jean. She annoyed him, he said. Well, perhaps. Perhaps her very kindness irritated him. Men were like that sometimes. But Jean had been so helpful during those first awful days, comforting Emily in her warm arms and clearing Caroline's room, which neither Lynn nor Robert could have borne to enter.

Somehow they had endured.

"If a marriage can survive this," people declared, "it can survive anything. Imagine the guilt!"

Yes, imagine it if you can, Lynn thought. But Robert had taken Bill White's words to heart. Through many cruel nights he had held her close. And for a long time they had moved softly about the house, speaking in whispers; she had walked on tiptoes until he had gently called her attention to what she was doing. It was he who had saved her sanity. She must remind herself of that whenever things went wrong. . . .

Yet how could a man as forgiving as he had been, so caring of his family, give way to such dreadful rages? Like this one tonight, like all the other sporadic outbursts through the years? To live with Robert was to dwell in sunlight for months and months; then suddenly a flashing storm would turn everything into darkness. And as quickly as it had come the storm would pass, leaving a memory growing fainter in the distance, along with the hope that this time had been the last.

The children never knew, nor must they ever know. For how could she explain to them the thing that she did not herself understand?

Annie especially, Annie so young and vulnerable, must never know! She had been different and difficult from the start. A red baby, dark, raging, squalling red, she was to some extent like that still, a child of moods who could be childishly sweet or curiously adult; one felt at such times that she was seeing right through one's slightest evasion or excuse. Yet she did rather poorly at school. She was overweight and clumsy at sports, although Robert, who did everything so well, tried hard to teach her. She was a secret disappointment to him, Lynn knew. A child of his, although not yet nine, to show not the smallest indication of doing anything well at all!

The full wealth of his love went to Emily, so like himself, tenacious, confident, competent in everything from mathematics to tennis. Beside all that, at fifteen she was already charming the boys. Life would be easy for Emily.

My children . . . Oh, God, if it weren't for them, Lynn cried to herself, I wouldn't go home at all. I'd get on a plane and fly and fly— anywhere, to Australia and beyond. But that was stupid. Stupid to dwell on the impossible. And if she had packed the suit none of this would have happened. It was her own fault. . . .

It was growing colder. A sharper wind blew in suddenly from the lake. Rushing through the trees, it brought the piercing scent of northern spring. Thrusting her hands more deeply into her pockets, Lynn drew the coat tighter against the chill. Her cheek throbbed.

She was a fool to sit here shivering, waiting to be mugged. But she was too sunken in spirit to move or to care. If only there were another woman to hear her woe tonight! Helen, or Josie, wise, kind Josie, the best friend either Helen or she had ever had. They called themselves the three musketeers.

"We've transferred a new man to be my assistant for marketing," Robert had announced one day more than seven years ago. "Bruce Lehman from Milwaukee. Jewish and very pleasant, but I'm not wildly enthusiastic. He strikes me as kind of a lightweight. No force. It's hard to describe, but I recognize it when I see it in a man. You'd like him, though. He's well read and collects antiques. His wife's a social worker. No children. You'll have to call and ask them over to the house. It's only right."

That was the start of their friendship. If I could only talk to her now, thought Lynn. Yet when the moment came, I probably wouldn't tell the truth. Josie would analyze, and I would shrivel under her clinical analysis.

As for confiding this to Helen, that's impossible. She warned me against Robert once long, long ago, and I will not go whimpering to her or anyone. I will handle this myself, although God knows how.

She stiffened. Her heart pounded. Out of the violet shadows beyond the lamplight a slatternly woman, drunken or drugged, came shuffling toward her and stopped.

"Sitting alone in the dark? And you've got a black eye," she said, peering closer. When she touched Lynn's arm, Lynn, shrinking, looked into an old, sad, brutal face.

"I suppose you ran into a door. A door with fists." The woman laughed and sat down on the bench. "You'll have to think of a better one than that, my dear."

Lynn got up and ran to the avenue, where traffic still streamed. The woman had given her such a fright that, in spite of the cold, she was sweating. There was no choice but to go back to the hotel. When the elevator stopped at her floor, she felt an impulse to turn about and go down again. Yet she could not very well sleep on the street. And maybe Robert was so angry that he would not even be in the room. She put the key in the lock and opened the door.

Fully dressed, he was sitting on the bed with his face in his hands. When he saw her he jumped up, and she saw that he was frantic.

"I looked for you everywhere. It's midnight," he cried. "Long past midnight. In God's name, where were you? I looked for you all through the hotel, up and down the streets, everywhere. I thought—I don't know what I thought." His face was haggard, and his hoarse voice shook.

"What's the difference where I was?"

"I didn't know what you might have done. I was terrified."

"There's no need to be. I'm all right." In one piece, anyway, she thought.

When she took the scarf off and moved into the full glare of lamplight, Robert looked away. He got up and stood at the window, staring out into the darkness. She watched his stooped shoulders and felt shame for him, for herself, and for the entity known as Mr. and Mrs. Robert Ferguson, respectable and respected parents and citizens.

Presently, still with his back turned to her, he spoke. "I have a quick temper. Sometimes I overreact. But I've never really hurt you, have I? Other than a slap now and then? And how often have I done that?"

Often enough. Yet not all that often. But the sting of humiliation far outlasted the momentary physical sting. The bruise of humiliation far outlasted the bruise on the upper arms where fingers had gripped and shaken. And a deep sigh came out of her very heart.

"When did it happen last?" he asked, as if he were pleading. "I don't think you can even remember, it was so long ago."

"Yes, yes I can. It was last Thanksgiving week, when Emily didn't get home till two A.M. and you were in a rage. And I thought, after we talked it over and you were so sorry, that it was to be really the last time, that we were finished with all that."

"I meant it to be. I did," he replied, still in the pleading tone. "But we don't live in a perfect world. Things happen that shouldn't happen."

"But why, Robert? Why?"

"I don't know. I hate myself afterward, every time."

"Won't you go and talk to someone? Get some help. Find out why."

"I don't need it. I'll pull myself up by my own bootstraps." When she was silent before this familiar reply, he continued, "Tell the truth, Lynn. You know I'm a loving, good husband to you all the rest of the time, and a good father too. You know I am." He turned to her then, pleading, "Don't you?"

She was silent.

"I did wrong tonight, even though some of it was an accident. But I told you how awfully important it was. I could only think of what it could mean to us. New York with a fifty-percent raise, maybe. And after that, who knows?" His hands were clenched around the wooden rail of the chair's back as though he would break it. The pleading continued. "It's hard, Lynn, a struggle every day. I don't always tell you, I don't want to burden you, but it's a dog-eat-dog world. That's why that woman steered you wrong about the suit. People do things like that. You can't imagine it because you're so honest, so decent, but believe me, it's true. You have to be alert every minute of your life. There's never a minute that I'm not thinking of us, you and me and the girls. We're one, a tight little unit in an indifferent world. In the last analysis we're the only ones who really care about each other."

At his urging she was slipping inch by inch back into reality, and she knew it. Children, family, house. And the man standing here to whom all these ties connected her. Impulsive thoughts of airplanes flying to the ends of the earth, of floating free and new, were not reality. . . . Home, children, friends, job, school, home, children—

A sudden thought interrupted this litany. "What did you tell Bruce?"

"What I told everybody, that the bag with my dinner jacket was lost."

She heard him making an easy joke of it. *My suit may be on a plane to the Fiji Islands, or more likely, it's still in St. Louis.* He was laughing, making everyone else laugh with him.

"That's not what I meant. What did you say about me?"

"Just said you weren't feeling well. I was vague about it."

"Yes, I daresay you would have to be," she said bitterly.

"Lynn, Lynn, can't we wipe the slate clean? I promise, promise, that I will guard my temper and never, never, so help me, God—" His voice broke.

Exhausted, she sat down on the bed. Let the night be over fast, she prayed. Let morning come, let's get out of this hateful room.

He sat down next to her. "I stopped at a drugstore and got some stuff," he said with a bottle of medicine in hand.

"I don't want it."

"Please let me."

She was too tired to struggle. He had taken a first-aid course and knew how to touch her cheek with care. Softly, softly, his fingers bathed her temples with coolness.

"Doesn't that feel better?"

Unwilling to give him satisfaction, she conceded only, "It's all right."

Relaxed against the pillows, she saw through half-closed eyes that he had unpacked her overnight bag and, meticulous as always, had hung up her robe and nightgown in the closet.

"Your poor, darling, lovely face. I wish you would hit me. Make a fist and let me have it."

"What good would that do?"

"Maybe you'd feel better."

"I don't need to get even. That's not me, Robert."

"I know. I know it isn't." He closed the bottle. "There, that's enough. There won't be any mark, I can tell. That damn door had a mighty sharp edge, though. The management ought to be told. It's so easy to trip there."

It was true. She had tripped. But would she have if his hand had not threatened? It was hard to be accurate in describing an accident. The event flashes past in seconds and the recollection is confused.

She sighed and mourned, "I'm so tired. I don't think I've ever been so tired."

"Turn over and let me undo your dress. I'll rub your back."

Anger still boiled in her chest, a sorrowful, humiliated anger. Yet at the same time, a subtle, physical relief was beginning to wear it down. Robert's persisting hands, slowly, ever so slowly and firmly, were easing the tension in her neck and between her shoulder blades. Her eyes closed. As if hypnotized, she floated.

How intimately he knew her body! It was as if he knew it as well as she knew it, as if he knew it as well as he knew his own, as if they were one body. One . . .

Minutes passed, whether a few or many or even half an hour, she could not have said. But as finally he turned her over, she felt no resistance. Half waking, half dreaming, her willing arms accepted.

When she awoke, he was already dressed.

"I've been up for an hour. It's a bright, beautiful day. I've been watching boats far out on the lake. Would you like to take a walk down there? We can always get a later flight home."

She saw that he was testing her mood.

"Whatever you want. I don't mind either way."

It was not important. She was testing her own mood, which was important. Last night the darkness had been a horror down there near the lake. But those were morbid, useless thoughts now. And something she had read only a short time ago now crossed her mind: A majority of Americans, even in these days, still see nothing so terrible about a husband's occasional blow. Surely this was a curious thing to be remembering now. Perhaps it was a lesson for her. What do you want of life, Lynn? She might as well ask. Perfection? And she admonished herself: Grow up. Be realistic. Look forward, not back.

Besides, you love him. . . .

He sat down on the bed. He smoothed her hair. "I know you must be thinking you look awful, but you don't, take my word for it."

Gingerly, she felt her cheekbone. It did seem as though the swelling had diminished.

"Go put on some makeup. I'll order room service for breakfast. You must be starved."

"I had a sandwich yesterday at lunch."

"A big breakfast, then. Bacon, eggs, the works."

When she came out of the bathroom, he was moving the table on which the breakfast had been laid. "These waiters never do it just right. You'd think they'd know enough to put the table where one can enjoy the view. There, that's better. As soon as we're finished, I want you to go out with me. We've an errand on the avenue."

"What is it?"

"A surprise. You'll see."

In the elevator they met Bruce Lehman.

"I thought you'd have gone home by now," Robert said.

"No, I've got to pick up something first. Remember? How are you feeling, Lynn? We missed you last night." He was carefully not looking straight at her.

Robert answered. "She fell and was too embarrassed to go to the dinner with a lump on her face."

"A bruise can't spoil you, as pretty as you are," Bruce said, now turning his full gaze to her.

Josie liked to say that she had married him because his eyes had a friendly twinkle, and he liked cats. This twinkle was visible even behind his glasses. He reminded Lynn of a photograph in some advertisement of country life, a sturdy type in a windbreaker, tramping a field, accompanied by a pair of little boys or big dogs.

"Mind if we go with you?" asked Robert. "You gave me a very good idea last night."

"Of course not. Come along. I bought a bracelet yesterday for Josie," Bruce explained to Lynn. "I wanted them to engrave her initials on it and it will be ready this morning."

"I was going to surprise Lynn," Robert chided lightly. "Well, no matter. We'll be there in a minute, anyway."

She was disturbed. There was a right time for gifts, a right mood for receiving them. And she remonstrated, "Robert, I don't need anything. Really."

"No one ever *needs* jewelry. But if Bruce can have the pleasure, why can't I have it?"

In the shop, which was itself a small jewel of burnished wood, velvet carpet, and crystal lights, Bruce displayed the narrow gold bangle he had ordered.

"Like it, Lynn? Do you think Josie will?"

"It's lovely. She'll be so happy with it."

"Well, it won't make up for the mastectomy, God knows, but I thought —a little something, I thought—" His voice quavered and he stopped.

Robert had gone to the other side of the shop and now summoned Lynn.

"Come here, I want you to look at this."

Set in a web of woven gold threads was a row of cabochon stones— rubies, sapphires, and emeralds in succession.

"This," Robert said, "is what I call a bracelet."

"Byzantine," the salesman explained. "Handwoven. The originals are in museums."

"Try it on, Lynn."

The price tag was too small to be legible, but she knew enough without asking, and so replied, "It's much too expensive."

"Let me be the judge of that," Robert objected. "If I'm going to buy, I'm not going to buy junk. Either the best or nothing. Try it on."

Obeying, she went to the mirror. Unaccustomed to such magnificence, she felt an awkwardness; she had the air of a young girl.

When Bruce came over, Robert commanded her, "Show Bruce what you're getting."

"It's Robert's idea. I really don't—" she began.

Bruce laid his hand on her arm and quite oddly, she thought, corrected her. "It's beautiful. Take it. You deserve it," and to Robert added, "We have good wives. They deserve our best."

So the purchase was concluded.

"Keep the bracelet in your pocketbook," Robert said. "It's not insured yet, and the suitcase might get lost."

"Like yours," Bruce said.

"You didn't want the bracelet," Robert said when they were flying home, "because you think I was trying to make up for what I did yesterday. But you're wrong. And it's nothing compared with what I'll be giving you someday." He chuckled. "On the other hand, compared with what that cipher bought for Josie—"

"Why do you call Bruce a cipher? He's one of the most intelligent people we know."

"You're right, and I used the wrong word. What I meant was that he'll never set the world on fire. That much I can tell you."

"Maybe he doesn't want to," she retorted with mild indignation.

"He does his work at the office all right and makes a good impression, but in my opinion he lacks brilliance, the kind that keeps a man staying late and coming back on Saturday when everyone else is taking it easy."

"He's had to be home a lot with Josie when she was so awfully sick, you know that. Now that she's so much better, it'll be different."

"Well, they're an odd couple, anyway. She effervesces like a bottle of fizz, while he has the personality of a clam."

"That's not true. He's just not talkative. He listens." And she said quietly, "You've never liked Bruce and Josie, have you?"

"Now, that's not true either." Robert clasped her hand, which lay on the armrest. "Oh, the dickens with everybody except us, anyway. Lynn, I've got a good hunch that there's a big change in the air for us. Things were said last night both to me and about me that make it fairly sure I'll be tapped for the New York post. What have you got to say about that?"

"That I'm not surprised. If anyone deserves it, you do."

"I'll be in charge of marketing the whole works from the Mississippi to the Atlantic."

She was having a private thought, vaguely lonesome: I shall miss Helen and Josie.

"They may be sending one or two others from here, under me, of course. There's a general switching going on all over the map."

"I hope Bruce goes."

"Because of Josie, naturally. You depend too much on her, Lynn."

"I don't depend on her at all. I don't know how you can say that."

"I can say it because I see it." After a minute he mused. "New York. Then, who knows? The international division. Overseas. London. Paris. Up and up to the very top. Company president when I'm fifty. It's possible, Lynn. Just have faith in me."

He was an exceptional man, not to be held back. Everyone knew it, and she, his wife, knew it most of all. Again he clasped her hand, turning upon her his infectious, brilliant smile.

"Love me? With all my faults?"

Love him. Joined to him, no matter what. From the very first day. No matter what. Explain it? As soon explain the force of the rising tide.

"Love me?" he persisted.

"Yes," she said. "Oh, yes."

Part Two

◇

Spring 1988

◇ 2 ◇

THE house lay comfortably on a circle of lawn and spread its wings against the dark rise of hills behind it. The architect, who had built it for himself, had brought beams from old New England barns and pine paneling from old houses to recreate the eighteenth century within commuting distance of Manhattan. The windows had twelve lights; and the fanlight at the front door was authentic.

Robert had found the property on his initial visit to New York and had come home filled with nervous enthusiasm. Connecticut was the place! It had charm. It had atmosphere. The schools were good. The neighborhoods were safe. There were wonderful open spaces. Imagine three wooded acres on a narrow, rural road with no one in sight except for the house directly opposite, and that, too, a treasure out of *Architectural Digest*.

Of course, it was expensive. But with his salary and his prospects a mortgage would be no problem. She had only to read the items about his promotion in *The Wall Street Journal* and in *Forbes* magazine to know where he was headed. Besides, a house like this one was an investment, a setting for entertaining—to say nothing of its being an investment in happy living for themselves. Once Lynn had seen the place, and if she liked it, then she must get busy right away and furnish it well. There must be no piecemeal compromises; a first-class decorator must do it all.

She would fall in love with it, he was certain; already he could see her working in the flower beds with her garden gloves and her big straw sun-hat on.

So they got out a bottle of champagne and, sitting at the kitchen table, toasted each other and their children and General American Appliance and the future.

Now in late spring, the evening air blew its fragrance through the open windows in the dining room. And lilacs, the source of this fragrance, reared their mauve heads and their healthy leafage above the sills.

"Listen, a mockingbird! I can't imagine when he ever sleeps," Lynn said. "I hear him the last thing when I fall asleep, and in the morning when I wake, he's still singing."

Josie's black eyes, too prominent in her thin, birdlike face, smiled at Lynn.

"You do love this place, don't you?"

"Oh, I do. I know I felt in the beginning that the house was too big, but Robert was right, we really do spread out so comfortably here. And as for its being too expensive, I still have a few doubts, but I leave all that to him."

"My wife is frugal," said Robert.

"A lot of men would like to have that complaint," Josie remarked. She spoke quickly, as was her habit. And again it seemed to Lynn that her remarks to Robert, however neutral, so often had a subtle edge.

Then again it seemed to her that whenever Bruce followed Josie in his so different, deliberate way, it was with an intention to smooth that edge.

"You've done a wonder with the house." His gaze went over Robert's head toward the wide hall in which rivers, trees, and mountains repeated themselves on the scenic wallpaper, and then beyond to the living room where on chairs and rugs and at the windows a mélange of cream, moss-green, and dusty pink evoked the gardens of Monet.

Lynn followed his gaze. The house had indeed been done to a refined perfection. Sometimes, though, when she was left alone in it to contemplate these rooms, she had a feeling that they were frozen in their perfection as if preserved in amber.

"As for us," Bruce was saying, "will you believe that after two years we still have unopened cartons of books in the basement? We left St. Louis in such a hurry, we just threw things together, we never expected to be transferred, it was all so unexpected—" He laughed. "The truth is that we aren't known for our neatness, anyway, neither Josie nor I."

Josie corrected him. "When you have work to do for the company, you're one of the most efficient people I've ever seen."

Robert shook his head. "We were completely settled in a week. I personally can't function with disorder around me. I'm internally compelled toward order. I know that about myself. If a sign says KEEP OFF THE GRASS, I have to obey, while there are other people who have to challenge the sign by walking on the grass." He sighed. "People are crazy."

"I can attest to that," said Josie. "The things I see and hear in my daily work—" She did not finish.

"I wish you'd tell me some of them, Aunt Josie. I keep asking you."

Everyone turned to Emily. There was a fraction of a second's silence, no longer than a collective indrawn breath, as if the four adults had simultaneously been struck by an awareness of the girl's beauty in her yellow dress, with her black silk hair flowing out under a cherry-colored bandeau and the shaft of evening sunshine on her eager face.

"I will, whenever you want. But so much is tragedy, sordid tragedy." And with gentle curiosity Josie asked, "What makes you so interested?"

"You know I'm going to be a doctor, and doctors need to understand people."

There was a fullness in Lynn's throat, a silent cry: How lovely she is! How dear they both were, her girls! And she was thankful for their flourishing; they had taken the move so well and found their places in the new community.

"Emily did incredibly on her PSATs," Robert said. "Oh, I know you don't like me to boast about you, darling, but sometimes I can't help it. So forgive me. I am just so proud of you."

Annie's round face under its halo of pale, kinky hair turned to her father. And Lynn said, "Our girls both work hard. Annie comes home from school, goes right to the piano to practice, and then to her homework. I never have to remind you, do I, Annie?"

The child turned now to her mother. "May I have the rest of the soufflé before it collapses? Look, all the air's going out of it."

Indeed the remaining section of the chocolate fluff was slowly settling into a moist slab at the bottom of the bowl.

"No, you may not," Robert answered as Annie shoved her plate under Lynn's nose. "You're fat enough. You shouldn't have had any in the first place."

Annie's mouth twisted into the square shape of tragedy, an outraged sob came forth, she sprang up, tumbling her chair onto its back, and fled.

"Come back at once and pick up your chair," commanded Robert.

In reply the back door slammed. Everyone took care not to look at anyone else until Emily spoke, reproaching gently, "You embarrassed her, Dad."

"What do you mean? We're not strangers here. Aunt Josie and Uncle Bruce knew her before she was born."

"But you know how she hates being told she's fat."

"She has to face reality. She is fat."

"Poor little kid," Lynn murmured. A little kid who didn't like herself, not her fat, nor the kinky hair that she had inherited from some unknown ancestor. Who could know her secret pain? "Do go after her, Robert. She's probably in the usual place behind the toolshed."

Robert stood up, laid his napkin on the table, and nodded toward the Lehmans. "If you'll excuse me. She's impossible. . . ." he said as he went out, leaving a dull silence behind him.

At the sideboard Lynn poured coffee. Robert had bought the heavy silver coffee service at Tiffany as a "house gift to ourselves." At this moment its formality in the presence of Bruce and Josie made her feel awkward; it would have been natural to bring the percolator in from the kitchen as they had always done. But Robert wanted her to use all these fine new things, "Or else, why have them?" he always said, which, she had to admit, did make some sense. Her hand shook the cup, spilling a few drops. It was an uneasy moment, anyway, in this humming silence.

It was Emily who broke through it. At seventeen she already had social poise. "So you're all going to the Chinese auction for the hospital tonight?"

"I've been racking my brains," Josie reported, "and the best thing I can come up with is to offer three nights of baby-sitting."

"Well, if you need references," Emily said gaily, "tell them to call me. You and Uncle Bruce sat for us often enough, goodness knows."

Lynn had recovered. "I'll give a 'dinner party for eight at your house.' "

"Dad's offering three tennis lessons. He's better than the coach we had last year at school."

"What's this about me?" asked Robert. He came in with his arm around Annie's shoulder and, without waiting for an answer, announced cheerfully, "We've settled the problem, Annie and I. Here it is. One luscious, enormous dessert, as enormous as she wants, once a week, and no sweets, none at all, in between. As a matter of fact, that's a good rule for all of us, no matter what we weigh. Good idea, Lynn?"

"Very good," she said gratefully. As quickly as Robert could blunder into a situation, so quickly could he find the way out.

He continued. "Annie, honey, if you finish your math homework tonight, I'll review it tomorrow and then we'll go ahead to the next assignment so you'll have a leg up on the rest of the class. You will surprise the teacher. How's that?" The child gave a nod. "Ah, come, Annie, smile a little." A small smile crossed the still mottled cheeks. "That's better. You staying with Annie tonight, Emily?"

"Going to the movies, Dad, it's Friday."

"Not with that boy Harris again?"

"Yes, with that boy Harris again."

Robert did not answer. Emily must be the only person in the world who can cause him to falter, Lynn thought.

"Eudora's going to sit tonight," she said. "Emily dear, I think I hear Harris's car."

"You can hear it a mile away. It needs a new muffler," Robert said.

An instant later Emily admitted Harris. He was a tall, limber youth with a neat haircut, well-pressed shirt, and a friendly, white-toothed greeting. It seemed to Lynn that health and cheer came with him. Now he was holding by the collar a large, lumbering dog whose long, ropy hair was the shape and color of wood shavings.

"Hello, Mr. Ferguson, Mrs. Ferguson, Mr. and Mrs. Lehman. I think your Juliet's got something in her ear. She was wriggling around outside trying to rub it on the grass. If somebody'll hold her, I'll try to take a look."

"Not in the living room on the light carpet, please," Robert said.

"No, sir. Is it all right here in the hall?"

"Yes, lay her down."

It was not easy to wrestle with Juliet. Emily held her legs and Robert pressed on her shoulders. Harris probed through the hairy tangle of her ear.

"Be careful. She may snap," Lynn warned.

Harris shook his head. "Not Juliet. She knows I'm trying to help." His fingers searched. "If it's inside the ear—no, I don't see anything, unless it's something internal, but I don't think so—if it is, she'll have to see the vet—sorry, poor girl—am I hurting you? Oops, I think I felt—yes, I did—hey, I've got it, it's a tiny burr stuck in the hair—ouch, that hurts—wait, old lady—I'll need a scissors, Mrs. Ferguson. I'll need to cut some hair."

"She won't miss it," Lynn told him, handing the scissors. "I've never seen such a hairy dog."

"You'd make a fine vet," Bruce said, "or M.D., either one."

Harris, still on his knees, looked up and smiled. "That's what I plan. Emily and I are both in Future Doctors of America."

"Well, you've certainly got a way with animals. Juliet even seems to be thanking you," Bruce said kindly.

"We've always had animals in our house, so I'm used to them," Harris explained, stroking the dog's head. "Just last week we lost one old dog. He was sixteen, almost as old as I am, and I do miss him."

Bruce nodded. "I know what you mean. What kind was he?"

"Just Heinz 57, the all-American dog."

"Juliet is a Bergamasco," Robert said. "I had a hard time finding one, I can tell you."

"I'd never even heard the name until Emily told me what she was."

"Not many people have. It's a very rare breed in this country. Italian."

Lynn laughed. "I don't think she gives a darn about being rare, do you, Juliet?"

The dog yawned, settling back under the boy's stroking hand. Harris spoke to her.

"You feel a lot better now that you're rid of that thing, don't you?"

"Oh, Juliet, we do love you, you funny-looking, messy girl!" Emily exclaimed. "Although I always did want an Irish setter."

"Everybody has an Irish setter," Robert said. He looked at his watch. "Well, shall we go? Leave your car here, Bruce. You can pick it up on your way home. And, Emily, don't be too late."

"That's a nice boy," Bruce remarked as always, when they were in the car.

Lynn agreed. "Yes, he's responsible and thoughtful. I never worry about Emily when he drives. Some of the others—"

"What others?" Robert interrupted. "It seems to me that she's always with him. And I don't like it. I don't like it at all."

"You read too much into it," Lynn said gently. "They're just high school kids."

"Emily is not 'just' anything. She's an exceptional, gifted girl, and I don't want to see her wasting her time. Yes, the boy's nice enough, and his family's probably respectable. The father's a policeman—"

"Is that what you object to?" Josie said bluntly. "That his father's a policeman?"

Lynn cringed. Intimate as she was with her old friend, the secret of Robert's and Josie's dislike for each other remained unacknowledged between them. Neither woman wanted to open this particular Pandora's box.

Bruce gave his wife a mild rebuke. "Of course he doesn't mean that."

It seemed to Lynn that Bruce and she were too often called upon to smooth rough passages. And she said impatiently, "What a waste of words! A pair of seventeen-year-olds."

"Well, I don't know," Bruce said somewhat surprisingly. "Josie and I fell in love when we were in high school."

"That was different," Robert grumbled. "Emily's different. She has a future in the world, and she can't afford to play with it."

"I thought you were still one of those men who think women are better off in the house," Josie told him.

Again Lynn had to cringe. It was a relief that before Robert could reply, the car arrived at the entrance to the country club.

The membership had gotten behind the hospital's gigantic fund drive. Actually, it had been Robert who had brought about the liaison between the club and the hospital's trustees. It was remarkable that after only two years in this community, he had become well enough known for at least ten people to stop and greet him before he had even passed through the lobby.

The auction, in the long room that faced the golf course, was about to begin. Flanking the podium, two tables held sundry donations: glass candlesticks, dollhouse furniture, and an amateurish painting of ducks floating on a pond. On one side there hung a new mink jacket, a contribution from one of the area's best shops.

Robert paused to consider it. "How about this?" he whispered.

Lynn shook her head. "Of course not. You know how I feel about fur."

"Okay, I won't force it on you. On second thought, if you should ever change your mind, I wouldn't buy this one. It looks cheap." He moved on. "How about the dollhouse furniture for Annie?"

"She hasn't got a dollhouse."

"Well, buy her one for her birthday. Let her fix it up herself. Annie needs things to occupy her mind. What's this? Do I recognize a menorah?"

"You do," said Bruce from behind him. "I inherited three from various relatives, and since we hardly need three, I thought I'd contribute one. It's a Czech piece, about a hundred years old, and should bring a very good price."

"I doubt it. There are no Jews in this club."

"But there are some in the neighborhood, and they always give generously," Bruce said, sounding unusually firm.

"That's well known," Lynn offered, worrying that Robert's remark might have sounded too brusque.

Robert moved on again. "Hey, look here. Two Dickenses from 1890. *Bleak House* and *Great Expectations*. These are finds, Lynn." He lowered his voice. "We have to buy something. It wouldn't look right if we didn't. Anyway, I want these."

With the appearance of the auctioneer the audience ceased its rustle and bustle. One by one, with approval and jokes, various offers were made and accepted: Josie to baby-sit, Robert to give tennis lessons, Lynn to give a dinner, and a few dozen more. All went for generous prices. A delighted lady with blue-rinsed hair got the mink jacket, the doll furniture went to the Fergusons, as did the two volumes of Dickens. And Bruce's menorah brought three thousand dollars from an antiques dealer.

Robert said only, "I could use a cup of coffee," as the crowd dispersed into the dining room, where dessert was to be served.

Robert and Lynn saved places for the Lehmans.

"It gets a little sticky," he whispered as they sat down. "We should be mingling with people here, and yet I should be with Bruce too."

"He seems to be doing all right," Lynn observed, for Bruce and Josie were standing in an animated little group. "They make friends easily," she went on.

"Yes, when he makes the effort. He should make it more often for his own good. Well, I'm not going to waste time sitting here waiting for them. There are a dozen people I ought to see, and I want to get the tally besides. We must have made over twenty thousand, at least. I want to get hold of a local editor, too, and make sure that my name is in the write-up and that General American Appliance gets credit."

Robert's fingers drummed on the table. "No. Tomorrow morning will be better for that. A few private words over the telephone away from this crowd will accomplish more."

Josie, Bruce, and another man had detached themselves from their group and now came over to the table. Bruce made introductions.

"This is Tom Lawrence, who bought your dinner offer, Lynn, so I thought you two ought to meet."

Robert said cordially, "Please join us, Mr. Lawrence, you and Mrs. Lawrence."

"Thanks, I will. But there is no Mrs. Lawrence. Not anymore." The man's smile had a touch of mischief, as if he were amused at himself. "You assumed I had a wife, or else why would I be bidding on a dinner party? I can't blame you, but the fact is that although I keep a bachelor's house, I like to entertain." He turned to Lynn. "Bruce told me that you're a fabulous cook and I ought to bid on your dinner. So I did."

"You bid more than it's worth," Lynn said. "I hope you won't be disappointed."

"I'm sure I won't be." Now Lawrence turned to Robert. "And you're the man, I noticed, who got my Dickens. A fair exchange."

"Not really. They're handsome books. I wonder that you parted with them."

"For the same reason that Bruce here parted with his candle holder— menorah, I mean. Both my grandfathers were book collectors, and since I'm not a collector of anything, it seemed to me that I didn't need duplicates. Also," he said somewhat carelessly, "one of my grandfathers helped found this club and the hospital, too, so the cause has extra-special meaning for me."

"Ah, yes. Lawrence Lawrence. The plaque in St. Wilfred's lobby."

Lynn, watching, knew that Robert was taking the man's measure. He would recognize assurance and alacrity. Now Robert was asking how Bruce and he had become acquainted.

"We met while jogging on the high school track," Lawrence responded. "We seem to keep pretty much the same schedule."

"You must live near the school, then."

"I do now. I gave up a bigger house after my divorce. I used to live out on Halsey Road," he said in the same careless way.

"That's where we are!" Lynn exclaimed. "We bought the Albright house."

"Did you? Beautiful place. I've been at many a great party there."

"You should see it now. We've done so much with it that you might not recognize it," Robert said. "It needed a lot of work."

"Really," said Lawrence. "I never noticed."

He doesn't like Robert, Lynn thought. No, that's absurd. Why shouldn't he? I'm always imagining things.

Suddenly Josie laughed. "Do you know something funny? Look at Lynn and look at Tom. Does anybody see what I see?"

"No, what?" asked Robert.

"Why, look again. They could be brother and sister. The same smooth sandy hair, the short nose, the cleft chin—it's uncanny."

"If so, I'm honored." And Lawrence made a little bow toward Lynn.

"I don't see it at all," Robert said.

The instant's silence contained embarrassment, as if a social blunder had been made. Yet Josie's remark had been quite harmless.

And Lynn said pleasantly, "You must tell me when you want your dinner for eight, Mr. Lawrence."

"Tom's the name. I'll get my list together and call you. Will the week after next be all right?"

"Don't forget we are taking Emily to visit Yale," Robert cautioned.

"I won't forget. The week after next will be fine."

Presently, the room began to empty itself. People looked at their watches and made the usual excuses to depart. The evening had played itself out.

"Who is this fellow Lawrence, anyway?" Robert inquired on the way home.

Bruce explained. "He's a bright guy, and partner in a big New York law firm."

"That doesn't tell me much. There are a lot of bright guys in big New York firms."

"I don't know much more than that, except that he's been divorced a couple of times, he's close to fifty, and looks a lot younger. And I know he comes from what you'd call an important family," Bruce added with what Lynn took to be a touch of humor.

"I'm not happy about having Lynn go over to a strange man's house."

"Oh," Lynn said, "don't be silly. Does he look like a rapist?"

"I don't know. What does a rapist look like?" Robert gave a loud, purposeful sigh. "My wife is still an innocent."

"It's a dinner party for eight. And I'm planning to take Eudora to help. So that should make you feel better. Really, Robert."

"All right, all right, I'll feel better if you want me to."

"People were saying some nice things about you tonight, Robert," Bruce said. "About the hospital, of course, and also the big pledge you got GAA to make to the Juvenile Blindness campaign."

"Yes, yes. You see, you people used to think all that had nothing to do with marketing electronic appliances, but I hope you see now that it does. Anything that connects the name of GAA to a good cause counts. And the contacts one makes in the country club all connect to these causes and their boards. You really ought to join a club, Bruce."

"You know I can't join this one."

"That's disgusting," Lynn said. "It makes me want to stand up and fight."

"You may want to but you'd better not. I keep reminding you," Robert told her, "that reality has to be faced. Bruce is smart enough to accept it. Join a Jewish club, Bruce. There are a couple just over the Westchester line. And the company'll pay. They'll be glad to."

Lynn, looking back from the front seat, could see Bruce's shrug.

"Josie and I never did go for club life, Jewish or not."

"It's time you began, then." Robert spoke vigorously. "You need to get on some of these boards, go to the dinners and have your wife go to the luncheons. You owe it to the firm and to yourself."

"I do what I can," Bruce answered.

"Well, think about what I'm telling you. And you, too, Josie."

Lynn interjected, "Josie works. And anyway, I can't imagine her exchanging gossip with company wives. You have to be careful of what you say. They judge everything, your opinions, your clothes, everything. Some of those afternoons can wear one out."

"It's the price you pay for being who you are and where you are. You'll think it a small enough price, too, if it leads to a big job in Europe," Robert declared.

A small chilly dread sank in Lynn's chest. She knew the pattern of promotion: two or three years in each of several European countries, then possibly the home office in New York again. Or else a spell in the Far East with another return. And no permanence, no roots, no place to plant a maple sapling and see it grow. There were myriads of people who would forgo a thousand maples for such opportunities, and that was fine for them, but she was not one of those people.

Yet Robert was. And he would well deserve his rewards when they came. Never, never, she thought as always, must she by the slightest deed or word hold him back.

As if he were reading her mind, at that very moment Bruce remarked, "When there's another big job in Europe, and with all that's happening abroad, there's bound to be one soon, you're the man to get it, Robert. Everybody knows that."

Later when they were reading in bed, Robert asked, "What are you doing tomorrow?"

"I'm taking Josie and a few friends to lunch, remember? It's her birthday."

"Missing the women's tennis tournament?"

"I have to. Josie works all week, so Saturday is the only day we can make it."

After a moment Robert, laying his book aside, said decidedly, "Josie's too opinionated. I've always said so. It's a wonder to me why he isn't sick of her, except that he's too much of a weakling, a yes-man, to do anything about it."

"Sick of her! Good Lord, he's no yes-man, he adores her! And as to being opinionated, she's not. She's merely honest, that's all. She's outspoken."

"Well, well, if you say so. I guess I'm just a male chauvinist who's uncomfortable with outspoken women."

Lynn laughed. "Our Emily's a pretty outspoken woman, I'd say."

"Ah, that's different." And Robert laughed too. "She's my daughter. She can do anything she wants."

"Except choose her own boyfriends?"

"Lynn, I only want what's best for her. Wouldn't I give my life for her? For all of you?"

"Dear Robert, I know that."

He picked up his book and she went back to hers. Presently Robert laid his down again.

"By the way, did you have the fender fixed where you scraped it?"

"Yes, this morning."

"Did they do a good job?"

"You'd never know there'd been a mark."

"Good. There's no sense riding around in a marked-up car." Then he thought of something else; it was as if he kept a memo book in his head, Lynn often told him.

"Did you send a birthday present to my aunt?"

"Of course I did. A beautiful summer bag."

"That's right, considering all those sweaters she knits for the girls."

There was a hurtful, grudging quality in this comment that Lynn was unable to ignore.

"Robert, I think you treat her very badly."

"Nonsense. I was perfectly nice to her last year at Christmas."

"You were polite, that's all, and it wasn't last year, it was the year before. The reason she didn't come last year was that she felt you didn't want her. You, not I. I actually like her. She's a kind, gentle lady."

"She may be kind and gentle, but she's a garrulous old fool and she gets on my nerves."

"Garrulous! She hardly opens her mouth when you're around."

He did not answer. And Lynn persisted.

"Emily's very fond of her. She had a lovely afternoon tea when Jean was visiting in New York last month."

"All right. Leave me alone about Aunt Jean, will you? It's unimportant."

He turned and, in pulling the blanket with him, dropped the book with a loud thump onto the floor.

"Sorry. Damn! I'm restless."

She put her hand on his arm. "Tell me what's really bothering you."

"Well, you may think it's foolish of me, you probably will think so. But I told you, I don't like the idea of your going to cook dinner in another man's house where there's no wife. I wish to hell you had thought of something else to contribute to the auction."

"But cooking is what I do best. It'll be fun. Didn't you watch the bidding? He paid a thousand dollars for my services, I want you to know."

"Bruce shoved him onto you. That's what happened."

"You're surely not going to be annoyed with Bruce. Robert, how silly can you be?"

"I don't like the man's looks. Divorced, and divorced again, and—"

Trying to tease him out of his mood, she said, "Apparently he looks like me, so you should—"

"So yes, he is something like you, and you—"

He turned again, this time toward Lynn, to meet her eyes, so that she could see close up his darkening blue irises, black lashes, white lids, and her own reflection in his pupils. "You grow more lovely with each year. Some women do."

She was pleased. "I do believe you're jealous."

"Of course I am. Isn't it only natural? Especially when I have never once in all our life together—I swear it—I have never been unfaithful to you."

The white lids, like shell halves, closed over the blue. And with a violent motion he buried his head in her shoulder.

"Ah, Lynn, you don't know. You don't know."

That he could want her still with such fierce, sudden spasms of desire, and that she could respond as she had first done when they began together, was a marvel that flashed upon her each and every time, as now. . . .

The wind fluttered the curtains, the bedside clock ticked, and a car door cracked lightly, quickly shut. Robert roused from his doze.

"Emily?"

"She's home. I kept awake to be sure."

"She stays out too late."

"Hush. Go to sleep. Everything's all right."

With all safe, Emily and Annie in their beds, now she could sleep too. Her thoughts trembled on the verge of consciousness, her body was warmed by the body beside which she had been sleeping for thousands of nights. Thousands.

There went the mockingbird again. Trilling, trilling its heart out without a care in the world, she thought, and then abruptly thought no more.

Tom Lawrence asked, "Are you sure I'm not in your way?"

Perched on a barstool in his glossy black-and-white kitchen, he was watching Lynn's preparations.

"No, not at all."

"This is a new experience for me. Usually when I have guests, I have a barbecue outdoors. Steaks, and ice cream for dessert. Fast and easy."

Since this was quite a new experience for Lynn, too, she had to grope for something to say, however banal, to avoid a stiff silence. "It's a pity not to use all these beautiful things more often," she remarked as she filled the cups of a silver epergne with green grapes.

"That's a great idea, putting fruit in that thing. I forgot I had it. You know, when we split up and I moved, my former wife and I agreed to divide all the stuff we owned, stuff from her family and mine, plus things we'd bought together. I didn't pay any attention, just let her do it all. The whole business was a mess. The move. The whole business." Abruptly, he slid from the stool. "Here, let me carry that. Where does it go?"

"It's the centerpiece. Careful, the arms detach."

The dining table stood at the side of a great room with a fireplace at each end. One saw that there was no more to the house than the splendid kitchen and what must be two bedrooms leading off this great room. A quick glance encompassed paintings, bookshelves, a long glass wall with a terrace, and thick foliage, dense as a forest, beyond it.

"What an elegant little house!" she exclaimed.

"Do you think so? Yes, after almost three years I can say I finally feel at home here. When I first moved in, my furniture looked alien. I hardly recognized it."

"I know what you mean. When the van comes and sets your things down in a strange place, they look forlorn, don't they? As if they knew and missed their own home. Then when the empty van drives away—oh, there's something final about it that leaves one just a trifle sad, I think."

And for an instant she was back in the little house in St. Louis—"little," contrasted with the present one—with the friendly neighbors on the familiar, homelike street. Then she said briskly, "But of course one gets over it."

His reply was wholly unexpected. "I imagine that you make yourself 'get over' things pretty quickly, though. You make yourself do what's right."

Astonished, she looked up to meet a scrutiny. Returning it, she saw that except for some superficial features, this man did not resemble her at all; he was keen and worldly wise, which she definitely was not; he would see right through a person if he chose to.

"What makes you say that?" she asked curiously.

He smiled and shrugged. "I don't know. Sometimes I get a sudden insight, that's all. Unimportant. And possibly wrong."

"Maybe you sense that I'm a little nervous about this evening. I'm hoping I haven't bitten off more than I can chew."

He followed her back into the kitchen. "Please don't be nervous. These are all real people tonight, a few old friends driving out from New York and not a phony among them. They'll be stunned when they see this table. I'm sure they're expecting Tom Lawrence's usual paper plates."

Arrayed on the counters were bowls and platters of food that Lynn had already prepared at home: a dark red ham in a champagne sauce, stuffed mushroom caps, plump black olives and silver-pale artichokes tossed into a bed of greens, golden marinated carrots, rosy peaches spiced with cinnamon and cloves. Back and forth from the pantry to the refrigerator she moved. Then to the oven, into which she slid a pan of crisp potato balls, and to the mixer for the topping of whipped cream on a great flat almond tart.

When all was finished and she was satisfied, full confidence returned. "This kitchen's absolutely perfect," she told Tom, who was still there quietly observing her work. "The restaurant-sized oven, the freezer—all of it. I'm really envious."

"Well, you deserve a perfect kitchen, you're that expert. Have you ever thought of going professional?"

"I've thought about it sometimes, I'll admit. I've even thought of a name, 'Delicious Dinners.' But what with a lot of volunteering and the PTA and our big house taking time out of every day, I don't know how—" She paused and finished, "Robert is very fastidious about the house." She paused again to add, "Anyway, I'm not in a hurry," and was immediately conscious of having sounded defensive. "I need a last look at the table," she said abruptly.

"Excuse me." Tom was apologetic. "But the silver—I mean, aren't the forks and spoons upside down, inside out?"

Lynn laughed. "When the silver's embossed on the back, you're supposed to let it show."

"Oh? Now I've learned something," he said. His eyes smiled at her.

They're like Bruce's eyes, she thought. There isn't another thing about him that's like Bruce, but that. Her hands moved, smoothing the fine cloth, rearranging the candlesticks. There aren't that many people whose eyes can smile like that.

"You've suddenly grown thoughtful, Lynn. May I call you that?"

"Of course. Oh, thoughtful? I was remembering," she said lightly, "when Robert bought the etiquette book so I'd learn how to give proper dinners when we moved here. I thought it was silly of him, but I find it's come in handy, after all."

The doorbell rang. "Oh, that's Eudora. She cleans and baby-sits for us. I've asked her to help. I'll let her in."

When Lynn returned, Tom said, "I wish you'd set another place at table, one for yourself, now that you've got help in the kitchen."

"I'm here to work. I'm not a guest," she reminded him. "Thank you, anyway."

"Why shouldn't you be a guest? There'll be all couples tonight except for me. And I really should have a female to escort me, shouldn't I?"

"That wasn't the arrangement."

His smile subsided as again he gave her his quick scrutiny. "I understand. You mean, if you were to be a guest, then your husband would be here too."

She nodded. "Anyway, I couldn't depend upon Eudora in the kitchen. She'll be fine to bring in the plates after I fix them and to clean up with me afterward."

She hurried away into the kitchen. Why was she flustered? Actually, the man had said nothing so startling. And she turned to Eudora, who was waiting for instructions.

"They'll be here in a minute. Turn the oven on low to warm up the hors d'oeuvres. Half an hour for drinks. I'll toss the salad. It goes on the blue plates—no, not those, take the other ones."

"They're having a good time," Eudora said much later. The swinging door opened and closed on genial laughter as she went in and out. "I never did see people clean plates like this."

"Good. Now carry the cake in so they can see it first. Then you can bring it back, and I'll slice it."

"You sure are some cook, Mrs. Ferguson. I'm old enough to be your mother, and I never even heard of the things you fix."

"Well, I'd never seen some of your good Jamaican dishes, either, until I knew you."

Although she had been standing on her feet all day, Lynn suddenly received a charge of energy. What had begun as a lark, an adventure, had become a test, and she had passed it. She had been paid for her skill, and she felt happy. So, when the door opened and Tom said his guests were demanding to see the cook, she was quite ready to go with him.

"Just do let me fix my face first. I'm all flushed from the stove."

"Yes, it's awful to be flushed like a rose," he retorted, pulling her with him.

In a moment she appraised the group: they were sophisticated, successful, bright New Yorkers, the kind who wear their diamonds with their blue jeans when they want to. They marry and divorce with equal ease when they want to. Good natured and accepting, it takes a lot to shock them. Robert would despise their type. All this went through her head.

They were most kind, heaping praise on Lynn. "What a talent. . . . You could work for Le Cirque or La Grenouille. . . . I ruined my diet tonight. . . . Absolutely marvelous."

The evening rose to a peak. Warmed by the food and wine, the group left the table in a high, restless mood. Tom turned on the record player, the men pushed back the scatter rugs, and dancing began.

He held his hands out to Lynn. "Come, join the party."

"It's rock and roll. I'm awful at it," she protested.

"Then it's time you learned," he answered, and pulled her out onto the floor.

At first she felt foolish. If Emily, who danced like a dervish, could see her mother, she'd die laughing. The best Lynn could do was to watch the others' dizzy twists and gyrations and try to imitate them.

Then after a while, the drumming, primitive, blood-pounding beat began to speak to her. Quite unexpectedly, she caught the beat.

"Why, you've got it!" Tom cried. "You've got it!"

This whirling, which should have been exhausting, was instead exhilarating. When Lynn became aware that Eudora was standing at the door to signal her departure, it surprised her to find that it was already almost eleven o'clock. She would have guessed the time to be no later than nine.

Pressing some bills into Eudora's hand, she whispered, "You remembered to leave the crystal?"

"Oh, I hate to leave you with it, Mrs. Ferguson, but I'd hate to be responsible for it too."

"That's all right, Eudora. I'll wash it fast and start right home."

Back in the kitchen with the apron on again, Lynn was rinsing the goblets when Tom, with eyes alight and in a merry mood, came looking for her.

"Hey! What are you doing in here?"

"Eudora was afraid to touch your Baccarat. She knows what it costs."

"Oh, leave it. We're all going to dance outdoors. It's a perfect night."

"I can't. Really. I can't."

"Yes, you can. I insist. For ten minutes. Come on."

The outdoor lanterns gave the effect of moonglow, barely glimmering toward the edge of darkness, where the hemlock grove fenced the little clearing on which the terrace lay. It had rained during the day, and the smell of damp grass was tart.

One of the men complained, "Age is creeping up, Tom, because I'm beat. How about some slow golden oldies for a change?"

"No problem. I've got all the tunes your parents danced to. Now, this is really nice," he said as his arm brought Lynn close. "When you come down to it, the old way is better."

Unlike Robert, he was not much taller than she, so that their faces almost touched. Their feet moved in skillful unison to the swing of the sentimental music.

"You have a sweet mouth," Tom said suddenly, "and sweet eyes."

An uneasy feeling stiffened Lynn, and he felt it at once.

"You didn't like me to say that, did you?"

"I didn't expect it."

"Why not? If a compliment is sincere, it should be spoken and accepted."

"Well, then, thank you."

"You still look uncomfortable. You're thinking I'm just a smooth talker. But you are really someone special, I have to tell you. Refreshing. Different."

She could feel his breath on her neck. The hand on the small of her back pressed her so close to him that she could feel his heartbeat. And the dreamy charm of the night changed into nervous misgiving.

"It's after eleven," she cried. "I have to go right away. Please—"

"So there you are!"

The harsh voice rang as Robert came from around the corner of the house into the light. Just then the music stopped, leaving the dancers stopped, too, arrested in motion, all turned toward the voice.

"I telephoned, I got no answer, I came over and rang the doorbell and still got no answer."

"This is my husband," Lynn said. "Tom Lawrence—but how stupid of me! Of course you know each other. I'm not thinking." And she moistened her lips, to which there had suddenly come a curious, salty taste, like that of blood, as if blood had drained upward from her heart.

"I'm so sorry. We've been out here, and the music's drowned out all the bells. Come in and join us," Tom said cordially. "Your wife made a marvelous dinner. You've got to sample some of the dessert. I hope there's some left, Lynn?"

"Thank you, but cake is hardly what I need. It's going on twelve, and I'm not usually out at this hour rounding up my wife at a dance."

Crazy thoughts went through Lynn's head: He looked sinister and black, a figure in mask and cape from an old melodrama, angry-dark, why can't he smile, I'll die of shame before these people. And in a shrill, gay tone not her own, she cried out, "What an idiot I am, I forgot to wear my watch, all these nice people made me come out of the kitchen and dance with them, I'll just get my bowls and things—"

"Yes, you do that," Robert said. "You do just that. I'll wait in front." He turned about and walked away through the shrubbery.

Tom and the whole company, men and women both, went into the kitchen with Lynn. Rattling and prattling, she let them help gather her possessions, and load her car, while Robert sat stiffly at the wheel of his car, and the hot, awful shame went prickling along her spine.

"You follow me home," he said.

Past quiet houses already at rest in the shadows of new-leaved trees, his car sped like a bullet aimed at the heart of the friendly countryside. She knew that he sped so because he was furious, and knowing it, her own anger grew. What right had he? Who did he think he was?

"Damn!" she cried. That an evening, having begun so nicely, could end in such miserable confusion, with Tom Lawrence's unwelcome attention and Robert's nastiness!

He had already driven his car into the garage and was waiting for her in the driveway when she arrived home. I want the first word, she thought, and I'm going to have it. Nevertheless, she spoke with quiet control.

"You were unbelievably rude, Robert. I almost didn't recognize you."

"Rude, you say? Rude? I went there as any other husband would, looking for his wife."

"You embarrassed me terribly. You know you did."

"I was concerned. Close to midnight, and no word from you."

"If you were so concerned, you could have telephoned."

"I did telephone, I told you. Where's your head? Didn't you listen to me? And then I went over to find you, not in the kitchen doing this ridiculous dinner, and where were you? Dancing, if you please. Dancing."

"I had been dancing for a couple of minutes, and I was just leaving that very second when you came."

"You had been dancing much longer than a couple of minutes. And don't try to deny it because I was there."

Caught in her lie, no, not a lie, a fib, an innocent fib, such an innocent business altogether in which to be embroiled, she lashed out.

"You were standing there behind the trees snooping? It's degrading. I should think you'd be ashamed, Robert. The way you just burst out of the dark, enough to scare the life out of people. Don't you think they all knew you must have been spying? You were horrible. You wouldn't have put on an act like that if any of them could be of use to you in your business. Otherwise, you don't care what you say to people."

"That's not true. But it is true that I don't give a damn about a lot of pseudosophisticated phonies. I recognize the type at a glance. I wouldn't trust one of them any farther than I can throw a grand piano, and that includes Lawrence."

"You're so critical. You're always carping. You don't approve of anybody."

The headlights of her car, which she had forgotten to turn off, blazed up on Robert. And he seemed, as he stood there, as strong as the dark firs behind him.

"Turn those lights off," he snapped, "or you'll have a dead battery." And turning his back, he climbed the steps to the deck at the back of the house.

She turned the lights off. She was too tired to put one foot ahead of the other, too tired to fight this war of words that she knew was far from over. But with a long sigh she followed him to the deck.

"Pseudosophisticated phonies," he repeated.

"What is it, Robert?" she asked. "Tell me what it is that makes you despise people you don't even know. What makes you so angry? Don't you like yourself?" And saying so, she felt the faint sting of her own tears.

"Please," he said, "spare me your pop psychology, Mrs. Freud."

He took out his keys and unlocked the house door. Juliet came bounding, barking fiercely, but, seeing who was there, jumped up on Robert and wagged her tail instead. He thrust her away.

"Not in the mood, Juliet. Down." And abruptly returning to Lynn, he demanded, "I want an apology. There'll be no sleep for either of us tonight until I get one."

How a handsome face can turn so ugly! she thought. In the half-dark his cheeks were faintly blue, and his eyes were sunk in their sockets.

"An apology, Lynn."

"For what? For overstaying my time by an hour? For having a little fun? You could have come in and joined the party. Tom asked you to."

"Oh, of course, if Tom asks."

"What does that sarcastic tone mean, I'd like to know?"

"It means that I don't like the way he was looking at you, that's what."

"The way he looked at me," she scoffed. "I don't know how he did because I wasn't studying his expressions, I assure you. But if," she cried indignantly, "if he or anyone should take it into his head to admire me a little, you'd have no right to object. Not you. You love it when women fawn on you. Don't tell me you don't, because I've seen it a thousand times."

"Now, you listen to me and don't change the subject. But no, on the other hand now that you've brought up the subject, I'll tell you this: I have never encouraged any woman. Never. Nor done anything in any way that I couldn't do right in front of you. I'll swear on the Bible."

"The Bible! All of a sudden the Bible. When were you last in church?"

"Never mind. I believe. I have my moral standards. One mistake, one misstep down a slippery slope, and you can't—"

"What is this? Who's made any missteps? What in heaven's name are you talking about? I can't figure you out."

"Damn it, if you'll stop interrupting me, I'll figure it out for you."

From the roof peak the mockingbird began a passionate crescendo, then a trill and a plaintive diminuendo. The sweetness of it went to Lynn's heart and pierced it.

"Let's stop this," she said, trembling. "I've had enough. There's no sense in it. I'm going inside."

He clutched her sleeve. "No, you're not. You'll hear me first."

She pulled, and hearing the sleeve rip, the fine sleeve of a cherished dress, she was enraged.

"Let go of me this minute, Robert."

"No."

As she wrenched it away, the sleeve tore off at the shoulder.

A muffled cry came from his throat. And he raised a menacing hand. His arm shot out, grasping her shoulder, and she spun, fled, and fell headfirst off the deck into the hawthorn hedge. She heard her own terrible scream, heard the dog going wild, heard Robert's outcry, thought, *my face!* and knew not to break the fall with her hands but to protect her eyes instead.

"Oh, God," Robert said.

When he lifted her, she screamed. She was flayed, stripped, skinned on the backs of her hands, her legs, her cheeks . . . She screamed.

"I have to get you up," he said, sounding as if he were speaking through clenched teeth. "If you can't bear it, I'll have to call an ambulance."

"No. No. We'll try. . . . Try loosening one at a time. I'll bear it."

Annie was out on a sleep-over at a friend's house. And Emily must not be home yet, or she would have heard by now and come running. And she gave thanks that they were not seeing this, a happening that must seem both hideous and absurd, with the dog now leaping, now howling, as if it, too, were in pain, shattering the quiet of the night.

Weeping and whimpering she lay and, while Robert brought a flashlight from the car and set to work on her torn arms and legs, tried not to scream. One by one the thorns were parted from her flesh. Only once or twice did she cry out loud.

When finally he raised her and she stood wavering on the grass, they were both sweating and stained with bloody droplets. Wordless, they simply stared at one another. Then she stumbled up the shallow steps, moaning softly.

"I've turned my ankle. I can hardly walk."

"I'll carry you."

He picked her up and bore her as lightly as he would have borne a child. He laid her on the bed and took her clothes off.

"Soap and water first," he said. "Don't be afraid, I'll be very careful. Then antibiotic cream. That'll do until you see a doctor in the morning."

"I'm not going to see any doctor. You don't need a doctor for a sprained ankle or a thorn."

"You had eighteen thorns. I counted."

"All the same, I'm not going," she insisted feebly, and was perfectly aware that this was masochism, that it was her intent to make him feel his guilt, guilt for the wounded hands clasped on her naked, wounded breast, for the ruined yellow dress that lay on the floor like dirty laundry, guilt for the whole horror of this night.

"Well, suit yourself," he said. "If you change your mind and don't want to drive, call a taxi. I can't take you. My desk in the office is piled with work, and work won't wait just because it's Saturday."

When she crept under the blanket, he was still standing looking down at her.

"What do you want?" she whispered. "Anything you want to say?"

He lowered his eyes and took a long breath. "Yes. I was angry. But I didn't throw you into the hedge."

"You pushed me. You were going to hit me, you were inches from my face."

"I was not."

"You were, Robert."

"Are you a crystal gazer or something, who can foretell what a person's going to do?"

"You grabbed my shoulder and shoved me. And I saw your face. It was ugly with rage."

"In the first place, it was too dark for you to see whether my face was ugly or not. This is garbage, Lynn."

All she wanted was to lie in the darkness and rest. "Why don't you let me alone?" she cried. "Haven't you any mercy? At least let me try to sleep if I can."

"I won't bother you, Lynn." He walked to the door. "I hope you can sleep. I doubt that I can. A miserable night. These miserable misunderstandings! Go downstairs, Juliet. Stop pestering."

"Leave the dog here. I want her."

Now darkness filled the room. The little sounds of the night were soft, a rustle in the oak near the window and the tinkle of Juliet's tags. The dog came to the bed, reached up, and licked Lynn's sore hand, as if comfort were intended; as always, then, comfort brought the most grateful tears. And Lynn lay still, letting them flow, feeling them cool and slippery on her cheeks. After a while the dog thumped down on the floor near the bed, the tears stopped, and she closed her eyes.

Still no sleep came. Emily was not home yet. It must be very late, she thought. But it was too painful to turn over in the bed and look at the clock. From downstairs there drifted the pungent smell of pipe tobacco, and she knew that Robert was sitting in the corner of the sofa watching television or reading, or perhaps just sitting. No matter. She didn't want to think of him at all. Not yet.

After a time she heard the small thud of a car door being closed, followed by Emily's feet creeping down the hall to her room. Where had the girl been so late? But she was home and safe.

At last it seemed that blessed sleep might come. It had not yet come when Robert entered the room and got into bed, but she pretended that it had.

In the morning, still feigning sleep, she waited until he had dressed and gone downstairs. Then she got up and limped painfully to the mirror, which confirmed what she had expected to see: a swollen face with small, reddened eyes sunk into bloated cheeks. The whole unsightly face was puffed, and there were dark droplets of dried blood on the long scratch. Merely to look like this was another undeserved punishment.

She was standing there applying useless makeup and trying to decide whether the wearing of dark glasses would help or whether it would be better simply to brave things out, when Robert came in.

"I hope you feel better," he said anxiously.

"I'm fine. I'm just fine. Can't you see?"

"I see only that you're hurt. And that hurts me, even though right now you may not think it does. But I am just so sorry, Lynn. So sorry it happened. I can't tell you."

"It didn't just happen: I'm not going to accept that stuff anymore. Somebody made it happen, and I'm not the somebody."

"I understand how you feel." Robert was patient now, and contrite. "I realize how it must appear to you. I was angry—we can talk about that some other time—I scared you with my anger, which was wrong of me, and so you ran and then—"

She interrupted. "And then I don't want to hear any more."

"All right. Come down and eat your breakfast. Let's keep things normal in front of the girls. Annie's just been brought home. I've told them about your accident, so they're prepared."

"My accident. Ah, yes," Lynn mocked, wiping off the eye makeup, which made her look like a sick owl. She would just honestly let the girls see she had been crying. They'd see the injuries anyway.

Emily had set the table in the breakfast room. Coffee bubbled in the percolator and bread was in the toaster. Evidently, she had gone outside and picked a spray of lilacs for the green bowl. Emily was a take-charge person.

"You're up early for someone who went to bed late," Lynn said pleasantly.

"A bunch of us are driving to the lake," said Emily, carefully not looking at Lynn's face, "where Amy's folks keep the boat. What's wrong with your foot? You've hurt that too?"

"It's nothing much. I just can't get a shoe on, so I'll stay home today."

Annie was staring at Lynn. "You look awful," she said. "You've been crying too."

Emily admonished her, "Mind your business, silly."

Robert spoke. "Your mother hurt herself. Don't you cry when you're hurt?"

No one answered. The silence was unhappy, restless with the awareness that it would have to end, and the fear that it would end badly.

"It was twenty minutes after twelve when you walked in last night," Robert said, addressing Emily. "Did you know that?" he asked, addressing Lynn, who nodded.

"I forgot to look at the time. A bunch of us were studying at Sally's," Emily explained.

"That won't do," Robert said. "You're damaging your reputation, if nothing more, coming home at that hour."

"We'll talk about it this morning, Emily," Lynn said.

"No." Robert looked at his watch. "I have to run. Emily, you are not to leave the house tonight. *I* want to talk to you. You and I are going to have a very serious talk, straight from the shoulder, one that you won't forget in a hurry. When I'm through, you'll know what's expected of you."

The emphasis on the "I" was directed at Lynn; she understood that clearly, having been told often enough that she wasn't firm, didn't consider appearances, and the girls would never learn from her.

"Oh, what an awful mood," Emily said when Robert had left.

Annie got up. "I promised Dad I'd practice this morning, and since he's in a bad mood, I guess I'd better do it," she said in a tone of resignation.

"That's not why you should," Lynn said gently. "You should do it because—well, because you should do it," she finished with a smile.

When Annie was in the living room drumming out a minuet, Lynn said to Emily, "Sit down while I have my second cup. You shouldn't stay out so late. You know that without my telling you. Were you really at Sally's all that time?"

"I was. Believe it or not, we were studying for finals, Mom."

Robert's blue eyes looked candidly back at her from Emily's face.

"I believe you." And thoughtfully, as if she had weighed whether or not to ask the question, she ventured it. "Was Harris there?"

"Yes. He brought me home."

"After twelve, your father said."

"He was sitting in the dark when I came in. Then he came to the hall and stood there just glaring at me. He didn't say a word, and neither did I."

"That was wrong of you."

"I'm sorry, Mom. But he needn't have looked so ferocious. I know I should have phoned, but I forgot to look at the time. That's not a crime."

"I suppose Sally's mother wasn't there, as usual?"

"Well, she's divorced, she goes on dates." Again the clear eyes met Lynn's. "So, no, she wasn't there."

"Wrong. All wrong," Lynn said. "And Harris—he's a fine boy, I see that, and it's not that we don't trust you, but—"

"But what, Mom?"

"Your father is very, very angry. You must try to do the right thing, you understand, or you'll be grounded. You really will, Emily, and there'll be nothing I can do about it."

There was a silence except for the balanced cadence of Annie's minuet.

Emily reached across the table and touched Lynn's hand. "Mom?" And now the clear, the honest, the lustrous eyes were troubled. "Mom? What's wrong with Dad? I wish he were like other people's fathers. He gets so mad. It's weird."

On guard now, Lynn answered as if she were making light of the complaint.

"Why? Because he's going to give you a scolding that you deserve?"

"No. It has nothing at all to do with that."

"What, then?"

"Oh, things. Just things. He gets so mad sometimes."

"Everybody gets cranky now and then. He works very hard. Sometimes he's terribly tired and as you say, it's only sometimes."

Emily shook her head. "That's not what I mean."

Lynn feared, although she did not want to think specifically of what it was that she feared. So she spoke with a touch of impatience.

"You'll have to give me an example, since I have no idea what you're talking about."

Still Emily hesitated, with a wary, doubtful glance at Lynn. Finally she said, "Remember when I met Aunt Jean in the city and she took me to tea? Something happened that I didn't tell you about."

"Yes?"

"Don't be scared, it's nothing awful. What happened is, we were talking and you know how she likes to tell about old times, when the neighbor's house burned down and what a cute little boy Dad was, and then suddenly she let something slip about Dad's first marriage—Mom, how is it we never knew he was married before?"

So that's all it was. Nothing, or comparatively nothing. . . .

Carefully, Lynn explained, "I don't really understand why it had to be such a secret, but it's your father's life and he wants it that way. That must have been a terribly hard time for him and he simply doesn't want to be reminded of it. People often do that; they just bury their bad memories."

"The second Aunt Jean said it she looked horrified, she was so scared that I felt sorry for her. She kept saying how sorry *she* was, and begged me to promise not to tell, to forget that I'd heard it. And of course I promised." Emily turned away for a moment and then, turning back to Lynn, admitted with shame that she had broken the promise. "I held back as long as I could, but last week I told Dad."

"Oh, that was wrong, Emily."

"I know, and I feel bad about it. You asked about Dad being so angry at me, though, and—"

"And?" Lynn prodded.

"He was absolutely furious. I've never seen him like that. Mad, Mom! I couldn't believe it. He glared at me. 'That's no business of yours,' he told me, 'and I don't want the subject to be mentioned ever again. Is that clear?' It stunned me."

"I hope he won't take it out on poor Aunt Jean."

"I made him promise not to let her know I had told on her. So I guess it will be all right. I hope so."

Now Lynn wondered whether Jean had said anything more, anything about Robert's boy, for instance. There must be more pain in that loss than he had ever admitted; it was natural, then, that he would want to forget the boy's existence. And, worrying, she asked, "Is that all Jean said?"

"Two or three words, and clapped her hand over her mouth. I told you." Emily frowned in thought, and shook her head in doubt.

"Don't you ever feel strange about it? If I were you—I mean, you might be passing each other on the street, and not know."

"Hardly likely. This is a big country. Besides, why should we know each other, in the circumstances? It's far better that we don't. Most times a divorce is a closed chapter—understandably."

"But aren't you even the least bit curious? I know I would be."

"You don't know. One doesn't know how to act in a situation, or how to feel, until it happens."

No, I never would have wanted to connect in any way with Robert's glamor girl, Lynn thought, as always with a slight bitterness, but this morning with an extra bitterness. She remembered when she had first known Robert, raw little girl that she had been, an innocent so unsure of herself, how she had flinched at the thought of Robert making love to her predecessor, so rich, so beautiful and careless, that she could afford to toss such a man away.

It was strange to be having these thoughts at the kitchen table this morning, on this particular morning.

Nervously, Emily played with a spoon. "All the same," she said, "Dad can be very odd."

"He's not, Emily. I don't want you to say that or think it."

And suddenly the girl began to cry. "Oh, Mom, why am I afraid to say what I really want to say?"

Again fear, hot as fire, struck Lynn's heart.

"Emily darling, what is it?"

"Something happened to you last night."

"Yes, yes, of course it did. I fell in the dark, fell into the hedge." She laughed. "It was a mess, falling into the hedge. Clumsy."

"No," Emily said. The word seemed to choke in her throat. "No. Dad did it. I know it."

"What? What?" Lynn's hands clenched together in her lap so that her rings dug into the flesh. "That's ridiculous. However did you get such an idea? Emily, that's ridiculous," she repeated in a high, unnatural tone.

"One time before we moved here, once when you came home from Chicago, I remember, I heard Aunt Helen say something to Uncle Darwin about how awful you looked. She said she thought maybe—"

"Emily, I'm surprised. Really, I am. I'm sure you didn't hear right. But even if you did, I can't help what Aunt Helen may have dreamed up."

"You wouldn't have cried so last night if it were only the pain. It's got to be more than that."

"Only the pain! All those thorns? Well, maybe I'm a coward and a crybaby. Maybe I am, that's all."

Emily must not lose faith in her father. It's damaging forever. A woman remembers her father all her life. My own dearest memories are of my dad. He taught me how to stand up for my rights and how to forgive; when he had to scold he was gentle. . . .

Lynn quieted her hands, resting them on the tabletop, and made a firm appeal.

"Trust me, Emily. Have I ever lied to you?"

But disbelief remained in the girl's quivering lips. Two lines formed on her smooth forehead.

"He was so ferocious this morning."

"Darling, you keep using that nasty word. He was in a hurry to get to the office, I told you. He was distressed." She spoke rapidly. "Your father's such a good man! Need I tell you that, for heaven's sake? And you're so like him, a hard worker, determined to succeed, and you always do succeed. That's why you've been so close, you two. You've had such a special relationship. It hurts me to think you might lose it."

"Don't you think it hurts me too? But you have to admit Dad can be very strange."

"Strange? After all the caring, the loving attention he's given you all your life?"

"You don't convince me, Mom."

"I wish I could."

"I feel something. It's stuck inside my head. But I can understand why you're talking to me this way."

The kettle whistled, and Emily got up to turn it off. She moved with elegance, even in jeans and sneakers; her slender waist, rounding into the swell of her hips, was womanly, while her skin was as unflawed as a baby's. Suddenly it seemed to Lynn that she was being condescended to, as if the young girl, out of a superior wisdom, were consoling or patronizing the older woman. Her very stance as she turned her back to stack the dishwasher, the very flip of her ponytail, gave rise in her mother to resentment. And she said somewhat sharply, "I trust you'll keep these unbecoming thoughts to yourself. And keep them especially away from Annie. That's an order, Emily."

Emily spun around. "Do you really think I would hurt Annie any more than she's already hurt? Annie's a wreck. I don't think you realize it."

This stubborn persistence was too much like Robert's. Lynn was under attack. Arrows were flying. It was too much. Yet she replied with formal dignity. "You exaggerate. I'm well aware that Annie is going through a difficult stage. But Annie will be just fine."

"Not if Dad keeps picking on her about being fat," Emily said, and added a moment later, "I wish things seemed as simple as they used to seem."

Her forced smile was sad, and it affected Lynn, changing the earlier flash of resentment into pity.

"You're growing up," she said wistfully.

"I'm already grown, Mom."

Across the hall Annie was still pounding at the minuet. Suddenly, as if two hands had come down in full angry force, the melody broke off into a cacophony of shrill chords, as if the piano were making violent protest.

The two women frowned, and Emily said, "She hates the piano. She only does it because he makes her."

"It's for her own good. She'll be glad someday."

They gave each other a searching look that lasted until Emily broke the tension.

"I'm sorry I said anything this morning. Maybe this is only a mood that will wear away." From outside came the light tap of a horn. "That's Harris. I'm off." The girl leaned down and kissed her mother's cheek. "Don't worry about me. I won't make any trouble. Forget what I said. Maybe I don't know what I'm talking about. But take care of yourself, Mom. Just take care of yourself."

The kitchen was very still after Emily went out. Then the screen door slammed on the porch. The dog rose, shook itself, and followed Annie outside. In the silence a plaintive repetition sounded in Lynn's ears. *Dad can be very strange. Take care of yourself, Mom.* And as if in a trance she sat with her fingers clasped around the coffee cup, which had long grown cold.

She tried to concentrate on errands to be done, the house to be tidied and clothes to take to the cleaners, all the small ways in which living continues even when the worst things have happened, for if the pipes break on the day of the funeral, one still has to call the plumber. And yet she did not rise to do any of these things.

The doorbell brought her out of her lethargy. Expecting the delivery of some packages, she put her sunglasses back on; they were light and concealed very little, but the United Parcel man would probably not even look at her, and if he did look, wouldn't care. Barefooted, in her housecoat, she opened the door into the glare of revealing sunlight and faced Tom Lawrence.

"You forgot this," he said, holding out her purse, "so I thought I'd—" His eyes flickered over her and away.

"Oh, how stupid of me. How nice of you." Absurd words came out of her mouth. "I look a mess, I fell, sprained my ankle, and can't get a shoe on."

He was looking at the tubbed geraniums on the top step. That was decent of him. He had seen, and was embarrassed for her.

"Oh. A sorry end to a wonderful evening. Ankles turn so easily. It takes a few days to get back to normal. I hope you'll feel better."

She closed the door. Mortified, she thought, I wish I could dig a hole and crawl into it. What can he be thinking! I never want to see him again. Never.

After a while, with main effort, she recovered. Alone in the house, she could admonish herself out loud.

"What are you doing, not dressed at eleven o'clock? Get moving, Lynn."

So, slowly and painfully, she limped through the house doing small, unimportant chores, raised or lowered shades according to need, wrote a check at the desk, and threw out faded flowers, allowing these ordinary acts to soothe her spirit as best they could.

Presently she went into the kitchen. For her it had always been the heart of the house, her special place. Here she could concentrate a troubled mind on a difficult new recipe, here feel the good weight of copper-bottom pots in her hands, and here feel quietness.

A lamb stew simmered, filling the room with the smell of rosemary, and an apple pie had cooled on the counter when, late in the afternoon, she heard Robert's car enter the driveway.

Robert's mouth was as expressive as his eyes; she could always tell by it what was to come next. Now she saw with relief that his lips were upturned into a half smile.

"Everybody home?"

"The girls will be home in a minute. Emily went to the lake, and Annie's at a friend's house."

"And how are you? You're still limping. Wouldn't it feel better with a tight bandage?"

"It's all right as it is."

"Well, if you're sure." He hesitated. "If that's Emily"—for there came the sound of wheels on gravel—"I want to talk to her. To both of them. In the den."

"Can't it wait until after dinner? I have everything ready."

"I'd rather not wait," he answered, walking away.

She thought, He will take out his guilt over me in anger at them.

"Your father wants to see you both in the den," she told the girls when they came in. As they both grimaced, she admonished them. "Don't make faces. Listen to what he has to say."

Never let them sense any differences between their parents about discipline. That's a cardinal rule for their own good. Rule number one.

Now again her heart was beating so rapidly that she felt only a need to flee, yet she followed them to the den, where Robert stood behind his desk.

He began at once. "We need more order in this house. It's too slipshod. People come and go as they please without having even the decency to say where they're going or when they're coming back. They have no sense of time. Coming home at all hours as they please. You'd think this was a boardinghouse."

The poor children. What had they done that was so bad? This was absurd. And she thought again: It is his conscience. He has to turn the tables to put himself in the right.

"I want to know whenever and wherever you go to another house, Annie. I want to know with whom you are associating."

The child stared. "The other fathers aren't like you. You think this is the army, and you're the general."

It was an oddly sophisticated observation to come from the mouth of an eleven-year-old.

"I won't have your impudence, Annie."

Robert never raised his voice when he was angry. Yet there was more authority in his controlled anger than in another man's shouts; memory carried Lynn suddenly back to the office in St. Louis and the dreaded summons from Ferguson to be "reamed out"; she had never received that summons herself, but plenty of others had and never forgot it afterward.

"You'd better get hold of yourself, Annie. You're no baby anymore, and you're too fresh. Your schoolwork isn't good enough, and you're too fat. I've told you a hundred times, you ought to be ashamed of the way you look."

Gooseflesh rose on Lynn's cold arms, and she stood there hugging them. It was unbearable to be here, weakened as she was today, but still she stayed as if her presence, silent as she was, was some protection for her children, although she was certainly not protecting them against these words, and there was no need to guard them from anything else. Never, never had Robert, nor would he ever, raise a hand to his girls.

Her mind, straying, came back to the present. He had been saying something about Harris, calling him a "character." That nice boy. She could not hear Emily's murmured answer, but she plainly heard Robert's response.

"And I don't want to see him every time I walk into my home. I'm sick of looking at him. If I wanted a boy, I'd adopt one."

Annie, whose face had turned a wounded red, ran bawling to the door and flung it open so violently that it crashed against the wall.

"I hate everybody! I hate you, Dad!" she screamed. "I wish you would die."

With her head high, tears on her cheeks and looking straight ahead, Emily walked out.

In Robert's face Lynn saw the reflection of her own horror. But he was the first to lower his eyes.

"They needed what they got," he said. "They're not suffering."

"You think not?"

"They'll get over it. Call them back down to eat a proper dinner in the dining room."

"No, Robert. I'm going to bring their supper upstairs and leave them in peace. But yours is ready for you."

"You eat if you can. I have no appetite."

She went upstairs with plates for Emily and Annie, which they both refused. Sick at heart, she went back to the kitchen and put the good dinner away. Even the clink of the dishes was loud enough to make her wince. When it grew dark, she went outside and sat down on the steps with Juliet, who was the sole untroubled creature in that house. Long after the sky grew dark, she sat there, close to the gentle animal, as if to absorb some comfort from its gentleness. I am lost, she said to herself. An image came to her of someone fallen off a ship, alone on a raft in an empty sea.

And that was the end of Saturday.

On Sunday the house was still in mourning. In their rooms the girls were doing homework, or so they said when she knocked. Perhaps, poor children, they were just sitting in gloom, not doing much of anything. In the den Robert was bent over papers at the desk, with his open briefcase on the floor beside him. No one spoke. The separation was complete. And Lynn had a desolate need to talk, to be consoled. She thought of the people who loved her, and had loved her: her parents, both gone now, who would have forfeited their lives for her just as she would do for Emily and Annie; of Helen, who—and here she had to smile a bit rue-fully—would give a little scolding along with comfort; and then of Josie.

But to none of these would she or could she speak. Her father would have raged at Robert. And Helen would think, even if she might not say, "You remember, I never liked him, Lynn." And Josie would analyze. Her eyes would search and probe.

No. None of these. And she thought as always: Marriage is a magic circle that no outsider must enter, or the circle will never close again. Whatever is wrong must be solved within the circle.

She walked through the house and the yard doing useless make-work, as she had done the day before. In the living room she studied Robert's photo, but today the rather austere face told her nothing except that it was handsome and intelligent. In the yard the two new garden benches that he had ordered from a catalog stood near the fence. He was always finding ways to brighten the house, to make living more pleasant. He had hung thatched-roof birdhouses in secluded places, and one was already occupied by a family of wrens. He had bought a book of North American birds and was studying it with Annie, or trying to anyway, for the child's attention span was short. But he tried. So why, why was he—how, how could he—

The telephone rang in the kitchen, and she ran inside to answer it.

"Bruce went fishing yesterday," Josie reported, "and brought home enough for a regiment. He wants to do them on the outdoor grill. How about all of you coming over for lunch?"

Lynn lied quickly. "The girls are studying for exams, and Robert is working at his desk. I don't dare disturb him."

"Well, but they do need to eat," Josie said sensibly. "Let them come, eat, and run."

She was always sensible, Josie was. And at that moment this reasonableness of hers had its effect on Lynn, so that she said almost without thinking, "But I'll come by myself, if that's all right with you."

"Of course," said Josie.

Driving down Halsey Road through the estate section, and then through the town past the sportswear boutiques, the red-brick colonial movie, and the saddlery shop, all at Sunday-morning rest, she began to regret her hasty offer. Since she had no intention of confiding in Josie, she would have to make small talk, or at least Josie's version of small talk, which would involve the front page of *The New York Times*. Yet she did not go back, but drove through the little town and out to where the great estates had long ago been broken up, where new tract houses stood across from the pseudo-Elizabethan tract houses that had been put there in the twenties.

It was one of these that the Lehmans had bought, a little house with mock-oak beams and leaded glass windows. It was a rather cramped little house.

"He can afford better," Robert had remarked with some disdain.

And Lynn had answered innocently, "Josie told me they couldn't afford anything better because of her medical expenses."

Robert had exclaimed, "What? Well, that's undignified, to say the least, going all over the neighborhood telling people about one's business."

"She's not going all over the neighborhood. We're friends."

"Friends or not, the woman talks too much. I hope you don't learn bad habits from her." And then he had said, "Bruce is cheap. He thinks small. I saw that from the beginning."

But Bruce wasn't "cheap." Josie's sickness had cost a small fortune, and as Josie herself had said, who knew what was yet to come? It was she who hadn't let him spend more. He would have given the stars to her if he could.

He was in the backyard when she drove up, sanding a chest of drawers, concentrating with his glasses shoved up into his curly brown hair.

He summoned Lynn. "Come, look at my find. What a job! I picked it up at an antiques barn way past Litchfield last week. Must have twenty coats of paint on it. I have a hunch there's curly maple at the bottom. Well, we'll see."

His enthusiasm was appealing to her. His full lips were always slightly upturned, even in repose; she had the impression that he could sometimes hardly contain a secret inner happiness. A cleft in his chin gave sweetness to a face that, with its high cheekbones and jutting nose, might best be described as "rugged." A "man's man," you could say; but then she thought, a "man's man" is all the more a woman's man too.

"You've really been having a great time with your antiques since you moved east," she said.

When she moved from the shade into the glare he saw her face. For an instant his eyes widened before he bent back over his work and replied, as though he had seen nothing.

"Well, of course, New England's the place. You can't compare it with Missouri for early Americana. You'd think that the old villages had been combed through so long now that there'd be nothing left, but you'd be surprised. I even found a comb-back Windsor. It needs a lot of work, but I've got weekends, and with daylight saving I can squeeze in another hour when I get back from the city. Where's Robert? Still working, I think Josie said?"

"Yes, as usual, he's at his desk with a pile of papers," she replied, sounding casual.

"I admire his energy. To say nothing of his headful of ideas. There's no stopping him." Smiling, Bruce turned back to the sander. "As for me, I'm driving my wife crazy with this stuff. She doesn't care about antiques."

"She cares about you, and that's what matters," Lynn told him, and went inside conscious of having blurted out something too serious for the time and place.

Josie was on the sun porch with the paper and a cup of tea. She looks thin, Lynn thought, thinner since I last saw her a week ago. Still, her bright expression of welcome and her strong voice were the same as always. The body had betrayed the spirit. And this thought, coming upon her own agitation, almost brought tears to Lynn.

"Why, whatever's happened to you?" Josie cried, letting the paper slide to the floor. "Your face! Your legs!"

"Nothing much. I slipped and fell. Clumsy."

"Is that why you've been crying?"

"That, and a silly mood. Forget it."

"It would be sillier to forget it. You came for a reason."

Lynn tucked her long cotton skirt over her spotted legs. "I fell into the hawthorn hedge in the dark."

"So it hurts. But what about the mood?"

"Oh, it's just been a bad day. The house is in turmoil, perhaps because they got upset over me. And we just don't seem to know sometimes how to handle the girls. Although it will straighten out, I'm sure. When you called, I suppose at that moment I needed a shoulder to cry on, but now that I'm here, I know I shouldn't have come."

Josie regarded her from head to foot. "Yes, you should have come. Let me get you a cup of tea, and then you can tell me what's on your mind. Or not tell me, as you please." She went quickly to the door and turning, added, "I hope you will tell me."

"We don't seem to know how to handle the girls," Lynn repeated. "But you know our problems already. I needn't tell you that Robert doesn't approve of Emily's boyfriend. And Annie won't try to lose weight, she stuffs herself, and Robert can't stand that."

She stopped, thinking again, I shouldn't have come here to dump all this on her. She looks so tired, I'm tired myself, and nothing will come of all these prattling half-truths, anyway.

"I do know all that," Josie said. "But I don't think you're telling me the whole story," she added, somewhat sternly.

Like my sister, Lynn thought, she can be stern and soft at the same time, which is curious. I never could be.

"They're good girls—"

"I know that too."

"Maybe I'm making a mountain out of a molehill. These are hard times in which to rear children. I'm sure lots of families have problems worse than ours. Yes, I am making too much of it," Lynn finished, apologizing.

"I don't think you are."

There was a silence in which Lynn struggled first with words that were reluctant to be said, and finally with words that struggled equally hard to be released.

"Yesterday Robert was furious because Emily came home too late."

"Do you think she did?"

"Yes, only I wouldn't have been so angry about it. And Annie, you know she wants to have her hair straightened and Robert says that's ridiculous, and there is always something going on between Robert and Annie, although he does try hard. Yesterday she screamed at him. She was hysterical, almost. She hates everybody. She hates him." And Lynn, ceasing, gave Josie an imploring look.

"Tell me, is it only Robert who is having this trouble with the girls? Just Robert?"

"Well, yes. It's hard for a man to come home from a trying day and have to cope with children, when what he needs most is rest. Especially a man with Robert's responsibilities."

"We all have our responsibilities," Josie said dryly.

For a moment neither woman said more. It was as if they had reached an impasse. Lynn shifted uncomfortably in the chair. When Josie spoke again, she was careful to look away from Lynn and down at her own fingernails, saying with unusual softness, "Isn't there anything more?"

Lynn drew back in alarm. "Why, no. What should there be?"

"I only asked," said Josie.

And suddenly Lynn began to cry. Muffled broken phrases came through her tears.

"It wasn't just the children this time. It was because of me—at Tom Lawrence's house—it was too late, and Robert came—and I was dancing —Robert was angry, really so awfully—of course I knew I shouldn't have been dancing, but—"

"Now, wait. Let me get this straight. You were dancing with Tom, and Robert—"

"He was furious," sobbed Lynn, wiping her eyes.

"What the hell was wrong with dancing? You weren't in bed with the man. What do you mean, you shouldn't have been? I've never heard anything so ridiculous," Josie said hotly. She paused, frowned as if considering the situation, and then spoke more quietly. "And so you went home and had an argument near the thorn hedge and—"

Lynn put up her hand as if to stop traffic. "No, no, it wasn't—" she began. For a red warning had flashed in her head. Robert is Bruce's superior in the firm. It won't do, no matter how much I care about Bruce and Josie, for me to undermine Robert at his work. I've said too much already. Stupid. Stupid.

It was just then that Bruce came into the room.

"I'm taking time out. You don't mind, Boss?" he began, and stopped abruptly. "Am I interrupting anything? You two look so sober."

Lynn blinked away the moisture that had gathered again in her eyes. "I was spilling out some minor troubles, that's all."

Josie corrected her. "They are not minor, Lynn."

"I'll leave you both," Bruce said promptly.

But Lynn wanted him. It would have been inappropriate and subject to misinterpretation for her to tell him: Your presence helps me. You are so genuine. So she said only, "Please stay."

"You've told me, and since I would tell Bruce anyway after you left, he might as well hear it from me now." And as Lynn sat like a patient, listening miserably while a pair of doctors discussed her case, Josie repeated the brief, disjointed story.

Bruce had sat down in an easy chair. His legs rested on an ottoman, while his arms were folded comfortably behind his head. This informal posture, and his deliberate, considering manner of speech, were reassuring.

"So you had a row over the girls. Does it happen often?"

"Oh, no, not at all. Annie and Robert—"

Bruce put his hand up. "I don't think you should be talking to me about Robert," he said gently.

Lynn felt the rebuke. She ought to have remembered Bruce's sense of ethics. And she stood up, saying quickly, "I've really got to run home and see about lunch. We can talk another time."

"Wait," said Bruce. "Josie, do you agree with me that Lynn needs advice? You're much too close to her to give it, but don't you think somebody should?"

"Definitely."

"What's the name of that fellow you knew who went into counseling, Josie? You had such a high opinion of him, and he settled in Connecticut, I think."

"Ira Miller," Josie said promptly. "You'd like him, Lynn. I can get you the address from my alumni bulletin. I'll just run upstairs."

"I'm not sure I want to do this," Lynn told Bruce when they were alone.

"You have lovely girls," he said quietly. "Your little Annie is my special person. You know that. And if they're a problem or making trouble, you need to find out why, don't you?"

He was trying not to look at her face or her dreadful legs when he repeated the question. "Don't you?"

"I suppose so."

"You know so, Lynn."

"Yes." They were right. She had to talk to somebody. There was a volcano in her head, ready to erupt in outrage and grief. Relief must come. It must. And it was true that to a stranger she would be able to say what she could not say to these old friends: My husband did this to me.

"I called him for you," Josie reported. "I took the liberty of making an appointment for you tomorrow afternoon. He couldn't have been nicer. Here's the address."

As they walked Lynn to her car, Bruce said, "I hear your dinner was a big success."

"Goodness, how did you hear that?"

"Tom Lawrence. I met him yesterday morning jogging."

"Oh, dear, I suppose he told you how awful I looked when he came to the house to return my purse? I was still in my housecoat, and—"

"The only thing he told me was that you should do something with your talent, and I agree."

"It'll be about half an hour's drive tomorrow," Josie said. She smiled encouragement. "And that's even allowing time for getting lost."

"Good luck," Bruce called as Lynn drove away.

Robert, finding the reminder on Lynn's writing desk, demanded, "Dr. Miller, three o'clock. What kind of doctor is this?"

These were the first words he had spoken to her that Sunday, and she gave him a short answer. "What are you doing at my desk?"

"I was looking in your address book for a periodontist that somebody asked about."

"I don't look at things on your desk."

"I never said you shouldn't. I have no secrets." He strode to the large flattop on the other side of the room. "Come on. Look. Open any drawer you want."

"I don't want to open any drawer, Robert. All right, I'll tell you. Dr. Miller is a therapist. That's what we've come to."

"That's not necessary, Lynn." He spoke quietly. "You don't need it."

"But I do. And you need to go too. Will you?"

"Definitely not. We had a disagreement. What's so extraordinary? People have disagreements all the time and get over them. No doubt this is some bright idea of Josie's."

"It is not," she answered truthfully.

"Bruce's, then."

Hating to lie, she did not answer.

"I'm not spending money on this stuff, Lynn. I work too hard for it. Paying some stranger to listen to your troubles." His voice rose now, not in anger but in plaint. "I've never prevented you from buying anything you wanted, have I? Just look around at this house." His arm swept out over the leather chairs, the tawny rug, and the golden light on the lawn beyond the windows.

"Furniture isn't everything, or rings either," she responded, twisting the diamond on her finger.

"I should think you'd be ashamed to go and spill out your personal affairs. You're overreacting, you're over emotional. A man and wife have a nasty argument, and you behave as if the end of the world had come. No, I don't want you to go. Listen to me, Lynn—"

But she had already left the room.

In midafternoon the turnpike was an almost vacant path through a pastel landscape, pink cherry bloom, white apple bloom, and damp green leafage. The station wagon rolled along so easily that Lynn, turning off at the exit, found herself an hour too early for her appointment.

She drew up before a square house on a quiet street of developer's houses, all alike, except that this one possessed a wing with a separate entrance. A dirt bike propped against the wall of the garage and a glimpse of a jungle gym in the backyard were encouraging; the man would be experienced, and his words would not all come out of books.

Thinking it absurd to sit in the car for an hour, she rang the bell. A nondescript woman in a purple printed dress, who might have been either the doctor's wife or his mother, opened the door. No, the doctor was not in yet, but Lynn might come inside and wait.

The wait felt very, very long. Now that she had taken this great step, now that she was actually here, an anxious haste overcame her. Let me get this over with, it pleaded. As the minutes went by so slowly, so slowly, a faint fear began to crawl up from the pit of her stomach, to quicken her heart and lump itself in her throat. And she tried to stamp the fear out with reassurance: It is like waiting for your turn at the dentist's, that's all it is.

But this office was too small. There was no willing stranger to talk with or even to observe.

Her heart was racing now. She crossed the little room, took a couple of magazines, and was unable to read. Nothing made sense, neither the summer fashions nor the economic development of Eastern Europe. Nothing. She got up to examine the pictures on the wall, skillful portraits and pictures of places where the subjects of the portraits had been. Here they were posed on beaches, in ski clothes, and smiling under the iron arches of the Eiffel Tower. When she had seen all these, she sat down again with her heart still racing.

What was she to say to this unknown man? How to start? Perhaps he might ask why she had come to him. How, then, would she explain? Opening sentences formed and reformed silently on her lips. Well, on Saturday night there was a terrible scene. Cruel, bitter words were spoken, words that I had not dreamed could be said in our home, where we loved—love each other. But on the other hand, don't all children sometimes say that they hate their parents? So that it means nothing, really? Really? But Emily said that Robert . . . that Robert . . .

A husky middle-aged man appeared at the inner door. They matched, he and the woman in the purple print, so she must be his wife, Lynn thought absurdly, and was at the same instant aware that she was not thinking straight.

"Will you come in, please, Mrs. Ferguson?"

When she stood up, the walls whirled, and she had to grasp the back of the chair.

"I'm suddenly not feeling well, Doctor." The words came brokenly. "Maybe it's the flu or something. I don't know. I'm dizzy. It just came over me. If you'll excuse me, I'll come again. I'll pay for this visit. I'm sorry," she stammered.

The man's eyes, magnified by thick glasses, regarded her gravely. And she was suddenly reminded of her bruises, the unsightly marks on which scabs had not yet formed.

"I had—you can see—I had a little accident. I fell. We have a thorn hedge, so pretty, but those thorns, like needles—"

"Oh? An accident?" He paused. "Well, you mustn't drive while you're dizzy, you know. Please come in and rest in a comfortable chair until you feel better."

Feeling forced to obey, she took her seat in a large leather chair, laid her head back, and closed her eyes. She could hear papers rustling on the desk, the opening and closing of a drawer, and the pounding of her blood in her ears.

After a while a pleasant voice caused her to open her eyes.

"You don't have to talk if you don't want to."

"It does seem foolish to sit here and say nothing. Really, really, I think I should go," she repeated, as if she were begging permission.

"If you like, of course. But I don't think you're coming down with the flu."

"The dizziness is gone at least, so perhaps not."

"I am curious to know why you came here at all. Can you tell me that much?"

"It's strange. I imagined you would ask me that."

"And did you imagine what your answer would be?"

"Josie—Josie Lehman said I should ask advice." She wiped her sweating palms on a handkerchief. "We don't, I mean, sometimes my husband and I don't seem to handle the children, I mean we don't always agree. We have a teenage daughter and a girl of eleven, she's very sensitive, too fat, and my husband wants her to lose weight, and of course he's right, and you see—well, this weekend there were, there were misunderstandings, a quarrel, you see, and Annie, she's the younger one, told Robert she hated him, and I didn't quite know what to do."

And Emily said: Dad did it to you.

I can't, I can't say that.

Lynn's eyes filmed. Fiercely she wiped the damned humiliating tears away. She had vowed not to cry.

"I'm sorry," she murmured.

"That's all right. Why not cry if you need to?"

"So. So that's what it is, you see. Maybe I'm exaggerating. Now that I hear myself, I think I probably am. It's one of my faults. I get too emotional."

There were a few moments of silence until the pleasant voice addressed her again.

"You haven't told me anything about your husband."

"Oh, Robert, Robert is an unusual man. You don't often meet anyone like him, a Renaissance man, you might say. People do say. He has so many talents, everyone admires him, his scholarship and energy, he does so much good in the community and takes so much time with the children, their education, so much time—"

I hate you.

Dad did it to you.

"Yes?" said the voice, encouraging.

"I don't know what else to say. I—"

"You've told me what your husband does for the children and for the community, but not what he does for you."

"Well, he's very generous, very thoughtful and—" She stopped. It was impossible; she was not able to say it; she should not have come here.

"Is that all? Tell me, for instance, whether you are often angry at each other."

"Well, sometimes Robert gets angry, of course. I mean, people do, don't they? And often it's my fault—"

Nausea rose into her throat, and she was cold. On a blazing summer afternoon she felt gooseflesh on her arms. And she stood abruptly in a kind of panic, wanting only to flee.

"No, I can't say any more today. No, no, I'm not dizzy now, truly I'm not. I can drive. It's just a headache, a touch of fever. I am coming down with something after all. I *know* I am. But I'll come back," she said. "I surely will. I know I should."

Asking no more, the doctor stood and opened the door.

"I'll give you an appointment, Mrs. Ferguson. I'm going away for three weeks. When I come back, if you want to keep the appointment, I will be glad to talk to you. And in the meantime it would be a good idea to keep a daily record of everything you all do together. Write it down, the happy hours as well as the other kind. Then we'll talk. If you wish," he repeated. "Will you do that?"

"Yes, yes, I will. And thank you, thank you so much," she said.

Safely alone in the car, safely away from the measuring eyes behind the thick glasses, she felt at first a deep relief. But very gradually, as the distance between herself and those eyes increased, and the distance between herself and home diminished, she began to feel instead the heat of a cowardly shame, as if she had been caught in some dishonorable act, a harmful lie, a demeaning theft, or as if she had been found wandering demented through the streets in her underwear. Why, why, had she not told the whole truth? The man had known there was something else. He had seen right through her.

The after-work traffic was heavy, so it was past the dinner hour when she reached home to find Robert's car already in the garage. Ready for a confrontation, she steadied herself and walked into the house. Well, I did it, she would say, and I'll face right up to him. Yes, I'll say, I'm going again, and there's nothing you can do about it.

They were all still at table. Robert got up and pulled out Lynn's chair, Annie smiled, and Emily said, "I put your chicken casserole into the microwave and made a salad, Mom. I hope you weren't saving the casserole for anything. I didn't know."

"Saving it for all of you, dear. And thank you, Emily. You're as helpful as my right hand."

"Annie set the table," Emily said pointedly.

"If I had two right hands, then you'd be the other one, Annie."

The atmosphere was tranquil. One could always sense something as palpable as wind or temperature in a room where any strong emotions, healthy or otherwise, had stirred the air. Here, now, a breeze rippled the white silk curtains, Juliet dozed under the table, and three calm faces turned to Lynn. Can they all have forgotten? she asked herself incredulously. It was true that Robert's black moods could quickly, with the flip of a coin, turn golden. Also it was true that, when in his own golden mood, he knew how to charm a person whom he had just hurt and angered. Besides, the girls had the wonderful, forgetful resilience of youth. For that at least, she should be thankful. Still, it was astonishing to see them all sitting there like that.

Annie inquired, "Where were you so late, Mommy?"

"Oh, I had the usual errands and didn't look at my watch."

Unconsciously, Lynn glanced toward Robert, whose glance, above the rim of his cup, met hers. He put the cup down, and she looked away.

"Aren't you going to tell Mom now?" asked Emily, addressing Robert.

At once alarmed, Lynn gave a little cry. "Tell Mom what? Has something happened?"

"Something very nice, I think," Emily said.

Robert, reaching into his jacket pocket, drew out a long envelope and, with a satisfied air, handed it to Lynn.

"Plane tickets," he told her.

"Kennedy to San Juan and transfer to St.—" she read. "Robert! What on earth?"

"Ten days in the Caribbean. We leave Saturday morning. That gives you a few days to get ready and to feel better. He wore a proud smile. "Now, what do you say to that?"

What I want to say, she thought, is: How dare you! What do you think I am? Instead, and only because the girls were present, she replied, "The girls can't miss school, Robert. I don't know what can be in your mind."

"They aren't going to miss school. This vacation is for you and me."

It was a cheap—no, an expensive—bribe. She could feel the heat in her cheeks. And still for the girls' sake, she said evenly, "It makes no sense. Who'll be in charge here? I'm not walking away and leaving a household to fend for itself."

"Of course not. That's all been taken care of. I've spent the whole day making arrangements. Eudora will sleep in while we're gone. The girls use the school bus, and if there's need to go anyplace, Eudora'll take them in her car or Bruce and Josie will, on the weekends. I talked to Bruce," Robert explained. "They'll be glad to take the girls to the town pool, and Bruce will drive Annie to her tennis lesson. I don't want her to miss it, and he doesn't mind."

Annie, who returned Bruce's love tenfold, now interjected a plea. "You know I like going with Uncle Bruce, Mommy. Please say yes, Mommy."

"So you see, it's all arranged. No problems. Nothing to do but pack a few clothes," Robert said positively.

Feeling trapped, Lynn pushed away from the table, saying only, "We'll talk about it later. I don't like having things sprung on me like this. Now, you have homework, girls. Leave the kitchen; I'll clean up by myself."

When she went upstairs, Robert followed. Once in their room, she turned on him.

"You think you can bribe me, don't you? It's unspeakable."

"Please. There's no bribe intended, only a cure. A cure for what ails us."

"It'll take more than ten days in the island paradise," she said sarcastically. "A whole lot more, to do that."

At the window she stood with her back to him. The view of trees and hill, always so restful to her soul, was melancholy now as the hill hid the lowering sun and shadowed the garden.

"The girls want us to go. You heard them."

Of course they do, she thought. It will be an adventure for them to lord it over the house with their parents away. Why not? And she thought, too, now with a twinge of unease, Emily will stay out too late with Harris.

Robert persisted. "I'm not worried about them, you know. Bruce and Josie are as dependable as you and I are."

Yes, she thought, when they can be useful, you will use the Lehmans, even though you don't like them. Still she said nothing, only, for some unconscious reason, turned up her palms, on which tiny dark-red scabs like polka dots had begun to form.

"I don't want to go," she said abruptly.

"You saw that man today," he said.

"I did," she retorted, "and what of it?"

"I didn't believe you would. I'm completely shocked. I didn't think you really meant to."

"I meant to, Robert."

"And what did he—"

"Oh, no!" she cried. "You don't ask a question like that. Don't you know any better? Unless you will consent to go with me."

"If it will satisfy you," he said, seizing her words. "I don't believe we need anything except to get away together. But if it will satisfy you, I will do anything," he finished humbly.

And she stood there still staring at her hands.

"We're tired, both of us." He, whose speech was always so deliberate, now rushed and stumbled. "This last year or two has been hectic, there's been no rest, you and I have scarcely had an hour alone together. The new house for you, new office and work for me. New faces for me, new schools, friends, all these hard adjustments—"

In the face of his distress she felt triumphant, and yet something in her had to pity that distress.

"Listen. I know my temper's hot, but I don't lose it often, you have to admit. And I'm always sorry as hell afterward. Not that that does much good, I know. But I'm not a bad sort, Lynn, and I love you."

From below came the sound of Annie's plodding minuet. Emily came bounding upstairs to answer her ringing phone. As if he had read Lynn's mind—as he almost always could—Robert said softly, "They need us, Lynn. Our children need us both. We can't punish them. Let's put this crazy business behind us. Please."

"Oh," she said with a heavy sigh.

He paced the room while again his words rushed.

"I was jealous, I was furious that night. The sight of you dancing with that man when I had been worried about you made me frantic. You looked so intimate together. I realize now how stupid it was of me. You're an innocent woman, you could never—" And he stopped while his eyes went bright with the start of tears. "Then you said there was something wrong with me."

"I was very, very angry, Robert, and I still am."

"All right. Angry or not, will you go? For the family's sake, will you go?" He laid the thick envelope on the dresser. "I was lucky to get these tickets. They're all booked up for honeymooners this time of year, but there was a cancellation. So you see, it was meant to be. Oh, Lynn, forgive me."

He was still standing there, with the tears still brilliant on his lashes, when without replying, she turned away.

Down the long road beside the marshes the plane sped, raised itself mightily into the bright air, and circled southward.

"Well, here we are," said Robert.

Lynn said nothing. Nothing was required. Resentment was still sore in her, burning like ill-digested food. Because of her wish to be finished with a hideous anger, to conceal from her children whatever could be concealed, she had been led and inveigled, tricked, into sitting where she now sat.

"You'll be glad you've gone," he said soothingly.

She turned the full force of her scorn upon him. "Glad? That'll be the day."

Robert, with a look of appeal, pursed his lips to caution: Shh. They were sitting three abreast. An old man, so hugely fat that his bulk hung over his seat into Robert's space, sat by the window. The aisle seat was Lynn's.

"Miserably cramped," Robert murmured. "First class was taken up, dammit."

Ignoring him, she took a book out of her carry-on and settled back. It had always been her way to "make the best" of things, and whether she liked to admit it to herself or not, there was, even in these circumstances, a certain anticipation of pleasure in the sight of palms and blue water. Having spent most of her life in the Midwest, she still found these a marvelous novelty; she had visited the lovely, lazy Caribbean islands only twice before. There's no point, she argued now, in wearing a hair shirt. I shall swim, I've brought three great books, and luckily for me, I'm thin enough so that I can afford to eat; I hope the food will be good. And I don't have to talk to Robert.

He mumbled again, "I'm going to try for first class going home. I can't tolerate this. It's worse than the subway."

When she did not comment, he made no further effort, and little more was said between them all the rest of the way.

From the balcony on the first morning, she looked out upon water and sky. There was no one in sight except for the beachboys, who were setting up a row of yellow umbrellas, and far out a little bobbing boat with a Roman-striped sail. I suppose, she thought idly, if one were to head straight east from here, one would land someplace in northern Africa.

"Why, you're up early," Robert said brightly. "You beat me this morning. Wonderful, isn't it?"

"Yes. I'm going for a walk on the beach."

"If you'll wait a minute, I'll go with you."

"Thank you, but I want to walk by myself."

"All right," he said agreeably.

The sun had not been up long, and the air was still cool. She walked easily on the firm sand at the water's edge, left the hotel's property behind, and continued along what seemed to be an unending stretch of beach edged by pine grove, beach grape, and clustered greenery nameless to her. Occasionally, she passed what must be the winter homes of American or British millionaires, low, gracious houses steeped in the shade of banyan and flamboyant trees.

Rounding an abrupt curve, she faced a grassy hill that blocked her path, steep as a ladder, with water on three sides. It would be a struggle to the top, but not daunted, she began the climb. Once there and breathless, she sat down to look about and gaze and was struck with the kind of wonder that fills the soul in some ancient, high cathedral.

No, not so. For here was a far greater splendor. Such blue! Almost green at the shore where the green hill was reflected, this water shaded into purest turquoise; then three quarters of the way to the horizon lay a broad band of cobalt so even as to have been drawn with a ruler. On the farthest outer edge the horizon was a thin, penciled line, above which there spread another blue, the calm, eternal blue of a sky without cloud.

The wind rushed and the tide in soporific rhythm splashed on the rocks below. Before her lay an immense dazzle, the mysterious power of brilliant light; so it had been for untold eons and would be for untold eons more, she thought, until the sun should burn itself out and the earth freeze. The thought was hardly original, but that made it no less awe-some.

Lying back on the rough sweet grass, she looked up at the shimmering sky. All the transient things, the injustice, the hurt, the unfairness, what were they in the end that we should waste our lives on them? My God, how short life was!

Now came a flock of seabirds, racing from nowhere, turning and turn-ing in their descent to skim the water and soar again upward. They were so joyous—could birds be joyous?—and she laughed at herself for think-ing so and at her own pleasure in watching them. And her first thoughts returned with a thrill of sorrow, repeating: How short life is. And we walk with blinders on.

For half an hour or maybe longer, she lay while the hilltop breeze cooled the sun's burning. Stretching, she felt how young and healthy her body was. Even her foot was beginning to ease, and the heat seemed to soothe her wounds. She felt a surge of strength, as if she had absorbed the power of the light, as if she possessed the power to do anything, to bear anything, to solve anything.

Then she lectured aloud. After all, Lynn, he didn't want, he didn't try, to hurt you. He's beside himself now with regret and guilt. This can go on forever, this rage of yours, if you allow it to. But it will corrode you if you do. Listen, he could have been eaten up with rage at you because of our tragedy, our Caroline. . . .

And she reflected, I shouldn't have stayed late at that damn-fool din-ner. That's what began it all. I should not have let myself be lured into staying. What if I had been waiting at home for Robert and then found him having a careless good time with a pretty woman?

She remembered Tom Lawrence's cheek so close to her own, almost touching, his mischievous, clever eyes, bright like his hair and his fresh skin, and the cheerful effects of this brightness. *You have such sweet eyes, a sweet mouth, Lynn.* Flattery, all flattery, possibly with the hope that it might lead to something, and possibly not that at all. How was she to know? I know so little, she thought. Married at twenty and sheltered ever since, when and where could I have learned about the world?

No, she said then to herself, and sat up. Naïveté like that is inexcus-able. I should have known better. I should at least have been smart enough to foresee consequences. My husband has a temper, that shouldn't be news to me. . . .

Our children need us, he'd said. It's true, she thought now, he is never too tired or busy to do something for them. Waiting in Washington between planes, he hails a taxi to the National Gallery of Art. *We can show them a good many pictures in ninety minutes,* he says, imbuing us all with his energy. He gets out of the hammock where he has been resting and runs into the house to fetch the encyclopedia because he wants to make sure he has given his daughter the best answer to her question. He sits up all night with Annie when she has her tonsils out.

He could also be harsh with them, and too demanding. Yes, yes, I know. But they were quite fine the last two days before we came here. Regardless of everything, they do love him. People say things they don't really mean.

Our children need us. They need us both.

There's nothing that can't be worked out by applying some simple common sense.

Back in the room, a note lay on a table next to a book. The note said, *Gone to breakfast. I'll be in the dining room or else on the beach.* The book was opened to a poem, a poem that Lynn did not need to read because she almost knew it by heart. Nevertheless, she read it again.

> *"O fierce and shy, Your glance so piercing-true*
> *Shot fire to the struck heart that was as tinder—*
> *The fire of your still loveliness, the tender*
> *High fortitude of the spirit shining through.*
> *And the world was young. O—"*

She laid the book down and shivered. He had given these poems to her when they were first married, and they had often read them together; sometimes he had read aloud in his grave, expressive voice; they had been so madly in love.

> *"The high fortitude of the spirit shining through.*
> *And the world was young—"*

"Oh, Robert," she said.

She found him reading on the beach. At her approach he looked up, questioning.

"I've come to bury the hatchet," she told him shyly.

Two poor tears sprang into the corners of his eyes, and he took her hand into his and held it. It seemed to her that a stream of common blood was running through their joined hands. She felt the pride and relief of calm forgiveness.

"You read the poem?" When she nodded, he cried anxiously, "Lynn, Lynn, you're everything in the world to me. Without you I'm nothing. You do know that, don't you? Are we all right again? Are we?"

"Let's not talk about it anymore. It's over."

"We can have our bad times, but at least they don't last. Right, darling?" He jumped up. "Well, as you say, enough. What shall we do first, now? Jog or swim?"

"Let's walk. There's something I want to show you, where I've been."

So they retraced her path between the incoming tide and the silver twisted branches of the sea grape, past the fine houses in their gardens, Robert speculating on the price of each.

"Hey! How far is this thing you want to show me? Aren't you tired yet? This is your second trip."

"No, I'm a walker, and it's worth ten trips. You'll see."

"You're as young as you ever were."

It was true. Her body in the scarlet swimsuit was as taut and limber as it had been when she was twenty. And rejoicing in this health, in the breezy morning and the decent peace she had made, she strode, ignoring her slight limp, up the hill.

They stood quite still at the top.

"I see what you mean," Robert whispered.

This time, though, there was a sign of life in view: a white yacht moving sedately on a line with the horizon.

"Look at that grand thing," he said. "Wouldn't you love to own it? We could go off to the South Seas, all around the world."

"No," she responded seriously, "even if we could afford it, which we likely never will, I wouldn't want it."

He shook his head as if she were beyond understanding.

"What do you want? Don't you ever want anything?"

Still very seriously, she told him, "Only peace and love, that's all. Peace and love."

"You have them. You shall have them." He dropped down on the grass. "Sit here. Let's stay a minute." When she complied, he turned serious too. "I know I'm not always easy to live with. I'm not home enough. I'm a workaholic. And you're very patient, I know that too. At the office and on the commuter train I hear stories that can make one's hair stand on end, about women having nervous breakdowns, drinking alone during the day, or else having an affair with a hairdresser." He laughed. "Imagine you having an affair! I think you'd flee in terror if a man were to lay a hand on you. And when I hear all this, don't think I fail to appreciate what you are, the time and effort you put in with the children, your solid health, your good cheer, everything. I should do more. I should take more upon myself."

"You do plenty. More than many fathers do. Much more," she said sincerely.

"No, I should do better. You don't play piano, so you can't help Annie with it. I was thinking she should switch to popular music. It will help her socially when she's a few years older." He sighed. "And I worry about Emily and that boy. I know you don't like to hear it, but—"

"Not now, Robert. It's too beautiful here to think of worries, even though I don't agree that Harris is a worry. Shall we go back?"

Half walking, half sliding, they descended the hill and trudged along the shoreline, their feet slapping through the wet sand.

For a time neither spoke, until Robert said, "Oh, I just want to say one thing more and then—you're right that this is no place or time for problems—but is Emily just being an average teenager, growing away as she's supposed to grow, or is there something else? Lately when we're together I've had the feeling that she's annoyed with me." And when Lynn did not reply at once, he said, sounding wistful, "I wish you'd be truthful if there's anything you know."

She hesitated. "She feels that you weren't always open with her and shut her out."

"Shut her out? From what?"

"Oh, things. Little things. For instance, she said—when she mentioned Querida a while ago you were furious. You shouted at her. You wouldn't tell her anything."

He protested. "Of course I wouldn't. Why does she need to know? That brilliant aunt of mine! It's a wonder she didn't let slip about the boy too. There'd be a hundred questions about that, wouldn't there? Well, my conscience is clear. I've done right by him, but he's no part of my life. The bank informs me that he lives in Europe. I don't even know in what country. I don't support him anymore. He's an adult. It's a complete separation. There's nothing unusual about that these days, with families dispersed over the globe." Stopping his agitated walk, he stood still, looking out over the water. "Why are we talking about this foolishness, anyway?"

"You asked about Emily."

"Yes. Yes, I did. Well," he said, looking down at her with a troubled expression, "is there anything else?"

I've gone partway, and I might as well go all the way, she told herself. And fixing her eyes upon Robert, she said quietly, "She thinks you did that to me the other night."

He took a deep breath, and she saw how her words had struck him.

"And what did you say? Did you—explain? Did you—"

She answered steadily, still with her eyes fixed on his. "I told her that was arrant nonsense. That I was astonished she could ever have such a thought."

Robert bowed his head. They were two people in pain. How odd, Lynn thought, to stand here in this streaming sunlight, with all this animated life around us, children on floats, people splashing into the waves, calling and laughing, while we have a dialogue so tragic, so profound. No one seeing them here could possibly guess. She pitied the man who stood there with bowed head, and she touched his arm.

"Enough, Robert. I've had no breakfast, and I'm starved. Is there a place on the terrace where I might get a cup of coffee and a roll?"

His response was a grateful, a humble, smile. "Of course. I've explored the whole place and all its hidden corners. There's a hidden corner with umbrella tables in the shade near the pool. Let's go. And after that, a swim. And after that," he said, recovering, "there's a fishing trip scheduled for this afternoon, a short one to an out island in a catamaran. Or we might sign up tomorrow for an all-day trip with snorkeling and a picnic lunch on one of the farther islands. Or would you like a water-ski lesson? I looked over the schedule this morning."

She had to smile. It was so like Robert to organize, to account for every minute.

"Swim first, then take the others as they come. Remember, you said we needed to relax."

"Right. Right you are."

Later in the afternoon they came back laughing at themselves after their first lesson on water skis, and took seats in the shade near the pool. Little groups of young couples were chatting at surrounding tables.

"Honeymooners, most of them," Robert observed. "You could be a bride yourself. You don't look any different from them."

"Brides are older these days."

"You're turning just faintly brown," he remarked.

"In spite of sunblock and a shady hat? I'll go home looking like a lobster. Ah, well, since that's the case, I might as well be fat too. I'll have ice cream."

She was aware as she ate that he was watching her, as if he were enjoying her enjoyment. She finished the ice cream with a feeling of satisfaction, thinking, How physical we are! The taste buds are satisfied, the stomach is filled, the air is fresh, not too hot and not too cool, and somehow all our troubles vanish—for a while, anyway.

A lizard, green as a gem, slid along a wall. Blackbirds stalked among the tables picking up fallen crumbs. A tiny yellow bird alighted on the table, paused on the edge, and then, on its frail, twiggy legs, hopped to the ice cream dish where lay a small, melted puddle. Totally still, Lynn sat watching the little beak thrust and thrust again; with the other part of her vision she was still aware of Robert watching her with the same affectionate concentration that she was giving to the bird.

"It's adorable," she said. "That little brain can't be any bigger than half a pea."

"It's you who are adorable," he told her.

An elderly couple sitting at the next table overheard him, for the man, catching Robert's eye, smiled and nodded.

"We were watching you two on water skis," he said with a heavy German accent.

"Oh, we were both awful," Robert answered. "It was our first time."

"So you were very brave, then. My wife and I"—he raised gray eyebrows in an expression of mock sorrow—"we are too old to learn new things."

And so a conversation began. Introductions were made, and brief biographical sketches drawn. The Hummels were from Stuttgart; he was a banker, semiretired, but only semi; they did a good deal of traveling, mostly in Eastern Europe of late, where so many astonishing changes were occurring. This trip, their first to the Caribbean, was purely for pleasure, to celebrate their fiftieth wedding anniversary. Later, at home, there would be a party with family and friends, but first they wanted this time alone.

"And is today the day?" asked Robert.

"Today is the day," Herr Hummel acknowledged, and his wife, a portly woman with beautiful upswept white hair and no devices behind which to hide her age, nodded and smiled.

"It's so lovely here," she said. "Usually we go to the Riviera for sun, but it is nothing like this. All these strange, wonderful flowers—" And she waved toward a clump of shrubbery that bore in clusters what looked like red beads, each the size of a pinhead. "What do you call those?"

"Ixora," Robert answered.

"Ah, you study flowers," said Mrs. Hummel.

"Not really." Robert laughed. "I just happened to pass some on my way to breakfast this morning and saw a marker with the name."

"He remembers everything," said Lynn.

"So you have," Mr. Hummel remarked, "a memory like—what is the word? Like a camera, you know."

"A photographic memory," Lynn said. "Yes, he has."

"Perhaps," said Mr. Hummel, "you will tell me if I go too far, intrude on your time, but perhaps you will have a drink of champagne with us tonight? It is tomorrow we leave. Perhaps you will have dinner with us, a table for four?"

"Why, that would be very nice," Robert answered cordially.

When they were alone, Lynn was curious. "Why did you say yes to dinner with them?"

"Well, he's a banker with connections in the new republics. It never hurts to pick up information and connections wherever you can. Besides, they're nice people, and you can see they're feeling a little bit lonesome."

She was amused. Even away on vacation his mind was with General American Appliance.

"It's dress up tonight," he said. "I read it on the bulletin in the lobby. Dancing and entertainment."

"Limbo and calypso, I'm sure. Funny, I keep loving calypso no matter how often I hear it."

"That dress is perfect, well worth the money."

White silk was even whiter and pearls more luminous against sun-tinged skin. She was pleased with herself.

"Where's the bracelet?" Robert asked.

"Which one?" she replied, knowing which one he meant because he always asked about it.

"The cabochons. The good one."

"It's much too valuable to take traveling," she told him.

It was indeed a special piece, always remarked upon whenever she wore it, and yet she wore it only when he reminded her to. It made her remember the sinking despair of that bleak windy night on the bench overlooking Lake Michigan. It wasn't healthy to relive a night like that one.

The Hummels had reserved a table near the dining-room balcony overlooking the sea. Champagne was already in a cooler. They were beaming, he in a summer dinner jacket and she in light blue chiffon, rather too fancy. A pair of solid burghers, Lynn thought, and felt kindly disposed to them. Fifty years married!

"It is so nice to be with young people for our little celebration," said Mrs. Hummel. "You must tell us more about yourselves. You have babies at home?"

"Not babies," Lynn answered. "Not babies. A daughter of seventeen and an eleven-year-old."

"My goodness, we have grandchildren older. A boy twenty-seven. He works in Franz's bank," she added proudly.

The conversation now divided, Mrs. Hummel describing to Lynn every member of her large family, while the men, led by Robert, pursued a different direction. With half an ear Lynn, who was hardly interested in the Hummel grandchildren, was able to hear some of the men's talk.

"I'm starting a course in Hungarian," Robert said. "I don't know where I'll get the time, but I'll have to make the time."

"A man of your type makes the time. I know your type."

"Thank you, but it's a difficult language. An Ugric language, related to Finnish, I'm told. I decided to start with it because, by comparison, Hungary is already somewhat prosperous. My firm deals in home appliances, as you know, and as the country gets richer, the demand will grow."

"Have you been in Hungary yet?"

"No, I want to prepare a team for Russia, Poland, and the whole area before I talk to the top brass—the president, that is. I've got to get a better handle on the languages, though. It makes an impression if you can show your contacts that you're at least making the effort to learn their language."

"You're right. It's true that not everybody speaks English. People seem to think that everybody does."

"—often think boys are easier to bring up," Mrs. Hummel was saying. "I suppose your husband would love to have a boy."

"I guess he would, but two are enough, and he adores our girls."

"Actually, I'm in marketing, but one needs to broaden one's scope. I have to know what they're doing in product development if I'm to do a competent job in marketing, don't I?"

"Ya, ya. Technology changes by the hour. You give me your card, I'll give you mine, and if I can be of any help, who knows, we may work some good things out together. No?"

"I'd be delighted. Now I think we're neglecting your great occasion. I'm going to order another bottle, and we're going to drink to the next fifty years."

"Your husband is a very ambitious, very intelligent young man, Mrs. Ferguson," Mr. Hummel told Lynn.

"It's heartwarming," Mrs. Hummel said, "to see a couple still young and beautiful together. All these discontented couples, I never understand, so many of them. Franz and I are seventy-three. I'm seven months older, but we never tell anybody." All four laughed, and Lynn said politely, "Neither one of you looks his age."

"Really?" Mrs. Hummel was gratified. "If it's so, it's because we have been so happy with each other. My mother always told me—there is a *sprichwort*—a saying, about not going to sleep angry."

"Never let the sun go down on your anger," Lynn said. "My mother told me that too."

"Ah, yes. And it works, it really does."

"Interesting types," Robert said when they got up to dance.

"Rather out of fashion these days in this world."

"Well, if they are, it's too bad about this world."

They were in the open courtyard. When the music paused, one heard the swish of the waves, hushed now at low tide. Into the perfumed night the music blended. "Smoke Gets in Your Eyes" and "Always and Always" they played.

It might be corny, Lynn said to herself, and yet the music is as lovely as the day it was written before I was born. And it still appeals to a longing that doesn't die, no matter what the style or the generation and whether people admit it or not.

"Do I dance as well as Tom Lawrence does?" Robert whispered.

She drew back and reproached him. "For someone who can be so tactful when he wants to be, I'm surprised at you."

"I'm sorry. It was meant to be funny, and it wasn't at all. I'm sorry." He kissed her ear and held her more closely. "Forgive me."

Passing the Hummels, who were dancing stiffly apart, the two couples smiled at each other.

"Never let the sun go down on your anger," Robert murmured. "We're going to remember that."

Yes. Yes. A whole fresh start. The champagne is going to my head. Such a lovely feeling. And above Robert's shoulder the sky was suddenly filled with blinking stars.

"Are there more stars here? Is that possible, Robert? Or am I drunk?"

"You may be drunk, but it does seem as if there are more because there's no pollution, and the sky is clear. Anyway, the constellations are different here. We're close to the equator."

"You know so much," she whispered.

And she looked around at the men moving to the music in slow circles. Not one could compare with Robert, so distinguished, so admired, so full of knowledge, with such marvelous eyes, now gazing into hers with that long, long look.

"I can't help falling in love with you." Their bodies moved to the nostalgia and the yearning, were led by it, slowly, closer and closer; as one body, they were barely moving, swaying together in one spot.

"I can't help falling in love with you," he sang into her ear. And she thought: I was so angry that I wished he would die. Oh, God, oh, God, and overcome with tears, she reached up to his mouth, and there on the dance floor, kissed him over and over.

"Oh, my dear, my dearest."

"Let's get out of here," he whispered. "Say good-night to those people and get out of here. Quick, I can't wait."

In the room he slammed and fastened the door, crying, "Hurry, hurry!"

"I am. Don't tear my dress."

"I'll buy you another one."

He seized her and carried her to the wide, cool bed. Palms rattled at the window and the sea wind blew all through the first time and the second, and then all night, long after they had fallen asleep.

They swam and went deep-sea fishing, then played tennis, took long runs on the beach, and lay resting in the shade. Others went to the free-port shops and returned with the usual bags of liquor and perfume, but Lynn and Robert went no farther than a sailboat could carry them. After the Hummels departed, they were always, by tacit agreement only, together.

In the mornings when the first tree frogs began to peep, they made love again.

"No work, no errands, no telephone, no clock, no kids," he whispered.

It was delicious, unhurried luxury. It was like being remade, like being married all over again. Robert had been right. This was what they had needed.

PART THREE

◇

Summer 1988– Spring 1989

3

No one was home when they arrived except Juliet, who gave them a tongue-licking welcome and then turned over to have her belly scratched.

"Where is everybody?" Lynn wondered.

"Maybe there's a note on the bulletin board in the kitchen."

She opened the kitchen door, stood a second in total bewilderment, and gasped.

"Oh, my God! What have you done?"

Robert came in grinning. "Like it? Like it?"

"How on earth did you ever do this?"

"It was easy. Just paid an arm and a leg for their guarantee to finish it in ten days, that's all."

A glistening new kitchen had been installed with a restaurant-sized stove, a double-sized refrigerator-freezer, a trash compactor, and a center island above which hung the best new European cookware. Closets and glass-fronted cabinets had been expertly reorganized and consolidated; a library of cookbooks stood in vivid jackets on the shelves, and African violets in lavender bloom flourished on the broad new windowsills.

"I think I'm going to faint," Lynn said.

"Well, don't do that. You're supposed to produce good meals here, not faint."

"It's perfect. It's gorgeous, you're a magician, you're Santa Claus, you're an angel."

"A talented worker deserves a good workroom. I've done some thinking, and I truly realize what this means to you, so if you want to do some sort of baking or catering on a small scale, if it will make you happy, why, now you've got the place to do it in. And if not, well, you've got a handsome kitchen, that's all."

"You couldn't, you absolutely couldn't, have given me anything more wonderful."

She was hugging him when the front door opened to a chorus, "Welcome home!" and the girls, with Josie and Bruce and Harris, came in with arms full.

"Chinese takeout," Emily said. "We didn't expect you to make dinner in this palace the minute you got home."

"I came over every day to watch the miracle take shape," Josie said.

"Girls, I hope you didn't make any trouble for Uncle Bruce and Aunt Josie," Robert said.

"We had a fine time," Bruce assured him. "We ate out, we ate at our house, and last Sunday Harris took us to the woods and made a meal from scratch. He started a fire without matches."

"Without matches," Lynn repeated, turning to Harris, who was actually blushing.

"Well, I was an Eagle Scout. You have to know how to survive in the wilderness."

"The Connecticut wilderness?" asked Robert.

Josie corrected him. "It's the same thing whether you're here or in the wilderness of Timbuktu."

Bruce laughed. "Timbuktu is not a wilderness, Josie."

"Harris," said Emily, "tell them about you-know-what at school."

"No, they're your parents, you tell them," Harris answered quietly.

"We both got an A in the advanced chemistry finals. The only ones in the class."

Harris corrected her. "You got an A, and I got an A-minus."

Robert put his arm about his daughter's shoulder. "I'm so proud of you, Emily."

Bruce spoke to Harris, who was standing a little apart. "You must be coming close to a college decision. Have you any special place in mind?"

"Wherever I can get the best scholarship," the boy replied seriously. "They're kind of scarce these days."

"Well, summer vacation's almost upon you, so just relax awhile and leave those worries for September," Lynn said cheerfully. "And you know what we're going to do? Next Sunday I'm going to inaugurate this kitchen. I'm going to make a big supper. All of you come. Annie, bring a friend or two, and, Bruce, if your cousin should be in town by then, bring him along. We'll eat on the deck."

"It's been raining all week," Annie said, pouting.

"Well, all the better. That means we're due for a long spell of sunshine," Lynn told her.

A long spell, a lasting spell of sunshine in many ways, she assured herself.

It was as she had predicted, the proverbial day in June, cool and blue. All the previous afternoon and all morning she had been working and humming to herself in the new kitchen, and the result was a summer banquet, "fit for the gods," as Robert put it.

On the big round table in the kitchen's bay window stood a lobster ragout fragrant with herbs, crisp green peppers stuffed with tomatoes and goat cheese, warm French bread, a salad of raw vegetables in an icy bed of lettuce, a pear tart glazed with apricot jam, and a chocolate torte garnished with fresh raspberries and *crème anglaise*. In a pair of antique crystal carafes, bought by Robert, were red wine and white, while for Annie and her friend Lynn had set out a bowl of ginger-ale punch in which there floated a few balls of vanilla ice cream.

"If you'd like me to grill a couple of hamburgers outside for the little girls, I'd be glad to, Mrs. Ferguson," Harris offered.

She looked at him and laughed. "You're just too polite to tell me that those kids won't like the lobster ragout, and you're right. I should have thought of that myself."

Harris laughed back. What a nice boy, she thought, handing him a plate of raw hamburgers.

Bruce had brought his cousin, who was visiting from the Midwest. He was a quiet man, much like Bruce himself, who taught physics at a high school in Kansas City. Harris and Emily immediately got talking to him about physics and premeds. Annie and her friend were full of giggles over some private joke. It gladdened Lynn to see Annie having an intimate friend.

Bruce's cousin admired the view. "You have a beautiful place here," he told Robert, who sat across from him.

"It needs a lot of work yet. I'm thinking of putting a split-rail fence along the boundaries. And of course, we should have a pool. I want a naturalistic pool, not one of those ordinary rectangular affairs, but something free form with woodsy landscaping. It'll be a big job."

"I'm perfectly content with the pool at the club," Lynn reminded Robert.

"My wife is easily satisfied," Robert said.

"You always say that," Josie remarked.

And Robert remarked, "Well, it's true."

"There's nothing wrong with the pool at the club," Lynn insisted, out of a certain consideration for the feelings of the schoolteacher, whose income, one could be sure, did not provide either for a private pool or a country club membership, adding, "especially when the company pays for the club. Otherwise, I wouldn't even want that."

"Let's all help carry things back to the kitchen," Bruce suggested. "Having stuffed ourselves like this, we need the exercise."

Robert sprang up. "After that, how about badminton, or croquet? I've just set up a game on the side lawn, so take your choice."

When the table had been cleared, Lynn sat down to rest.

"Do you know the best thing about vacations, Josie? That they stay with you. Here I am, happy to be home, and yet a part of me is still down on the island. I can still feel that soft, damp air."

"I'm glad," said Josie.

"I can't thank you and Bruce enough for taking care of the girls."

"Don't be silly. We love them, and they were wonderful."

Juliet, having been unlawfully fed with hamburger scraps, came sniffing to Josie now in hopes of more.

"Yes, yes, you're a good dog," she said almost absently, while her hand played in the thick ruff of hair around the dog's neck. "A good dog," she repeated, and then suddenly she raised her hand to confront Lynn with what Lynn knew she had been meaning to say all the time. "So. You have an appointment with my friend, I think."

"I'm not going to keep it. I must call him."

"I think you should keep it," Josie said.

"Things change, Josie. Being away together, you get a different perspective. Robert's right. When we moved, we all had too many adjustments to make. It's been especially hard for the girls, unsettling, bad for the nerves, even though on the surface they handled it well. It's foolish to take every blow-up too seriously, as if the end had come. In this last week alone since we've been home, why—I can't tell you how good it's been. Robert's even been so nice to Harris. I convinced him that he shouldn't worry, that they're just kids having their first crush, and he finally agreed that I'm right, that Harris is a very fine person. And Robert's gotten the girls interested in the hospital fund drive, so they're selling tickets to everybody they know. They'll be calling you next, I'm sure."

"It's nice to hear all that, but I still think you ought to go, Lynn."

"I wouldn't know what to say to the man. I'd feel like a fool," Lynn said firmly. "No. I'm canceling the appointment. To tell the truth, I forgot about it or I would have done it already."

So she closed the subject. She regretted the day she had run to Josie and complained. She was a big girl, for heaven's sake, and would solve her own problems. She already had solved them.

June was a crowded month, a month of rituals. Annie had a birthday party complete with pink crepe-paper, pink icing, and a new pink dress. Friends had weddings and proud commencements. It was a time of graceful ceremonies, set about with flowers. And through these festive days Lynn moved with a fresh sense of well-being.

On a hot Saturday, the last in the month, Robert went to the city for a morning's work. Lynn, knowing that he would never alter his habits, agreed to meet him later in the afternoon at the club's pool. Arriving early, she found a chair in the shade and, glad of the privacy afforded by Annie's and Emily's occupation elsewhere, settled down to read until Robert should arrive. She was somewhat irritated, therefore, when she saw a man approach carrying a folding chair, and more than irritated when he turned out to be Tom Lawrence.

Lawrence was dressed for golf, wearing a light straw hat, which he now tipped to her, replaced, and removed again, this confusion giving her the impression that he was as discomfited as she was.

"In this heat you've got to be crazy to go out on the fairway," he complained. "I need to cool off in the shade. Do you mind?"

"Not at all."

He sat down, and she returned to her book with a finality intended to discourage any further conversation. For a few moments he waited, saying nothing, and then spoke.

"Actually, I was on my way out, when I caught a glimpse of you. I wanted to talk to you. I wanted to apologize."

She raised her eyes from the book and looked at him. The happy thought came to her that this time, unlike the last, she could face him confidently; she was wearing the scarlet swimsuit that had been so successful on the Caribbean beach; her body was unblemished and her face unmarked by having wept.

"What for?" she asked.

"I was to blame for making you late that night and making your husband furious."

"He wasn't furious," she said, resenting the man's intrusion.

"Oh, come." The tone was gentle. "He was furious. Everyone saw it."

"I can't help what everyone saw," she said coldly. "And it was none of their business, anyway." To her shame angry tears began to form, as they always did whenever her emotions, grieving or joyous, were stirred. Damn tears. She blinked them back, but not before he had seen.

He shook his head. "It's a pity for you to be unhappy."

She turned upon him then. "How can you talk to me this way? What do you know about me? I'm not unhappy. Not."

"You were miserable when I saw you the next morning. And I do know something about you. I know that your husband lays a heavy hand on you, and I don't mean just psychologically either."

She was appalled. She was totally shocked. She had a positively Victorian impulse to say something like "How dare you?" and then flounce off in seething indignation. But of course, that would be ridiculous. There were people sitting all around the pool who would notice. All this rushed through her head, and she said only, "I have never heard anyone talk so outrageously in all my life. You're making a fool of yourself too. You don't know what you're saying."

"But I do know. I used to do divorce work, and I've seen the signs too often to be mistaken."

Her heart was pounding. She pulled herself up into a haughty posture and said, making each word sharply distinct, "My husband happens to be a useful, respected citizen with a good name. He's a senior officer with one of the world's largest corporations, General American Appliance. Perhaps," she added sarcastically, "you have possibly heard of it?"

"Yes, I've been a stockholder for years. As a matter of fact, the president, Pete Monacco, is a friend of mine. He married my cousin. A sort of third cousin, I believe."

"Well, good for you. With connections like that you should know better than to cast aspersions on a man who does what Robert does, in this community alone. The hospital, AIDS, the new town library—" She was almost sputtering. "You ought to be ashamed of yourself!"

Lawrence was undaunted. "The one has nothing to do with the other. A man can be a distinguished citizen and still be violent toward his wife."

His voice and face were kind. He sat there, easily, cradling the straw hat on his knee. He might have been talking about something as trivial as the heat. But his words were blunt and hard as a hammer.

"You don't know how good Robert is, how totally devoted to his family. You don't understand."

For answer Tom simply shook his head. And this stubborn refusal to retract his words made her anger boil afresh.

"What's the matter with me? What kind of a fool am I? Why am I even *talking* like this to a stranger? Allowing you to say such things to me. It's degrading to us both. And I'll tell you something: If you're still around, we'll invite you to our fiftieth anniversary and dare you to come. Dare you."

He stood up. "I admire you for your defense, Lynn. I know your kind of woman. You have a vision of romance. 'Till death do us part,' no matter what. It's the 'no matter what' that's wrong. Otherwise I'm all in favor of fiftieth anniversaries, I assure you."

She got up and walked toward the pool. Only a dive into the water would silence this man.

"Romantic visions of everlasting love. That's what you're living by."

"Yes," she said over her shoulder, "yes, I believe in that. I live by it."

"Take care you don't die by it, Lynn."

Those were the last words she heard before the water splashed over her.

"You seem disturbed about something," Robert said, when, not long afterward, he joined her.

"This sickening heat is enough to disturb anybody."

Later he remarked, "I thought I saw Tom Lawrence leaving the club when I drove in."

"Yes, he was here."

"Did you talk to him?"

"A few words. Not much more than hello and good-bye."

Still later, at dinner, he said, "The company president is flying in on Monday to give a talk. He's some impressive guy. Powerful. It's easy to see how he got where he is. Funny how things change, though," he mused. "A generation ago nobody with an Italian name would have headed a company like ours."

"What's wrong with an Italian name?"

"It just didn't use to happen, that's all. Now it happens every day."

What made her say what she next said, Lynn could not have explained. "Tom Lawrence is related to him."

"How do you know that?"

"He told me so today."

"You must have had quite a talk with him, then," Robert said after a moment.

"Not at all. I told you that we said a few words. And he happened to mention Mr. Monacco."

Robert looked amused. "I don't mind that you talked to him, Lynn, since that's what you're thinking of. So he told you he's related to Monacco? That's odd. I had the impression that Lawrence was old American stock."

"It's his second cousin who's married to Monacco."

"Oh." Robert looked reflective. "I wish I had a connection like that, distant or not. Business is contacts, it's channels. I've got a head full of ideas, but how to get to the right ears with them? One department overlaps another—" With a small, self-deprecating frown he paused. "Too bad. I would have done differently if I had known about Lawrence. But I'll make up for it. We're certain to run into him again at the club."

Lynn was aghast. "You surely aren't going to ask for an introduction to Mr. Monacco, are you?"

"No, no, no. That's not the way things are done. You get acquainted with somebody, invite him to dinner, get talking, and after a while—after a while, who knows what can happen?"

What can happen, she repeated to herself, is too awful to think about.

Still she could not help but think about it. The unmitigated gall of that man! Who was he to play detective-psychologist, and to pry into the innermost heart of a stranger's life? She could only dread the next time she would have to see Tom Lawrence.

Indeed, she was so agitated for a week or more that she kept waking up in the middle of the night to relive the scene at the pool's edge. She felt actually ill. Her stomach churned. And suddenly, one morning as the kitchen warmed with the pungent smells of coffee and bacon, she had to run from the room.

"I can't stand the smell of food," she complained when she came back. "Even the sight of it makes me sick."

"That certainly doesn't sound like you." Robert looked at her thoughtfully. "I don't suppose you could possibly be—"

She stared at him. "Oh, no. What are you saying?"

"We had some pretty good times down on the island."

She was barely able to absorb the possibility. Why, Emily was already seventeen!

"Would it be awful if I were? Would you mind awfully?"

"Do I look as if I would mind?" He chuckled.

"Maybe I am a little late," she admitted. "But since I often am, it hasn't occurred to me that it could be anything."

"Don't look so terrified. We always wanted three, and would have had them if we hadn't lost Caroline." Robert kissed her cheek. "It may be nothing, but see a doctor tomorrow, anyway. Or this afternoon, if you can."

She went to the doctor, received an affirmative answer, and came home in a state of shock despite what Robert had said. Her head was full of troublesome possibilities. How would Annie take the news? And she'd heard that at Emily's stage of life, a mother's pregnancy could be a painful embarrassment.

But Robert held her close. "Darling, darling. I'm delighted." Back and forth, he strutted, across the bedroom. He laughed. "Maybe it will be a boy. Not that it wouldn't be wonderful either way, but it would be fun to have a boy for a change. This is absolutely the best news, Lynn. You'll have to postpone your business venture for a while, but I guess there couldn't be a better reason. And don't you worry about the girls. Annie will have a live toy, and Emily's a real woman. She'll be a help, you'll see. Let's go downstairs and tell them."

"Oh, let it wait, Robert, this is much too soon."

"Why wait? Come on," he insisted.

His delight overflowed and was contagious.

"Well, Annie, you've been wanting us to let Juliet have puppies, so will this do instead?" He swung the heavy child off the floor and hugged her. "Room for one more, hey, girls? Always room for one more and plenty of love left over."

"Wait till I tell people in school," said Annie. "I'll bet I'm the only one of my friends who'll be having a new baby."

"Not yet, dear," Lynn warned. "It's not till the end of February. I'll let you know when you can talk about it. And, Emily, are you sure you don't feel 'funny'?"

She was moved when, unknowingly, Emily repeated Robert's words about Caroline, the little sister whom she could barely remember. "There would have been three of us if Caroline hadn't died."

The little white coffin, the overwhelming scent of white roses, enough to make you faint, hushed words meant to comfort, and arms supporting her.

Now again it was as if all of them, husband and children, were rallying to support her. She felt a sudden strong sense of unity among them, and a surge of excitement, a physical vibration, went through her body. On all their faces she seemed to see a look of curiosity, of respect and tenderness. And it came to her that, in this roundabout way, she might possibly be making up to Robert, in part, for the child who through her fault had been lost.

"Let's drive over to tell Josie and Bruce," she said suddenly.

"No, no. This is private talk between women. You run to see Josie, since I see you're bursting to tell. Just don't stay too long."

Bruce was in the backyard putting the finishing touches on the chest of drawers.

"That's beautiful," Lynn said.

"I was right. It's curly maple." He shoved his glasses up into his hair and looked at her quizzically. "Josie didn't expect you, did she? She's got a late meeting at the office."

"No. I was passing nearby and remembered something. Not important. That's a beautiful piece," she repeated. "What are you going to do with it?"

"Darned if I know. Maybe keep it and give it to Emily someday when she gets married. She likes old things. Feel the wood." He guided her hand over the top of the chest. "I've been working two months on this. Feels like satin, doesn't it?"

She smiled. "Like satin."

He was so steady, so relaxed, working there near the shed in the cool of the late afternoon. She wondered what it would be like to live with a man who moved and spoke without haste. He never seemed to be *going* anywhere, but rather to be already *there,* and content to be there. She imagined that he must be a considerate lover.

"You look preoccupied," he said while his hand moved up and down with the waxing cloth.

"I am, somewhat."

"Nothing bad, I hope."

"Not at all." A smile, quite involuntary, spread across her face and quickly receded as she told herself: It is utterly selfish of me to bring this news with such pleasure when they have—at least I know Bruce has—always wanted children so badly.

He had seen the quick flash of her smile. "What is it? Tell me."

"I'm going to have—I'm pregnant."

His wide mouth opened and shut. He laid the cloth down. And because his face went blank, with no readable expression, she was puzzled and vaguely hurt.

"Aren't you going to say anything? Is it so startling that you can't?"

"Well, it is a bit of a surprise."

Naturally, he would be remembering the day when she had come here with tear-swollen eyes and a pathetic story of trouble at home. But that was past. This baby was testimony to the start of a new understanding, a whole new era. And she said lightly, almost frivolously, "Why? I'm not that old."

"That's not what I meant."

"Oh, that! That's old business. It's over, Bruce, completely healed."

"Josie and I only want you to be happy, Lynn."

"I am happy."

"Then let me congratulate you." He gave her a quick hug. "I'll tell Josie the minute she comes in."

When she got back into the car, he was still watching her with that first blank look on his face. And as the car moved away, she heard him call after her, "God bless you, Lynn."

Now came a time of bloom. Nausea went as abruptly as it came. She felt strong and able, animated by good health. Because it had been so unexpected and because she was older, this new life seemed more marvelous than any of the others had. When, after amniocentesis, the doctor asked her whether she wanted to know the sex of the baby, she declined. She wanted to have all the delights, the suspense, and the surprise.

Once Robert told her she looked "exalted." He had come upon her in a quiet moment listening to music, and she had laughed, making light of her own profound feeling.

"It's only hormones," she had answered.

In the garden, working through a drowsy noon, and in the beautiful new kitchen, she often sang. From time to time she had a recall of that almost mystical experience when, on the top of the cliff, she had stood looking out upon the silence of sea and sky.

For Josie and Bruce's anniversary Robert proposed taking them to the dinner dance at the country club. This suggestion surprised Lynn because it was always she who arranged their social times with the Lehmans, and she remarked upon it.

"Well," he replied, "they were so nice to the girls while we were away, so it's only right to do something for them in return. I don't like being indebted. Wear that white dress again," he said. "Maybe it was the dress that got me started on Robert junior one of those nights."

"You really do want it to be Robert junior, don't you?"

"Or Roberta, or Susie, or Mary, will be just as wonderful. Wear the bracelet, too, will you?"

"Of course." For the first time she clasped it on without any ugly memory. After all, it was stupid, it was almost superstitious, to let such memories persist. Chicago was long past. Her heart—or whatever it is that makes a person different from every other person on earth—was glad. And Robert owned it.

But she never entered the club without feeling a small dread of encountering Tom Lawrence. The very thought made her face burn. And for some inexplicable reason she had a premonition that tonight was to be the night.

So it was. They had just sat down when she saw him in the dining-room doorway. Unaccompanied, he hesitated as if he were looking for somebody. She could only hope that Robert would not catch sight of him, but of course, Robert was too alert to miss anything.

"I was standing there hoping I'd see somebody I know," Tom said when Robert hailed him. "My date had to leave town in a hurry, a family illness, and at the last minute I thought I'd come alone anyway. How are you all?"

His light, skeptical eyes roved around the table, skimmed past Lynn, who was doing her best to look indifferent, and came to rest on Bruce, who replied. "I can answer for Josie and myself. It's our anniversary and we are feeling absolutely great, thank you."

"Congratulations. How long?"

"Twenty years."

"That's marvelous. Nice to hear that in these days."

I wonder, Lynn thought, whether he is remembering my invitation to our fiftieth?

"Do you care to join us?" Robert asked. "Since you and Bruce are old friends, or I should say old jogging companions, at least."

"Yes, pull up a chair," Bruce said.

The evening was ruined at the outset. Unless she could contrive to keep her eyes down on her plate, she would be looking straight at Tom, who now sat across from her. And she was furious with him for foisting himself upon them; surely he knew what he must be doing to her.

When the three men took over the conversation, the two women subsided into listening. First came the usual generalities about the state of the economy; then almost imperceptibly, talk veered to the personal as Robert skillfully led it where he wanted it to go.

"I understand you're related to our boss, Bruce's and mine."

"Yes, we're good friends," acknowledged Lawrence. "I don't see him that often unless I happen to be in San Francisco or I'm invited to their Maine camp in the fall, which I generally am. They like to go for the foliage season. There isn't much of a foliage season in California, as we all know," he finished agreeably.

"I have to admire a man like Monacco," Robert said, "working his way up from the bottom to where he is today. These modern heroes amaze me, these men who create jobs, make the country strong, and let people live better. Heroes," he repeated.

No one contradicted him, and Robert continued, "I heard him speak in New York not long ago and was vastly impressed. He talked about what we're all concerned with, the future of the European community, especially the new eastern republics. I've been exploring a lot of ideas myself. The rapidity of change is astounding. Who could ever have predicted it?"

Lawrence said that no one could have, not to this extent, anyway.

"Establishing a company, a brand name, isn't going to be as easy as some think. We're talking about a huge, backward area with poor transportation, and it's all so fragmented. Czechoslovakia is different from Hungary, and they're both worlds removed from Romania. Worlds apart." And Robert made a wide gesture. "But I find it all fascinating, a history book in reverse, the future unfolding before your eyes. Fascinating."

Lawrence agreed that it was.

Lynn could only wonder about the thoughts that Tom must be having as he listened, with head politely inclined toward Robert. And Robert, all unaware of the other man's opinion of him, continued smoothly.

"I'm having fun with some ideas of my own. One thing I'm doing is studying Hungarian, and that's not the easiest language in the world."

"Where do you get the time?" asked Lawrence.

"It's not easy. I have to squeeze it in somehow, mostly on Saturday mornings."

"That's when I go jogging with your colleague here." Lawrence motioned toward Bruce. "We're out conditioning our flab, while you're in town conditioning your brain." He laughed.

Bruce defended Robert. "He watches his flab, too, as you can see. He watches everything. He's known for it in the firm."

Tom said, "You've got a fine name there yourself, Bruce. Monacco's aware of it. I told him you were my jogging partner, and he recognized your name, your good name."

"Thanks," Bruce said. "I like my work, but I also like to forget business over the weekend, stay home or go out into the country, picking up old furniture. Then I spend Sunday afternoon puttering around restoring it. I'm teaching myself to weave cane. Maybe I should have been a cabinetmaker. Who knows, I might end up being one when I retire."

"You can't be serious," Robert said.

For the first time Josie spoke. "He could be. I guess you still don't know Bruce that well."

Here we go again, Lynn thought. What is it about those two? Impatiently, she twisted in the uncomfortable chair while trying to avoid Tom Lawrence's eyes.

"Well, maybe I don't know Bruce." And Robert demanded of him, "Do you mean to say you'd leave one of the biggest firms in the world to become a cabinetmaker?"

"Probably not," Bruce replied mildly. "Just a thought. But there is something rewarding about working with your hands. I love the feel of old wood. It almost comes alive under your fingers." And he looked around the table with his wide, slow smile.

And Lynn thought, as always, So cheerful, never in a hurry, and still he gets things done.

"I have never been especially ambitious," Bruce said as if he were thinking aloud. "I just keep going step by step."

"For someone who's not especially ambitious, I should say you've come mighty far," Josie remarked, with the combination of affection and gentle rebuke that was so typical of her.

For answer Bruce took her hand, and they sat united, content with each other. He is thankful that she's here, Lynn knew. She's had four good years. If you can get through five, you're home free, they say.

When the dance band struck up, Bruce rose. "Excuse us. It's not the anniversary waltz, but it will do just the same."

Tom's eyes followed them. "I like them," he said simply.

Robert acknowledged the remark. "Yes. Salt of the earth."

"You two go and dance. Don't mind me." For the first time Tom addressed Lynn. "I always do seem to lack a partner, don't I?"

Compelled to make some reply, she gave him a faint smile. Then Robert said hastily, "Why don't you dance with Lynn? I want to make some inquiry about the cake I ordered for the Lehmans and check on the champagne."

"You're sure you don't mind?" asked Tom.

Asking Robert whether he minds, as though I were an object that can be borrowed or lent! She was hotly indignant.

"No, no. Go ahead," Robert said. And a second later she was on the dance floor with Tom Lawrence's arm around her waist.

"Why are you doing this?" The final word emerged with a hiss. "It's not even decent, what you're doing tonight."

"Why? I want to apologize, that's all."

"What? Not again?"

"Yes. I've been making too many bad mistakes involving you. When I left you at the pool that day, it didn't take me long—as a matter of fact, I was only halfway home—to realize that I had said some horrendous things. I've been hoping to meet you so that I could tell you I'm sorry. I hurt you. I interjected where I had no business to be."

"No, you didn't have any business."

"I am dreadfully, dreadfully sorry."

He drew far enough away so that he could look into her face, and she saw in his an expression of genuine contrition and concern. She thought wryly, I've had so many apologies these past months, Robert's and now this. And she wondered, too, whether it could be the body contact while dancing that made it easier for people to make these intimate revelations. Who would think now that these two people, strangers to each other, were saying such serious things to the tune of a society dance-band?

"In my work I seem to have acquired a kind of intuition. It works like a flash, and as a rule I find I can depend on it. But that's no excuse for using it. I must learn to keep my mouth shut even when I'm sure I'm right."

"But you were wrong that time. Your intuition failed you. Look at me," she commanded with a proud lift of her head. "How do I look to you?"

"Very, very lovely, Lynn."

"Robert treats me very, very well, Tom."

"Does he?"

"I'm going to have a baby."

The skeptical eyes looked straight into hers while two pairs of feet moved expertly, not missing a step. Then the music stopped and Tom released her.

"God bless you, Lynn," he said.

The blessing jolted her. It was what Bruce had given her when she had brought him the news, and it had seemed fitting on his lips. But on Tom Lawrence's it seemed ironic.

Nevertheless, the evening turned out not badly after all.

Bruce and Josie received their cake and their champagne toast. At Robert's request the band played "The Anniversary Waltz," Bruce kissed Josie, everyone applauded, and then they all went home.

"Very smooth, that Lawrence," Robert remarked on the way back.

"Does that mean you don't like him?"

"I can't make up my mind."

"That's unusual for you. You generally know right away what you think about people."

"Maybe that's a failing. Maybe I shouldn't be so sure of my judgment. Oh, he's sharp as a tack. Congenial, a thorough gentleman, but somehow I can't make up my mind what he thinks about me. I almost think he dislikes me. But that's absurd. Why should he? Oh, but that Bruce! He makes such an idiot of himself with his remarks about furniture when, if he were more attuned to what's going on, he should have seen that I was leading the conversation somewhere. I looked up Lawrence's law firm. They have offices in Brussels, London, and Geneva. You never know what might come of that. Besides, the connection with Pete Monacco is no bad thing. Good Lord, a man has to keep his eyes wide open! That's Bruce's failing. I saw it the first day he came to the St. Louis office. Remember when I came home and told you? A lightweight, I said. A nice guy who'll never get very far. Oh, he's done all right, but he's stuck where he is. Stuck."

"That's not what Tom Lawrence said. Remember? He said Bruce has a very good name in your firm."

"Fine. But I'm there on the spot and I think I should be a better judge than Lawrence is."

Jealous. Jealous of Tom because I was foolish that night, and of Bruce because he is a handsome man. He wants to be the only handsome man, I suppose. Lord, men can be such babies!

"All the same," Lynn said amusedly, "if I had a brother, I'd want him to be like Bruce."

"As long as you wouldn't want your husband to be like Bruce. Or like anyone else, including Tom Lawrence. Right, Mrs. Ferguson?"

"Right," she said.

Josie telephoned with thanks for the anniversary celebration.

"It was lovely, perfect. They even played our songs, our specials."

"That was Robert's doing. You know he never forgets anything."

They gossiped briefly, and then Josie said, "Tom Lawrence really admires you."

"How can you know that?"

"He told Bruce."

"Oh, he admires my cooking."

"No, you."

"Well, that's generous of him."

"He's a generous person."

"I didn't realize you knew him that well."

"I don't know him *that* well. He stops in for a cold drink or a hot drink after he's met Bruce on the track. I find him interesting. Hard to pin down, like quicksilver. But very decent, very honorable."

"How can you know if you say you don't know him well?" Lynn asked, wanting for some reason to argue the point.

"I just know. It's not important either way. I only wanted to pass on a compliment."

When the conversation ended and she hung up the phone, she sat for a moment or two staring into the mirror on the opposite wall. An odd little smile flickered over her lips.

A few weeks later Robert telephoned from the office at midday. He never called from the office, and she was startled.

"Is anything wrong?"

"Wrong? I should say not." There was glee in his voice. "In a million years you'd never guess. I got a call from California from the big boss. I almost fell off the chair."

"Not Monacco? He called you?"

"Himself. I can't imagine what Tom told him about me. He seems to have described me as some kind of genius, some sort of phenomenon. So, Monacco says he'd like to meet me and have a talk. We've been invited for the weekend to his place in Maine. His wife will call you."

Robert was chuckling; she knew that he was wearing an enormous smile and that his eyes would be brilliant with excitement.

"I haven't mentioned it to anyone here. It's a bad policy to seem boastful. Being casual about it is much the better way."

"Does that mean not to tell Josie?"

"Oh, they'll know. We'll have to ask them to keep an eye on the girls again, anyway, won't we? But, uh, keep it light, as if it's nothing much. It'd be nasty to rub this under Bruce's nose, since he wasn't invited. Now I'm beginning to get nervous. I do have some good ideas, it's true, but I hope the man won't be expecting so much from me that I'll fall flat on my face. Well, at least you'll be there to help charm him. I think you must have charmed Lawrence."

"Don't be silly."

Robert laughed. He was absolutely euphoric. "In a nice way, I meant."

"I didn't charm him, any way, nice or not. I danced with him once, at your behest, if you remember, and we hardly spoke."

"Okay, okay. Don't keep the phone tied up too long in case Mrs. Monacco should call."

When she hung up, her feelings were mixed. Of course this was a marvelous thing for Robert, an unprecedented summons to the man's home. Small wonder that he was ecstatic. She could only be glad for him, and she was glad. Yet at the same time she was slightly vexed and vaguely troubled.

She made excuses to avoid the country club, although she knew Robert liked to go there for dinner. But apparently Tom Lawrence also liked to go there. . . .

Robert urged her. "As new in the community as we are, it's important to keep being seen. Otherwise, people forget you're alive."

"Your name's all over this community, on practically every committee. They couldn't forget you if they wanted to," she told him.

"Speaking of remembering people, we really should show some appreciation to Tom Lawrence. Let's have him over for dinner one night. I mean, when have you heard of anyone's doing such an extraordinary favor for a man he scarcely knows? Of course I called him at once to thank him, and I mentioned that we'd like to have him come over soon."

"I will, but first I want to get a few things out of the way. That root canal's been bothering me, which means a few visits to the man in the city. And I want to get the baby's room finished, too, before I get so big that I won't want to go into the city. But I will," she promised.

It disturbed her to think of seeing Tom again; it was disturbing in itself that she should feel that way. She was a literal person, one who needed a clear explanation for everything, even for the workings of her own mind. So it was with some dismay that one afternoon not long afterward she encountered him on a New York street. Having done her errands, she was on the way to Grand Central Terminal and home. She had stopped in front of a small picture gallery, attracted by a painting of sheep on a hillside, as well as by the name above the entrance: Querida. An unusual name. The name of Robert's first wife. It gave her a small, unpleasant flutter. And then, turning away from the window, she had seen Tom Lawrence.

"What are you doing in the city?" he inquired, as though they were old friends who reported their doings to each other.

She replied casually, "I go to a dentist in the neighborhood. And today I bought nursery furniture."

"That must be a happy thing, although I wouldn't know, would I?"

Again, she had a sense of being brightly, although not disagreeably, scrutinized.

"You're looking wonderful. They tell me there are women who actually thrive on being pregnant. Are you buying pictures?"

"No, just admiring." And wanting to divert that scrutiny, she remarked, "These sheep are lovely."

"She does have nice things. I've priced some, and the prices are very fair, but she's a cranky kind of oddball. Are you on your way home? Yes? So am I. We'll go together. Are you walking or cabbing?"

"I always walk as much as I can when I'm in the city."

"Yes, it's wonderful this time of year. Everything seems to be waking up. And the shops! I can see why women go crazy in the shops."

Tweeds and silks, silver, mahogany, and burnished leather made a passing show of the windows as they walked down Madison Avenue. The most brilliant blue, as deep as cobalt, overhung the towers, and where distance disguised grime, the towers shone white.

"Am I going too fast for you?" Tom asked.

"No, I'm fine."

They were keeping an even pace. Always with Robert she had to hurry to keep up with his long strides, but then, she thought idly, Robert was half a head taller than this man.

"I never take the train home this early," Tom explained, "but I made myself take time off to do some shopping today." He went on making small talk. "My days are pretty long. I take the seven-thirty every morning, so I guess I'm entitled to treat myself now and then."

"Robert takes the six-thirty."

"He's a hard worker."

And suddenly she cut through the small talk, saying, "I must thank you for that incredible invitation to Maine. I know Robert's told you how much it means to him."

"Oh, that. It was all Pete's idea. He says there's never much time during his flying visits to New York, what with all the meetings and stuff, so Maine's a much better place to talk."

"I didn't mean Maine, specifically. I meant the whole business." She raised her eyes to Tom, inquiring directly, "Why did you do anything at all for Robert? Did he," she asked, not flinching, "did he by any chance ask you to?"

"Lord, no. Don't you know he wouldn't do that? But I knew he wanted something all the same."

Troubled, she went further. "Was he so obvious?"

"I suppose not really. I guess maybe it was my famous intuition that I told you about," Tom said rather mischievously.

"No, really. I'm serious. Because you don't like Robert."

"Robert's very smart, very competent, very diligent. I knew I wouldn't go wrong by recommending him."

"But Bruce wasn't invited."

"I didn't mention Bruce."

"Why not? You like him very much. You said so; I heard you."

"Ah, don't ask so many questions, lady!"

Embarrassed, she murmured only, "It was awfully good of you."

In the train Tom read the newspaper, and Lynn read her book, until the train had passed the dark brown tenements in the uptown reaches of the city, then the cheerful towns with their malls and parks, and crossed the Connecticut line. At that point he laid the paper aside and spoke.

"Lynn . . . I have another apology to make."

"Oh, no, not another! For what this time?"

"For that first night at my house. If your husband could have read my thoughts, which fortunately he couldn't, he'd have had a right to be furious." Tom paused. "The truth is, I was hoping that you and I'd get together. Oh, not that night," he amended quickly, "of course not. But I thought perhaps the next time."

She turned her face away toward the window to hide her exasperating blush. Naturally, it was flattering to be propositioned after all these years, to know that she could tempt someone else beside Robert. She supposed, though, that she ought to feel angry; whatever had made this man dare to think that she would be open to his proposition? And she felt guilty because she was not angry.

Rather mildly, she said, "But you knew I had Robert."

"I made a mistake. I misread you, which I don't usually do. Maybe it was the wine or the spring night or something. Anyway, a sexual attraction doesn't have to disrupt a man's or a woman's other life. Do I shock you?" For she had turned to him and saw now his rueful smile. "Yes, of course I do. You'd eat yourself alive with guilt if you ever—you'd say 'cheated.' Well, I respect that. Maybe someday you'll feel different about it."

"Never." She shook her head decisively. "Robert and I are permanent." She looked down at her little swollen belly and repeated, "Permanent."

Tom followed her glance. "I understand. And I've made my apology for my thoughts and intentions that night. I wanted to clear my own mind. So—" She remembered that he had that funny way of saying "so" when he changed the subject. "So. You'll have a good time in Maine. Pete and Lizzie are easygoing, not formal at all. Paper-plate people like me. And it's beautiful this time of year. Over near the New Hampshire line the mountains turn red and gold. I'll be sorry to miss it."

She was surprised. "You're not going?"

"No. I've too much on the fire at the office."

She was not sure whether she was sorry or glad that he would not be there.

Robert laid careful plans for the weekend. "We'll need a house gift, you know."

"Wine?" she suggested. "Or I'll find something suitable for the country, a rustic bowl for flowers or fruit or something like that."

"No, definitely not. That's banal. Besides, they already have their own wine and no doubt a couple of dozen bowls or whatnots too."

"Well, what then?"

"I'll tell you what. An enormous box of your best cookies. Those almond things, you know the ones, and the lemon squares, and some chocolate brownies. Everybody loves them. That will be just the right gesture, friendly, simple, and elegant. As for clothes: sweaters, naturally, and heavy shoes. They'll probably take us tramping through the woods. And raincoats, and don't forget an umbrella. Something silk for the two nights in case they dress for dinner."

"They won't dress for dinner up in the woods, and besides, I haven't a thing that fits anymore. I never did show this early, but I do show now."

He regarded her thoughtfully. "You look like a woman who needs to lose a little weight around the middle, that's all."

"That's just it. My things don't fit around the middle, and it's too early for maternity clothes."

"Well, buy something. For myself, tweed jackets, not new. A relaxed, used look." Robert unfolded his plans systematically. "We'll start the afternoon before and stay overnight on the road. Then we'll arrive rested and fresh before noon. And we'll take the station wagon. The Jaguar might look—I'm not sure, but it might look overdone. If the boss drives one, it certainly will. Yes, the station wagon."

In midmorning they arrived exactly as planned. A long log house set about with cleared fields lay on a rise above a small lake. At the side were two tennis courts. On a wide veranda looking down on a bathhouse and a dock was a row of Adirondack chairs. The driveway was a rutted dirt road with a worn, grassy circle for parking; half a dozen cars were already there, station wagons, plain American sedans, and not an import in sight.

Lynn looked at Robert and had to laugh. "Are you ever wrong?" she inquired.

"Ah, welcome, welcome," cried Pete Monacco, descending the steps. "How was the trip?" His voice boomed, his handshake was painful, and his smile showed square teeth that looked as granite hard as the rest of his large body. "Beautiful scenery here in the East. I wouldn't miss this for the world. California is home and we love it, but for color you've got to see New England. Just look out there! My wife, she's Lizzie and I'm Pete, we're all first-name folks when we're up here, has taken everybody sailing, but they'll be back for lunch. Here, let me give you a hand with the bags."

In their room Robert beamed. "I don't know what the hell that fellow Tom can have said about me. Call him 'Pete'! You wouldn't guess he's the same man as the one who flies in with an entourage like the President's, gives a talk that's part pep and part scolding, leaves his commands, shakes your hand in the reception line, and then flies back across the Mississippi. Well, here we are. Can you believe it?"

He looked around the sparsely furnished room. A rag rug covered the floor, the walls were pine, the bed had Indian blankets and a huge comforter folded at the foot. The only ornament was the view that was framed by the single window.

"There's a sailboat coming in," Lynn said.

Robert peered over her shoulder. "Pretty sight, isn't it? Yes, all you need is money. Well, and taste too," he conceded. "Knowing how to use it."

"We ought to go down and meet everybody," she said as Robert began to unpack.

"No. Tidy up first. It'll take five minutes, if that. Let's get a move on."

Hot coffee and doughnuts were being served on the veranda when they came downstairs. Lizzie Monacco, in jeans and a heavy sweater, shook hands.

"Excuse my freezing hands. There's a real wind out there. But it's great fun. Would you people like a ride around the lake this afternoon?" Like her husband she was voluble, with curly gray windblown hair and a candid expression. "My goodness, how young you are! Lynn, isn't it? You are the youngest female here, and we shall all feel like old hags next to you."

"No, no." Lynn smiled. "I have a daughter who'll be going to college next year."

"For goodness' sake, and you're pregnant too. I hope it's not a secret, but Tom told me, anyway. I hope you're feeling well, but if you're not, don't feel you have to keep up with our crazy pace. Just take a book and relax."

Robert answered for her. "Lynn's in good shape. She plays a great game of tennis too."

"You do? Good. We're all tennis freaks here. So maybe after lunch and a hike—there's a lookout place just down the lake where you can climb and see for miles, really splendid—maybe when we come back, we can play."

"This is what you love. Busy, busy, busy," Lynn murmured later to Robert.

"I know. It makes me feel like a kid. And the air, the pine smell. I feel great."

These men came from the company's top echelon, chiefly from Texas and points west of Texas. If there were any women in the top echelon, they weren't at this party; these women were all wives. They didn't, Lynn noted, wear the same anxious look that she had so often seen on the women at the country club, whose husbands were still on the way up and always fearful of falling back down. These people seldom fell back or fell very hard if they did; there was always a golden parachute. She listened as the older women talked of volunteering, of the Red Cross and the United Way. Those slightly younger had gone to work in real estate or travel agencies and were pleased with themselves, since they did not have to work and yet did so.

"Tom told me that you're a fabulous cook," said Lizzie Monacco, drawing Lynn into the conversation. "I took a look at that gorgeous box of cookies. We're going to serve them at dinner tonight. It was darling of you."

Lynn was thinking: Tom has surely done a lot of talking. He had put effort into this weekend. Pete Monacco was not a man who was readily open to suggestion, that was obvious. So Tom must have been very, very persuasive.

After the hike, tennis, and cocktails, they dressed for dinner. Lizzie had been most tactful.

"We do change for dinner. But nothing fancy, just anything you'd wear to your club on a weekday night. Anything at all." And she had given Lynn her candid smile.

"You were right again," Lynn said as she took a dark red silk dress off the hanger. She laid a string of pearls and the bracelet on the dresser.

"Don't wear that," Robert cautioned.

"Not? But you always want me to."

"Not here. It looks too rich. The pearls are enough. Modest. Sweet. I'm sorry you wore your ring, come to think of it. Ah, well, too late."

"You beat him at tennis. Should you have?" she asked.

"That's different. People respect a winner. They respect sports. It may seem silly, and I suppose it is when you really think about it, but the idea of excelling in a sport sort of stamps a man. He won't forget me." With his head tilted back he stood knotting his tie and exuding confidence. "That's what I keep telling the girls. That's what I shall tell him." He pointed at her abdomen, laughed, and corrected himself. "Sorry, I don't want to be sexist. But I don't know why I'm sure it's a him. Come on, you look lovely as always. Let's go down. I'm starved."

In the long dining room on a pine sawbuck table, pewter plates were set on rough linen mats. The utensils were plain stainless steel. But the candles were lit, and the dinner was served by two maids in uniform. A pair of handsome golden retrievers lay patiently in a corner.

"The great thing about the airplane," Lizzie said contentedly, "is that you can bring your household across country, dogs and all."

The airplane? No, the private company jet, thought Lynn, and was amused. A variety of conversations crossed the table, and she tried to catch some of them. There was talk of travel, not to London or Paris, but to the Fiji Islands and Madagascar. One couple had been on an expedition to the South Pole. It was like peering through a crack in the door, to a new world. Robert wanted to push the door open and walk into that world. It seemed to her as she overheard him at the other end of the table that he had already gotten one foot through the crack.

His rich voice and his eager expression were very attractive. At any rate, three or four of the men were paying attention, leaning to catch his remarks, which were addressed, of course, to Monacco.

"—we should, I've been thinking a lot about it, and we should train our own people in languages before we send them over. We should do our own public relations. Our outside PR in one office alone costs twenty-five thousand a month, minimum, and it won't be any less over there. I've been getting some figures together. Seems to me we know our own product best and should be able to do our own PR."

Then Monacco asked something that Lynn, caught in the crossfire of conversations, could not hear. But he had asked a question; that meant he was listening carefully.

"—met a German banker recently from Stuttgart. He's just the man to give us the answer to that. He travels all through the new republics. Yes, he's a good friend of mine. I can get in touch with him as soon as I get back to the office."

"Oh, that house where the light's on?" Lizzie was saying. "Across the lake, you mean. That's the caretaker's light." Through the autumn dusk there sparked one point of fire; it danced in the black water. "They left, and the place is for sale. We had a real scandal around here," she explained to Lynn. "This perfectly wonderful couple—we've known them for years and their place is really beautiful—well, she left him. It seems he knocked her around once too often. All those years it had been going on and none of us ever had the faintest suspicion. Isn't that amazing?"

Lynn's neighbor, with eager eyes and voice, supplemented the story. "They were a stunning couple. How could we have guessed? He had the best sense of humor too. He absolutely *made* a party. You'd never think to talk to him that he could do things like that."

"Well, it goes to show, doesn't it? You never know what goes on behind closed doors."

"No," said Lynn.

Her heart had leapt as though a gun had sounded. Now, just calm down, she said to herself. Just stop it. That business is all past. It ended months ago on the island. It's finished, remember? Finished.

Robert's voice sounded again over the chatter. "Of course, advertising's cheapest during the first quarter of the year, we know that. Television and radio are hungry then. I think we should find out how that works abroad before we make any definite commitments."

Almost unconsciously, Lynn glanced toward him, and at that very instant he glanced toward her, so that she caught his familiar, endearing smile. Things are going well, it declared.

"Oh, here come your marvelous cookies," cried Lizzie.

"You didn't make these yourself?" asked Lynn's neighbor.

"Yes, she did. I know all about her. She's professional."

Lynn corrected her. "No, no, I'd only like to be."

"Well, why don't you? I have a friend whose daughter—she must be about your age—makes the most exquisite desserts for people, bombes and—"

"Lynn's pregnant," Lizzie interrupted. "She'll have other things to do."

"Really? Congratulations! You have a daughter ready for college and you're having another. That's marvelous."

All eyes were on her. An earnest woman said, "You set an example, starting again just at the age when practically everybody's breaking up. Your baby's lucky."

"I hope so."

"One thing's sure, between you and that handsome husband of yours, it'll be good looking."

Presently, everyone got up and went into the living room for drinks. A vigorous fire flared under the great stone mantel, drawing Lynn to stand and gaze at it.

"You're looking thoughtful," said Pete Monacco.

"No, just hypnotized. Fountains and fires do that, don't they? And this has been such a lovely day."

He raised his glass to her as if making a toast. "We're glad you came. Robert's got interesting ideas. I'm glad he was brought to my attention. Unfortunately, some very bright guys get lost in the crowd—not often, but it can happen. He'll be making his mark in the firm. Hell, he has made it."

"I think I've left an impression," Robert said later. They were in bed under the quilt. "He asked me to put some of my ideas in writing and send them to him. What was he saying to you?"

"Nice things. That you were going to make your mark on the firm."

The window was low. When she raised her head, she had a clear view far down to the lake, where the diamond point of light still glistened from the vacant house that belonged to "the perfectly wonderful couple."

Robert stroked her stomach. "It won't be long before this fellow will be kicking you."

"Who is he? What will he be?" she wondered. She had also begun to think of the baby as "he." "It's all so mysterious. When I look back upon where we've been and then look ahead, even only as far as a year from now . . . Yes, it's all so mysterious."

It had grown very cold outside, and the wind had risen, sounding a melancholy wail through the trees. Even under the quilt it was cold, and Robert drew her close.

"Listen to that wind," he whispered. "It's a great night for sleeping, all snug in here. And it's been a great day. Things are really looking up for us, Mrs. Ferguson." He sighed with pleasure. "I love you, Mrs. Ferguson. I take it you're aware of that?" He chuckled, drawing her even closer.

"I am," she answered, thought following swiftly: It is absurd to let a piece of gossip affect me. What have Robert and I to do with those people? I know nothing about them, anyway. I am I and Robert is Robert.

He yawned. "Can't keep my eyes open. Let's sleep. Tomorrow'll take care of itself."

That was certain. They unfold, those unknown tomorrows, with their secrets curled like the tree that lies curled within the small, dry seed.

They started home right after dawn on Sunday. That way, Robert said, they'd be back before dinner with some time left over to be with the girls.

The house was deserted when they arrived. There wasn't even a light on.

"Ah, poor Juliet! They left her in the dark," said Lynn as the dog came forward into the dark hall. "They're probably over with Bruce and Josie. I guess they didn't expect us back this early."

"I never asked you what Josie said about our going up to Monacco's place."

"She didn't say much."

"I wonder what they really thought. You can't tell me there isn't some sort of envy, in a nice way at least."

"I don't think so. You know Josie is the last person to disguise her feelings, especially to me. So I'd know if there were."

"Did you know we've been invited to Monacco's in Maine?" Lynn had asked her, wanting no cat-and-mouse game between them, no dishonesty posing as tact.

And Josie had replied that yes, Robert had told Bruce, and she had said, "Don't feel uncomfortable on account of Bruce. I know you." She had smiled. "Bruce wasn't made to shine or sparkle. He knows himself."

That was true. You could see that Bruce knew who he was and didn't need to measure his worth by other people's accomplishments.

"Robert's exceptional," Josie had said. "He works like a demon and deserves whatever he may get."

Robert said now, "I did feel a little sorry, a little uncomfortable, when I told him."

"Well, you needn't have. Josie told me you deserve whatever you get."

Robert laughed. "One can take that in two ways."

"They mean it in one way only."

"Of course. Just a joke." He started upstairs with the two suitcases. "Come on, let's unpack before they all come home."

"I'll do it in the morning."

"You always say that. Who wants to wake up and find suitcases staring you in the face? Never put off till tomorrow what you can do today. That's my motto."

She followed him. The first room at the top of the stairs was the new nursery, and she couldn't pass it without peering in. The furniture had arrived, the crib and dresser in light yellow; the walls matched; there were large Mother Goose pictures in maple frames and spring-green gingham curtains, a refreshing change from pink and blue. A large, soft polar bear sat in one corner of the crib. At the window there was a rocking chair, where she would sit to nurse the baby. The thought of doing this again brought a renewal of youth, an affirmation of womanhood. None of the theories that one read, with all their political or psychological verbiage, could come within miles of describing the real sweetness of the fuzzy head and the minuscule splayed fingers against the breast.

In the bedroom, where Robert had already begun to unpack, the telephone rang. He was standing by the bed holding the phone when she came in.

"What? What?" he said. A dreadful look passed over his face. "What are you saying, is she—"

And Lynn, seeing him, turned ice cold.

"We'll be there. In the parking lot. Yes. Yes." He put the phone down. He was shaking. "That was Bruce. Emily's had a hemorrhage. From menstruation, he thought. She's in the hospital. Hurry. He'll meet us there."

The car squealed around the corner at the foot of the drive.

"Take it easy, Robert. Not so fast. Listen, listen, it was just her period, that's all it was. . . . But why a hemorrhage?" She babbled. "But it can't be anything too bad. She's in perfect health. . . ."

"They don't admit people to the hospital for nothing at all," he said grimly.

She wrung her hands in her lap and was quiet, while, in a frenzy, they rode through the town and into the hospital parking lot, where Bruce was waiting. Robert slammed the car door and began to run toward the entrance.

"Stop, I have to talk to you first," Bruce cried. "No, no, she's not—you're thinking she died, and I'm breaking it to you easily—but no, no, she's upstairs and she'll be fine, only she's terrified." The kind, earnest eyes matched the kind, earnest voice. "The fact is—well, I have to tell you, Emily had a miscarriage."

There was a total silence, as when the sounds of the world are drowned by a heavy snowfall. Traffic on the avenue and bustle in the parking lot all receded, leaving the three in that pool of silence, looking from one to the other.

"She's terrified," Bruce repeated, and then begged Robert, "don't be hard on her."

"How—" Lynn began.

Bruce resumed steadily. "She telephoned us around noon. She was more worried about Annie than about herself. She didn't want Annie to know. So Josie took Annie to our house, and I brought Emily here. The doctor says"—Bruce laid his hand on Lynn's arm—"he said she was in the third month. Are you all right, Lynn?"

Robert groaned, and at the piteous sound she turned to him. So he had been justified, more than justified, in his fears. And she cried inwardly: Oh, Emily, I trusted you! And she cried: Was this my fault? Robert will say it's my fault.

"Shall we go?" asked Bruce.

On the long walk from the parking lot she rallied. I'm the one who is good in emergencies, remember? Say the mantra: Good in emergencies . . . Her legs were weak, yet they moved. Then it seemed as if the elevator would never come. When it did, they shared space with a patient on a stretcher; so Mom had been carried that day with the white sheet drawn up to a drained white face. No one spoke as they ascended, then stepped out into a foreboding wave of hospital smells, of disinfectant and cleaning fluids. Ether too? No, it couldn't be, not in a corridor. But it sickened her, whatever it was, and she swallowed hard.

"I asked for a private room," Bruce said when they stopped at the end of the corridor. His voice rose half an octave, cheerfully. "Emily, your dad and mom are here."

A hot sunset light lay over the bed where Emily lay. Her body made only a slight ridge under the blanket, and the one arm that was exposed was frail; nothing of Emily had ever before seemed frail.

Lynn took a cold, sweating hand in hers and whispered, "We're here. Darling? We're here."

She wanted to say, It's going to be all right, it's not the end of the world, nor the end of you, God forbid. There's nothing that can't be solved, can't be gotten over, nothing, do you hear me? Nothing. She wanted to say all these, but no sounds came from her dry lips.

Emily's beautiful eyes wandered toward the ceiling. Tears rolled on her cheeks. And Robert, who had been standing on the other side of the bed, said faintly, "I have to sit down."

He's going to be sick, Lynn thought, while Bruce and the nurse, who had been at the window, must have had the same thought, because the nurse shoved a chair across the room, and Bruce took Robert's arm.

"Put your head down. Sit," he murmured.

Robert laid his head on Emily's coverlet, and the others walked toward the door out of his hearing.

"Poor man." The nurse clucked her tongue. "It's funny how often men take things harder than we do. She's going to be fine, Mrs. Ferguson. Mr. Lehman called Dr. Reeve. He's the chief of gynecology here, you couldn't get better."

Lynn's voice quivered. "I'm so scared. Tell me the truth. She looks so awful. Please tell me the truth."

"She's very weak, and she's in quite some pain. This is like giving birth, you know, the same pains. But there's nothing to be afraid of, you understand? Here, rest till the doctor comes back."

Rapid steps came purposefully down the hall. Dr. Reeve looked like a doctor, clean shaven, compact, and authoritative. He could play the part in a soap opera, Lynn thought hysterically; a foolish laugh rose to her throat and was silenced there. Were they really in a hospital room talking to this man about Emily?

Robert stood up. "Bruce you talk, you do it," he said, and then sat down again.

Bruce conferred briefly with the doctor, who then turned back to the parents.

"She's losing a lot of blood," he said, wasting no words. "We'll need to do a D and C. She says she hasn't eaten since breakfast. Can I rely on that? Because if she's had food within the last few hours, we'll have to wait."

Lynn replied faintly, "I don't know. We've been away. We just got home."

"You can rely on it," Bruce said.

"Fine. Then we'll take her up right away." Dr. Reeve looked keenly at Robert and Lynn. "Why don't you two go out with your brother and—"

Bruce prompted. "I'm just a friend."

"Well, take them out and get something to eat." He looked again at Robert, who was wiping his eyes with the back of his hand. "Have a drink too. You can come back later in the evening."

"A good idea," said Bruce, assenting. "We'll do just that."

"No," Robert said. "I'm not leaving here. No, we'll stay."

"All right," Bruce said quickly. "There's a sun parlor at the end of the hall. We'll sit there. And if you need us for anything, Doctor, that's where we'll be."

"Fine. I suggest you go there now, then." The professional smile was sympathetic, but firm.

He means, Lynn knew, that we are not to stand here watching them wheel Emily into the operating room. It's plain to see that Robert can barely cope with this. Poor Robert. And she took his hand, twining her fingers through his as they went down the hall with Bruce.

In restless, forlorn silence they waited. Bruce and Lynn thumbed through magazines, not reading, while Robert stared through the window wall at the treetops. It was long past visiting hours, and steps were few in the hall, when a familiar, distinctive clicking sound approached: Josie's high heels, worn because Bruce was so much taller than she.

"I got permission to come in," she whispered. "I tracked Eudora down, and she went straight to your house, so I could bring Annie back there. Eudora's a princess. Annie was having her bath and getting ready for bed when I left."

Josie was wise. She gave no comforting words, no warm hug that would have brought on tears. She simply did whatever was needed.

Robert, with head in hands, was huddled in the sofa. All six feet four of him looked small. Lynn got up and caressed his bent head.

"Our beautiful girl, our beautiful girl," he moaned, and clearly she recalled his cry when Caroline's tiny body lay before them. Our baby. Our beautiful baby.

"She's going to be fine. I know. Oh, darling, she will."

"I'd like to get my hands on that rotten little bastard. I'd like to kill him."

"I know. I know."

Time barely moved. Eventually it grew dark. Bruce stood up and turned on the lights, then returned to sit with Josie. They spoke in whispers, while Lynn and Robert sat hand in hand. No one looked at his watch, so no one knew what time it was when Dr. Reeve appeared in the doorway. He looked different in his crumpled green cotton pants, with a pinched face and circled eyes. Authority had come from the suit and the tie and the brisk walk. Now he looked like a tired workman. Such scattered thoughts went through Lynn's head as he came toward them.

"Your girl is all right," he said. "She's in the recovery room, but she'll be back in her own room shortly. Mr. Lehman asked for a nurse through tonight and as long as needed. Good idea if you can afford it. Now, I suggest that you go home and come back again in the morning. Emily won't know you for hours, and it's already close to midnight." He glanced at Robert. "If—it's highly unlikely—if it should be necessary to call anyone, shall—" He glanced toward Bruce.

Robert got up. It was as if the news had brought him back to life. "No, we're the parents. We're over the first shock, and we can handle whatever comes next. You can imagine what a shock it was, being away and finding this when we got home."

"Of course. But it must be good to have friends like these to handle an emergency for you."

"We appreciate them. Bruce and Josie are the best."

"Well," Bruce said brightly now, "all's well that ends well. What I suggest is that we get something to eat. I personally could eat shoe leather at this point."

Josie went considerately on tiptoe through the corridor. "Darn heels sound like hammers," she whispered. "Listen. We're all too tired to go home and forage for food. What about the all-night diner on the highway? We can get a quick hamburger or something."

When they were settled in a booth, she explained, "I told Annie that Emily had a sick stomach, a little problem. She was scared at first, but then she accepted my story and seems fine."

"She mustn't ever know, of course," Lynn said.

"I knew you would feel that way about it, and that's why I told her what I did."

The emphasis on *you* prompted Lynn to ask, "Why? Wouldn't you feel that way?"

"I'm not sure. Kids know much more about what's going on around them than you may think."

"I'm sure Emily didn't tell her about—about what was going on between herself and Harris, for God's sake!"

"I'm sure Emily didn't, but as I said, kids are smart, and Annie is especially so. Smart and secretive," Josie added. "Annie could say a lot of things if she wanted to or dared to."

Robert, who had said nothing since he sat down, now burst out. "Never mind what Annie knows or doesn't know! It's Emily who's tearing me to shreds. The thought of her—" He turned upon Lynn. "I want you to know, I blame you as much as Emily. I told you when she was only fifteen years old that you were too lax with her. You have no backbone. You let people walk all over you. And you're not alert. You don't look around and watch what's going on. You never did."

Caroline, Lynn thought, and her will ebbed hopelessly.

"Now here we are," Robert said. "Yes, here we are."

"That's hardly fair, Robert," Josie protested angrily, "and not true. I don't know of a wiser, more caring mother than Lynn. You mustn't do this to her."

"I don't care. This was all avoidable. Is this what I work for, to see my daughter ruined, thrown away on a penniless bastard? Ruined—ruined."

The fluorescent bulbs above them glared on Robert, turning his exhausted face dark green.

Bruce said quietly, "You mustn't think of Emily as being ruined, Robert. This is a terrible thing, I know it is, but still, at seventeen she has a wonderful long life ahead. You mustn't," he said more sternly, "allow her to think otherwise."

Robert flexed his fingers. "I want to get my hands on the bastard. I just want to get my hands on him."

Despair sank like a stone in Lynn's chest. A few hours before they had been feeling—or she had been feeling on Robert's behalf—the glow of his success. They had been driving home through the bright fall afternoon with music on the radio, the new baby on the way, and—

"I could kill him," Robert said again. "Home now, sleeping like a log, not giving a damn, while Emily is—" He broke off. "Does the bastard even know, I wonder?"

"Of course he does," Bruce said. "He's quite frantic. He wanted to go to the hospital, but I told him he couldn't. I told him to call me for information. As a matter of fact, I will telephone him when we get home. He's waiting up."

Lynn was inwardly saying her mantra again: Good in emergencies. Now she made inquiry. "The third month. What was she—what were they—intending to do? Did she say? I don't understand," she whispered.

Bruce answered her. "On the way to the hospital Emily told me that she hadn't known really what to do. She had intended to get up courage to talk to you both this week, but she didn't want to spoil her father's important trip to Maine, to get him upset before the big meeting."

Robert made correction. "It wasn't a big meeting. I don't know where she got that idea. It wasn't that important."

"Well, anyway, that's the story. They were, I gather, quite beside themselves this last month, the two of them. They didn't know where to turn."

Lynn burst into tears and covered her face. "Poor baby. The poor baby."

Bruce and Josie got up. "Let's go. Get whatever rest you can," Josie commanded. "I have to go to work in the morning, although I suppose I could phone in."

Lynn recovered. "No. Go to work. You've done enough. You've been wonderful."

"Rubbish," said Bruce. "If you need either of us, you know where we are. You two will come through this all right, though, and so will Emily. Only one thing: Be kind to each other tonight. No recriminations. This is not your fault. Not yours, Robert, and not Lynn's. Have I got your word?" he asked, leaning into the car where Robert had already started the engine. "Robert? Have I got your word?" he repeated sternly.

"Yes, yes," Robert muttered, and grumbled as he drove away. "I don't know what he thinks I'm going to do to you."

That you are going to go on blaming me, she said to herself. That's what he thought. But now you won't, thank God. I don't think I can bear a harsh word tonight. And yet, was any of it my fault? Perhaps. . . .

Home again, she walked restlessly through the house. Setting the table for breakfast, she thought: Disaster strikes and yet people eat, or try to. She let the dog out and, while Juliet rummaged in the bushes, watched the stars. The sky was sprinkled with them; far off at a distance beyond calculation, could there be some living, thinking creature like herself, and in such pain?

She went upstairs to Emily's room, wanting to feel her presence, wanting to find some clue to her child's life. The closet and the desk were neat, for Emily was orderly, like Robert. There hung the shirts, not much larger than a hand towel. There stood the shoes, sneakers next to a pair of three-inch heels. On the bedside table lay a copy of *Elle* and a book: *Studies of Marital Abuse.*

Lynn opened the book to the first chapter: "The Battered Woman in the Upper Middle Class." She closed the book.

Are we now marked by this forever? Is it engraved on Emily's mind forever?

"Come," Robert said from the doorway. "This won't do you any good." He spoke not unkindly. "What's that she's reading?" And he took hold of the book before Lynn could hide it. "What the devil is this trash? The battered woman! She'd have done better to read about the pregnant high school girl."

"The one has nothing to do with the other."

Yet perhaps it had. Things are entwined, braided into each other. . . .

"Somebody comes out with a 'study,'" Robert scoffed. "Then somebody else has to write another. It's all a money-making, publicity-seeking lot of trash. Exaggerations. Lies, half of it. Throw the damn book out."

"No. It belongs to Emily. Don't you touch it, Robert."

"All right," he grumbled. "All right. We've got enough trouble tonight. Come to bed."

Neither of them slept. It began to rain. Drops loud as an onslaught of stones beat the windows, making the night cruel. Turning and turning in the bed, Lynn saw the hall light reflected upward on the ceiling. Robert would be sitting downstairs in his usual corner, his "mournful" corner, alone. If anything were to happen to Emily, it would kill him. But she had poor Annie—why did she always think "poor Annie," as if the child were some neglected misfit, disabled and deserted, when she was none of these? And then there was this baby, the boy Robert wanted. But nothing would happen to Emily, the doctor had said. He'd said it. Her thoughts ran, circled, and returned all night.

The doctor was just leaving Emily's room after early rounds when Robert and Lynn came down the hall. He spoke to them quickly in his succinct, flat manner. For after all, Emily could mean no more to him than another problem to be solved as skillfully as he could.

"She's still in some pain, but it's lessening. She has anemia from the blood loss, and we've just given her a transfusion, so don't be shocked when you see her. It's all to be expected." He swung away, took a few steps, and turned back. "I have a daughter her age, so I know." He stopped. "She'll have her life," he said then with an abrupt smile, and this time walked away.

A lump in Lynn's throat was almost too painful to admit speech, but she called after him.

"Thank you for everything. Thank you."

The nurse, who had been sitting by the bed, stood up when, with questioning faces, they entered the room.

"Come in. She's not sleeping, just resting. She'll be glad to see you."

Lynn stood over the bed. Glad, she thought bitterly. Glad, I doubt. Bruce said she was terrified.

The girl's face was dead white, frozen, carved in ice.

Robert said softly, "Emily, it's Dad. Dad and Mom."

"I know. I'm very tired," Emily whispered with her eyes shut.

"Of course you are. Emily, we love you," Robert said. "We love you so." His voice was so low that he repeated the words. He wanted to make certain that she had heard him. Kneeling on the floor, he brought his face level with hers. "Emily, we love you." Then he put his face down again on the coverlet.

Everything spun too fast. The way life moved and sped was extraordinary. It was fearful. One was, after all, quite helpless. First there was Emily trying for Yale with all the honors. And then there was this scene. A sudden vertigo overcame Lynn and she grasped the back of the bed to steady herself.

The nurse whispered, "She'll sleep now. The night nurse said she was up most of the night in spite of the medication."

So they waited all day in the room. Late in the afternoon Emily awoke and stirred in the bed.

"I'm better," she said clearly.

And indeed, some faint color flowed under her skin, and her eyes were bright, their pupils large and dark as after recovery from fever.

Next she said, "You're very angry."

They spoke in unison. "No, no."

She sighed. "You need to be told."

"Not now," Robert said. "You don't need to talk now."

But Emily insisted. "I want to." In a tone of bewilderment, as if she were telling a stranger's story, one that she did not really understand, she began. "At first I didn't know. I didn't think, it was only about the middle of the second month. I didn't know. And after that, I was so scared. I couldn't believe it."

Her thin hands clung together on the coverlet. On her little finger she wore the initialed gold ring that had been too large even for her middle finger when it was new. She had been eight, seven or eight, Lynn thought; my sister gave it to her for her birthday; we had a clown at the party, I remember.

"I—we didn't know what to do. We kept talking about what to do. I was going to tell you, honestly. I just couldn't seem to get my courage up."

And Lynn thought of the day she had learned about the baby who, it now seemed, was at this minute making its first movements within her, of how she had brought the news home and the house had turned into a holiday house.

"I didn't want an abortion, I couldn't do that."

"What then would you have done?" Robert asked softly.

"We thought—I'll be eighteen this month, we'll be in college next year. They have married couples in college, lots of people marry that young. We'd want to be married, we'd want the baby to have proper parents." Emily's eyes turned toward the ceiling for a moment, reflecting. "You see, we're not that modern. Maybe I am, but Harris isn't. He comes from a very religious family. They go to church every Sunday. He does, too, and they'd want things done right. They're very good people, really. Harris wouldn't be what he is if they weren't."

Robert raised his head, looked across the bed toward Lynn. His lips formed a sneer; she understood the sneer. But he said nothing. And she herself was as yet incapable of making any judgment at all.

"You won't believe this," Emily said, "but it was only one time. I swear it." When neither parent answered, she continued, "I loved him. I love him now. So it happened. It was one day when we were going to the lake, and—"

"No." Robert spoke roughly. "No. We don't have to hear about that."

He did not want to imagine his daughter with a man, to think of Emily and sex at the same time. Well, that was understandable, Lynn supposed.

Now Emily reached for her hand. "You know, Mom," she said. "You understand about loving, even when there are times one shouldn't." And she gave her mother a serious, meaningful look, holding her so long with that look that Lynn, struck by painful memory, was the first to turn away. It was as if Emily wanted to remind her of something, as if there were some complicity between her daughter and herself.

Then the nurse came back. It was five o'clock, dinnertime, and visiting hours were over until the evening, she said, apologizing.

"Anyway, now that Emily's doing fine, you must feel better yourselves."

"You must be awfully tired, Mom." Emily smiled. "You're starting the fifth month, aren't you? Go home and rest."

When they were halfway home, it occurred to Lynn that Emily had not spoken one direct word to Robert.

A car was parked in front of their house when they entered the driveway. Two men got out and walked toward them. One was Harris in his neat chinos, and the other, of equal height, with the same thick brown hair, but older and broader, was undoubtedly his father, wearing a policeman's uniform.

"Oh, no," Lynn said aloud.

Robert heard her and gave an order. "Be quiet. I'll handle this."

They met beside Robert's car. The boy, like Lynn, was afraid, but his father came forward frankly.

"I'm Lieutenant Weber. My son has come to talk to you. Speak up, Harris."

Robert gave a stop signal with his raised hand. "There is nothing you can tell me that I want to hear. Nothing."

The boy flushed. The blood, surging from neck to scalp, looked as though it must burn him.

"I'd like to beat you to a pulp," Robert said, making a fist with the raised hand.

"Mr. Ferguson," the father said, "perhaps if we go inside and talk together—"

"No. My little girl is in there, and anyway, I don't want you—him—in my house. I don't want to talk to him."

"Let him speak here, then. Please, Mr. Ferguson. It'll only take a few minutes."

"I just want you to know," Harris said, "it's hard to find the words, but —I am so terribly sorry, I'll never forget this as long as I live." His whole body was shaking, but he raised his head and threw his shoulders back. "I'm ashamed. I am so terribly ashamed, and so sad for Emily because I love her. I don't know what else to say, Mr. Ferguson, Mrs. Ferguson." He gave a little sob, and his Adam's apple bobbed. "You've always been so nice to me, and—"

His father continued for him. "I have always told him, always since he was grown, that he had two little sisters and that he must treat girls as he'd want somebody to treat them."

Robert interrupted. "Look, Lieutenant, this is all very sweet talk, but there's no point in it. Talk can't undo the facts or make us feel any better. The facts are that Emily came close to dying—"

"No, Robert," Lynn said softly. "No, don't make it worse than it is."

"My wife's a sentimental woman. She doesn't want to hear the truth spoken. It's all right for you to talk sweetly, young fellow. You're not the one lying in pain."

Harris's eyes glistened, and with her eyes Lynn tried to communicate with him. Certain thoughts were taking shape in her mind. He hadn't raped Emily, after all. And it did take two.

Lieutenant Weber said it for her. "It does, after all, take two," he reminded them gently. He gazed out toward the hill where darkness already lay on the trees. "And it's not the first time this has happened, God knows."

A dialogue spun itself out between the two men while Lynn and Harris stood by.

"That doesn't concern me. I'm only concerned about this time."

"Of course. As the father of girls I surely understand. The question is, what is to happen now to these young folks?"

The man was sorrowful and yet not humble, Lynn saw. Somehow the onus is always put on the boy, so it must be hard to be standing in his shoes. Yet he does it honorably. And Robert was making it harder, offering no way for minds to meet.

"He's heard plenty from me and his mother, too, about this, you can bet, enough so he'll never forget it," Lieutenant Weber persisted.

"He didn't hear enough. If he were my son, I'd break his neck."

The father laid his hand on his son's arm. "What good would that do?"

"Let him suffer a little, that's what."

"Don't you think he is suffering? He's a good kid, same as Emily. She's been at our house, and we know her well. She's a fine girl, the finest. They made a mistake, a bad one, but not the worst. Now it's up to us to help them."

"I'm going inside," Robert said coldly. "We've been through hell, my wife and I, and we're wasting our strength listening to drivel. If you'll excuse us." The gravel crunched under his heel as he moved.

"I'm sorry you think it's drivel, Mr. Ferguson. Harris came here like a man to face you. In our family he's been taught to have respect. Never mind this modern stuff. He goes to church, he's not the kind who goes banging—pardon the expression"—this with a bow toward Lynn—"every girl he—"

Robert's anger blazed. "No," he said, "not every girl. Only a girl from a family like this one, a home like this one." He waved his arm toward the house. "Not such a dumb idea to come snooping and sneaking around a place like this so he can raise himself up from the bottom."

Lynn cried in horror. "Robert! Robert!"

"You stay out of this, Lynn. People like him there think they'll better themselves by creeping in where they don't belong."

"Now, wait a minute, Mr. Ferguson. Don't you take that superior tone with me. I won't stand for it."

"Dad! For God's sake, don't! Please don't argue," Harris pleaded.

"Don't you worry, son. You go sit in the car. Go now. I won't be long."

When the boy was out of hearing, he resumed. "I came here like a gentleman with my son. I planned to go into your house so your neighbors across the road wouldn't recognize me in my uniform. I wanted to spare you again, the way I spared you before. I wasn't going to tell you this, for Emily's and Harris's sakes I wasn't, but you've asked for it. On the bottom, are we? You're hardly one to talk."

"Explain yourself," Robert said. "And lower your voice while you're at it."

"Yes, that would be a good idea," replied the other man, and lowered it. "It would have been better for you if you had lowered yours that night a while back when you were battering your wife."

"Oh, Lieutenant, oh, please," Lynn begged.

"Mrs. Ferguson, I'm sorry, but I have to. I'm a man too. Maybe it's just as well that Mr. Ferguson hears the truth."

Lynn's heart raced. It crossed her mind that even at her age, one could have a heart attack. How fast could a heart beat before it gave up?

"Let me tell you," Weber said, "I was called here, I was on duty, when a call came a while back in the summer. The people across the road were out taking an evening walk when they passed your house and heard something going on. So they phoned the station, and up I came. I stood in the dark, and I heard enough to know what it was, all right. I could have taken you in right then and there. But I wasn't about to make trouble for Emily. I figured she already had enough because it can't be the greatest thing for a girl to grow up here, grand as it is."

Robert was breathing heavily, and Weber continued.

"We're very fond of Emily. We know what she is. True blue. I wouldn't hurt her for the world. So I told the people across the road that it was a mistake, and back at the station I buried the record. Buried it. So don't you talk to me about fine family, Mr. Ferguson, or coming up from the bottom." He turned to Lynn, who was crying. "I know you're expecting, Mrs. Ferguson, and this isn't good for you. I'm awfully sorry about it. About everything. If there's anything I can ever do for you, you know where I am, where we are, Harris and—"

"Yes, you can do something," Robert said. He was shaking. "You're a lying bastard, cop or no. You saw nothing when you were here, and you know you didn't. You're trying to intimidate me. Well, it won't work. Now get out of here, you and your precious son. And never come back, either one of you. That's what you can do, and that's all I have to say."

"That's just what I intended to do all along, Mr. Ferguson. Good night, Missus."

For a minute the two were speechless. Lynn was as shocked and immobile as in that first second when Bruce had told them about Emily. The sound of Weber's chugging old engine died away down the road before Robert spoke.

"Stop crying. Cry about Emily, not about that garbage." He bent down in the dusk to stare at her. "Don't tell me you're feeling sorry for that wretched kid. Yes, I wouldn't be surprised. I suppose you are."

"Yes, Robert, I am."

"It figures. That's you."

"Maybe it is."

Pity, like a wave, flooded over her, pity for everything, for a child lost in the crowd and crying for its mother, for a shivering dog abandoned on the roadside, for Emily, so afraid, so ashamed, and for that young fellow, too, with his scared eyes, paying such a price for his few moments of a natural passion. And now, unmistakably this time, the baby moved within her, flexing its tiny arm or leg, stretching and readying itself for a hard world.

"We've seen the last of them, at any rate," Robert said as they went toward the house. "If he ever comes here, you're to throw him out. But he won't dare." They went inside, where Robert poured a drink. His hand was shaking. "My heart's pounding like a trip-hammer. This sort of thing doesn't do you any good, that's for sure."

"No," she said, wiping her wet cheeks.

There was a terrible shame in the room, as if two strangers, a man and a woman, had blundered into a place where one of them was naked. It was not quite clear to her who the naked one was here, Robert, so painfully proud, or she herself, who had for the first time seen another human being stand up to Robert and win. For Weber had won; there could be no doubt of that.

He swallowed the drink and went to the foot of the stairs, calling Annie.

"We're home, honey. What are you doing?"

"Homework," came the answer.

"What homework?"

"Geography."

"Have you got the atlas up there with you?"

"Yes."

"Good. Good girl. Well, stay up there and finish it."

Returning, Robert said, "We need to talk before she comes down."

"About what?"

"About what we're going to do, naturally. I'd like to take her out of that school. Put her in private school, where she won't have to see him. I don't want her to see him even passing in the halls."

"You can't do that to her, you can't break up a term in senior year, Robert!"

He considered, then conceded, "I suppose you're right. But I'm going to have a talk with Emily—oh, don't worry, I see the worry on your face. It's going to be very peaceable, with no recriminations, because she's been through enough. But I'm going to make things quite clear, all the same. I want her to rest at home for a week or so, and when she goes back to school, she'll say she had the flu." He walked back and forth across the room with steps so firm that the crystals on the wall sconces made a musical tinkle as he passed. "I want you to keep a strict watch over her free time, Lynn. I want to know where she's going, with whom, and when she'll be home, and no nonsense about it. You get the idea." He increased his pace so that the crystals complained. "Damn! Damn! And life was looking so good. The fates just can't let you enjoy what they give without taking something away at the same time, or so it seems. However, there's no use lamenting about the fates."

Lynn agreed that there was not, and he continued, "I want to keep up with what I started in Maine, keep up the momentum. If it weren't for all that, I'd like to take the lot of us away over Thanksgiving and again at Christmas, and again in February, spend every damn school vacation away from here. But as it is . . . well, we'll have to find other things to do, a ski weekend, theater tickets, Saturdays in the city, anything to keep that girl out of harm's way."

So he walked the length of the room like a general organizing his campaign. That which had been darkly, safely buried, that which Weber had dug up and brought into a cruel glare, had been dismissed from Robert's mind: It was an outrageous lie, it had never happened.

At least, Lynn thought wryly, at least Weber's done one thing; he's had a sobering effect; Robert hasn't said anything more about my being to blame for Emily's trouble.

The words repeated themselves in pitying silence: Emily's trouble.

"I am so terribly tired," she said involuntarily.

Robert gave her a glance. "Yes, you do look done in. Go to bed. I'll see how Annie's doing."

She moved heavily. It was an effort to raise her arms and slip the dress over her head, to pull the spread back and get into the bed. Yet it was not long before she fell into a thick, dark sleep. Toward morning when the windows turned gray, she dreamed. She tumbled, hurling from some great height while grabbing in terror at the empty air, while below, sharp, pointed things—knives, sticks, thorns?—were aimed at her open eyes, and there was no way, no way she could—

She screamed, screamed, and was jolted awake. Robert was holding her, saying softly, "What is it?"

"Nothing, nothing," she whispered.

He comforted her shaking body, stroking the back of her neck.

"Nerves. Nerves. And why not? You've been through too much. Take it easy. I'm here. I'm here."

"Then I have your promise, Emily?" Robert asked.

"I have already given it to you," she answered, lying back on the pillowed sofa.

"It is for your own good, Emily. You've had a very narrow escape. As terribly hard as it was, the miscarriage"—here he seemed to gulp over the word—"was easier than the other way would have been. Your whole life, your ambition, everything, would have turned inside out." He made a gesture of hopeless dismissal. "So now the rest is up to you," he said, standing up and producing a smile meant to encourage. "I have to run for the late train. My desk must be loaded." At the door he turned back again. "Oh, yes, I meant to tell you, I've bought tickets to the opera, Saturday matinees. But you'll be able to squeeze in your homework all day Sunday. And Annie will too."

"He's so well oiled," said Emily when Robert had gone. "Everything planned. You press a button and the answers to all your problems just pop out. Quick and easy."

"That's nasty, Emily. Your father means so well. You never thought he'd be so understanding, now, did you?"

"Does he think I don't see through him? Do your homework all day Sunday, meaning, Don't leave this house. I'm keeping an eye on you."

"That's not true. You heard him say you should go out with other boys."

"I don't want to go out with other boys. I want to be with Harris. I want to be trusted."

Lynn raised an eyebrow. "Trusted? Well, really, Emily."

"It happened once, Mom. We're hardly ever alone together in the first place. All summer we were at the lake with a crowd, you know that. You believe me, don't you?"

Her blue eyes, moist as petals, are so beautiful, that it's a wonder he could resist her at all, Lynn thought.

"You believe me?" the girl repeated.

"Yes. But you see what happened from just that once."

"We want to get married."

"Oh, my God, Emily, you're much too young."

"Eighteen! You were only twenty."

"That was different. Your father was older."

"My father? Yes, and look what you got."

Lynn, choosing to ignore the sarcasm, said only, "Harris, or you, or both of you, may change your minds, you know."

"Not any more than we'll change our minds about medical school. And it was horrible, what Dad said about Harris wanting to better himself because our family has more money," Emily said bitterly. "It was a cheap and cruel and stupid thing to say. Harris phoned me at the hospital just before you got there to take me home, and he told me."

"Your father was beside himself with worry over you. I've never seen him so desperate. People say things when they're desperate."

Lynn felt as if she were being driven toward a trap. But Harris had not been present, he had been sent to wait in the car when his father had talked about that night last spring. Her mind moved swiftly in recollection. Obviously, then, Weber hadn't wanted Harris to hear that part. He was a decent human being who had done his best to conceal what had happened. "I buried it," he had said. "Buried it." No, he would not have told Harris. And Lynn's fear subsided.

"Harris said his parents have told him he mustn't see me, that he must even avoid me in school."

"They're right, Emily. It's wiser that way."

"It's all Dad's fault. It goes back to him."

Lynn protested, "There's no logic in that remark. I don't understand it at all."

"Don't you? I could tell you, but you wouldn't want to hear it. There's no use talking when you won't be open with me, Mom."

Lynn, folding her hands on her lap, looked down on the backs that had been covered with puncture wounds. What Emily wanted was a confirmation, an admission about those wounds, now long healed. But she was not going to get it. A mother hides her private pain from her children. For their own good she does this.

For my own good, too, she thought. Abruptly a tinge of anger colored her feeling for Lieutenant Weber. He should not have said those things! He should have known how they would hurt. But then, there were the things that Robert had said . . . Her head throbbed.

"I'll tell you, Emily," she said somewhat crisply, "I can't play verbal games with you. You say you're a woman, so I'll talk to you as one woman talks to another. I'll tell you frankly that I'm not feeling my best right now, and I don't want to argue about anything. I only want to help you, and I want you to help me too."

Emily got up and took her mother into her arms. "All right, Mom, we won't talk about this anymore. Just have a wonderful, healthy baby and be well." She smiled at Lynn. "Don't worry about me. I'll work hard the rest of the year and graduate with honors too. You'll see. And I won't make any trouble for anybody. I've made enough already."

4

"**W**HAT'S the matter with Emily?" Annie asked again. "Why won't anybody tell me?"

"There's nothing to tell. She's just working terribly hard these days. She has to keep her grades up if she wants to get into Yale," Lynn answered cheerfully.

"She cries a lot. Her eyes were red last night." Annie's own small, worried eyes were suspicious. "Didn't you see?"

"She has a little cold, that's all."

The weight of Emily's sadness lay heavily on Lynn. Of course she cried, why wouldn't she, poor child? The double shocks, to the body and to the spirit, had aged and changed her. Hardened her too? she wondered.

She hesitated at the door of Emily's room. Conscious of her own pregnancy's pronounced visibility, she could not help but think of its effect on the wounded girl.

But she opened the door, and in the cheerful, artificial tone that had by now become a habit, inquired, "Busy? Or may I come in?"

Emily put the book down. "I'm busy, but come in."

"I don't want to disturb you. I thought—you've been isolated lately with all this studying. Of course, it's necessary, I know." Floundering so, she came suddenly to the point. "Tell me. Do you need to talk about your feelings, about Harris? Because if you want to, I'm here. I'm always here for you."

"Thanks, but there's nothing to talk about."

Emily's shoulders appeared to straighten, and her chin rose a proud inch or two. This small display of pride seemed to shut Lynn out, and she repeated gently.

"Nothing?"

"No. We stay completely away from each other, so if that's why you're worried, don't."

"I'm not worried about that. I know you'll keep your word."

"He sent me a birthday card with a lace handkerchief in it. And we do talk on the phone." Emily paused as if, Lynn thought, she expects me to protest about that. When no protest came, Emily said proudly, "He works every day. He even has a Sunday job. I suppose it's part of his punishment."

"Oh! I shouldn't think punishment was necessary. I mean . . . Our feeling is that you should have fun, you know that." And when Emily was once more silent, Lynn continued, "I know boys call you."

"Because they know Harris and I are through."

"But you never accept."

Emily gave her a twist of a smile. "If I wanted to, and I don't, there wouldn't be time, would there? My days are filled up. Aren't they?"

Indeed. True to his word, Robert had provided an activity for every available hour; they had gone to the opera, to country fairs, and the local dog show; they had skated on the season's first ice at Rockefeller Center and seen the exhibit at the Metropolitan Museum. Vigorously, tenaciously, he fulfilled his plan, and with equal tenacity and her new cool courtesy, Emily had complied.

But how she must ache!

So the autumn passed, a long, slow season this year, the ground covered with black leaves rotting under steady rain, a season sliding downhill toward a frozen winter, as if the chilly gloom wanted to reflect the cold that underlay the sham politeness in the house.

By tacit agreement the trouble was covered over. At meals Robert led the talk to current events, the day's headlines. Alone with Lynn the talk was chiefly about the firm. It was as if, for him, nothing else of any import had happened or was happening.

"They're thinking of sending me abroad," he told her one night. "There's a group from the West Coast going, from Monacco's office, and they want me to go with them for a meeting in Berlin. After that I go alone to meet the people whom we've contacted in Budapest." Excited, stimulated, he paced the bedroom floor and came to rest behind Lynn, who was brushing her hair at the mirror. "It'll take two weeks probably, if

I go. I'm pretty sure I will, though. It'll be some time in December. I hate to leave you." He studied her face. "You look tired."

"I'm fine. We'll be fine."

"You're pretty heavy this time, that's what it is. By March you'll be yourself again."

She agreed. "I'm sure."

Yet she felt a weakness that she had never felt before. It was hard to get out of bed in the morning, and so hard to keep running between activities, the train to New York, the car to the country fair, going, going all the time. With Robert away there would at least be some rest.

Josie said, "It's not the pregnancy. You're emotionally wrung out. Emily's trouble was enough to do it, God knows."

But you don't know the half of it, thought Lynn. Involuntarily, she sighed.

Josie remarked the sigh. "You never went back to my friend—Dr. Miller, I mean." The tone was accusatory.

"No." Go back to tell him about Lieutenant Weber and—and all the rest? Wake that up yet again? And for what? What could he do, that man, except make her feel like two cents, sitting there? And biting the thread with which she was mending Annie's skirt, she remarked only, "That child tears everything. She's always bumping into things."

"How do she and Robert get along these days?"

"All right. No problems."

Not on the surface, anyway. He kept them all too busy, she thought. But perhaps that was healthy? Healthy and wholesome. You want to think so . . . but is it?

"Robert's leaving for Europe on Tuesday, you know," she said, feeling slightly awkward because Bruce was not leaving. Yet to ignore the fact before Josie would be more awkward.

"Yes, I know."

No more was said about that. Then Josie asked about Emily.

"She never mentions Harris, and I don't ask anymore. 'It's over,' she told me. So maybe Robert was right when he said it would pass and the scars would fade. I guess so. I don't know." She reflected. "Anyway, she's working long hours, half the night, for the science fair. It's all voluntary. I think she's doing too much, but Robert says I should leave her alone. Well, of course, he's so proud of her achievement. And I am, too, but mostly I want her to be happy. I feel"—Here Lynn put the sewing down and clasped her hands—"I feel so terribly sorry for her, Josie, and for the boy too."

"Bruce has seen him a few times when he passes the soccer field on the way to the jogging track. He asks about Emily."

"Yes, I'm sorry for him," Lynn repeated, and, with a little laugh, added, "You can imagine that Robert isn't. His anger over this has gone too deep. There's no forgiveness in it."

"Robert's an angry man to begin with," Josie said. "Listen, Lynn, I don't want to come after you with a sledgehammer, but I wish you would listen to me. You *need* to talk to somebody. Keeping your secrets—and I know you do—will only harm you in the end. God only knows what may happen." And she repeated, "Robert is an angry man."

Her comments only offended Lynn; Josie's comments always had. They were exaggerated, and anyway it was unseemly to disparage a woman's husband to her face, no matter what you thought.

Yet this was the only flaw in the long friendship. She had always to consider that. And she had also to consider the nasty things Robert said about Josie. So she made her defense a calm one.

"Robert has always worked under very high pressure. Right now he's got his heart set on building a future for this baby, for the son he's convinced it is."

"Oh, naturally he'd want a son."

"Well, we already do have two girls, Josie. Anyway, Robert's a workaholic. I worry sometimes that he'll work himself to death."

"If he does, it'll be by his own choice."

"Oh, no, he plans to live and rear this boy. He's got such plans, it's really amazing to hear him; you'd think having a baby was the grandest thing that can happen. Well, I guess it is, after all." Stricken with embarrassment before this barren woman, she stopped.

Josie's response was quick. "Don't be sorry about me. I've long accepted that other women have babies and I don't. You have to face the realities, one right after the other, all through life."

Lynn was immediately sober. "Well, you surely face them," she amended. "I remember how you were when you had your operation. You were amazing." She smiled. "Thank goodness, you're fine now."

"Is that a statement or a question?"

"Well, both, I guess." Lynn was startled. "You are fine now, aren't you?"

"You can't know that positively," Josie answered quietly. "Can you ever know anything positively?"

"I suppose not. But are you telling me something—something bad about yourself?"

"No. I'm only telling you that facing reality isn't the easiest thing for most of us to learn."

There was a silence until Josie rose to depart. She left a vague discomfort in the room, a hollow space, a chilled draft, an enigmatic message. Lynn felt as if she had been scolded.

On Monday, the night before he was to leave, Robert came home early. He had bought new luggage and laid it on the bed ready to pack. His passport and traveler's checks were on the dresser, the new raincoat hung on the closet door, and his list was at hand.

They had dinner. He was euphoric, filled with a sense of novelty and adventure.

"This is much more than a question of profits, you understand. The world's peace, its future, hang on whether we can make the European Community work. We need to take all these eastern republics into some sort of attachment to NATO. That's why it's so important to lay an economic foundation." He talked and talked. His eyes were brilliant.

Upstairs again after dinner, he went on talking while folding and packing; he would not allow Lynn to do it for him, preferring his own method. As he called out, she checked off the list.

"Notebook, camera, film, dictionary. There, that's it." He turned to her. "God, I'll miss you."

"You'll be too busy to miss anyone."

"Only you," he said gravely. "Hey, I guess the girls have gone to bed. I'll kiss them good-bye in the morning unless they're still asleep."

"They'll be up."

"I'm leaving at the crack of dawn. Where's Juliet?"

"Right there on the other side of the bed. I'll go put her out."

"No, no, I will. Come on, girl, let's go," he said as the dog, stretching and yawning, lumbered behind him.

It was not half a minute later when Lynn heard the voices exploding in the kitchen, and she raced downstairs. Robert was standing over Annie, trembling in her nightgown, with a face all puckered in tears. In front of her on the kitchen table was a soup bowl piled high with ice cream, whipped cream, fudge sauce and salted almonds; the base of the tower was encircled by a ring of sliced bananas, and the peak was adorned with a maraschino cherry.

"Look! Will you look at this!" Robert cried. "No wonder she can't lose weight. You're a pig, Annie. You're worse than a pig because you're supposed to have some intelligence. You're disgusting, if you want to know."

Annie sobbed. "You—you've no right to say things like that. I haven't murdered anybody. If I want to be fat, I'll be fat, and it's my business."

Lynn mourned, stroking the child's head. "Oh, Annie. You had a good dinner. You were supposed to be in bed."

Robert interrupted. "Stop the coaxing and caressing. That's been the whole trouble here anyway. No discipline. No guts. Anything they want to do, they do."

He snatched the soup bowl, Annie snatched, too, and the contents slopped over onto the table.

Annie screamed. "Don't touch it! I want it!"

"Oh, this is awful," Lynn lamented. "I can't stand this! Robert, for heaven's sake, let her have a spoonful, a taste. Then she'll let you throw it away, I know she will."

" 'Let' me? What do you mean? Nobody 'lets' me do anything in this house. I'm the father. Here," he shouted with the bowl now firmly in his grasp, "this is going where it belongs, into the garbage pail."

The lid clanged shut, and Annie howled. "That was mean! You're the worst father. Mean!"

"I may be mean, but you're a mess. A total, absolute mess. A disappointment. You'd better get hold of yourself."

Lynn protested, "Robert, that's cruel. It's true that Annie needs to watch her weight, but she is not a mess. She's a lovely girl, and—"

"Lynn, cut out the soft soap. It's sickening. I gag on it."

"Don't you yell at Mommy! Leave Mommy alone!"

The two confronted each other, the trim, tall man opposed to the square little girl whose stomach bulged under her nightdress and whose homely, pallid face was mottled red with rage. Lynn summoned every ounce of control.

"Come upstairs with me. Come to bed," she repeated quietly. "There's no sense in this."

When she had pacified Annie and seen her into bed, she went to her own bedroom, where Robert was reading.

"Well," she said, "a nice good-bye on your last night. Very nice to remember."

A stack of Christmas cards waiting to be addressed lay on a table beside his chair. He held up a photograph of the Ferguson family, standing in front of the holly garlands on the living room mantel; they were all smiling; even Juliet, with lolling tongue, looked happy. Then he snapped the card back onto the pile and mocked:

"The perfect American family. There they are. Perfect."

"Losing your temper like that over a dish of ice cream," she protested.

"You know very well it was more than that. It was the principle of the thing, the disobedience, her defiance."

"You called her a 'mess.' That was unforgivable. Brutal."

"It's the truth. I work with her, you see how much time I spend trying to lift her out of her slovenly habits, I try my darnedest, and still she comes home with C's on her report card. I don't know what to say anymore."

Robert stood up, walked to the dresser, where he arranged his combs and brushes in parallels, then walked to the window, where he brought the shade even with the sill.

The baby made a strong turn or kick inside Lynn. Its weight pulled her so hard, she had to sit down.

"I can't stand this," she said.

"Well, what do you want me to do? Go around pussyfooting, pretending not to see what I see? Maybe if you kept better order here—"

"Order? What's disorderly? Do you mind giving me an example other than the ice cream tonight?"

"Okay. That business last week when she went to school with a ten-cent-store ring on each finger. She looked ridiculous, and I said so, but you let her do it anyway."

"Oh, for heaven's sake, it's the style in her grade. So it looks ridiculous —what difference? So I let her do it, and now I'm a failure as a mother."

"Don't put words in my mouth. I didn't call you a failure."

But you've thought it. I know. Ever since I let the baby drown.

"You implied it," she said.

"What's all this quibbling? What are we doing here?" Exasperated, he punched his fist into his palm.

She should really not argue with him. Just don't talk back, she told herself. He's tense, he has to leave early in the morning, he needs his rest. Annie will forget about this, I'll forget, and it will all pass if I just keep quiet.

Yet a quick answer leapt from her mouth. "I don't know what you're doing, but I know what I'm doing. I'm trying to cope."

He stared as if in astonishment. "You? You are? Coping? While I'm working my head off on the brink of the biggest opportunity of my life— of our lives—calmly keeping myself together and doing an expert job in spite of the disaster here at home, the disaster that you allowed to happen—"

She sprang up. "Back again to Emily, are you? This is too much. It's insane."

"Insane? You don't want to hear it, I know. And if you notice, I haven't talked about it. Purely out of consideration for your condition, Lynn. Purely."

"Louder! Speak louder so she'll be sure to hear this."

He strode to the door, closed it, and said in a lower voice, "I warned you and warned you about her and that bastard, but in your laissez-faire way you did nothing. You didn't watch her, you ruined a beautiful girl, you ruined her life."

Lynn's anger mounted. "Listen here, you with your phony accusations. I could have done some accusing, too, in my time if I'd wanted to, and my accusations wouldn't have been phony either. You know darn well what—"

Robert sprang up, grabbed her arms, and shook her. "If you weren't pregnant, I know what I'd—"

"Take your hands off me, Robert. You're hurting me. Now, you let me alone, you hear?"

"Goddamn crazy house," he muttered, walking away. "I'll be glad to get out of it in the morning."

She lay down, hoping for sleep. Anger was disaster. Some people throve on it, but it sapped her; some bodies just were not programmed for anger. She lay awake while Robert undressed and did his small last-minute chores. She heard his shoelace break as he sat on the side of the bed removing his shoes; she heard him fumble in the weak lamplight, searching for another lace.

When at last he got into bed, she did not turn to him, as was their custom, nor did he turn to her.

In the morning when she woke, he was gone.

It was a brilliant morning. It turned the view from the kitchen window into a Japanese print: Brittle black branches on the hill's crest cut patterns against the sky. Lynn stared at it, unseeing; on this day it could give her no pleasure. Nothing could. A faint nausea rose to her throat, and she pushed her cup away. Too much coffee. Too many heavy thoughts.

The house was quiet, and the hum of its silence was unbearably mournful. She got up, moving her clumsy body to the appointment book on the desk. There was nothing much for today except the monthly visit to the obstetrician, who would scold her for not having gained weight;

years ago they used to scold you for gaining it. Other than that, there were just a few little errands and marketing. Lunch with Josie had been crossed out because Josie had a cold, and that was just as well, for she was in no mood for sociability.

Dr. Rupert having been called away, Lynn was to see an associate, a young man, younger than she, his curly hair hanging almost to shoulder length over his white coat. The look had gone out in the eighties, but now, in the nineties, it was apparently coming back. Wrapped in white sheeting, she sat on the examining table observing him while he read her record.

"Nausea last month, I see. How is it now?" he asked her.

"I still have it now and then."

"It's not usual in the sixth month."

"I know. I didn't have it the other times."

"It says here that you feel unusually tired too."

"Sometimes." She didn't feel like talking. If he would just get on with it and let her go! "I'm much larger than I was with my other babies, so I guess there's just more to carry."

He looked doubtful. "Could be. But your blood pressure's up this morning. Not terribly, but definitely up. Is there any reason that you can think of?"

Alarmed, she responded quickly. "Well, no. Is it bad?"

"No. I said not terribly. Still, one has to wonder why it's up at all. Has anything upset you?"

His smile wanted to persuade her, but she would neither be persuaded nor tricked into any admission. Yet, some answer had to be given.

"Perhaps it's because my husband has just left for Europe, and that worries me a little. I can't think of anything else."

He was looking straight into her eyes. His own were shrewd, narrowed under eyebrows drawn together as they might be if he were doing a mathematical computation or working a puzzle.

"I was wondering," he said slowly. "Those marks on your upper arms—"

"Marks?" she repeated, and glancing down, saw above her elbows the blue-green spots where Robert's thumbs had pressed last night.

"Oh, those." She shrugged. "I can't imagine. I bruise easily. I'm always finding bruises and can't remember how I got them."

"Symmetrical bruises. Somebody made them," he said, flashing the same easy smile.

As if she didn't see through him! His deliberately casual manner, coaxing, as if he were speaking to a child!

The father said to the new bride, "Somebody made those marks. Lynn, I want to know."

"Is there something you want to tell me?" the doctor asked her now.

Thinking she heard a note of curiosity in his voice, she felt the hot sting of indignation. It was the new style these days; you got it on television and in print, people saying whatever came into their heads without manners or tact, prying and snooping with no respect for privacy; *just let it all hang out.*

"What can you mean?" she retorted. "What should I possibly want to tell you?"

The young man, catching her expression, which must have been fierce, retreated at once.

"I'm sorry. I only asked in case you had something else on your mind. So, that's all for today. Next month Dr. Rupert will see you as usual." And he turned back to the chart.

Her heart was still pounding when she left the office. Meddler. Officious busybody. She wondered whether he would write, *Two bruises, upper arms,* on the chart.

Even as she pushed the cart through the supermarket a little while later, she was still aware of her heartbeat. Then, in the parking lot as she was unloading the cart, she caught sight of Harris Weber and his mother in the next row of cars. And her heart began its race again. They hadn't seen her yet, and she bent lower over the bags so that they might leave without noticing her. This avoidance was not because of any ill feeling toward them, for she had almost none toward Harris and certainly none at all toward his mother; it was because the unknown woman knew things about her, about her and Robert. . . . And she wanted to hide, not to look the woman in the face and have to see there—what would she see there? Curiosity? Pity? Contempt?

But they were taking so long that by now the boy must have recognized her car and would know she was leaning ostrichlike over the groceries in order to avoid them. Something told her to look up, not to hurt the boy.

"Hello," she said, and raised her arm in a slight wave.

He gave her his bright, familiar look, that candid look with the masculine sweetness in it, whose appeal she had felt from the very first.

"Hello, Mrs. Ferguson."

"How are you?" she called across the car's hood.

"Fine, thanks. And you?"

She nodded and smiled; the mother nodded and gave in return a smile that said nothing; it was merely polite and perhaps a trifle shy. That was all. And they drove away, the old car sputtering out of the parking lot.

There, Lynn told herself, that wasn't so bad. It had to be done. Yet the little encounter had given her another kind of sadness—not for herself, but for Emily. She went home, put the groceries away, sat down to read the mail, mostly bills and Christmas cards, and with the sadness still in her, listened to the drowsy hum of the silence.

The telephone rang. She must have been dozing, for it startled her, and she jumped.

"Hello," said Robert.

"Where are you?" she cried.

"In London. I told you, we took the day flight so we're staying the night here, and we leave for Berlin in the morning. It was a fine flight."

"That's nice," she said stiffly.

"Lynn, it's night here, but I couldn't go to sleep without talking to you. I waited till you'd be back from the doctor's. How are you?"

"How is my health, do you mean, or my state of mind?"

"Both."

"My health is all right. The other is what you might expect."

"Lynn, I'm sorry. I'm so awfully sorry. I said it was a good flight, but it wasn't, because I kept thinking about us all the way. About us and Annie. I didn't want to hurt her feelings, God knows. I never do."

"You hurt her because she isn't Emily. She isn't beautiful, and—"

"No, no, that's not true. I do everything for her, everything I can. But I'm not as patient as you are, I'll admit that. I always do admit when I'm wrong, don't I?"

She wanted to ask: Shall I count the times you do, the times you don't, and give you the ratio? But that kind of hairsplitting led nowhere. It was like jumping up and down on the same spot.

She sighed. "I suppose so."

"I get frustrated. I want so much for her, and she doesn't understand. Annie's not easy."

There she had to agree. Yet she fenced with her reply, saying sternly, "Nobody is, Robert."

"That's not so. You are. You are the kindest, the gentlest, the most reasonable, sensible, wonderful woman, and I don't deserve you."

Was this the frowning, hostile man who had shouted last night in the kitchen, hurt her arms, and turned his back on her in the bedroom? Yes, of course he was. And somewhat scornfully she admonished herself: Don't tell me again that you're surprised.

"Lynn, are you there?"

"I'm here, I'm here."

"Tell Annie I'm sorry, will you?"

"Yes, I'll tell her."

"The whole thing was stupid, the way we turned away from each other without saying good-night as we always do, or without saying good-bye this morning. What if one of us should have an accident like the Remys and we were never to see each other again?"

The Remys, who had lived across the street. Linda and Kevin. The words pierced her. She could still hear Linda's terrible cry when they called to tell her of the accident; the sound had rung down the block so that people had come running, and Linda had gone mad.

"He left for work an hour ago!" she screamed, and had kept screaming. "He left for work an hour ago!"

"That angry night would have been our last one. Think about it," Robert said.

A heart attack. A plane crash, or a car crash on a foreign road in fog and rain. His mangled body. They would return it to America. He would never sit in that chair again.

"Lynn, are you all right? What is it?"

"I'm all right."

But he had pierced her. It felt like internal bleeding. She was seeing herself in the house alone—because what are one's children, more than an extension of oneself? These vulnerable girls, this unborn infant to care for, and he not coming back. No man's voice, no man's dependable step coming up the stairs at the end of the day. No man's strong arms.

"I guess my nerves wore thin," she said. "I should have brought you and Annie together before night. But I was just plain mad. And then, I'm not twenty years old anymore," she finished ruefully.

"Yes, you are, as you were when I met you. You'll always be twenty. Tell me you love me a little. Just tell me that, and it'll hold until I come back. Tell me you're not angry anymore."

Her very flesh could feel the vibrations in his voice, the quiver of his pain.

"I love you all so much, but you first of all. I'm nothing without you, Lynn. Forgive me for the times I've hurt you. Forgive me, please."

"Yes. Yes."

The marks on the arms, the hot-tempered words so dearly repented of

—what are they in the end compared with all the goodness? Nothing. Nothing.

Thousands of miles apart, we are, and still this tie renews itself as if he were in this room or I in that strange room in London, and we were touching one another. Astonishing!

So her anger dissolved. It lifted the chill that had clung like a wet pall all that day, and comfort began to warm her.

"And you love me, Lynn?"

"Yes, yes I do."

In spite of everything, I do.

"Take care, then, darling. Give my love to the girls. I'll call again in a couple of days."

Relief was still flooding, and she was still sitting there cradling the plastic instrument in her hands as if it could still hold some essence of that relief, when it rang again.

"Hello, this is Tom Lawrence. How are you?"

"I'm fine, thank you." And she actually heard the lilt in her own voice.

"I'll tell you why I'm calling. I wonder whether you can do me a favor. My sister's in town with her daughter. They live in Honolulu, and she thought it was time for Sybil to see what lies beyond Hawaii. Sybil's twelve. Don't you have a girl about twelve?"

"Yes, Annie. She's eleven."

"That's great. May we borrow her? Do you think she'd like to go into the city? We'd see a show, maybe a museum or maybe the Statue of Liberty. How does that sound?"

"It sounds lovely."

"Well, then, we'll pick Annie up tomorrow morning, if that's all right, and we'll take the train in."

"Annie'll be thrilled. She loves New York."

"It'll be a new experience for me, with two ladies that young. My sister wants the morning off by herself to do the shops, so I'll be on my own with the girls for a while."

"You'll do very well, I'm sure."

"She'll like Sybil. A nice kid, even if she is my niece."

A faint worry passed through Lynn. For some reason she imagined the sister to be like the excessively smart young women whom she had seen at that party in Tom's house. She would be incredibly thin, and her daughter would be, too, dressed in French clothes, and looking sixteen years old. There were plenty of girls like that, but Annie was not one of them.

So it was with some relief that she greeted the party at the door the next morning. Tom's sister, who might have been his twin, was pretty and proper and friendly. Sybil, like her, was neither thin nor fat, although not as pretty as her mother. Annie would have a good day.

Lynn's prediction turned out to be right. Annie had a wonderful Saturday. At dinnertime she repeated triumphantly, "I had chocolate cake with raspberries and cream. I told them my father says I'm too fat, and Tom said when I'm older I'll want to diet and not to worry too much in the meantime."

" 'Tom'? You called Mr. Lawrence 'Tom'?"

"He told me to. Because Sybil calls him 'Uncle Tom.' "

Light snow, mixed with rain, had begun to freeze. In the moment of quiet it could be heard tinkling on the windowpanes.

"It's nice eating here in the kitchen," Emily said. "Cozy."

It was true. In the dining room with only four at the table, it always seemed that ten or twelve more were missing, for the table, an original Sheraton, was long enough to seat eighteen. The room always seemed to echo. Robert said, though, that a dining room was meant to be dined in.

Annie was still full of her day. "I told him I hate my hair, it's so kinky. And he said I can have it straightened if I want to. I said my father won't let me, and he said I could do it when I was grown up because I could do whatever I wanted then. He said he knew a lady who had it done, and she loved it afterward." Annie giggled. "I'll bet he meant one of his wives."

Lynn and Emily glanced at each other. And Emily scoffed, "You don't know anything about his wives."

"Yes, I do. Sybil told me. He's had two. Or maybe three, she thinks." Annie, looking thoughtful, stopped the fork midway to her mouth. "You know what? If you ever divorce Dad, I think you should marry Tom."

"Why, Annie! As if I would ever divorce Daddy."

"I should think you would pick Uncle Bruce," Emily remarked. "You love him so much."

She had a twitch at the corner of her mouth as she spoke, that might have been humorous, or cynical, or both. Lynn looked away.

And Annie said seriously, "Yes, of course I love him, silly, but he has Aunt Josie."

Lynn rebuked them. "This is all silly. And don't you dare say anything as idiotic as that in front of Daddy either. He's coming home the week after next on Wednesday."

"Eleven more days. Only eleven more days," Annie said. "I thought he was going to stay longer."

"Well, he'll be finished with his work by then," Lynn explained, "so it will be time to come home."

Annie grumbled. "He just left. What's the use of going away when he just turns around and comes right back? He can't be doing very much. I hope they give him a bigger job next time."

"Go let Juliet out. She needs to go," Lynn said.

On the Monday, when school reopened, Emily came home without Annie, grumbling, "That kid! She missed the bus again. Now I suppose I'll have to get in the car and go back for her. And she'll be soaked, too, standing outside in this mess."

Lynn looked out of the window where sleet was slanting as if it, too, like the trees, were leaning against the wind. A high, dangerous glaze lay on the white slope.

"No, I'll go, Emily. The roads are slippery, and you haven't been driving long enough to manage."

Emily looked at her mother's enormous belly. "And if the car gets stuck and you have to get out and you fall? No, I'll go, Mom. I'll be careful."

When you come down to it, she is still the most responsible girl, Lynn thought as she watched the car move cautiously down the drive, slide into the road, and move almost inch by inch out of sight. Nevertheless, she remained at her anxious post by the window, mentally timing the trip to the school and return.

When the telephone rang—always at the most inconvenient moments, it seems, the telephone has to ring—she picked it up. An unfamiliar voice came over the wire.

"Lynn Ferguson? This is Fay Heller, your sister Helen's neighbor in St. Louis. Do you remember me?"

Lynn's insides quivered. "Yes, yes. Has anything—Where's Helen?"

"Helen's fine. The whole family's away on a ski trip. I'm calling because they're away, and your little girl Annie's here at my house."

Lynn sank down onto a chair. "Annie? There with you? I don't understand."

A very calm, soothing voice explained. "Don't be frightened. She's quite all right, unharmed. She arrived in a taxi around three o'clock. I saw her ringing Helen's bell, and naturally getting no answer, so I went over and brought her here. She doesn't want to explain herself, and so I haven't pressed, but—"

Oh, my God, she's run away. What else is going to happen? To run away makes no sense. . . .

"I can't imagine whatever got into her head!" Lynn cried, the trite words coming automatically, while her thoughts ran opposite. You don't have to imagine, you know. Robert is coming home. . . .

The ice cream episode had been horrible, and yet . . . To run away . . . Annie, Annie . . .

Her head pounded. Her sweaty, cold hand shook, holding the receiver.

"Kids do surprise us sometimes, don't they?" The woman was trying to make light of the affair, trying to console. "I guess we did the same to our parents in our time."

Lynn's thoughts were racing. However had Annie bought a ticket and gotten onto the plane? An unaccompanied child, going all that distance? They would never sell her a ticket.

"May I talk to her, please?"

"I did suggest that she call you right away, but she was a bit upset, naturally, so I thought it better not to insist."

"She's not afraid to talk to me? Tell her I won't scold her. I only want to know how she is. Tell her, please, please."

"Well, the fact is, I wouldn't say she's afraid, but she was really awfully tired, and I sent her upstairs to lie down. After she ate, I mean. She was hungry."

Now the woman is being tactful. The truth is, Annie doesn't want to talk to me.

"She wants to go home. Do you want me to see whether there's a plane we can get her on this evening?"

So she does want to come back! Oh, thank God for that.

"No, in the circumstances, I don't want her to fly alone. I'll find out how I can fly from here instead."

"Actually, the weather's very bad on this end. Why don't you let me keep her overnight? It's late in the day now, anyway."

Tears were gathering; Lynn's throat was tightening. And the other woman, apparently sensing this, said gently, "You're thinking she's a trouble to us, but she isn't. And she's quite fine here. You remember my three, don't you? They're grown and gone, but I still know what to do with a young girl. So don't worry."

A little sob broke now. "I'm terrified thinking what might have happened if it hadn't been you who discovered her. God knows who else might have come along."

"Well, no one else did. Wait a minute, my husband's saying something.

Oh, I'm right. Nothing's flying out of here tonight. You'll have to wait till tomorrow."

"All right, then, I'll take the first plane in the morning. And, oh, I want to thank you. How can I even begin?"

"Don't bother. You would do the same for someone. Just get a good night's sleep if you can."

She must wipe her eyes and compose her face before Emily came back. The mother is strong in emergencies, not shaken. A mother hides her fears and hurts. But she hadn't been able to hide them from the doctor that morning. . . .

In the back entry Emily stamped snow from her boots and called, "Mom? Mom? She wasn't there. I looked all over. The darn kid must have gone home with one of her friends. You'd think she could at least call up. Why, what's the matter?"

"What on earth do you think that foolish child has gone and done?" Lynn wanted to express, instead of her total dismay, a kind of mock exasperation as if to say, with hands thrown up, What will she do next?

But Emily did not respond in kind. "She's very frightened. Her dark thoughts frighten her," she said gravely.

The two women looked at each other. It occurred to Lynn that they, too, were exchanging such rather enigmatic looks quite often lately. It occurred to her, too, that it was always she herself who first dropped her eyes or turned away.

"Annie was never an easy child, not like you," she said, since a comment of some kind was needed.

That, of course, was just what Robert had said when he called from London. And Emily's reply was the very one that she, Lynn, had given to Robert.

"Nobody's easy."

She was not up to a philosophical argument, not now. "I'll fly out tomorrow on the first flight I can get." Since Emily still stood there looking uncertain, she added, "I remember the Hellers. They're good friends of Aunt Helen's. So let's try not to worry too much."

Emily said only, "Well, I've a ton of work. I'd better get to it."

Sometimes, not often, it can seem that there's no comfort in Emily, Lynn thought. In fact, she even has a way of making me feel uncomfortable, almost as if, right now, I'm the one who made Annie run away.

The dog whined to go out. She stood at the kitchen door while Juliet ran to the shrubbery, where each twig was now glassy with ice. The dog squatted, ran back, and shook the wet from her fur, sprinkling the kitchen floor. On sudden impulse, oblivious of the wetness, Lynn knelt and hugged her. She needed living warmth.

"Oh, God," she said, letting the dog lick her hand.

But she needed words, too, warm words, and these the animal could not give. So she went to the telephone. She had to tell Josie.

"Are you all right?" asked Josie when she had finished her short account.

"Yes, yes, I only needed to talk. I'm sorry to be dumping on you when you're sick."

"It's only this nasty cold that I still can't shake, and you are not dumping. Hold on a minute. Bruce is here and he wants to know what this is all about."

First Lynn heard them conferring in the background. Then Bruce came to the telephone.

"Lynn, take it easy," he said. "I'll go bring her back. The weather's bad, and you can't risk a fall. I'll go in the morning."

She protested, was overruled with utmost firmness, and, suddenly exhausted, went upstairs to lie down on the bed.

In a rowboat, alone and terror stricken, struggling and straining somewhere on turbulent high seas with no land in sight, she suddenly saw the flare of light and heard someone speak. Emily was standing beside the bed.

"Mom dear, wake up. You've been asleep for more than an hour. You've got to eat something. I've made dinner."

In midmorning Tom Lawrence called with an invitation to Annie for a good-bye dinner with Sybil, who was going back home. The normalcy of this request, made in Tom's jocular way, but arriving in these abnormal circumstances, made Lynn's answer choke in her throat.

"Annie's not here." Her voice slipped into a high falsetto. "Annie's run away."

There was a pause. What should, what could, anyone reply to news like that?

He asked her quietly whether she could tell him anything more.

"Yes. She went back to St. Louis to my sister. Only, my sister wasn't there—" Her voice broke, and he had to wait for her to resume. "Bruce has gone to bring her home."

"Robert's not back, then?"

"No. The day after tomorrow."

"Who's with you, Lynn?"

"Nobody. I made Emily go to school, and Josie has a terrible cold, flu or something. And I don't want anyone else to know."

"Of course not. You shouldn't be there by yourself, though. I'm coming over."

"Oh, no! You needn't. I'm all right, really."

She must look frightful, a pregnant elephant with dark circles under the eyes. . . . Strange that she should care at all, at a time like this, how she would appear before this man. "Your work, your office—"

"I'm coming over."

The pile of logs in the fireplace was ready to be ignited. For a moment she regarded it uncertainly, feeling a little foolish for even having the thought, as though she were being a hostess preparing for guests. Then, deciding, she lit the fire, went to the kitchen to prepare coffee, took a cup of violets from the windowsill and put it on the tray with the cups and the coffeepot. By the time Tom arrived, the fire was lovely, the coffee was fragrant, and a little plate of warm muffins lay on the table before the fire.

In jeans and a flannel shirt he looked like a college boy, belying his years. Robert never wore jeans. Her thoughts were disconnected.

"Do you want to talk about it?" he asked. "Or shall we talk instead about the day's headlines? Or shall we not talk at all?"

She put out her hands, palms up, expressing confusion, and began to string together the adjectives that seemed to come automatically with every description of Annie. "I don't know how to say it. . . . She's a difficult, secretive, moody child." She had to stop.

Tom nodded. "She's a great little kid, all the same. My sister couldn't get over how much she knows compared with Sybil."

And Robert complains that she's stupid.

"She's a sweet little girl, your Annie."

There was a very gentle compassion in Tom's face. His eyes were leaf shaped; funny, she had not noticed that before.

"You gave her a wonderful time. She loved it."

He took a muffin. "Banana. It's different. What's in it?"

"Orange peel. I thought I'd try it. Is it any good?"

"Wonderful. I told you, you ought to be in business. But of course, this is hardly the time."

The fire crackled, drawing them with its ancient lure to watch its tipsy dance. Presently, Tom spoke again.

"May I talk frankly? Annie's worried about herself, isn't she? About her weight and her hair?"

"Yes, you were very kind to reassure her."

And as she remembered Annie saying, "You should marry Tom," a tiny smile, in spite of herself, quickly came and went.

He opened his mouth and closed it.

"You were going to say something, Tom."

"No, I changed my mind."

"Why? Please say it."

He shook his head. "I got in a lot of trouble with you once, remember?"

"Yes, because you said things that weren't true."

She had to tell him that. Had to. Framed in silver on the table beside the sofa, Robert was regarding her gravely. On his hand the wedding band showed prominently. It had been his idea to wear joint rings.

Tom had followed her gaze. And, as if he had made a resolve, continued. "I was only going to say that Annie repeated several times that her father was upset about her weight. That's all I was going to say. I thought it might be a useful clue to what's happened."

Upset. That dreadful scene. *You're a mess.* The child's blotchy, tear-smeared face. And then: *I would never hurt her feelings. I love you all.*

"I don't know what to think," she murmured, as if Tom weren't there.

He took a swallow of coffee, put the cup down, took it up again, replaced it once more, and then said, "I'm your friend, Lynn. We haven't known each other very long or closely, but I hope you feel that I'm your friend."

Clearly, he was trying to pull from her some admission, some confession of need, and some appeal for his help. Even in the midst of this day's turmoil she was alert enough to be aware of that. Yet she felt no resentment toward him for trying, which was strange, and because it was necessary to respond to his generosity, she murmured, "I know you would help if you could. The fact that you're sitting here is enough to tell me that."

"And you're sure I can't help?"

She shook her head. "It is something we shall have to work on with patience. Robert always used to talk Annie out of her—her moods—but lately, they've been having their troubles. Well, she's growing up, and growing up is harder for some children than it is for others."

"Oh, yes. Well, I wouldn't know, not having had any children, only wives."

She leapt toward the change of subject. "How many, may I ask?"

"Two and a half."

"A half!"

"Yes, I lived with one for a year. You might call that having half a wife." He laughed. "Oh, it was all very friendly. We made a mutual decision to call it quits."

Lynn thought: If I had him, I don't think I would, or could, easily let him go. And she remembered how when she first had seen him, she had felt a kind of lightness about him, a bright illumination, shedding happiness.

He gave her now a quizzical look, saying, "You don't approve?"

"I? I don't judge. But Robert wouldn't—" And she stopped.

That was wrong. Her mention of Robert's trouble with Annie was wrong. One kept one's problems to oneself, within the family. And she looked again at Robert's photograph, which, although it was of ordinary size, dominated the room. This time, Tom followed her glance.

"I talked to Pete Monacco the other day. He wanted me to know how much they're all impressed with Robert. Of course, he thinks Robert and I are very close friends."

At the "close friends," Lynn flushed. She said quickly, "Well, Robert's impressive. I don't know where he gets all his energy. In addition to everything else he does, he's taken on a new project, fund-raising for AIDS research."

"Incredible energy."

There was a pause, as if they had both been brought up short at a line that neither one must cross. Then a telephone call came, easing the moment.

"Yes, Bruce? Oh, thank God. Yes, hurry. Don't miss it." She hung up. "That was Bruce, phoning from the airport. They're on the way home. Annie's cheerful, and I'm not to worry." She wiped her eyes. "Not to worry. Imagine."

"But you do feel a lot better."

"Yes. I'll talk to Annie very, very seriously. As you say, she's a bright girl. We'll talk heart to heart. I can reach her." As she spoke, it seemed to her that this was a reasonable attitude. You talk things out, you reached understanding. True, Annie had run off on a crazy impulse, but she had come back; it was not the end of the world.

"Yes, I do feel better," she repeated.

He stood up, saying, "That being the case, I'll leave you. It's my sister's last day."

"Of course. You were wonderful to come at all."

"You're a lovely woman, Lynn. But you're all out of style. Oh, I don't mean your clothes. When you're a normal shape you look like Fifth Avenue. I mean, you still have a sort of old-fashioned, small-town trustfulness. I'm not making myself clear, am I?"

Answering his smile, she said, "Not really."

"What I mean is, trust is out of fashion now."

He took her hand and raised it to his lips.

"Something I learned last year in Vienna. They still do it there. 'I kiss your hand, honored lady.' "

At the front door, puzzled and slightly embarrassed, she could think of only one thing to say, and repeated, "It was wonderful of you to come. Thank you so much."

"I'm here for you anytime you need me. Remember that," he said, and went down the path.

She was left with the same puzzlement. Was this just unusual kindness on his part, or was there anything more to it? She was, after all, so inexperienced. She had hardly spoken to another man or been alone in a room with any man but Robert since she was twenty years old. But she let herself feel flattered anyway. For a pregnant woman with a burdened mind it was a pleasant feeling.

"Well, here we are," cried Bruce when Emily opened the front door.

Lynn held out her arms, and Annie rushed into them, hiding her face against her mother's shoulder. Bruce looked on, his smile combining triumph with relief, while a gleam of moisture fogged his glasses.

"Why did you do it, darling?" Lynn cried. "You scared us all so terribly. Why? You should have talked to me first!"

"Don't be angry at me. I was scared too." Annie's plea was muffled in Lynn's sweater. "I was scared when I was on the plane. I wished I hadn't done it, but I couldn't get off the plane, could I?"

"No, no, darling, not without a parachute." And Lynn pressed the child closer. Then she cried, "How ever did you get a ticket at your age?"

"There were some big girls going to college and they let me say I was their sister. Then when I got there I wanted to go back again, only I didn't have enough money. I used up everything in my piggy bank for one way. So I had to go to Aunt Helen's house. And I rang the bell, and nobody was there, and"—the recital ended in a wail—"I wanted to go home!"

"Of course you did. And now you are home."

But the courage of the child! To make this plan, to carry it out by herself, took brains and courage.

Annie drew away, wiped her running nose with the back of her hand, and shook her head. Tears had streaked her face. Her rumpled collar was twisted inside the neck of her coat. If the girl were beautiful, Lynn told herself in that instant, one would not feel quite so much anguish, such protective pity. And she repeated softly, "Why didn't you tell me, Annie, whatever it was?"

Annie burst out. "You wouldn't answer. Anyway, it's awful here. It's so full of secrets in this house. You're sick—"

At that Lynn had to interrupt, protesting, "Darling, I'm not sick. Sometimes when a woman is pregnant, her stomach acts funny, that's all. That's not being sick. You know. I've explained it to you."

"But that's not the kind of sick I mean. And besides, there's something wrong with Emily too. She's different. She's always in her room. She hardly talks to me anymore."

Now it was Emily who interrupted. "That's not so, Annie. I have to study in my room. And anyway, I do talk to you."

"You won't let me come in, and I know why. You're crying, and you don't want me to see it. Nobody ever tells me the truth. When you went to the hospital, you said it was something you ate, infectional flu or something."

"Intestinal flu," said Lynn.

"And that's all it was," said Emily.

"I don't believe you! Do you want to know what I think? It was something Dad did."

"Oh, what a dreadful idea!" Lynn cried.

Perhaps they ought to have listened to Josie and told the truth to Annie. These days kids knew everything. They knew about abortions and miscarriages, homosexuality, AIDS, everything. But Emily would not have wanted it. And it was Emily's life, after all.

"How can you think such a thing?" Lynn cried out again.

"Because he's mean, that's why. You never want anybody to say things about him, but I don't want him to come home. I don't. I don't."

And this was what his tumultuous angers had produced. What mattered all his steady, persistent efforts to teach tennis or piano? Lynn wanted to cry again, but knew she must not.

Like strangers on an unfamiliar street, uncertain which way to turn, the little group stood hesitantly in the hall.

Bruce broke into the uncertain silence. "Let's get our coats off at least and sit down."

"You must be hungry," Emily said promptly. "I can fix something in a couple of minutes."

"No," Bruce answered. "We had dinner on the plane. I think we should talk instead."

They followed him into the den, where Lynn had kept the fire burning all day. He walked toward it and stood with head down and an intent expression, as if he were seeing something hidden in the fire's ripple and flare. Then he turned about and, still with the same grave face, began rapidly to speak.

"We had a few words about all this on the flight home. But then I realized it wasn't the place for the things I wanted to say. So let's have an open talk now. What I want to explain to Annie is something she has already found out, that people, every one of us, are a mixture of all the people who came before us. This one's eyes and hair, that one's talent for the piano, another one's sense of humor or short temper or patience or impatience."

Except for the jingle of Juliet's collar as she scratched herself, the room had gone very still. Not used to seeing him so solemn, they were all drawn to Bruce.

"And when you get people together in a family, in the same house, you come up against these differences every day. In my house Josie thinks I'm messy, and I am. I get sawdust on my clothes and in my pockets. Then I come in and sit down on the sofa and leave sawdust between the pillows. Josie can't stand that. I think she makes too much of a fuss because I don't think the sofa is that important, but she does, and she thinks I ought to see that it's important. So we're just different, that's the way we are."

He paused with his eyebrows drawn together and looked them over keenly. "And every one of you here does things that the others can't stand." He raised his hand as if to halt anyone who was about to speak. "No, I'm not looking for confessions. I just wanted to make my point. Annie, have you any idea what my point is? I mean, why Josie and I don't pull each other's hair out over the sawdust? Or one of us doesn't run away?"

Annie gave a small smile.

"Makes you want to laugh, doesn't it? Tell me. Why do you think we don't?"

"I guess," she said weakly, "because you love each other."

"You guessed right, Annie. That's the whole answer. You say your father's 'mean.' Maybe he seems so, but I'm not here, and I don't know.

But if he does say mean things, the truth is he also says very good things, too, doesn't he? And does good things for you too?"

Receiving no answer, Bruce pressed again. "Come now. Doesn't he?"

"I guess so."

"Ah, Annie, you know so. I've been here often enough. I've seen you two play piano duets together, and that's wonderful. I've watched him teach you to play tennis, too, and I've met you both at the library on Saturday mornings, getting books. Do you think he does all those things because he's mean?"

Lynn had seldom heard Bruce speak at such length and with such intensity; he was known for his brevity. When they were together, it was Josie who, earnest and positive, did most of the talking.

"So maybe, I'm not saying he has, but you say he has a terrible way of scolding. But, Annie, what can you do about it? He isn't likely to change. People rarely do, Annie. Most of us stay pretty much the way we're made. So running away won't help. This is your home, here's your mother, here's your sister. You'll have to make a go of it right here."

Emily was looking straight ahead. Her face held sadness; the parted lips were tired. And what were the thoughts that had drawn a line across her forehead? Lynn's own head was heavy with scattered recollections. Did Bruce really mean what he was saying?

"It comes back to love, as you just said about Josie and me. You have to remember that people can scold and yell and still love. Your father loves you, Annie. He would do anything for you. Always think of that, even if it's sometimes hard to do. Try not to let words hurt you, even if they seem unfair and perhaps really are unfair. If it's his way to speak harshly sometimes, well then, that's his particular fault, that's all, and you'll have to live with it."

All this time Bruce had been standing, and now he sat down, wiping his forehead as if he had been making a great effort. Again Lynn saw the gleam of moisture behind his glasses. Today is a day, she thought, that I'd like to forget. This desolate day. And yet, he has managed to put some heart into it.

"I was wondering," he said now slowly, his remark directed at Lynn as much as to Annie, "whether it might not be a good thing for Annie to have someone to talk to when she feels troubled? There's a Dr. Miller, a friend of Josie's—"

"It would be a wonderful help to you, Annie," Lynn said. "I agree with Uncle Bruce."

Immediately, Annie objected. "No! I know what you mean. A psychologist. I know all about that, and I'm not going, not, not, not!"

Lynn waited for Bruce to respond. It seemed quite natural to trust the decision to him.

He said gently, "You don't have to decide this minute. Think about it carefully, and when you change your mind let your mother know."

"I won't change my mind," Annie said.

This defiance sounded exactly like Robert. Curious thought. If Annie should agree, though, there would be another tussle, strong objections from Robert, almost impossible to override. And yet, Lynn thought fiercely, if need be, I will override them.

"Okay, okay," Bruce said. "Nobody's going to force you to do anything. We're just glad you're home. Your family can't get along without you, Annie, even Aunt Josie and I can't. We depend on you for those Sunday mornings when you help with the furniture."

Bruce had a project, repairing old furniture that had been donated for the needy, a quiet project that brought no acclaim. And Lynn recalled again, as she so often did, her father's old expression: He is the salt of the earth.

The fire had died into a pile of white ash, yet its friendly heat seemed to linger. Bruce was standing before it with hands outstretched toward the warmth. And a bizarre thought flashed into Lynn's head: What if I were to get up and put my arms around him? Bizarre! Have I lost my mind? The man is Josie's husband, for God's sake. And I am Robert's wife. And it is Robert whom I love.

She said cheerfully, "You're hungry, no matter what you say. Stay a minute. I made vegetable soup this afternoon while I was waiting for you."

"That sounds good after all," Bruce admitted. "Airline food leaves you hollow."

So they came to a little spread in the kitchen, soup and biscuits, a dish of warm fruit and a plate of chocolate chip cookies. To Lynn's surprise Annie refused the cookies. Could it be that when sweets were freely offered, Annie found that she didn't want them as badly as when they were refused? One had to ponder that.

At the front door she took Bruce's hand between both of hers.

"This is the second time you've been a lifesaver. Do you realize that?"

"It's what friends are for, Lynn."

"I am so very rich in friends." And for no known reason she told him that Tom Lawrence had come that morning too. "I was so surprised."

"Why? He thinks the world of you," Bruce said. "But then, we all do."

When he had gone and Annie was upstairs, Lynn asked Emily, "What was Bruce saying while I was in the kitchen?"

"Nothing much."

"You all suddenly stopped talking when I came in. Don't hide anything from me, Emily."

"Okay. He only said that you need us at this time. That it's not right for you to be under stress, not good for you or for the baby."

Lynn frowned. "I hate to seem like an invalid, for heaven's sake. As if you shouldn't feel free to express yourselves naturally. I don't want that."

"Is it true about the baby?"

"I don't really know. They say it may be."

"I've never seen him so stern," Emily said. "He seemed almost angry at us."

"Why, what do you mean?"

"He said we are to keep this house peaceful no matter what anyone— what anyone says or does. Ever. We are to keep things smooth and happy." Emily reflected. "It's true, I have never seen him so stern. He actually commanded us. It didn't seem like Uncle Bruce talking." She laid her cheek against Lynn's. She was taller than Lynn, who had not been aware until this instant how much taller. "We—both of us—took him very seriously. Annie won't do anything wild again. He helped her a lot. Don't worry, Mom."

"If you say so, I won't."

"Promise?"

"I promise."

But it is all too simply said, Lynn told herself. How many of Bruce's own words he really believed, she thought again, or what he truly thought, she could not know.

Nevertheless, when Robert came home, it was as if the two previous days had been wiped out of memory.

Having been delayed at customs to pay for all the gifts he had bought, he was late in arriving. It took two men, the driver and Robert, to maneuver a tall carton up the walk and set it down in the hall.

"Why, what on earth have you brought?" Lynn cried.

"You'll see."

His eyes sparkled; the long trip, the exertions, had only lifted his high spirits. He had hugs and kisses for them all. For an instant, as Annie was pulled to him, Lynn, watching and inwardly imploring, thought she saw refusal in her eyes, but it vanished, and perhaps she had only imagined it. Laughing, he held Lynn's hands and stepped back at arm's length to examine her.

"Oh, my, you've grown! Look at your mother, girls. I swear it looks as if she had twins in there, or triplets. If so, we'll have to build an addition onto this house, or move. But how are you, darling?" And not waiting for an answer, "How is she, girls? Has she been feeling well? Because she'd never tell me if she hadn't been."

"She's been fine," Emily assured him.

"Then you've been taking good care of her." He rubbed his hands together. "It's freezing outside, but nowhere near what it is in Central Europe. Oh, I've got a million things to tell you. It's hard to know where to begin."

"How about beginning with dinner?"

"Ah, dinner! Ah, good to be home."

Lynn had prepared a feast of rich, hot food for a winter's night: mushroom soup, brown slivers floating in the golden broth, duckling with dark cherries, spinach soufflé with herbs and onions, and apple pudding in wine sauce. Champagne stood in a nest of ice, and everyone drank except Annie, who tasted and made a face. Even Lynn, in spite of her pregnancy, took a sip. The table was set with the best china and the Baccarat crystal that Robert had bought. In the center Lynn had arranged a low cluster of white roses. All this excellence did not go unappreciated.

"Your mother!" Robert exclaimed. "Your mother. Just look at all this." He was exultant.

"What a fantastic experience! Of course, it was hard work, late hours, talking and translating, meeting all sorts of people, some cooperative and eager, some stubborn—but that's life, isn't it? All in all, though, I should say it was a great success. Budapest, as you walk through the old quarter, is somewhat dark and dingy to our eyes, but wonderfully quaint, all the same. And then suddenly you come up against a modern glass tower. The company's office is as modern as anything we have in New York. You walk away, and there's a Chinese restaurant, next a pizza place, and there you see what's ahead, you see the future."

Robert paused to cut off a piece of duckling, swallowed it, and could barely wait to continue his tale.

"Hungary is a full democracy now. Knowing some history of its past, you can only feel the marvel of what's happening. Eventually, they'll be in NATO, or in some sort of association with it. No doubt of that. What the country needs now, what all these countries need, is management training, and that's where the West, where we, come in. Oh, say, I almost forgot. I brought a real Hungarian strudel. I bought it yesterday morning. It's in my carry-on. Well, we can eat it tomorrow. It'd be too much with this dessert too. You should see the little coffeehouses, Lynn. All the pastries! You would get recipes galore. I sat in one of them and looked out onto a square with palaces and a huge Gothic church. Marvelous. You're going to love it, girls."

"What about college?" Emily asked anxiously.

"Don't worry, just you get into Yale. Nothing's going to interfere with that." Robert smiled. "You'll just fly over whenever there's a vacation. I'll be earning enough to afford it, don't worry."

"And what about me?" inquired Annie.

"Don't you worry. We'll have a fine school for you, with diplomats' children and all sorts of interesting people and—"

He had brought home his full vigor and his old magic. It was contagious. And in her daughters' faces, Lynn saw that they were feeling the contagion too.

"And of course we won't be limited to Hungary. It's so quick and easy to get around Europe, and you'll have a chance to see it all. You'll see Greece and the Parthenon, and you'll know why I wanted you to study the Greek gods, Annie. Rome, Paris, of course, and"—he made a wide sweep of his hand—"the world! Why not?"

After dinner they opened the packages. Standing in the center of a circle of chairs, Robert unwrapped and displayed his finds. He had bought with care. For Annie there was a cuckoo clock. "I remember you said once that you wanted one, and this one's a beauty." For Emily there was a watercolor of a castle on a hill. For Lynn there were Herend figurines, all in green and white and large size: a kangaroo, an elephant, and a unicorn.

"I thought awhile about whether I should get them in the red or the green. What do you think, did I do right, Lynn?" he asked.

And without waiting for her reply he set them on the mantelpiece, then stepped back, regarding them with a slight frown. "No, not that way." He moved them. "They should be clustered at the side. Symmetry is boring."

Lynn remarked, "I don't know where you got the time for shopping."

"I don't know myself. When you want to do something, you make the time. That's about it."

The evening went on long past Annie's bedtime and usurped Emily's homework hours.

". . . and we should have at least a few days' skiing in Chamonix. From what I've read the French Alps have a special charm. Oh, I'll manage to get days off." Robert laughed. "The boss of the office can always wangle a few days, especially when he's overworked all the rest of the time. Say, look at the clock. All of a sudden jet lag has got to me. Shall we go up?"

In their bedroom as he undressed, Robert said, "Things are looking so good, Lynn, so good. You know what they say about getting sand in your shoes, so you'll want to return? Well, there may not be any sand over there, but I can't wait to go back."

As he emptied the suitcase and sorted the contents, he moved fast and spoke fast, leaping from one subject to the next.

"I faxed a report to Monacco and got a very pleased reply. . . . I noticed something different about Emily tonight. That sort of remote look she's been having is quite gone. She seemed warmer toward me. Yes, as I predicted, she's gotten over that fellow. Thank God. . . . And Annie, too, was really sweet, I thought. . . ."

He hung his ties up on the rack and, turning, suddenly exclaimed, "Oh, but I missed you all so much, hectic as it was. Did you miss me as much, Lynn?"

She was telling herself: He's bound to find out, so I might as well get it over with now. So as briefly as possible she began to relate the story of Annie, making sure not to disclose any of Annie's remarks about him.

Robert was startled, vexed, and dismayed, all together.

"Good God," he said, "the minute my back is turned some disaster befalls my children."

Lynn's heart sank.

"I didn't want to spoil your homecoming, and I hope this hasn't, because, as you see, we're all right now." And she improvised, for to tell the tragic story with complete accuracy would only provoke an argument. "It seems she had been worried about me. Well, I suppose it's only natural for her to have mixed feelings about this pregnancy. And then she was upset about Emily last summer. She thought Emily was terribly sick and we were hiding the truth. It all seems to have been preying on her mind, and so she just—"

And why am I hiding the truth myself? she asked now as she fell suddenly silent. Am I still so torn about Caroline that I fear to take any more blame for anything? He has already said that Emily's trouble was my fault. . . .

Robert had sat down heavily. "And Bruce brought her home," he said.

"Yes, it was wonderful of him, wasn't it?"

He slumped in the chair. In the weak light of the lamp on the bedside table, his face went sallow, as if the vigor had just drained out.

Anxiously, Lynn explained, repeating herself, "He was wonderful. He talked to Annie, to both of them, so beautifully."

"What did he talk about?"

"Oh, life in general, meeting challenges, optimism, understanding one another. He did them a lot of good."

"That may be, but I'm not happy about it."

"No, there's nothing to be *happy* about. I really do believe, Robert, that Annie should have some help, some counseling. And so should we."

"That's nonsense. I've told you my opinion of that stuff. Anyway, Annie's not the first kid who got a notion in her head and ran off. It happens all the time. I'm sure she was sorry before she was halfway there."

Well, that much was true. . . .

"But I'm thinking about Bruce. He's my subordinate in the office, and he knows my family's most private affairs, Emily's mess last summer, and now this. Dammit all."

"He was very kind," Lynn said, and then, wanting to clear the record entirely, she added, "Tom Lawrence was very kind too. He came over that morning."

"Oh, for God's sake, he too? How did that happen?"

"He didn't want me to be alone when he heard. You shouldn't mind, Robert. These are good friends."

"Good friends, but they know too much."

"They're fine men. They would never talk about our children. You know that."

"The fact that they themselves know is enough," he grumbled.

As she leaned to take off her shoes, she could barely reach her feet. Seeing her struggle, he got up to help her. The baby was active; its movement under her sheer slip was visible to him, and she saw that he pitied her; he would not argue.

"Poor girl," he said. "What a time you've had with me away! Poor girl. Now I'm home, you relax and let me take care of things."

The baby turned and turned. Through these last frantic days she had scarcely been able to give thought to it, but now awareness of its imminent arrival shocked her. Only another eight or nine weeks from now, it would be separated from her, separated and yet in another way closer, because of its demands, which would and should come before any others. She must, she must, keep calm and hopeful for its sake.

Calm and hopeful. All right, then. Relax and let Robert take care of things. He wants to, anyway.

Robert V. W. Ferguson, Jr., was born early on a windy morning in between winter and spring. Rough and tough as he had been in the womb, his exit from it was remarkably easy. He weighed nine pounds, came with a full head of hair, and was the first of the Ferguson babies not to be bald. His hair was sandy like Lynn's; his face gave promise of length and would probably be aquiline like Robert's.

"All in all a nice compromise," said Robert. He stood against a background of spring bouquets arrayed on the windowsill. "Have you counted the flowers? That basket of green orchids on the end is from Monacco. He wired it from California." He watched his son feeding at Lynn's breast. "What a bruiser!" he cried. "What a bruiser. Just look at that boy."

Scarcely containing his jubilation, he made Lynn feel like a queen.

Back at home she lay in bed like a queen.

"You're going to take it easy, you're going to rest and be waited on at least till the end of the week," Robert insisted.

The bassinet, skirted in white net, stood beside the bed, and Lynn thanked Josie for its blue bows.

"The minute we heard from Robert that it was a boy," Bruce said, "she came over here. And I want you to know that I'm the one responsible for the bows being blue."

"So sexist," Josie said.

"You surely weren't going to put pink ones on, were you?" asked Lynn.

"Why not?" was Josie's cheerful reply. "Still, I did what my husband ordered."

Their funny mock bickering amused Lynn. The short hour that she had been home had already filled her with a fresh sense of well-being. New books in their bright jackets were stacked on the bedside table, next to the box of chocolates—now no longer on the forbidden list—and a cluster of lilies of the valley in a tiny cup. Husband, friends, and daughters, all of them fascinated by the baby in his soft wool nest, were gathered around her. Annie and Emily spoke in whispers.

"You don't have to whisper, darling," Lynn told them. "Talking won't disturb him a bit."

Annie asked anxiously, "When can we hold him?"

"When he wakes up, I'll let you hold him."

And shyly, Annie said, "Isn't it funny? I don't know him at all, but I love him already."

Lynn's eyes filled. "Oh, Annie, that's lovely."

"Why? Did you think I wouldn't love him? I'm much too old to have sibling rivalry with the baby."

Everyone laughed. Bruce patted Annie on the back, and Emily said, "Annie, where are the boxes that came this morning?"

"Right here, behind the door. Open them, Mom. They're probably more sweaters. He's got seven already. And there's a big box downstairs that came yesterday. I haven't opened it."

Robert went down and a few minutes later returned with a child-size wing chair upholstered in needlepoint.

"Queen Anne! Isn't that adorable? A formal chair for our living room," cried Lynn. "Whoever thought of that?"

"Tom Lawrence's card, with best wishes." Robert frowned. "Why such a lavish present? We hardly know him. He's not an intimate."

Lynn, feeling the rise of heat, hoped it wouldn't flow out on her cheeks. Tom had outdone himself; the gift was original, in perfect taste— and expensive.

As if Bruce had read her mind, he came to the rescue.

"It's not so lavish for a man in Tom's position. Expense is relative. And obviously he likes you both."

"Well, it's only that I don't like feeling beholden," Robert explained.

A puzzled look crossed his face. Lynn knew that he was thinking back to the weekend in Maine, and to all the things Lawrence had done for him, the good words he had put in for him.

"You'll have to write to him tomorrow at the latest, Lynn."

"I don't feel up to it. I'm more tired than I thought I was," she said untruthfully.

A letter to Tom, if indeed he had any ideas—and the more she thought, the more certain it appeared that he might have some, even though she had certainly made her own position quite clear—might be unwise. The situation was a little bit exciting, but it was also disturbing. No, not a letter.

"You write," she told Robert, "and I'll sign it along with you." And she turned to Emily as if she had abruptly remembered something. "Hasn't Aunt Helen even phoned?"

Annie, Emily, and Robert all looked around at each other.

"No? How strange. I don't understand it."

"Oh," Robert said, "it was supposed to be a surprise, but we might as well tell you. They're on the way, both of them. They should be here in an hour or two. They're renting a car at the airport."

"Darwin too?" Lynn was touched. "How good of him to take the time!"

"His time." Robert laughed. "Bathtubs and toilets. Important business."

"I shouldn't care to be without either one," Bruce remarked, laughing.

Josie said firmly, "I like Darwin. I always did. He's kind."

"Oh, kind, yes," Robert agreed. "A diamond in the rough."

If only Robert would not always, always, say things like that!

And Robert said, "I might as well break the news. Aunt Jean has taken it into her head to come too."

"Don't look so glum! I think it's darling of her to want to see the baby. I'm glad she's coming, and I'm going to show her I'm glad." But then immediately Lynn worried. "Where's everybody going to sleep? And what's everyone going to eat? They'll be here for a couple of days, I'm sure, and—"

"Not to worry." Emily assured her. "I've fixed a nice bed in the little third-floor room for Aunt Jean, Uncle Darwin and Aunt Helen will have the guest room, and we've a ton of food. Uncle Bruce went marketing with us this morning before you got home, to help carry all the stuff. Enough for an army."

"And the dinner table's set already," Annie said. "We even made a centerpiece out of the flowers you brought home."

So they all came and went, up and down the stairs all day, in and out of the room where the queen lay back on embroidered pillows, the best set, kept for sickness in bed and so, fortunately, never used before.

Annie brought Juliet up to let her sniff at the bassinet. "To get used to the baby's smell," she explained. Robert brought a supper tray. "Don't I make a good butler?" he asked, wanting praise. And then came Helen and Darwin, he as pudgy and beaming as ever, she as welcome as ever.

"I feel as if I haven't seen you for a century," Lynn cried as they hugged each other.

"Well, it's been almost two years. No matter what they say about planes getting people back and forth in a couple of hours, it's a big trip. It's traveling."

"This family's going to get used to traveling," announced Robert, who in his pride was standing with a hand on the bassinet. "This little boy is going to see the world." And when Helen looked blank, he asked, "Do you mean to say Lynn hasn't told you? Yes, we're going to be living abroad for a while. Two years, three, five—who knows?" And he gave an enthusiastic account of his project.

"How is it that you never told me about all this?" asked Helen when the two were alone. Then, before Lynn could reply, and in her quick, penetrating way that so much resembled Josie's way, said, "You had too much else on your mind, that's why."

"Well, it wasn't the easiest pregnancy, I'll admit. But isn't he darling? His head is so beautifully shaped, don't you think so?"

Helen smiled. "He's lovely. Mine looked like little monkeys for the first month or so. But I wasn't thinking of the pregnancy. I meant—you must know that I meant Annie."

Lynn had no wish to reveal the doubts and worries that, even though Annie did seem to be much steadied, still flickered in her consciousness. She especially did not want to admit them to Helen. So she spoke lightly, in dismissal.

"Annie's over all that."

"Yes, until the next time."

Helen was always reaching for clues, for signals and alarms; of course it was because she had never liked, and still didn't like, Robert. But she was too decent to say so.

There was a note of petulance in Lynn's voice when she replied. She heard it herself and even knew the reason for it: I've said things are different now, but I've said it often enough before too; I don't want to be reminded of that today; I just want a little time to be purely happy with my baby.

"Annie's fine, Helen. Delighted about Bobby. Can't you see?"

Helen's silence told Lynn that she did not believe her.

"You can ask Bruce if you don't trust me," Lynn added stubbornly. "He knows Annie well."

"I want to trust you," Helen said, her lips making the tight pucker that always gave a shrewd look to her pretty face. "I want to. But I know that if things were bad, you would never admit it."

Probing, probing, Lynn thought resentfully.

"You've always been so secretive. One has to worry about you."

Lynn's impatience mounted. "Look at me. What do you see? Look around at the house. What do you see?"

"I see that you look the same as ever and your house has everything of the best."

From downstairs there came the sounds of a piano accompanying lively song.

"That's Robert playing, and the girls are singing. They made up a funny song to welcome me at the door when we came home from the hospital. Doesn't that tell you anything?" demanded Lynn.

"Well . . . It tells me that we all love you." And Helen, apparently accepting defeat, changed the subject. "Do you know what? I'm starved. I'm going down to see what there is to eat."

"May I come in, or will I tire you?" Jean hesitated, as was her way. At least it was her way when she was in Robert's house.

"Of course come in. I'm not the least bit tired and it's ridiculous for me to be lying on this bed, but the doctor said, 'Two days rest, positively.' "

When Jean had admired the baby for the second time, she sat down in the rocking chair by the bed. For a few moments she said nothing, merely smiling at Lynn with the expression that Robert called "meek"; instead Lynn had always seen, and saw now, not meekness but a stifled sorrow.

Jean folded her old, brown-spotted hands together; lying in her flowered lap—did she never wear anything but flowers?—they were patient and strong.

"It's nice to have a time alone with you, Lynn," she said. "And this is likely to be the last time. I'm moving to Vancouver."

"But so far away! Why?"

"I'm going to live with my brother. We're both pretty old and all we have is each other."

"You have us. You could move here, near us."

"No, dear. Let's be truthful. Robert doesn't like to have me around."

There was nothing meek about the statement. It had been delivered with a rather stern lift of the curly gray head and an expression that, although grave, was yet without rancor.

The statement demanded an honest reply. Or a more-or-less honest reply.

"Robert can be irritable sometimes with anyone, Aunt Jean, when he's in the mood. But you must know, his bark is worse than his bite."

"I know. He was a darling little boy, and so smart. We used to play games together, checkers and dominoes. He loved to beat me, but, oh, his temper was terrible when he lost! We had fun together . . . but things change. It's a pity, isn't it? After my sister was gone, and he moved away. . . . You would have liked Frances," Jean said abruptly. "She was a gentle person. And she would have loved having you for a daughter. You've always reminded me of her. You're soft and you're kind, like her."

Very much touched, Lynn said simply, "Thank you."

The rocking chair swayed; there was a quaintness in its regular creak, an old-fashioned peacefulness as in the presence of the old woman herself.

"I'm sorry you and I haven't seen more of each other, Lynn. But I'm glad to see how well things are going for you. They are going well, aren't they?"

"Why, yes," replied Lynn, wondering.

"And Robert is still a good husband to you."

Was that a question or a statement?

"Why, yes," Lynn said again.

Jean nodded. "I'll think of you here in this lovely house and it will be a pleasure to me. I've put that photo of Emily and Annie into a flowered frame. I like to have flowers everywhere. I guess you've learned that about me, haven't you? I do hope you'll send me a nice photo of Bobby sometime."

"As soon as he grows some more hair. I promise."

"And that you'll still call me every week—even in Vancouver."

"Of course we will. You know that."

"I like your sister," Jean said, "and your friends Josie and Bruce. There's something special about him, although I don't know yet what it is."

Lynn smiled. "You like everybody, I think."

"No, not everybody. But I do try to find the good in people if I can. Frances was like that—too much so for her own good—oh, well, tell me, does the baby need an afghan for his carriage?"

So the conversation veered away from people into the neutral area of things, things knitted, woven, cooked, and planted. The comfortable ease that Jean had brought into the room was ever so vaguely troubled when she left.

I wish people wouldn't be so—so enigmatic, Lynn said to herself.

Now Emily came and sat on the edge of the bed.

"Mom, you're so especially beautiful when you're happy," she said.

She had a charming way of widening her eyes to express emotion. Today her hair was twisted and piled on top of her head; she wore the heart-shaped gold earrings that Robert had given her on her last birthday. Just to look at her brought an undiluted joy that Lynn needed just then.

"I'm happy when you all are." The baby grunted in his sleep. "Turn him onto the other side of his face for a change," she said.

"Oh, Lord, I don't know how. I'm scared to touch him."

Lynn laughed. "I know. When you were born, I was afraid to pick you up, afraid you'd break. Just raise his head gently," she directed, "and turn it. He's not that fragile."

"He sighed," Emily said. "Did you hear him? It sounded just like a sigh when I turned him."

"He's probably worrying about the international situation," Lynn said cheerfully.

But Emily was grave. "Mom," she said, "I never realized what a serious thing it is."

"Serious?"

"To care for a baby, I mean. A person should think about it very, very long before doing it."

She spoke very low, not looking at her mother, but away toward the window where a dark blue evening was coming on. And Lynn understood her meaning: that what had happened last summer must not happen again.

Still speaking toward the darkness, Emily continued, "All the plans you must have for him, his health and his school, the cozy room that he was brought to, and the quiet home. You have to plan, don't you? And keep to the plan."

Lynn was putting herself into her daughter's place, trying to imagine her remorse, to feel the fright that must still be hers when she considered some of the turns her life could have taken. And hesitating, she said softly, "There will be a right time for you, Emily. You know that now, don't you?"

Emily turned back to her. "I know. And I'm fine, Mom. I really am. Believe me."

She was an achiever, competent and strong. A young woman with purpose, Lynn thought as always, certainly not your usual high-school senior.

"Yes," she said. "Yes, I do believe you." And then to relieve the poignancy of the moment, "But have you had your dinner?"

"Half of it. I thought you might not like being alone."

"I don't mind at all. Go down and finish. Just hand Bobby to me first. He's going to be hungry in a minute, I can tell."

And sure enough, the boy woke just then with a piteous wail.

"Turn on the lamps before you go. Thanks, darling."

When Emily walked out she left no suspicions and no enigmas behind to fog the air. Lynn took a deep, pure breath. From belowstairs came the pleasant buzz of talk. She could imagine them sitting at the table; Robert at its head was carving and serving the meat in the old-fashioned style to which he kept. The back door banged; somebody was letting Juliet out. Someone was walking through the halls; heels struck the bare floor between the rugs. These were the sounds of the family, the rhythms of the house, the home.

Let Helen peer and delve; she means well, but never mind it. And never mind poor, dear old Jean's *And Robert is still a good husband to you?* It is the natural curiosity of a lonesome woman, that's all it is.

These last few days, these last few months, had been so rich! Before then it had been a cruel year, God knew, but was pain not a part of life too? Miraculously now, a new spirit seemed to have come over them all, over Robert and the girls, and because of them, over herself.

And she lay with the hungry baby at her breast. Little man! Such a little creature to have, by his simple presence, brought so much joy into this house! Lynn was feeling a cleansing gratitude, a most remarkable peace.

PART FOUR

◇

Spring 1989–
Fall 1990

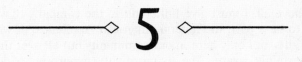

5

THE enormous room was packed. Every table had been taken, and, reflected in the mirrored wall of this somewhat typically gaudy hotel ballroom, the audience was impressive in its size.

"This man," said the mayor, "this man on whom we gratefully bestow the Man of the Year Award, has accomplished more for our community in the few years he has been among us than many, including myself, who were born here, have done for it."

Affectionate and friendly laughter approved of the mayor's modesty. Nevertheless, thought Lynn at the pinnacle of pride, it is true.

"The list of his activities fills a long page of single-spaced type. There's his work on behalf of the hospital, the cancer drive, the new library, so sorely needed, for AIDS, education, for the whole recycling program that has set an example to the towns around us. I could go on and on, but I know you are waiting to hear from Robert Ferguson himself."

Robert had grace. Beside him on the podium the town's dignitaries, three men and a pleasant-faced woman with blue-white curls, looked nondescript. It was always so. Wherever he went, he was superior.

"Mayor Williams spoke of a list," he said. "My lists are much longer. They contain the names of the ones who are really responsible for the success of whatever good causes I have been helping. It would take hours to tell you who they are, and I might miss some, and I mustn't do that. So I'll simply tell you that we owe a debt of hearty thanks to all those people who manned telephones, gathering the funds we needed, who stuffed envelopes, gave benefit dinners, wrote reports, and stayed up nights to get things done."

His voice was richly resonant, his diction clear and pure, but unaffected. There wasn't a cough or whisper or creaking chair among the audience.

"And above all, I must give full credit to the company of which I am fortunate to be a part, to General American Appliance, of whose magnanimous gifts, not only here in our community but all over the country, you are certainly aware. The extraordinary generosity of such great American corporations is the wonder of the world. And GAA has always been outstanding for its public service. *We care.* And here in this relatively little corner of the United States, you have been seeing the fruits of our caring.

"And so I thank my superiors at GAA for encouraging my little undertakings here and covering for me whenever necessary, so making it possible for me to find the time I need.

"Last—my family. My wonderful wife, Lynn—"

All eyes turned to Lynn in her daisy-flowered summer dress; Robert had been right to insist on a smashing new dress. Across from her at the round table sat Bruce and Josie, flanked by town officials. Bruce smiled as he caught her eye; Josie, who seemed to be regarding the chandeliers, had no expression. And a thought fled through Lynn's mind: Robert has not mentioned Bruce.

". . . and my lovely daughters, Emily and Annie, who never complain when I have to take some of the hours I owe them to go to a meeting. Emily will be graduating from high school on Tuesday, and entering Yale in the fall."

Emily, serene in white, inclined her head to acknowledge the applause with the simple dignity of a royal personage. Her father's dignity.

". . . and our Bobby, four months old today, has been very cooperative too. He tolerates me—"

Laughter followed, then more applause, a concluding speech, a shuffling of chairs, and the emptying of the room. In the lobby people crowded around Robert; he had charmed them.

"How about a drink? Come back to our house. It's early yet."

"Thanks, but my wife's a real mother, a nursing mother, and Bobby's waiting," Robert said.

He was glowing. It was as if there were a flame in him, heating his very flesh. She felt it when she stood beside him at the crib, watching the baby settle back to sleep after feeding. And surely she felt it when afterward in bed he turned to her.

"All those months we've missed because of the baby," he whispered. "We have to make up for them."

In the close darkness of the bed, without seeing, she yet knew that his eyes were thrilled, that their blue had gone black with excitement. She put her hand out to feel his racing heart, the heat and the flame.

The graduates, in alphabetical order, came marching down the football field through the lemon-yellow light of afternoon.

"Good thing that kid's name begins with *W*," Robert whispered.

He may be at the end of the line, Lynn thought, but he's still the valedictorian.

It was the finality of all this ceremony that was so moving. Childhood was indisputably over. These boys and girls would all disperse; these young ones, a little proud, a little embarrassed in their gowns and mortarboards, would be gone. The bedroom would be vacant, the customary chair at the table unoccupied, and the family diminished by one. Nothing would ever be the same. Two weak tears gathered in Lynn's eyes. Reaching for her purse to find a tissue, she was touched on the arm.

"Here, take mine," said Josie. "I need one too."

Josie knew. Bruce knew, too, for he had taken Josie's other hand and clasped it on his knee. Last year at this time things had looked rather different for Emily, alone and desperate with her secret. Now they were calling her name, handing the rolled white document: "Emily Ferguson, with highest honors."

But Robert was chuckling, bursting. His girl. His girl. He was the first to scramble down from the benches to take her picture and rejoice.

Everywhere were cameras, kissing and laughing and calling. The PTA had set up tables on the grass for punch and cookies. People crowded in knots and got separated, parents making much of teachers, younger brothers and sisters finding their own friends.

Lynn, as she stood at a table to replenish her cup of punch, heard Bruce's voice a few feet away.

"Yes, of course it's a science and an art. You're lucky at your age to be so sure of what you want to do."

"Well, it's useful," she heard Harris say. "That and teaching are the only truly essential things"—and then, so apologetically that she imagined his fair skin flushing—"I don't mean that business isn't useful, Mr. Lehman. I don't express myself very well sometimes."

"Don't apologize. I quite agree with you. If I'd had the ability, I would have wanted to be a doctor or perhaps a teacher of some sort."

They caught sight of Lynn, who had filled her cup. Sure enough, Harris was brick-red.

"Congratulations, Harris," she said.

"Thanks. Thanks very much. I seem to have lost my folks. I'd better run."

They watched him dart back into the crowd.

"It touches you to see a boy like him. You just hope life will be good to him," Bruce said.

"I know. I feel the same."

"Robert would slaughter us if he heard us."

"I know."

She oughtn't to have agreed; it was complicity with Bruce against Robert. And as they stood there drinking out of their paper cups, she avoided his eyes. It occurred to her suddenly that they had never had a dialogue; they were always in a foursome or more.

Presently, Lynn said, "Emily's having a little party tonight. Want to come and supervise the fun? They're all over eighteen, and Robert's allowing one glass of champagne apiece. One small glass."

"Thanks, but I think not. We'll call it a day."

That was strange. She was wondering about the refusal, when she met up with Robert.

"Did you see Bruce talking to young Weber?" he demanded.

"Only for a second."

"Well, I watched. Bruce deliberately sought him out. Your fine friend. I consider that disloyalty. Unforgivable."

Not liking the sarcasm of "your fine friend," she answered, "But you'll have to forgive it, won't you, since there's nothing you can do about it."

"More's the pity."

"It's all over, anyhow. Emily's started a new chapter. Let's go home for her party."

The next day in the middle of the afternoon, Bruce telephoned, alarming Lynn, who thought at once of Robert.

He understood. "Don't be frightened. It's nothing to do with Robert, and I'm not at the office. I didn't go in today." His voice was clearly strained, as if there were something wrong with his larynx. "Josie was operated on this morning. I'm at the hospital in her room. She's still in recovery."

"Why? What is it?" Lynn stammered. "It's not—"

"Yes," he said, still in that strangled voice. "Yes. The lymph. The liver. It's all through her."

A wave of cold passed through Lynn. *Footsteps on my grave,* my grandmother had used to say. No, Josie's grave. And she is thirty-nine.

She burst into tears. "I can't believe it. You wake up suddenly one morning, and there's death looking into your face? Just like that? Yesterday at the graduation she was so happy for Emily. She never said . . . There's no sense in what you're telling me. I can't make any sense of it."

"Wait. Hold on, Lynn. We have to be calm for her. Listen to me. It wasn't sudden. It's been going on for months. All those colds she said she had, that time I went to St. Louis last winter to fetch Annie, all those were excuses. She was home, too sick to move; she almost didn't get to the graduation yesterday. She wouldn't have chemo—"

"But why? She had it before and came through it so well!"

"This is different. We went to New York, we went to Boston, and they were all honest with us. Try chemo, but without much hope. That's what it came down to, underneath the tactful verbiage. So Josie said no to it, and I can understand why, God knows."

Lynn asked desperately, "Then why the operation now?"

"Oh, another man saw her and had an idea, something new. She wanted to refuse that, too, but you grasp at straws and I made her try it. I was wrong." And now Bruce's voice died.

"All these months. Why did she hide it? What are friends for? You should have told us, Bruce, even if she wouldn't."

"She absolutely wouldn't let me. She made me promise not to worry you. She said you had enough with the new baby and . . ." He did not finish.

"But Josie's the one who always says you should face reality."

"Your own reality. She's facing hers, and very bravely. She just didn't want to inflict *her* reality on other people as long as she could face it alone. Don't you see?"

" 'Other people'! Even her best friend? I would have helped her. . . ." And afraid of the answer, Lynn murmured the question, "What's to happen?"

"It won't be very long, they told me."

She wiped her eyes, yet a tear slipped through and dropped on the desk, where it lay glistening on the dark leather top.

"When can I see her?" she asked, still murmuring.

"I don't know. I'll ask. Maybe tomorrow."

"Does Robert know?"

"I called him this morning at the office. They needed to cancel my appointments. I have to go now, Lynn."

"Bruce, we all love you so, Emily and Annie. . . . I don't know how to tell Annie."

"I'll talk to her. Annie and I, you know we have a special thing."

"I know."

"I have to go now, Lynn."

She put the receiver back and laid her hand on the desk, saying aloud, "I am heartsick." And the words made literal sense, for her chest was heavy, and the cold tremble would not stop. Josie, my friend. Josie, the sturdy, the wise, fast moving, fast talking, always there. Josie, aged thirty-nine.

She might have sat in a fog of sorrow all that afternoon if Bobby's cry had not rung through the fog. When she had taken him up from his nap and fed him, she carried him outdoors to the playpen on the terrace. With a full stomach and content in his comfortable, fresh diaper, he lay waving a rattle. Dots of light flickering through the emerald shade seemed to please him, for every now and then his babble broke into something that sounded like a laugh. At four months! She stood looking down at his innocence, knowing that there was no way on earth he could ever be shielded from heartbreak.

After a while she rolled the playpen over to the perennial border, where he could watch as she knelt to weed. A different reaction had begun in her, a need to move, to assure herself of her own vitality.

From a tough central root, purslane shot its multiple rubbery arms and legs like an octopus, crawling like cancer among the phlox and iris, peonies and asters, all the glad and glorious healthy life. With fierce hatred she dug out the roots and threw them away.

The sun had gone behind the hill, and the grass had turned from jade to olive when tires crunched the gravel. Robert, on his way from the station, had called for the girls at the pool, and the three were coming toward her as she rose from her knees. By their faces she saw that he had given the news to the girls.

"Is she going to die?" asked Annie, never mincing words.

The truth was as yet unspeakable. She could think it and know it, but not say it. So Lynn answered, "We don't know anything except that she's very sick."

"Perhaps," said Emily, "the operation will have cut it all away. My math teacher in junior year had cancer when he was thirty-five, and he's old now."

"Perhaps," said Robert. "We shall hope."

Alone with Lynn he gave a long, deep sigh. "Poor guy. Poor Bruce. Oh, if it were you . . ."

"Are we maybe rushing to a conclusion?" She clasped her hands as if imploring him. "Is it really hopeless?"

"Yes. He told me the only hope left is that it may go fast."

Measured by the calendar it went fast, covering as it did only the short span of summer. And yet it seemed as if each day contained twice the normal count of hours, so slowly did they move.

Once on a weekend they tried bringing Josie home. She was so light that Bruce, carrying her, was able to run up the steps into the house. At the window, where she could look out into the trees, he set her down and brought an ottoman for her feet. The day was warm, but she was shivering, and he put a shawl around her frail shoulders.

The cat bounded onto her lap and she smiled.

"He hasn't forgotten me. I thought maybe he would have."

"Forgotten you? Of course not," Bruce said heartily.

We are all acting, thought Lynn. We know we dare not show tears, so we talk loud and briskly, we fear a moment's silence, we bustle around and think we're being normal.

A fine rain had begun to fall, so that the summer greenery was dimmed behind a silvery gray gauze. Josie asked to have the window opened.

"Listen," she said. "You can hear it falling on the leaves." And she smiled again. "It's the most beautiful kind of day in the most beautiful time of the year."

This time next year, Lynn thought, and had to look away. She had brought a dinner, light, simple food, white meat of chicken in herbs. Josie took a few mouthfuls and laid the fork down.

"No appetite," she said, apologizing, and added quickly, "but as always, your food is marvelous. Someday you'll do something really big with your talent. You should be trying it now."

Robert corrected her. "She has her hands full at home. Right, Lynn?"

"I don't know," said Lynn, thinking that Josie's skin, her lovely skin, was like old yellowed newspaper.

"But I know," said Josie, wanting her way.

In the evening she asked to go back to the hospital, and Bruce took her.

Her flesh fell off, leaving her eyes sunken into their round bony sockets and her teeth enormous in the cup of her jaws. Yet in a brief spurt of energy a lovely smile could bring harmony to this poor face. More often, it seemed as though the medication was loosening her tongue. Indeed, when she was lucid, she admitted as much.

"Yesterday I said something I perhaps should not have said," she told Lynn one afternoon. "I remember it now quite clearly, isn't that odd?"

"I don't remember anything," Lynn assured her, although she did remember and quite clearly too.

"It was when I showed you the roses that Tom Lawrence brought. I was so surprised. I didn't expect a visit from him. We don't know him all that well."

"He likes Bruce, that's no mystery."

"That's what you answered me yesterday. I said, 'No, he likes you, Lynn.' We are his contact with you, since he can't very well see you when Robert's not there, and he doesn't want to see you when he is there. That's what I said, and it upset you."

"Not at all. Why should it upset me, since it's so silly?"

"It's you who know the answer to that. But you would never tell me what you think about Tom. You would never tell me anything that really touches you in the deepest part of your heart. You're too secretive, Lynn."

"Secrets, Josie?" Lynn queried gently. "What about you? You've been sick for six months and never said a word."

"There was nothing you could do!" And as Lynn began to protest, she cried, "Now, don't scold me again about that!"

The plaintive tone, so unlike Josie's clear, brisk way of speaking, was hopeless and, like the wasted hands on the coverlet, helpless.

And Lynn burst out, "Was I so wrapped up in myself, my new baby, my own life, that I didn't see what was happening to you? How can I have been so blind to your need?"

"Lynn dear, no. I had good days and bad ones. I just didn't let you or anyone see the bad ones. And you are the last person to be accused of self-absorption. It would be better for you if you did think more about yourself."

"But I do," Lynn protested.

"No, you don't. You've built a wall around yourself. Even your sister knows that. No one can really get through to you. But a person can't do what you're doing forever." Josie turned in the bed, seemed to find a more bearable position, and resumed, "That's why I wish—I wish you had a man like Tom. I could die knowing that you were being treated well. That you were safe. . . ."

"Josie, Josie, I'm fine. I'm safe, dear. And don't talk about dying!" And don't talk about Robert. . . .

"Yes, now I must. There's a right time to speak out. Six months ago it wasn't necessary. Now it is."

Lynn looked at the walls, the depressing hospital-green walls that, if they could talk, would tell of a thousand griefs and partings. Now here was another. It was too hard to imagine a day on which she would pick up the telephone to call Josie and have to tell herself that Josie was no longer here.

"You've been my support," she said, ready to weep. "Whenever I'm worried about Annie, and I worry so about her, you're my support. You've borne all my troubles."

Josie's wan smile was faintly bitter. "No, not all. You skirt around the truth about Robert."

"About Robert?" Lynn admonished gently. "But we are very happy, Josie. . . . Everything's fine now."

"No, no." Josie's head rolled back on the pillow. "I'm a social worker, you forget. I see things you could never imagine. I see things as they really are." Suddenly her fingers clawed at the sheet, and her body writhed. "Oh, why can't you be honest with me when I'm in such pain, when I have to die and leave Bruce? Oh, God, this pain!"

Lynn's heart was bursting. "I'll get the nurse," she said, and ran, and ran.

Even now, half raving, Josie probes, she thought on the way home. Josie and Helen.

It was all too much to contend with. Her deep thoughts ran like an underground river.

The summer plodded on, creating its own routine. At Robert's insistence Bruce came almost every evening for dinner before going to the hospital.

"He must have lost fifteen pounds," Robert had observed. "We can't let him go on like that. It's a question of decent responsibility. He's part of the firm of GAA, after all."

Annie left for scout camp, and Lynn said, "I'm glad she's gone. It would be too hard for her when—" and glancing at Bruce, she stopped.

He finished for her. "When the end comes? Annie and I have had some very truthful talks about that, and I don't think you need to worry about her. She's quite prepared," he said firmly, "as I must be." He smiled. "And am not."

No one at the table spoke until Emily said gravely, "This makes everything else in the world seem small, doesn't it?"

A heat wave, striking the countryside, struck the human body with intent to draw its breath out. Petunias went limp in the border, and birds were still. Even the dog, after a minute or two outside, panted to get back into the house. And in the air-conditioned house the air was stale. It was as if the very weather had conjoined with events to stifle them all.

"It takes too long to die," said Emily.

And then one morning at breakfast Emily had something else to say, something very serious.

"You'll be shocked. I'm scared to tell you," she began.

Two startled faces looked up from their plates.

"I don't know how to begin."

"At the beginning," Robert said impatiently.

The girl's hands clung to the table's edge as if she needed support. Her eyes were darkly circled, as if she had not slept. She gulped and spoke.

"I'm not going to go to Yale."

Robert stood up, his chair screeching on the floor, and threw his balled napkin onto his plate.

"What? What? Not going to Yale?"

"I wrote to them. I want to go to Tulane."

My God, Robert's going to have a stroke, Lynn thought, while into her own neck, the blood came rushing. She could see the beat of the pulses at his temples and put her hand on his arm to warn him.

"Tulane? Why," he said, "of course, it's the southern climate, isn't it? You like that better. Oh, of course, that must be it." And he made an elaborate sweep of his arm in mocking courtesy.

Emily said quietly, "No, Dad. It's because Harris got a scholarship there." And she looked without flinching at her father.

Robert stared back. Two pairs of steady eyes confronted one another, and Lynn glanced toward the girl, so frightened yet firm, and back to the furious man and back to the girl. How could she be doing this to them? She had given her word. How could she be doing this to herself? After all that had been said, all the reasoned explanations, the kind, sensible advice; had it all passed into deaf ears and out again?

As if she were reading Lynn's thoughts, Emily said, "I have not lied to you, since that's what you must be thinking. I have not seen him even once since—since what happened. We do talk on the phone. You know that, Mom."

"What?" cried Robert. "You knew they had telephone communication and you allowed it!"

His anger, like a diverted stream, now rushed torrentially toward Lynn. She braced herself. "Why, yes. I saw no harm in it." His eyes were hot and were cold; the cold burned like dry ice. "I thought, I mean—"

"You didn't think and you don't know what you meant. It's just another example of your ineptitude. This whole affair was mismanaged from the start. I should have done what I wanted to do, sent her away to a private school."

"A school without telephones?"

"That could have been managed," Robert said grimly. He picked up the ball of napkin and hurled it back onto the plate. If it had been hard, it would have shattered the plate. "Dammit, I don't know how I manage to keep my head. A thousand things on my mind, and now this! If I should have a stroke, you'll have a lot of questions to ask yourselves, both of you. That's all—"

"No. Don't blame Mom," Emily said, interrupting. "That's not fair. The fault is mine. The decision is mine. Dad, I'm nineteen. Please let me have some say in my own life. I'm not trying to defy you, I only want to be happy. We don't want to be away from each other for four years. No, please listen to me," she said hurriedly. "There won't be a repeat of what happened last year. I understand that's what you're afraid of. We'll be very careful, we'll be so busy keeping our grades up, that we'll keep all that to an absolute minimum, anyway—"

Robert roared. "I don't want to hear about your sex life."

"We haven't had any for a year. I only meant—"

"I'm not interested, I said!"

"This is disgusting!" Lynn cried.

She closed her eyes. How ugly, the three of them on a summer morning filling the blue light with their dark red rage! Her eyelids pressed against her eyeballs, wanting to shut the rage out.

The dining-room clock struck the half hour.

"Good Christ," Robert said. "I've got fifteen minutes to get to the station. With luck maybe a truck will hit me on the way, and you'll all be free to take the road to hell without my interference." He picked up his attaché case and, at the door, turned around. "You did say you wrote to Yale, didn't you?"

"Yes. I gave up my place."

"Well. Well, I'll tell you what. I'm not going to pay your bill anywhere but at Yale. Is that clear, young lady? You just write to them again and phone or go there and straighten the mess out with them, or you won't go anywhere. I'm not paying my good money so that you can go and shack up with that boy again."

"We won't. . . . I told you. . . . I promise. I've kept my promise, haven't I? If only you would listen . . ." Emily whimpered.

"And I told you: no tuition. I hope that's clear. Is it clear?"

Wordlessly, Emily nodded.

"Fine. So don't waste your energy or mine asking me again. No tuition. Not a penny. That's it. And it's your own doing. Now let me get out of here."

They stood, each behind her chair, as if frozen there, while the front door sounded its solid thud, and the car's engine raced, its tires spurted gravel on the drive and squealed around the curve.

Lynn sat down again, and Emily followed. A conference, it seemed, was called for, although Lynn was too distraught, too confused, to begin one. Emily, with her head down, fiddled with the silverware at her place. Its tiny clash and clink were unbearable, and Lynn scolded.

"Do stop that." Then more quietly, she said, "Well, you've managed to set the house on fire once again, haven't you?"

It was rotten of Emily. Rotten.

"It's Dad. He's unforgiving," Emily replied.

"No. He's crushed, that's what it is. And don't dodge the issue. Giving up Yale! After all your effort and our hopes. Why weren't you at least open about it? We could have talked it over. This is really—it's really unspeakable. I trusted you. Now you've put me in the position of a fool. No, what am I saying? I don't mean to talk about myself, about your father and me. Never mind us. What about you? What are you doing with your life, you foolish, foolish, capricious, thoughtless girl?"

"I don't think I'm foolish or thoughtless, Mom." The tone was earnest and reasoned, belying the tears that, unwiped, rolled over reddening eyelids. "We want to be married. Oh, not yet. We know it's much too soon. But we mean it, Mom. Why didn't I talk about this before I canceled Yale? Because you know as well as I do that Dad would have talked me out of doing what I want to do. He's so powerful, he gets his way. Oh, I wish our family was like Harris's family!"

How that hurt! What else had Lynn ever wanted but to build a life for her children that they would happily remember? And now this girl, across whose face and therefore in whose mind there passed the most delicate and subtle feelings, could wish that they were "like Harris's family."

"Yes? What are they like?" she asked in a dull monotone.

"Well, we told them how we feel. They aren't exactly thrilled about our being at college together, but they think we're old enough to make our own mistakes. His mother said we made one mistake, so probably that would be a warning not to make another. And she's right. Oh, you think—"

"You don't know what I think," Lynn said with bitterness. And it was a bitter thing to stand between this enmity, daughter against father.

"Well, Dad thinks—"

"Yes, try to imagine what he thinks. He works so hard for us all."

"He works for his own pleasure, Mom. The way you put it, anytime a person opposes Dad, you lay guilt on the person because Dad 'works hard.' Harris's father works hard too. Do you think a policeman's life is easy?" Emily's words came tumbling. "And you needn't think they're eager to have Harris marry me. They think too much of their son to have him marry into a family that doesn't want him. They're pleased that we're going to wait. But they do understand that we don't want to be separated. Is that so bad? Is it?"

Yes, it was pretty bad, a pretty bad trick this canny girl had played.

"This is all academic," Lynn said, "since without money you can't get to Tulane or any other place." At that her voice caught in a little sob. "So there go college and medical school. Both. Just like that."

"Won't you give it to me, Mom?"

"Money? I haven't got any."

"He would really do that," Emily said, asking a question and declaring a fact at the same time.

"You know he would."

"Then will you give me the money, Mom? Even though you don't approve?"

"I just told you, I have none. I haven't a cent of my own."

"Not a cent? None!" Emily repeated in astonishment.

"I never have had. Your father gives me everything I need or want."

The girl considered that. And Lynn, who knew so well the nuances of her daughter's expression, saw unmistakable distaste and was humiliated by it.

"Aunt Helen, maybe? For the first semester, at least!"

"Don't be silly. Aunt Helen can't afford it."

That was not true. Darwin had been doing well of late, well enough for them to buy a bigger house in a prettier suburb. But she wasn't going to exhibit her dirty linen to Helen.

"If I have enough for the first semester, I'm sure I could get a student loan. And I'd find work. I'd take any kind I could get."

"It's not so easy to get a loan. When they find out your father's position and income, you'll never get one."

"Oh, Mom, what am I going to do?"

"If I were you, I'd go back to Yale and be thankful."

"But you see—I can't! It's too late. They've already filled my place from the wait list."

Stupid, stupid girl . . . This crushing disappointment, this disaster, made Lynn hard.

"Then you've burned your bridges, so I guess that's the end of it."

Emily stood up. "Then there's nothing you can tell me."

"What can I tell you? Except," she added, knowing it was cruel to her, "that I'm on my way to visit a dying woman. You may come if you want to."

"No. I'm going upstairs."

Lynn sat with her face in her hands. She was furious with Emily, and yet felt her daughter's pain as if it were scarring her own flesh. I suppose, she thought, eventually I will have to go crawling to Helen. I will have to endure her sardonic questions: *What are you telling me? That Robert refuses?* But it was also likely that Helen would refuse. They had their own children to educate; one son was going to graduate school. The new house was certainly mortgaged; Darwin couldn't be doing *all* that well. . . . Her thoughts unraveled. Maybe as long as it wasn't where that boy was going, Robert would pay for some other place. But no, he wouldn't; he had had his heart set on Yale for this brilliant daughter. Robert never changed his mind.

She got up from the table and went to the window. Outside in the yard Eudora was singing while she hung clothes on the line. Eudora believed that white goods should dry in sunlight. Bobby was sitting up in the playpen. Falling backward, he would struggle up again, as if proud of his newfound ability to look at the world from a different angle. Eudora bent to talk to him. The scene was cheerful. It was wholesome. Wholesome. A good word.

The house inside was unwholesome. From the bottom of the stairs she could see the closed door to Emily's room and could well imagine that behind the door, Emily was lying facedown on her bed in despair. A part of her wanted to go up and give comfort, to stroke the poor, trembling shoulders. Meager comfort that would be! cried the part of Lynn in which anger was still stone hard.

She grabbed her car keys and started for the hospital. In the rearview mirror she practiced a noncommittal face, the only decent face to present to a sufferer, surely not tears, not even gravity.

And yet her resolution failed her. Josie, this day and for a brief hour, was wide awake. Bruce was telling her something about the new cat when Lynn came in.

"I'm so furious at myself," she began. "It's beastly hot, and I made a sherbet for you with fresh raspberries. It even looks cool, and I thought you'd love it, but then I went and forgot it. My mind—" And she clapped her hand to her forehead.

Josie looked quizzical. "So? What's your trouble? You never forget things, especially things for me. What is it?"

"Oh, nothing much, really."

But she was bursting; the trouble could scarcely be confined.

"Tell us," said Josie.

So Lynn did. When she had finished her account, Bruce and Josie were somber.

"She's tenacious, all right," Josie said. "You have to admire that much, anyway."

Lynn sighed. "Yes, like Robert."

"No." Josie corrected her. "Like herself."

It was clear that she didn't want Emily to resemble Robert. Now in some way, Lynn had to defend him.

"Emily tricked us into thinking she was finished with Harris. She lied to us."

"I don't remember," Bruce remarked calmly, "that she ever said she was 'finished.' She said she wouldn't see him all year, and she hasn't done so."

"A lie by omission, then, wasn't it?"

"When you were a year older than Emily is now, and someone had told you to stay away from Robert for another four years, and probably lose him in doing so, would you have obeyed?" asked Bruce.

Her glance fell under his chastisement. "No," she said, and then, recovering, protested, "but that was different. Robert was older. He was a man."

"Nonsense," said Josie. The voice was tired, but the word was crisp.

"Nonsense." She raised herself on the pillow. "If I've ever seen a real man, I've seen one in young Harris."

"But Yale," Lynn lamented. "To give that up! It has crushed Robert." She appealed, "Don't you understand that?"

"But Emily," said Josie. "It is a question of priorities."

Bruce's eyebrows drew together in his familiar expression of concern as he spoke.

"Yes, I can understand Robert. She should have told you, she should have been candid, but she wasn't. She was afraid to be candid, and that has to be understood too."

"You are leaving her alone with her mistake," Josie remonstrated. "Leaving her alone to pick up the pieces by herself."

In their quiet way they were scolding Lynn.

"She's an extraordinary girl," Josie said, making a little show of vigor. "Of all people Robert knows that. I must have heard him say so a thousand times at least. Does he want to take everything away, her chance at medical school, all that, so he can have the miserable satisfaction of saying later: 'I told you so. You transgressed, so you've paid for it, paid for it with the rest of your life'?"

How she hated Robert! Hatred had given her strength enough to speak out, and now having spoken, she lay back, exhausted.

And something happened to Lynn that had never happened before in her life: Thoughts that should not have been revealed took shape in speech, and she heard herself saying without any rancor at all, "You have always despised Robert."

"Yes," Josie said simply. "I have," and closed her eyes.

Lynn was feeling faint. It was the overpowering scent of gardenias, a little pot of them on the window ledge. Josie would not have said that if it were not for the medication and the pain. Bruce, shaking his head and with silent lips, spelled out the same: It is the medicine.

"Let her go," said Josie, faintly now.

They had to lean toward her, not sure they had heard correctly. Lynn stroked the hot forehead and pushed back the tousled hair.

"What did you say, darling?" Bruce asked.

"Let her go. She had highest honors. . . ." Josie's breathing was hard. "A good girl . . . woman. . . . Let her get away. . . . She needs . . . Take my money for her."

Lynn struggled against tears. "No, darling. We can't do that. You are an angel, but we can't do that."

"Yes, I said!" Josie's hands went frantic as pain struck again. "Bruce, listen to me."

"Dearest, I'm listening. We'll do what you say. I promise I'll give whatever Emily needs. She'll take it from me."

"No," Josie gasped. "Mine . . . Power of attorney . . . Not your name . . . Not you involved . . . at office. Not you."

Bruce turned helplessly to Lynn. "She means that my interference would complicate things between Robert and me. Yes, I see. And it would be terribly hard for you too. Lynn, will you let me take it for Emily out of Josie's account? Will you?"

Past reasoning about what was right, and yet feeling somehow that it probably was right, confused and troubled and in anguish for Josie, she bowed her head in assent.

As she went out and met the nurse who came hurrying in, she heard Josie's anguished cry repeated. "Let Emily go!"

Robert was beaten. Emily, swollen eyed and half sick, had taken a bowl of cereal to her room, so that Lynn sat alone with him at the dinner table. Unspeaking, they sat over the barely eaten food.

Only once he groaned, "Ruined her life. Ruined it."

"Would you consider another place, someplace where Harris wasn't?" Lynn asked.

"No. Maybe in a year or two. I'll see. She must learn a lesson. Parents cannot be defied. No."

Lynn's father had been full of old-time sayings: *The rigid tree breaks in the storm, but the soft one bends and bounces back.*

She would have liked to tell that to Robert out of compassion, to console and warn, but it would have been useless this night, so she said nothing and waited instead until he had fallen asleep before going in to Emily.

The girl wept when Lynn told her what Josie was going to do. She wept and was glad and grateful. Also, she was hesitant.

"Does Dad know?"

"I hadn't the heart to tell him tonight."

"The heart?"

"The strength, I should have said. He will be very, very angry."

The two looked at each other. And Lynn said honestly, "I was angry, too, you know that. It was Josie and Bruce who said, mostly Josie—" She could not go on.

"I know, Mom. I understand."

"Do you, Emily?"

"More than you have ever realized."

The morning began with dread. In the kitchen Lynn made the coffee and orange juice, moving on tiptoe, moving the utensils without a sound, to let Robert sleep another minute and to postpone the moment when he would appear and she would have to speak.

Perhaps with the same motive Emily came in on tiptoe, whispering.

"Uncle Bruce called on my phone. I have to rush over now with the college bill to get the check before he leaves for the hospital. They are so good to me, Mom! I don't understand why they want to do this for me."

"They love you, that's why." And she said also, "They trust you."

"And you? Do you trust me too?"

"You're old enough to be trusted, so I will have to."

"You won't be sorry, Mom. I promise. And I'm going to pay back every cent. I can't tell how long it will take me, but I'll do it."

So young and so sure of herself! Well, the world wouldn't survive for very long if people weren't sure of themselves at nineteen. And her heart ached over Emily's youth and courage.

"If I had money of my own I would do anything and everything for you. You know that, Emily. Oh, I wish I had money of my own! But—" She stopped before completing the sentence in her head. Your father never let me, he said it wasn't necessary because he gave me whatever I wanted, which was true, but it was being treated like a child, an imbecile, damn it—

She took a deep breath and spoke aloud.

"You'd better leave if Bruce is waiting."

"Was that Emily going out?" asked Robert as he entered the kitchen. "I heard her phone ring a while ago. That young bastard, I suppose."

"No, it was Bruce. Josie is going to pay for Emily at Tulane." And she waited for the explosion.

He sat down. "You can't really have said what I think you said. Maybe you should say it again."

She drew a deep breath. "When I was at the hospital, I told them about Emily. Josie can't bear"—she must be careful not to bring Bruce into this affair—"Josie can't bear to have Emily waste a year, and so she offered, she insisted on paying."

Robert's right hand made a fist. "That damnable woman! That damnable, interfering witch of a woman! I had her number the first time I saw her, and you know I did." The fist came down hard on the table, rattling the empty cups. "I'd like to smash this fist into her. I hope she rots. I'd like her to tell me to my face how I should deal with my own family."

"She's dying. She can hardly talk."

"Hardly talk? Then who masterminded this scheme? It must have been Bruce."

"No, it was Josie. She asked him, since he has power of attorney, to write a check, and he simply agreed. It was her idea, not his. She meant so well," Lynn pleaded.

"The hell it was only her idea! It was his too. And yours too. You could have put a stop to it. You're only the girl's mother, aren't you? You could have said, if you had any respect for your husband's judgment, for his wishes, you could have said no. Positively no. Well, say something. Why don't you?"

"Because I've been thinking, probably we were too harsh. It's Emily's life, after all," she said disconsolately. "Her life."

"God, I'm cursed! My wife, my daughter, the whole lot of you. The only one who hasn't disappointed me is the boy, and who knows how he'll turn against me when his time comes?" Robert sprang up so abruptly that he upset the coffeepot, which, as it smashed, sent a brown river meandering across the floor. And Juliet, who had been lying under the table, ran with her tail between her legs. "The humiliation! Think of it: that weakling, that excuse for a man, comes into my home and takes over. The next thing, he'll be sleeping with my wife."

"You're revolting, Robert. Let me tell you, I have no desire to sleep with Bruce. But if you had a few of his qualities, it might be better for us all."

"His qualities! You have the gall to say it would be better for the family if I were like him?"

"Yes, and better for you too."

Robert's eyes burned right through Lynn. He took a deep breath, a long step, and slapped her. Pressed as she was against the wall, she had no room to evade him, but could only twist helplessly. His open palm struck swiftly, stinging one cheek, then the other, and then the first, in succession; his ring, his marriage band, grazed her cheek as her head slammed against the wall, and she cried out. The dog came flying and yelping back into the kitchen. The backyard gate swung shut with a clang. Eudora's key turned in the lock at the kitchen door, and her face appeared in the upper half. Robert fled. Lynn fled. . . .

Panting and groping in the closet for his attaché case, he mumbled, "Fine condition for the commuter train. Smile the good-morning greeting, read the newspaper, act like all the other men, after a scene like this. Yes, fine condition," he repeated as the front door closed upon him.

On the sofa in the back den she sobbed. The attack had pained, but that was not the whole reason for her sobs. Not at all. A sudden light had flared in her head. It was so hot that it hurt.

For this attack was different from all the others. It had brought an end to the excuses and dodges, the concealment that had made the reality tolerable. There was no doubt that Eudora had seen, and now she knew. And it was this knowing that would take away Lynn's dignity. It had stripped her at last. It had damaged her very soul, or whatever you wanted to name the thing that, apart from blood or bone, was your self.

So she lay, and cried, and tried to think.

There came a knock at the door and a call. "Mrs. Ferguson? Are you all right? Is anything the matter?"

"Yes, thank you, I'm all right."

The door opened, and Lynn was revealed in her rumpled wet-eyed state. Now she had to sit up and make the best of it.

"I'm upset," she said. "I've been crying because of Mrs.—of my friend, Josie."

"Oh, sure, it's awful hard." Eudora's face was kind—she was a kind woman—but her eyes spoke, too, and they were saying plainly, "I know the truth, but I will pretend for your sake that I don't."

Kind as she was, she would talk at her other jobs. It was only human nature. The story was too juicy to be withheld. It would be all over the country club. It would be whispered behind Lynn's back. Whispered.

Up and down she walked now, past Robert's austere face framed in sterling silver, and past her own soft, childish face, her dreaming eyes beneath blond bangs and a bridal veil held by clustered lilies of the valley.

"I will leave him," she said aloud. And the sound of her voice, the sound of those daring, impossible words, those unthinkable words, stopped her in her walk, and the shock chilled her bones.

Eudora was singing as she carried Bobby down the stairs.

"Big fat boy. Beautiful, big fat boy, Eudora's boy. You beautiful—"

They went into the kitchen. And Lynn stood listening, asking herself, How much should I bear? How much can I bear? I shall have to keep my head. Am I to tear the roof down over his head?

"Beautiful big fat boy—"

Josie is dying. Emily is leaving. Let me take one day at a time. That's it. One day at a time.

She went into the kitchen, into the light near the window, and inquired anxiously, "Do I look all right, Eudora? I don't want Josie to see that I've been crying because of her."

Eudora considered. "You look all right. Put a little powder on, maybe. Up on your left cheek," she explained with tact.

In the hospital's corridors there are the smells of antiseptics and anxiety. So many large things are compressed in a narrow space, in a short time, as one walks: the night they came in their terror, rushing to see Emily, the gusty morning when Bobby came squalling into the world, and now, as the door opens off the corridor, there is Josie on the high bed with her wasted hands, on which the plain wedding band has been tied with a string.

Bruce got up from his chair in the corner.

"She went into a coma last night," he said, answering Lynn's unspoken question.

The sorrow in him was tangible. It made her chest ache to look at him. All the clichés were true; the heart does weigh heavily in the chest, heavy and sorely bruised.

"Why? Why?" she asked.

He shook his head, and they sat down together on either side of Josie's bed, where she lay as in peaceful sleep. As if a loving hand had passed across her face, the agony and torment were wiped away.

After a long time the noontime sun came glaring into the room. Someone pulled the shade, making a watered-green gloom on the walls. When later the room became too dark, the shades were raised again to let in a tawny summer afternoon.

A doctor came, murmuring something to Bruce, and then more audibly, he addressed them both.

"This can go on for days, or it may not. We can't tell. In any case, there's no point in staying here around the clock. I think you should go home, Bruce. You were here until three o'clock this morning, they tell me. Go home."

At the hospital's front steps they met the other world where cars passed, glittering in the light, and small girls played hopscotch and a couple strolled, thoughtfully eating double ice cream cones.

"Can you give me a lift?" Bruce asked. "My car's in the shop. I was lucky to get a taxi last night."

"Of course."

There was little to talk about until Lynn was compelled to say something about Emily.

"How can anyone say thank you? Thank you for saving a person when he was drowning, thank you for curing a person's blindness? How does one say such things?"

"How do I say thank you for being my support? We don't need words, Lynn."

Numbed by her dual sorrow, she drove without thinking, as if the car, like an obedient, well-trained horse, knew the route by itself.

"We go back a long time," Bruce said suddenly. "Eighteen years. Emily was a baby." He placed his hand over Lynn's. "Don't worry too much about her. I have a feeling that she will do very, very well."

"Perhaps. But do you know," she said sadly, "that I am glad she's leaving? I never thought I could say that, but I can." And a little sob escaped from her throat.

The car had stopped in front of his house, and he gave her a quick look, saying, "You don't want to go home like this. Come in and we'll talk."

"No, I'm not going to burden you with my troubles. You have enough and far more."

"Let's say I don't want to be alone."

"In that case, I will."

The house, though tidy, had the abandoned air that comes when there is no woman in it. The curtains that were usually drawn at night were still drawn, and the philodendron on the mantel were turning yellow. Lynn shuddered in the gloom and pulled the curtains back.

In the bay stood Josie's prize gardenias that she had nourished and brought all the way here when they moved.

"Gardenias need water," Lynn said. "It would be a pity to lose these."

That was a foolish remark. What could it matter to this man if the plant should die? But she was restless, and it soothed her at this moment to fuss with it.

"Bruce, I see a couple of mealybugs. I need cotton swabs and some alcohol. Where does Josie keep all that stuff?"

"I'll get it."

A nervous exchange of trivia came next.

"You can't ever seem to get rid of them," said Lynn as she rubbed each dark leaf.

"Josie told me."

"It's her pet plant. A miracle that it survived the move at all."

"So she says."

"I've never had any luck with gardenias. Josie has a green thumb."

"That's true."

In the bay, when Lynn had cleaned each leaf, topside and under, they stood looking out at the yard, where a flock of pigeons had taken possession of the bird feeder.

"See that one?" Bruce pointed. "The white one? It's her favorite. She claims it knows her."

He can barely see the bird, Lynn thought, with those blurred eyes.

"I want a brandy," he said, he who scarcely drank even wine. "What about you?"

She smiled wanly. "It wouldn't hurt."

They sat on either side of the fireplace, she on the sofa, he in his easy chair. He removed his glasses; she did not remember having ever seen him without them, and it seemed to her now that perhaps she had never really seen him before. The glasses had in some way given him a benevolent look; the simplicity of the man she had pictured in her head, striding on a hill alongside a bevy of large dogs, or else the one whom she had actually known, as he sanded old wood and looked up with that benevolent smile, was gone. This man was bitter.

He caught her studying him.

"What is it?" he asked.

She could say only, "I'm so sorry for you. My heart hurts."

"No, feel sorry for her. She gave so much to everybody. Everyone who really knew her . . . And now they're taking her short life away. Feel sorry for her."

"Oh, God, I do! But you, she worries about you, Bruce. She told me. About leaving you alone."

"She worries about you too."

"There's no need to," Lynn said, wanting to seem, and wanting to be, courageous.

He did not answer. Perhaps it was the positioning of the furniture and the fireplace and the same tension of immediate grief that restored abruptly the day when Bruce had brought Annie home. And she told him so, saying, "You have always been there when I needed you. I know that you talked to the girls when I was out of the room that day."

"I only tried to mend, to find a way for you all to survive together."

He swirled the brandy, tilting and tipping and studying the little amber puddle.

Then abruptly he inquired, "Has it worked?"

Lynn's courage left. She felt herself broken. She saw herself backed against the kitchen wall this morning, so small and weak, so insignificant in the face of Robert's anger. No one must ever know of that insignificance.

Bruce's eyes were studying her with a gravity almost severe. He asked again, "Has it?"

Faltering, she replied, "Yes, but now because of Emily, he—"

The cat came in, Josie's exquisite white cat; curling itself around Bruce's ankle, it made a diversion for which Lynn was grateful.

He smoothed the cat's fur and looked over again at her.

"What did he do?"

"He was quite—quite furious. He—" And now she was truly broken, unable to go on.

"He struck you, didn't he? This morning, before you came to the hospital."

She stared at him.

"Dear Lynn, dear Lynn, do you really think we don't know? And haven't known for I can't remember how long? That day in Chicago I knew, and even before that we both did. Oh, when first we suspected, we told ourselves we must be wrong. It's hard to think of Robert's using force; he's always so coldly polite when it's plain that he has a rage inside. One doesn't imagine him being common enough to be violent."

Bruce's laugh was sardonic. And Lynn could only keep staring at him.

"I remember when we first met. We were invited to your house. You had made a wonderful dinner, coq au vin. And we had never had it before, although it was a fashionable dish then. How trustful you were! It was what we both thought of you. The way you looked at Robert. How can I put it? I'm floundering. It's hard to make clear what I mean. Josie and I, we are—how shall I say it—more equal in our marriage. But you seemed so tender to him, and there's so much love in you, even for that plant over there."

"But there's love in him too," she said, choking. "You don't know. I've loved him so. You don't know—or maybe you do have some little idea how good he was when I let Caroline die. He never blamed me, although anybody else would—"

"Now, stop right there. Anybody else would say it was an accident. Accidents happen. A child pulls away from you and runs into the street. An adult stumbles and falls down the stairs in front of your eyes. Are we supposed to be infallible? And as for not blaming you—ah, Lynn, admit it, in a hundred subtle ways he lets you know it was your fault, but he— he the magnanimous—forgives you! Crap, Lynn. Crap. Stop the guilt. You did not kill Caroline!"

Bruce was on a talking jag. It was as if all the pent-up fear and grief and anger at the fates that were taking Josie away were storming within him, lashing to be released.

"Maybe I'll be sorry to have talked to you like this, but right now I'm sorry I didn't do it a long time ago. Only, if I had you wouldn't have listened and then you'd have ended up by hating me."

"No," she said truthfully, "no, I could never hate you. Not you."

For there was something about him that had always touched her heart: the candor, the simplicity, the vigorous bloom of a man who was healthy in body and in mind.

"That day you came over," he continued, "that morning when you told us you had fallen into the thorn hedge, don't you think we knew what had really happened? Tom Lawrence told us about the dinner at his house, and how he found you when he brought back your purse the next day. Oh, don't worry!" He flung up his hand. "Tom never talks. He's too decent for that. He was only concerned that you were in trouble."

Lynn put her face into her hands. And he went on relentlessly.

"The day when you came to tell us you were pregnant, we could hardly believe that you would tie yourself up again. Josie was sick over it."

"Why are you doing this to me, Bruce?" she burst out.

"I don't know. I suppose I hope you will start to think."

"Oh, my God, oh, my God!" she cried.

He jumped to his feet and, sitting down on the sofa, took both her hands in his.

"Oh, Lynn, I've hurt you. Forgive me, I'm clumsy, but I mean well. Don't you think I'm glad you had Bobby? That's not what I meant at all."

Her baby. Her little boy. She wanted to hide. And in her despair she turned and put her head on Bruce's shoulder.

"Yes, he struck me this morning. We had some words about Emily, and he was furious."

"I'm sorry, I'm sorry. Poor little Lynn."

"It wasn't—it wasn't so much that my face was hurt, it was that I felt, I feel, like nothing. Can you understand? Like nothing."

His big hands smoothed the back of her head softly, over and over.

"Yes," he murmured, "yes."

"Maybe you can't. It's so different with you and Josie."

"It is. It is."

His voice was bleak. Like an echo, it came from far off, detached from the warm, living shoulder to which she clung, detached from the warm hand that cradled her head.

"This morning I hated him," she whispered. "His filthy temper. And still there is love. Am I crazy? Why am I so confused? Why is living just so awfully hard?"

"Lynn, I don't know. I don't know why dying is so hard either. On this day, all of a sudden I don't know anything at all."

She raised her head and looked into his expressive face, on which, over the short season of this summer, deep lines had been written. And it seemed to her that they two, on this hollow, emptying day, must be among the most miserable people in the world.

He pushed her bangs aside and stroked her forehead, saying with a small rueful smile, "How good you are, how sweet. You mustn't give up, you mustn't despair."

"Please don't be kind to me. I can't bear it."

Yet, how clearly she needed the kindness of encircling arms, of human warmth! And so, impulsively, she raised her arms around his neck; he pulled her to him, and she lay against his heart. It was consolation. . . .

So they held to each other, each sunk in grief, not speaking. In unison they felt the rise and fall of breath, and in unison heard the beat of the other's heart.

The room was still. From the yard came pigeons' throaty gurgles, a peaceful sound of untroubled life. A clock somewhere else in the house struck the half hour with a musical ping, leaving a sweet, glittering chime in the air. Neither moved. In this quiet, one could simply float, assuaging against each other's limp and weary body the need for comfort.

Then, little by little, there began a response. Up and down her spine, perhaps unconsciously, his hand moved. It was so soft, this fluttering touch, this delicate caress, and yet from it a subtle pleasure began to travel through her nerves. After a time—how long a time she could not have said and never afterward remembered—there came from the deepest core of sensation a familiar fire. And she knew that he was feeling it as well.

It was as if, outside of the self that was Lynn Ferguson, she was observing ever so curiously a film in slow motion.

The film gathered speed. The actors moved inexorably, his lips on her neck, his fingers unfastening her blouse, her skirt falling into a yellow heap on the floor. Neither of them spoke. She lost all thought. He lost all thought. Desperate and famished, they hastened; it was a kind of collapse into each other, a total fusion. . . .

When she awoke, he was gently shaking her. Startled, disoriented in time and place, it was a moment before she understood where she was.

In that moment, as she later recalled it, she was free of care; the knot of tension at the nape of her neck had disappeared; she was *normal.*

That moment ended, and she knew what had happened, knew that after it had happened, she had dozed, resting in this man's arms as if she belonged there. Appalled, she met his eyes and saw in them a duplication of her own horror.

He had dressed himself, but she was naked, covered only by the plaid knit throw that he had put over her. Through long evenings and on rainy afternoons she had watched Josie knit that throw. Knit, cable, purl, rose and cream and green.

"I have to get to the hospital," he said dully.

"You have no car," she said.

"They've brought mine back."

This dialogue was absurd. It was surreal.

The afternoon had faded. From the window where Josie's beautiful white cat slept on the sill came an almost imperceptible movement of air and a creeping shade. The room became a place where, helplessly, one waited for some onrushing, unstoppable disaster.

"Oh, God," she groaned.

He turned away, saying only, "I'll let you get dressed," and left the room.

Shaking, with nausea rising to her throat, she put on her clothes. On the opposite wall there hung a mirror, one of Bruce's antiques, with a surface of wavy glass that distorted her face as she passed it. This ugly distortion seemed fitting to her, and she stopped in front of it. Ugly. Ugly. That's what I am. I, Lynn, have done this while she lies dying. I, Lynn.

And Robert said, "On the health and lives of our children, I swear that I have never been unfaithful to you." He would not have sworn it so if it were not true. Whatever else he was, he was not a liar.

She had expected Bruce to be in a hurry, but when he returned, he sat down on the chair across from the sofa. So she sat down, too, neat, proper Lynn Ferguson with the shaking stomach, the knot as tight as ever it had been at the nape of her neck, and her feet neatly placed on the floor. She waited for him to speak.

Several times he began, and as his voice broke, had to stop. Finally he said, "I think we must forget what happened, put it out of our minds forever. It was human. . . . We are both under terrible strain."

"Yes," she said, looking down at her feet, the suburban lady's nice brown-and-white summer pumps.

His voice broke again. "That this could happen—I don't know—my Josie—I love her so."

"I am so ashamed," she whispered, looking not at Bruce but at the white cat.

"We will have to forget it," he repeated. "To try to forget it. But before that, I must apologize."

She gave a little shrug and a painful frown as if to say, There is no need, the burden is just as much mine.

"And something else: I should never have told you what I did about Robert and forced your answer."

"It doesn't matter. What you said was true."

"All the same, you will be sorry you admitted it. I know you, Lynn. I know you very well."

"I have admitted it to no one but you, and I trust you."

He put on his glasses, restoring the old Bruce, the one she had known, the brotherly friend with whom such a thing as had just passed between them would have been an impossibility. And he said, "Perhaps that's your mistake."

"What? Trusting you?"

"Oh, God, no, Lynn. I meant your mistake in not admitting it to anyone else."

"Such as who?"

"Well, once I would have said—I did say—a counselor. But now I would say 'Tom Lawrence.' "

To ask for advice, for help, from Tom? And she remembered the scene at the club pool, remembered the humiliation and her own defiant invitation to the golden wedding.

"A lawyer? No."

"He's not only a lawyer, Lynn. He would care. He admires you. Believe me, I know."

He is also the man who thinks I belong in the nineteenth century, an anachronism, part charming, part absurd. That, no doubt, is what he finds interesting, only because it's different from what he sees around him, those blunt, independent women at his party that night. If he knew what I have done just now in this room, he would have to laugh through his amazement. "The joke's on me," he would say. She could hear him say it and see the crinkles forming around his light, bright eyes.

Her mind leapt: What if Robert knew! And terror seized her as if she were alone in a stalled car at midnight, or as if, alone in a house, she heard footsteps on the stairs at midnight.

She stood up, fighting it off. "I've been gone all day. The baby . . . And Emily, I must talk to Emily."

He saw her to the door and took her hand. "Go home. Drive carefully." The lines in his forehead deepened with anxiety. "Are you all right? Really?"

"I am. I really am."

Naked with a man who wasn't Robert. With Josie's husband . . .

"We've done no harm, Lynn. Remember that. It was just something that happened. We're both good people. Remember that too."

"Yes," she said, knowing that he hoped she would forget because, not believing it himself, he needed to have someone else believe it. But he himself would remember this betrayal of his darling Josie.

"I have to get to the hospital," he said.

"Yes, go."

"I'll call you if anything—"

"Yes, do."

So she left Josie's house.

It was Bobby who relieved the silence at the table, which Eudora had thoughtfully set before leaving, although it was not her job to do so. From the freezer she had taken one of Lynn's pot pies and heated it. Lynn thought, It is because she pities me.

Emily had eaten earlier by herself and gone to her room.

"Emily said to tell you she has a headache. But you're not to worry, it's nothing," Eudora said, while her eyes told Lynn, I pity you.

Eyes told everything. Eyes averted told of guilt or shame or fear. Robert's glance fell on Lynn's cheek, where the split skin showed a thin red thread. Lynn looked down at her plate. Robert fed soft pieces of potato to the baby.

The baby bounced in the infant seat. When he dropped his toy, Robert retrieved it; when he threw his toy, Robert had to get up and fetch it from under the table.

"Toughie," Robert said. "Little toughie."

Lynn said nothing. The boy was beautiful; the hair with which he had been born and that he had lost soon after birth was now growing back, silky and silver white.

She imagined herself saying to this child: Your father, whom I loved— love still, and God alone can explain that—I wish He would because I am incapable of understanding it myself—your father has struck me once too often.

Is it Josie who has made this time different from the other times? Or Eudora who has made it seem like the last straw? Or simply that it is, it truly is, the last straw for me, and me alone.

The telephone rang. "Shall I take it or will you?" asked Robert.

"You, please."

Any hour the phone could bring the news of Josie's death. Her legs were too weak to carry her to the telephone; her hand would not be able to hold it.

But it was only from the PTA. "A Mrs. Hargrove," Robert reported as he sat down again. "You're asked to be class mother for Annie. I said you'd call back."

He spoke without inflection or tone. Then he stretched his arm to reach the basket of bread, as if he could not bring himself to ask for the bread, he who was contemptuous of anyone who had poor table manners, of what he would call "the boardinghouse reach." So she handed the basket to him, their hands grazing, their eyes meeting blankly.

The evening light lay delicately on mahogany and turned the glittering pendants on the chandelier to ice. The baby, out of some secret bliss of his own, spread his adorable arms and crowed. And Emily was hiding in her room. And Annie, fragile Annie, would soon be coming home.

It was unbearable.

Emily looked up from the open suitcase on the bed when Lynn came in. The doorknobs were hung with clothes and the chairs were strewn with more; sweaters, shoes, skirts, and slacks were heaped together. On the floor along with Emily's Walkman were piles of books, and her tennis racket leaned against the wall.

"So soon?" asked Lynn.

"Mom, I wanted you to know beforehand, not shock you by having you walk in like this. The thing is, I delayed telling about Tulane, I delayed because I dreaded it, and now I'm at the last minute. Freshman indoctrination starts the day after tomorrow, and I'll have to leave tomorrow morning. Oh, Mom!"

"It's all right," Lynn said, swallowing the inevitable pain.

"I tried to call you at the hospital this afternoon, but you weren't there. I didn't know where else to try."

"It's all right."

"The nurse in Josie's room said you and Uncle Bruce had left."

"We didn't leave, we only went to the cafeteria for coffee and a doughnut." And Lynn, suddenly aware of exhaustion, shoved a shoe aside and sat down on the edge of a chair.

"I was hoping you'd get home early so we could talk."

"I went back to Josie's room and stayed late."

Emily's eyes filled. "Poor Josie! She was always so good to me, now more than ever. It's not fair for her to die."

Youth, youth, still astonished that life can be unfair.

"I wish I could see her again to tell her how much I love her and how much I thank her for what she's doing. But I did thank Uncle Bruce. I thanked him a thousand times."

"Josie wouldn't hear you if you did go. She's in a coma."

"Like a deep sleep."

"Like death."

On the pillow lay the face, the head so small now that the hair had fallen; under the blanket lay the body, so slight that it barely made a displacement. And while she lay there, where had her husband been, where her dearest friend?

With enormous effort Lynn pulled her mind back from the edge of the cliff. "Have you talked to your father at all?"

"I tried to, but he wouldn't answer me, wouldn't even look at me. I don't like to leave home this way, Mom," Emily said, now crying hard.

Lynn stood up to put her arms around her daughter. "Darling, this isn't the way I planned it either. Things will work out. They always do. Just have patience. Believe me."

How often, not knowing what else to say, you had to rely on platitudes!

"Patience isn't going to help you, Mom."

"I don't understand," Lynn said.

"I know he hit you this morning. Eudora told me."

"Oh, my God!"

A shiver passed along Lynn's spine and ran like cold fingers through her nerves. Her arms dropped; like bewildered rabbits or deer caught on the road at night by the sudden glare of headlights, unsure whether to stand or run, the two women paused.

"She said I mustn't let you know she told me."

"So why did she do it?" Lynn wailed.

"Well, somebody ought to know, and I'm your oldest child."

"How could she have done this? She had no right."

"Don't be angry at her, Mom. She feels so bad for you. She told me you're the nicest, kindest person she ever worked for."

Lynn was not mollified. What a terrible thing for Emily to be leaving home for the first time with this fresh information in her poor young head! This unnecessary information! It was mine to give when I was ready to give it, and not before, she thought.

"Promise you won't be angry at Eudora?"

Emily knelt at the chair onto which Lynn now fell and laid her head on her mother's knee, her wet cheeks dampening the thin silk skirt. Over and over, Lynn smoothed her daughter's hair, from the beating temples to the nape where the ribbon held the ponytail. A scent of perfume came from the hair, and she had to smile through her tears; Emily had been at her bottle of Joy again.

She stroked and stroked, thinking that this was to be another home broken in America. A statistic. This girl was a statistic, as were Annie and the baby in the crib across the hall. And her mind, as it went back to the beginning, asked almost reproachfully: Who would have believed it could end like this?

Her mind turned pages in an album, the pages rustling as they flashed disjointed pictures. Their first dinner, his wonderful face in candlelight, and she herself bewitched. People praising him, and she in a kind of awe that he belonged to her. The wedding music, the double ring, and the blaze of sunshine on the church steps when they came out together. The hotel room in Mexico and his dark rage. The death of Caroline and his arms around her. Slaps and shoves, falls and tears. The snowman on the lawn, hot chocolate afterward, and Robert at the piano with the girls. The bench in Chicago and the half-crazed beggar woman laughing at her. The rapture of the night when Bobby was conceived. This morning. Now.

Again Emily asked, "You won't be angry at Eudora?"

"No, I won't be."

What difference did it make, after all? When the end came, Emily would find out a whole lot more. And a great sigh came out of Lynn's heavy chest.

The unthinkable was happening, or was about to. Leaving Robert! Just yesterday she would have said, would have said in spite of everything, that there is always a way; there is so much good here too; there is always hope that the last time really was the last. But today was different. A great, unheralded, unexpected change had taken place within her. She was a good woman, deserving of a better life, and she was going to have it from now on.

Ah, yes! But how to do it? Ways and means. She calculated: In a short while, a few months, Robert would be sent abroad. It would be quite logical then for him to go ahead to prepare for their housing while she stayed behind to settle last-minute business here at home. Then, from a safe distance, she would let him know they were not going to follow him, and that she was through. Finished.

But where to go, with a baby still in arms and without a penny of her own? How to prepare? Bruce had said: Talk to Tom Lawrence. Well, perhaps she would. But she could see his bright, ironic face. He would be remembering, although surely he would never say, I told you so. Bruce had said: He admires you. Tom had said that brutal morning when Annie ran away: When you need help, I will be here for you. In a queer and subtle way, and in spite of the anguish of this day, she felt now a faint touch of self-esteem.

Emily got up, wiped her face, and began to fold sweaters.

"Let me help you," Lynn said. This movement, the physical action of emptying drawers and packing a suitcase, was a physical pain. It was too final for them both.

"Oh, Mom, I can't bear to leave you like this. Why do you put up with it? Why?" Emily cried, her tone high and piercing.

The tension had to be eased, the girl must get a night's sleep and leave in relative calmness to take the plane. So Lynn said softly, "Honey, don't worry about what Eudora told you. I'm sure she exaggerated."

"It isn't only what happened this morning. Before Bobby was born, something happened. I know the truth about that too."

Startled, Lynn stopped folding. "What do you mean?"

"The night you got into the thorn hedge and the people across the road, the Stevenses, called the police."

"Who told you that? Did Lieutenant Weber?" And a terrible anger rose in Lynn. Was the whole world conspiring to spread the news?

"No, no, he wouldn't do that, ever. Harris heard his father telling his mother. They didn't know he was sitting on the porch and could hear them in their living room. And when they found out that he'd overheard, his father asked him not to let me know. He said I mustn't be embarrassed or hurt in any way. But Harris did tell me. I suppose he shouldn't have, but he was worried, and he thought I ought to know. Not that I didn't already have my own ideas about it."

"I see," Lynn said.

She glanced at the wall where Emily's camp photo hung. Eight girls sat on a cabin's steps with Emily in the middle of the row, eight girls who perhaps knew more dreadful things than their naive expressions revealed. My girl, my Emily.

"I was sick. I was so ashamed before him when he told me. I was so ashamed for all of us, for the family that's supposed to be so respectable, with people all impressed by Dad's awards and his charities and this house and everything. I was so ashamed, I was sick. How could my father do that to you? But I'd been right the morning after when I didn't believe your explanation. Why didn't I believe it? Why ever did I suspect that there was something more? When I love Dad so? Then you denied it so strongly and I thought I mustn't think about my parents this way, it doesn't make sense. And when you came back from your trip and seemed so happy together, I thought surely that I'd been all wrong. I was even ashamed of myself because of the thoughts I'd had.

"You were already pregnant with Bobby when Harris told me. We were walking in the woods up at the lake. I guess I fell apart, and he took me in his arms to comfort me. He was so strong and kind! That's when it happened, when we made love. We'd planned not to do it until we were older, honestly we had. A lot of the kids start sex even in junior high, everybody knows that. But you never see things in the papers or on TV about all the kids who don't, even in high school." And Emily, giving a little sob, continued, "It's funny, Mom, when I go over it in my mind, how making love just seemed to grow out of the comfort and the kindness. It just seemed to be all one thing, do you know? And it happened just like that. I guess I'm not explaining it very well. I guess maybe you can't understand how it was."

Lynn was still looking at the photograph; that was the year Emily got braces on her teeth; there were elastic bands on the wires, and she'd gone around to show them off to her friends. She could not look at Emily when she answered.

"I understand," she said.

"It took so long for your hands and your arms to heal last summer, and every time I saw the scabs, I wanted to tell you that I knew. But I'd made so much trouble for you already, that I felt I had no right to make more. And that time Annie ran away, you remember that Uncle Bruce told us both to keep things peaceful for the baby's sake, for all our sakes?"

"You told me."

"And then," Emily said, "when Bobby came, he was so darling. You looked so beautiful holding him. And Dad was so nice, too, really himself. I thought, well, just forget what happened and keep your secret. It's the best you can do. Keep the peace, as Uncle Bruce said you should."

"And how well you have done it."

"I tried. But now that I'm going away, there's something I want to tell you. You were looking at that camp picture a minute ago. Now I have a picture I want to show you."

From a folder in her desk drawer she drew a photograph, evidently an enlarged snapshot, of a little boy not more than a year old. He was sitting on the floor; holding a striped ball three times the size of the tiny face under its full head of straight black hair.

"He looks like an Indian," Lynn said. "He's cute."

Emily turned the picture over.

"Read the name."

"Jeremy Ferguson, with love from Querida," Lynn read, and paused. It was a long pause. Then, "Where did you get this?" she asked.

"When Bobby was born and Aunt Jean came to visit, she brought me a box of pictures. There was Dad from birth to college, there were my grandparents and their grandparents, taken in the eighteen eighties, really interesting, and then I found this, which looks modern. When I asked who the boy was, she said very quickly, 'Oh, some distant cousin in your father's family, I'm not sure who. I cannot think how it ever came to me,' and changed the subject. But she was flustered and of course there has to be more to it. Who is he, Mom?"

Lynn was unnerved. There was too much happening all at once, too much to endure without adding a long, fruitless explanation and questions that she was in no mood to answer.

"I have no idea," she said.

"Mom dear, look me in the eye and tell me that's the truth."

Lynn closed her eyes, shook her head, and pleaded, "What difference does it make? Do we need any more trouble? Don't complicate things. You have no need to know."

Emily persisted. "Well, you're telling me in spite of yourself. You're telling me Dad has another child."

Lynn sighed and gave up. "Yes, all right. There was a boy born to his first marriage. I'm surprised Jean kept the picture. She must have been very fond of him."

"And Querida? Is she his mother?"

"Yes. Listen, Emily, if your father finds out that Jean gave this to you, he'll be wild."

"She didn't give it to me. I distracted her, and later when she looked for it, she couldn't find it."

"Emily! Why on earth do you do these things?" Lynn lamented.

"Because I want to understand. I have a half brother and I never even knew it. This secrecy makes no sense, unless there's a whole lot behind it, in which case it may make sense."

"You're looking for trouble. Your father's angry enough without your making things worse. Besides, he has a right to privacy, regardless of anything else. So do put that thing away. Please."

"All right, Mom, since it upsets you." With a swift tear Emily destroyed the photo. "There, that's over. But I have one more thing to tell you. Querida is in New York."

"How on earth do you know that?"

"I don't know it for a fact, but I'm making connections, Sherlock Holmes stuff. That time in New York before Bobby was born, when I met Aunt Jean there, we were in a taxi on my way to Grand Central to go home, and she got out first a few blocks before. We stopped at the corner for a red light, so I was able to see where she went. It was a store with the name 'Querida.' Mom, it's got to be the same person."

Lynn had a sudden picture of herself standing on the street with Tom on the day they had ridden home together on the train. In the window of the shop there had been a painting of sheep, and the name on the sign was QUERIDA. And she remembered the twinge of recognition, the stab of jealousy and curiosity, the wanting to know, the wanting not to know. But all that meant nothing, after this morning.

She said so now. "It means nothing, Emily. I don't care where she is or who she is. So please forget Sherlock Holmes, will you?"

"Okay."

Emily was packing a small stuffed polar bear among the sweaters. Her profile was grave, and her face when she turned back to Lynn was suddenly older than her years, so she questioned.

"May I ask you something, Mom?"

This child with the stuffed animal, this little woman . . .

"Anything, my darling. Ask."

"Why didn't you ever call the police?"

As if by an automatic reflex Lynn had to attempt a defense.

"Your father's not some drunkard who comes home and beats his wife every Saturday night," she said quietly, realizing in the instant that these had been Robert's very own words.

"But that night? That one night? The neighbors heard, and they called, so it must have been pretty bad."

"I couldn't, Emily. Don't ask for an answer I can't give. Please don't."

In a flood came the terrible sensation of the night when Weber had confronted Robert. Her one thought then had been that her children must be spared this hideous shame. Beyond her understanding were the women who could let their children watch their father being taken away by the police, unless of course they had been beaten most awfully. . . . This was not Lynn's case, and Emily knew it was not.

"I feel sorry for all of us," said Emily. "And in a queer way, for Dad too."

In a queer way, yes.

"Tell me, Mom, may I ask what you are going to do?"

"I am going to leave him," replied Lynn, and burst into tears.

The polar bear's black eyes looked astonished. The very stillness was astonished.

"When did you decide?"

"This morning. It came to me this morning. Why today and not the other times? I don't know. I don't know anything."

"It had to be sometime," said Emily with pity.

Lynn covered her face again, whispering as if to herself alone, "He was —he is—was—the love of my life."

The sentimental, melodramatic words were the purest truth.

"Sometimes I think I'm dreaming what's happened to us all," Emily said.

Lynn raised her head, pleading, "Don't commit yourself and your free will to any man. Don't."

"To no one? Ever? You can't mean that, Mom."

"I suppose not. Certainly don't do it yet. Don't let Harris disappoint you. Don't let him hurt you."

"He never will. Harris is steady. He's level. There are no extremes in him."

Yes, one could see that. There was no sparkle in him, either, thought Lynn, recalling the young Robert, who had lighted up her sky.

"If I tell you something, you won't laugh?" And before Lynn could promise not to laugh, Emily continued, "We made a list, each of us did, of all the qualities we'd need in the person we marry and whether the other one had those qualities. Then we read the list aloud to see how they matched. And they did, almost exactly. Now wasn't that very sensible of us? Harris said his parents did that, too, when they were young, so that's how he got the idea. They're really such good people, the Webers. You can feel the goodness in their house. I think a person's family is so important, don't you?"

"It's not everything."

"It helps, though," said Emily, as wisely as if she had had a lifetime's experience with humanity's woes.

The confident assertion was a childish one, and yet, perhaps . . . I knew really nothing about Robert, Lynn told herself. He came as a stranger. And comparing the wild, thoughtless passion she had felt for him with her daughter's "sensible" list, she felt only bafflement.

"I think Bobby's crying," said Emily, tilting her head listening.

"He's probably wet."

"I'll go, Mom. You're too upset."

"No, I'll go. You finish packing."

"I want to hold him. He might be asleep when I leave in the morning."

The night-light sent a pink glow into the corner where the crib stood. While Lynn watched, Emily soothed the baby, changed him, and cradled him in her arms.

"Look at his hair! I should have been the blonde," she complained with a make-believe pout.

"You'll do as you are."

So these were her children, this young woman in all her grace, and this treasure of a baby boy, the son of Robert, from whom she was about to part.

Emily whispered, swaying lightly while Bobby fell back to sleep on her shoulder, "When are you going to do what you said?"

"I have to think. I have to think of Annie and you and him."

"We'll be fine. We'll still be a family, Mom."

"Oh, my God!" Lynn exclaimed.

"It must be awful for you, but you have to do it. Eudora said it was terrible—"

Lynn raised her hand for silence. A sudden vision of the scene with Bruce that afternoon, a recurring shock, had produced the exclamation. If Emily knew *that*! If Robert knew it! And yet in a curious way, she wished he could be told and be wounded in the very heart of his pride, wounded and bloodied.

She steadied herself. "I'll drive you to Kennedy in the morning. Have you called Annie at camp to say good-bye?"

"No, I'll phone her when I get there. And I'll write often. I'll be so worried about you all, Mom."

"You mustn't be. I want you to concentrate on what you have to do. I want you to see yourself as Dr. Ferguson in your white coat with a stethoscope around your neck." And Lynn forced a smile. Then she thought of something else. "Will you talk to your father too? I'm sure his anger will fade if you give him a little time. And he is still your father, who loves you, no matter what else."

When they closed Bobby's door, the hall light shone on Emily's wet eyes.

"Just give me a little time first too," she said, "and then I will."

A familiar smoky scent drifted up the stairs. Robert must be smoking his pipe. Without looking Lynn knew that he was sitting in the corner chair by the window, brooding in the meager light of one lamp, in a room filled with shadows, and with a mind filled with shadows too. At the top of the stairs she hesitated; a part of her wanted to go down and tell him, in what is called a "civilized" fashion—as if anything as brutal as the termination of a marriage begun in passion and total trust could, no matter how many fine words were summoned, be anything but a devastation—that she was unable to continue this way. But another part of her knew that the attempt would lead to a horrified protest, to apologies and promises, then to tears—her own—and perhaps even more frantic blows. Who could be sure anymore? So she turned about and went to bed.

Every muscle, every nerve, was stretched. There was no sleep in her. Her ears picked up every sound, the swish of a passing car, the far high drone of a plane, and Emily's slippered steps from the bathroom back to her room. Clearly, she constructed tomorrow's departure, the final embrace, the giving of the boarding pass to the attendant, the ponytail and the red nylon carry-on disappearing down the jetway.

"I shall not cry," she said aloud. "I shall send her off with cheer."

And she reminded herself that Emily knew twice as much about the world as she had known at Emily's age. . . .

The screen door clicked shut as Robert brought Juliet inside. A moment later they came upstairs, the dog with tinkling collar tags and Robert with a heavy, dreary tread. Always, his footsteps had revealed his mood, and she knew what was to follow: He would sit down in the darkness and talk.

He began, "I'm sorry about this morning, Lynn. It was nasty, and I know it."

"That it was. Very nasty, and that hardly describes it."

He was probably waiting for her to say more, probably bracing himself for an attack of rage such as she had made in the past; he could not know that she was beyond such agonized rage, far beyond it, that she had reached a tragic conclusion.

Breathing hard, he began again. "It was Emily. I don't think my spirit has ever sunk so low in all my life. It crushed me, Lynn. And so I lashed out. I was beside myself. That's my only excuse."

Yes, she thought, it's your only and your usual excuse. When haven't you had a reason for being "beside yourself"? It's never been your fault, but always somebody else's, usually mine.

"Aren't you going to say something? Yell at me if you want to. But try to understand me too. Please, Lynn. Please."

"I don't feel like yelling. I've had a terrible day."

"I'm sorry." Sighing, he said, "I suppose we just have to tell ourselves that Emily will survive her mistake. What else can we do? What do you think?"

"I'm too tired to think."

Yes, but tomorrow she would weep storms. Weep for Emily, for the turmoil that had thrown her into the arms of Bruce, and for the collapse of this marriage that had been the focus of, the reason for, the central meaning of, her life.

"Maybe I can give you a piece of good news to make up for the rest," Robert said now, speaking almost humbly. "Monacco flew in today. He told me they'll be sending me back across the pond right around the start of the year."

And he waited again, this time no doubt for some enthusiasm or congratulations, but when she gave neither, he resumed, letting his own enthusiasms mount.

"I've been thinking that I should go a month or so ahead of you and get things ready. They have some very comfortable houses with gardens in back, very pleasant. We'd need a furnished place, naturally. I'll have it all cleaned up and ready by the time you arrive with Annie and Bobby. And maybe by that time Emily might—" He broke off.

"I'm tired," Lynn said again. "I really want to sleep."

"Okay."

He turned on the night-light and quietly began to undress. But he was too charged to be still for very long; he was a quivering high-tension wire.

"I've been thinking, too, that we could rent this house. We're not going to spend the rest of our lives in Europe, and we may want to come back right here. We can put everything in storage. What do you think?"

"Fine."

Emily's departure had "crushed him," and yet here he was, hale and strong enough to make his rosy plans. That's called "putting things into perspective," I suppose, thought Lynn. I am so bitter. I am so bitter.

"Did you know that our government sponsors a training program for bankers in Hungary so they can learn investment methods? They have no personnel. No accountants, for instance, a handful in the entire country. It's shocking to us how ignorant they are. Well, a whole generation lived under communism, after all, so all the more of a challenge, I say."

The bed creaked as Robert got in. He moved so near to Lynn that she could smell his shaving lotion. If he touches me, she thought, shuddering, if he touches my breasts, if he kisses me, I'll hit him. I will not be tricked into anything anymore. I will remember my head being slammed against the wall. I will remember Bruce this afternoon. No . . . no, I don't want to remember that.

"Sleeping?" murmured Robert.

"I would if you didn't keep waking me up."

"I'm sorry," he apologized, and turned over.

Yes, tomorrow she would weep storms, tomorrow she would weep for the waste, for the loss of the central meaning of her life. She would set free all the grief that was imploding within the little bony cage where her heart lay, and let it explode instead, to shatter the very walls of this house.

Then, somehow, she would pick herself up and keep going. If Josie could face death with quiet courage, surely she, Lynn, could face life.

On the third day Josie died. On the fourth day they saw her home to her grave. It was Josie's own kind of day; the air was soft after recent rain, pearl-gray clouds hung low, and the smell of wet grass rose among the tombstones. Lynn, almost blindly, read names that were meaningless to her and inscriptions that could only be ineffectual: BELOVED WIFE, DEAR FATHER. For how can a mere adjective describe wretched pain and endless loss?

And always, always, came the pictures: rain pelting the hearse when they followed her mother through the town and uphill to the burial ground; white flowers on Caroline's tiny coffin . . .

"Astonishing," Robert whispered as the crowd gathered. "The whole office staff is here. Half the country club, too, it seems, and they didn't even belong."

"Josie had friends," Lynn said. "Everybody liked her and Bruce."

Bruce's name caught on her tongue. She winced and feared to look at him. He looked like a man of seventy, like a man stricken and condemned.

"My heart, my right hand," she overheard him say to someone offering condolences.

"I know what this means to you," Robert whispered.

"How can you know? You never liked her. You were furious with her."

"Well, she loved you, and I can appreciate that, at least."

Up the small rise people streamed from the parking lot, all kinds and colors and ages of them, the fashionable, the workers and, too, the poor, who must have come to Josie in their need and been comforted, so that they remembered her.

The many voices were muted. All was muted: the spray of cream-colored roses on the coffin, and even the simple language of the prayers, giving thanks for the blessing of Josie's life and the memories she had left to those who loved her.

The brief service came, then, to an end. Too shaken to cry, Lynn looked up into the trees where a flock of crows were making a great stir. And turning her head, she met Tom Lawrence's somber gaze.

"If you need help," Bruce had advised, "ask Tom Lawrence."

"I know women inside out," Tom had told her once. "You'd eat yourself alive with guilt if you ever—"

And Robert took her arm, saying, "Come. It's over." They got into the car and he said, looking almost curious, "You really loved her, didn't you? Funny, I should still be mad at her because of Emily, but what's done is done, and why waste energy? Besides, you'd have to be heartless to look at Bruce's face just now and not feel something. Who knows what goes through a person's head at a time like this? I suppose people recall the times they fought and the things they said that now they wish they hadn't said. But that's only natural. Nobody's perfect. Anyway, he looks like a cadaver. He looks as if he'd been starving himself. He hasn't come to dinner these last few days, and maybe we should keep asking him over for a while until he can straighten himself out."

"That's kind of you," she said, somewhat surprised. And then, induced perhaps by this compassion that he now showed for a man whom he had never liked, she had a sudden insight into herself: If Eudora hadn't been a witness, if Bruce hadn't revealed that he and Josie had always known, might she not have gone on as before, burying the memory, denying it, as indeed she had been doing for years? Maybe she would even have gone on making love to Robert, as he had wanted her to the other night before Emily left, when she had by her silence and immobility rebuffed him. It was an odd, uncertain insight.

They drove on, while Robert ruminated: "I wonder what he'll do now. He's the kind who may never marry again. God forbid, if anything were to happen to you, I never would."

She had to say something. "You can't know that," she said.

"Yes, I can. I know myself. If I had to stand there in that awful cemetery the way he just did and watch you—I can't even say it."

She was thinking: He will suffer when I leave.

"I suppose he'll just go back to the office in a couple of days, back to his old plodding routine."

She thought then: But Robert will have his work. He will get the news, be stunned and furious, and suffer most awfully. She saw him now as clearly as if it had already happened; standing in some strange room on a strange street with a view, perhaps, of cobblestones and medieval towers, he would open her long, sad, careful letter; in expectation of loving words, he would start to read and, not believing his own senses, would read again. . . . And someday he would become the head of the company and have all the glory he so dearly wanted.

Her hands, faintly brown, lay on her lap. When she turned them over, the scars, smooth, white pinhead spots, were unmistakable. And on her cheek this morning, the thin red cut was just closing.

She turned her head to look at Robert, at the lean, fine face. He had scarcely changed. He was as fascinating as he had been when she first had seen him. For her there was something aphrodisiac about the white collar and the dark suit as, so many women admit, there is about a military uniform.

What you have done to me, to us! she thought. You had so much, we had so much, and could have kept it, but you have thrown it away. What you have done with your filthy rage!

The house was bleak. Almost it seemed a dangerous place with hazards and avoidances, as if one were walking through a minefield.

First there was Annie, who, fresh from scout camp, where unfortunately she had not lost a pound, had to be faced with two stupendous changes, the departure of Emily and the death of Josie. The matter of Emily was eased by some telephone calls, but the matter of Josie could only be eased, it seemed, by Bruce.

Lynn drove her to his house, where she spent the day and came out looking relatively cheerful in spite of her swollen eyelids.

"Uncle Bruce said it's all right to cry. He said after I've cried, I'll feel better, and I do. He said Aunt Josie wouldn't want me to be too sad. She'd want me to remember nice things about her, but she'd mainly want me to do good work in school and have friends and be happy. Why didn't you come inside, Mom?"

"I had a lot of errands, and Bobby's cutting a tooth. He's cranky."

"I think you should tell Uncle Bruce to come to dinner. There's nothing in his refrigerator."

"No? What did you have for lunch?"

"He opened a can of beans."

"He hasn't got his appetite back. It's much too soon."

"Aren't you going to tell him to have dinner with us?"

"He'll come when he's ready."

If Lynn knew anything at all about Bruce, she knew he would never be ready. The prospect of sitting down to dinner, the two of them facing Robert, would be as dismaying to him as it was to her.

"Do you suppose he'll get married now that Aunt Josie's dead?" asked Annie.

"How on earth should I know that?" And then, because she had shown such irritation at the question, Lynn made amends. "How about taking Bobby up the road in the stroller? He'd like that. He adores you."

The adoration was mutual, for Annie's reply was prompt. "Okay! You know I'm still the only person in my class who's got a new baby at home?"

"Oh? That makes you sort of special, doesn't it?"

That night Robert said, "I've been making inquiries about schools for Annie. We should really prepare her now and get her used to the idea. We don't want a too sudden disruption at midterm."

Lynn replied quickly, "Not now. She hasn't been back at school a week yet. Leave her alone for a while."

"I suppose you've heard from our other daughter?"

The tone had a knife edge, a serrated knife edge, she thought, saying calmly, "Yes. She likes the place. She's taking biology, of course, sociology, psychology—"

Robert stopped her, raising the newspaper like a fence in front of his face.

"I don't want the details of her curriculum, Lynn."

"Are you never going to relent?" she asked.

The newspaper crackled angrily as he shifted it. "Don't pin me down. 'Never' is a long time."

A bleak house indeed.

As she drove back from a PTA meeting, Lynn's mind was filled not with its agenda, the school fair and back-to-school night, but with her own uncertainties. Would she be staying in this house? Almost certainly not, for Robert would hardly support a place like this one after she had left him. So there would be a new home to prepare; should it be here where the family's roots had gradually been taking hold, or would it be better to turn to the older, deeper roots in the Midwest?

And then there loomed the larger, ominous problem: the severance itself. She had no experience at all with the law. How exactly did one go about this severance? Here on the road, dancing ahead of the car, she seemed to see a swirling cloud of doubt and menace, rising like some dark genie released from its jar.

The road curved. She was not often in this part of town, but she recognized a turreted Victorian house.

"It has two hideous stone lions at the foot of the driveway," Tom Lawrence had said. "Take the next left after you pass it. I'm a quarter of a mile from the turn."

The genie threatened to tower over the car, to descend and crush it. . . . Lynn broke into a chill and a sweat; she drove left beyond the lions and drew up in breathless fear before Tom's house.

It had not occurred to her, unthinking as she was just then, that he might not be home. But his car was there, and he answered her ring. She was taken aback at the sight of him. It had been crazy to come here, yet it would have been crazier to turn now and run.

"I was just passing," she said.

That was absurd, and she knew it as she was saying it.

"Well, then, come in. Or rather, come in and out again. It's too beautiful to be indoors. Shall we sit in the sun or the shade?"

"It doesn't matter." The chill wanted sun, while the sweat wanted shade.

He was wearing tennis whites, and a racket lay on a table alongside an open book. A bed of perennials, of delphinium, phlox, and cosmos, pink and blue and mauve, bordered the terrace; from a little pool lying in a grotto came the cool trickle of a tiny fountain. Upon this peace she had intruded, and she was too embarrassed to explain herself.

"An unexpected visit. An unexpected pleasure," Tom said, smiling.

"Now that I'm here, I feel a fool. I'm sorry. I don't really know why I came."

"I do. You're in trouble, and you need a friend. Isn't that so?"

Her eyes filled, and she blinked. Considerately, Tom gazed out toward the garden.

When she was able, she said in a low, tremulous voice, "I am going to leave Robert."

Tom turned quickly. "A mutual agreement, or are you adversaries?"

A lawyer's questions, Lynn thought, and said aloud, "He doesn't know yet. And he will not agree, you may be sure."

"Then you'll need a very good lawyer."

"You told me once that if I ever needed help, I should call you."

"I meant it. I don't take matrimonial cases anymore, but I'll get you somebody who does."

"You don't seem surprised. No, of course you aren't. You're thinking of my invitation to our golden wedding."

Mechanically, she twisted the straps of her handbag and, in the same low voice, continued, "He struck me. But this time something different happened. I knew I couldn't—I know I can't—I can't take it again."

He nodded.

"I know you think I'm stupid to have put up with what I did. One reads all those articles about battered women and thinks, 'You idiots! What are you waiting for?' "

"They're not idiots. There are a hundred different reasons why they stay as long as they do. Surely," Tom said gently, "you can think of some very cogent reasons yourself. In your own case—"

She interrupted. "In my own case I never thought of myself as a battered woman."

"You didn't want to. You thought of yourself as a romantic woman."

"Oh, yes! I loved him. . . ."

"From a woman's point of view I daresay he's a very attractive man. A powerful man. Admired."

"I wish I could understand it. He can be so loving and, sometimes, so hard. Poor Emily—" And briefly she related, without mention of the pregnancy, what had occurred.

Tom commented, "That sounds just like Bruce's generosity. You've seen him since the funeral, of course."

"No."

"Now I am surprised, close as you've been."

Close, she thought, wincing.

"I don't think he wants to see me," she said, and at once corrected this slip of the tongue. "To see anyone yet, I meant."

Tom inquired curiously whether Bruce knew of her plans.

"I haven't really made them yet," she evaded. "I've only been thinking about them. Robert will be sent abroad in a couple of months. He will go ahead of the rest of us, and I thought I would send him a letter with my decision."

"That gets complicated. Wouldn't it be better to have it all out now and have the wheels turning before he leaves?"

"No. He'll be crushed as it is—but if I do it now, he'll never leave, and his chance will be lost. This chance is all he talks about. I can't be that cruel. I can't destroy him utterly."

She was still twisting the strap of her purse. Tom reached over and put the purse on the table.

"Let me get you a drink. Liquor or no liquor? Personally, I think you could use a stiff drink."

"Nothing. Nothing, thank you."

They had sat on either side of the fireplace. The white cat had wound itself around his ankle. He had stirred his brandy. And after the brandy . . .

"So in spite of everything you don't want to hurt him. You still feel something," Tom said.

"Feel! Oh, yes. How can I not, after twenty years?" She had not expected to weep, to make a scene. Nevertheless, tears came now in a flood. "I can't believe this is happening. These last days have been a nightmare."

Tom got up and went into the house. When he returned, he held a damp washcloth, with which, most tenderly, he wiped Lynn's face. Like a child or a patient she submitted, talking all the while.

"I should be ashamed of myself to come here and bother you. I should solve my own problem. God knows I'm old enough. It's ridiculous, it's stupid to be talking like this. . . . But I'm miserable. Though why shouldn't I be? Millions of other people are miserable. Am I any different? Nobody ever said life is supposed to be all wine and roses."

She started to get up. "I'm all right, Tom. See, I've stopped crying. I'm not going to cry anymore. I'm going home. I apologize."

"No, you're too agitated." Tom pressed her shoulders back against the chair. "Stay here until you wind down. You don't have to talk unless you want to."

A cloud passed over the sun, dimming the garden's colors, quieting the nerves. And she said more calmly, "The truth is, I'm afraid, Tom. How is it that I'm determined to do this, and at the same time I'm so scared? I don't want to face life alone. I'm too young to live without love. And there may never be anyone else who will love me."

"What makes you think that?"

"I'm almost forty, and I have responsibilities, a baby, a teenager who can be troublesome, and Emily. And it's not as if I had a career or were free with an independent fortune and were a ravishing beauty besides."

Tom smiled. "I know one man who thinks you are. Bruce thinks so."

A flush tingled up Lynn's neck into her face. If Tom had told her this two weeks ago, she would have shrugged. "Oh," she would have said, "Bruce is as prejudiced in my favor as if I were his sister." But such a reply would have stuck in her throat if she were to try it now.

"I just realized," Tom said, "that I've made a tactless remark. I've said 'one man'—although," he added with his usual mischievous twinkling around the eyes, "I myself wouldn't really call you 'ravishing' either. It sounds too rouged and curly, too flirtatious, to suit a lovely woman like you."

"I'm not lovely," she protested, feeling stubborn. "My daughter Emily is. You saw her. She looks like Robert."

"Oh, yes, oh, yes. Robert's your standard, I see that." The rebuke was rough. "Get your mirror out."

She was puzzled. "Why?"

"Get it out. Here's your purse. Now look at yourself," he commanded, "and tell me what you see."

"A woman's who's distraught and dreary. That's what I see."

"That will pass. When it does, you will be—well, almost beautiful. It's true that your face is a shade too wide at the cheekbones, at least for some tastes. And maybe your nose is too short." Tilting his head to study her from another angle, he frowned slightly, as if he were criticizing a work of art. "It's interesting, though, that you have dark lashes when your hair's so light."

"Don't tease me, Tom. I'm too unhappy."

"All right, I was teasing. I thought I could tease you out of your mood, but I was wrong. What I really want is to rejoice with you, Lynn. You're finally going to end this phase of your life, get strong, and go on to something better."

"I'm going to end this phase, that's true. But as to the rest, I just don't know." She looked at her watch. "I have to go. I like to be home when Annie gets out of school."

"How's Annie doing?"

"Well, I worry. I always feel uneasy. But at least there haven't been any more episodes. No running away, thank God. She seems calm enough. And Robert has been doing all right with her. As a matter of fact, he's so tired and busy, so preoccupied these last few weeks with his big promotion, that he doesn't have much time for her or anything else."

Not even for sex, she thought wryly, and I don't know what I shall do when he does make an attempt.

Sunk as she was in the deep lounge chair, she had to struggle upward. Tom pulled her and, not relinquishing her hands, admonished her.

"I want you to be everything you can be. Listen to me. You're too good a human being to be so unhappy." Then he took her face between his hands and kissed her gently on the forehead. "You're a lovely woman, very, very attractive. Robert knows it too. That's why he was so furious when he came here and saw you dancing that night."

"I can barely think. My head's whirling," she whispered.

"Of course it is. Go home, Lynn, and call me when you need me. But the sooner you leave him, the better, in my opinion. Don't wait too long."

In a state of increasing confusion she started for home. What did she feel for Tom? What did he feel for her? Twice now her need for comfort and support had led to a complication—in Bruce's case rather more than a "complication"!

But then, as she drove on through the leafy afternoon, she began to have some other thoughts, among them a memory that loosened her lips and even produced a wan little smile.

"I wish you would marry Tom," Annie had said once when she was at odds with Robert. "Of course, you could marry Uncle Bruce if he didn't already have Aunt Josie."

It was the babble of a child, and yet there was, for a woman in limbo, a certain sense of security in knowing that at least two men were out there in the great unknown world of strangers who found her attractive, and she would not be going totally unarmed into that world.

And she asked herself whether anyone, at the start of this short summer, could have imagined where they would all be at its waning. On graduation day Emily had been on a straight course to Yale, or so it had seemed; Josie had been smiling her congratulations, and now she was dead; Robert and Lynn, husband and wife, had sat together holding hands.

Robert, home early, explained, "I decided to call it a day at the office and shop for luggage. We haven't nearly enough. I was thinking, maybe we should buy a couple of trunks to send the bulk of our stuff on ahead. What do you think?"

It was strange that he could look at her and talk of normal things without seeing the change in her. "We have plenty of time," she said.

"Well, but there's no sense leaving things to the last minute either."

A while later Emily telephoned. "Mom, I just got back from my sociol-

ogy lecture, and what do you think the subject was? Abused women."
Her voice was urgent and agitated. "Oh, Mom! What are you waiting
for? The lesson is: They never change. This is *your life,* the only one you'll
ever have, for heaven's sake. And if you've been staying on because of us,
as I believe you have, you're wrong. I have nightmares now, I see your
scarred hands and the bruise on your face. Do you want Annie to find
out too?"

"I told you what I'm going to do," Lynn said. "And if you have any
feeling that you're responsible for my staying, you're mistaken. I've
stayed this long because I loved him, Emily."

Neither spoke until Emily, her voice barely breaking, said, so that
Lynn knew she was in tears, "My father, my father . . ."

There was another silence until Lynn responded, "Darling, if it's the
last thing I do, I'll take care of you all. I will."

"Not me. Don't worry about me, just Annie and Bobby."

"All right, darling, I won't worry about you."

Nineteen, and she really believes she doesn't need anybody anymore.

"Have you seen Uncle Bruce? How is he?"

She dreaded a face-to-face meeting with Bruce. It would be stiff and
strange. . . . It would be guilty. . . . "Not for the last few days. He's
doing as well as one might expect," she answered.

"Be sure to give him my love."

When she had hung up the phone, Lynn sat for a little while watching
darkness creep across the floor. From upstairs in Bobby's room came the
sound of Annie, singing. Bobby, delighted with this attention, would be
holding on to the crib's railing while he bounced. Annie's high voice was
still childish, so that its song at that moment was especially poignant.

A juggler must feel as I do now, Lynn told herself, when he steps out
onto the stage to start his act. One ball missed, and they would all come
tumbling. . . .

"But I shall not miss," she said aloud.

Eudora was waiting for her in the garage when Lynn came home with the
groceries.

"Mrs. Ferguson! Mrs. Ferguson," she called even before the engine
had been shut off. "They want you at the school, somebody telephoned
about Annie—no, no, she's not sick, they said don't be scared, they need
to talk to you, that's all."

Everything in the body from the head down sinks to the feet; so went
Lynn's thought. Yet she was able to speak with uncommon quietness.

"They said she's all right?"

"Oh, yes. They wouldn't lie, Mrs. Ferguson."

Perhaps, though, they would. They might well want to break bad news gently. . . .

But Annie was sitting in the principal's office when Lynn rushed in. The first thing she saw was a tear-smeared face and a blouse ripped open down the front.

Mr. Siropolous began, "We've had some trouble here today, Mrs. Ferguson, a fight in the schoolyard at recess, and I had to call you. For one thing, Annie refuses to ride home on the school bus."

Lynn, with her first fears relieved, sat down beside her child.

"Yes, you look as if you've been in a fight. Can you tell me about it?"

Annie shook her head, and Lynn sighed. "You don't want to ride home in the bus with the girl, is that it? I'm assuming it's a girl."

Annie folded her lips shut.

"Don't be stubborn," Lynn said, speaking still mildly. "Mr. Siropolous and I only want to help you. Tell us what happened."

The folded lips only tightened, while Annie stared at the floor. The principal, who looked tired, urged with slight impatience, "Do answer your mother."

Lynn stood up and grasped Annie firmly by the shoulders. "This is ridiculous, Annie. You're too old to be stubborn."

"It seems," Mr. Siropolous said now, "that some of the girls were taunting Annie about something. She punched one of them in the face, and there was a scuffle until Mr. Dawes managed to separate them."

In dismay Lynn repeated, "She punched a girl in the face!"

"Yes. The girl is all right, but of course we can't allow such behavior. Besides, it's not like Annie. Not like you at all, Annie," he said, kindly now.

Lynn was ashamed, and the shame made her stern.

"This is horrible, Annie," she chided. "To lose your temper like that, no matter what anyone said, is horrible."

At that the child, clenching her pathetic little fists, burst forth. "You don't know what they said! They were laughing at me. They were all laughing at me."

"About what, about what?" asked the two bewildered adults.

"They said—'Your father hits your mother all the time, and everybody knows it. Your father hits your mother.'" Annie wailed. "And they were laughing at me!"

Mr. Siropolous looked for an instant at Lynn and looked away.

"Of course it's not true," Lynn said firmly.

"I told them it was a lie, Mom, I told them, but they wouldn't listen. Susan said she heard her mother tell her father. They wouldn't let me talk, so I hit Susan because she was the worst, and I hate her anyway."

Lynn took a handkerchief from her purse, with a hand that shook wiped Annie's face, and said, still firmly, "Children—people—do sometimes say things that hurt most terribly and aren't true, Annie. And I can understand why you were angry. But still you shouldn't have hit Susan. What is to be done, do you think, Mr. Siropolous?"

For a moment he deliberated. "Perhaps tomorrow you and Susan, maybe some others, too, will meet in my office and apologize to each other, they for things they said, and you for punching. We'll talk together about peace, as they do at the United Nations. In this school we do not speak or act unkindly. How does that sound to you, Mrs. Ferguson?"

"A very good idea. Very fair." The main thing was to get out of there as quickly as possible. "And now we'd better get home. Come, Annie. Thank you, Mr. Siropolous. I'm awfully sorry this happened. But I suppose you must be used to these little—little upsets."

"Yes, yes, it's all part of growing up, I'm afraid," said the principal, who, also pleased to end the affair as quickly as possible, was politely holding the door open.

"She's such a good child," he murmured to Lynn as they went out. "Don't worry. This will pass over."

"Susan," Lynn reflected aloud when they were in the car. "Susan who? Perhaps I know her mother from PTA?"

"She's awful. She thinks she's beautiful, but she isn't. She's growing pimples. Her aunt lives across the road."

"Across our road?"

"Mrs. Stevens," Annie said impatiently. "Mrs. Stevens across the road."

Lynn, making the swift connection, frowned. But Lieutenant Weber had told the Stevenses that night that there was nothing wrong. . . .

"She's afraid of dogs, the stupid thing. I'm going to send Juliet over to scare her the next time she visits."

Needing some natural, light response, Lynn laughed. "I don't really think anybody would be afraid of our clumsy, flop-eared Juliet."

"You're wrong. She was scared to death the day Juliet followed Eudora to the Stevenses. She screamed, and Eudora had to hold Juliet by the collar."

"Oh? Eudora visits the Stevenses?"

"Not them. The lady who comes to clean their house is Eudora's best friend."

Was that then the connection, or had it been only Weber, or was it both? It surprised her that no hot resentment was rising now toward whomever it was who had spread the news. People would always spread news; it was quite natural; she had done it often enough herself.

Then came a sudden startling query. "But, Mom—did Dad ever?"

"Ever what?"

"Do what Susan said," Annie mumbled.

"Of course not. How can you ask?"

"Because he gets so angry sometimes."

"That has nothing to do with what Susan said. Nothing."

"Are you sure, Mom?"

"Quite sure, Annie."

An audible sigh came from the child. And Lynn had to ask herself how she would set about explaining the separation when it came, how she might explain it without telling the whole devastating truth; some of it, yes, but spare the very worst.

Well, when the time came, and it was approaching fast, some instinct would certainly show her the way, she assured herself now. But for the present she could feel only a deep and tired resignation.

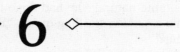

6

THE baby was being dried after his evening bath when Robert, hours late, came home. Lynn, stooping beside the tub, was aware of his presence in the doorway behind her, but did not turn to greet him; the time for loving welcomes was past, and she waited for him to speak first, after which she would give her civil response.

"I'm home," he said.

Then some quality in his voice made her glance up, and she saw that he looked like death. He had opened his collar and loosened his tie; he, Robert Ferguson, to be disheveled like that in the commuter train!

"What's the matter?" she cried.

"You will not believe it," he said.

"I will believe it if you tell me."

"Ask Annie to put Bobby to bed. She won't mind. And come downstairs. I need a drink."

He's ill, she thought, that's what it is. They've told him he has cancer or is going blind. Pity, shuddering and chill, ran through her.

"Glenfiddich. Toss it down," he said, as if he were talking to himself. "And toss another."

The bottle made a little clink on the silver tray. He sat down.

"Well, Lynn, I've news. General American Appliance and I are finished. Parted. Through."

"Through?" she repeated, echoing the word that had, in the instant, no meaning.

"I didn't get the promotion, so I quit. That's why I'm late. I was cleaning out my desk."

"I don't understand," she said.

He stood up and walked to the long bow window that faced the road and the lighted lantern at the foot of the Stevenses' long drive. Like a sentry on duty he spun around, walked the length of the room to the opposite window, and stood there looking out into the dark lawn and the darker bulk of the hill beyond. When he turned again to face Lynn, she saw that his eyes were bright with tears. Then he sat down and began to talk in rapid, staccato bursts.

"Yes, cleaning out my desk. Twenty-three years of my life. And do you know how I got the news? In the elevator coming back to the office late in the afternoon. I hadn't been there all day. I'd gone straight from the train to an appointment. And a couple of kids were talking, clerks or mailroom kids; they didn't even recognize me. They were talking about Budapest, and Bruce Lehman going there to head the office. It sounded crazy. I didn't pay any attention to it, except to be amused. And then Warren called me in. He showed me a fax from Monacco, and I saw it was true. And still I couldn't believe it."

Robert put his hands over his face. His elbows rested on his knees, and his head sank. She was staring at a beaten man, as out of place in this rich room as any beggar sprawled upon marble stairs.

"I told him there had to be some ridiculous mistake, that everybody knew it had been promised to me. Why Lehman? It made no sense. I said I wanted to speak to Monacco then and there. So Warren phoned California, but we didn't reach Monacco. I demanded that Warren tell me what he knew. I wasn't going to spend a sleepless night trying to figure out what had gone wrong. Damn! It'll be a sleepless night anyway."

And again, Robert got up to pace the length of the room. At the mantel he paused to adjust the Herend figurines, which Eudora had moved when she dusted.

"I remember the day I bought these," he said. "I thought I had the world at my feet. I did have it too. Excuse me. These damn tears. I'm ashamed that you should see them."

"There's nothing to be ashamed of, Robert. A man has a right to show his grief too."

She spoke softly, not out of compassion alone, but also out of her own bewilderment in the face of this stunning complication.

"And Warren? Did he tell you why?"

"Oh, yes. Oh, yes. He was delicate about it, you know, very much the gentleman. But how he was enjoying it! He's home now, I'll bet on it, regaling his wife or maybe the crowd at the club, with the story. God, as hard as I've worked, brought marketing farther along than anyone else had ever done; and what has Lehman ever accomplished compared with me? A drudge, without imagination—"

"You haven't told me the reason," Lynn said patiently.

"The reason? Oh, yes. I said he was delicate about it. Very tactful. It seems that people—that someone has been saying things, personal things, exaggerations—God! Everybody, every marriage, has problems of one sort or another, problems that people overcome, put behind them. I told him the stuff bore no resemblance to reality, none at all. What right anyway do strangers have to draw conclusions about what goes on between a man and his wife? You'd think a man like Monacco would have more sense than to listen to idle gossip."

"Idle," Lynn murmured, so faintly that he did not hear her.

All the whispering had united into one tearing shout, loud enough to reach to California. It was a confirmation of sorts, but useless to her, for to what end would it lead? And her path that had seemed so clear, though painful, had brought her into a blind alley.

"Would you believe a man like Monacco could stoop so low? What have I done that's so terrible, after all?" When she was silent, a note of faint suspicion came into his voice. "I wonder who could have spread this dirty stuff. You couldn't—you didn't ever run to the Lehmans with anything, did you?"

She interrupted. "Don't dare say such a thing to me!"

"Ah, well, I believe you. But then, how and who?"

The question hung between them, and he was expecting an answer, but she was numb and could give none. In all this horror there was the kind of fascination that draws a person unwillingly to look at an accident, to stare at bloody wreckage.

Robert resumed, "Warren said—and he was speaking for Monacco 'according to instructions,' he said, that of course I was free to stay on in my present position. 'Of course,' " Robert mocked.

"And you're not going to," she said, recognizing the mockery.

"Good God, Lynn! I wrote out my resignation then and there. What do you take me for? After a slap in the face like that, do you think I could stay on? While Bruce Lehman enjoys the reward that belongs to me?"

"Bruce never wanted it," she said.

"He's damn well accepted it now."

The world is spinning around me, and I make no sense of it, Lynn thought. Then, for want of something to say, she inquired, "Are you sure you're doing the right thing by leaving?"

"No doubt of it. Anyhow, they want me to go, don't you see that? They'd find a way to ease me out. They'd make it so miserable that I'd want to leave." Robert's face contorted itself into the mask of tragedy, with cheeks puffed, brows upward drawn, and mouth gaping. "I'm ruined, Lynn! Destroyed. Disgraced. Thrown out like trash, a piece of trash."

It was all true. He had done it to himself, but it was still true. What could she, what should she, say? She could think of nothing but some trivial creature comfort.

"Shall I fix you something? You've had no dinner."

"I can't eat." He looked at the clock. "It's half past eight. Not too late to see Bruce. Come on."

"See Bruce? But why?"

"To offer congratulations, naturally."

Dismayed, she sought a sensible objection. "He won't want us to visit. We'll be intruding, Robert."

"Nonsense. He'll appreciate congratulations. We'll bring a bottle of champagne."

"No, no. He's in mourning. It's not fitting," she protested.

"This has nothing to do with Bruce's mourning. It's a question of Robert Ferguson's honor and good taste, of his sportsmanship. I want him to see that I can take this like a man."

"Why torture yourself to make a point, Robert? A phone call will do as well."

"No. Get the champagne. He can chill it in his freezer for half an hour."

Silently she asked: Whom are you fooling with this show of bravado? By your own admission you're dying inside.

"If it's a celebration you want," she said, not unkindly, "button your collar and change your tie. It's stained."

Bruce wouldn't care, but Robert would see himself in a mirror and be appalled.

She had not been in Bruce's house since that day. He had been reading when they arrived; the book was in his hand when he opened the door. The evening was cold and windy, a harbinger of winter, and apparently he had been using Josie's knitted afghan on the very sofa where they had lain together, where he had covered her nakedness with that afghan.

And she wondered whether the same thought was in his mind, too, and could not look at him or at the sofa, but made instead a show of greeting the white cat.

Bruce asked whether they would mind if he saved the wine for another time together, explaining, "I am not quite up to it. It's been a rather bad day for me, Robert."

"Now, why should that be?"

"It's very simple. The post was yours. You earned it, and it should have gone to you."

Robert shrugged. "That's generous of you, Bruce, but it wasn't in the cards, that's all."

The remark was almost flippant; it could have aroused compassion for its attempt at bravery, or, given the fact that the others present knew why "it wasn't in the cards," it could arouse anger.

Bruce, though, was compassionate. "I have to tell you that I'm overwhelmed. It won't be easy to follow in your footsteps, Robert. I only hope I can do the job."

"I'll be available for advice if you need it anytime. It might be a good idea for you to come over one night soon and let me give you some background on what's already been done over there."

"Well, thanks, but not just yet. This has come down on me like a ton of bricks, while I'm still buried under a mountain of bricks. I'm not thinking very clearly."

"I understand," Robert said sympathetically.

"At least, though, this will force me to get away. I'd been wishing there was someplace where I could get away from myself, Outer Mongolia, maybe, or the South Pole. So now it's to be Hungary. Not that it makes any difference where. I'll still be taking myself with myself, and myself's pretty broken down."

Bruce had not given Lynn a glance, but now he turned fully toward her and made a request.

"I'm worried about Barney." The cat, lying curled in front of the fireplace, looked like a heap of snow. At hearing his name he raised his head. "I can't take him with me, and Josie would haunt me for the rest of my days if I didn't get a good home for him. So do you suppose you could take him, Lynn? I don't want to give you any more work or any problem, but I'm stumped."

"You don't know Lynn if you can say that," Robert declared. "She'd take in any four-legged creature you can name."

"Of course I will," Lynn said quickly.

"No, you don't know Lynn," repeated Robert.

But he does know Lynn, and very well too. The words, on the tip of her tongue, came so close to slipping out that she was shocked.

"What's your schedule?" Robert asked.

"Sometime in December, I think." And Bruce said again, "It's all so sudden. . . . I'll keep Barney till I go. . . . It's good of you. . . . I'm grateful. . . . Josie would be grateful."

"He's in a fog. He'll never measure up. Doesn't know what he's in for," Robert said when they left.

At home he resumed his agitated pacing, saying, "He'll never measure up."

Annie came quietly into the room, so quietly that they were startled by her voice.

"What's wrong? Has something awful happened? Is Emily sick again?"

Robert made a choking sound. "Oh, Annie. Oh, my little girl, no, Emily's well, thank God. Thank God, we're all well." And pulling Annie to him, he kissed the top of her head and held her, saying tenderly, "I'll find a way to take care of you. They think they've ruined me, but they can't crush my spirit, no—" He began to weep.

"You're terrifying her!" Lynn cried. "Daddy's upset, Annie, because of some trouble at work. He's leaving the firm. He's upset."

The child wriggled free of Robert and stared at him as if she had never seen him before. A variety of expressions moved across her face, ranging through curiosity and distaste to fear.

"I need to talk to Emily," Robert said. "Get me her number, Lynn."

"You'll scare her to death too. Wait till you calm down."

"I'm calm," he said through his tears. "I'm calm. I need to talk to her, to tell her I'm sorry. We're a family, we make mistakes, we have to stand together now. What's the number, Annie?"

If I hadn't seen how little he drank of it, I would have said it's the Scotch, Lynn thought.

"Emily, Emily," Robert was saying into the telephone. "No, don't be frightened, we're all right here, it's just that I quit GAA. It's a long story, too long to explain over the phone, but—excuse me, I'm very emotional at the moment, I feel that the stars have fallen—But I'm going to pull myself together and I—well, I want to apologize, to straighten things out between you and me. I've been heartsick over the situation. I want to apologize for not understanding you, not trying to understand. I just want to say, don't worry about the tuition, I'll pay it, I'm not broke yet. You just stay there and do your work and God bless you, darling. I love you, Emily. I'm so proud of you. Tell me, how's Harris?"

Later, in their bedroom, he became subdued, sighing and questioning, "Tell me, do I—do we—deserve this? I wanted everything for you, and now—now what?"

In bed he turned and, pulling her gently from where she had been lying with her back toward him, drew her close. And she knew it was assurance that he wanted, a bodily relief from tension, some sweet recompense for loss. He wanted proof that he was still a man, her man. Had he asked this of her even a few hours ago, before disaster had befallen him, she would, she knew, have scratched and fought him. Now, though, she hadn't the heart to inflict another hurt; what did it matter, after all? A woman could lie like a stone and feel nothing. In a few minutes it would be over, anyway.

So often during these past weeks she had imagined the humbling of Robert Ferguson, and yet now that he had been humbled beyond imagining, the sight was almost too dreadful to be borne. And she felt his pain as if she were herself inside his skin.

In the tight little world of the company, many of whose officers lived in the town, news spread. On Saturday in the supermarket a group of women had obviously been talking about the Fergusons, because when they saw Lynn, they stopped and abruptly gave an unusually cordial greeting.

Not that it makes any difference, she thought, and it's probably absurd of me to ask, yet I have to know how this happened. And going to a pay phone, she telephoned Tom. Perhaps he would know; if he did not, he would find out.

"It's about Robert. Have you heard that he's left the firm? They found out that . . ." Her voice quavered.

"Yes, I know. Come over, Lynn. I'm home all morning."

In the large room where the table had glittered on that night from which the present trouble had stemmed, she felt suddenly very small. She felt like a petitioner.

"How did you hear?" she asked.

"Monacco phoned me. He's always had the impression, for some unfathomable reason, that Robert and I are close friends."

"But why did he phone you? To ask or to tell?"

"Both. He told me that a letter had come to him, and he asked me whether the accusations in it were true, whether I knew anything about them."

"A letter," Lynn echoed.

"I don't know who sent it. It was a woman's letter, anonymous. But it sounded authentic, Monacco said, as if the wife of one of the firm's officers had written it. It had a good deal of corroborating evidence, one thing being a report from some neighbors."

Tom lowered his eyes to study his shoes before saying anything further. Then, looking directly at Lynn, as if he had had to consider the decision to say more, he continued, "It was about what happened the night you came here to make dinner."

"An anonymous letter. How dirty!"

She was thinking rapidly: Who, except the Stevenses, could have known what happened that night? And they were related to that child Susan's family. And Eudora, who had seen too much, was a friend of the woman who worked for the Stevenses.

"And since the letter said there'd been a call to the police, Monacco had a check made."

Weber. He hadn't "buried" it, after all. Weber had wanted to get back at Robert for the things Robert had said.

"So they made the check and found that there had indeed been a complaint, and that somebody in the police department had tried to hide it, had actually hidden it, as a matter of fact."

Then she had misjudged Weber. At once guilty and pitying, she asked Tom, "Did he get into trouble, the man who had hidden it?"

"No. The police chief is a friend of mine, and we had a talk."

"Then you know about Emily and his son," she said softly.

"Nothing except that they've been going together." Tom smiled. "Do they still say 'going steady'? My teenage vocabulary is definitely out of date."

"I don't really know. It's all a tangle," lamented Lynn.

Tom nodded. "*Tangled* is the word. Even the cop at the club knew all about it. He used to be my gardener before he joined the police force, and he tells me things. You'd be surprised how many people know about Robert, things true and untrue. That's what happens in these towns; you find your way into the stream of gossip, and soon everybody knows what kind of breakfast cereal you eat."

"The meanness of it!"

It seemed to her as if, in exposing Robert, the slack-tongued mob, inquisitive and gloating, had exposed them all, herself and the girls and even the baby boy. Anger exploded, and she protested, "You would think people might find better things to do than to probe into other people's trouble!"

"You would think, but that's not the way it is." And Tom added, "Monacco won't tolerate scandal, you see, not even the slightest."

"It isn't fair! The thing's all blown out of proportion. It's between Robert and me, anyway, isn't it? Not GAA, or the town. Why should any wrong done to me affect his job? Why?" she ended, demanding.

Tom's expression, as he raised his eyebrows and shook his head, seemed to be saying, I give up!

"Oh, you think I'm naive?"

"Yes, very. Corporations have an image, Lynn. There's morale to maintain. How can you get respect from a subordinate when your own behavior is—shall we say 'shady'?"

"All right, it was a silly question. All right."

Then, following Tom's glance, she became aware that she had been twisting her rings, working her nervous fingers on her lap. And she planted her hands firmly on the arms of the chair. But she ought to go home; having heard what she had, there was nothing more to wait for.

"Monacco was really distressed," Tom said gently. "This isn't anything a man likes to do to someone he admires. And of course he said what you might expect, that this was the last thing he would have believed of Robert, as brilliant as he is, with such a future ahead."

"Like seeing a murderer's picture in the paper, I suppose. 'Oh, my, he's got such a nice face!' Is that it?" And Lynn's fingers went back to the rings, twirling and twisting.

Tom reached over and held one of her hands quietly. "It's the devil for you, I know."

"One has to ache for Robert, regardless of everything. He can't sleep, just walks around the house all night, upstairs and down. He barely eats. He looks older by ten years. The rejection . . . The humiliation . . ."

"Especially because Bruce is the one who got his place?"

"Well, naturally. He certainly never thought that Bruce, of all people, could be his competition."

"Why do you say 'of all people'?"

"I didn't say it, Robert did. He always said Bruce was not competitive."

"He was dead wrong. When the Hungarian project was first conceived, Bruce was right up among the top prospects."

"How do you know all this? Even if you're connected with Monacco, you still don't work for GAA. So how do you know?"

"I never did know or care about GAA. But this one time I made it my business to. I wanted Robert to get a promotion. I did it for you."

At that Lynn slipped her hand out of his so quickly that he, too, spoke quickly.

"I knew, it didn't take much to see, in spite of your protests, Lynn, that the marriage wouldn't last. And then you'd be needing a decent settlement. Courts aren't giving much to wives these days."

The room was absolutely quiet. A phone rang somewhere in the house and stopped when Tom did not answer it. A man passing on the walk outside gave a rumbling laugh, and a woman laughed in return. Then the sound faded. So people were still finding humor in the world! The thought came to her that she might never again have anything to laugh about. And another thought came, a questioning: If I were free now, unencumbered by events, would I accept this humorous, quirky, kindly man who's sitting here carefully looking at his shoes again and not at me? Surely his last words meant something: *I did it for you.*

"How good you are!" she exclaimed, and would have said more, but was fearful of tears.

"Well," he said. "Well, I like to set things straight. Lawyers, you know. They're orderly. So tell me, where do we go from here? Or I should say first, where do you go?"

"Where can I go, Tom? The man is ill. He begs forgiveness—oh, not only for the bad things, but for his failure. There's been very little money put aside. I was surprised how little. He needs a position, he'll need one soon, but first he'll have to get back some pride and courage. He wants to move away from here, to start fresh. I don't know. I don't know anything. I'm sick at heart myself, Tom. It's a whole strange, sad new page. He's so humble, so changed."

"No, Lynn. He's not changed."

"You can't say that. You haven't seen him. On the telephone, talking to Emily, he sobbed."

"I don't need to see him. You're too good," Tom said. "That's the trouble."

"Does one step on a person when he's already fallen down?"

Tom did not answer, and she hid her face in her hands, thinking that Tom, after all, couldn't know what was churning inside her. Twenty years together, with so much good! Oh, yes, bad too, bad too. And yet grown together, one flesh even when he hurt her, so that now she could feel his suffering as no outsider, no matter how sensitive or how subtle, could ever feel.

She raised her face, appealing for understanding. "I can't leave a sinking ship, Tom. I can't leave."

He nodded. "But you will eventually," he said.

It was a time of waiting, an uneasy suspension of customary life. The days went slowly, and although it was autumn, they were long. From this house, surrounded by heavy foliage, Lynn looked out into a haze of faded colors, of greens gentled into gray and reds turned rusty, mournful yet lovely in their melancholy. It seemed to her that the earth was reflecting the mood of the house, for the fall should be bright and blazing. But it is all in the mind, she told herself; one sees what one needs to see.

On the far lawn under a maple Annie was doing her English assignment, reading *Huckleberry Finn*. Robert, kneeling on the grass, extended his arms toward Bobby, who, now going on ten months old, had already taken a few independent steps. Robert was proud; the boy would be athletic; the boy would be a strong tennis player, a swimmer, a track star.

If that gives him comfort, Lynn thought, let him have comfort. It was strange to see him here at home in the middle of the afternoon. Eudora, as she passed now between the garage and the grape arbor, must think so too.

Poor woman, only a week ago she had come, hesitant and shy, to make a confession.

"There's something I have to tell you, Mrs. Ferguson. All Mr. Ferguson's trouble, I heard about it from my friend, she shouldn't have talked, but I shouldn't have talked, either, I know I shouldn't. It was just that we were all having lunch at church, and you know when people work in other people's houses, they hear things, and they talk. I didn't mean to hurt you all, honestly I didn't. Even Mr. Ferguson, he's a gentleman, and I really liked him until he—"

Lynn had stopped her. "Dear Eudora, I understand. And it wasn't just you or your friend at the Stevenses'. Even the policeman at the country club knew, it seems that a great many people did. Oh, don't cry, please. Don't make it harder for me."

There had been no stopping the contrition. "I wouldn't hurt you for the world, you've been so good to me, all those clothes, and not just your old ones, but the new things for my birthday and last Christmas. You've been my *friend*. I couldn't stand it that morning when I came in and saw what he was doing to you, such a little thing you are, can't be more than a hundred pounds. Such a little thing."

The mild, anxious eyes had been asking a question that Eudora dared not ask aloud: "Are you staying, Mrs. Ferguson? Are you really?"

Lynn, raising her chin ever so slightly to show determination, had replied to the unspoken question. "We always need to look ahead in life, not back. What's past is past, isn't it?"

And in the saying she was conscious of maturity and strength.

"It's between Robert and me, our affair alone," she had told Tom Lawrence.

But of course, it was not. It was the proverbial stone thrown into a pond, with the widening ripples. It was Emily and Annie. . . .

Annie had been the surprise. The resilience of this so-often-troubled child was always a surprise. Unless she was holding it all in . . .

"Uncle Bruce told me not to believe what the kids said. He told me not even to answer them. 'They want you to cry and get angry,' he told me. 'But if you don't do either, you'll spoil their fun, and they'll stop.' We talk on the phone a lot." And she had finished with assurance, "Uncle Bruce gives me good advice." Then abruptly switching, she had demanded, "Why doesn't he come here anymore?"

"He's been busy getting ready to go away," Lynn had explained.

It was a question whether Bruce was more concerned to avoid Robert or to avoid her.

She wished Bruce would talk to Emily, but then was almost positive that his remarks to her would be quite different from his advice to Annie. Anyway, Emily was determined not to be moved.

Speaking to her sometime after the day of Robert's first frantic telephoned appeal, Lynn had come up against a wall of resistance.

"Mom, you're making a dreadful mistake," she had said in a sorry tone of disapproval. "Dreadful. I've done a lot of reading about marriages like yours."

"I know. I saw a book in your room. Those statistics don't fit every case. Emily. *People* aren't statistics."

"But there's a pattern, no matter how different each case may seem. We're still discussing wife abuse in my sociology course and I tell you, I've felt cold chills. You've got to take care of yourself, Mom. You can't depend on Dad anymore. You need to leave, and soon, Mom."

"No. If you could see your father, you'd know what I'm seeing. He's a different man. This has done something drastic to him, something terrible."

"You may be looking at him, but you're not seeing him."

"Have you no mercy or forgiveness, Emily? No pity?"

"Yes. Pity for you." And at the end Emily had said, "Well, Mom, you have to do what you think best."

Offended and defeated, Lynn had replied rather coolly, "Of course I must. Don't we all?" Then, softening, she had tried again. "In spite of his worries Dad's looking forward to Christmas, to the family being together. Would you like to bring Harris to dinner too? I'll make a feast, a *bûche de Noël* and everything."

"Harris has his own family dinner," Emily had replied, in the dry tone she seemed lately to have acquired.

"Well, one other day during vacation, then."

"We'll see," said Emily.

Stubborn! When Robert was really trying so hard to make amends!

"Don't tell Emily I'm worried about what I'm going to do," he kept saying. "I don't want her work to be affected. She needs a clear mind."

"But what are you really going to do?" Lynn had asked again only last night.

"I don't know yet. I need more time to think. In the meantime we can manage with my severance pay." The tone was dispirited, and the words were certainly vague. "Something, I'll find something."

On her birthday he had laid a long-stemmed rose at her plate.

"It's the best I can afford right now. I won't buy jewelry unless it's flawless, you know that. So, a flawless rose instead." Straightening his shoulders, and with a smile intended to be brave, he had said, "But next year at this time there'll be a shiny box tied with ribbon."

Something within Lynn had been displeased with this image; she had picked up the rose, so alive in its perfect simplicity, and held it against her cheek, saying only, "This is perfect, Robert. Thank you."

She could have said, "I don't measure things by shine and ribbon, don't you know that?"

But it would have come out prissy and righteous-sounding, which was not her intent at all, so she had just let him go to the piano, where, while she ate her breakfast, he played a birthday song.

Yesterday when it rained, she thought now, watching the baby stagger across the grass and fall into Robert's arms, he had spent the whole afternoon at the piano playing dreamy nocturnes. How long could the man go on this way? He went nowhere, not even on simple errands to the shopping center, where he feared to meet anybody he knew.

"You have to go out and hold your head up," she kept saying. "After all, you're not a murderer out on bail, are you? This is a seven-day wonder, anyhow. There's something new every week for people to chew over. Already, I'll take a bet on it, your departure from GAA is old stuff, forgotten."

But that was not true. At the supermarket there were no more curious glances and conversations broken off at her approach, but the telephone at home, an instrument that had once rung steadily, was now silent. And she recalled the conversation at Monacco's dinner table, the caretaker's light in the vacant house across the lake where had lived that couple about whom "you'd never guess it was possible."

Now Robert, seeing her at the window, waved, and she opened the casement.

"Bruce phoned while you were out," he called. "He's cleaning the house out and has some stuff he wants to give us, though I can't imagine what. Will you go over in the station wagon? He'd bring it himself, but his car's too small. Can you go now?"

"Can't you do it?"

"I'd rather not get into conversation with him in the circumstances," Robert pleaded.

Dismay was her instant reaction. Clothed though she was, she knew that she would feel naked in that room with Bruce, with no third person there to draw attention away from her. And yet, as she closed the casement, another thought came: I have neglected him, and he was, he is, or he and Josie were, our dearest friends. Shameful to have been so engrossed in her own trouble when his loss was so much greater! Yes, on one hand, came the argument: You have to remember that afternoon; how can you face each other, Lynn, tell me how? But on the other hand . . . So she stood, fearing to go, not wanting to, then in a queer, shamefaced fashion, wanting to.

Some time ago, before Josie's death, she had meant to give her a collection of pictures that they had taken together over the years. In the hall chest lay this folder, this record of the radiant hours that people want to save, the picnic on the Fourth of July, the birthdays, the company outing, and the silly hats on New Year's Eve. Surely Bruce would want this treasure. He would want every scrap and crumb of memory. Yes.

He was standing in a house half stripped when Lynn arrived. The first thing she noticed was that the living-room sofa was gone. A pair of early American matching chests were all that remained in the room.

"The new owners bought the best stuff," Bruce said. "The tall clock under the stairs, the stretcher table—stuff. The rest I gave away to the homeless project. Come, I'll show you what I thought might look nice in your garden. The new people don't want it."

Through the garden door, which stood open, he pointed to the bird-bath that had been bought during his and Josie's only trip abroad. It was a large marble basin, on the rim of which there stood a pair of marble doves, drinking. Bruce laughed about it.

"Damn thing cost more to ship home from Italy than I paid for it! But Josie fell in love with the doves. And it is rather nice, I have to admit."

Now he added, "Would you like to have it? If you do, I can ask my neighbor's boy to help me load it into your car."

"It's beautiful, Bruce. But are you sure—?" she began.

"That I won't ever use it? Yes, Lynn. Quite sure. I've had my time for a home, and my time's passed."

What a pity, she thought, to feel so old at his age. He was beginning to look himself, though; the haggard desperation that had marked his face during these hard months had lessened; the body tries to heal even when the spirit cannot. Rest healed, and so did the sun that was now glinting on his curly, summer-bleached hair. Funny, she thought, I never noticed his lashes are golden.

They were standing in the doorway. A white butterfly fluttered and poised itself on a clump of dead, still-yellow marigolds.

"Butterflies," murmured Lynn, "and it's almost Thanksgiving."

He, apparently not inclined to speak anymore, stood there with his hands in the pockets of his jeans, his glasses thrust up into his curly hair, and eyes that seemed to be seeing, not the quiet surrounding afternoon, but something different, something far away.

And she, feeling superfluous, made a move to leave, asking hesitantly, "Did you say your neighbor will help carry?"

"Yes, his son. They're across the street. I'll go out the front door and get him."

The kitchen cabinets had been almost all cleaned out, Lynn saw as she followed him. The floor was littered, a broom stood in a corner with a new trunk next to it, and a pile of books stood waiting to be packed into stout crates.

"I'm taking my books and Josie's, the only things I want to save."

"Oh," Lynn said, "I almost forgot, I've got a collection of pictures that you'll want. I left them in my car. They go all the way back to when you first came to St. Louis. Oh, my head's a sieve."

"You've had a few other things to fill your head with," Bruce said. "How is Robert these days?"

"Subdued. You wouldn't know him. Subdued and worried, but nothing like what he was in the first days, thank God. I'll never forget how he cried on the telephone to Emily. I'd never seen a man show grief that way, although there's no reason why men shouldn't. But still, my father, even after my mother's funeral—" Abruptly, shocked at her own tactlessness in mentioning funerals, she stopped.

"I take it that you're staying, Lynn." And when she nodded, he said quite gently, "I thought you probably would."

"He's changed," she told him, aware as she spoke it that she had used the same word, *changed,* both to Emily and to Tom.

Unlike either of those two he made no protest but looked at her with an expression of utmost sweetness. Leaning against a kitchen counter, he faced her as she leaned against the counter opposite, the two of them standing among the disarray of an abandoned home. Neither one would venture to speak of what surely must have been in each of their minds; she was thinking, as she regarded him, that it had always been a total impossibility for her to have sex with any man but Robert, and yet it had happened with this man.

"It is your loyalty," Bruce said suddenly, as if he were thinking aloud. "You feel his pain as if it were your own."

"Yes," she said, surprised that he had expressed her feelings so exactly. "I suppose it makes no sense to you. You can't understand it. And Josie would be furious with me if she could know."

"You're mistaken. Josie would try to talk you out of it, but she would understand. There are very few things that Josie failed to understand or forgive."

He meant what had happened between the two of them, on that day when she lay in such pain that even morphine could not assuage it. That's what he meant.

"Oh, she was no saint," Bruce said. "I don't want to draw false pictures. She deserves to be remembered as she really was."

Indeed, not saintly, with that sharp scrutiny of hers and that peppery tongue! Only good, purely good, to the very last day.

Bruce made a little gesture with both hands, a movement implying emptiness.

"They say an amputated limb still aches. So I suppose it doesn't really do any good to go away, since the ache will only go along with me. Still,

I'm relieved to be given this chance, although not at Robert's expense, it's true."

"When are you going?"

"Next week. Tuesday."

"And how long will you be gone?"

"Years, I hope. They tell me I'm climbing up the ladder. I don't know. If I do well in Budapest, there'll be more places, they say. Moscow, maybe. I don't care, Lynn. But the communists have left a lot of ecological cleaning up to be done, and I care about that." He smiled. "For the Emilies and the Annies and the Bobbies of the world, I care."

The cat roused itself from where it had been sleeping in an empty box, crossed the room, and rubbed against Lynn's ankle. Extremely moved by the words and the memories that had just passed, she stooped to stroke its back, and the cat, to acknowledge the soft stroke, raised its small face, its pink mouth, and its astounding periwinkle eyes.

"You did ask us to take him, didn't you, Bruce?"

"If you still want to."

"He can come with me now," she said, wanting a reason not to have to see Bruce again, only to leave quietly now, to say the last good-bye and have it over with. "I'll take good care of him. Don't worry."

"Do you remember how she used to say she married me because I liked cats?"

"I remember." And she thought, but did not say, It was because your eyes smiled too. She said instead, "Are there—do you have instructions about Barney's food and things?"

"I'll write them out. Where's a pencil?" He went rummaging and, in an obvious attempt at cheer, kept talking. "Let's see: litter box, carrier, collar and leash, almost never used but good to have, some canned food, his favorite kind. Of course, he likes scraps whenever you have fish for dinner."

"Dover sole?" she asked, forcing a laugh, needing to seem light-hearted.

He responded in kind. "Oh, naturally. Only the best. And you might let him have a couple of spoons of ice cream now and then, any flavor but coffee. He doesn't like coffee."

Standing on the walk, she watched while Bruce and the neighbor's son put the birdbath and the unprotesting cat with his belongings into the station wagon. Then the moment of departure came, and suddenly there was nothing to say. Uncomfortable with this vacuum, she remarked that the neighbor's son seemed to be a fine boy, rather mature for fifteen.

"That's what you have to look forward to with Bobby," he replied.

"I hope so. I'll do my best."

"I know you will."

"So, I guess it's good-bye," she said, and, absurdly, held out her hand.

"A handshake, Lynn?" Holding her face, he softly touched her lips with his own. Then he put his arms around her, held her close, and kissed her again.

"Take care of yourself, Lynn. Take good care."

"And you. You do the same."

"I worry so about you. I have for a long time."

"There's no need. I'm fine. I'm strong."

"Well, but if you ever need anything, call Tom Lawrence, will you?"

"I won't need anything. Honestly. Believe me."

"Tom cares about you, Lynn."

Tom, she thought, says the same about you. It would be comical if things weren't all so mixed up. And, turning from him so that he might not see her wet, blinking eyes, she climbed into the driver's seat.

"Be sure to write to us now and then, especially to Annie."

"My special Annie. I'll always be there for her."

"You are the best, the kindest," she said, and, able to say no more, started the engine.

The last she saw of Bruce as the car moved off was the sunlight striking his glasses and his arm upraised in farewell. The last she saw of the little house was the kitchen window, where Josie's red gingham curtains still hung. Her eyes were so wet that she could barely see to drive.

Robert is probably right about him, she thought. He's the kind who really may never marry again. He's lost. And the word echoed: lost. It was a tolling bell, grave and sorrowful and final. She would probably never see him again. He would drift and she would drift, and they would not meet.

At home there was hustle and bustle. Annie at once took over the care of the cat.

"Barney knows me best," she insisted. "He should be my cat. I'll be responsible for his food and his vet appointments and everything."

"And will you clean the litter box too?" Lynn asked.

"Absolutely. Now I have to introduce him to Juliet. I really don't think there'll be any trouble, do you?"

"I don't think so. If there is, we'll learn how to handle it."

Robert was still in the yard with Bobby. At the moment the little boy was stretched on the grass with Juliet, and both were watching Robert hammer a playhouse into shape. He does everything well, Lynn thought, observing the swift competence and the masculine grace.

Seeing her, he called, "Like it? He'll be able to use it before you know it."

"It's time for his bath." She walked out and picked up the baby. "Oh, my, wet through. You do need a bath."

The boy laughed and caught hold of her hair. Robert gave them a look of such intensity that she had to ask curiously, "What is it?"

"You. Both of you together. Your lovely, tranquil spirit. I don't deserve you."

She did not want her heart to be touched or moved. She wanted just peace, calm and practical and friendly.

"Dinner will be heating while I bathe Bobby. Then I have Annie's scout meeting tonight. It's for mothers and daughters, so will you put him to bed?"

"Of course I will."

"Come see when you're finished there," she called back from the kitchen door. "I've brought Bruce's cat."

Then she closed the door and carried Bobby upstairs. *I worry about you,"* Bruce had said, with the implication that she was somehow in peril. But it was not so, for she was going to be in control. I can run this house and this family like clockwork, she told herself, holding her child. I can keep a happy order here, and I can cope with anything.*

She was strong, and she was proud.

A few days later she went to New York for the pre-Christmas sales. Now that their financial future was uncertain, she had to shop with a particular care, to which for a long time she had been unaccustomed. Hurrying homeward past Salvation Army Santa Clauses and shop windows festooned with glass balls and tinsel arabesques, she worried whether the coat and skirts would fit Annie properly.

But there was something else on her mind, something that, because of her preoccupation with Josie's death and Robert's depression, she had locked away in the dark. However, it did not accept the darkness, but struggled out again and again, as if to force her to examine it.

There was something odd about Aunt Jean's connection to Querida. Or there would be, provided that Emily's report was correct. Or provided that the name over the shop's door belonged to *the* Querida—which it might well not, she thought now, summoning common sense and probabilities.

She was passing through the neighborhood, and it gave her immediate recall, such as follows a chord, a flavor, or a scent; it brought back the day when events had crashed upon each other like cars on a foggy highway; there had been Robert's attack in the kitchen, her flight into Bruce's arms, and Emily's sorrowful leavetaking. And it seemed to her that all these were somehow linked in ways that she could not fathom, that these things had their origin in one place, one time.

I have to know, she thought, as she came to the street, to the shop, and, with a thumping of the heart like a pounding on a door, stood there looking in the window.

A row of dog paintings was on display. They were all the fashion these days; the English-country-house look was the right look, casual elegance among rural acres for the homes of people who had never owned either an acre or a dog and possibly would never want to, she thought, surveying the haughty pugs, Queen Victoria's favorites, and the sporting setters, flaunting their proud tails. But there among them hung an unfamiliar creature, a strange beast, looking so much like Juliet that it could have been Juliet.

Abruptly her feet made the decision to enter and she found herself inside.

A small, dark woman limped across the room and took Juliet out of the window.

"It's not old," she said in reply to Lynn's query. "I've put it with the old ones because it has a nineteenth-century look. Actually, it's the work of a man who simply likes to paint dogs, any kind."

"It's charming."

The dog, sitting on a doorstep, had the same alert, faintly concerned expression that Juliet wore whenever the family drove away without her.

"Yes, I see by your face how much you like it," the woman said.

"It's the image of our dog."

Lynn's heart was pounding, and while she was seeing the painting, she was also seeing the woman. Had Robert not spoken about "a job in a gallery," and "a dabbler"? Still, his "beauty" could certainly not be this person, whose angular face with its flat black eyes was topped by a dome of coarse black hair. Relief and disappointment met and mingled. In one way she "had to know," she wanted to behold the woman who had first occupied her place; but in another way there was dread.

She returned to the picture. It would be a fine surprise for Robert, something to enliven him. They might hang it in his den at home or better still in his office. For an instant she forgot that at present he did not have an office.

"It's not expensive. The price is on the tag."

The price was most fair. Since the painting was small enough, she could carry it home right now. And she handed over her credit card.

The woman looked hard at the card and slowly turned her eyes up toward Lynn.

"Robert V. W. Ferguson. So now you've come too," she said. "I was wondering whether you would."

Lynn's knees went so weak that she had to perch on the stool that stood beside the counter, and she stammered.

"I don't understand."

"Your daughter Emily was here a while back, the day after Thanksgiving."

Emily in New York? But Emily was in New Orleans! We talked on the phone on Thanksgiving day. She must have flown in to see this woman, and gone back to college without telling us. . . .

The woman was staring at Lynn in open curiosity.

"She had a lot of questions, but I didn't answer them. She's too young, sweet and young. Besides, it's up to you to tell her whatever you want her to know."

Lynn's voice came in a whisper. "I know nothing."

"Nothing?"

"Not much. Only that you didn't get along."

"Didn't get along! There's a bit more to it than that, you can be sure." The black eyes bored into Lynn. "You're a pretty woman. He liked blondes, I remember."

Lynn was in panic. She had come here wanting to find out—what? To find out something about Robert that other people—Aunt Jean—knew and had kept hidden. And now that she was here she was in panic.

"He must have told you something about me."

"That there was a child, a boy," Lynn whispered again.

"Yes. He's a man now, living in England. He's had a good life: I saw to that. And you? Do you have other children?"

"Another girl, and a boy ten months old."

"A nice family."

The air in the confined and cluttered space held bad vibrations; there was an impending intimacy from which Lynn now shrank. What she must do was to stand up and leave the place, picture and all. But she was unable to move.

Querida's eyes roved over her, coming to rest on the fur coat and the fine leather bag. "I see that he has accomplished what he wanted to."

And Lynn, mesmerized, submitted to inspection. The brusque remark, that could have been offensive, was somehow not. It was merely odd. Whatever could Robert have seen in this woman? Two more ill-matched people one could hardly imagine.

As if she had read Lynn's mind, Querida said, "I don't know how we ever got mixed up. It was just one of those things, I guess. He was brilliant, won all the scholarships, and God knows he was good looking. I was Phi Beta Kappa, and I suppose he was impressed by that. I was no beauty, although somewhat better looking than I am now, that's for sure. We were together only three or four times and I got pregnant. I didn't want an abortion, and I'll say this much for him, he did the right thing for those days, anyway. He married me."

Had she no inhibitions? Why was she telling these things to a person who had not asked to hear them?

"We were dirt poor, both of us. Hadn't anything, never had had anything."

Poor? The trips to Europe and Querida's prominent family? What of them?

"Why do you look surprised? Are you surprised?"

"Yes," Lynn murmured.

"I suppose he told you I was beautiful. He always liked to tell me about his former lovers, how exceptional they were. And I suppose he drew you a picture of his distinguished patrician background. Poor Robert. He did it so often that he really believed it. Anyway, by your time they were dead, so what difference? But I knew. I knew the mother with the doilies and the tea wagon. The genteel poor. Pretense, all pretense. She was pathetic, a decent little woman, half the size of her husband, and helpless under his fists."

"I don't want to hear this!" cried Lynn, shuddering.

"But maybe you should."

You could feel the anger burning in this queer woman, as if her very skin would be hot to the touch. She was eccentric, neurotic, or even perhaps a trifle mad . . . And still you had to listen.

"Jean worries about you. Oh, yes, she's kept in touch with me over the years. She's a good soul, like her sister, and she's never been sure about you and Robert."

This was too much, this infringement of the decent privacy that Lynn had guarded all her life.

"People have no right—" she blurted, but the other, ignoring her indignation, continued.

"Do you know how Robert's mother died? They were in their car on the turnpike, the two of them. A man at a tollbooth notified the police when he saw what was wrong, but by the time the police caught up with them it was too late. She had been trying to jump out of the moving car, away from him. The people in the car behind had seen it. The car swerved and hit a tree. They were both killed. Good for him, and none too soon. And those," Querida said, "are the distinguished Fergusons."

Oh, the horror! And the woman would not stop the gush of words. Perhaps she could not.

"Do you see this leg? My hip was broken. Yes, the story repeats itself, although not all the way, because I knew enough to get free. Yes, Robert did this to me."

Now Lynn recognized that she herself was in a state of physical shock; her mouth went dry, her palms wet, and her heart was audibly drumming in her ears. She sat quite still, not having moved from the support of the counter at her back, sat and stared as the nervous voice resumed.

"It wasn't the first time, although it was the worst. We were ice skating. He asked me what there was for dinner, and I said we'd pick up some fast food on the way home. I wasn't a good housekeeper. I'm still not, and that infuriated him. But he infuriated me with his compulsive ways, so neat, so prompt, so goddamn perfect. So he went absolutely mad about the dinner. A thing like that could trigger him."

Lynn's dry lips formed a statement: *I told you I don't want to hear any more.* Yet no sound came out.

"It was almost dark, and we were the last ones on the lake. So he slapped my face, and his gloves had buckles on the wrists. He shoved me, and I fell on the ice. He kicked me, and I couldn't get up. Then he was scared, and he ran to a public phone to call an ambulance. When they came, I was almost fainting with the pain. I heard him say, 'She fell.' "

If she would just stop and let me get out of here, Lynn thought, and then rebuked herself: You know you have to stay to the end, to hear it all.

"A neighbor woman cared for the baby while I was in the hospital. When he came and started talking about the 'accident,' I told him I never wanted to see him again. So I took my child and left. I had a friend in Florida who gave me a job, and I let him get the divorce on the grounds of desertion. I didn't care, I wanted no part of him. I said if he ever came near me or the child, I would expose him and ruin him forever." Again there came that forced, grim laugh. "I must say he has supported the boy generously—not me, because I wouldn't take a penny of his anyway. Now my son is twenty-four and independent.

"My hip wasn't set right. They tell me it should be broken again and reset. But I don't want to go through all that. I keep it this way as a remembrance of Robert."

Why was she revealing this terrible story after all these years? It was to take revenge for her suffering. It was to destroy Robert's marriage, especially if it should be a good one.

"And do you think it does any good to go to the police? Do you? Well, I'll tell you. It doesn't. I went once. They didn't even take me seriously. I came in a nice car. We both had jobs then, and we had pooled our money for it. We had a neat apartment in a decent neighborhood. 'What are you complaining about?' they asked me. 'The guy can't be all bad. You should see the things we see. Straighten it out. Don't make him angry. Of course, if you want to swear out a complaint, we can arrest him and make a big stink. Then maybe he'll lose his job, and where'll you be? Nah, think it over. You women don't know when you're well off.' That's what they told me. I see I've upset you."

"What did you expect?" Lynn's pity and horror collided. Her head reeled, and her voice filled with tears. "You had no right to dump all this stuff on me. I came in to buy a picture, and—"

The other woman's tight face softened. "I suppose I shouldn't have talked," she said. "I shouldn't be involved in this at all. But when your daughter came I suspected—never mind. Do you still want the picture? I'll let you have it for nothing. My way of apologizing."

Lynn slid off the stool. "Yes, I want it. And I want to pay for it."

"As you wish. I'll wrap it."

Although her heart was still pounding, she was beginning to recover and take command of herself. With a show of casual dignity she walked around the walls as if to examine the paintings hung there, yet, in her agitation, scarcely seeing them at all.

After a moment the voice pursued her. "You don't believe me."

Lynn turned and went back to the counter. "Whether I do or not," she said quietly, "doesn't matter. Just give me the picture, please, so I can go."

In the silence, now throbbing with the words that had been spoken there, she waited while the package was being wrapped. Querida's fingers delicately handled paper, cardboard, and twine; she had oval nails and a strong profile as she bent over the work. An intelligent face, thought Lynn.

The silence broke abruptly. "He made her life a hell. I'm talking about Robert's father and mother. Her people hated him. They begged her to leave him, but she wouldn't. A little bit proud, a little too ashamed. I know. I've seen them, the soft ones who listen to the sweet apology and believe it won't happen again. You, too, I'm thinking."

Now words came, choking in Lynn's throat. "You don't know anything about me!"

"But I do. I know that lovely girl of yours wouldn't have sought me out unless she had a great trouble on her mind. She knows plenty, but she wants to know more. I saw. Pull yourself together, my dear; take care of yourself and your children. I know you think I'm queer and maybe I am, but I mean well."

The door slammed and cold air struck Lynn's face. A blast of wind from Canada rounded the stone corner and almost knocked her over as she ran toward Grand Central. Her legs barely held her.

The soft ones—the sweet apology . . .

A strange woman, with those wild eyes. How they must have hated each other! Not like Robert and me because we—in spite of all, we—

But he lied to me. All those lies. And yet she—is everything she said true?

Faintly dizzy, she struggled through the wind and the crowds. Within the vast cavern of the terminal "Good King Wenceslaus" reverberated heartily. People returning to their suburban homes were normal; there was reassurance in the cheerful sound of greetings; a fat man clapped another on the back and two matrons squealed with delight at seeing one another. These were common, everyday noises. These were ordinary, everyday people.

The train clicked over the tracks. It's true, it's not, it's true, it's not, said the wheels. This had been the worst day . . . Lynn laid her head back against the seat. And the woman next to her, young and fashionable with no troubles on her face, asked anxiously, "Are you not feeling well?"

"It's only a headache, thank you. I'm all right." Embarrassed, Lynn smiled.

The car was parked at the station. When she got in and drove through the town, which looked the same as it had that morning, it seemed astonishing that everything should be the same. Station wagons were parked in the supermarket lot, the yellow school buses were returning to the garage, and the windows were prepared here, too, for the holiday as if nothing of any importance had happened since the morning.

It seemed too early to go home. Actually, it was early, for she had wanted to make another stop in the city on the way to the train. But after what had happened, she had needed only to rush away. So she stopped the car at a dingy luncheonette on the fringe of the center and sat down to order a pot of tea with a bun. Tea was soothing.

He kicked me while I lay on the ice with my hip broken. Now, that, that's hard to believe. Yes, he had bursts of rotten temper—how well I know! But sadism like that, never. No, that's hard to accept. Out of a kernel of truth, a large kernel, she has developed this sickly growth, this enormous exaggeration.

She's odd, filled with rage and, in some way that I can't diagnose, disturbed. But if she were more, let's say for want of more accurate words, more reasonable, temperate, sweeter, *acceptable,* then would I be more apt to believe her?

Yet even if only some of it is true, how terrible and sad it is that he has needed to conceal it all these years! Why, when I would have tried to help him? Didn't he know that I would have tried?

But weigh the sin of his concealment against all our years together, all the good, all the good. . . .

The warm cup, held between Lynn's hands, brought remembrance of her parents, sitting at the kitchen table on other winter afternoons. They had used to hold their cups just so, and the cups had had daisies around the rims. It had been a simple time. . . . Her eyes flooded, and she thrust the tea away.

Someone put money in a jukebox left over, probably, from the fifties, and canned voices, moaning over love lost or remembered or found, swelled out into the gray, depressing room. Lynn got up and paid her bill. It was time to pull herself together and go home. It was time, Josie would say, to face reality. Go home and, making no fuss, ask him what you want to know, and tell him what you have found out.

Robert had put a candle bulb in each window, so that the house appeared to float through the early darkness like a ship with lighted portholes. Through the bow window, where the curtains were still open, she could see him sitting in his big leather chair with Bobby on one knee; they were looking at a book spread on the other knee.

The little boy adored the man: His dark blue eyes were rounder than Emily's and Robert's; they were round like his dear head and his little fat hands. She felt a twinge of pain, like a tender wound, a soft something that was both merciful and sorrowful. For a moment she was almost within their skins, that of the vulnerable baby, and that of the man who perhaps had once known such grievous hurt that he was unable to admit its existence.

Opening the door, she heard Annie practicing her piano lesson at the other end of the hall, and she paused a moment to listen. Annie was really doing better, doing better at everything. It might be that the new quietness in Robert, the slowing of the house's rhythm, had affected the child too. It was a strange irony that the father's most cruel defeat should have brought about a subtle kind of peace that had not been there before, whose absence she had not even been aware of until it occurred.

The dog jumped to announce her presence and Robert looked up in surprise.

"Hello! We didn't hear you come in."

"I've been watching you. You're so cozy, you two."

"We're halfway through Mother Goose, up to Little Jack Horner." He got up, set the baby in the playpen, and kissed Lynn. "You've been shopping, I see. Did you buy anything nice?"

"I hope you'll think so. It's your Christmas present."

"Didn't we promise each other just books this year? And now you've gone and broken your promise," he said with a rueful smile.

"This wasn't horribly expensive, honestly. It's a picture. Open it."

"Why not wait till Christmas?"

"Because I don't want to wait."

Bobby, attracted by the crackle of paper as Robert cut the string, stretched out his arms as if he could reach the bright redness and the crackle. And something caught again in Lynn's chest, in her heart and throat, at the sight of the merry child and the father's dark head bent over the package.

Surely this family's path would straighten and all the past evil be forgotten! This was only a sharp turning in the path, a crooked obstacle to be got over, and she would get over it. There was so much else to be thankful for; no one had cancer, no one was blind. . . .

"Wherever did you find this?" Robert cried. "It's Juliet to the life. Fantastic!"

"I thought you would love it."

"It's wonderful. Dog portraits are always the same, spaniels or hounds or faithful collies. Thanks a million, Lynn."

"You'll never believe where I found it. Quite by accident, I saw it in a window on the way to the train, in a tiny gallery called 'Querida.'"

Robert's face changed. As if a hand had passed over it, the eyes' lively shine, the smile crinkles at their corners, the smile pouches of the cheeks, and the happy lift of the lips were wiped away. And she saw that he was waiting for the words that would come next, saw that, quite understandably, she had stunned him.

"The odd thing is that it really was she. I couldn't believe it. It was when I showed the American Express card and she recognized the name."

Say nothing about Emily having been there. Be careful. Nothing.

"Very interesting." He clipped the words like a stage Englishman. "Interesting, too, that you didn't turn right around and walk out."

"But I wanted the painting," she protested, and was aware, even as she spoke them, that the words were too innocent. Then she added, "Besides, it would have been awkward just to turn on my heel and leave."

"Oh, awkward, of course. Much easier to stay and have a cozy chat with the lady."

Robert's eyes narrowed, and he straightened his posture. As always, it seemed that he grew taller when he was angry. And in dismay she knew that he was very, very angry.

This was not what she had expected; perhaps she'd been foolish to think he would defend himself. Instead he was on the attack.

"There was no chat. I was only there for the time it took to pay and have this wrapped. It was only a minute. A couple of minutes," she said, stumbling over the defense.

"So you didn't open your mouths, either of you." He nodded. "After that astonishing revelation there was total silence, I'm sure."

"Well, not exactly."

"I suppose you got quite an earful about me."

It was he who was to have been on the defensive, he who was to have been scared. How had the tables been turned like this? And she murmured, almost coaxing now, "Why no, Robert, not at all."

"I don't believe it. Your curiosity would have kept you listening, with your ears open and your mouth hanging open, while your husband was smeared with filth. Don't tell me not, Lynn, because I know better." He was trembling. "Talk about loyalty! If you had any, you wouldn't have entered there in the first place."

"How would I know? How could I have known?"

"You knew damn well that that—creature—played around with art and worked in a gallery. You didn't forget that, Lynn. And the name— you didn't forget that either. You could have thought, when you saw that name—it wasn't Susan, it wasn't Mary; do you see it on every street corner? You could have thought, Well, maybe it's possible, I won't take a chance. But your curiosity got the better of you, didn't it?"

The iota of accuracy in what he said brought a flush of heat that ran up her neck and scorched her cheeks.

"Well, didn't it?"

His voice rose and filled the room so that Bobby, hearing the unfamiliar tone, turned a puzzled face to his father.

Now Lynn had to go over to the attack. "You're impossible! How can you have so little understanding, when my only thought was to bring you something that might make you a little bit happy in these hard days? And I did cut her short. I didn't want to hear anything, so I walked out when she—"

"You cut her short? But you just told me nothing was said. You'd better get your story straight."

"You get me all mixed up. You tie my tongue. When you're like this, I can't even think straight. I get so muddled, I don't know what I'm saying."

"You're muddled, all right. Now, listen to me—I want to know exactly what was said, and you had better tell me exactly."

Like a whip he sprang and grasped her arms at the place where he had always grasped before, in the soft flesh above the elbow. His hard fingers pressed his thumbs against the very bone.

In the playpen the baby now pulled himself up and stood swaying against the railing. His wide eyes stared at them.

"Let go," Lynn said, keeping her voice low for Bobby's sake.

"I want an answer, I said."

The pain was horrible, but she still spoke evenly. "Keep your voice down, Robert. The baby's terrified. And do you want Annie to hear this too?"

"I want to know what that crazy woman said, that's what I want. Answer me!"

He shook her. There was a fierceness in his expression that she had never seen there before, something desperate and grim, something fanatical. And, more frightened than she had ever been, she began to cry.

"Ah, the tear machine. Don't answer a simple question. Just turn on the tear machine."

He shook her so violently that her neck jerked.

"Robert, let go! I'll have to scream, and everybody will know. This is insane. Look at the baby!"

Bobby's wet pink mouth hung open and his round cheeks were puckering toward tears. "Look what you're doing to the baby!"

"Then talk."

"All you do is find fault with me! I can't stand it!"

In a nasal whine he mocked her. "All I do is find fault with you. You can't stand it."

The baby rattled the playpen, fell on his back, and wailed. And Lynn, frantic now with fright and pain and concern over Bobby, screamed out, "Let go of me, Robert! Damn you—"

"Talk, and I will."

There was a tumult within her, the desperation of a captive who has been wrongly accused, a victim of terror. And this desperation exploded.

"All right, I'll talk! Enough of lies! Let the truth blare! Why have you hidden yourself from me all these years? I had thought to talk to you in a civil way and ask you why you never trusted me enough to be open with me. Why did you hide what your father did to your mother? Oh, I see now why Aunt Jean was never welcome! It's you! You didn't want her around for fear she would say too much. And why? Did you think so little of me as to believe I wouldn't understand about your family? Did you think so little of yourself that you had to invent a family? Why do you feel that you have to be without flaw, descended from saints or something?"

She saw the pulses throbbing in his temples, where suddenly on each a crooked blue vein had swelled. And now that she had begun, now that the pressure of Robert's hands was unbearable, she, too, screamed, not caring or able to care who heard.

"Why did you tell me Querida was beautiful and rich? To make me jealous? Why didn't you tell me about her broken hip? Why have you lived with all these lies, so that I've had to live with them too? Now I see, I see it all. My life, my whole life . . . What's the matter with you? What have you done?"

Her words tumbled and raced and would not cease.

"A sham, a cover-up, all the excuses I made because I wanted not to admit anything. I needed to keep the dream. She told me everything you did to her, Robert, everything. She said—"

He let her go. He picked up the painting, raised it high, and brought it down hard, splintering the frame and ripping the canvas from top to bottom over the back of a chair. The baby screamed; in a distant room the piano sounded a smashing discord and stopped. The vandalism was atrocious. He was panting like an animal.

"You disgust me!" she cried. "People should know this, should see what you can do! Yes, you disgust me."

He struck her. A violent blow landed on her neck, and she fell back, crashing into the playpen. When she picked herself up, he struck her again, grazing her eye as she turned, gasped, and tried to flee. With his left hand he seized her collar; his right fist smashed her nose so hard that the crack was audible, as bone met bone. Blood gushed; she reached for support, but there was only empty air. The room slowly circled and tilted around her as she fell, and was still.

She had fallen or been laid upon the sofa. Vomit and blood had smeared her white silk shirt, and for some reason that later she was to find incredible, this damage to the shirt was the first thing she saw. It was a terrible humiliation. She heard herself wail, "Oh, look!" She sobbed. In a confusion of sound and sight she seemed to see Eudora clutching Robert's coat and screaming at him, "What the hell have you done?" At the same time she seemed to see Eudora holding Bobby on one arm while Annie, somewhere at her side, was crying.

Next came the pain in a wave of fire, so that, as if to cool it, she pressed her hands to her face, then drew them away in revulsion over her own sticky blood.

The room was filled with a swelling crowd of many people, many voices making a vast, low roar. But after a while she knew that the roar was only in her head. When she opened her eyes again, she began to distinguish among the faces. Eudora was still holding Bobby. Annie was at the foot of the sofa. Somebody was wiping her face with a cold towel; the hands were gentle and very careful. She focused her eyes. The room had stopped circling, and things had righted themselves so that she began to see quite clearly. It was Bruce who stood over her holding the towel.

"What are you doing here?" she whispered.

"Annie called me." He took his glasses off and wiped them. His eyes were moist, as though they might have held tears; yet at the same time they were fierce. His mouth, his full-lipped, easy mouth, was a hard line. "You fainted," he said.

Annie knelt and laid her face on Lynn's shoulder, whimpering, "Mommy. Oh, Mommy."

"Careful, dear. Her face is sore," said Bruce.

Now came Robert's voice. "I've got the ice bag. Move away a little, Annie."

"Don't you touch her," Bruce commanded. "The ice bag can wait a minute."

"I have a first-aid certificate," protested Robert.

"You know what you can do with your goddamn certificate! She'll see a doctor after she's pulled herself together. You keep away from her, hear?"

Now Robert moved into view, his eyes and his voice making joint appeal.

"Oh, God, Lynn, I don't know how to say what I feel. I never intended . . . But things just got out of hand. . . . We were both angry. . . ."

Bruce shouted, "Oh, why don't you shut up!"

"Yes, why don't you?" Annie repeated. Her head was buried in her mother's shoulder while her mother's arm held her.

"Annie dear," Bruce said, "your mother will be happier, I think, if you go upstairs. I know this is awfully hard for you, but if you'll just try to be a little patient, we'll talk about it in the morning, I promise."

Robert coaxed. "Don't worry about Mom. It looks worse than it is. I'll see that she's taken care of. Do go up, darling."

When he moved toward her, as if to take her away from the sofa, Annie scrambled up out of his reach and, with her hands on her chubby hips and her eyes streaming tears, defied him.

"I'm not your darling. You're an awful father, and Susan was right. You do hit Mom. I saw you just now, I saw you. And, and—I never told anybody, but sometimes I have a dream about you, and I hate it because it wakes me up and I feel so bad, and I tell myself it's only a dream, but now, now," she sputtered, "look what you did! It's as horrible as the dream!"

"What dream, Annie? Can you remember it?" asked Bruce.

"Oh, yes. I see Mom in a long white dress, wearing a crown on her head and he—he is hitting her."

This blow, this other kind of blow, struck Lynn again between the eyes. And it had struck Robert hard, too, for, dazed as she was, she was able to see how clearly he was recalling that night of the New Year's Eve costume party, so long ago. Annie had been no more than three. . . .

And she gave Robert a terrible look. She wanted to say, So, this explains a good deal about Annie, doesn't it?

But instead she whispered, summoning the top of her strength, "You're *my* darling. So will you do something for me and go up with Eudora? Tomorrow I'll tell you about the dream, about everything."

"Come, Annie," said Eudora, "come up and help give Bobby his bottle. I'm going to sleep on a cot in your room with you. I'm staying here tonight."

Annie raised her head, and Lynn, too miserable to speak, gave the child a look of appeal.

"Juliet has to sleep in my room too."

"Of course she will," said Eudora.

And the little group shuffled out, the woman holding the baby and the girl, for comfort, holding on to the dog.

And we were sure, thought Lynn, silent in bitter grief, that we had kept the children from knowing.

The doorbell rang just as Eudora started up the stairs.

"That's Tom Lawrence," Bruce said. "I called him."

"What? He has no business here. Don't open the door, Eudora," commanded Robert.

Bruce countermanded the order. "Yes, please open it, Eudora. I'd do it myself, only I don't want to step away from Mrs. Ferguson."

"What in blazes—" said Tom. Stunned, he stood in the doorway and stared at the scene. "What in blazes—"

He walked over and looked down at Lynn, grimaced, shut his eyes for an instant from the sight, and turned to Robert.

"So, you bastard, it's finally happened. It took a while coming, but I knew it would. You ought to be strung up."

"You don't know what you're talking about! We had some upset here, an argument, and I only meant—"

The words diminished and faded. As shocked and foggy as Lynn's brain was then, still there came a lucid thought: He is considering that Tom is a lawyer, and he's scared.

"You 'only' nothing, Ferguson." Tom walked toward Robert, who drew back. It was strange to see him drawing back from a man whose head barely reached past his shoulder. "I'm calling the police."

Lynn struggled up against the pillows. Her eye throbbed. When her tongue touched her front teeth, one moved. She tried again. Definitely, it had been loosened. And she spoke through swollen lips.

"No. No police. Please, Tom." She wanted him to understand that Annie had already seen horror enough. "All I want is for—him," she said, motioning toward Robert, "for him to get out." She lay back again. "I'm so dizzy."

"Ah, you see? Even Lynn doesn't want the police," said Robert.

"I'd like to overrule you, Lynn," Tom said gravely. "This is a public matter now. A man can't be allowed to get away with this kind of thing."

"Stay out of it, Lawrence," Robert said. "Nobody invited you here."

Bruce jumped to the attack. "I invited him. Lynn needs friends, and she needs legal advice, which I can't give."

"My advice again is to call the police," Tom urged. "They need only to take one look at her, and it'll be worth a thousand words for future use."

Robert pounced. "Future use?"

"It would be in the newspapers," Lynn murmured. "My children have been hurt badly enough without that too."

"You're not thinking," Bruce said quietly. "Everyone knows about it, anyway. In the office now—"

At that Robert shouted out. "In the office? Yes, yes, do you think I don't know about the lies you've spread? You wanted to tear me down, you wanted to take my place."

Bruce pointed to Lynn. "Lies? Look at your wife's face. If I had talked, and I never did, which you know quite well, there would have been no lies. No. Robert, if I had ever wanted to talk, I could have done it long ago, that morning in Chicago, or maybe even before that, and you would never have gotten as far as New York. Let alone Europe," he shouted. His rage and contempt had set him on fire. "You aren't fit to live, after what you've done here tonight. You ought to be taken out and shot."

I'm not here, Lynn was saying to herself. All this has nothing to do with me. It's not happening to me.

Tom took her hand, which was cold, as one chill after another began to shake her.

"What do you want us to do, Lynn? Tell us. There's no point in arguing who said or did not say what. You're too exhausted."

She answered him softly, as if she feared Robert's wrath if he should overhear. "Just make him go. I don't want to see him ever, ever, ever."

But Robert had heard. "You don't mean that, Lynn," he cried. "You know you don't."

Tom gave an order. He was a small, active terrier badgering a Great Dane. "You heard what she said. Go! Get your coat and get out."

Robert, clasping his hands, beseeched her. "Lynn, hear me. These people, these strangers, are egging you on. I'll spend the rest of my days making up to you for this, I swear I will. And telling me to go is no solution. These people—it's no business of theirs."

"Tom and Bruce, whom you call 'these people,' are my friends," she answered, finding voice. "I wanted them here. I need them. And I want you to go. It's I who want it. I."

He beat his clenched hands on his breast. "You and I have lived a life together. Can any third person know what we have had, you and I? The things that have been between us? I'll change. I'll go anywhere you want, talk to anyone you want, take any counsel. I promise, I swear."

"Too late," she cried. "Too late."

"I beg you, Lynn."

His shame and his agony were contagious; absurd as it was, as her intelligence told her it was, he could still elicit pity. It was odd that when he was angry, he could seem so tall; now between the other two men, pleading, he shrank.

Bruce held out his hand, commanding, "Give me your house keys, Robert. Does he have duplicates?" he asked Lynn.

Still overcome with the shame of this, she told him, "In the drawer of the table behind you."

"I'll take them." Bruce put them in his pocket. "I'll throw them out when I get home. You'll change your locks tomorrow. Now get out of here, Robert. Now. This minute."

"You may come back tomorrow morning at nine o'clock for your clothes," Tom said. "But you heard Bruce, so go, and hurry up about it. Lynn needs rest and attention."

"I want to hear that from Lynn," Robert answered.

His face had gone gray. She thought: He knows I pity him, even now. But I am not wavering. If I had any tendency to do it, and I do not, the thought of Annie alone would stop me.

And drawing herself upright, she said sternly, "I will tell you, Robert. Leave now, or weak as I am, I shall take Annie and Bobby and sit at the airport until the first plane leaves for my sister's in St. Louis, and you'll have the damned house to yourself."

Tom cried, "Oh, no! This house is yours as much as his. You'll stay in it until your lawyer says you may leave it. I'm getting a fine Connecticut lawyer for you tomorrow. And you had better get going, Ferguson," he threatened. "Otherwise, no matter what Lynn says, I'll have the police here in ten minutes."

The two men stood side by side in front of Robert. He looked them up and down, then looked at Lynn for so long that she had to shut her eyes. His face was like that of a man who has come upon a ghastly slaughter and is helpless. She supposed that her expression might be the same. Then he turned on his heel and went rapidly from the house.

The door closed. There was the sound of wheels on the gravel drive, and then nothing.

* * *

The two men took charge. First came a doctor, a friend of Tom's who, in a situation like this one, was willing to make a house call.

Bruce explained. "Mrs. Ferguson doesn't want to press charges, and if she goes to the hospital—"

The doctor understood. "There would be questions. As long as there's no damage to the retina, I think we'll be able to manage here at home." Plainly shocked, he bent over Lynn and flashed a light into her eye. "No, there's not. You're lucky. It almost—" And he shook his head.

When he had gone, Tom and Bruce made decisions for the morning. New door locks must be installed. Appointments with a dentist and an attorney must immediately be made. Bruce would talk to Annie and assess the damage to her.

"I'm staying all night," he said. "I can stretch out on the sofa in the den."

He would certainly not stretch out on this one. Lynn's blood had ruined the moss-green damask, ruined it forever. And Robert had always worried about their guests' palms on the armrests.

"Your flight's tomorrow night. You need some sleep," she protested.

"It doesn't matter. There's no sleep in me now, anyhow. I'll make up for it on the plane."

Until long past midnight they talked. Bruce wanted to know what had led to such horror, and she told him everything, starting with the painting, which still, in its innocence, lay wrecked on the floor.

His comment, when she had finished, was thoughtful and sorrowful. "He was afraid that, after what you had heard, you would leave him. He was terrified. Don't you see?"

"I see that he went into an insane rage. It was unimaginable," she said, shivering again. "He could have killed me."

Bruce said grimly, "He might well have if Eudora hadn't been here."

"Such rage! I can't comprehend such rage."

Bruce shook his head. "You have to look deeper. Robert has always been filled with fear. He's one of the most fearful people I've ever known."

"Robert?"

"Oh, yes. He doesn't think much of himself. That's why he has always had to be the dominant one."

She thought. Doesn't think much of himself? But it was I who looked to him! I who always felt, so secretly that I could hardly acknowledge it even to myself except in a pensive moment now and then, that I was never quite good enough, neither accomplished nor beautiful enough for him.

"Have you just thought of this now, Bruce? Tell me."

"No, it was clear a long time ago, almost at the beginning."

She raised her swollen, tired eyes to Bruce and asked him quietly, "So that's what you saw in Robert. What did you see in me?"

"That you were always too terribly anxious to please. That you deferred to him. It was plain to see, if one looked only a little beneath the surface."

"And you looked."

"No, strictly speaking it was Josie who looked and saw. I learned from her. I learned a great many things from Josie."

"Did she think it would ever come to what happened here tonight?"

"We both feared it very much, Lynn."

"And yet you must have seen so many of our happy times, our good times."

Lamplight struck her ring when she moved her hand, so that the diamond came to life; absently, nervously, she twirled it around and around her finger, playing, as was her habit, with needles and sparks of light. Good times and undercurrents . . . Annie playing duets with Robert and Annie having nightmares, concealing her nightmares . . .

"What is to become of Annie?" she asked, lifting her eyes from the ring. "I am so afraid, so worried about her."

"I think now you really must take her for counseling. I have always thought so, anyway. You know that."

"Yes, but will you talk to her too?"

"In the morning, I told you."

"We shall all miss you so, Bruce."

"I'll miss you too." And in a familiar gesture he pushed his glasses up into his hair. "But I'm ready to go, Lynn. I couldn't even wait to get the furniture out of the house. The chairs she sat in, the address book in her handwriting, everything—I can't look at the things."

It would be years before he got over Josie, if ever. But I, too, Lynn thought, in my very different way I, too, face loss. I am opening a door and stepping into darkness, to a flight of stairs and a fall into darkness.

"I have lost my courage," she said suddenly. "This morning I still had it, and now it's gone."

"And no wonder. But you haven't really lost it. You've been under attack. Your good mind will recover and pull you through. I know it will."

He stood up. "Go on to bed, Lynn. It's late. Do you need help up the stairs?"

"Thanks, I'll manage." Stretching her sore cheeks, she tried to smile. "I must look awful. I'm afraid to look in the mirror."

"Well, you certainly don't look your best. But you'll mend. By the way, you should sleep in some other room, in Emily's. He'll be coming for his clothes, and they're probably in your room, aren't they? I want to keep him out of your way. And, oh, yes, you should take a sleeping pill. Are there any in the house?"

"Robert kept them for the times when he felt keyed up. But I've never taken one."

"Well, take one tonight."

Painfully, she pulled herself upstairs and got into bed. It crossed her mind, as some hours later she fell into the mercy of sleep, that she had quite forgotten to be ashamed before Bruce.

A stream of sunlight had already crossed the room at a noontime angle when Lynn awoke. Groggy and unwashed, she had fallen into bed, and now, still groggy and unwashed, she got up to go to the mirror.

The sight stunned her. She could hardly bear to look, and yet she had to keep on looking. That a human being could do this to another human face! One's identity, one's face that is like no other among all the billions on the earth! This violation of the most intimate property—it's rape in a dark alley, it's a sleeping household entered through a broken window, it's a freight car filled with half-crazed refugees, a prisoner led to a torture cell, it's every hideous thing that men do to one another.

She sobbed: Oh, my life . . . I wanted to make everything so beautiful for all of us. I did. I tried. I did. . . .

And then, a terrible fury took over. If he had been in the room and she had had a knife, she would have plunged it into his heart. Thank God, then, that he wasn't there, for she must preserve herself, get well, and be strong. She had brought three dependent lives into the world. *She* had. Not *he*. She, alone now. He had forfeited those lives, whether he knew it or not, had given them up forever. And Lynn gritted her teeth on that.

Then she ran the shower. Gingerly she cleansed her swollen, livid face of the blood that had dried black around her lips and nostrils. Carefully she pried open the eye that was half shut and bathed it. Then she powdered herself all over, put on scent, and fastidiously cleaned her nails. Let the body, at least, be presentable, even if the face was not. This was a question of self-respect.

When she came out into the bedroom, Eudora was straightening the bed. Most tactfully, she did not focus upon Lynn, but reported instead the events of the household.

"Mr. Lehman said to tell you good-bye. He had a long talk with Annie before he left, I didn't hear it, but Annie was willing to go to school, I didn't think she would be, but she was, and he drove her himself. Mr. Lawrence phoned, the doctor's coming again this afternoon, unless you need him sooner, then Mr. Lawrence will send a cab to take you to the office. Bobby's fine, he's already had his lunch, and I put him down for his nap. And Emily's on the way, she phoned from the airport, Annie called her last night, I couldn't stop her. So I guess that's about all."

"Oh, dear. She's in the middle of exams."

"Well, they'll wait. You're her mother," Eudora said firmly.

The house trembled when Emily arrived. The front door banged, and feet clattered up the stairs; she plunged into the room and, halfway toward Lynn, stopped.

"Oh, my God," she whispered, and began to cry.

"Oh, don't," said Lynn.

Poor child. She shouldn't have come, shouldn't see this.

"Emily darling, don't cry so. It looks worse than it is. Honestly."

"You would say that! I don't believe you. What are you doing, protecting him again?"

"No, no. That's over."

"Oh, my God, this is a nightmare! But it was only to be expected. It was only a question of time."

"Was it? I suppose so."

"Oh, Mom, what are you going to do?"

Emily sat down on the edge of the bed. There was such anguish in her question that for an instant Lynn had to turn away without answering.

"Do? Many things. My head's swimming with all I have to do."

"How did it happen? What led to it this time?" Emily asked, emphasizing *this time*.

"I'll tell you the whole thing, but first tell me how you came to that place. I was there too. I bought a picture, and she told me about you. You were in New York without letting me know. What happened? Why?"

So many secrets. So much going on behind each other's back.

"You knew what my thoughts have been, Mom. Suddenly I wasn't able to rest any longer while they were whirling in my head. So I took a plane to New York, spent a couple of hours, and flew right back."

"Whatever was in your mind when you went there? What did you expect to learn?"

"Maybe I felt there was some dark secret, I don't know. I was curious about Jeremy, though, and there wasn't any other way to find out about him."

"Well, did you find out anything?"

"He lives in England, and in a nice enough way, terse but still nice, she made it clear that he should be let alone. Obviously she doesn't want Dad to learn where he is. But who knows? Maybe someday—or maybe never—he'll want to know Annie and Bobby and me."

The winter afternoon was closing in and Lynn pulled the lamp cord to lighten the gloom.

"You're wondering what brought me there," she said, conscious that each of them had avoided saying the name "Querida." "When I considered what you had learned through Aunt Jean—it took me a while—I knew I had to reach back into the past. I had deliberately closed my mind. I realize that. And so I had to open it. Perhaps," Lynn said ruefully, "perhaps in a way I hoped, when I went in, that the woman would turn out not to be—to be Querida, and then I would not have to face facts. If there were any facts. And of course there were."

Now, having made herself say the name, Lynn made herself continue to the end of the horrifying story.

There was a long silence when she'd finished. Emily wiped her eyes, got up, walked to the window, and stood there looking out into the oncoming night. Lynn's heart ached at sight of the girl's bowed head; revelations like these are not what you want your nineteen-year-old daughter to hear.

"Poor Aunt Jean," Emily said. "She must have struggled all these years with herself: to tell or not to tell?"

"She couldn't possibly have told. There are some things too awful to let loose. It would be like opening a cage and letting a lion out."

"The lion got out anyway last night."

And again there was a silence; it was as if there were no words for the enormity of events.

Lamplight made a pale circle on the dark rug, laying soft, contrasting shadows in the far corners of the flowery room, with its well-waxed chests, its photographs and books.

And almost absently, Emily remarked, "You love this house."

"I don't know. I love the garden." The roof had caved in. Everything was shattered. "It will be sold."

"What's going to happen to Dad, do you think?"

"It's a big world. He'll find a place, I'm sure," Lynn said bitterly.

"I meant—will he go to jail for this?"

"No. He could, but I don't want that."

"I'm glad. It's true that he deserves it. Still, I should hate to see it."

"I know. I guess we're just that kind of people."

There was a tiredness in the room. They were both infected with it. They were people who had come, breathless after a steep climb, to the top of a hill, only to find another hill ahead.

"I had to come and see you." Emily spoke abruptly. "I thought I would lose my mind when I heard last night."

"But you have exams this week."

"I'll take a makeup on the one I missed today. Once I've seen the doctor, if he says you're all right, I'll go back. Harris came with me," she added.

Lynn was surprised. "Harris?"

"He insisted. He wouldn't let me go alone."

Lynn considered that. "I always liked him, you know."

"I do know, and he knows it too."

"So then, how are things with you both?"

"The same. But we're not rushing."

"That's good. Where is he?"

"Downstairs. He didn't think he ought to come into the house, but I made him."

"What, freezing as it is? Of course he should have come in. I'll put on some decent clothes and go down."

"Downstairs?" Emily repeated.

"It's just my face that's awful, not my legs."

"I meant—I thought, knowing how you are about yourself, that you wouldn't want anyone to see you like this."

Go down, put out your hand, and don't cringe. Don't hide. That time's over, and all the burden of pride is over too.

"No," Lynn said. "I don't mind. It's out in the open now."

7

SHE had spent so many hours in this chair across from this man Kane, whose ruddy cheeks, gray-dappled hair, and powerful shoulders were framed by a wall of texts and law reviews, that she was able to feel almost, if not entirely, comfortable.

"It's funny," she said, "although I know perfectly well that it's not true, I still, after all these months, have the feeling that something like this only happens among the miserable, helpless poor. How can it have happened to me? I ask myself. Ridiculous of me, isn't it?"

Kane shrugged. "I guess it is, although most people like you would be surprised to learn that twenty percent of the American people, when polled, believe it's quite all right to strike one's spouse on occasion. Do you know that every fifteen seconds another woman is being battered by her husband or her boyfriend in this country? There's nothing new about it either. Have you ever heard of the 'rule of thumb'? It's from the English common law, and it says that a man may beat his wife as long as the stick is no thicker than his thumb."

"What a fool I was! A weakling and a fool," she said softly, as if to herself.

"I keep telling you, stop the blame. It's easy enough for the world to see you as having been weak, for staying on so long. You saw yourself, though, as strong, keeping the home intact for your children. You wanted a house with two parents in it. In that sense you really were strong, Lynn."

Her mind was racing backward into a blur of years, as in an express train, seated in reverse direction, one sees in one swift glimpse after the other where one has just been. At the same time her passive gaze out of the window at her side fell upon a street where a cold, late April rain was sliding across a stationer's window, still filled with paper eggs and chicks, although Easter was long past. Holiday decorations were inexpressibly depressing when the holiday was over. . . . Robert had used to dye the eggs and hide them in the garden.

"And besides, in your case," Kane was saying, "one could say you had plausible reason for hope. One could, that is, if one hadn't the benefit of knowledge and experience with these cases."

His fingers formed a steeple; the pose was pontifical. Men in authority liked to make it, she thought, observing him.

"He is an extraordinarily intelligent man, according to Tom Lawrence and to his own counsel. And of course, there was his status. I don't mean that status was anything you sought, but he was admirable in the public's eyes, and that had to have had its effect on you."

"I guess so. But how unhappy he must have been in his youth!"

"Yes, but that's no excuse for making other people—a wife—pay for it. *If* that's the explanation at all."

"When he lost that promotion, he lost everything. I had an idea that he might even kill himself."

"More likely to kill you, it seems."

Kane shrugged again. It was an annoying habit, and yet she liked the man. He was sensible and plain spoken.

"I understand he has the offer of a job with some firm that's opening an office in Mexico. He's probably glad enough to go, even with a deal less money. But he's lucky, and his counsel knows it. You've let him off easily. No criminal charges and no publicity."

"I did it for my children. They have a terrible memory of this as it is. Annie's still having bad dreams, even with therapy."

"Well, he's out of their lives, even without Mexico. His attorney says he's satisfied about custody—he damn well better be! Your children are all yours. He said he thinks it will be better for them and for himself not to see them."

"My daughters don't want to see him. But it's a terrible thing for a man to lose his children, so if they should ever want to see him, I would not stand in the way. Right now, though, they refuse."

"He knows that. I believe he meant the little boy."

The little boy, now surefooted, could run all over the house. The first week or so after Robert's disappearance he had called "Daddy," but now whenever Tom came, he seemed to be just as comfortable playing on the floor with him as he had been with Robert.

"Bobby will not remember," she said, thinking, This is the second time that Robert has lost a son.

"So there being no contest, this will move along easily. You'll be free before you know it, Lynn." He regarded her with a kindly, almost fatherly smile. "How's the baking going? That cake you sent for my twins' birthday was fabulous. They're still talking about it."

"I've been doing some. One friend tells another and I get orders. But my mind's been too disturbed to do much of anything."

"And no wonder. Is there anything else you want to ask today?"

"Yes, I have something." And from the floor beside her chair she picked up a cardboard box and, handing it over to Kane, said only, "Will you please give this to Robert's lawyer for me? It belongs to Robert."

"What is it? I need to know."

"Just jewelry, some things I no longer want."

"All your jewelry?"

"All."

"Come, Lynn. That's foolish. Let me look at it."

"Open it if you want."

Each in its original velvet container lay the diamond wedding band, the solitaire, pearls, bracelets, and earrings, twenty years' worth of shimmering accumulation.

"Heavy. The best," he said as he spread the array on the desk.

"Robert never bought anything cheap," she said dryly.

Kane shook his head. "I don't understand you. What are you doing? These things are yours."

"They were mine, but I don't want them anymore."

"Don't be foolish. You'll have a pittance when this is over, you know that. There must be over one hundred thousand dollars' worth of stuff here."

"I couldn't wear any of it. Every time I'd touch them, I'd think"—and she put her finger on the bracelet, on the smooth, deep-toned cabochons in a row, emerald, ruby, sapphire, emerald, ruby—"I'd remember too much."

She would remember the diamond band on the white wedding day: flowers, taffeta, and racing clouds. She would remember the earrings bought that week when Bobby was conceived, when the night wind rustled the palms. She would remember the bench by the lake in Chicago, the cold windy night, the despair, and the crazy woman laughing. And she withdrew her finger as if the jewels were poisonous.

"Then sell the lot and keep the cash. You won't have anything to remind you of anything." Kane laughed. "Cash is neutral."

"No. I want to make a clear, clean break. Just get all you can for my children from the man who fathered them. For myself, I will take nothing except the house, or what's left of the sale after the mortgage is paid off."

Kane shook his head again. "Do you know you're incredible? I can't decide what to think about you."

He looked at Lynn so long and hard that she wondered whether he was seeing her with admiration or writing her off as some sort of pitiable eccentric.

"I've never had a client like you. But then, Tom Lawrence told me you were unique."

She smiled. "Tom exaggerates."

"He's always concerned about you."

"He has been a true friend in all this trouble. To me and to my children. Annie adores him."

Annie asks: "Will you every marry Tom, Mom? I hope you do."

And Emily, even Eudora, too, put on such curious expressions whenever his name is mentioned, just as Kane is doing now.

Well, it's wonderful to be wanted, she thought, and I daresay I can have him when I'm free, but right at the moment I am not ready.

"By the way, his lawyer mentioned something about Robert's books. He'll want to come for them. I'll let you know when. Perhaps you can have them packed so he can remove them quickly. And you should certainly have someone in the house when he comes."

"I'll do that."

"The house should sell fast. Even in this market the best places are snapped up. It's a pity that the mortgage company is going to get most of it."

"A pity and a surprise to me."

She stood up and gave him her hand. When he took it, he held it a moment, saying kindly, "You've had more surprises in your young life than you bargained for, I'm afraid."

"Yes. And the mystery is the most surprising."

"The mystery?"

"That when all is said and done, all the explanations asked for and given, I still don't really know why."

"Why what, Lynn?"

"Why I loved him so with all my heart."

"You need to get married again," said Eudora some months later. "You're the marrying kind."

"Do you think so?"

Eudora had gradually become a mother hen, free with advice and worries. She had taken to sleeping several nights a week at the house, ostensibly because she "missed Bobby," but more probably because she feared that somehow, regardless of new locks and burglar alarms, Robert might find his way in.

It was natural, then, that a pair of women in a house without a man should develop the kind of intimacy that enabled Eudora to say what she had just said.

"I was thinking maybe you shouldn't sign any papers to sell the house just yet." She spoke with her back turned, while polishing Lynn's best copper-bottomed pots. "You might want to stay here, you never know," she said, and discreetly said no more.

Of course they all knew what she meant. Tom Lawrence was in all their minds, as in Lynn's own. The two girls, Annie and Emily, home for Thanksgiving, were having lunch at the kitchen table and giving each other a sparkling, mischievous look.

"I shall never stay in this house," Lynn said firmly. She was breaking eggs for a sponge cake. "Eight, nine—no, eight. You've made me lose count. I have only stayed here this long because I've been instructed to until everything becomes final."

Divorce was a cold, ugly word, and she avoided it. *Everything* said it all just as well.

"And when will that be?" asked Emily.

"Soon."

"Soon," shouted Bobby, who was pushing a wooden automobile under people's feet.

"He repeats everything. And he knows dozens of words. Do you suppose he always understands what he says?" asked Annie.

Eudora's reply came promptly. "He certainly does. That's one smart little boy. One smart little boy, aren't you, sweetheart?"

"He's crazy about Tom," Annie informed Emily. "You haven't seen them together as much as I have. Tom spends half an hour on the floor with him every time he comes to take Mom out."

They were pressing her for information, and Lynn knew it. What they wanted was some certainty: along with the relief of knowing that the shock, the plural shocks, they had undergone were never to be repeated, they were feeling a certain looseness. There was neither anchor nor destination; the family was merely floating. So they were really asking her what was to come next, and she was not prepared to answer the question.

"I'm trying out a new recipe with the leftover turkey," she told them instead. "It's a sauce with black Mission figs. Sounds good, doesn't it?"

"Why, what's the celebration?" Emily wanted to know. "Who's coming?"

"Nobody but us. It's celebration enough to have you home. Do you want to invite Harris for leftover turkey?"

"Oh, thanks, Mom, I'll call him."

"Is Tom coming?"

"No, but he's coming tomorrow afternoon. It's the day your father will be here for his books."

In spite of herself Lynn felt a tremor of fear. She had not seen Robert since that horrendous night. And dread mounted now even as she stood stirring the yellow dough. Still, Tom would be there. . . .

"Eudora's going to put Bobby in his room while he's here, and I'd like you two to be out of the house. Go visit friends, or maybe there's a decent movie someplace."

Emily said cheerfully, "Okay." She got up and laid her cheek against Lynn's. "I know you worry about us. But we're both, Annie and I, pretty solid by now. As solid as we'll ever be, I guess, and that seems to be good enough."

"Thank you, darling, thank you."

As solid as they'd ever be. No, one never "got over" what they had seen. It would be with them for the rest of their lives, and they would just have to work around it. That was what they were doing; now in her second year, Emily had a 3.6 average, and Annie—well, Annie was trudging along in her fashion.

Alone in the kitchen a short while later, Lynn's thoughts found a center: Tom. No man could be more attentive. All through this troubled time he had been there, solid as a rock, for her to lean on. And as the trouble began, ever so gradually, to recede into the past, during these last few months especially, she had begun to feel again the stirrings of pure fun. They had danced and laughed and drunk champagne to commemorate the day when her last scar faded away. He had brought her again the brightness that had surrounded him on the fateful night of the dinner in his house.

He never made love to her, and that puzzled her, for how many times since they met had he not told her that she was lovely? It was not that she wanted him to attempt it; indeed, she would have stopped him, for something had died in her. Perhaps it was that that he sensed, and he was simply being patient. But it troubled her to think that she might never again be the passionate woman she once had been.

And Robert had always said, "Funny, but to look at you, no man would guess."

Yet she felt sure that ultimately Tom would ask her what the girls were hoping he would ask. Sometimes it seemed that when that moment came, she would have to say no to him, for what was lacking, she supposed, was the painful, wonderful yearning that says: *You and no other for the rest of our lives.* Yet, why not he, with his intelligence, his humor, charm, and kindness? A woman ought to have a man, a good man. It was a terrible thing to be alone, to face long years going downhill alone.

She would have to make up her mind, and soon. For only this morning on the telephone, he had answered her invitation to stay for lunch after Robert's coming: "Yes, I'll stay. I've been wanting to have a talk with you."

The day was bright. She had carefully considered what she was to wear, dark red if it should be raining, or else, in the sun, the softest blue that she owned. When she was finished dressing, she examined herself from the pale tips of her matching blue flats to the pale cap of her shining hair, and was more pleased with herself than she had been in a long time. Simplicity could be alluring without any jewels at all.

Eudora appraised her when she came downstairs.

"You look beautiful, Mrs. Ferguson." And she nodded as if there was complicity between the two women.

Eudora thought the dress was for Tom's benefit, which it was, but in a queer way, it was also to be for Robert's; let him see, especially with Tom in the house, that Lynn was still desired and desirable.

The books had been packed, and the cartons put in the front hall. Tom was already there when the car stopped in the driveway.

"He's got a driver with him to help him carry," he reported to Lynn, who stood half hidden in the living room. "Are you afraid? Why don't you go back into the den?"

"No." She could not have explained why she wanted to look at Robert, other than to say it was just morbid curiosity.

He wore a dark blue business suit out of the proverbial bandbox. She did not know whether it was surprising or not that he should be as perfect in his handsome dignity as he had ever been.

No greeting passed between him and Tom. It took several trips from the house to the car before the books were removed, and they were all accomplished in silence. She had thought and feared that perhaps he might try to talk to her and to plead, but he did not even seem to notice where she was standing.

On the last trip Eudora came out of the kitchen to give him a vindictive smile as she passed.

Ah, don't, Eudora! It is so sad. So very sad. You don't understand. How can you, how can anyone, except Robert and me?

At the doorstep Juliet came from the back of the house, wagging her tail at the sight of the man who had been her favorite in the family. When Lynn saw him stoop to caress the dog, she ran to the door. Something compelled her, and Tom's wavering touch did not restrain her.

"Robert," she said, "I'm sorry, so sorry that our life ended like this."

He looked up. The blue eyes, his greatest beauty, had turned to ice; without replying he gave her a look of such chilling fury, of such ominous, unforgiving power, that involuntarily, she stepped back out of his reach.

Tom closed the door. She went to the window to watch Robert walk down the path; it was as if she wanted to make sure that he had really gone away.

When Tom put a comforting hand on her shoulder, she was whispering, "To think he was my entire world. I can't believe it."

With his other hand on her other shoulder he turned her about to face him.

"Listen to me. It's over," he said quietly. "Let it be over. And now, I believe you promised me some lunch."

On a little table in front of the long window, she had set two places with a bowl of pink miniature chrysanthemums between them.

"If I can't eat outdoors when cold weather comes, I can at least look at the outdoors," she said, to start conversation.

And she followed his gaze across the grass, which was still dark emerald, although the birches, spreading their black fretwork against the sky, were quite bare.

They talked, and Lynn knew it was prattle, that, comfortable as they appeared to be, there was an underlying nervousness in each of them. The moment was approaching. At some time before they were to leave this room, she was certain, a momentous question would have been put.

It was incredible that even now, she could be still uncertain of her answer, although it seemed more and more as the minutes passed that her answer ought to be yes.

Thoughtfully, Tom peeled a pear, took a bite, pushed it aside, and began.

"We've had a rather special understanding, a feel for each other, haven't we?" And he paused as if waiting for confirmation, which she gave.

"That's true."

"There are things I want to say, things I've thought about for quite a time. What's brought it all to a head is that you've reached a turning point. Kane told me the other day that you're about to be free." He picked up the pear and then put it back on the plate. "I'm being really awkward. . . ."

Lynn said lightly, "That's not usual for you."

"No, it's not. I'm usually pretty sure of myself. Blunt, like a sledgehammer."

"Oh, yes," she said, still lightly, "I found that out one day at the club pool."

He laughed, and she thought, He's acting like a boy, a kid scared to be turned down.

"Well," Tom resumed, "perhaps I should organize my thoughts, begin from the beginning. You remember, I think I've told you about that night at my house when we were dancing and I confessed I'd had the intention of dancing you right into bed—you were so blithe, so sweet, so fresh-from-the-farm, and I had always been rather successful with women. That's an awful thing to say in 1990, so forgive me for saying it, will you? I hope you're not going to take it too badly."

"No, go on."

"Well, aside from that, I was mistaken in being so sure of you that night. I knew that later and was ashamed of myself, too, especially when on the very next morning I saw what trouble you were in. I surely wasn't going to add any other complications to your life. I suppose you're wondering what the point of all this rambling talk can possibly be."

"That you want to be honest about your feelings. Isn't that the point?"

"Precisely. Honest and open, which brings me to the present."

He stopped to take a drink of water that she knew he must not really want; it was only a means of delay. His forehead had creased itself into three deep, painful lines.

"So what I want to say is—oh, hell, it's difficult—I think we've come to the time we should stop seeing each other."

"Stop?" she echoed.

"Oh, Lynn, if you could know how I have anguished over this! I've thought and thought. Probably I should have ended this months ago but I couldn't bring myself to do it because I didn't *want* to end it, and I still don't *want* to now. But I know I must. It wouldn't be fair to you—or to myself—to go on misleading us both."

Tom took another drink of water and, to cover his agitation, adjusted his watch strap. Lynn was tingling and hot with shame; the blood beat in her neck.

"You haven't misled me, not at all," she cried. "I can't imagine how you ever got such an idea!"

Suddenly he reached and grasped both her hands. She tried to wrench them away, but he held them fast.

"You wouldn't want an affair, Lynn, while I would. But I don't want to get married again. I'm not the man to start another life rearing an adolescent girl and a toddler. Playing with Bobby for an hour is something very different. It wouldn't be right for any of us."

The irony of this, she was thinking. How foolish of me to have been so sure, to have misread—

He was tightening his hold on her hands; his voice was urgent and sad.

"Lynn, if I were starting life again now without all these experiences I've had, I would look for a wife like you. There's no one with whom I'd rather have spent my life. If I had met you in the beginning, I would have learned things about myself. . . . I've had two divorces, as you know, and other involvements besides. I live a certain way now, without obligations. It's a long story. No, don't pull your hands away, please don't. I know you haven't asked me to psychoanalyze myself, but I have to tell you. . . . I wouldn't do for you, Lynn, not in the long run. In the kind of life I lead, with the people I know, we are wary with each other. We don't expect things to last."

"I don't expect anything either. Not anymore. And you don't have to tell me all this."

"I wanted to. I did have to, because someday, I hope you'll find someone steady and permanent, not like me. I could have been that, I know that much about myself. But now—well, now I'm not the faithful type, and I know that too."

"Robert was faithful," she said for no reason at all, and her lips twisted.

"Yes. Confusing, isn't it?"

She pulled her hands away, and this time he released them.

"I've hurt you. I've hurt your pride, and that's not at all what I intended to do."

"Pride!" she said derisively.

"Yes, why not? You have every reason for it. Oh, I knew I'd be too damned clumsy to make this clear! But I couldn't simply stop calling or seeing you, could I? Without any explanation? It would have been far worse to leave you wondering what was wrong."

She said nothing, because that much was true.

"I only want you to move on now, Lynn, and you can't very well do that with me or any one man hanging around."

Still she said nothing, thinking, I have been rejected, and the thought stung hard. *A woman scorned.*

Yet he had not scorned her.

"Lynn? Listen to me. I only wanted not to mislead you, even though you say you expected nothing."

"That's so," she said with her head high.

"Then I'm glad. You've had betrayals enough."

When he stood up from the table, she rose, too, asking with dignity whether he was leaving now.

"No. Let's sit down somewhere else if you will let me. I have more things to say."

He took a chair near the unlit fire and sighed. She had never seen him so troubled.

"I told you once, didn't I, that I used to do matrimonial work? I quit because it wore me down. Too many tears, too much rage and suffering. The price was too high. But one thing it did was to teach me to see people, and that includes myself, far more clearly than I ever had."

"So you've told me I must find a man to marry me who will be faithful and permanent, ready to cope with my children. But that's not what I want. Right now I don't ever want to depend on a man again."

"Right!" The syllable exploded into the room. "Right! What I was going to tell you is that you shouldn't look for any man at all. Not now. You should look to yourself only. Put yourself in order. You don't *need* anyone. That's been your trouble, Lynn."

"What are you doing, scolding me?" The day was awful, first seeing Robert and now undergoing this humiliation, for say what one would, it was humiliation. "If you are scolding, it's inhuman of you."

"I'm sorry. I don't mean it that way. It's only that I know what you are and what you can be. I want you to be your best, Lynn." He finished quietly. "Robert didn't. He wanted you to be dependent on him."

Her right hand, reaching for her left, tried to twirl the rings that were no longer there. Remembering, she put her hands on the arms of the chair. And, meeting Tom's look of concern, admitted, "Until he left, I had never balanced a bank statement. I had hardly ever written a check."

"But now you do both."

"Of course. I've had to."

"Tell me, whatever happened to Delicious Dinners?"

"You know what happened. I had Bobby instead."

"Why can't you have both?" he asked gently.

Lynn shook her head. "The very thought is staggering. Money and child care, a place and time—I don't know how to begin."

"This very minute you don't, but you can learn. There are people who can tell you how to start a business, where to get the right child care, everything you'd need to know. Step out into the world, Lynn. It's not as unfriendly as it often seems."

For an instant the crinkles smiled around his eyes, until the look of concern replaced them again, and he asked, almost as if he were asking a favor, "Don't you think you can try? Look squarely at the reality of things?"

She smiled faintly. "Yes, that's what Josie used to say."

"And she was right."

The cat plodded in from the kitchen, switched its tail, and lay down comfortably at Tom's feet.

"He's made himself at home here, hasn't he? What do you hear from Bruce?"

The change of subject relieved Lynn. "Postcards with picturesque scenery. He writes to Annie and me, he tells about his work, which seems to be going well, but doesn't really say much, if you know what I mean."

"I had a card from him, too, just a few lines, rather melancholy, I thought."

"He'll never get over Josie."

"I don't think I ever felt anything that intense," Tom said soberly. "I suppose I've missed something."

"No. I'd say you're fortunate."

"You don't really mean that."

"Well, maybe I don't."

"Will you think seriously about what I've just said? Will you, Lynn?"

It was his look, affectionate and troubled, that finally touched her and lessened her chagrin. Aware that he was making ready to leave, she got up then and went over to take his hand.

"You are, when all is said and done, one of the best friends a person could ever want. And yes, I will think seriously about what you said."

So it ended, and for the second time that day she stood at the window to watch a man walk out of her life.

He had told her some rough truths. *Put yourself in order. Be your best.*

In a certain way these admonitions were frightening. Indeed, she could, she wanted, and would need to be an earner again. She had already been thinking about refreshing her secretarial skills, renting an apartment, and squirreling away for the inevitable emergencies whatever might remain to her after the mortgage company got its share.

It would be a meager livelihood for a woman with a family, yet it would be manageable; the hours would be regular, which meant that good day care for Bobby would not be too hard to find. But this was not at all what Tom had meant by "be your best."

She walked into the kitchen and stood there looking around. Everything sparkled, everything was polished, from the pots to the flowered tile, from the wet leaves of the African violets to the slick covers of the cookbooks on their shelves. Peaches displayed their creamy cheeks in a glass bowl on the countertop, and fresh, red-tipped lettuce drained from a colander into the sink. It came to her that this place was the one room in the house that had been completely her own; here she had worked hour upon hour, contented and singing.

For no particular reason she took a cookbook from a shelf; it fell open to the almond tart that she had made for that fateful dinner at Tom Lawrence's. And she kept standing there with the book in hand, thinking, thinking. . . .

Le Cirque, they'd said, applauding. The finest restaurants in Paris . . . Well, that's a bit of an exaggeration, a bit absurd, isn't it?

She walked back into the hall and through the rooms and back to where Tom had sat. "Put yourself in order," he said. So possibilities were there. You started simply, took courses, studied, learned. People did it, didn't they? You took what you might call a cautious chance. . . .

And after a while she knew what she must do. The thing was to move quickly. Hesitation would only produce too many reasons not to move. She went to the telephone and dialed her sister Helen's number.

"I have a surprise for you," she said.

Helen's voice had the upward lilt of eager curiosity. "I'll bet I know what it is."

"I'm sure you don't."

"It's about a man named Tom. Emily and Annie have both told me things. Isn't he the one who sent the needlepoint chair for Bobby?"

"You have a memory like an elephant. No, it's not about him or any other man. It's about me and what I'm to do with my life. I'm going into business for myself."

And a kind of excitement bubbled up into Lynn's throat. It was astonishing how an idea, taking shape in spoken words, could become all at once so plausible, so inevitable, so alive.

She could almost feel Helen's reaction, as though the wire were able to transmit an intake of breath, an open mouth, and wide eyes, as Helen shrieked.

"Business! What kind, for goodness' sake?"

"Catering, naturally. Cooking's what I do best, after all. I've been baking cakes to order, but we can't live on that."

"When did you decide on this?"

"Just an hour or two ago."

"What next? Out of the blue, just like that?"

"Well, not exactly. You know it's been in and out of my mind for ages. I've toyed with it. And now things have come together, that's all. Opportunity and necessity."

"And courage," Helen said, rather soberly. "It takes money to open a business. Is your lawyer getting any more out of Robert or something?"

"Nothing more than you already know."

"It's not much, Lynn."

"I wouldn't want more from him even if he had it."

"Well, I would. You are the limit, you are. Where's this business going to be, anyway?"

"Somewhere in Connecticut. Not this town, though. I want to get away."

There was a silence.

"Helen? Are you there?"

"I'm here. I'm thinking. Since you want to get away from where you are, why not make a big move while you're at it?"

"Such as?"

"Such as coming back here. You've been away only four years, and everybody knows you. People will give you a start here. Doesn't that make sense?"

Lynn considered it for a long minute. It did seem to make practical sense. She had perhaps not thought of going "home" because it might seem like going back for the refuge of family and a familiar place. But then, what was wrong with that?

"Doesn't it make sense?" Helen repeated.

"Yes. Yes, I believe it does."

"It will be wonderful to have you here again! Darwin," Lynn heard her call. "Come hear the news. Lynn's coming home."

The house, with its furnishings, was sold overnight. A formal couple, impressed by Robert's formal rooms, walked through it once and made an acceptable offer the next day.

Except for the kitchen's contents and the family's books, there was little to take with them. There were Emily's desk and Annie's ten-speed bicycle; to Lynn's surprise she also asked to keep the piano, although she had not touched it since the night when that final dissonant chord had crashed. Carefully, in a carton lined with tissue paper, Lynn packed pictures and photographs, treasured remembrances of her parents on their wedding day, of her grandparents, and her children from birth to graduation. When these were done, she stood uncertainly, holding the portrait of Robert in its ornate silver frame. As if they were alive, his eyes looked back at her. She had an impulse on the one hand to throw it, silver and all, into the trash, while on the other hand she reflected that posterity, perhaps at the end of the twenty-first century, might be curious to behold a great-grandfather. By that time probably no one alive would know what Robert Ferguson had really been, and his descendants would be free to praise and be pleased by his distinguished face. So she would let the thing lie wrapped up in an attic until then.

Two unexpected events occurred just before moving day. The first was a Sunday-afternoon visit from Lieutenant Weber and his wife.

"We weren't sure you would welcome us," said the lieutenant when Lynn opened the door. "But Harris said you would. He wanted us to come over and say good-bye."

"I'm glad you did," Lynn answered, meaning the words, meaning that it was good to depart from a place without leaving any vague resentments behind.

When they sat down, Mrs. Weber explained, "Harris thought, well, since you are moving away, he thought we ought to be, well, not strangers," she concluded, emphasizing *strangers* almost desperately. And then she resumed, "I guess he meant in case he and Emily—" and stopped again.

Lynn rescued her. "In case they get married, he wants us to be friends.

Of course we will. Why wouldn't we? We've never done each other any harm."

"I'm thankful you feel that way," Weber said. "I know I tried to do my best, but I'm sorry it didn't work."

"All of that is beginning to seem long ago and far away." Lynn smiled. "Can you believe they're already halfway through their sophomore year?"

"And doing so well with their A's," said Weber. "They seem to kind of run a race with each other, don't they? On the last exam Emily beat, but Harris doesn't seem to mind. It's different these days. When I was a kid, I'd've been sore if my girlfriend ever came out ahead of me."

"Oh, it's different, all right," Lynn agreed.

Talking to this man and this woman was easy, once the woman had recovered from her first unease. Soon Lynn found herself telling them about her plans, about the store she had rented and the house that Darwin had found for them.

"My brother-in-law's aunt and uncle have moved to Florida, but they don't want to sell their house in St. Louis because the market is so bad. So they'll let me stay there for almost nothing, just to take care of it. We'll be house-sitters."

Almost unconsciously, Mrs. Weber glanced around the living room, which was as elegant as it had ever been except for the slipcover on the blood-stained sofa. The glance spoke to Lynn, and she answered it.

"I shan't miss this at all, not even the kitchen."

"Yes, Emily told us about your kitchen."

"I'll show it to you before you leave. Yes, it's gorgeous. I'm taking my last money, my only money, to fix one like it in the shop. It's a gamble, and I'm taking the gamble."

So the conversation went; they talked a little more about Emily and Harris, talked with some pride and some natural parental worry. They admired the kitchen and left.

"No false airs there," Lynn said to herself after the couple had gone. "If anything should come of it, Emily will be in honest company. Good stock."

The second unexpected event concerned Eudora. She wept.

"I never thought you'd go away from here. I was sure that you and Mr. Lawrence—"

"Well, you were wrong. You all were."

"I'll miss my little man. And Annie too. And you, Mrs. Ferguson. I'll think of you every time I make the crepes you taught me to make. You taught me so much. I'll miss you."

"We'll miss you, too, don't you know we will? But I can't afford you. And the house isn't at all like this one. It's a little place that any woman can keep with one hand tied behind her back."

For a moment Eudora considered that. Then her face seemed to brighten with an idea.

"You'll need somebody in the shop, won't you? How can you do all the cooking and baking and serving by yourself?"

"I can't, of course. I'll need to find a helper, or even two, if I should be lucky enough to see the business grow that much."

"They wouldn't have to be an expert like you, would they? I mean, they would be people to do easy things and people you could teach."

There was a silence. And suddenly Lynn's face brightened too. Why not? Eudora learned fast, and she was so eager, waiting there with hope and a plea in her eyes.

"Eudora, are you telling me that you would—"

"I'm telling you that I wish you would take me with you."

The day arrived when the van that was to take the piano and the sundries rumbled up the drive. It was a colorless day under a motionless sky. The little group, almost as forlorn as the gray air, stood at the front door watching their few possessions being loaded into the van.

"Wait!" Lynn cried to the driver. "There's something in the yard in back of the house. It's a birdbath, a great big thing. Do you think you can make room?"

The man gave a comical grin. "A birdbath, lady?"

"Yes, it's very valuable, it's marble, with doves on it, and it mustn't be cracked or chipped."

"Okay. We'll fit it in."

"Mom, what do you want with it?" asked Annie.

"I don't know. I just want it, that's all."

"Because Uncle Bruce gave it to you?"

That canny child was trying to read her mind.

"Maybe. Now bring out Barney in the carrier and put on Juliet's leash. Don't forget their food and a bowl for water. We've a long way to travel."

So the final moment came. The van rumbled away, leaving the station wagon alone in the drive. For a moment they all took a last look at the house. Aloof as ever, it stood between the long lawns and the rising hill, waiting for new occupants as once it had waited for those who were now leaving it.

"The house doesn't care about us," Lynn said, "and we won't care about it. Get in, everybody."

The station wagon was full. Annie sat in the front, Eudora and Bobby had the second row, and in the third, alongside Barney in his carrier, sat Juliet, so proud in her height that her head almost touched the roof.

"We're off!" cried Lynn. And not able, really, to comprehend the tumult of regret and hope and courage that whirled through her veins, she could only repeat the cry, sending it bravely through the quiet air: "We're off!"

The car rolled down the drive, turned at the end, and headed west.

PART FIVE

◇

Winter 1992–1993

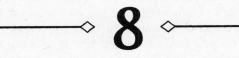

E MILY, who was home for spring break, propped her chin in her hands and leaned on the kitchen table as she watched Lynn put another pink icing rosebud on a long sheet cake.

"It seems so strange to have it still cold in March," she remarked. "Right now in New Orleans the tourists are sitting in the French Market having a late breakfast, beignets and strong, dark coffee. Do you know how to make beignets, Mom?"

"I've never made any, but I can easily find out how."

"That cake's absolutely gorgeous. Where and when did you ever learn to be so professional?"

"At that three-week pastry course I took last year."

"I'm so in awe of what you've done in just two years."

"Two years and five months. But talk about awe! Harvard Medical School! I'm so proud of you, Emily, that I want to walk around with a sign on my back."

"Wait till next September when I'll actually be there."

Cautiously, Lynn inquired, "How is Harris taking it?"

"What? My going to Harvard? He wasn't admitted there, so I'll go to Harvard and he'll be at P & S, which is mighty good too. I don't feel happy about it, but I certainly wasn't going to turn down an opportunity like this one."

You turned Yale down, Lynn thought, but said instead, "I wouldn't expect you to. And if you still keep on loving each other, the separation won't alter things."

"Exactly," agreed Emily.

She had come a long way. Yet she still looked like a high school girl with her jeans and sneakers and the red ribbon holding her hair back from her radiant face. From her father she had received some intellectual gifts and the handsome bone structure, but thank God, nothing more. She would do well with or without Harris or anyone else.

Never tell a daughter, Lynn thought now, that she'll find a wonderful man who will love and take perfect care of her forever. That's what my mother told me, but then it was in another time, another age.

With the last rose firmly affixed she stepped back to appraise her work.

"Well, that's finished. I like to do jobs like this one here in my own kitchen. There's too much going on at the shop for me to concentrate on fancy work."

The kitchen smelled of warm sugar and morning peace. It was quiet time while Annie was in school and Bobby in nursery school, time for a second cup of coffee. And she sat down to enjoy one.

In their big basket five puppies squealed and tumbled, digging at their mother in their fight for milk.

"They're so darling," Emily said. "Are you going to keep them all?"

"Heavens, no. Annie wants to, of course, but we'll have to find homes for four of them. I've consented to keep one. Then we'll have Juliet spayed."

Emily was amused. "How on earth did such a thing happen to our pure-bred Bergamasco lady?"

"She got out somewhere, maybe before I had this yard fenced in. Or maybe somebody got in. I have my suspicions about a standard poodle who lives near here, because a couple of pups have long poodle noses. They're going to be enormous."

One of them fell out of the basket just then and made a small puddle on the floor. Lynn jumped, replaced the pup, and cleaned the puddle, while Emily laughed.

"Mom, I was thinking, wouldn't Dad be furious that Juliet had mongrel puppies?"

"He wouldn't approve, that's sure. He wouldn't approve of this whole house, anyway."

She looked out into the hall, where Bobby's three-wheeler was parked and a row of raincoats hung on an old-fashioned clothes tree. How relaxing it was not to be picture perfect all the time, neat to the last speck of dust, prompt to the last split second. . . .

Emily remarked, "I rather like old Victorians with the wooden gingerbread on the front porch and all the nooks. Of course, this furniture's pretty awful."

"If I buy the house, I'll certainly not buy the furniture. And I might buy it. They've decided to sell, and since they're Uncle Darwin's relatives, they've offered easy terms. Maybe I shouldn't do it, but the neighborhood's nice, the yard's wonderful for Bobby, and I am finally meeting expenses with a little bit left over. So maybe I should." Lynn smiled. "Live dangerously! Have I told you that I've given Eudora a ten percent interest in the business, plus a salary? She's my partner now, and she's thrilled. She learns fast when I teach her. And, of course, she has her own Jamaican dishes that people love, her rice-and-peas, her banana pies, all good stuff. She can oversee the shop while I'm home baking or, if I'm busy at the shop, she'll come back here to let Annie and Bobby in after school. So it's been working out well for all of us."

Emily, absorbed in this account, marveled at the way the business had just "leapt off the ground" and "taken flight."

"There's a big demand," responded Lynn. "With so many women working now, it's not just a question of dinners and parties, it's also all the food we freeze and cook daily to sell over the counter. Besides, it was a good idea to come back here where dozens of people remembered me."

Emily asked, "Does Uncle Bruce write often?"

"Well, I wouldn't say often, but he certainly writes."

His friendly chatty letters. His work, his travels. And nothing more.

"The latest news is that they want him to open a new office in Moscow. He's been taking lessons in Russian."

Emily opened her mouth, made a sound, and closed her mouth.

"What is it? What is it you want to say?"

"I wanted to ask—to ask whether you ever heard from Dad."

"The only contact I have or will ever want to have is with the bank, when they forward his remittances for all of you. Apparently he has a very good job." Lynn hesitated over whether to say anything more, and then, deciding to, went ahead. "Have you heard from Dad?"

"A birthday present, a check, and a book of modern poetry. He didn't say anything much about himself, just hoped I was happy."

His girls, his Emily, Lynn thought, and, in a moment of painful empathy, felt Robert's loss. But it was done, there was no undoing it. . . .

She stood up and removed her apron, saying briskly, "I have to go to the shop now. Oh, Aunt Helen's going to come by to pick up the cake."

"Twenty-five years married!"

"Yes, and happily."

"Dad always thought Uncle Darwin was an idiot, didn't he?"

"He thought a lot of people were, and he was wrong."

It was uncomfortable to be reminded of Robert's scorn, the twist of his mouth, the sardonic wit at other people's expense, the subtle digs about the Lehmans' being Jewish or even about Monacco's being Italian. And it was obvious that Emily, too, had been uncomfortable asking.

On sudden impulse Lynn bent to stroke her daughter's forehead. "What are you going to do while I'm gone, honey?"

"Nothing. Just be lazy. It's vacation."

"Good. You need to be lazy. Enjoy it."

Let life be sweet, let it be tranquil, Lynn thought as she drove through the quiet suburban streets. As best we can, we must plaster over the taint and the stain. Bobby would not remember that night, and Annie always would; but her intelligence, which Robert had so disparaged, would help her. It had already helped her. And therapy had helped, but chiefly she had improved because Robert was gone. It was as simple as that. She had lost twenty pounds, so that her face, no longer pillowed in fat, had developed a kind of piquant appeal. Her hair had been straightened, and now, for the first time, she was pleased with herself. She had even gone back, entirely unbidden, to the piano!

They had come far since the day the station wagon had crossed the Mississippi and they had spent their first night in the strange house. It had been after midnight, raining and very cold. Darwin had started the furnace, and Helen had made up the beds into which they had all collapsed.

The rain had beaten at the window of the strange room where Lynn lay. From time to time she had raised her head to the bedside alarm clock. Three o'clock . . . Her heart had jumped in a surge of pure panic. Here she was, responsible for all these people, for her children and even for Eudora, so hopeful, so faithful, and so far from home. Panic spoke: You can't go it alone. It's too much and too hard. You don't know anything. All right, you can cook, but you're no five-star genius. What makes you think you can do this? How dare you think you can? Fool, fool, you can't. And the rain kept beating. Even the rain, as it told of the relentless world outside, was hostile. Then dawn came, a dirty gray dawn, to spill its dreary light upon the ugly furniture in the strange room.

What are you thinking of? You can't do it alone.

But she had done so. She had admonished herself: Head over heart. You won't accomplish anything lying here in bed and shivering with fear. So she had gotten up, and in that same dreary dawn, had taken pen and paper to make a list.

First there was school registration and continued counseling for Annie. Then a visit to the store that was, she had thought wryly, to make her fortune, to see there what needed to be done. Next, a visit to one of those volunteer businessmen's groups where someone would show her how to go about starting a business; she had read that these groups could be very helpful.

"The world is not as unfriendly as it often seems to be," Tom had assured her. Maybe, she had thought in that gray dawn, maybe it's true. I shall find out soon enough.

And now Lynn had to smile, remembering how very friendly it could be. For the man who had helped her the most, a fairly young man, retired in his mid-forties, had been sufficiently admiring of what he called her "enterprise," to become very serious, serious enough to propose marriage.

"I like you," she had told him, "and I thank you. I like you very much, but I am not interested in getting married."

It was one thing and very natural to desire the joy of having a man in the bed; it was one thing to welcome the trust and commitment of a man as friend; but to be *possessed* in marriage, to be *devoured* in marriage as she had been, even discounting Robert's violence, was another thing. He had *devoured* her. It was this that she feared. The day might come when equality in marriage might seem a possibility and she would have lost her fear, but not yet. Not yet. At least not with any of the men she had been seeing.

There had been men to whom Helen and their old friends had introduced her, men decent, intelligent, and acceptable. Some of them had been fun in many ways. Yet that was all. She was not ready.

She liked to say, laughing a little at the excuse, although it was obviously a true one, that she simply hadn't the time! When people, usually women, inquired and urged, "Why don't you? George or Fred or Whoever is really so nice, so right for you," she would protest that she had Annie and an active little boy, she had the business, she hadn't an hour; couldn't everyone see that?

Sometimes—often—she thought of Bruce. She relived the day, the only day, they had made love. Time had faded the guilt and left her with the memory of a singular joy. She thought about it long and deeply now, wanting to relive it and to understand it. And, ultimately, she came to understand the subtle difference between sex that was giving and sex that was all taking, sex that was ownership. Robert had *owned* her, while Bruce had not. And she knew in her heart that Bruce would never want to own a woman; he would want her to be free and equal.

But it was useless to be thinking at all about him. Except for those brief letters and postcards with pictured castles from Denmark or Greece, he had disappeared into another life, vanished from the stage on which Lynn's life was being played.

Once, a month ago, she had been surprised by the appearance of Tom Lawrence. He had been in St. Louis to take a deposition and had telephoned the shop.

"I took a chance on 'Delicious Dinners' and looked it up in the phone book," he said. "Will you have dinner with me?"

And she had gone, feeling both gratitude and pride in being able to show him how well she had carried out his advice. Gratitude and pride, but nothing more.

She had been completely honest with him.

"I would have married you if you had asked me that day. I was prepared to," she said. "Now I thank you for telling me it would have been a mistake."

He answered seriously, "As I told you then, it would have been different if I had met you when I was twenty years younger and maybe wiser."

She laughed. "You would have spared me a ton of trouble if you had."

"Why? Would you have taken me then instead of Robert?"

Considering that with equal seriousness, she shook her head.

"No. At that time the Prince of Wales probably couldn't have gotten me away from him."

"Lynn, it's so good to see you! And you're looking so lovely, younger; all the tension seems to have been wiped away."

She said playfully, "You don't think running a business is tension?"

"Yes, but it's a very different kind." He smiled at her with the old brightness, not mischievous now, but affectionate. "I like your suit. I like your pearls. I thought you had given back all the jewelry."

"I did. I bought these myself."

"They're handsome. Pure white, European taste. Americans prefer creamy ones. You see how much I know?"

She had been passing a jeweler's on the day that her bank loan, obtained through Darwin's willingness to cosign the note, had been paid off. She was then in the black. And she had stood for a minute staring at the marvelous blue-white pearls, struggling with herself. She didn't need them. But she loved them. She wanted them. So she went in and walked out with the pearls in hand, *her* pearls, for which there was no reason to thank anyone but herself.

"What do you hear from Bruce?" Tom had inquired.

It had seemed that everyone in town who had ever known Bruce was always asking that, and now she replied as always, "Not very much. He seems to be frightfully busy."

"He is. I happened to mention him the last time I saw Monacco and he told me. Actually he said Bruce is a 'brilliant guy. Quiet, with no brag about him.' "

"I'm glad for him. At that rate I don't suppose we'll ever see him again."

Tom had looked at her keenly. "What makes you say that?"

"The paths life takes. You meet, you stay for a while, and you part."

"He was very fond of you."

"And I of him."

"I understand you went back a long time together."

"That's true."

A long time. Back and back into the dimmest corners of the mind and memory. Young days in the sun, easy and familiar as brother and sister. Snatches of memory popping like switchboard lights. The morning Robert bought the bracelet and Bruce said, "Take it, you deserve it." She had not known then what he meant. The day he phoned from the hospital where he had taken Emily. The day he fetched Annie after she had run away. The day they had made love in Josie's house; wrong as it had been, it had been comforting, it had been voluptuous, it had been happy. It had been right. And then had come the night when, awakening from unconsciousness, she felt him washing her damaged face.

Memory, going back and back.

But she had not wanted to speak of these things to Tom, had herself been troubled because she was not sure what they really meant, and because, after all, they were useless.

The car came to a stop on a pleasant street bordered with prosperous shops and trees that would in a few months give summer shade. Between a florist's and a bookstore hung a bright blue sign on which in fine old-fashioned script was written DELICIOUS DINNERS. Beneath the sign, in a bow window, stood a table, beautifully set with a spring-yellow cloth, black-

and-white china, and a low bowl of the first daffodils. Customers were going in and customers were coming out at the bright blue door.

Two young girls in starched white were busy at the counter when Lynn went in. At the rear, behind swinging doors, the work was being done; a woman was cleaning vegetables, and Eudora was arranging a fish platter for a ladies' luncheon.

"Well, I finished the cake," Lynn said. She looked at her watch. "Plenty of time for me to do the salad bowl and the cornbread sticks. I told her that a French bread would be better, but she wanted the sticks. Is that my apron on the knob?"

An hour later she was taking the corn sticks out of the oven when one of the salesgirls opened the swinging door.

"There's a man here who insists on seeing you. I told him you were busy, but he—"

"Hello," Bruce said.

"Oh, my God!" Lynn cried, and dropped the pan on the table.

"Yes, it's who you think it is." And he opened his arms.

She was laughing, she was crying, as he hugged her and the astonished onlookers gaped.

"I thought you were in Russia! What are you doing here?"

"I was supposed to go to Russia, had my things ready, had my tickets, but then I changed my mind, changed the airline, and arrived at Kennedy this morning instead. Then I made this connection. I didn't have time to shave. Sorry."

"Who cares? I can't believe it. No warning, nothing." She babbled. "Emily's here on spring break. Guess what! She got into Harvard Med. She'll be so glad to see you. She'll be bowled over. And Annie keeps wondering whether you'll ever come to see how well she's taking care of Barney. Oh," she repeated, "I can't believe it." And pulling away from the hug, she cried, "And look who's here! Eudora!"

"Eudora? What are you doing here in the Midwest?"

"She's my partner," Lynn answered before Eudora could get the words out. "She has an interest in this place."

Bruce looked around. "You never told me when you wrote that it was anything like this. I had no idea."

He saw the shelves, the enormous, gleaming stove and freezer, the trays of cookies, the people at the counter waiting to be served.

"Why, it's stupendous, Lynn. I expected you would be doing, oh, I don't know. I expected—"

"That I'd be making dinners single-handedly? Well, I started that way.

There were only Eudora and I the first few months, but business grew. It just grew."

In his excitement Bruce had pushed his glasses back into his hair, and she had to laugh.

"You never keep them on your eyes."

"What? These? Oh, I don't know why I do it. Tell me, can we have lunch? Can I drag you away from here?"

Lynn appealed to Eudora. "Can you manage without me? I don't want to run out on you, but—"

"No, no, it's fine. I only need to toss the salad and make some pea soup. You go." Eudora was enjoying the surprise. "Better take off your apron before you do, though."

"I'll use my car," Bruce said. "I rented one at the airport. I've already taken my stuff to the hotel. I got a suite. I had too much stuff to fit into one room. Let's go back there for lunch, I'm starved. I only had coffee this morning."

"You brought all your things out to St. Louis? I don't understand."

"It's a long story. Well, not so long. I'll tell you when we sit down."

He was all charged up; it was entirely unlike him to talk so fast.

"Well," he began when they were seated in the dining room, quiet and hushed by carpets and curtains. "Well, here I am. It feels like a century since I was last in this place. Remember our farewell party here before we all left for New York? You look different," he said quizzically. "I don't know exactly what it is, but I like it. You look taller."

She was suddenly self-conscious. "How can I possibly look taller?"

"It's something subtle, perhaps the way you stand, the way you walked in here just now. Something spirited and confident. Not that I didn't like the way you looked and walked before. You know that, Lynn."

She did not answer. Tom, too, had given many a compliment, and she no longer took much stock in compliments.

"You look peaceful," Bruce said, studying her face. "Yes, I see that too."

"Well, I've made peace with a lot of things. I think you'll be glad about one of them. A while back I went with some of the women to a tea at that house where Caroline fell into the pond. I made myself go to look at the pond, and for the first time I was able to remember what happened without blaming myself. I accepted, and felt free." She finished quietly, "That was your doing, Bruce, that afternoon in your house." She smiled. "Now tell me about yourself, what's been happening."

He began. "I took the position, as you know, because I wanted to get away. And I threw myself into the work. It was a godsend. We worked like beavers, all of us did, and I do think we've made great strides. The company was pleased. I even got a letter from Monacco, offering me the post in Moscow. Well, I almost took it. But then I decided to go home."

"What made you do that? You were on the way to bigger things, like wearing Monacco's shoes one day," she said, thinking of how Robert had coveted those shoes.

"That's the last thing I'd want, heading an international corporation, with all its politics. It's good that some people want it, just the way some people want to be President of the United States, but I don't want either. I told them I'd like to go back to my old place here in St. Louis, only this time I'd be the boss. That much authority, I'd like."

"Why not New York, at least?"

"I never liked New York. Again, it's a fine place for some people, for the millions who live there and love it and for the millions more who would like to be there. But millions more, including me, wouldn't," he ended firmly.

Curiosity drove Lynn further. "So why did you go there in the first place? You didn't have to."

This time he replied less firmly, almost sheepishly, "I guess I wanted to show I was as good as Robert. It was pride, but I think I wanted to prove that I could do whatever he could, and do it just as well. I knew he never liked me and had a low opinion of me."

Astonished, she pursued him. "But why should you have cared about Robert's opinion?"

"I told you. Pride. Human beings are foolish creatures. So now that I've proved what I can do, I don't care anymore."

This strange confession touched her heart in an unexpected way. She felt hurt on his behalf, hurt for him.

He looked down at his plate and then, raising his eyes, said somewhat shyly, "I had a letter from Tom Lawrence after he came here to see you a couple of months ago."

"Yes, he was here."

And still shyly, Bruce said, not asking a question but making a statement, "Then you and Tom have something serious going."

"I don't know what makes you think that. He didn't come to see me. He had business in the city and looked me up, that's all. He's a fine man, and he has his charm." She smiled. "But he's not for me, and I'm not for him either."

"Really?" The brown eyes widened and glowed. "I thought he had come on purpose to see you. Not that he said anything definite, but anyway, I'd been expecting something of the sort." Bruce stumbled. "I always thought you and he—"

She said stoutly, "For a while I had some fleeting thoughts, too, but it was very halfhearted, a sort of desperation, I guess, still thinking that a woman can't survive without a man. I've got over that. God knows it took me long enough."

"You can't mean that you're writing men off because of what you've been through?"

"I didn't say that."

They were sparring. If they had been fencing, they would have just tipped their weapons and retreated, tipped again and retreated. She became aware that her heartbeat was very fast.

"I'm glad it's not Tom," Bruce said suddenly.

"Are you?"

"Is it—is there anybody else?"

"No. There could be, there could've been more than one, but I didn't, I don't, want any of them."

She looked away at the tables where people were talking in low voices about the Lord knew what, the movie they had seen last night or maybe what they were going to do with their whole lives. And as she sat with her forlorn hands resting on the table, she wished that Bruce had not returned to live here where she would be bound to encounter him, bound to treat him like a cousin or a good old friend. Until this moment, in spite of her intermittent longings, she had not realized how deep those longings were; they had always been stifled. Here she sat and there, only inches away, were his warm lips and warm arms. They would have their lunch and smile and part until the next time, and that would be all.

She wanted to get up and run out. But people don't do things like that. They conceal and suffer politely.

"A few weeks ago I went over that batch of pictures you gave me," he said. "I spread them out so I could travel through the years. I had—I guess I had—an epiphany."

Startled by the word, Lynn raised her eyes, which met a long, grave gaze.

"I saw everything, saw you and saw myself quite clearly. I shocked myself with my sudden knowledge of what I had to do." Leaning over the table, he placed his hand on hers. "You've always been very dear to me, I don't know whether you felt it or not. But don't misunderstand; I don't need to tell you how I loved Josie. So how could I admit that there was still room for you? How could I?"

Her eyes filled with tears and she did not answer.

"Tell me, am I too late? Or perhaps too early? Tell me."

Very low, she replied, "Neither. Neither too early nor too late."

A smile spread from his mouth to his eyes; they radiated an amber light. The smile was contagious; Lynn began to laugh while her tears dropped.

"How I love you, Lynn! I must have loved you for years without knowing it."

"And I—I remember the day you left. I turned the corner and you were waving—"

"Don't. Don't cry. It's all right now." He shoved the coffee cup aside. "Let's go upstairs. It's time."

And to think that only this morning on the way to work she had been thinking of him, with such desire and so wistful a sense of "never again"!

"Love in the afternoon," she whispered. This time there was no sorrow, no search for comfort, no guilt, only the most honest, trusting, naked joy. Tightly together, they lay back on the pillows.

"I'm so contented." Bruce sighed. "Let's not go back to your house this minute. We need to talk."

"All right. What shall we talk about?"

"I'm just letting my mind wander. Maybe someday when we're tired of doing what we're doing we could open a country inn. What do you think?"

"Darling, all the options are open."

"We could furnish it with antiques. I got some old things in Europe, Biedermeier, it's being shipped. You'd be surprised how well it looks with other things, I never liked it before, but—"

Suddenly he laughed his loud, infectious laugh.

"What's funny?"

"I was thinking of the times I must have been gypped. Those old pieces that I so lovingly restored . . . A fellow told me of a place in Germany where they manufacture them and send them over here, all battered and marred with five coats of peeling paint. I used to spend hours removing it to get down to the original. Remember how Annie used to help me? Oh, Lord!" He shook with laughter. "Lynn, I'm so happy. I don't know what to do with myself."

"I'll tell you what. Let's get dressed after all and go back to the house. I want you to see everybody, and I want them to see you."

"Okay." He kept talking. "You know, I think another reason why I took that post in Budapest was that I had always envied Robert for having you without deserving you. I was pleased to see him punished when he saw me take his place. Very small minded, I know."

"Very human too."

And she pondered, while combing her hair before the mirror, "I wonder, do you believe Robert became what he did because of his father?" The name "Robert" sounded strange when spoken in her own voice. She had no occasion anymore to use it. "Of course he could easily have done just the opposite to prove himself different, couldn't he?"

"He could have, but he didn't, and that's all that matters."

Bruce came behind her, and the two faces looked back out of the mirror.

"Bruce and Lynn. It's funny how there's really never any one person for any of us. In my case, if it hadn't been Josie, it could have been you."

She thought, Tom Lawrence said something like that, not quite the same, but almost.

"But Josie and I are so different," she replied.

"That's what I mean. Tell me, if it hadn't been Robert, could it have been me?"

She answered truthfully, "I don't know what I would have done then. Someone else once asked me that question, and I answered that not even the Prince of Wales could have gotten me away from him. I was bewitched—then. I wasn't the person I am now."

"But if you had been the person you are now? Or is that an impossible, a foolish, question?"

"Foolish, yes. Because, can't you see, don't you know, that if I had had my present head on my shoulders—" She turned about and took his face between her hands. "Oh, my dear, oh, my very dear, you know it would have been yes. A thousand times yes."

In the living room Annie was practicing scales. Downstairs in the makeshift playroom that would have to be made over, Bobby and two four-year-old friends were playing some raucous game.

"I hope," Lynn said, "you think you can get used to a very noisy household."

"I lived in a very quiet one for a long, long time. I will get used to it with gratitude."

They were standing in the little sun parlor overlooking the yard. She had shown him around the house, he had been welcomed by the family, who, perhaps guessing what was afoot, had left them in this room by themselves.

"Look out there," Lynn said. "What do you see?"

"Don't tell me you moved the birdbath with you."

"At the last minute I couldn't leave it."

A mound of grainy, half-melted snow lay at the marble base, while the rest of the lawn was bare, ready for spring.

"I have it heated in the winter. Birds need water in the winter too."

"It's like you to think of that. Nine out of ten people wouldn't."

"Look, look at that lovely thing! It's the first robin, first of the season. Watch it drink. It must be tired and thirsty after its long flight from the south."

The bird fluttered into the water, shook itself, and flew away into the trees.

"I wonder what it thinks. That there's a whole bright summer ahead, maybe."

"I can't imagine, but I know what I'm thinking."

She looked up into the dear face. The glasses were pushed back again into the curly brown hair, and the eyes sparkled.

"I'm thinking of our own bright summer, and all the years ahead."

HOMECOMING

CHAPTER

1

The desktop was always covered with mail, incoming and outgoing. Appeals from charities, politicians, whether federal, state, or town, bills and letters from scattered friends, all came flowing. Sometimes it seemed to Annette that the whole world made connection with her here and asked for response.

She picked up the pen to finish the last of the notes. Her precise backhand script lay between wide margins, the paper was as smooth as pressed linen, and the dark blue monogram was decorative without possessing too many curlicues. The whole, even to the back of the envelope, on which her name was engraved—Mrs. Lewis Martinson Byrne, with her address beneath—was pleasing. E-mail might be the way these days, but there was still nothing as satisfying to send or to receive as a well-written letter; also these days, "Ms." might be the title of choice for many, but Annette still preferred to be "Mrs.," and that was that.

Having sealed the envelope, she placed it on top of the tidy pile of blue-and-whites, sighed, "There—that's finished," and stood up to stretch. At eighty-five, even though your doctor said that you were physically ten years younger, you could expect to feel stiff after sitting so long. Actually, you could expect almost anything, she thought, knowing how to laugh at herself.

Old people were amusing to the young. Once when she was less than ten years old, her mother had taken her to call on a woman who lived down the country road. It seemed, as most things did now, like yesterday.

"She's very old, at least ninety, Annette. She was a married woman with children when Lincoln was president."

That had meant nothing to Annette.

"My nephew took me out in his machine," the old woman had said. "We went all the way without a horse." Marveling, she had repeated, "Without a horse."

That had seemed ridiculous to Annette.

"So now it's my turn," she said aloud. "And yet, inside, I don't feel any different from the way I felt when I was twenty." She laughed again. "I only look different."

There she was between the windows, framed in gilt, eternally blond and thirty years old, in a red velvet dress. Lewis had wanted to display her prominently in the living room, rather than here in the more private library. But she had objected: portraits were intimate things, not to be shown off before the world.

Facing her and framed in matching gilt on the opposite wall was Lewis himself, wearing the same expression he had worn in life, alert, friendly, and faintly curious. Often, when she was alone here, she spoke to him.

"Lewis, you would have been amused at what I saw

today" (or saddened, or angry). "Lewis, what do you think about it? Do you agree?"

He had been dead ten years, yet his presence was still in the house. It was the reason, or the chief one, anyway, why she had never moved.

It had been a lively house, filled with the sounds of children, friends, and music, and it was lively still. Scouts had meetings in the converted barn, and nature-study classes were invited. Once the place had been a farm, and after that a country estate, one of the less lavish ones in a spacious landscape some two or three hours' drive from New York. They had bought it as soon as their growing prosperity had allowed. The grounds, hill, pond, and meadow were treasures and had already been promised after Annette's death to the town, to be kept as a green park forever. That had been Lewis's idea; caring so much about plants and trees, he had built the greenhouse onto the kitchen wing; all their Christmas trees had been live, and now, when you looked beyond the meadow, you saw in a thriving grove fifty years' worth of Scotch pines and spruce.

Of course, it was all too big, but Annette loved it. Especially she loved this room. It was—what was the word for it? Cozy, perhaps? No, that was a poor word to describe it. *Cozy* meant too much stuff: too many afghans, plants, and pillows. This room's walls were covered with books: novels, biography, poetry, and history. The colors were many quiet shades of blue. Today, in winter, one dark red amaryllis flourished in an earthenware pot on the desk.

In the corner there was a large dog-bed for the two King Charles spaniels. They had always kept spaniels. Roscoe, a gangly, homely mongrel with sorrowful eyes, had a mat of his own. He was completely dependent on Annette, who had found him deserted and hungry on a Caribbean beach. And she wondered whether, after having lived all these years in comfort, he had any memory of his past misery. She wondered about animals. She wondered, in fact, about everything. . . . But she had better get moving with this pile of letters if they were to be picked up today.

The morning was mild, one of those calm, cold winter mornings without wind, when the pond lay still and lustrous as stainless steel. Soon, if this cold were to last, it would freeze over. Wearing a heavy jacket and followed by the dogs, she went down the drive to the mailbox at the end.

CHAPTER

2

I didn't say I wouldn't go, Dad. I only said I didn't feel like going."

"Cynthia, I understand. Our hearts ache for you. You can't know how much."

Across the miles she heard his sigh and saw him seated in his wing chair, high above the Potomac, with the telephone in his hand and a view of the Jefferson Memorial before him. She knew that her parents suffered as people suffer for a bomb victim or an amputee, yet still with no true knowledge of his pain.

Gran's note lay on her lap, written, of course, on the familiar paper that had accompanied every greeting and every birthday present going back to the year when Cynthia had learned to read.

Come Saturday whenever it's convenient for you,

spend the day with me, have dinner and stay overnight.
Stay as long as you like, if you've nothing you'd rather do.

Gran was wonderful, with her sweetness, humor, and old-fashioned foibles. But Cynthia was not in the mood for them. To pack an overnight bag, to sleep in a different bed, even these simple efforts were too much right now.

"Is Mother there?" she asked.

"No, she's at one of those charity teas. Your mother, the confirmed New Yorker, has made this move from the city with no trouble at all. It's taken me, the dollar-a-year man, a whole lot longer. Government is mighty different from the business world, let me tell you."

She understood that he was making conversation because he did not want to hang up the telephone, to lose that link. He wanted to have answers to questions that usually he was reluctant to ask. Now he asked.

"I hate to bring up the subject, but have you heard anything from Andrew?"

"No," she said bitterly. "Not since the last useless apology, and that's over a month ago, when I got my unlisted number. Apparently he hasn't gotten a lawyer yet. And my lawyer says we can't wait much longer to file for divorce."

"What the hell's delaying him?" And when she did not reply, "The bastard! And I always liked him so much."

"I know. He was likable, wasn't he? More's the pity for me."

"Tell me, are you still seeing that—doctor?"

"The shrink, you mean? No, I gave it up last week. Frankly, I find that working on meals for the homeless does as much for me, or maybe more."

"You're probably right."

Dad would think so. As a perfect exemplar of the work ethic, he disapproved of self-pity, weakness, and failure. Especially did he deplore a failed marriage. The Byrne

family had never had a failed marriage. But he was always far too kind to say so. She knew that too.

"You may not think it, but this visit will do you good,
Cindy. We'll take our old, brisk walk around the pond
with Gran's dogs, then down to the village and back.
Your mother and I really want you to go. Will you?"

"What's the occasion? It's not Gran's birthday."

"She misses us. Simple as that. If you have time, pick
up a box of those chocolate macaroons that she loves,
will you? Your mother's bought a silk shawl for her, even
if it's not her birthday. We'll take the shuttle early Friday.
I'm afraid you'll have to rent a car. It's a pity you let
Andrew keep the Jaguar."

"He's welcome to it. Who needs a car in New York?
Anyway, he bought it, it was his money."

"Well. Well, all right, dear. We'll see you next Friday."

What was the use of arguing? It was easier to accede
and go.

She sat there. Her limp hands lay in her lap. The
fourth finger on the left one showed a band of white skin,
as did the right hand where the engagement diamond
had once flashed. You would think that after four
months, skin would have darkened. And she kept sitting
there, looking at her hands.

"They should be photographed," Andrew always said,
"or even sculpted. You have classical hands."

He had thought she was beautiful. She knew very well
that she was not, certainly not in any classical sense. She
was only slender, with plentiful dark hair and fine, clear
skin. She was well groomed. Working as she did on the
editorial board of a fashion magazine, she understood
how to make the best of herself.

"You startled me," he told her on that first evening. "I
didn't want to go to another boring cocktail party, but it
was an obligation. And there you were, the first person I

saw when I entered the room. I just stopped and stared. You were standing there in the middle of that jostling, chattering, overdressed crowd, tall and calm in your dark-blue dress. Do you remember?"

She remembered everything. Everything. As usual she had been wearing dark blue. It was her signature. Sophisticates in New York wore black, so she would wear dark blue, different, but not too different.

"You were twinkling," he always said, liking to repeat the story, "with that look you have when you are amused and too polite to let it show. It wasn't a superior look—it isn't like you to be superior—just faintly curious, as if you were wondering what the competition and all the nervous tension were about."

Curious. Grandpa Byrne had had that look.

"I love your poise," Andrew said, "the way you don't shriek out greetings with all that fake enthusiasm people have. I love the way you can sit with your hand in mine and keep silent until the very last note of the music dies."

He had the most wonderful face, a strong nose, a soft, olive complexion, and, in contrast, light eyes, green, dark lashed and pensive. Remembering was unbearable now. A metamorphosis had taken place. What had been sweet, was gall, bitter and angry. . . .

She stood up and went to the window. New York with all its splendor was merely a jumble of towers and steeples this afternoon, a forbidding stone wilderness under the gloomy rain-soaked sky. If the rain had not been torrential, she would have gone outdoors and walked in it for miles, walked to exhaustion.

"What shall I do?" she asked aloud. "I am becoming a nuisance to myself and must not become a nuisance to other people. Must not."

Turning, she looked around the room, searching there

as if, among the remnants of a life destroyed, she might somehow find a signpost, an explanation, or a direction. But the fruitwood chests, Persian rugs, and paintings of the Hudson River School with their round hills and snowfields, these tasteful possessions that befit the home of a rising young banker, all these had no explanation for the wreckage. None.

She walked down the hall. It was long, thirty-one steps to the end. Or more, if you counted from the far wall of the living room. Starting at two o'clock in the morning you could easily measure off a mile before dawn, and if you were lucky, the urge to sleep might come.

Past the bedroom where now, in a sumptuous moss-green bed, she slept alone, were the two closed doors; the people who came to clean this pair of rooms were instructed to close the doors when they were finished and to keep them so. Suddenly, she needed to open them and look in. The rooms, except for color, pink in one and blue in the other, were mirror images; each had a crib, an adult-sized rocking chair, a toy chest, and a row of stuffed animals on a shelf. Now the window shades were down, so that the light was dim, restful, and mournful, as in rooms where the dead lie. It was fitting. . . .

Remember? Yes, remember it all from beginning to end.

"Twins," the doctor said with a happy grin. People always seemed to smile at the subject of twins, as if having them were somehow, in a nice way, comical, one of nature's jokes. Well, maybe they were, she had thought, going home. And thinking so, began to chuckle.

It was an energetic fall day, and she walked briskly. In the bright air she imagined a smoky scent, although goodness only knew where it could come from, for surely here on the east side of Manhattan there were no leaves being burned in anyone's backyard. But there were chrysanthemums in the florists' windows. And she bought a bunch of miniature whites. Then, at the bakery, she bought a box of chocolate chip cookies, which would be her last such indulgence until the twins should be born. At home, having arranged the flowers on the table, she laid out their wedding silver, lighted candles, poured wine, and waited for Andrew. Working late at the magazine as she often did, she was not usually able to greet him at dinner with such a formal display.

Andrew cheered. "Great! Great! And so that's why you've begun to look like a baby elephant. To think when I married you my fingers were almost able to meet around your waist."

Kissing her lips, her neck, and her hands, telling her how happy he was and how blessed they were, he almost at once began to take charge of things.

"You are to go by taxi to and from work every day. I insist. Winter will be coming on, and the streets may be slippery, even with the slightest dusting of snow."

"You're bossing me," she protested, not meaning it.

But he was serious. "Yes, and I shall keep doing it. You take too many chances. Next thing, I swear you'll want to go skiing."

"I love your frown. It's so stern." She stroked the two vertical lines between his eyes. "I love your nice, level eyebrows and the way your hair keeps falling over the left side of your forehead. Why always the left side? And I love—"

"You silly woman. You could have found a really handsome guy if you had looked a little longer."

Plans were taking shape in his head. If we're smart, we'll start looking right now for a larger apartment. Two cribs will never fit into that little room.

Two cribs, blankets, a double carriage, and another entire layette, eventually another high chair and a double stroller, all these and more became the various grandparents' excuse to go back again to the infants' department.

Cynthia had always been gratefully aware of her good fortune. Never having been surrounded by anything else, she was nevertheless able to imagine very vividly what it was like not to have it. Going away to an Ivy League school, she felt in the first place lucky for being able to pass the entrance examinations, and after that, for being able to go without the financial pressures that bore so heavily on so many other students. Coming home at vacation time, she saw keenly how comfortable and beautiful that home was.

And there were no impediments when she and Andrew came together. Their two families, being similar, blended easily; each was pleased with its child's choice. The marriage took place promptly; since they were sure, there seemed to be little need to try each other out by first living together. So, in traditional ceremony, with Cynthia wearing her mother's lace and carrying white roses, in a grand old Gothic church, to the measures of a trumpet voluntary, they were married.

Now, with equal ease, they were planning for the arrival of their twins.

One day as spring approached, the doctor had more news. "You know what, Cynthia? You have a boy and a girl in there." He was an old man with an old man's forgivable twinkle. "You've planned it well, haven't you? That's the way to do it."

She was ecstatic. "I can't believe it. Are you sure?"

"Sure as can be."

Now there would have to be two extra bedrooms, since you wouldn't keep a boy and girl together forever. Her mind's eye, as she walked home through that warming afternoon, saw how the rooms might be decorated: cowboys in one, perhaps, and ballerinas in the other? No, too banal. As to names: both to begin with the same letter, as for instance in *Janice* and *Jim*? No, that was corny. How about Margaret, or just Daisy, which was what her mother was called, or perhaps Annette after Gran? Let Andrew choose the boy's name. There were so many lovely problems to be worked out.

This time she had a bunch of crimson tulips next to the wine cooler when Andrew came home.

"We'll need a pretty big place," he said. "Don't forget the nanny's room."

Certainly, because she would be returning to work, there would have to be a nanny, though both parents were decided that weekends were to be spent entirely with their children.

The remaining months were devoted to the new apartment. High on an upper floor from which you could see the park, this new home was one of the city's most coveted luxuries, and maybe, thought Cynthia, a greater luxury than they should have undertaken. But Andrew thought otherwise.

"It's not out of line," he assured her. "Both of us are working and doing well. And even if you didn't work, we could manage. We'd just cut way down on something else. This is an investment, a permanent home for the four of us, or maybe more?"

The birth, as predicted, went smoothly. Timothy and Laura, weighing together a total of nine and a half pounds, arrived on a breezy June day, conveniently, as Cynthia said, between four-thirty and five, allowing their father and their already doting grandparents to celebrate at dinner. Obviously, they were not identical twins, but they looked it, having Andrew's eyes, Cynthia's dimpled chin, and an unusual amount of her dark, lavish hair.

On the second morning they were brought to their pretty rooms and to the care of a good-natured nanny, Maria Luz, who had reared three babies of her own in Mexico. For the first few days there was a kind of pleasant confusion in the house, as friends arrived to coo and marvel, leaving behind them a mountain of tissue paper and shiny boxes out of which came enough tiny sweaters, embroidered suits, and dresses to outfit six babies. But eventually the house grew quiet, order was established, and a routine emerged so smoothly that you might almost think Timothy and Laura had always lived there.

They were easy babies, according to Maria Luz and the books on Cynthia's night table. They did a minimal amount of crying, soon slept through the night, gained weight on schedule, and sat up when they were supposed to.

On Sunday afternoons in the park, people turned their heads as the double carriage passed. And Cynthia, healthy and vigorous with new clothes and a flat stomach, felt that she, that all of them, had been blessed.

"I never thought," Andrew said, "I'd be so foolish about my children. I always thought that people who dragged snapshots out of their wallets without being asked were idiots. And now I do it myself."

The months went by. The first birthday came with a party, presents, paper hats, and smeared icing, all joyously recorded by the video camera. Sooner than you would imagine, the carriage was stored, and a double stroller took its place. Laura and Tim were halfway through their second year.

And now into Cynthia's mind there came a faint, unspoken shred of thought: Perhaps two were not enough? Perhaps it would soon be time to think about another? Why not? She had just been given a nice raise. Life was so good. . . .

It felt marvelous to be going home on a rare half day off with the first whiff of winter in the air. Walking fast in her sneakers while swinging the bag that held, along with her purchases, her smart, high-heeled office shoes, she would get there in time to give the baths, or one bath, at least, while Maria did the other. Tim was so active now that you had to wear a rubber apron, or you'd be drenched.

When she reached the front entrance of her building, she was still smiling at the thought. Joseph, the doorman, did not smile back, which was unusual. He looked, actually, stern. Angry about something? she wondered, and, dismissing the matter, went into the lobby. At the elevator her neighbor from the apartment across the hall came quickly forward on seeing her, and she, too, had a queer expression on her face, so queer that alarm ran down Cynthia's back.

"Cindy," the woman said.

Something had happened. . . .

"Let's go up. They were looking for you, but—"

"What is it? What is it?"

"An accident. Cindy, oh, darling, you'll need to be—"

The elevator stopped, the door slid open, and a low thrum of many voices surged toward them. Crowding there were her parents, Andrew's parents and his brother, her best friend Louise, their doctor, Raymond Marx, and—

"Where's Andrew?" she screamed and ran, pushing them all aside.

He was bowed on the sofa with his face in his hands. Hearing her, he looked up, weeping.

"Andy?" she whispered.

"Cindy. Darling. An accident. There's been an accident. Oh, God."

And so she knew. She thought she was tasting blood in her mouth.

"The babies?"

Somebody took her arm and sat her down beside

Andrew. Dr. Marx was murmuring while he clasped hands tightly on her shoulders.

"There was a car, a taxi. Going around the corner, it jumped the curb."

"My babies?"

The soft murmur cut like a blade into her ears. "My babies?" she screamed again.

"It struck the stroller."

"Not my babies?"

"Oh, Cindy, Cindy . . ."

Those were the last words she remembered.

When she awoke, she was in bed. Andrew, fully dressed, was lying across the foot of the bed, which was odd. When she stretched her arm out, the sleeve of her nightgown fell back, which was normal. Sunlight fell over the ceiling, and that was also normal.

Yet there was something different. Then it all flooded; great waves of anguish and disbelief broke over her. "No! It didn't happen! It's a crazy dream, isn't it? It's a lie, isn't it? Where are they? I have to see my babies."

Andrew, trying to take her into his arms, knelt beside the bed. But she was frantic; she pushed him away and ran to the door. When it opened, a nurse in white came in with a bottle and tumbler in her hand.

"Take this," she said gently. "It will quiet you."

"I don't want to be quiet. I want my babies. For God's sake, can't you hear me?" The cry was a howl. It shattered her own ears. I am going insane, she thought.

"You must take it, Mrs. Wills. And you, too, Mr. Wills. You need to sleep. You've been awake since yesterday morning."

"Cynthia," her mother said, "darling, take the medicine. Please. Please. Get back to bed. The doctor said—"

"I want to look at them. They need me."

"Darling, you can't see them."

"Why? Why?"

"Oh, Cindy—"

"Then they're dead. That's it? Dead?"

"Oh, Cindy—"

"Who did it? Why? Oh, God, let me kill him too. Oh, God."

"Please. Think of Andrew. He needs you. You need each other."

Whether they gave her another pill or a hypodermic needle, she did not know. She knew only that the sunlight faded.

When she awoke, it was night. The lamps were lit. A few people were talking in low voices. Now she was alert enough to understand what they were saying.

The taxi, going, as witnesses said, much too fast, had smashed the stroller, which had just left the curb. The twins had died instantly. Poor Maria Luz, injured, had been taken to a hospital, treated for shock, and released. She was now staying with relatives. The children would be buried in the Byrne family plot in the country.

These were the facts. This was all. So it ended. The charmed life was over.

On the third morning Cynthia was awakened by the sound of hangers rattling on the rods in her closet.

"I'm looking for something she can wear. It will be cold." That was her mother's voice.

"You'll have to ask her. I don't know," said Andrew.

"The doctor gives her too much stuff. She's half asleep all the time."

"Just till the funeral's over. No more after that, he said."

"Well, I suppose—oh, there you are! Darling, I'm searching through your things for something black."

They were both in black, her mother in a correct black

suit and Andy in the same, with the tie that he had needed to buy for his uncle's funeral. What sense did it make to care what one wore? The only appropriate thing was sackcloth and ashes, anyway.

"I never wear black," she said.

"Darling, navy blue will do very well. This wool dress, with a warm coat, will be fine. Shall I help you dress?"

"No, I'll be all right, Mom. Thanks."

"Then I'll leave you. Your father's arranged for the car. There's just time for a quick bite before we start."

"I'm not hungry."

"You must take something. Andrew, make her eat. And you eat something too."

"They've taken care of everything. They've been wonderful," Andrew said when Daisy left.

"Have they—I mean, are Tim and Laura—do we—"

"They're up there already. Oh, God, Cindy."

For long minutes they held on to each other. It was as if one or the other, alone, would have fallen. When at last they straightened themselves he fastened the back of her dress, she brought him an extra handkerchief, and they went out together.

In the limousine silence held almost all the way, broken briefly when Cynthia's father gave directions to the driver. Andrew's right hand, joined with her left, rested on the seat between them. Once she spoke.

"Does this seem real to you?"

In answer he shook his head. For her, reality kept flickering in through a dull sense of detachment that was equally terrifying. Was she about to lose her mind?

Reality was the memory of another time in another long limousine, not grim black like this one but white, festooned by one of their friends, a practical joker, with a JUST MARRIED sign: she had worn a pale green linen suit and they had, as now, been sitting on the backseat holding hands. Reality was coming home from the hospital with one wrapped-up baby in her arms and another in Andrew's.

And she blinked hard, forcing the pictures to fade. This was no time for such pictures, going now where they were going.

"We're almost there," her father said suddenly.

The car rounded a turn and passed a parking lot filled and overflowing onto the roadside. It stopped at a walk that overflowed with people. And she wanted to flee, to hide from sympathetic eyes and soft, murmured words. Yet it was very kind of all these people to be here. So she understood what was expected of her.

She was expected to take Andrew's arm, to walk in and go straight down toward the two little white caskets. And she did so.

An odd other and outer self that had been observing her for the last two days took note of the flowers that lay in wreaths and baskets and sheaves on the floor. They, like the sprays of lilies on the caskets, were white. For purity and innocence, they stood.

But Tim had not been innocent! He had been a rogue, a rascal who stole Laura's cookie right out of her hand and made her cry. Andrew was—no, had been—boastful about his boy. "Tim is one tough guy," he always says— no, used to say. One tough guy.

The other self was watching her carefully. It told her to remember everything because this was the last day she would ever touch them or touch, rather, the flowers and the smooth white lids. She leaned forward to put the tips of her fingers on the lids. The wood was smooth as satin and cold. The lily petals were cold too.

An organ was making soft, tentative sounds like whispers or footsteps in a room where a child is asleep. When it stopped a rich, manly voice began to speak. The words were poetic and half familiar, all about mercy and love.

Prayers. Beautiful, gentle words. Well-meaning. At her back there were crowd sounds, the light occasional coughs and tiny rustlings of polite, well-meaning people. She wondered when it was all going to be over.

And suddenly it was. The organ resumed its quiet song, men appeared to bear the little caskets away, and somebody said, "Come, Cynthia." Two by two people moved toward the door with Andrew and Cynthia in the lead.

Daylight burst into their faces. Following it eastward, they walked on the graveled path between last summer's stalks of dead brown grass and entered the burial ground.

Many generations of Byrnes and others among the forebears of Laura and Tim lay here in this old place. It had never been a sad place, just vaguely interesting when you were a child brought to it on Memorial Day and then most interesting when you were old enough to be curious about history. So many children were buried under these gray, time-ravaged headstones with their worn inscriptions. Molly, aged three, now with the angels. Susannah, aged two. A second summer death, most likely the result of drinking unclean cow's milk after her mother weaned her. Ethan, aged eighteen months and sixteen days. Eighteen months, thought Cynthia. Like mine. I must remember to count the days. But I can't think this minute and there is no time.

For they had reached the hole in the ground, the hole with the green drapery that was meant to conceal the stony, clodded earth which, considerately, would not be shoveled in until everyone had walked away.

The crowd had dwindled to relatives and intimates: Gran with swollen, pink eyes, Andrew's people, cousin Ellen who wept behind a handkerchief, the boss and staff from the magazine and—and I can't believe it, thought Cynthia, there's poor Maria Luz with a relative who somehow found the way here. All come to say good-bye to Laura and Tim.

Oh, my Tim, my Laura, you weren't here very long but you will never be forgotten, not your smiles, your first teeth, your long eyelashes, your cries and red cheeks and fat hands—

"Amen," spoke the fine voice, and the circular gathering responded, "Amen."

Someone, Andrew's mother or her own, or someone else, said quietly, "It's over, Cynthia."

Once more she took Andrew's hand. It was wet on the back where he had used it to wipe his eyes. The little crowd parted to let them proceed to their car. Low comments floated past them as they walked. "I heard it was the taxi's fault." "I was at their wedding." "Remarkably brave." "Saddest thing I've ever seen." A woman looked into Cynthia's face as though she wanted to say something and didn't know how to say it.

At the end of the path they got into the car and went home the way they had come.

For a long time they held on to each other. No matter how their parents loved them and mourned with them, this agony was still Cynthia's and Andrew's. They became very solitary. They took long walks in the snow through the park, where once they had so proudly wheeled their twins, where and when the future was theirs and the world a field of flowers.

In the evenings they listened to music together. The broadcast news meant nothing to them. The apartment was completely quiet now. No more did they keep their ears open for a cry or a call. Only the great, solemn music broke the silence. Friends telephoned with tactful invitations to dinner or a movie; with equal tact they accepted refusal.

Once every week they went for a counseling session. Everyone knew that was what you did when tragedy struck. Andrew was the first to stop going.

"It's only rubbing salt in the wound," he said. "Nobody needs to tell me that I have to get on with my life. Don't I know well enough that there'll be a line waiting for my good job if I lose it?"

"What good job? We don't need any job."

"We have to eat, Cindy."

"Do we? I don't know why. I'm never hungry, and I don't care where I live. I don't need anything."

"I know. But we can't kill ourselves."

"If it weren't for you, I would."

He sighed. "Don't say that, Cindy."

"Why not? It's true." She got up and began to pace the floor, from the window to the bookshelves and back again.

"I shouldn't have been working. I should have been taking care of my own children. I'll never forgive myself, never. I look at myself in the mirror, and I see guilt written on my forehead. Yes, believe it, in big red letters: *G-U-I-L-T*."

"Darling, that's foolish. It was a ghastly accident that could have happened to you, or me, or anybody."

"You know what? I'm going to quit the stupid job. That's what I'm going to do."

"I wouldn't do that so hastily. You've taken a long leave of absence, so wait till that's over and then decide. It's too soon after—after everything to make such a big change."

It was impossible to imagine going back to that office, receiving condolences and pitying looks, being chic, being "with it," and brave. She would have to find something completely different, where there were no reminders, among people she had never seen before.

Certainly she would find something else, but not yet.

She was not ready yet. And anyhow, my job is ridiculous, she thought. It has no real meaning. Fashion! Silly dresses for women who don't know what real life is all about. Hemlines are longer, or are they shorter again this season? I don't know. I know that jackets have to be fitted this year, so of course you must throw last year's jackets away, mustn't you?

She saw that Andrew was filled with pity for her. But then, her heart was broken over him too. He didn't pace the floor for relief of tension as she did. He did not because no doubt he felt he must not. He was a man; men did not give way to grief. So they had been taught, poor souls.

At night they lay close with their arms around each other. When they needed to turn, they lay back to back, feeling the comfort of simple contact, and wanting, in their despair, nothing more than to be one.

Then, after a while, Andrew began to feel the rise of desire, but she felt nothing. "I can't," she said. "Not yet." And he complied. It was incomprehensible to her that he could feel the need for pleasure. What pleasure could there be ever again? Inside of her there was a poison, corrosive as acid, a savage hatred for the man who had killed her children and was still alive to breathe the good air; a terrible rage at unjust suffering; rage at the world.

There came a time when Andrew did not willingly comply.

"How can you feel pleasure?" she cried.

"It's not just pleasure, as you put it. It is an act of love between you and me. We are still alive, you and I."

"How soon you have forgotten!" she exclaimed.

" 'Forgotten'?" he repeated. "How can you even think that about me?"

Then she apologized. "I didn't mean it as it sounds."

"It was pretty clear to me. A simple word."

"I'm sorry," she said again, and sighed. "It's just that I can't think of anything else. I see them in the stroller, their pink faces, their little hands in mittens, so precious, and in one second—"

"Don't, don't, Cindy. You have to stop this sometime," he pleaded.

He was not always so patient. "That doctor you're seeing doesn't seem to be doing you much good."

"No? He has only saved my sanity, that's all."

There was a pause before Andrew said, "Soon it will be six months."

Six months since we last made love, he meant. And that night, when he approached her, she did not turn away, but gave herself, lying like a stone, feeling nothing.

She did not fool him, and he told her so without reproach, only with sadness.

"I can't help it," she answered.

She intended her answer to be true, and although in a measure it was true, there was another measure by which it was not true, by which she actually could have helped it but did not want to. How could they, how could Andrew, think that they would ever resume the life that had been before the tragedy destroyed it? Perhaps after all, men were different. . . .

They began to drift. When he came upon her sitting one day at the window with her hands in her lap and her red eyes swollen, he upbraided her.

"Sooner or later you will have to stop crying. I don't know how to help you anymore. We can't go on like this. I can't."

His words and his tone offended her. "And you will have to stop thrashing around all night," she cried. "I don't ever get a night's sleep. Speaking of wearing on somebody's nerves, do you realize that you're constantly cracking your knuckles? Every night we sit in front of the television, and I have to hear the sound of your cracking bones."

They went to bed and lay far apart. An emotional storm was sweeping through Cynthia. For months she had been lethargic and numb; now instead there came these storms, panic and fear of confronting love or life; panic and fear of being shut out of life. She felt a terrible, inexpressible loneliness.

She knew she must get hold of herself. She knew that they had been living like hermits, and that it was terribly wrong. So one day when a friendly couple, Ken and Jane Pierce, invited them to dinner at their country club, she accepted.

"I'm so glad," Jane said. "Frankly, I didn't think you would say yes, but I thought I'd try."

The two couples rode out of the city together, which was agreeable because conversation had to be impersonal. At the club there would be many people they knew, people from whom Cynthia had long retreated, and so, for this first appearance, she had considered her dress with special care. Is this the return of pride? she asked herself ironically. Or is it the slow return of mental health? The doctor said it was.

In the mirrored hall at the club, she saw the reflection of a dreadfully thin young woman, with tired eyes, wearing a flowered silk dress. She had bought the dress for a vacation they had never taken; they were to have gone to Florida with the babies.

"You look wonderful," someone told her, speaking with the kindness that is reserved for people who have been dreadfully ill and who do not look wonderful.

The tables were set outdoors on a broad terrace. Without interest she ate the food that was placed before her, as without interest she heard the chatter that passed over her head. Vaguely she knew that the women were discussing a hotly fought school-board election. The men, talking business as usual, were mostly grouped at the other end of her table, while Andrew was in between, with Ken on one side and a rather animated young woman wearing a rather deep décolleté on the other.

It amused her a little to see how skillfully Andrew was managing to divide his attention. He always behaved so well and had such presence. And in spite of being wan and weary he was the best-looking man here tonight. She felt sad for him. He didn't deserve what had happened to them. They must, she must, somehow turn their minds away from it. . . .

In front of Cynthia the golf course swept into the creeping dark, while to the left a wooded tract sloped gradually downhill. The day's heat still lay upon the grass and rose into the air, while overriding the hum of human voices was the clear, unending chirp of crickets.

We should have gotten out of the city long before now, she thought. It would have helped to go up to Gran's place and walk in the woods together. We must do that soon. There, we might heal. We could be what we have always been.

And thinking so, her shoulders eased; she had not realized before how rigid they were. She looked out into the distant space where twilight had turned now to full night, cobalt-blue except where Japanese paper lanterns drew their small gold circles on the darkness. How good it would be to stretch out and drowse beneath the trees! It was a long time since she had felt so sweet an urge. A curious peace had touched her, a country peace.

Andrew was laughing. It was so long, too, since she had heard him laugh. It was so long since she herself had seen anything in the world to laugh at. Had her behavior helped to drag him farther down? Yes, probably, it had.

The woman next to him must have told a joke because

all the men were laughing. She was a pretty woman, but flashy, not Andrew's type, with that heavy makeup and that dress. Not that she had ever worried about other women—for they were *married,* she and Andrew, really married.

But I have been very ill, she thought. I have certainly given no care to how I look. I need to revive, to come back to life and open my arms to Andrew.

Tonight I will break down the barrier. Tonight.

A little wind rose now, swishing through the leaves, and she pulled her shawl around her shoulders. Pale yellow wool and softly fringed, it gave her a sense of femininity and grace that she had not felt for too long. The sudden warmth within her was more than a warmth of the body; it was a lifting, a release.

And wanting to give him a look or a touch that would say, *Darling, it's going to be all right again, I'm sorry it's been so long but really, really something's just happened to me and—*

She was stopped by a long wail from Andrew's neighbor.

"My God, do you know what I've done? I've lost my best bracelet! And it wasn't insured. Oh, I'm sick."

From all sides came advice and commiseration, while people searched in the grass and under the table.

"Where did you last see it? Think."

"Are you sure you wore it tonight? Sometimes we think we had something on, and didn't."

"How did you enter the clubhouse?"

"I parked the car myself in the far lot and walked up through the front door and the dining room."

"That's easy enough. Start at the car and retrace the whole way."

"I'll go with you," offered Andrew. "We'll begin right here in the dining room. It has to be somewhere."

"Oh, how sweet of you! Two pairs of eyes should surely find it."

The men returned to their conversations. The women talked about children, those learning to walk and those applying at colleges. And Cynthia, listening, was not devastated. It hurt, but not quite as deeply as such talk had been hurting. She was mending. . . .

Twenty minutes went by. A few people were preparing to leave.

"Baby-sitters, you know."

"Have to get up at the crack of dawn tomorrow."

"Where can your husband have gone?" Ken asked.

"I'm wondering where myself," she replied.

"Well, they went in that way," somebody said doubtfully.

Cynthia went inside to look. There were only some youngsters dancing the macarena. From the front steps she had a clear view of the parking lots. That woman's red dress would be visible. . . . She went back to the table. Fear, even as she knew how unreasonable it was, began to throb through her chest. He might have fallen somewhere or been suddenly taken ill. You never knew. The world was filled with unanticipated dangers. Who could be more aware of that than she was?

More time went by. One of the men walked to the edge of the golf course, calling a long, drawn-out "Andrew . . ."

Silly of him. What would anyone be doing out there?

"It's a puzzle," Ken said.

Jane moved restlessly. She had children at home, and there was an hour's drive ahead.

"It's fine for the people who live around here, but for us poor folk who stay in the city all summer—" She broke off. "Well for Pete's sake, we've all been looking for you."

Andrew, with the owner of the lost bracelet, was walking out of the woods, she flourishing the bracelet and laughing.

"Guess what? It was on the seat of my car. I always take it off while I'm driving. The charms get in the way."

"But where on earth were you?" Cynthia heard Jane ask, and heard another woman adding under her breath, "Where do you think? It's only Phyllis's usual little disappearing act."

And Andrew, who had certainly heard, too, was standing like a bashful boy, startled by the sudden fall of silence.

Ken said quietly, "Let's go get the car. It's late."

"I need the ladies' room first," said Cynthia.

Jane followed her. "Don't let him see any tears, don't give him the satisfaction," she counseled.

Cynthia, replying with some defiance, for a soft response would surely have brought tears, said quietly, "You don't see any, do you?"

And she bent toward the mirror, running a comb through and through her hair, which did not need combing. A terrible shame flushed her face; she had been publicly humiliated.

"That Phyllis person is really a bitch. She can't keep her hands off a good-looking man. I don't know why anyone would want to invite her here; she's not a member."

"Oh, please—"

"All right, I'll say no more. Only, listen, Cynthia, you two have been through hell. Don't let this throw you back down. It's rotten, but it's not the worst. You just have to close your eyes sometimes."

It was unbearable. "We'd better go. They're waiting."

"If you're ready. Otherwise let them wait."

"I'm ready."

"Don't worry, you look fine."

"Do you know what? I don't care how I look."

"Men." Jane sighed as they walked to the car. "Men. They're all the same."

Andrew and Ken, together in the front seat, talked their way back to the city, while the two women were silent, Jane out of consideration and Cynthia in turmoil. She was a pitied woman whose value had been cheapened in front of strangers. The armor of marital dignity had been stripped away from her.

All these feelings came rushing into words the moment the apartment door was closed. On shaking legs she stood leaning against the wall.

"You were gone for three quarters of an hour from the time you were missed, and God knows how long before that. With that—that cheap thing that even Jane said can't keep her hands off a man—and you, you made a fool out of yourself." She was maddened. She thumped her chest. "You did this to me? To me?"

"I didn't mean to make a fool out of you or myself. It's—you're exaggerating. It was harmless," Andrew said, stumbling over the word. "I meant, I didn't mean any harm. Foolish, I meant."

She stared at him. Never before had he, a man of confident pride, appeared so flustered, so inept.

"Foolish," he repeated, looking not at Cynthia's face, but at her shoes.

"What were you thinking of? What were you doing there?"

"We—it was—a walk. We took a little walk."

"I'm sure. It wasn't a little walk, it was a long one, unless—unless you spent a good part of it lying down."

"I admit I used poor judgment, but you're making too much of this, Cynthia. You're carrying it too far."

"Am I? I don't think so."

Everything about his posture spoke to her and drew a

picture in her head. She threw her words at him. "You had sex with her."

"That's ridiculous. You have no grounds for thinking so."

"I simply feel it. There are times when you feel things. Anyway, what else would you have been doing, discussing philosophy with her?"

"We were just talking. Talking, about nothing in particular."

"Out in the dark bushes for almost an hour talking about nothing in particular. Do you think I'm an idiot? What's all this about, Andrew? I want to know. And don't lie. I want the truth. I can take it."

There was a silence. There were voices in the corridor as people came out of the elevator. There was silence again.

And then suddenly, Andrew raised his head. He looked straight back at Cynthia. "You said you wanted the truth. Well, what you feel—well, you're right."

All her nerves jumped. One, at the corner of her temple, shot a single, dreadful pain, and she had to sit down.

"It's probably best that I admit it, that I tell you the worst. Then you'll believe me when I say that I've never done it before."

She began to sob. "I think I'm losing my mind."

He spoke humbly. "I never have done it, Cynthia, I promise. I must have been crazy tonight."

"Why? Why? Were you drunk? You're never drunk."

"I had a few glasses of wine, but I won't blame it on that. It simply happened. I'm so sorry, Cindy. I wish to God it hadn't."

" 'Just did.' You bastard. What would you say if I had done it?"

"I would be furious. Frantic."

"No doubt. The mother of your children. Your dead children."

"It was crazy. I don't know how else to say it, it was crazy. Because I love you, Cindy, and I always will."

She saw that his eyes were filled with tears. He moved to the chair as if to touch her hand or caress her head, asking pardon. She picked up her white evening purse and hurled it at him. It fell on the floor, breaking the fancy little frame. She was inflamed, burned alive with outrage, the image of him lying on the grass—with whom? A glittering dress and a raucous laugh.

"I hate you," she screamed. "After what we've been through, you can do this—after what we've been to each other—or so I thought."

"Cindy, please. Nothing's changed. I've done an awful thing. But can't you forgive an awful thing, an aberration, a crazy moment?"

You never know about men. They all swear they don't do it, even the best of them.

"I admit it was inexcusable. But you have been so cold to me—"

"Cold! When my heart's been crushed! What sense are you making? Don't you hear yourself? No, you don't. You don't have the faintest idea of anything that—"

"And *my* heart? It's you who haven't the faintest idea of what it means to come together and comfort each other. I tried so, I tried all these months. I needed a little human warmth. That's all I needed." He stopped, and wiped his eyes. "I'll keep trying if you will, Cindy. Please. I'm so damned sorry about everything."

An actor, he was. Walks back to the table nice as you please after he's dusted the grass from his trousers.

"I can't look at you," she said. "You sicken me. Go inside and get a pillow for yourself. You'll sleep here on the sofa."

"If it'll make you feel better tonight," he began.

"Tonight, you say? Don't bother counting the time until I let you back in any bed with me."

Never. Oh, God, never. Period. I'm looking at someone I don't recognize. I wish I were dead. God, let me die.

He had wrecked everything. Just when they were starting to see light, he had turned the light off. How would she ever trust a human being again? The world that had once been decent and rational made no sense. Hatred solidified into a hard mass around her heart. She floundered among moods, among sobbing grief, fury, and despair.

"But I've apologized over and over," he kept saying all through those first awful days. "I tried to explain something that's probably unexplainable. I beg you, Cynthia. I beg you now."

"A wife sitting at the other end of the table, and a man calmly walks off into the bushes. No. Beg all you want. I'm deaf to it. I don't want to hear you or see you. In fact," she said one morning after another bitter session, "the sooner you leave here, the better. Let me alone. Leave now."

"You can't mean that, Cynthia."

"But I do. I'll give you a day. I'll give you till tomorrow. You can spend today packing your things. Then, as soon as the apartment can be disposed of, I will leave it too."

"My God," Andrew said, "you do mean it." And his temper rose too. "Then sit here and stew. Cry your eyes out instead of pulling yourself together. I've lost patience. I can't do anymore."

So it ended. Now she was trying to make a new life for herself at work in a settlement house for homeless mothers and children. It was a joyless life, but a useful one at least. Often she thought when she saw a young woman holding her baby that she would be willing to change with her. Poverty was cruel and dreadful, but with compassionate help it could be overcome; it was not final.

Again she went to the window as if out there might lie some answer to her questions. The sky was a dirty pink, the nighttime sky that hides the stars above great cities. It was time to leave this costly view and things that filled these rooms, the shining, pretty gadgets that once had been so joyfully assembled for a lifetime home. Gran's letter lay open on the desk. *Come and spend the day. Spend the night. Stay as long as you want to. I love you.*

Once more she read the loving words and imagined Gran at her desk writing them.

How could anyone refuse?

CHAPTER

3

In Washington, Lewis Byrne put down the receiver and sat quite still, thinking about his daughter.

He had always, in the privacy of his thoughts, called her his gift of joy. Tall and calm as Cynthia was, he could see himself and his kin in her; piquant and graceful, she was also like her mother, having Daisy's quick wit and strong, athletic body. Repeated in Cynthia these qualities seemed to have been intensified; as you watched her, you could imagine a bird in flight. A wounded bird now, he thought, and was heavy with that thought, when the door opened and Daisy came home.

"How was it?" he inquired.

"Nice. I surprised myself by finding how many women I already know in Washington."

"Looking at you, nobody would ever guess your worries."

She had brought a brisk air into the room, as if she had just returned from a swim or a horseback ride or tennis. There was energy in her stride and her direct blue gaze.

Ruefully, she replied, "What's the use of showing them?"

"None, I suppose. I talked to Cynthia."

"Anything new?"

"Nothing, except she's going with us to Mother's."

"Oh, that's good. I was afraid she wouldn't."

"She loves my mother."

"Well, of course. What I meant was, having to go through the town, seeing the church where they were married, and then the cemetery."

"How Andrew can have done this to her! Men have their moments, God knows, but this! It's unforgivable. After all they had been through, and just when we really thought she was beginning to recover." Lewis shook his head, sighing. "No matter how old your children are, it's never over, is it? Remember the shock we had when she broke her arm in three places? And when she was seven, and got lost at the Brownie picnic—or we thought she was lost, anyway?"

"Remember when she was fifteen and madly in love with that awful boy?"

For a few minutes they were silent, until Daisy said gently, "Get up. Let's have dinner and go to a movie, a comedy, if there is one. This sort of thing doesn't help either us or Cynthia."

"You're right. But I hate December," he said as he rose.

On a short, gloomy afternoon that call had come, rushing them to their daughter, to their dead grandchildren and the anguish.

"I know it's a bad month altogether. But come on, dear, get your coat."

For Daisy's sake he must try. They had dinner and it

was good, but he was not hungry. The movie flickered before his eyes without registering. Back at home when she went to bed, he pleaded work.

"I'll come in a little while. I've got to read some material on public housing."

In the chair by the window he settled down again. The apartment must certainly be warm, he thought, since it always was, yet tonight it felt as if a chill were seeping through the walls. The Jefferson Memorial looked like a carving in ice, and the world froze. He got up, shivering, to pour a glass of wine. Perhaps it would not only warm him, but put him to sleep. These days he always felt short of sleep.

Yes, December. I shall always hate the month. As if Cynthia's catastrophe were not enough, this week is the sixth anniversary of another death: on a Saturday night the firm of Byrne and Sons died. One of the finest architectural engineering firms in the country came to an end. Smashed. Wiped out.

And at this recollection Lewis's hands shook, spilling the last few drops of wine on the unread public-housing report. A disaster like that must live forever in one's mind, he thought. He could still see the headlines in the newspapers, black letters dancing a crazy, evil dance.

"Three concrete balconies in the new Arrow Hotel International collapse. Eighty-three killed and more than six hundred injured. Rescue workers fear many more trapped inside. Toll may go much higher."

The horror. And Gene, my brother, my partner, still blames me. No forgiveness, no understanding, just blame.

That structure—and it, too, he saw as clearly as if he were now standing in front of it—that elegant, milk-white luminescence between the palm groves and the Atlantic, was to have been, if not the firm's crowning work, then at least another triumph in its list of successes from coast to coast. Arrow Hotels International had, for the past twenty years, engaged no other firm but Byrne to design their projects. And now the glory days were over.

It had all begun with that scruffy-looking kid, Lewis thought, having an exact recollection of the morning when his secretary had announced that "some young fellow" was insisting upon seeing Mr. Byrne.

"Some kind of a nut, is he?"

"I don't think so, Mr. Byrne, although you can't always tell, can you?"

Jerry Victor was his name. The matter was very important, of great concern to the firm, and a matter of conscience.

"All right, I'll see him and get it over with."

"That's not a bad idea. He looks like the type who'll keep coming until you do see him."

He was some sort of high-level clerk in the office of Harold Sprague and Company, the contractors. Deliberately untidy, with typically uncombed hair in a ponytail, he was well spoken, very earnest, and obviously educated. You could tell almost from his first few words that he was also a crusader. Some people, and Lewis was one of them, would say at once that he was an agitator. Admittedly, Lewis was a conservative whose tolerance for what he called "cranks" was low. Nevertheless, he listened politely to what Victor had to tell.

He worked in a small space at the end of a narrow corridor between two offices. On a recent day sometime after working hours, he had gone back to his desk to get some important keys that he had mislaid. Except for a cleaning crew the offices were vacant, so it surprised him to overhear two men in conversation across the passage. He was certain that one of them was Mr. Sprague. The voices were low, but the walls were thin. While he was searching and unfortunately not finding his keys, he could not help but overhear. He was, he said, not accustomed to eavesdropping, but he had been so shocked by the first few words, that he had then concealed himself to hear the rest.

"Then eight percent, is it?" asked one man.

"Yes, isn't that satisfactory?"

"We had talked of ten."

"That's a bit steep."

"You have to consider volume. We have two more jobs for you after this with Byrne. You'll find it worth your while."

"How about nine percent back? How does that sound?"

"Okay, okay. We'll compromise. You won't lose anything. There are more ways than one to mix concrete, right?" And someone laughed.

That, then, was the incredible story. Good God! Harold Sprague had been a friend at Yale, and before that, a friend at prep school. They had traveled in Europe together, and their families had been summertime neighbors in Maine. It was impossible to associate him with a dirty kickback scheme. This kid, this Jerry Victor, had most certainly not understood correctly and had probably not even heard correctly. Most likely he had some agenda of his own; he had perhaps been reprimanded and was seeking revenge; or he was simply a radical who lied because he wanted, on principle, to undermine a company, that being the true motive of many a whistleblower these days. So Lewis reasoned.

Or so he had reasoned then. Time and events had tempered that first certainty. Reflecting, he gazed out now upon the lights that dotted darkened Washington. No doubt, he could admit, he had been somewhat dazzled by the name of Sprague and should not have been. He winced as he recalled that day.

"This is a preposterous accusation!" he had said. "You didn't even see the men."

"I know Mr. Sprague's voice."

" 'Know his voice'! No, young man, that's pretty flimsy evidence. I suggest you forget about it, do your job, and take care of yourself."

After admonishing and then dismissing the fellow with proper dignity, he had mentioned, as if it were a joke, the absurd affair to Gene.

"All the same, it should be looked into," Gene said.

"What? You can't be serious. Do you actually want me to insult Harold Sprague with rot like that?"

"When you come down to it, what do we know about him or his suppliers? This is the first contracting job we've ever given him."

"We know his reputation up and down the West Coast."

"We shouldn't have changed. We've had the same reliable contractors for the last twenty years."

"I wanted to give him a chance, now that he's expanding in the East. His price was competitive, wasn't it?"

"I don't agree. We definitely ought to speak about this. I'll go if you feel uncomfortable about it."

"Gene, I forbid you from doing it."

Nevertheless, Gene did it.

"I was tactful," he reported a week or two later. "I said that I thought he should know there was a rumor, not that I believed it, just that he should know it. Of course he was indignant, furious—oh, not at me, don't worry—"

"I think you've made a big mistake because of a disgruntled crank."

"I don't know about that. The kid came to see me a few days ago. He's been having a tough time, and he's leaving his job."

"Good riddance. He's an arrogant troublemaker. I've

asked around and found that nobody likes him. He even stirred things up in the union."

"As to that, I don't know. But I do know that I can look at a man and most of the time I can tell whether he's an honorable, truthful human being or not. I believe that boy is."

"That's a doubtful statement, Gene. Think about it."

"No more doubtful than your belief in a man because you went to Yale together."

And so, a slight distance grew between the brothers. It was nothing overt, rather a subtle coolness, as when a draft stirs the air in the corner of a room that is otherwise tight and warm. It was still remembered when, two years later, the grand hotel was finished. . . .

And what a jewel it was! Here was grandeur without ostentation, which he despised. When the lines were right, there was no need for fussy ornament.

Standing at the place where a blooming low hedge divided the lawn from the sand, he looked beyond the great arch, all the way through the depth of the structure, to the opposite arch and the alley of royal palms that stretched from the front entrance to the road. If you were standing at the front entrance, you would see only blue water and, at this moment, the black nighttime sky, in which mountainous clouds hid a few blinking stars.

It will rain soon, he had thought, probably all day tomorrow, too, and was glad for her sake that Daisy had not been able to come along this time. She had been at so many engineers' meetings, anyway. As for him, this one was rather special, since most of the members were having their first look at Byrne and Sons' achievement. He moved to go inside to the music, the champagne, and, frankly, to the congratulations.

A thunderous clap shook the air. Like lightning as it splits and fells a tree, striking unholy terror in animal or man, it crashed again. And instinctively, Lewis ran for shelter. Then in an awesome fraction of a second as he reached the door, he saw, not shelter, but chaos—and it was inside.

It struck his heart. He thought he was having a stroke. He thought he was dying.

Chaos was concrete boulders, contorted steel, and shattered glass, lying at the bottom of the five-storied atrium. The balconies had fallen. Even now, the last one on the second floor, struck by the one above, was giving way, and shrieking, flailing, tumbling human bodies were falling with it.

Now he knew he was dying, and wanted to die.

There was, among all who saw this, one long, audible intake of breath; then universal screams, sobs, and curses, and after that an instant, violent, impulsive rush to aid. Lewis pulled a girl from under a girder; she had lost an arm. A man lay with blood pouring from his mouth; his eyes were open, and he was dead. Human beings, their heads barely visible beneath the rubble, cried and pleaded in terror, while groups in twos and threes strained to move the debris that covered them. Lewis thought of his brother, but there was no time or way to look for him. There was scarcely any space in which to walk through the mass of ruins.

Water came gushing from broken pipes onto the slippery floor. An enormous chunk of concrete too heavy for human arms to shove lay over a pair of legs, and yet he tried; the man was screaming in his agony and begging; then suddenly his cries ceased, and Lewis walked away to steady an old woman who, though bloody, was able to stand. A child's face was torn; he had fallen onto the sharp end of something, most likely onto a piece of the delicate iron filigree that had adorned the balconies. A gush of vomit came from out of Lewis's mouth.

On one side of the lobby little tables were still set with

cutlery, flowers, and pink cloths. On the other, in the cocktail lounge, the piano stood unscathed. Beyond it you could glimpse the Blue Room, where on sofas and carpet those victims who could be extricated from the destruction were already being laid.

Chambermaids, chefs in white, and men in maroon uniforms came running in from all over the hotel. Someone said, "Come here, grab her legs," and Lewis obeyed as they picked up a heavy woman who had fainted. People ran in from the street. It must be raining, he thought, for their clothes were streaming. Dazed, he moved from aid to aid, from place to place, through the turmoil of dust and splintered glass. In one vague moment he thought he was seeing the carnage of a battlefield, read of in countless books and watched through countless movies. Only here in this place there had been music a few minutes ago, and women in evening gowns. . . .

The wail of an ambulance broke into his daze. Police, firemen, and paramedics began to take charge. More help came. In the mirrored ballroom a temporary morgue was set up for the many dead. There was a frenzy of newsmen carrying cameras.

How many hours all this went on, Lewis was never able to recall. It seemed as if days must have passed until, pushed to the limit of shock and exhaustion, he went up to the suite that had been reserved for himself and Gene.

The lobby had been cleared of the dead and injured. They had done all that they were able to do that day. What remained was the work of the hospitals. What he did recall perfectly, though, was the terrible quarrel with Gene.

Gene had opened a bottle of brandy. "Because God knows we need it. That scene downstairs in the lobby— hell couldn't possibly be worse."

Rain spattered on the balcony. A high wind had risen, clattering in the royal palms. It had blown the outer doors open.

"Some idiot didn't latch the doors," Lewis said. He got up and locked them. "I feel angry at the world, Gene. Things like this shouldn't happen. Music one minute and amputated legs the next. Listen to that wind. All we need is a hurricane."

Gene filled his glass and sat staring at the wall. Lewis still stood at the window, trembling, staring at nothing. After a while, hearing Gene's mumble, he turned around.

"What are you saying?"

"Just mumbling. Trying to figure the count. How many do you think? Dead and injured altogether."

"I don't know. Too many, that's all I know. God almighty!" he cried. "How and why? Why?"

"I'll tell you. Because we should have taken action at the start when young Victor came with his story about Sprague. I suppose you see now that I was right two years ago. I hate having to say it, but it's the truth."

"You're jumping at conclusions. We don't even know yet what went wrong, and you've already fixed the blame for it."

"We know very well what went wrong. The concrete was no good. All you have to do is feel it. Cheap stuff. Not enough aggregate. I searched as best I could in all the mess tonight, and I'll swear there weren't nearly enough iron bars for reinforcement either. We trusted. Or you're the one who trusted. Not I! And now we'll be blamed for the disaster. The fact is, we deserve the blame."

"Well, if the supplier gypped Sprague and you're sure about the concrete, I don't see—"

"I'm sure. Go downstairs now and see for yourself. I never wanted Sprague, anyway," Gene muttered. "You know I didn't. And now we're through, finished, washed up. Do you understand?"

"You're jumping at conclusions, as I've already said, and you're drunk. That's brandy you're drinking, not water."

"I need to be drunk. Do you realize how many people died tonight? And how many may live who will never walk again on account of your stupidity?"

"God damn it, how dare you!"

"I dare. Your fancy friend, heaven help us. Let's not offend him. Oh, no, never. No social conscience, that's your trouble."

"You're out of your head. I'm not going to let you get away with this when you sober up, brother or no brother."

Toward dawn the telephone rang, bringing down upon both their heads the raving rage of the hotel's owners, Arrow Hotels International.

"You were hired because you're supposed to be the cream of your profession. What in hell have you done or not done with this job? You'll hear from our lawyers at ten o'clock your time, and we'll be at your door ourselves as soon as the Concorde lands tomorrow."

So then we entered the prickly thickets of the law, thought Lewis now, a dark wilderness where we strayed for months and years, looking for some light beyond.

It's all a matter of passing the buck, distributing the guilt. The supplier cheating the contractor (oh, yes, I admit, Gene was right, and the concrete was inferior). The contractor is an innocent victim, or else he is criminally negligent. The architect engineers at the top of this pyramid have the same choice, as does the owning company. Victimized or responsible? Which is it? So they all sue each other. And the families of the dead and injured sue everyone in sight.

Then into the fracas steps Mr. Jerry Victor, a few years

older now, with a respectable suit and haircut this time, plus an interesting story for an investigative reporter. And where does the reporter go after interviewing Victor? Of course he goes to Lewis Byrne. And Lewis Byrne is called upon to explain himself in the courtroom, to give as best he can his foolish reason for not pursuing an inquiry. And Eugene Byrne must explain his part in the affair, how he did ask his brother to speak with Sprague, and how his brother refused.

Thank heaven the business had finally come to an end.

Not, he thought now, that it ever really will. Shall I ever stop seeing the terrible face of that girl with the bloody, mangled shoulder and missing arm? Was she dying, dead, or in shock when I picked her up? I don't know enough about the human body to tell. And I still hear that old man going mad, screaming a woman's name: "Julia! Julia!"

"What on earth are you mumbling about?" asked Daisy. "I was just falling asleep when I heard you. Come to bed, it's almost twelve."

"I was thinking of things. Of my rotten brother, for one."

"Honey, you've got to stop. He's not worth your thoughts."

"All right, I made a bad mistake. But he has no understanding, no mercy. Testifies against me. Accuses me of having no social conscience. Can you imagine? Me, a dollar-a-year man? While he's still raking in consulting fees?"

"Lewis, please. You get yourself so worked up."

She was pressed warmly against his back, with her arms around him, her lips moving on his neck. After all these years she could still give him everything he wanted. Yet tonight he was too filled with his distress to respond.

Feeling this, she withdrew, saying gently, "The last

few years have been too tough. We're due now for some good years. I'm sure we are."

"Social conscience," he repeated as though she had not spoken. "That snob. He and his wife, Susan, the *Mayflower* descendant. Neither one of them ever got over that, did they? And look at the way he treated Ellen when she fell in love with Mark. Believe me, I'd choose Mark any day over our son-in-law, with all his fine family background. Even if Mark is Jewish. The things Ellen's told Cynthia about what they had to go through because of Gene! Good lord, Arthur Roth's Jewish and he's been my accountant for thirty years, and my father's before me, and he's the salt of the earth."

"Come, come, for heaven's sake, you're out of breath. This isn't doing you any good, or me either."

"I didn't tell you I saw Gene the last time we were in New York to visit Cynthia. I guess I didn't want to upset you. I saw him approaching me at the end of the block. It's a good thing I'm farsighted. It gave me time enough to cross the street and look into a shop window. I tell you, Daisy, the sight of him makes me boil."

"Then it's good that you don't have to see him. Let's try to do something about our Cynthia instead. We're going to have a good visit at your mother's. I always feel as if I've stepped back into an easier, slower age when we're there at your old home. The mahogany is cared for, there are flowers on the table, the dogs are brushed, old George still does the gardening, Jenny's still in the kitchen, and your mother's always cheerful."

At this Lewis did finally have to smile. "Yes, there's something about her that draws people. Jenny told me last time that she and George plan to stay as long as Mother lives." Then, frowning again, he exclaimed, "Poor Mother. She shouldn't have these family troubles at her age. I wonder—do you think maybe she's asked us to come because there's something wrong with her?

She's the last person to complain, but if there is anything wrong with her health, I'm glad it's me that she wants to see. God knows she wouldn't get the same help from Gene."

"Darling, I'm sure there's nothing the matter. She simply wants to give Cynthia a little change. It's going to be lovely for the three of us. Come on to bed."

CHAPTER

4

The first thing Gene Byrne noticed when he came home from his office was the topmost envelope in the pile of mail on his desk. Anna, his day worker, had known he would be interested first in his mother's letter.

Sitting down at once to read it, he had to smile. An invitation to spend the day and stay for dinner! It could just as well have been given over the telephone. But then, that would not have been like his mother to do.

"I would appreciate your not mentioning this to Ellen. I don't want to hurt her feelings. Do I have to tell you how I adore your Ellen and her babies? I do plan to have them come soon, but this time I'd like to have just you."

The indefatigable Annette Byrne is finally showing her age, he thought. Young children, especially his darling granddaughter Lucy, can wear even a young person's nerves out after a full day of their constant dartings, spillings, and questions. He understood that, and yet he was disappointed. Although his days were filled with welcome work, and although, living as he did in New York, he could have filled his evenings, and often did so, with drama and music, he had his lonely hours too. His life had changed when his daughter married, his son moved to London, and his wife died. He had to expect some lonely hours and had no right to complain. He never did complain. Still, he was disappointed.

Anna had put his dinner in the warming oven for him and, knowing his tastes, had set a place at the little table overlooking the East River. It was pleasant while eating to watch boats going by, pleasant to be snug here high above the windy streets, pleasant to take his drink out of a crystal goblet. The embroidered place mat was initialed *SJB*, for Susan Jane Byrne, and was still in use even though it had been bought for her trousseau some thirty-two years ago.

Susan had left him much too soon. Cancer wasn't choosy about the ages of its victims. It would be ten years next week since he had taken up what they used to call "bachelor quarters," directly after her death and Ellen's marriage, which had come a few months later. He often thought that if she had to die, she had at least been spared some unlooked-for troubles: the woeful marriage and the disaster of the grand hotel.

He himself tried not to think about those things. Fortunately, he was busy, unlike that brother of his, who had, he supposed from the little he heard, relapsed into idleness. One had to accept accomplished facts. Ellen's marriage, for instance, could have been much worse than it had seemed at the beginning. The children, of course, were wonderful. As to the other blot on his reasonably fortunate life, having had good parents and a beloved wife, he knew that it could never be wiped out. He must simply not look back at it.

That would be difficult this anniversary week, however. Yesterday, coming home in a torrent of rain, he had had a total recall of the tropical storm that night, the dripping ponchos on the cops, the shine of wet pavement where the ambulances were being loaded, the frenzied bustle, calling, shouting, and the clatter of helicopters overhead.

No more room in the morgue. They're laying them on the floor.

It should never have happened. It was, when you came down to it, simply a question of honor and truth. If only Lewis had listened to him when Jerry Victor came with his story, it never would have happened. But Lewis was too impressed with the Spragues and the château in France, where the elder Hanson-Spragues entertained ambassadors and financiers each summer, to open his mouth and investigate.

No one will ever convince me, Gene thought now and probably for the thousandth time, that Victor wasn't telling the truth. It's not as if he was looking for trouble. He could have filed a complaint for violation of the whistleblower law. He'd been promised a raise, and then all of a sudden it was denied. He'd been given some work that he'd never been taught to do and that he was bound to bungle. They wanted him to bungle it. He knew he was being prepared for a fall. Why didn't he sue? Because, as he said, he had a life to make. I admired him.

The funny thing is, if he had looked the way he looked in the courtroom a few years later, Lewis might have paid more attention to him.

He gets a lot of this snobbery from Daisy too. And who on earth does Daisy think she is? Her family never amounted to a hill of beans. Nobody ever heard of them. When I think of Susan, so unassuming even though she was the closest we come in this country to an aristocrat, going back to the *Mayflower*—

Yes, but it's Daisy's daughter who made the good marriage, not ours. Life's little quirks. You never know what's around the corner. That was a terrible, unspeakable thing that happened to those twins. I was relieved to be in London when it happened; the funeral must have been awful. Ellen said it was. I can imagine. Or rather, I can't. Suppose it had been Lucy and Freddie, I think I'd go out of my mind.

They're so beautiful and so smart and so sweet. They look like Ellen. Not that Mark isn't a nice-looking young man. He dresses neatly, very well, in fact. Of course, you have to make a proper appearance when you work in a fine midtown art gallery. I wonder how much he makes. It can't be much, I think, or why would they live in a remodeled loft way downtown instead of up here in this neighborhood, near the park, where Cynthia lives? It's so depressing downtown among those lofts and factories, so gray and grimy, with all the trucks and cluttered sidewalks. You feel as if the air is poisonous, and it probably is, from the exhausts, and no trees to absorb anything. Where in heaven's name are the children going to play? And whom are they going to meet?

But Ellen's apparently quite content, so maybe the choice is her idea. I don't know. She always was an independent. Like most artists. Maybe she'll actually make a name for herself someday after the children are both in school. I saw something rather good on the easel that she keeps on the north side of that big room. Good Lord, they cook and eat, she works, the children play, and they all do everything but sleep in that one room. Still, they're obviously happy together.

That elopement almost gave me a heart attack. Why, with all the contacts and opportunities she had, did she have to pick anybody named Mark Sachs? Not that I have anything against Jews. Well, maybe I do, a little. They're peculiar people. I never know what they're thinking. I don't feel at ease with them. It's just—it's just— Actually, though, it's not Mark whom I mind so much. No one could say fairly that Mark is not a gentleman. But his parents, especially his father! Never mind that he's a doctor and supposedly chief of some staff somewhere or other, I can't look at him. The one time I saw him, nine years ago, was more than enough. I never want to look at that black beard again. Sat there with a sour face; didn't eat anything. Ellen promised I wouldn't have to see him, and thank heavens, she's kept her promise. I daresay the doctor isn't eager to see me either. Hah! It was mutual hatred at first sight, especially on his part. I sensed it the minute he walked into the room. The mother isn't quite as bad, except for her loud, whiny voice. Overemotional. Orthodox. Not pleased with my daughter. Not good enough for him. I can imagine how they must have ranted at home. To be mixed up with people like those. And my grandchildren related to them, tied to them for life.

I'll bet he hasn't given them a cent because he disapproves of the marriage. At least I've set up trusts for my family that they don't even know about. I'd like to give them things now, but they won't accept anything. Ellen doesn't want anything, and Mark's very independent. Well, I give him credit for that. So they'll get theirs when my time comes. Except for Susan's jewelry. Ellen already has it all, some handsome pieces, too, although goodness knows when she ever wears them. At least she has them. It wouldn't have hurt those people to make a gift to the mother of their grandchildren, even though they don't like her. Oh, well. As long as I never have to have any contact with them, and I won't. That's one thing you can be sure of.

Gene drank his coffee. Again, his glance fell on his mother's letter. And again he wondered whether there was any reason for concern.

Come early, she had written. *I'll expect you not later than ten.*

Well, that was all right. An early riser, he would have a quick breakfast and start. But why specifically at ten? Unless she was expecting a conference of some kind with a doctor or lawyer, perhaps. It hurt him to think of her with either one, for doctors and lawyers almost always meant some kind of trouble. She had enough worries already: Cynthia's troubles, and then the irreconcilable breach between her sons.

He got up and wrote a memorandum: *Stop at bookstore for Mother. New book on English castles, plus a good novel. Also, chocolate macaroons, large box.*

CHAPTER

5

On the other side of Central Park, Aaron Sachs and his wife, Brenda, were having their supper.

"We'll have to start early to pick up Mark and Ellen downtown before we get on the road," she said.

"Why they don't have a car, I'll never know. You'd think he could at least afford a cheap car."

"I'm sure he can. But what does anyone want with a car on Manhattan Island?"

"Right as usual, dear wife." And Aaron winked at her.

She was so reasonable that she sometimes, when he was in a bad mood, annoyed him. Still, after all these years, she was his treasure, his "woman of valor," good natured, vigorous, and almost as pretty as she had been on their wedding day.

At present he was not exactly in a bad mood, but he was tired. He had had some tough surgery and a sorry case that was bound to go wrong. Now this letter from Annette Byrne was a complication in his busy life. Who wanted to drive out into the country in the middle of winter to visit a woman one scarcely knew? They had been in her house only once before, and that was nine years ago. He picked up the letter and, propping it against his dinner plate, stained it with tomato sauce.

"Oh, that beautiful stationery," Brenda said.

"Never mind the stationery. *It would mean a great deal to me if you would all come,* she says, *and it will be fun for Lucy and Freddie. We have a new family of swans to show them. So please do come.* Now, why should it mean a great deal to her? Why?"

"What's so puzzling? She's old and alone. She wants to have some time with her grandchildren and her granddaughter's family. Personally, I think it's very gracious of her to include us."

"We are Mark's parents, aren't we?"

"Even so."

Aaron sighed. "I won't be able to eat the food, you know. It'll probably be baked ham."

Brenda laughed. "Of course it won't be. But whatever it is, we can eat vegetables. That's what we always do, isn't it? And we can do it again."

"They don't know how to eat, anyway. The food has no taste."

"That's why everybody goes to French restaurants, the food's so bad."

"I was only kidding, my literal wife." And they both laughed.

"She's a lovely woman, very simple in her manner, as I remember her. I have to admit, though, that I'm a little intimidated. I'm not used to grandeur. Not that the house is palatial, just the reverse. It has the kind of simplicity that costs a fortune, you know? And then the grounds, the gardens—"

"Anybody would think to hear you that you live in a hovel. Five rooms on Central Park West. Not too bad."

"I didn't say it was bad, idiot."

"Then act accordingly. Don't be humble. You're an aristocrat, aren't you?"

"Some aristocrat."

"You grew up in a house in the suburbs, you went to a private school, and your grandparents were born in this country. I lived in Washington Heights with the rest of the refugees, and borrowed the money for medical school. So by my standards you're an American aristocrat."

He loved to tease her. She was so earnest, so literal minded, that he could always count on at least four or five seconds between the time she heard what he said and the time she realized that he was joking.

"Mark loves her, you know. He's mentioned her lots of times."

"Who? Ellen? He should love Ellen. He married her."

"Oh, Aaron, you know very well I meant the grand-mother. She's very close to them. But the two sons haven't spoken to each other for years, Mark says. It must be a very difficult kind of balancing act for her."

"WASPs. They've no sense of family."

"That's ridiculous. You shouldn't use that word, any-way. A wasp is a mean insect."

"Well, Anglo-Saxons, then. I've nothing against them—well, maybe I have. Some. They're a cold people. And stingy. They don't do a thing for their children once the children are grown and out of the house. I wonder whether her father knows about the pearls you gave Ellen, and what we've set aside for the grandchildren. Living in one of their homes must be like living in an ice-box. They don't express themselves. They walk around whispering politely, all buttoned up. No feeling."

"Nonsense, Aaron, you don't know anything about them. Those are ugly stereotypes; that's all they are."

"I know about people."

"No, you don't. You only know about people's broken bones. How can you talk like this when your own daughter-in-law is the sweetest soul on earth? And you know she is."

Brenda's fine, dark eyebrows rose, as, waiting for a response, she watched him. Yes, he did like Ellen. She was making his son happy. . . . But how much different it would be if, for example, Mark had married the Cohens' daughter. She was a beautiful girl, and he had always hoped that something might come about. Or if not Jennifer Cohen, at least somebody from a family that could be joined to theirs. They'd celebrate the holidays together and feel at ease. What was he going to talk about up there at that fancy country estate? And he grumbled something inaudible to Brenda.

"You're tired," she said.

"I am not," he answered, never wanting to admit that he was.

"Yes, you are. I can tell by your grumble. You're tired, and this invitation has upset you besides."

"Well, it's made me think. It's brought back things that I've tried to bury. Why, Mark doesn't even go to the synagogue anymore. I asked him."

"Mark knows who he is. He discusses it freely. He's Jewish, but secular."

"Secular! Where in blazes is the good in that?"

Brenda sighed. "Where the good is, I can't answer. It doesn't seem like much good to me. But it's life, the world today, or part of it. And there's nothing you can do about it."

"I wonder what's going to happen to the children. Look at them. So beautiful."

In a double frame on the piano, they sat: Freddie, not yet two, was holding a ball, and pleased with it, smiled, showing his tiny teeth; Lucy, just six, had light, ruffly hair and a ruffly dress; her smile was piquant, already feminine.

"They both look like my mother," Brenda said. "Take after her side."

"So beautiful," Aaron repeated, his eyes going moist. "Yes, but what's to become of them, what will they be?"

"I suppose Ellen's side thinks about it too. At any rate, there's nothing we can do about that, either, Aaron."

For a few minutes neither spoke. The little table on which they had their meals had been placed at the window so that they might look down at the park. From this height the skating rink looked like a mirror speckled with moving black dots.

"It doesn't seem cold enough to be skating," observed Brenda.

"Artificial ice."

"Did I mention that Ellen's painting is going to be shown in one of those galleries near their apartment?"

"You told me."

He knew she was making conversation. His morose humor, his dwelling on the old subject, were not fair to her. And forcing a bright tone, he said, "I think she has talent. Those landscapes she does are really pretty."

"That's just what's wrong with them. They're too pretty. They're only skillful imitations of Winslow Homer's country scenes. She even has a deer in the last one."

"Don't disparage it. I liked it."

"Darling, excuse me, you're a marvelous surgeon, but you really don't know the first thing about art."

Aaron waved his arm toward the farther wall, on which, above a grouping of stainless-steel-and-leather chairs, there hung an enormous painting of acid-green and bloody-purple tubes, snaked around each other.

"And you do? And that's art? It looks like intestines."

"Aaron! It happens to be very, very fine art."

"Bunk. You're reacting against a reaction. You like this abstract stuff because your parents ridiculed it." And he laughed, glad to have something to laugh about.

"Well, laugh away. It's good to see you being funny."

"Incidentally, how is it that you admire Annette Byrne's things? If you like the stuff in this room, you can't like her Chippendale."

"Well, I don't like Chippendale. But her things are good of their kind, and they're put together with taste." She reflected, "Ellen has taste, too, along with her other good qualities."

Aaron nodded. "True. True. Listen, you don't have to persuade me to go. Save your energy. I'm going next week. I don't look forward to it, but I'll do it. Call up and tell her we'll be there."

"No, I'll write. When you receive a letter, you answer with a letter. That's proper. They're very proper people." And suddenly, a dark expression passed across Brenda's face. "You know what? It's only the father who puts a bad taste in my mouth."

"You just met him once."

"Yes, and that was once too often. I felt such anger, the only time in my life I felt such anger. It stuck in my throat. I hated him."

"The feeling was mutual, you can be sure."

"Shriveled like a prune, his dry lips, and his eyes like pins pointed into my eyes. Who does he think he is, the duke of Westminster or somebody? The duke would be more gracious."

"Not if his daughter had run off and married our son, Brenda dear."

They both laughed. Then Brenda said seriously, "If I should ever run into him someplace, I'd—I'd make a scene. I don't know what would happen."

"You'd get your name in the papers, that's what would happen. Not that I wouldn't mind joining you. He looks down on our Mark! Mr. Hitler. He only needs a mustache to look like him."

"Tell me. How does a girl like Ellen come from such a father? And how does a woman like Annette have such a son?"

"God knows. Maybe it's in the genes. Don't ask me, I'm not a psychiatrist, or God either." Aaron stood up and shoved his chair toward the table. "Come on, enough of this. If you still want to go to the movies, I'll stack the dishes in the washer while you repair your face. Hurry, or we'll be late."

"Aaron, I just had a horrible thought. You don't think she'd have that man there, would she?"

"What man?"

"Ellen's father."

"Are you out of your mind? Of course she wouldn't. By the way, don't forget to pick up a little something to take along."

"I know. Mark told me what bakery to go to on the East Side. Annette likes chocolate macaroons."

CHAPTER

6

At four o'clock in December, the short, dark afternoon was over. Electric light filled the enormous room, glaring above the rug on which Freddie played with his blocks and Lucy, sprawled on her stomach, studied the first-grade reader. It shed a softer light on the easy chairs and bookshelves at the far end of the room, brightening the easel with the unfinished painting at the north window. And, at the opposite end, it brightened, too, the stove, the sink, and the ironing board, where Ellen was at work.

Despite the short afternoon it had been a long day. The days began around six o'clock when, from the other side of the partition that divided one space into three small sleeping rooms, there sounded Freddie's early stirrings in his crib. First came a chirping sound, part speech and part song; what thought could he be expressing and from what heard music came those few sprightly notes? Next came the rattle and pounding of the crib as he propelled it back and forth against the partition. Last came his demanding call for attention, meaning a diaper change and breakfast. There was no use, even on a holiday or Sunday, in covering one's head with the blankets, no escape from that demanding call. It was time to get up.

"Rise and shine," Ellen's father used to say when it was time for school. And now that was her own morning greeting to her own children. Funny, she reflected, how you trail all these tag ends, this miscellaneous baggage, along, even when you move from your first life into another one that's removed one hundred eighty degrees.

She still used her mother's linen place mats, even though she had to iron them herself. They were too precious to bring to the Laundromat, as were the handmade dresses that Gran bought for Lucy. Lucy had few occasions to wear them, but they were lovely. Ellen had worn such dresses herself when she was growing up in a long-ago time of children's concerts and Upper East Side birthday parties with crepe-paper hats and loot bags to take home.

This was another world in which she lived now. It was hardly a world of poverty—not by any means—but it was surely different. Here expenses mattered very much. You had to watch them, to make some careful calculations before spending anything at all. It bothered her father, who was always questioning, always offering to buy, to pay for this or that, and always meeting with refusal. Mark's parents did the same and, in the same way, met refusal.

For Ellen and Mark had need to prove themselves. When people marry each other in stubborn defiance of a hundred earnest objections and dire warnings of failure, they must go it alone. They must show—and always she had to smile at the old, trite, true slogan—that "love conquers all." Well, of course, sometimes it did not. And she would think, then, of her poor cousin Cynthia. But for Mark and herself, love had conquered.

And she looked over at her children. Born of love, they were blessed besides with intelligence and good looks. Their savory dinner of chicken pie and vegetables was baking in the oven. Their father would soon be coming home. What more could anybody ask for?

Her ears, as evening approached, were always alert to the sound of the rising elevator, which had once, when this building was a warehouse, carried freight and was slow. Mark's footsteps would rush through the outer hall; he seldom walked, but almost always ran to any of his destinations. She would open the door, and there he would be with his kiss, his smile, and his tie already torn off.

He was the kind of person who was most comfortable in jeans and sneakers. Anybody who knew him well would be amused to think of him or to see him at work in that uptown gallery, wearing the fine dark suit and striped tie of a banker or Wall Street lawyer. But he loved the work, and as he said, "The clothes go with the territory." As it happened, he wore them very well. He was tall and slender, with a serious expression; he was cordial and serious, with a well-modulated voice. In a word, he was elegant.

Gran said that they made a handsome couple. No one but Gran had told them that; friends do not usually make such comments among themselves; and from their respective families, given the circumstances, they could hardly expect such a compliment. Nevertheless, Ellen knew it was true. They did make a handsome couple.

She also was tall, and had once been as blond as Lucy now was. She wore her tan hair with its few clever streaks in a ballerina's upsweep, revealing her long neck and graceful profile. On her various errands around the neighborhood, marketing, walking Lucy to and from school, and taking Freddie to play in the pocket-sized park, she wore jeans as almost everyone else did. Otherwise, she wore simple clothes in vivid colors, for she loved color: aquamarine, apricot, and lapis lazuli. She wore little jewelry, inexpensive earrings that she bought in novelty shops, the plain wedding band that matched Mark's wedding band, and, on appropriate occasions, the splendid pearl necklace that his mother had given to her. It had been in essence a kind of peace offering from Brenda when Lucy was born. She liked Brenda, who had, in spite of all, a fundamental tolerance and heart.

Her own mother's jewels, which had naturally come to her, were in a safe deposit box at the bank. They were too formal and too precious to fit into Ellen's life as they had into Susan's. Lately she had come to think and speak of her mother as "Susan"; it made her seem young and filled with the happiness she must once have had. People had always described her with the word *sunny* before the long illness that filled Ellen's memory of her as "Mother" or "Mom."

If Susan had lived long enough to see us married, Ellen thought, I would have asked her some questions. And I believe I know what she would have answered. Or maybe, given the pressure that Dad would have put on her, she would not have answered. Yet I do think she knew what was happening and simply did not have the physical strength to take a stand for me. I really sensed that, didn't I? And wasn't that why we waited, Mark and I, until she died? She had enough to bear without the addition of a social scandal, absurd and minor as it was. . . .

After working hours, or on a free Saturday that first year after her graduation from college with a degree in fine arts, she used to tour the art galleries from the tail end of Manhattan to the treasure houses of the Upper East Side. Sometimes she merely glanced into a window and, seeing nothing to tempt her, walked on. At other times when tempted, she went in without any intention of buying, merely of satisfying her avid eye.

In particular she loved old landscape paintings or current works that gave the feel of a quiet world without industry—although such a fondness reflected only an impractical nostalgia—a world of greenness and space, of domestic animals, and crops and changing seasons. This nostalgia had probably to do with long summers in her childhood at Gran's house. No matter. And so it happened one spring day that she walked into a certain gallery on Fifty-seventh Street.

A very nice-looking young man came forward and addressed her. "May I show you anything?"

Ellen hated that. She had simply wanted to look, and she said so.

"Very well. I'll be happy to answer any questions you may have."

She walked around. The walls were hung with superb paintings, sparkling out of exquisite gold frames that in themselves cost more than Ellen could afford. At home they had expensive paintings, but they were not her taste. And anyway, they belonged to her parents, not to her. Standing in front of a woodland brook under falling snow, she thought: Now, I would give my eyeteeth to own that—or better still, to be able to paint it.

There were two rooms. After she had slowly and carefully passed around all their walls, she returned to the brook and was still standing there absorbed in the winter light and the stillness through which she seemed to be hearing the trickle of water over rocks, when a voice in back of her spoke.

"That really talks to you, doesn't it?"

"Yes, and I'm answering it," she said.

He laughed. It was a small, discreet laugh, professional sounding as befitted his role. There was a dignity
about him, a bit formal, a quality that she took to be
British. She knew very little about things British except
for what she had seen on her only visit to Britain, and,
naturally, what one saw on television or in the movies.
Later she learned that indeed he had been wearing an
English suit, bought for him by his parents on their trip
to Britain. But that was another story.

"Is there anything you would care to know about it?"
he asked.

"Well, yes, the price," she said, which, having been a
fine arts major and having recognized all the names on
all those walls, she could easily estimate.

"It is thirty-five thousand dollars. An exceptionally
fine example of his work. He died last year, you know."

"Yes, I know."

"His prices are bound to go up, so this is actually a remarkably good investment."

She did not reply. The young man had lovely eyes, extraordinary eyes, brown, but yet almost gold around the
pupils. Or perhaps it was the light slanting in from the
street?

"Of course I understand that you would only purchase
a work like this out of love for it, but still, it is always nice
to know that your investment will hold up."

He wanted so much to sell it! Naturally; they worked
on commissions. The place was hardly busy, either, and
there were two other men standing and sitting, the latter
idly turning the pages of the catalog. It must be a difficult life, very frustrating.

"I'll think about it," she told him, aware that he must,
hundreds of times, have heard the same words from
people who were only looking.

For an indecisive moment they stood there; she saw
his glance fall to her hand, to the dazzle of Kevin's four-

carat round-cut diamond engagement ring. When he spoke, there was a touch of hope in his tone. After all, a young woman who owned such a ring—might she not also do more than just think about that snow falling in the woodland brook? Bowing almost imperceptibly, he gave her his card.

Mark Sachs, she read.

"Ellen Byrne. I'll think about it," she repeated. "And thank you so much."

She walked slowly home up Fifth Avenue, where there were no shops, only the summery park on the left with its carriages, beautiful babies in fashionable strollers, and beautiful dogs being led by professional dog-walkers. On the right, all the way to the museum and beyond, rose the limestone walls of apartment houses with green awnings and doormen in maroon uniforms. In one of these she still lived with her parents, there being no sense in setting up an apartment of her own when she was so soon to be married anyway.

It occurred to her that most likely she would be spending her life in just such an apartment, spacious, quiet, and filled with valuable possessions in simple good taste. Her children would be reared as she had been, sledding in the park and sailing a marvelous boat, given for her seventh birthday, in its pond. Late in the afternoons they would do their homework in their little bedrooms above the side street; the important rooms, living room, library, and master bedroom, would face the park.

The master bedroom. The term had a masterful sound, almost patriarchal, when you thought about it. And thinking further, it seemed to fit Kevin, who was authoritarian, competent, and very kind, as well.

On first meeting him her father had observed, "That young man will go far."

He had already done so. Although not yet thirty, only

four years out of law school, he had been offered a place in the firm's Paris office. At this moment he was in Paris getting some orientation, after which he would return, they would be married, and go abroad to live for two or three years; then after that, following the usual track, he would return to the New York office and a promotion.

The prospect of living in France had thrown Ellen, as in a sudden analytic mood she now saw herself, into a kind of rapture. An adolescent rapture. Ever since having been there once with her parents, she had sustained a long love affair with France. She had also sustained a love affair with Kevin.

They had been casually introduced on the campus of the university at which she was an undergraduate senior and he a graduate of its law school. He had come back that day on a visit. A group of five or six, Ellen's roommate among them, was on its way to the coffee shop, and she went along. Beside Kevin there was one other man, but he was uninteresting. It was Kevin, blue eyed and bold of feature, who held attention, not only the women's, but even the men's in the class.

He had already entered the world, that world which often, at worst, appeared like a dangerous jungle, or at best, like a game of musical chairs, where everyone scrambled, knowing that there were not enough seats to go around and that somebody was bound to be left out. Looking at Kevin, you felt almost certain that he would not be one of those left out.

Ellen had never expected to be noticed. She had indeed gone out a great deal with many differing types of men on the campus—fraternity men, athletes, and poetic loners—but they had all been her own age or close to it, so it was with a little well-hidden gasp of surprise when, under cover of some loud general conversation, she heard Kevin ask for her telephone number.

Her roommate was equally surprised. Her quick, appraising glance at Ellen seemed to be saying: Why you? What is it about you that's so special? She was, however, in possession of some interesting facts about Kevin, which she gave to Ellen. He came from an Ohio family that had something to do with steel. In New York, where he lived alone, he had an apartment near the World Trade Center.

"He will probably never call you," the roommate predicted. "He's too full of himself to bother with an undergraduate. You're too young for him."

But he was not "full of himself"; he was, as it turned out, most modestly understated, and he did call. When the telephone rang a few days later, it was to ask her when she would be back in the city. For Christmas vacation, she told him, and gave him her number there. Her father noted with unusual approval that he did not "pick her up" in the lobby downstairs, but came straight to the apartment to introduce himself to her parents.

"Which is what a man was always expected to do, you know."

Things moved with remarkable speed after that. On the first time they went to a Broadway show. On the second they danced in the Rainbow Room. On the third time they had dinner quite far downtown in one of the newest French restaurants that had gone to the top of the critics' list. The lights were hazy, the murals transported you, depending on where you looked, to the shores of Brittany, or southward to the Alpilles, and the tables were far enough apart for intimate conversations to be held in private.

It was not that their conversation was what you would necessarily call "intimate." It was explanatory. Ellen learned that he was already fluent in three languages and was trying to find time for the study of Mandarin, because China, whether we liked it or not and he did not, was sure to become the dominant force on the planet. Kevin learned that she was hoping to get a wonderful position in a major museum of art somewhere, practically anywhere, because such jobs were hard to get. At any rate, she was bound to enter the world of art; she loved it ardently, and though really she had no talent to speak of, had even tried drawing and painting on the side. They had kindred interests and some acquaintances in common.

All these things in an odd, vague way made him less a stranger, so that when they could no longer keep sitting at table drinking wine, of which Ellen was not particularly fond because it made her sleepy, followed by coffee, which woke her up—when they positively had to leave to stand outdoors in a blast of icy wind and he suggested that they warm themselves in his apartment, it seemed like a perfectly reasonable thing to do.

In those years, she often thought later after she was married, people had been amazingly casual about having sex. Quite simply, going to bed together after a few days' acquaintance was expected, even if you did not especially want to do it. Ellen really did not want to; no one had moved her deeply, as you were supposed to be moved; she wondered whether possibly no one ever would.

Kevin was gentle, yet not too gentle. He thought she was absolutely beautiful, absolutely wonderful, and told her so, over and over. Then he took her home in a taxi, saw her to the door, kissed her, and the next day sent her a magnificent bouquet of two dozen roses.

Maybe the roses were really too obvious. If I were a parent, she thought, I would put two and two together. But her mother had just had another chemotherapy treatment and was too miserable to notice anything, while her father, she guessed, was so taken with Kevin Clark's person and status that he would question nothing. Anyway, there was nothing he could do about the situation, and undoubtedly he knew it.

You grow quickly attached to a person who glorifies you, provided, naturally, that the person is otherwise attractive. When she was back at college Kevin's nightly telephone calls gave her something to anticipate all day and something to look back upon with a sense of fulfillment. As often as possible she now went home for weekends, which was something she had never done before. Once Kevin drove up for a weekend, and they spent a few hours at a motel, which was also something she had never done before.

"Ellen's a simple girl," said those who knew her best. "She has always had very few wants."

Now suddenly she wanted life to be lavish, not in any material sense, but in the amorous and sensual. Reliving evenings that her parents assumed were being spent at the theater or similar places, she bought expensive underwear and perfume. She knew she was envied, except perhaps by her radical feminist friends.

She went through finals, did very well, and was graduated in May. She had invited Kevin because he said he wanted to come, so there he stood with her parents and Gran, among the crowd that saw her go past with the robed academic procession. Everyone knew, yet properly, no one ventured a word about what was coming next.

It came in Kevin's apartment later that week. On the twenty-second floor she was looking out at the view, the spread and sparkle across the Hudson, north to the bridge that spanned it and south toward the tip of the island, where it met the bay.

"It seems," she murmured, "that in this city, the first thing people want in an apartment, if they can afford it, is a view."

"That depends. This has been nice for me, but for the long pull I like the kind of place where you live, lower down and near the park, so our children could play there, the way you did."

She turned about. This was the greatest moment in her life, she thought. Why didn't she cry or feel something incredible? She felt merely pleased, quite pleased. But it was, after all, no surprise. She threw her arms around him, and they kissed, a very long kiss.

"I take it the answer is yes. And with that in mind I came prepared. Here it is."

"It," of course, was the brilliant ring, the family ring that had been kept for Kevin's bride. Now everything was sealed, sealed and soon to be signed. They would have to wait not quite a year until he should be established in Paris. In the meanwhile he would have to be traveling back and forth for the firm to other parts of Europe. And in the meanwhile there was great rejoicing. His parents arrived from Ohio, were invited to a celebration dinner, and to another one at Gran's place in the country. There were champagne and flowers; there were toasts. A lucky man, Kevin was. A lucky woman, Ellen was.

She was very well aware of all that on the day she walked home after the encounter in the gallery on Fifty-seventh Street.

Her mother was resting on the sofa in the library. Almost every afternoon during this past year she rested. And still, not wanting to admit the extent of her illness, she pretended surprise at herself. Her apology hurt Ellen's heart.

"I don't know what got over me today. The drowsy spring weather, I guess. Kevin phoned from Paris, dear. I told him you weren't home yet. He'll call back at five."

At five precisely as always, the call arrived. "I'm missing you terribly," he said.

"And I you."

"What did you do today? Don't you get off earlier on Wednesdays?"

"Yes, but I took a walk afterward."

"Where did you go?"

Kevin had a habit of wanting detailed explanations for everything, which was sometimes bothersome to Ellen, but still, since he willingly gave such explanations for his activities, shereally should not let it be bothersome to her.

"Went around looking into galleries."

"Did you see anything you liked?"

"Yes, for thirty-five thousand dollars."

"Well, I can't promise you anything in that range, darling. But I'll tell you, there's an art gallery in almost every fair-sized town in France, and they're not always too high priced either. Wait till you get here. You'll see a lot of landscapes, the kind you'll love. What's the weather like over there?"

"A wonderful spring afternoon, warm and soft."

"That's a perfect description of you. It's rained here all day, and it's still pouring tonight. What are you doing this very minute?"

"I was just emptying my handbag. It's full of junk."

"I was counting the minutes until five o'clock. Now I'm going to turn off the light. Big busy day tomorrow."

When she hung up, Ellen sat with the handbag on her lap, tossing things into the wastebasket: a worn-down lipstick, a torn handkerchief, a piece of a candy-bar wrapper, and a card. *Mark Sachs,* it read, under the name of the gallery.

Momentarily, she felt a tiny pang of regret. Wouldn't the young man have been astounded if she had said, "Yes, I love it, I'll take it?" She would have enjoyed seeing his face, but that was absurd. She tore up the card and tossed it, too, into the basket.

About two weeks later Ellen walked through Fifty-seventh Street carrying a pair of shoes that she had just bought. The shop windows were filled with colorful objects; adult toys, she called them, even while enjoying them. There in the gallery's window was "her" painting. Really lovely, she thought, and was wondering to herself whether, ridiculous as it was, she might try to paint something like it: a brook in falling snow, dark water, dark bare trees, the sky to be light gray, almost white—

"So you're still thinking about it?" And there was her salesman, coming through the door.

"No, I can't possibly do it. The only reason I said I'd think about it was that I wanted to make an easy exit."

He smiled. "People do that all the time. It's understandable."

"What I'm really thinking about is how I might try to paint something like it."

"You're an artist?"

"I don't dare say that. I'm a would-be artist."

"Even the greatest had to start."

There came then a pause with nothing to fill it, and she moved away from the window.

"Going east or west?" he asked.

"West to Fifth and then uptown."

"So am I."

They walked to the corner, waited at the red light, and turned north. She felt awkward and foolish to be keeping step with this total stranger and having nothing to say.

Mark Sachs was his name. She remembered how it had looked on the card, discreet and refined, almost like engraving.

"Nice to get through early," he said. "We're not all that busy this time of year. Nice to get some air."

"It's not too hot to walk, for a change. I'm going to get off the avenue and go through the park."

"So am I. Whenever I visit my parents on Central Park West, I like to cut through the park and out at the natural history museum. That gives me about a mile and a half's worth of exercise, anyway."

The dialogue was now slowly starting up.

"They've done wonders over at that museum. But my love is always art museums. I thought that after graduation I'd get a great job in one right away, but the great job hasn't turned up. They never tell you how hard it is to find one. So I'm working in the museum shop, which is fun, and I'm hoping it will—who knows?—lead to something."

"I took my job the same way. I knew I wanted to do something in the art world. I didn't want to be a doctor or a lawyer or a teacher. Maybe if I'd grown up in the West, I'd be a sheep rancher, I don't know. So I got an MBA with the thought that I'd eventually own an art gallery."

Some little boys were playing with toy boats at the pond. For a moment they stood watching.

"What would New York be without the park?" Ellen wondered aloud. "I played with boats right here. I actually grew up in this park. It feels like home, as if I owned it."

"Same with me, from roller skates to baseball."

"You must live right across from me. I'm near the art museum, and you're near the Natural History."

"No, I have an apartment in the Village with two friends from college. It's just my parents who live uptown. I try to visit them on Wednesdays."

"That's nice. I've been living at home since graduation last May because I—" And with a feeling that these explanations, made to a stranger, were really uncalled for, she stopped.

He looked at his watch. "Well, I'm early for dinner. They'll be surprised." Their paths were branching, yet he still was not walking away. "It's been nice talking to you."

"Yes," she said with a smile, and, looking at her own watch, remarked, "yes, early for dinner, but there's nobody home to be surprised. They're in Maine."

"So you'll prop up a book while you eat alone? That's what I like to do."

This situation was absolutely ridiculous. Two strangers having a stilted, silly dialogue instead of going along on their ways.

"No," she said, "I missed the morning paper. I'll pick one up and read it in the sandwich shop."

"A sandwich? Is that all you're going to eat?"

"Oh, they have more stuff if I want any. There's a great place on Madison. It's really much more than just a sandwich shop."

And still they stood there where the path forked. He seemed to be studying her face, then seemed about to speak, closed his mouth, and at last, did speak. "Would you mind—I mean would you mind if I went along?"

Ellen had, then, a moment of doubt. Wasn't this, when you came down to it, nothing else but a pickup? On the other hand, where was the harm? You might look at it as an hour's worth of adventure, a small, insignificant adventure, a little fun.

In front of the restaurant there were a few tables beneath an awning. When they had sat down and given their orders, they fell again into awkward silence until Ellen broke it, saying frankly, "I'm sorry I took so much of your time for nothing that day. You thought I was really going to buy it, didn't you?"

"You can always hope. And if people look—well, look as if—"

She laughed, interrupting him. "It's this ring. People see it and naturally assume things. I can't blame them, though I hate the idea of it."

"Then why do you wear it?"

"It's my engagement ring."

He seemed to be embarrassed, as if he had committed a social blunder, although, as she was well aware, it was she who had brought up the subject.

"He's working at his law firm's branch in Paris right now."

"So you'll be living in Paris."

"For a year or two. I'm hoping to learn things there that might add to my job résumé when I come back."

"I spent a year abroad while I was in college. Then I went there again for two summers and wrote an article about how architecture changed when Hausmann rebuilt the city."

"Was it published?"

"In a small, a very small, magazine. It didn't amount to much. Hardly original. But someday I'd like to do a book on how to remake a whole city, the way Hausmann did."

She asked curiously, "Do you like what you're doing now?"

"I'm saving money for that art gallery and the book I want to do, so I have to like it. In the meantime I'm learning things. I'm out in the real world meeting people. Something interesting happens every day. Sometimes sad, sometimes funny."

Her glance met his eyes, in which she was startled to see again a lovely glint of gold around the iris. It was a lively glint, and yet if you were asked, you would say his eyes were thoughtful.

"What happened today? Something funny or sad?"

"I'll tell you and you can tell me which it is. An old couple came in and walked around for a long time. They were country people, and this was their first trip to New York. He wanted to buy her a present. She said she'd like a picture to hang above the sofa. The one she liked was your snow on the brook. Good judgment. 'You like it, Mother?' he said, although quite obviously she was not his mother. And he asked the price. So I told him it was thirty-five. 'That's pretty steep,' he said, 'but since it's her birthday, she's entitled to it.' And he took out his wallet. 'Might as well pay cash.' I saw my colleague's face grow red with silent laughter. I told the man very gently that there'd been a misunderstanding, that I should have explained he'd need to add some zeros. He was astonished. 'You mean you'd charge over a thousand dollars for that? Excuse me, sir, I don't mean to be impertinent, but that's highway robbery.' The poor lady was disappointed and they went out still shaking their heads. So what do you think about that story?"

"It touches my heart. It's far more sad than funny."

"Of course it is."

For some reason the simple anecdote had moved her excessively. She had a curious awareness of sharpened senses: of the afternoon sun's painful glitter on metal, of ice cubes squirming in her glass, of a passing woman's anxious face.

"Tell me a funny one," she said.

So, as if she had given a command, he did. He was a raconteur, an entertainer. They had drunk a second tall glass of iced coffee and the sun had gone behind the buildings across the avenue before they realized that it was late.

"You're really a humorist," she told him. "You're really a wit."

"Thank you. If I have any wit at all, I get what little I have from my father. Dinnertime was fun when I was a kid. It still is. Which reminds me, I'd better run."

Ellen went home thinking about Mark Sachs. He was an interesting person, so very alive. She had a feeling that he never wasted a living moment. Then another thought fled across her mind. *What is he like when he makes love?* She felt unspeakably foolish, and, ashamed of her foolishness, crushed the thought at its birth. Who was he, anyway? She would never see him again.

Another Wednesday arrived. It was very hot, the kind of day when you think of doing nothing but being near water or, if that is not possible, of reading somewhere in the shade. The perfect spot in the park was the place where the walk forked toward the West Side. It was even breezy there, and very quiet.

From time to time, as people passed, Ellen glanced up over the book. Some boys came by on Rollerblades. Two nursemaids pushed baby carriages. An old man scattered crumbs for birds as he walked. Then suddenly, there was Mark Sachs.

He sat down beside her and looked at her book. "French. You're preparing yourself. Are you leaving pretty soon?"

"The date's not been set, but soon. He—we have to find an apartment."

"My favorite place is the Place des Vosges."

"Expensive tastes!"

"Just idle talk. What's your choice?"

"That depends on how soon and how far Kevin moves up in the firm." And suddenly, conscious of an obligation, she said loyally, "He's very bright. Someone told me he's shot up like a rocket."

"So eventually you will afford the snowy brook, or something like it."

"I told you I'm going to paint one of my own."

"Are you really any good? Seriously?"

Ellen shook her head. "I don't believe so, although once they hung something of mine in our church hall in the country."

He nodded, then said abruptly, "I'm Jewish. Orthodox. That is, my parents are."

"So? I'm an Episcopalian. What about it?"

He shrugged. "I don't know. I just like to set things straight, I suppose."

She wondered why he wanted to set things straight. . . .

Now she pursued the subject. "That sounds interesting. Tell me about yourself"—adding quickly—"if you want to."

"There's nothing much to tell."

"Oh, no. There always is. For instance, why aren't you Orthodox, like your parents?"

"Just never rubbed off on me. My father's a good man, sometimes hard to live with if you don't agree with him on certain things. He wanted me to be a surgeon too. He wanted it badly, so that's been a big disappointment to him, although he never says so anymore, so he's evidently forced himself to accept me as I am. Mother accepts things more easily." Mark smiled. "Or at least she pretends to. She's a social worker, trained to unravel the knots and make peace. Anyway, her background is very different from Dad's. She's never had to struggle, and that's a big part of the difference."

This candor touched Ellen. It was not that he had revealed anything very intimate, but rather that he had responded so easily, so confidently, to a stranger. And suddenly, without plan, words came out of her mouth.

"I waited for you here today. I remembered you said you pass here on Wednesdays."

"I thought you did," he said.

This was not making any sense. Why had she admitted such a thing? The man would think she was pursuing him. In the first place it was only half true.

"I meant," she said to correct herself, "I come here anyway. It's a favorite spot of mine. And then it crossed my mind that it would be such a funny coincidence if we were to meet here again."

He was looking at her lips, which today were coral, to match her summer dress. Then he looked up straight into her eyes. His own were smiling.

"Can we perhaps have dinner one evening?" he asked. "If that's an inappropriate question, please say so."

"Inappropriate?" she repeated.

"Yes, because you are engaged."

"I go out with friends. Kevin doesn't mind. What does a dinner mean?"

"Well then, I'll call you. But I want you to do something first. Look in the telephone book for my father's name and office address. Dr. Aaron Sachs. You will see where I come from and that I have a respectable past, at least."

"Don't you think I can see for myself that you're respectable?"

"No, I could be Jack the Ripper in a good suit. You should be more careful."

She laughed. "All right, Jack. I will be."

When he left her, she sat looking after him. At the turn in the path he looked back at her, did not wave, and went on.

The sun had gone in and the air was sultry. It was an effort to lift her feet as she walked home. And a heavy tiredness overcame her. At home on the answering machine there was a message from her father.

"Your mother's not feeling well. It's nothing acute, but we both think she'll be better off at home. We're driving back tomorrow."

The subliminal message was clear: her mother's time was approaching. It had been long in coming and was no longer a shock, but perhaps a mercy. And yet, when she passed her mother's photograph on the piano, she had to turn away.

The telephone rang, making an alien noise in the silent room. "Where've you been?" Kevin asked. "I've made three tries in the last hour."

"In the park, reading."

"Poor girl. I know it's an awfully lonely time for you."

"Well, I have the job, and I read a lot." There seemed to be nothing else to say.

"You sound so distant, Ellen. What is it?"

"Mom's troubles have come back. Dad's bringing her home tomorrow."

"Oh, Lord, I'm sorry. But you knew that it was coming. You'll be brave. I'll help you any way I can."

"I know you will, Kevin."

"Now I have a bit of good news for you. I'm coming home for Thanksgiving, and I'll be in the U.S. for two months, so we can be married and return to France together about the first of February."

"Yes, but if something happens to Mom?"

"We'll plan a quiet wedding whatever way things go. Just the family. Very simple. Actually, I like that better than a lot of fuss."

When they hung up, she began to cry. It wasn't only because of Mom. What was it? It was confusion. It was everything.

Mark and Ellen had dinner together. They went to a concert in the park, and then to another. One rainy night they saw a movie, took a taxi to her door, and talked very seriously all the way about the movie. He seemed to have lost his humor and wit.

Her father was cheerful when she came in. Everybody was cheerful in Mom's presence these days.

"How was the picture?"

"Interesting. Very well done, I thought."

"Did your friend like it? Your friend—what's her name again?"

"Fran. She was in my class."

"Kevin phoned," her mother said. "I think he was a little annoyed when I told him you had gone to the movies. He had told you to expect his call."

"Oh, I'm sorry! I must have misunderstood." But she had not misunderstood; she had forgotten.

After her father left the room, her mother asked a strange question. "Are you happy, Ellen?"

"I'm fine, Mom. Or almost fine. I'll be really perfect when I see you feeling better again."

Her mother smiled faintly and was silent.

She went to her room and got ready for bed. When she had removed her ring, she laid it on the night table and stood looking at it. Her heart seemed to be shaking in her chest.

One day her mother said, "Our dentist saw you at the concert with a young man."

"Really? Yes, I was there with one of the women at the shop and her boyfriend. The three of us."

By October it was almost too chilly to meet in the park. When Mark came uptown on a Sunday afternoon, he was prepared with a heavy sweater and heavy shoes for a walk in the woods. Ellen was dressed the same way. This was the first time they had seen each other wearing anything but office clothes.

"You look so different," she cried.

"And so do you. More real. No, that's not quite what I meant. More natural, maybe? Except for the ring."

She flexed her hand and stared at it, saying slowly, "It's very beautiful . . . but I'd just as soon not have it."

"Then why have it?"

"Things happen. Sometimes you don't know why they happen."

He was looking over her shoulder into the trees when he spoke. "Your parents like him."

"Very much."

"It isn't fair for you to be here." And when she failed to answer, he said angrily, "If I were engaged to marry a girl, I wouldn't want to know that she was meeting another man this Sunday afternoon in Central Park."

She only looked at him.

"Come here," he said, pulling her by the arm.

In the thicket that might have been miles away instead of a mere few yards from Fifth Avenue, they had their first kiss, a kiss that did not want to end.

"Oh, God," she said. "Oh, God." And cried.

They had to go somewhere, so the following week Mark took a room in a luxurious hotel, where, like any pair of tourists, they entered with their luggage.

"It's too expensive," Ellen protested. "You can't afford it."

"No, we deserve a beautiful place. You," he said, "you. I would die for you. Do you know that?"

They lay awake in each other's arms, not wanting to sleep, not wanting the night to end.

"God, I love you," he said.

There were tears in his eyes. Kevin had never been so moved, nor had she. This love and this lovemaking were entirely new. Different people, she thought, and I never had any idea how different it might be. How could I have known? This man is like me in every way. We are the same.

Each week they changed hotels, and Ellen made excuses for her nights away from home.

"This won't do," Mark said. "I should go to your house and tell the truth."

"You can't do that. I'm still engaged. Anyway, my mother's too sick to go through what she'd have to go through with Dad. And what of your people? Will your father tear his clothes when he hears this? I've heard that they do."

"No," Mark said grimly, "but he'll feel like doing it."

"We couldn't help it, could we? When you're growing up, you always ask how people can tell whether it's the real thing or not. And no one is ever able to give you a satisfying answer. 'Oh, you'll know,' is all they say. But it's true. You do know."

On the first of November the shops put pumpkins on

display, real ones, or chocolate, or paper. And Mark commented as they were walking that Thanksgiving was around the corner.

"Yes, I can't sleep for dreading it."

That evening her mother asked again, "Are you happy, Ellen?"

"You've asked me that before," she said gently.

"You wouldn't tell me if you weren't."

That's right, I wouldn't, Ellen thought. These are your last weeks, the doctors warned, perhaps your last days. I wonder whether you know it. If you do, you don't tell us either. We all want to spare one another.

When Susan died, Kevin flew home for the funeral. Afterward and for the next few days the house was besieged with visitors and telephone calls. Toward the end of that hard week Kevin decided that Ellen needed some respite and must come with him to his apartment for a few hours' peace.

She thought, as he turned the key in the lock, that this was going to be the worst hour of her life. Often as she had rehearsed this scene in every possible variation, she had still no clear idea of what she could possibly tell him that would not hurt him too much.

When he put his arms around her, she did not resist, but stood stiffly with her own arms at her sides. She had clearly intended to be very, very kind, yet it had suddenly become impossible for her to respond to the pressure of his body.

Drawing a step back and with a puzzled, anxious frown, he said, "I don't understand. Aren't you happy to see me?"

"Yes, but—but there's been so much," she stammered. "It's so hard for me to talk, I—"

"I know. Your mother," he said gently.

There was a choking lump in her throat. Her glance

went toward the window, toward black night and a scattering of lights.

"Not only that. I—oh, Kevin, I don't know how to say it. I feel like a thief, a betrayer, a liar. . . . This is nothing I ever dreamed would happen. But it did. It just did. I never wanted—"

He was staring at her. She saw him reach out and hold to the back of a chair. And for a few moments they both stood facing each other in disbelief.

"Who is he, Ellen?"

"It doesn't matter, does it?" she pleaded.

"I'm not going to kill him. Tell me."

"I met him one day this summer. He's a decent, good man, as you are. Neither one of us wanted to deceive or to hurt. We couldn't help it. That's the truth, the whole truth, I swear."

"And of course you have been sleeping with him while I was away, missing you."

She saw his hand grip the chair. White knuckles, that was the expression, and they really were white.

"I could call you names. I could say plenty of things, but I won't. You aren't worth the effort."

Now, so many years later, that scene was still alive, its colors, its sounds and silence, still fresh, that scene and the others that followed it.

Kevin went back to France with the ring in his pocket. Through mutual friends she learned that he had taken the break very hard, yet no harder than her father had done.

"Where's truth and honor, Ellen? My daughter, hiding away, lying, cheating on a good man. It's an incredible outrage."

"If you would only see Mark. It's not fair to condemn without seeing him," she said, not pleading, but with effort keeping her head high.

"I know enough without seeing him. You don't belong

with him. That's all. For your own good I've asked you to reconsider, and you won't. You are a fool, a willful little fool, and I have no more to say to you."

The same drama had been played out at Mark's house. So Ellen packed her belongings, left a loving note for her father, and married Mark at City Hall.

Eventually, they all had to meet. It was Gran who, more than half a year later, had engineered the meeting in the guise of a wedding reception. A few elderly relatives and some of Gran's neighbors had been the buffers on the great lawn, which was so great that certain people—the two fathers—needed to have no contact with each other.

"Contact at glaring distance," Mark said.

Despite the summer day, the roses and garden party punch, it had been really horrible. Only the elderly ladies, enthralled by the Romeo-and-Juliet occasion, had valiantly kept the conversational balloon from leaking all its air and shriveling onto the ground.

Brenda had been the first to soften, and for that Ellen would thank her forever. It was the birth of Lucy that finally had softened the two fathers enough to accept the marriage as long as they never had to see each other.

By this time, Ellen thought as she put the ironing board away and got ready for dinner, the hatred can only be called pathological. Well, so be it, she was thinking when Mark came in.

"I'm starved," he said after he had put his briefcase down, kissed first Ellen and then the children. "What's this here?"

"An invitation from Gran. She wants us to come up next week and stay overnight."

Mark read aloud, *"Don't mention this to your father, Ellen. I'm inviting Mark's parents too. Next time it will be your father's turn."*

"Are my parents going?" he asked.

"Yes, we're to ride up together."

"We really should see your gran more often. She's a sweet old soul. I always think she must have been like you when she was young."

"When Freddie is just a bit older, it will be easier and we'll do it."

"Remember that wedding reception? What an ordeal! I came home in a sweat because of those two men. Nine years ago! I'll tell you right now, I couldn't go through it again." And he laughed at the recollection.

CHAPTER

7

Annette had a habit that had taken root as long ago as her childhood. It was her custom, no matter what might have occurred during the day, to look ahead each night before falling asleep to something happy in the next day. More often than not the something was simple, such as a trip to browse in the local bookstore, or an afternoon with an old friend. It might even be something quite trivial, like having pancakes and sausage for breakfast on a winter morning. Small comforts, she often thought, do help to soften large griefs, no matter what anyone says. Not, she would mentally add, that I am any great authority on grief. I have had very few of them: my husband's death, and the deaths of poor Cynthia's twins.

This present sorrow could not possibly compare with those. Nevertheless, the breach between her sons had gone on far too long, and it hurt. Consider all those expressions fixed in the language, like *blood brothers,* and *brotherly love;* those two men were too old and too intelligent to cast such precious bonds away.

Then there were other things that offended her sense of rightness: the impending and, in her opinion, entirely unnecessary divorce between Cynthia and her nice young husband was one. The in-laws' feud that burdened Ellen's household was another. What on earth was happening to people who should know better? Why couldn't they just behave themselves like adults? Act your age! she wanted to say to them.

But that was not so easy. In a brief, inspired moment she had believed it might be, and so had written those tricky invitations. Now, tomorrow morning, her chickens would be coming home to roost. And she was scared to death.

She stood now in the library, talking to the portrait of Lewis. His keen brown eyes paid attention; on his left hand, resting upon an open book, the wedding band gleamed. For a moment she had an old, familiar impression that he was teasing her: *Oh, Annette, what a meddler and busybody you are.*

"No, I'm not," she replied aloud. "If you were still here, you yourself would give your sons what-for."

Two boys who played in the bathtub together. And she almost had to laugh at the memory of the day when, half grown and old enough to bathe themselves, they had let the water overflow.

Loud shrieks, as glee turned into rage, had brought both parents running. A small lake was forming on the floor while the boys wrestled in the tub.

"He got soap in my eyes!"

"He punched me!"

By the time the slippery, protesting pair had been lifted out and pacified, by the time the floor had been mopped and order restored, both Lewis and she had been almost as wet as the boys. And how had it ended? They had all gone out for ice cream, as sweetly and happily as you please.

If only today's troubles could be so easily tidied away!

Cynthia. All these tragic divorces, instead of putting some effort into marriage.

"It wasn't all champagne and roses for us, was it, Lewis? And then those kids Ellen and Mark. Were they supposed to fall in love to please their parents? We didn't. You didn't have a bean when we were married, and I know my parents weren't delighted about it, either, but they never said so."

When Annette's voice ceased, the room was too quiet. The dogs in their baskets slept deeply, without twitching in dreams of the hunt. The sleep of the old, she thought. They're old like me. I hope they won't outlive me, for who will take care of them? I wish I knew how long I have, so I could make plans. People do live into their nineties these days, though. Still, you can't count on it. It seems as if you can't count on anything, although I suppose it's age that makes me take that point of view. Age that makes me want to lecture to the young. And yet, I'm afraid of them. What kind of a mess are we going to have here tomorrow?

It was then, as she sat down in front of the telephone, that she knew she must ask for help. To do otherwise was nothing but foolhardy.

Marian Lester lived halfway between the Byrne house and the high school, where she taught. Only in her late forties and looking ten years younger, she was an unusual person to be a friend of Annette Byrne. But Annette had been active in community affairs, even on the board of education for many years after her grandchildren, let alone her children, were grown. And so they had had a long acquaintanceship. Then suddenly a friendship had begun.

One Saturday morning Annette had been surprised to see Marian in the group of kindergarten children who were having their nature walk through Byrnes' woods.

"Don't tell me you're tired of teaching teenagers," she said.

"No way. But I'm on the board of our local wildlife committee, and they ran short of helpers for this morning's outing. So here I am, filling in. It's rather fun for a change."

Marian looked wistful, Annette thought. She had been a widow for several years and lived alone, her children being adults and faraway. The little town was hardly overfull of desirable single men, and anyway schoolteachers had scant time to go out searching. Such a pretty woman too! It was a waste. . . .

On impulse Annette suggested dinner.

"That is, if you have nothing better to do one night this week," she said, with tact. "I know an old lady isn't the most exciting company."

Marian smiled. "That depends on who she is. And you don't have to specify midweek. I'm not often busy on weekends either."

"Then what about tonight?"

"I'd love it, thank you."

They had a very pleasant evening, the first of many. They were both bookworms, music lovers, and nature lovers. They were passionate about causes. Like all women who are mothers, they had their own stories to relate.

Annette had the advantage of means that had enabled her to travel the world, yet she seldom talked about the things she had seen.

"I always say that the worst bores are people with

travel tales about their hotel bargains and sick stomachs."

"You never bore me. I *want* to hear about the Ganges. Do you really see floating bodies? Did they serve fermented mare's milk in Mongolia? No, you never bore me."

There was an unusual serenity about Marian. At least, it seemed outwardly to be so. What was within, of course, one could not know. The thoughtful, listening expression and calm voice, even the smooth curve of the dark hair from the center parting to the ears, were all soothing to hear and look at. It seemed to Annette that Marian must never have had any of both Cynthia's and Ellen's busyness—inherited, most probably, from me, she would think with a grin.

So they admired each other, and exchanged the small favors that friends do. Marian knitted a handsome sweater for Annette, while Annette gave books and a matinee in the city. And they confided things, as friends do.

Therefore Marian knew all about the tangled quarrels in Annette's extended family. Therefore Annette was now at the telephone.

"I need your help, you see. I want to have things straightened out. It's ridiculous for these people to waste life like this." And then, as a doubt rose, she asked, "Tell me the truth. Am I wrong, Marian? Am I sticking my nose into other people's business?"

"Well, of course you are, but that doesn't mean you shouldn't do it. Some of the best things in the world happen because people stick their noses in."

"So you'll come? You can sit comfortably in the snuggery—that's my little office where I pay bills and read mail—you can read there. Then if you hear any loud argument, and I'm sure you will, come out and be a buffer."

"I'll be there early. It sounds interesting."

Hearing the smile in Marian's voice, Annette felt her dread recede. At least she would have an ally.

"Go to sleep, Annette, and think of something nice for tomorrow, the way you always do."

Promptly at ten o'clock Gene's tires crunched over the gravel drive. From his earliest years when he had first learned to tell time, he had always been either right on the dot or else five minutes early. His reliability had been a family byword ever since his childhood. Perhaps, Annette thought, this time will be different and I shall be able to reach that strong sense of what is required and right.

Coffee and his favorite cinnamon rolls were set on a tray in the sunroom, where he liked to sit on a wicker garden chair among flowering plants.

"You've had the chairs painted," he observed the minute he walked in.

"I thought white would be a nice change. Do you like it?"

"Very nice. You've never lost your touch with African violets, I see. It looks like summer in here."

"The light's good. That's all you need, no particular skill."

"You'd never think it was twenty-five degrees above outside."

"I got a feel of it when I let the dogs out."

"Old Roscoe keeps going, doesn't he?"

"Yes, he's in fine shape for his age. Look at him. He loves the sun."

Gene looked at the dog, who was bathing in a pool of heat beside Annette's chair. He looked at his mother, who was also in fine shape for her age, slender and beautifully groomed, from polished shoes and pale blue country woolens to wavy white hair. Then he looked at the tray with its two cups and two plates. So she was not expecting anyone to join them, he reasoned, and was relieved of his earlier vision of doctors or lawyers come to discuss alarming news.

"I've been rummaging around in the attic," she said. "It's amazing how things accumulate almost before you know it. And I found some surprises. You know, I thought we'd given your trains away years ago, but here they are, in perfect condition, each piece wrapped in tissue paper. Your father must have done it. There's a huge layout—do you remember?—bridges, tunnels, a river, villages, and trees. It will be a real treasure for Freddie in a couple of years."

"It certainly will be," Gene agreed, although where they would put the huge layout in that place where they were living was surely a puzzle.

He wondered about this conversation, too, and why he had been invited just today. Invited? Was not *summoned* perhaps a better word? For the letter, when he thought about it, was in a way rather strange. Again, why just today? And be prepared, if possible, to stay overnight? It would have seemed more natural if she had said, *I'd love to have a visit from you soon. How about next week or the week after?*

On the other hand, there was probably nothing to it at all except a normal desire, very normal at her age, to be with her son very soon.

"And how's Lucy? I haven't seen her since Labor Day weekend, and I miss her."

"She's an absolute joy. I took her to see the *Nutcracker* last week. The place was packed with children, but even so, I saw people looking at her and making comments. She had on a black velvet dress that Ellen said you gave her, and with that blond hair and all her chatter—"

Annette laughed. "You're nothing but a proud grandfather."

"I'll admit that. But she really does attract attention. She's the image of Ellen, don't you think? And Ellen looks a lot like you."

"Undeserved credit. Ellen looks just like her mother."

Susan. Sometimes he went for days in quiet acceptance of his loss, and sometimes the very mention of her name, a face, or a fraction of song were enough to send a thrust of pain through his chest.

And he could not help but say, "I miss her terribly."

"I know. It comes at moments, doesn't it? Like a jab in the heart."

Neither one of them spoke. She was gazing into the space above his head. She's remembering my father, Gene thought, and felt her sadness.

"Yes, yes," she said, "you look back and back. . . . It's like looking in a telescope, seeing things recede, the front lawn, the meadow, the hill, the mountain, and beyond that, each smaller and smaller the farther out you can see. As in one's life . . . things that happened long ago get smaller and smaller too."

He became alert. Annette was not given to philosophical platitudes. But since she was evidently not finished, he listened politely.

"There's another thing about time, another aspect. It's unfortunate, really quite sad, that more often the good things, when you're looking back through the years, seem to melt into a vague, rosy blur. It's the bad things that stand out like black stains. Have you noticed? I had a bad argument with my sister once, and even though we made it up, when she died, I remembered it. I didn't want to remember it, but there it was. And I was so thankful that we had made up."

So that was it, the old business again. He reached over to pour a second cup of coffee and was trying to think of an inoffensive way to keep his mother from continuing the painful subject, when Roscoe jumped up and barked. From the front hall sounded the spaniels' hysterical yapping. Then there were voices.

"Jenny, how are you?"

Oh, my God, that was Lewis!

"Jenny, you look wonderful. You never get old."

That was Daisy, dear sister-in-law with the phony English accent.

"I'll hang up your coats. Go on in. Your mother's in the sunroom."

That was Jenny, undoubtedly in on this business and bursting with curiosity.

There were three of them, including Cynthia, at the doorway looking in. Gene half rose from his chair and sank back. There was a total shocked silence; even Annette, who had risen all the way, seemed for an instant unable to move.

You've gone too far, he thought instantly. Now that you've done it, you don't know how to handle it. Poor Mother. And pity surged in his chest.

Of course it was clear now why she had been so definite about ten o'clock. She had wanted to make sure that the cars might not pass each other on the narrow country road and have a reason to turn back.

Annette collected herself admirably. As if this were any ordinary arrival, she greeted, kissed, offered chairs, and suggested fresh coffee. But still no one moved.

Lewis spoke first. "What is this, Mother? Is this your idea of a joke? It's a very bad one, if that's what it's meant to be."

"Not at all. Plainly and simply, I wanted to see my sons together." Her heart was trembling, but her voice was steady.

"With all respect," said Daisy, "this was a very bad idea. Lewis and I have come all the way from

Washington. We've been worried. Frankly, we thought you were ill."

"Does a person have to be ill to deserve a visit from you?"

"Of course not. But you have made a dreadful mistake."

"Let the men speak for themselves, please."

There they were, the brothers, not looking at each other, not saying anything, just standing there ready to flee. They were handsome men, much alike in their dignity, their dark hair slightly silvered at the temples, as if they were playing the role of distinguished citizens in an advertisement for an investment bank. Their heavy eyebrows, straight and thick, and their rather sensitive, expressive lips were like their father's. Handsome men, but still not as handsome as their father, Annette thought loyally. He would have a few thoughts for them if he were here. If they think I'm going to let them leave this room, they have another think coming. . . .

"A dreadful mistake," repeated Daisy. "I'm sorry to say so, Mother. It hurts me."

Annette was angry. Daisy was making her more angry, with her frosty courtesy. A long time ago she had spent a year at an English boarding school and had never gotten over it, in her kilts with the safety pins and her make-believe accent. You tried to like her and mostly you did like her well enough, but there had been times when you didn't, and this was one of them.

"And I'm sorry you feel that way, Daisy. But I am their mother, and I want peace between them."

Then Lewis spoke up again. "It's too late."

"Nothing's ever too late while you're still alive."

"Water over the dam, Mother."

"That's ridiculous." She was surprising herself by being able to talk straight and stand straight, while her heart was performing so madly.

"Ridiculous?" Gene repeated. "I don't know how you can say that." The last time he had seen Lewis, they were leaving the courthouse with their lawyers. They were not speaking then and would certainly not speak now. At any rate, he thought, not after what I've been through. "When people testify against each other in a courtroom, it is hardly a laughing matter."

"You're right, Gene. I withdraw the word. *Tragic* is the right one."

"Oh, please," said Cynthia, addressing nobody in particular.

She was pitiful. Gene wanted to catch his niece's eye to show, although she already must know it, that this feud with her father had nothing to do with her. But she was looking down; her face was shadowed, and terribly thin. Her fashionable suit—so unlike Ellen's conservative choices—seemed only to emphasize the change in her. He had seldom seen her since her unspeakable tragedy and then only on those few occasions when they happened to be visiting Ellen at the same time. He supposed that her visits to Ellen were rare because they were too painful. Freddie was almost as old as those twins were when—

"Come, Cynthia," Daisy commanded. "You don't need this on top of everything else."

When they left, Annette stood barring the door. "Now I ask you two to listen to me. You owe me that much. Please sit down."

"Out of love for you, I will sit," said Lewis. "I don't want to upset you any more than you already are, but—please, Mother, this is very painful, very unfair. Surely you can't have forgotten what I've been through! Between lawyers and newspaper reporters, I've had more than a fair share of misery. I've been pilloried. Must I go over it all again this morning?"

"You're missing the whole point," Annette replied

softly. "What I'm asking you both to do is to put all that away. It was a—a disease. Yes, a time of sickness and suffering. Would you want, if you had been sick in the hospital, to keep reliving those weeks for the rest of your life? Wouldn't you rather try to forget about them?"

"That's exactly what I've been doing. That's exactly why Daisy and I moved to Washington, where I'm working on something very worthwhile, I hope, for the general good. So I am already putting it all behind me."

"You can't have put it all behind you while you're still estranged from your brother."

"Oh, but I can! That's been my cure. Are you asking me to forgive and forget what he did to me?" Sharp, sarcastic lawyers had shamed him, portraying him as a culprit, a careless incompetent who had not bothered to investigate a serious complaint, indifferent to the possibility of the terrible consequences that had indeed occurred and would torment his dreams forever. Indifferent? Hardly. But Gene had not helped. "Am I supposed to forget the guilt he heaped on my head? It haunts me. I didn't deserve to be torn to shreds by lawyers and reporters."

"The newspapers came to me, too, after you sent them."

Lewis's voice rose hoarsely. "I sent them? That's idiotic."

From his chair, which was as far from Lewis's chair as was possible, Gene retorted, "It's very simple. You didn't like it when I told the truth about your refusal to check on Sprague after what Victor had reported. Very simple."

"You could have toned down your remarks instead of making me look like a deliberate criminal."

What could I have toned down? Gene thought. Victor had laid the facts out on the table, and I was under oath. I should have followed up on Sprague myself right at the beginning. But I always deferred to Lewis because he was the elder who'd been in the business three years before I was.

Fresh anger flared, and Gene cried out, "You expected me to lie for you, did you? Oh, it was only a little matter of truth—"

"And honor," Lewis finished for him. Honor, from the man who had put his own daughter through hell when she dropped the man he wanted for her and made another choice.

It was all so ugly. And so terrible, coming to a head here in their mother's house. They might as well be thrusting a knife into her.

"Those poor innocents who died," Gene said. "And all you think of is yourself, how you suffered—"

"You make me sick. You're like all these high-sounding talkers whose hearts bleed easy tears for the world, while at home, with your own daughter, you—"

Gene lurched forward in the chair. "Damn you! What has Ellen got to do with all this? You don't know what you're talking about. Leave her out of it, understand?"

Flinging out his arm in his agitation, he knocked the fruit bowl off the table. It shattered to slivers, while apples and tangerines rolled away on the floor.

"Oh, I'm sorry! Sorry!" he cried, stooping to pick up the mess. "I'll buy you another bowl. Watch the broken glass, you'll cut yourself."

It was not glass; it was crystal, Lalique, to be exact, and Annette's favorite, with its delicate birds perched around the rim. They had bought it on their twenty-fifth anniversary, when they had gone abroad on the S.S. *France*, and this was the memento of those lovely days.

"Never mind," she said. "We'll clean it up later. It's nothing. No, really," she repeated, for he, the meticulous, considerate Gene, was red with embarrassment.

"I need to get out of here. Let me get some newspapers and take it off the floor before somebody gets cut."

Then, "I'm sorry, Mother, but let me go home. I'll see you another time. Next week positively."

If she did not catch them both now, she never would. Of that, Annette was certain.

"No," she said harshly. "No. You are two grown men, and I can't believe that you want to behave like children. If your father were here—" She stopped, feeling the sting in the back of her nose that always preceded the gathering of tears.

"I'm glad for his sake that he isn't," Lewis said sadly.

"But I'm here! So for my sake, can't you—" she began.

"Mother, try to understand. We've lived through disaster. It broke us. You might as well try to put the pieces of that bowl together as to do what you want us to do. Mother, it can't be done, and the sooner you recognize it, the easier it will be for you."

She saw them again—so often did the same images recur—in the bathtub together, and dressed on Sundays in matching sailor suits, and wearing mortarboards at their college commencements. She saw them, too, as they must have looked on the terrible night when the hotel crumbled apart.

Why did it matter so much that these men in late middle age were at loggerheads? She did not have any good explanation for why it mattered so much to her. It simply did. Perhaps it was just that life was so short.

"Hate," Lewis said, "takes a lot of energy, and I need all my energy now to help my daughter. Nothing else can be as important to me except you, Mother. Certainly not my brother. Now if you'll excuse me, please, I'll go find my family."

"Good riddance," Gene said when the door closed. He had put the fruit on the tray and was picking up shards with a paper napkin. "That's about the only thing he said that I can agree with."

"Beautiful! A beautiful, worthy sentiment. God help me, could I ever have dreamed I'd live to hear it?"

"Mother." He held her shoulders and spoke softly. "I know what this must do to you. I never thought I'd live through anything like it either. But it can't be helped. It's too deep and has lasted too long. And you still have each of us whenever you want us, you know that. Only, not at the same time, that's all."

Annette searched Gene's decent, intelligent face and shook her head. "I'm ashamed of you," she said in her bitterness, "ashamed, do you hear? And you both ought to be ashamed of yourselves."

Then she wrenched herself free of his hands and went out.

In the meantime Daisy and Cynthia were in the library. Daisy was seething.

"I can't get over your grandmother. Of all people, so tactful, so Old World, really, to do a thing like this. God knows whether those two men will come to blows in there—I don't mean that—or maybe, who knows, maybe I do. They could. Anything can happen. In this world we have to be prepared for any crazy thing."

"Yes," said Cynthia, a trifle sharply, as one who should know very well about that.

She was at the window, staring out at gloom, wintry land, frozen pond, and lowering, dark sky. "It looks like snow or sleet or something."

"Oh, great. I'd like to get back to the city before it starts. I hate driving on ice. Stop twisting your necklace; you'll break it."

"If it wants to break, let it."

Daisy scolded herself: Here I talk about a necklace, when it's her heart that's broken. From having had everything, she has nothing. It's like being bombed, or burnt out, or beaten to death. Damn Andrew for giving her this last blow. Damn him to the ends of the earth. If only there were something we could do for her. We talk and talk, Lewis and I. We think and try to imagine a miracle, of walking in and finding her standing calmly again, in that quiet way of hers, with that touch of a smile at the corners of her mouth.

It had been a bad idea to bring her here today. This old town had too many memories, the church, the wedding, and the party in this house when they came back from the honeymoon, she coming down the stairs in her lavender dress . . . And then, the cemetery.

"This is a beautiful room," she observed. "When your father's finished in Washington and we're home again, I think I'll redo our den in these colors. Annette won't mind if I copy her, I'm sure."

"Mom, I'm all right." Cynthia spoke without turning from the window. "You don't have to work so hard to cheer me up."

"It's not hard work. It comes naturally, darling. And you do seem to need cheering up."

"I know I'm dull company. I shouldn't have come. I'm better off working. At least I'm helping people, and that helps me."

"Well, that's true." Daisy, hesitating over a question, decided to proceed with it and ask whether there was anything new happening, any word of Andrew.

"Wouldn't I tell you if there were?"

"I should think his parents would try to get in touch with you. After all—"

"I suppose they've given up. You and Dad haven't gotten in touch with Andrew either."

"I wouldn't care to be there when your father meets him."

"As far as I can see, he never will, so you needn't worry."

Sometimes, when she was unable to fall asleep and lay still counting her heartbeats, Cynthia's thoughts churned, inventing situations in which she would have to confront Andrew: on the street, in a bus where he would take the seat next to hers and try to argue her into letting him come back, or at the theater where he would be sitting directly behind her and she, feeling his eyes on the back of her head, would be waiting for some vengeful, humiliating move or words from him. And as she imagined that scene, her muscles would tense in dread.

Perhaps, inevitably, she would have to see him in the divorce court. She had no idea whether the parties did have to meet there. If they did, she would act as if he were invisible.

The pond was dark blue. Out in the center beyond the ice, two swans and their young were swimming, their young now, in December, having grown to be as large as the parents. This was the time of year when, like little birds being driven out of the nest and made to fly, the cygnets were to be sent forth into the world. And Cynthia, who had known about swans ever since her grandfather had raised the first pair, wondered how many generations this present family was removed from that first. She watched now as the big one, the father, rose into the air, flew low and returned to his huddled family, rose again, and repeated the flight. He was teaching them how to fly.

Swans were monogamous, faithful.

Then, as she turned her head to follow the great white wings, she saw a car come up the driveway. Now who? Who else was coming? Surely not Mark and Ellen?

"Oh, no! Mom, you won't believe this. Come look, it's Ellen with Mark and the children and, yes, they've got his father and mother with them too."

Daisy peered out. "Of all the senseless, confused, and

idiotic messes, this gets the first place. What can have possessed Annette? If I didn't know she wasn't, I'd say she must be senile."

"Do you realize that those two fathers despise each other? They haven't been in the same room for the last— it must be eight or nine years!"

There was a slight bustle in the hall, and then a short procession, with Jenny at the head, appeared around the corner and paused for a moment of astonished recognition.

Jenny was in a red-faced fluster. "You'll all be comfortable in here. There are plenty of chairs. Can I get you anything?"

"I think we have everything. Thank you, Jenny," Ellen replied.

Indeed, they seemed to be laden; they had a tote bag full of toys, a diaper bag, and an armful of sweaters. Mark held a partially consumed bottle in one hand, while with the other he juggled Freddie onto his knee.

Now Gene has two enemies, Daisy thought. This should be interesting.

"This is quite a surprise," Mark said brightly. "We were wondering whose car that might be."

"We rented it," Daisy said.

"Do you remember each other?" asked Ellen. "My aunt, Daisy Byrne, and Mark's parents, Aaron and Brenda Sachs. Dr. Sachs."

"How do you do?" said Daisy, who only remembered black whiskers.

Lucy had run to Brenda and was being hugged. "Grandma's little doll. Somebody loves Grandma and Grandma loves somebody."

"Where's Gran?" asked Lucy.

The question floated for a moment until Daisy replied, "She's in the sunroom with Gene and Lewis."

Ellen gasped. "What's happening? Is it working out?"

"I doubt it. Personally, when I left there, I was thankful that neither of them is armed."

"Oh, what can Gran have been thinking of?"

"Only Gran can answer that, I'm afraid."

"It's all so sad and so unnecessary," Cynthia said.

Ellen smiled at her. Regardless of their fathers they were fond of each other. But their paths had led them far apart. It must be agonizing for her to see me with my children, she thought. I understand why she doesn't visit.

"I think Freddie's wet," Mark said.

"What, again? Stick your hand in and feel."

"No, my mistake. I apologize, Freddie. Now get down and play with your blocks."

He's a sweet man, Cynthia thought. She watched the blocks tumble into a little pile on the floor. She hadn't seen Freddie in months, which was wrong of her. It made her sorry and ashamed to think that she, living in the same city, had been staying away. She could have come to the party when he turned one. Sending a good present was not the same. He was a cute little boy, still pudgy, like a baby.

"Do you live nearby?" asked Brenda, who, having caught Daisy's eye, felt it necessary to say something to her.

"No, we're in Washington now."

Brenda nodded. "I thought I remembered Ellen's mentioning that you had moved out of New York, but I didn't recall where to."

She was making conversation. It's like being at a funeral, waiting for the service to begin; you always feel that you have to make some remark to the stranger who's sitting next to you. What an odd thought to be having, Brenda said to herself, and looked toward Aaron for solidarity.

But Aaron had gone down on his knees beside Freddie

and the blocks. He was feeling signals in the room. They seemed to stream like electric currents speeding through the world, filling the air with messages from man to man. He sensed the vibrations in this room. Brenda was feeling out of place; his son was uneasy; that young woman—Cynthia, wasn't that her name?—was grieving; and her mother was suppressing a boiling anger.

Ah, stop it, he admonished himself. None of this concerns you.

Lucy asked Brenda, "Is Papa Gene here?"

Brenda's glance consulted Mark, who did not see the glance because he was, in like silent fashion, consulting Ellen.

"I don't know," replied Brenda.

Lucy slid down from her lap and went to Daisy. "You said he was here with Gran. Why doesn't he come to see me?"

"I don't know," Daisy said.

"I want to see him."

"Well, you can't right now."

Spoiled, thought Daisy. When a child's that pretty, it gets too much attention. And she really did have a doll's face. You couldn't help wondering how Laura would have looked at this age. You wonder too much, she told herself.

"You have to wait," Ellen said.

"But I want to see him," insisted Lucy.

"Not now, Lucy." And without thinking Ellen explained to Daisy, "She really loves my father so much."

"Apparently so," Daisy said. The child was appealing, but she was in no mood to cater to any child, however appealing. And what a stupid remark for Ellen to make, to her of all people.

Ellen was restless. When to the room at large she remarked, "I wonder whether they plan to stay in there all day," no one answered.

Aaron built a tower of blocks, which Freddie, with great glee, overturned. He kept building more until Freddie lost interest and began to forage in the bag of toys for something else, whereupon he got up, brushed off his trousers, and looked out of the window, observing that the sky was threatening.

"It's a good thing we're staying overnight," Mark said. "I wouldn't want to be on the roads with the kids if it should get as bad as it looks."

"Are you invited for overnight?" Ellen asked Cynthia.

"We—" Cynthia started to say, when Daisy interrupted.

"We were supposed to, but we are definitely not going to. As a matter of fact, I'm ready to start right now."

"Don't you like Gran's house?" asked Lucy, turning wide blue eyes up at Daisy. "Don't you like Gran?"

Daisy liked children, but at the moment this one was really a bit much. Her parents, considering the situation, should make her keep quiet. They should see that we are all nerves here.

Lucy was still surveying Daisy from top to toe. Apparently, she was fascinated by Daisy. "You have flowers on your shirt," she observed.

"I do."

"They're pretty."

"Thank you."

"Why does that man hate Papa Gene?"

This child was too smart. And why, Daisy wondered, must she fasten on me?

"I don't know. I don't know anything about it," she countered, giving Lucy the smile that often, but not always, can placate a persistent child.

"You do know. You said the man in the sunroom."

The adults looked from one to another. *Did you ever? You have to watch everything you say in front of them.*

"Grandpa," asked Lucy, losing interest in Daisy, "you don't hate Papa Gene, do you?"

Suddenly, Aaron had a coughing fit. And Mark said hastily, "Come, Lucy. Come over and take a toy out of your bag and play."

"They're all baby toys, Daddy. I don't like any of them."

"You're being awfully stubborn," he said impatiently.

Brenda corrected her son. "Mark, anybody can see she's bored. She's only six. What do you expect?"

She would, Daisy thought. A social worker, I heard. Overindulgent. Crammed with pop-Freudian psychology. Just tell the child to be quiet. My head is splitting.

The message came clearly to Aaron: She doesn't approve of Brenda. Country-club Republican. Captain of girls' hockey in school. Champion golfer. Champion hang-glider, for all I know. God, I'd like to get out of this place. Can't breathe in this atmosphere.

"What on earth is going on in there?" Daisy cried.

"They'll have to be out soon," Ellen soothed. "I'm sure everything will be all right."

You think so, Cynthia thought not unkindly, because everything turned out all right for you.

"That Gene," Daisy began to protest. "There's never any telling what that man—" and stopped.

"You're forgetting yourself, Mom," Cynthia told her. "He's Ellen's father."

"I'm sorry, Ellen," Daisy said at once. "I did forget myself."

"You see, we're not the only ones who think he's a bastard," Aaron whispered to Brenda, who whispered back, "Stay out of this, Aaron."

Cynthia clasped and unclasped her hands. Unbearable hostility surrounded her. Even her grandfather, looking out of his gold frame, seemed suddenly to be cold and angry, which was, she knew, absurd, for he had been a kindly man who worked in his fancy little garden and gave her his prize strawberries, warm from the sun, for breakfast.

She had to get out of this room. "I'm going for a little walk," she said.

Daisy cried, "No, Cindy, no! The minute your father comes out, we're leaving. I don't want to have to go looking for you."

"I'll only go as far as the pond. You can see me from this window. Excuse me, everyone, please."

On their broad black feet two swans slid over the ice as if they were on skates. The remains of cut-up bread lay on the grass at the pond's edge. Gran fed them all winter when, because the pond was frozen, they were unable to reach underwater to feed themselves. Cynthia watched them until they reached a circle of water where those few of their young who had not yet been sent away to fend for themselves were floating. The tranquillity of these creatures and the peace of the wintry silence relieved her tension. A strong wind blew, but there was no rustle of leafage. There were no birdcalls. And she stood still, hearing the silence.

Sometimes she thought of going away to a place where she knew no one and no one knew her. She imagined a cold place, in Alaska perhaps, near a glacial lake where eagles nested in the trees. She thought of a warm place on an untouristed island, where the surf rolled and broke on a quiet beach. Like a primitive person you would just live there, simply live out each day; and all the days would roll on with little memory of the past or need to care about what was to happen in the future.

Naturally she knew, even as she was having these es-
capist daydreams, that they were foolish. She knew as
well as anyone could that the best, maybe the only, way
to be rid of such malaise is to work and be involved with
other people. But she had been doing just that, she had
not been thinking only of herself or feeling sorry for herself; self-pity was disgusting.

Yet she had not been healed. . . .

The wind was rising. It was terribly cold, so that she
drew her coat tightly about her. It was a fine, warm coat
of gray cashmere, so enormously expensive that she had
hesitated to buy it. But when you worked in the fashion
world, you could not avoid some extravagances; they
were part of the job. All of that was long ago in another
life, to which she never wanted to return.

And she started back toward the house, thinking that
something must have been resolved in there by now,
most probably for the worst. She felt so sorry for Gran,
naive, hopeful Gran, who was trying so hard to arrange
everything for the best.

Another car, a black Jaguar, had been added to the
three in the driveway. At the sight of it she stopped short.
It could not possibly be Andrew's car. . . . But of course, it
was. She went weak with outrage. Impulsively, she went
toward the kitchen door with the intention of hiding, but
that made no sense because they would be looking all
over for her in order to start home. And straightening her
shoulders, she marched boldly through the front door
into the hall.

Andrew was standing there with Jenny. Evidently he
had just arrived because he was still wearing his fleece
jacket. She had a flash of recall: a windy Saturday, a
search for a double stroller, and after they had bought it,
the purchase of the red fleece jacket. Now she had a
quick flash of his startled face, flushed by the wind, with
dark circles under his eyes.

Furiously, she demanded, "What do you think you are doing here?"

"I don't know. I was invited to come. Your grandmother telephoned. I had no idea what she wanted. She didn't say."

"Fine story. You didn't know I'd be here?"

"No, I didn't." He gave her a tentative smile. He was being conciliatory, as if he were not sure what she was going to do. And she could have struck the smile off his face.

"I don't believe you," she said. "You and my grandmother, who seems to have lost her mind, cooked this up between you."

"I can't help it if you don't believe it, but it's the truth. I'm staying for the weekend at Jack Owens's house, and your grandmother happened to meet Mary Owens in the village. That's how she knew I was with them, and she phoned me."

"Well, now that you've come, you should turn right around and go."

"I can't very well do that until I've seen your grandmother, can I, now, Cindy?"

"I am not Cindy to you, I am Cynthia. Or better still, I am nobody at all."

"Cynthia—can't we please talk quietly and sensibly?"

"No. No. Was there anything 'sensible' in what you did that night? I was down, as I thought you were, too, all the way down in a dark hole after we lost our children—and I was just beginning to climb up and see a trace of light, just beginning—"

"You were? But you never told me. I never saw—"

"I never got the chance that night when you thrust me back down with my face in the mud. In mud! You did that to me. And you—now you come using words like *sensible*."

"Cynthia!" Daisy's voice rang from the guest closet at

the back of the hall. "We're just getting our coats—why, what on earth are you doing here?" she cried, seeing Andrew.

Lewis strode down the hall, his voice booming. "What the devil are you doing here? Haven't you done enough to my daughter without following her?"

Now Annette came running with her glasses sliding down her nose. "Stop, Lewis! He's not doing anything to Cynthia. I invited him."

"You what? Now I've heard everything. You have done more harmful mischief this morning, Mother. I'm speechless."

Suddenly the hall, which was long and almost as wide as an average room, was as crowded as a highway at rush hour; there could not have been more than a dozen people in it, but they all, even Ellen with Freddie in her arms, came jostling out of various doors toward the little group at the front, toward the loud anger.

"Oh, Gran," cried Cynthia, "oh, Gran, what have you done to me? Why did you do this? You knew all about—"

"Yes, I knew. That's why I did it."

Mortified by this public display of her most private emotions, Cynthia began to cry.

Daisy put her arms about her daughter. "This whole morning has been a circus. Disgusting. We're leaving. This is it. Your presence, Andrew," she said icily, "is the last straw." And she turned toward Annette. "We have to take Cynthia home. Right now. And, Andrew, you stay away from her. You came here snooping, for what I don't know, but stay away from her. I mean it."

"That's between Cynthia and me, Mom."

"What right have you to call her 'Mom'?" demanded Lewis. "You forfeited that right when you behaved like an animal that night—"

"Please, please," Annette pleaded. "All right, I made a

bad mistake. I meant well." Her eyes filled, and she took a white lace handkerchief out of her cuff to wipe them.

"I'll go," Andrew said. "This is too much for you. For everybody."

But Annette seized his lapel. "No, I asked you to come, and I don't want you to go like this. You haven't done anything wrong. No."

Aaron was feeling pity. It was a shame to see an old person attacked. He saw that sometimes in his practice, and he was never able to keep his mouth shut.

" 'Be not hasty in thy spirit to be angry,' " he said now, loud enough for everyone to hear.

Lewis snapped. "Most of us are well acquainted with the Bible, thank you very much."

"This is a crazy house." This time Aaron whispered. "I told you, Brenda, I didn't want to come here."

Brenda sighed ruefully. "Ah people, people. It's tragic, that's all it is."

"Disgraceful. Yelling like savages."

"Don't you think you ever did some ranting and yelling?"

"Well, maybe, but not like this."

"Honey, you were so loud when Mark ran off and married Ellen that I was afraid the neighbors would hear. The people across the hall, if you want to know, did hear."

Annette wiped her flowing eyes. As tall and erect as she was, she seemed suddenly very small.

"Papa Gene," Lucy cried, for Gene had come out of another door under the stairs. "Gran is crying."

"Good God, Brenda, here's my best friend," Aaron muttered as he and Gene caught sight of each other.

"Do hush," said Brenda. "We're stuck here till tomorrow."

"Why can't we leave now?"

"Drive all that way back with Freddie? The trip up was too long as it is. And besides, they're predicting a storm."

Gene called over somebody's head, "Did you know about this assemblage, Mark?"

"Only that we were invited. We and my parents."

"Interesting," Gene muttered. "Very interesting."And then, turning to Annette, he put his arm around her. "Don't cry, Mother. Everybody knows you meant well. It just hasn't worked, but that's no fault of yours. I think it's best now that we all go home and let your house be peaceful again. Go take a rest and don't make yourself sick over a failed experiment. It's not worth it. I told you, I'm coming next week to spend the day with you. I promise."

You don't have to keep your promise as far as I'm concerned, she thought, but did not say, being at the stage in which a sorrowful, defeated person throws up his hands and cries: *I don't care. Now let everything go to smash. It doesn't matter tome anymore.* She had tried tough love with her sons, but it had not worked. She had hoped that within Andrew and Cynthia, as they saw each other, a bit of their original fire would spark again. Nothing had worked, they were all going away, and let that be the end of it.

At that moment Marian came almost flying out of the dining room.

"What's this?" she cried. "People are leaving? Why, lunch is already on the table."

In spite of her tears Annette recovered her dignity as a hostess. In a most gracious tone she said, "Some of you know my dear friend Marian Lester."

"I do! I do! You gave me that doll with the straw hat on. I was going to bring it, but Mama said it was too big to fit in the bag and wouldn't let me." Lucy chattered on.

"I'm getting a boy doll just as big for my birthday. Papa Gene's giving it to me, aren't you, Papa Gene? Why are you putting your coat on? Aren't you going to stay for lunch? Grandpa and Grandma are staying. We're going to be here until tomorrow morning. Aren't you?"

"Well," Gene began, thinking, What a fine pickle, damn it, when Marian mounted the first step and clapped her hands.

"You people can't walk out like this. You simply can't do this to Annette," she said like the schoolteacher she was. "Jenny has made a beautiful lunch, to which you were all invited. You all accepted the invitation, so do, please, put your coats away."

Well, well, thought Daisy, and just who does she think she is, to order us around as if we were in her kindergarten?

Gene chuckled to himself. Hasn't she got nerve, though? I seem to remember she's a teacher. Claps her hands like one. But pretty. That tilted, pert little nose . . .

"Mrs. Lester," said Lewis, "I do understand, but my daughter isn't feeling well, and we really need to get her home."

Marian was not to be deterred. "It's after twelve, and you've a long ride back to the city. You'd certainly need to stop off on the way for something to eat. So you'd do a lot better to have a nice lunch now before you leave."

"Yes, do," urged Ellen, who was hoping that maybe Cynthia and Andrew would make some move, although it certainly didn't look now as though they ever could.

"You can't do this to Annette, or to Jenny, either, after all her work." Marian spoke sternly. "You simply can't. If some of you can't stand one another—you see, I know all about many things—you can go separately into the dining room. It's a buffet lunch. Take what you want and go wherever you want to eat it. Some of you are talking to each other and you can get together. There are enough rooms in this house so you can all spread out."

"I guess we'll have to stay, Mother," said Cynthia, who was pained by the sight of Gran's woebegone face.

"I don't see how you can forgive her for this trick," replied Daisy, tossing her head in Andrew's direction.

"I don't forgive her, exactly, but I feel terribly sorry for her."

"Then you're more tolerant than I am. If she were not so old, I would give her a piece of my mind. Does she think it amusing to do this sort of thing?"

Lewis upbraided his wife. "Don't be absurd. You know her better than that. Now, come on," he said irritably, and, propelling his wife and daughter ahead of him, marched them into the dining room.

A few minutes later he marched them out again. Holding their plates, the three retired to eat by themselves in Annette's snuggery.

In the dining room the long table was set with bowls and platters bearing sliced cold meats, a hot chicken pie, a huge, crisp vegetable salad, warm breads of three different kinds, molasses cookies, peach cake, and a mélange of fresh fruit. The bowls and platters were old porcelain, Annette's best. At the heart of their arrangement was an overflowing cluster of cream-colored roses.

"Done herself proud, as they say," remarked Andrew to himself. There had been some slight confusion in the hall as to who would go to the table after the first three and how some of them would avoid each other. Shaken by seeing his wife again—Andrew still thought of Cynthia as "my wife," not only because under the law she still was, but also because he still felt attached to her—Andrew stood at the foot of the stairs with his plate, uncertain of where he was expected to go. He was pulled about by ill-assorted emotions, sadness, a certain amount of anger, and a miserable embarrassment over feeling superfluous. If he could decently have fled from the house, he would have done so.

Just then Gene had given him a warm greeting. "Andrew! Haven't seen you for too long," he cried, thinking at the same time that it was a pity that Lewis wasn't near enough to see the warmth of the greeting. "Come join us. Ellen and Mark are going to eat in the sunroom. Stone floor, you see, so in case Lucy spills, as she usually does, it won't do any damage. Come on, let's hurry."

Even in his present frame of mind Andrew had been able to feel amusement at the "hurry," which clearly meant, "Hurry before Mark's parents get there first and shut me out."

Those parents of Mark's were the last to go to the table.

"Heaven only knows what they'll have to eat," Aaron grumbled. "Shrimp salad, most likely."

"Well, you're fat enough to go without one lunch if you have to," Brenda told him. At this point she had begun to feel the prevailing nasty mood.

But to Aaron's great relief, since he had had a very early breakfast, he found plenty of salad and fruit that he could eat.

These they took to the library, which, because they had already spent time there, seemed a little familiar. Nevertheless, they were feeling rather forlorn, when Mark came in with Lucy. He sat down and took a mouthful of food before he looked up over the plate and smiled at them. The smile, as both of them knew very well, was his way of telling them that he understood their discomfort. They were thinking how different it would be if he had married Jennifer Cohen. Well, it would be different for Ellen, too, if she had married that other guy. She would probably be living in Paris, on the Place de Something-or-Other.

After a minute he said, "We're all feeling dreary. It's a very strange situation, to say the least."

"There seems to be more than one strange situation," Aaron responded.

"Weird," Brenda said. "That young couple. You would think that after their tragedy, they would cling to each other."

Aaron objected. "It's not that simple. You're a social worker, and you don't know about complex relationships?"

"Well, of course I do. Something else must have happened afterward. Of course."

"It did, but not now." And Mark looked significantly toward Lucy.

Brenda shuddered. "It feels as if somebody has just died in this house."

"Don't worry," Mark said. "They'll all be rushing home in a few minutes. They want to beat the weather."

The room was growing noticeably darker, and he got up to turn on the lights. Outside, the sky was iron-gray, hard and somber. Conversation seemed to wilt as the little group, with their plates on their laps, contemplated that sky. Even Lucy, thoughtfully chewing molasses cookies, was drawn into the silence.

They all looked up when Annette came in. She was traveling from one room to the other, trying to act as though it were perfectly natural for people to be thus dispersed. Having powdered her nose and removed all signs of tears, she had resolved to see things through with dignity to the end. Admittedly, she had been saved by Marian, who now, in the dining room, was presiding over the tea- and coffeepots.

"How are you all doing?" she asked cheerfully. "Is everyone having enough to eat?"

Lucy jumped up. "I'm not. I need some cake."

"Well, of course you do. Come on with me, and I'll get some for you."

"Grandpa, you come too. We'll get some for Papa Gene. He likes cake."

For a moment no one answered, and then Mark said quickly, "Grandpa's still eating. You and Gran go do it."

Now Lucy directed her frown toward Aaron. "You never want to go see Papa Gene. You never do."

At that Annette took her hand. "Come on," she said firmly. "The cake will be all gone if we don't hurry."

"We forget what children observe," Brenda remarked when they left. "Without actually understanding, they can detect so much that we think we're hiding. It's even said that infants can sense moods from indifferent handling or angry voices. . . ." Her own voice dwindled away. Neither her husband nor her son refuted her.

Not at our house, Mark was thinking. Our children are safe from all that. His plump baby boy and his spirited, small Lucy were safe.

"Let him go, dear," Ellen said, for Lucy, kissing Freddie, was smearing the remains of a chocolate bon-bon on his cheek.

It was really remarkable, considering all you heard and read about sibling jealousy, that Lucy had accepted Freddie's arrival so well. Spunky and rough as she could be when playing with her friends, with him she was gentle and affectionate. Perhaps, Ellen thought, it is because she sees and receives so much affection at home.

"I'm bored," Lucy said.

Gene chuckled. "Now, where did she ever get that?"

"I can't imagine. She certainly hasn't heard it from me. I never have time enough to get bored."

"What's this?" Annette, still on her room-to-room tour, had just come in. "Bored? Well, naturally she is.

Now that she's had lunch, there's nothing for her to do. Why don't you take her to see the swans, Ellen?"

"It's freezing outside," said Gene, protective as usual.

"Nonsense. As long as she's warmly dressed, a little fresh, cold air will be good for her. It'll be good for Freddie too."

Ellen, agreeing and glad to get out of the house, went for the clothes. She had been feeling too uneasy for comfort, uneasy and even apprehensive, as if something were going to *happen*. It was not usual for her to exaggerate worries, but today was exceptional. As long as so many enemies were under one roof, there could be an explosion.

Here sat Andrew, watching Freddie with a wistful smile on his serious face, and God only knew what anguish within; Andrew, the cause of Cynthia's disillusionment and the object of her parents' wrath.

An overheard remark might ignite either Lewis or Ellen's own father, who in turn might do or say something that would inflame Lewis or Aaron; or Aaron might in some way offend her father.

There was no end to it. With all that pain and anger, even people who thought themselves civilized were capable of doing crazy things. . . .

Outdoors she took a long breath of cold air. The brown, frozen grass crackled under her feet as, walking carefully, she carried Freddie downhill toward the pond. Lucy, as usual, ran far ahead.

Even in December it was beautiful here. When trees were bare, one saw the true grace of their branches, upraised like arms. Crows, surely not pretty birds, had their own grace, too, as they rose from their perches and sped down the sky. In the woods that framed Gran's property there was, to an eye aware of colors, among the pines and spruce, the hemlock and firs, an abundance of greens: olive and grass and moss; there was even the dusty blue of a single Colorado spruce, an exotic loner among all those native greens. It could not have grown there by natural accident; her grandfather must have planted it. I should paint that sometime, she thought, exactly as it is, or maybe, better still, in the flicker of summer sun and shade.

All those people cooped up in the house right now could be taking a hike through the woods on the trail that Gran kept cleared for the Scouts. But no, they were nursing their grievances instead, some of them so old that they would never be uprooted. It would be easier to uproot that spruce with a toy shovel.

Near the edge of the pond there was a rock, remembered from Ellen's childhood, with a flat ledge on which one could sit. From there you could see the whole pond as far as the juncture with the larger lake.

"Sit down for a minute with me," she said to Lucy, "and look around. Tell me what you see."

After making a full circle turn Lucy said, "You told me the leaves all fall off when it's cold, but that tree has leaves."

"It's called a pin oak, and it's the only one that loses its leaves in the spring, when all the other trees are getting new ones."

"Why?"

"I really don't know. I'll find out, though, and then I'll tell you."

And she would have to find out, because Lucy would be sure to remember and ask her. She was an intense little girl, eager and curious. They had not needed the school psychologist to tell them how very bright she was. Ellen smiled to herself, thinking that it required a deal of energy to keep up with this first-grader. Freddie, on the other hand, was quite different; a much more placid baby than Lucy had ever been, he was sitting comfortably on her lap with the pacifier in his mouth.

"It's too cold," Lucy said.

"You're right. It's growing colder. Let's walk around the edge, nearer to the swans, and then hurry back to the house."

It was so quiet and calm here alone with her children! She was reluctant to leave it. But a fine sleet was now starting to fall, stinging one's face.

"Come on, let's run. See? The swans made a long path, breaking the ice, so they can swim. They do it pushing with their chests. It's hard work."

Three floated, their orange beaks proud and high, their ruffle-edged white wings like ballet skirts.

"Those must be the father and mother with one of their grown children who hasn't flown away yet," Ellen explained. "Aren't they beautiful?"

"I want to pet one."

"Oh, you can't. They're swimming."

"But if they walk over here on the ice?"

"You mustn't. They don't like it. Swans can be fierce. Even the dogs are afraid of them."

"Do they bark at the dogs?"

"No, these are mute swans. That means they don't make much noise, just grunts sometimes. When they're babies, they peep a little, that's all."

"Where do the babies live?"

"In a nest, the same as little birds do. You remember the nest they showed you at school."

"A swan's nest has to be much bigger," Lucy observed.

"Much bigger. About as big as our sofa at home."

"Where is it?"

"Way over on the other side. I don't think it's even there anymore in the winter."

"Let's look for it."

"Not now. Hey, the sleet's really coming down. Let's run."

"I want to see the nest."

"No, Lucy. I said no."

"But I'll be right back, I promise."

"No, Lucy!"

"Right back, Mommy!" And she was gone, racing over the ice toward the swans.

"Come back! Back, Lucy!" screamed Ellen.

In horror, screaming, tearing her throat, she stood there as Lucy ran; the swans, with a great splash and spread of wings, rose into the air when Lucy plunged and disappeared. Black water closed over her. . . . For an instant Ellen looked wildly about. Then, setting the heavy baby down on the grass, she ran onto the ice, slipped, fell, got up, and slid into the water.

In the library Mark and his parents were still a group apart. He was on the window seat looking out toward the pond, musing to himself.

"What a queer situation I'm in today. I've always liked Cynthia, and I like Andy too. We used to play tennis sometimes, singles on Sunday mornings. But I can't very well go talk to either of them without hurting the other."

Brenda sighed. "Poor souls. To lose a child—that's the worst of all."

Half hearing, Aaron shuddered. "Two of them."

He had been absorbed in his own thoughts, feeling the atmosphere of this house, this room with its portraits and books. He was thinking about the people who had lived here, old-line Americans, at home for generations in the same neighborhood among trees that were centuries old. It must be a good feeling, he thought without envy, merely ruminating. In a locked glass-fronted bookcase apart from the rest of the books in the room, he read titles: Dickens, Balzac, Thackeray. . . . How is it that a man brought up with all these good things can be as hateful as Gene Byrne?

Then at once came the retort: And what made you so

hateful toward him, Aaron? You were never brought up to hate.

"Look," he said, beckoning to his son. "These must be first editions, don't you think? What a treasure! All these great minds—"

It was exactly then, in the middle of a sentence, that he heard his son's dreadful cry.

"What— What?"

"In the pond. Oh, God, they've fallen in!"

Brenda screamed and ran to the window. "Where? Where? I don't see—"

But Mark and Aaron were already fleeing through the hall and out, down the steps to the lawn.

In the hall, doors were opening. From the kitchen, the snuggery, the sunroom, and from everywhere, people were staring.

"What is it? What happened?"

"What on earth?" Gene cried. Brenda's screams had annoyed him. "What's all this racket?"

"Ellen!" Brenda screamed back at him. "Ellen— they've fallen into the pond!"

Then everyone ran. Without coats they ran out into the falling sleet, stumbling and sliding down the hill behind Mark and Aaron.

The channel of water was narrow, not much wider than the swan who had forced it open. One edge was jagged, where the ice had broken under Ellen's weight as she plunged in. Now Mark plunged into grasp Ellen as, in her thick down jacket and heavy shoes, she struggled.

"Lucy! Lucy!" she implored.

"Rope! Rope!" Lewis cried helplessly.

Under his weight a piece of ice had cracked, and he jumped backward. On either side of the channel the ice was crumbling.

Andrew came running with rope. "In my trunk." He

gasped. "Can you reach—" And he held the rope out to Mark.

"No! No! It's Lucy." He was weeping. "She wouldn't—"

At once Andrew grasped his meaning. *She wouldn't know enough to catch or hold on to the rope.* The pond was fifteen or twenty feet deep. The child was at the bottom. What if the rope were not long enough anyway?

The four men, for Gene had come up behind the others, stood for a second as if mesmerized by despair until Andrew, prepared to jump in, took off his shoes and was then abruptly pushed aside.

"Let me. Tie the rope around my waist," Daisy commanded. She dropped her shoes and her skirt. "Pray God it's long enough. Tie it as low as you can. Give me three minutes. If I haven't jerked the rope, pull me up."

Ellen had collapsed onto Mark's shoulder. Aaron and Gene were trying to pull them both up onto the ice, but without a rope it was almost impossible. Meanwhile, Andrew was holding with both hands on to the rope, which had by now grown taut. The rope was either too short, or else Daisy had reached the bottom and perhaps—only perhaps—found Lucy.

There was no sound except for the steady tinkling of sleet upon the ice. The horrified little group of watchers on the rapidly whitening grass stood speechless and unmoving in the arctic cold. Like people watching a disabled plane attempt a landing while emergency equipment was prepared for disaster, their eyes were large and their lips hung open. Even the dogs stood still, as if they knew that something out of the ordinary was happening.

After who knew how long, Andrew felt a tug on the rope. "She's pulling!" he shouted. And when Lewis sprang to help him, protested, "No, let me. I'm younger than you, and you've got a bad back."

Instantly, Gene sprang to help, leaving Mark with one

arm around Ellen and the other forearm resting in a vain attempt to lift himself onto the slippery ice. Together, gradually, Andrew and the two brothers pulled, fought for footing, slipped, fell, got up and pulled some more, until at last Daisy's head appeared above the water. She was blue in the face. Her hair streamed and she had no breath left, but she was holding Lucy to her chest.

From the huddled group of women on the grass came a cry. All, even Jenny, came running. Gene seized Lucy, while Daisy, her chest heaving, sank down on the ice.

"Get back, all of you," warned Andrew. "It's not solid so near the edge. Get back."

The little girl lay lifeless, her long hair dripping and her legs dangling in Gene's arms. "Oh, God," he groaned, "she isn't breathing."

Aaron snatched her away from Gene. "Give her to me." And he began to run toward the grass.

"If someone, for Christ's sake," Mark yelled, "will take Ellen, please? I can't hold on much longer."

Andrew and Lewis, who had been tending Daisy, ran with the rope, tied it tightly around the two of them and pulled. Mark, faint from exhaustion and cold, stumbled onto the ice. Ellen was unconscious.

"My God," Andrew murmured, "the water's got to be thirty-two degrees."

All was helter-skelter. Then Aaron, tense and brusque, laid Lucy on the grass and took command.

"Lay Ellen down. Somebody get Daisy back to the house. Quick! She needs warm, dry clothes, blankets, and hot drinks. Right now!" The words came out like bullets. "You—what's your name—Andrew, can you do mouth-to-mouth resuscitation?"

"No, but if you show me, I can—"

Lewis broke in. "I've done it. Where shall I—"

"Then let Andrew take your wife to the house. You, Lewis, do Ellen. I'll take the baby. Hurry, hurry, hurry!"

Neither mother nor child, lying side by side, was breathing. "Do what I do. Look. Move the head back and forth as far as you can. Watch me. Back and forth. Back and forth. Open the airway. Pinch the nose. No, like this. Pinch. Now fit your mouth on hers, tight fit, blow. Get the air flow. . . ."

Sleet poured over Aaron, who knelt there trying to pour life into his little grandchild, and over Lewis, who was doing the same for his brother's child.

Gene and the women stood waiting, trembling in their light clothing. No one stirred. Annette wept silently. Mark was supine on the grass. Cynthia, clutching the baby, watched her father. In awe Brenda watched her husband; she was confident; if it could be done, Aaron would do it.

Time passed; whether it measured two minutes or twenty, no one there would ever be able to estimate. They would say only that it was an eternity.

Suddenly, Lucy struggled and coughed. A stream of water flew out of her lungs; she began to cry, and vomited. Mark forced himself to his tottering legs and took her, wet, sobbing, and shaking, into his arms.

A few minutes later Ellen brought up a stream of water. In confusion she tried to rise, and then, as she opened her eyes and reality flowed back, she became hysterical.

"Lucy! Where's Lucy? Where's Freddie? Oh, for God's sake, what happened to Freddie, I left him—"

"Freddie's fine. Cynthia has him. And Lucy's right here. Look. She's all right too. Take it easy, Ellen. Take it easy," Lewis whispered. "There she is with Mark. And here's your father."

"We need a car, we need help," Aaron said. "They can't walk back."

But Marian, practical Marian, had thought of that and was already partway up the hill toward the parked cars.

A few moments later her four-wheel drive came bumping over the grass, and Ellen, with Lucy clinging to her, was lifted in.

"The rest of us had better hotfoot it to the house," Aaron said. "We've been out here for a good twenty minutes or more, and hypothermia is no joke."

Soaked and shivering, with frozen fingers and feet, all those who could not fit into the Jeep ran toward the house.

An hour later everyone was gathered in the library, where Jenny, while the survivors were being cared for upstairs, had built a grand log fire. Close to its heat and crackle a big chair held Ellen with Lucy on her lap, both of them drowsing under a thick red blanket. On the other side of the fireplace, in a pair of similar chairs and also covered with blankets, sat Mark and Daisy, with Freddie and a pile of blocks on the floor between them. On a table within easy reach was a large tray with a varied assortment of hot drinks, ranging from brandy to coffee to cocoa for Lucy. Annette, remembering that sugar was the quick remedy for exhaustion, had added a plate of sugar cookies.

"What else can a person like me, at my age, do but give food?" she asked Marian. "I should be doing something more, but I don't know what. I'm still trembling, and I feel useless."

"Useless? You're the last person to say that about herself."

"My loyal friend is speaking."

"No, it's the truth."

"I couldn't have managed today without your help, Marian."

"It wasn't much, but I'm glad I could do it. Now I'd better go home."

"You're sure you won't stay to dinner?"

"I'll stay another half hour. But the weather's getting worse, and I want to get back before dark."

The room was very still except for the sound of the fire. Those near to it were recuperating, and the others, Annette thought, were naturally respecting their rest. But it also occurred to her that this was the first time since any of them had entered the house today when they had all been in one room together. They were still scattered over a large space. Gene was on the sofa next to her. Andrew had drawn a straight chair near to the sofa, with the dogs at his feet. Cynthia, as far away from Andrew as she could get, was with her father on the other side of the room, near Daisy; they made a loose grouping with Aaron and Brenda. Such remarks as were made among them all were murmured and inaudible at Annette's end of the room. After the day's shock, she supposed, when during those awful minutes at the scene we all stood in total silence wondering whether Ellen and Lucy were alive, this would be a normal reaction; or would it be more normal now to let one's emotions bubble and bubble over? She really did not know. She only knew that somebody must eventually say something.

So she raised her voice loud enough to be heard by everyone and inquired, "Are you all feeling any warmer?"

Aaron Sachs responded, "I know I am, but how are you, Mrs. Byrne?"

"Daisy," said Daisy in her crisp fashion. "And I'm fine, thank you."

"You're my all-time heroine, Aunt Daisy," Mark told her. "For the rest of my life . . . I don't know . . . I can't express it."

"Two and three quarter minutes by my watch without taking a breath," Andrew said. "Right up to the limit."

"A heroine," Aaron echoed. "A heroine with good lungs."

Annette glanced at Gene, who cleared his throat and leaned down to stroke Roscoe's head. When he looked up, he spoke almost shyly. "Yes. It seems that there are no better words than *thank you,* Daisy. Two syllables to weigh against a child's life." His voice broke. "Thank you. Thank you, Daisy."

For another few minutes no one spoke. Then Lewis was heard.

"There were a couple of young fellows at the club who went in for swimming under ice. Kind of crazy—very crazy. But Daisy did it one day. They showed her how. I was angry at her. She'll dare anything, Daisy will."

A little prickle of shame went down Annette's back. What right had she had in the first place to sniff, even mentally, at Daisy's "boarding school and country club" athletics? Just because she isn't like me, she scolded, I felt myself superior, a more "serious" person. My God, if we all would just take a good, honest look at ourselves, we might not always like what we see.

"Hypothermia can put you in the hospital in a few minutes," Aaron was saying. "That's all you need."

Andrew mused, "Funny. When I cleaned the trunk of my car, I was going to take the rope out. I had it there from the time I got stuck in a snowbank. It was on a ski trip in Vermont," he added irrelevantly, and added again, "Lucky thing I didn't."

"I never learned to swim underwater," said Mark. "Never learned to resuscitate either. Now I mean to do it."

"Red Cross," Lewis advised. "Daisy and I took a course. Very enjoyable too."

They were all speaking without looking at one another. It was as if, Annette thought, they were addressing a public gathering, or perhaps simply talking to the air, or maybe just thinking out loud.

Cynthia was silent. She was watching Freddie, who,

after many patient trials, had managed to build a tower of three blocks. And she tried to remember what she had read in one of her many books—long since given away—about the various stages of child development. What foolish worries we have! As if it matters whether a beautiful, healthy baby like this one is a bit smarter or a bit slower than the baby next door. His cheeks that had been red from the cold were now red from the heat. With a happy laugh he knocked the tower down. Then he began to build it again. She could not take her eyes away from him.

Yet she was aware that Andrew had craned his head in her direction. Whether he was looking at her or at Freddie, she was unable to tell, but it made no difference either way. He didn't belong here.

I should see more of Ellen and Mark, she thought. Somehow, God only knows how, this sight of Freddie, my picking him up when he was crying there on the grass, has changed me. I never thought I could bear to hold a baby again.

"It's time for his supper," Mark said, standing up.

Cynthia said quickly, "If you'll tell me what he eats, I'll give it to him."

Mark smiled. "You want to, don't you?"

"Yes. May I?"

She saw, when he nodded, that he understood her. "He gets junior food, and after that a bottle. Everything's in our tote bag in the hall. Wait. I'll give it to you."

"No, I'll find it. He'll go with me. He likes me."

"Jenny has the high chair," Annette called.

On Cynthia's lap in the snuggery Freddie was already having his bottle when Marian, in coat and boots, passed the door.

"Pretty sight," she called.

"Come in for a second. I want to thank you for helping Gran today. And for all the rest too."

"Wasn't it a horrendous day? And yet, crazy as it sounds, maybe some good will have come out of it."

"I have a feeling it will. Uncle Gene and my father have got to do a lot of thinking after this. In fact, it seemed to me in there that they already have begun."

"Death, or even the prospect of it, has a mighty powerful effect on people. I never realized how powerful until it hit me."

"I think Gran said you're a widow?"

"A sudden widow. We went to the city for a weekend vacation, had a wonderful dinner, saw a wonderful play, and went happily to bed in our hotel room. Toward morning I heard him get up, walk across the room, and fall."

Marian sat down on the edge of a chair. Her face was without expression, and strangely, that seemed to move Cynthia more than tears might have done.

"He was tall, thin, and blond, part Scandinavian, and athletic. One of those people who you think are made to live long."

"How awful for you."

"Sometimes I was angry at him. So many hours, so many days wasted . . . And now gone. Forever. Never." She threw out her hands, palms up. "And that's it." Then she rose, and, suddenly brisk and businesslike in her customary way, she concluded, "I don't know why I got started on this. I'm sorry. That's a sweet boy. Lovely eyes. I'd better run. It's already dark."

Why I got started. Cynthia smiled wryly. You wanted to teach me a lesson, that's why. But it won't work, Marian. No, because my situation is entirely different. Entirely.

When she carried Freddie back into the library, Ellen, awake now, took him from her, leaving her with empty hands. A bad feeling of utter detachment swept over her.

And she stood uncertainly, hearing the fierce wind shake the windowpanes.

"I wouldn't want to be out in a car tonight," Annette remarked.

Andrew said promptly, "That reminds me. I'd better say good-bye to you all and start right now."

"Absolutely not," Annette protested, thinking: He wants to leave because Cynthia won't even look at him. "That's a ten-mile drive, and Jenny just heard on the radio that the roads are all ice. There's plenty of room for you. This house is elastic. It stretches to fit." And as he hesitated, she added with deliberate tactlessness, "You know that. You've been here often enough. Just sit down, Andrew."

There came a restless stir in the room, as if everyone had sat too long or, having said all they were capable of saying, were uncomfortably aware of what was still unsaid.

Brenda was folding the red blankets that were no longer in use. And Annette made an announcement.

"Brenda has been making up beds for all you people tonight. Can you imagine? When I went upstairs, I found her working. You shouldn't have, Brenda."

"Well, Jenny is busy enough in the kitchen, and this really is a mob. Don't worry, your linen closet is still neat. I am the original fusspot—Aaron, don't sit in that chair, what are you thinking of? Your suit is still wet."

Aaron bounced up. "I know it, but what am I going to do? I didn't bring another suit."

"Oh, my, you're soaked," cried Annette. "Doesn't anyone, can't anyone—" And she looked around the room in appeal. "You're the nearest to his size, Gene."

Embarrassed, Aaron laughed. "Only a six-inch difference."

Gene, fidgeting, fussed over Roscoe, which was something that, not being a dog person, he did not usually do. "I keep a few things here. I'll find something," he said, looking self-conscious.

"So that's solved," said Annette.

We'll see what happens at dinner, she thought. I'm not sure of anything, but we have made some progress, at least. . . .

"Why don't we go up and rest?" she said cheerfully. "If you want to, I mean. I think we all deserve a rest. As for me, I need a nap before dinner. It's at seven."

The lunch table had been transformed for dinner, thought Andrew, who noticed such things, much as a woman wearing a sweater and skirt, however becoming, is transformed by a ballgown. Candles in silver holders glowed on pale yellow china edged in the Greek key pattern. The cream-colored roses in the large bowl had been augmented by smaller clusters going down the center of the table. Once again Annette had "done herself proud." She might as well, he thought somewhat bitterly, have been adorning a wedding reception. . . . As indeed, she had once done.

With her customary attention to household details Annette surveyed the table and was satisfied. Very infrequently these days were festive meals served in this lovely room that had for so many years been used to bright lights and bright conversation. Life was quiet now in this house where she lived with Jenny and the dogs. And she thought again, Okay, there's been progress since our near disaster today. But let's see what happens next.

"We'll serve ourselves from the sideboard and then sit wherever we want," she said. "Gene, will you do the wine? And, Lewis, you're a good carver, so please do the roast."

"Ah, roast beef," sighed Lewis. "The cholesterol special. But I love it. The first I've had in six months."

"Aaron and Brenda, there's pasta for you. Jenny makes a marvelous red sauce without meat. And we've lots of vegetables," Annette assured them. At the same time she could scarcely keep from laughing because Aaron looked so ridiculous in the borrowed suit.

"If you want to laugh, go ahead," Aaron said. "I had a glimpse of myself in the mirror on the way downstairs."

"Are you some sort of mind-reader? Well, to tell the truth—"

Now Aaron laughed. "You don't have to say so, everyone can see it."

The trousers, at least six inches too long, were fastened up with safety pins. At the waist another large blanket pin, borrowed from Freddie's tote bag, kept the trousers from falling down.

"Of course, as long as I sit no one can see it, so that saves my dignity."

"Tell me, how is the pasta?"

"Perfect, thank you."

"You went to so much trouble for us," Brenda said.

"It was no trouble at all. It was a pleasure."

Mark, observing from the other end of the table, had a sudden surge of pride in his mother. She was a gracious woman. He had never given any thought to her public persona, to how she might look to other people—not counting his father-in-law, and well he knew what that man's prejudice had been! There she sat, quiet and confident in her fine dark dress and her narrow necklace of sculptured gold. And he felt a great tenderness for her.

Tenderness overflowed in him. Here were Ellen, his darling, and Lucy sitting high on Annette's two-volume *Oxford English Dictionary*, and Freddie safely asleep upstairs in the portable crib; it went without saying that these had always been far more precious to him than was his own life. Tonight, though, it seemed as if his capacity to feel a unity with other human beings had expanded, too, so that, in varying degrees, he felt able to say that he "loved"—however you wanted to define *love*—every soul in the room.

Annette, reading his expression, was moved by it. And again she thought she felt a kind of loosening in the atmosphere: people—twelve of them, a nice tidy number around the table—were beginning to converse a bit. She became suddenly aware that she had been sitting with strained, tight muscles, and must relax.

They all looked so *civilized.* And these were the same people, the same group, that had been so *savage* in the front hall this morning. Maybe they had been having some serious reflections during that little nap time. . . .

Her eyes roved from her two sons—was it purely an accident that had brought them to be sitting next to each other?—to Lucy in her pink dress, to the bronze lights in Ellen's hair, to Aaron Sachs's neat beard, and her eyes were satisfied.

When they reached Cynthia—ah, that was another matter! Perfect in gray silk and appropriate pearls, she sat like a statue, cool, remote, and without expression. And in Annette's heart there was a painful contest between compassion and impatience. Cynthia's father and mother, apparently, had taken steps toward Andrew. And yet, who was a mere grandmother to judge?

"Did you know that I fell into the water?" Lucy's voice rang out, addressing nobody in particular. "I don't remember how I got out, but I did."

"It was Aunt Daisy who rescued you," Ellen said. "You should thank her properly."

Lucy scrambled down, knocking the dictionaries to the floor, ran toward Daisy, gave her a tight hug, and proclaimed, "I'm going to tell everybody in my class what you did."

A handful, thought Daisy, returning the hug. Enough spunk for two her age. Must keep Ellen hopping. Very, very sweet, all the same. Silly of me, but in a way now, I feel possessive about her.

"With every minute it becomes more incredible," Gene was saying. "What Daisy did! How can I ever express or thank . . . all of you . . . If I live to be a hundred . . . Excuse me." And with some embarrassment he wiped his eyes.

Awkwardly, Lewis patted his brother's arm. "That's all right. You already did, and we all know. We know."

Aaron, who sat across from the two men, was surprising himself with his own reflections. Funny, I never imagined that men like these would show tears. All that stiff-upper-lip business. Of course, I don't ever get this close. It's another world. Same city, but another world. And yet, here we sit with the same feelings—that little girl, that little mother today—we sit here feeding ourselves, all hungry, same stomachs, same bones, as I should know. The few times I ever saw the older one, I had no particular opinion one way or the other. He was a gentleman, that was all. Cool. Both brothers the same, I see. The only difference is, the first one's daughter didn't marry my son. It looks as if they're getting together. I hope so for Annette's sake. Their sakes too. This business in a family is wrong. Wrong.

"For the rest of my life," Gene was saying, "I'll have nightmares about what could have happened."

"Well, it didn't," Lewis said. "And as for nightmares, we've both had our share of them, I guess."

As his words carried, talk ceased. Annette, who had been talking to Brenda, pricked up her ears. Daisy, who had begun to say something cordial to Andrew—for although she had been so furious with him, he had been so kind to her today, as she had already told Cynthia—now stopped.

"Yes," Lewis repeated, "we've surely had plenty of them."

I admit to myself, he was thinking, that perhaps I was foolishly influenced after all. If it hadn't been for the Sprague family, the grandfather a judge, with all the prestige, I probably would have gone right in and demanded the truth. I would have raised hell.

"I seem to be having some second thoughts about things today," he said.

Gene nodded. "Yes, yes, I know what you mean. I guess circumstances alter cases, don't they? Cliché. But clichés are true."

And he wondered whether it was indeed possible that Jerry Victor really was a troublemaker with his own private agenda. Not that, if he had been, it would have altered the fact that Sprague had obviously been guilty; it would only in part have explained some of Lewis's reluctance to challenge Sprague. Perhaps, if Sprague had been my friend, I, too, would have hesitated. I have been quick to condemn. I have been closing my mind against Lewis, without even trying to understand, or forgive.

Annette watched her two sons. It must have been hard for Gene to be second all the time, always having to wait, being the younger, for the privileges of age, even to wait to go into the business. Of course, it couldn't have been otherwise, but still, that can put a chip of envy on a younger brother's shoulder. Then the older one sees the chip . . .

And suddenly words came out of her mouth, words she had certainly not intended to say.

"You've been too proud to talk things out, both of you. Too proud. Your father was like that too."

"The first time you ever said anything critical about Dad!" exclaimed Lewis.

"Well, what did you think? That he was perfect? Who is, pray tell me? Pride," she repeated, almost angrily.

" 'A man's pride shall bring him low,' " said Aaron, " 'but he that is of a lowly spirit shall attain to honor.' "

"Aaron!" Brenda wailed. "What on earth is wrong with you?"

"There's nothing wrong with him. That's from the Bible," Daisy said. "My father always quoted from the Bible."

"But the time and place!" Then, in spite of herself, Brenda had to laugh. "I'll tell you what, he's had too much wine."

" 'Wine is a mocker and strong drink is riotous,' " retorted Aaron with a wink.

At that the laughter was so loud that Jenny peeked through the kitchen door, smiled, and shook her head in amazement.

"I want to dance," said Lucy. "We always dance."

Ellen explained. "Mark and I like to dance sometimes. We put on a CD and roll back the rugs. Lucy has her own CD. She wants to be a ballerina."

"What's Lucy's music?" Annette asked.

" '*Gaîté parisienne.*' Have you got it?"

"Oh, yes, but this rug doesn't roll back."

"That's all right, I'll dance in the hall," said Lucy.

She was getting too much attention, Ellen knew, but today, why not? Today, she could have anything.

So the music started. Everyone stood up and watched Lucy perform. Filled with a sense of her own importance, but even more so with rhythm, she twirled her skirt and curved her arms above her head.

"Who'll dance with me?" she cried.

"I will," said Aaron in prompt response.

And, adorned with safety pins, with one hand holding

his trousers up and the other hand in Lucy's, he whirled with her down the length of the hall and back.

"What a good sport!" Daisy whispered to Annette in the midst of the general laughter. "I have to take my thoughts back. Both of them seemed so awkward and out of place this morning in the library, as if they resented being here."

"You never know about people till you know them," Annette responded.

She was thinking about Daisy. Who could say what quirk or insecurity had made Daisy put on what Annette called her "airs"? But so good, so incredibly brave . . . And she took Daisy's hand in a warm squeeze.

"Come, Mark and Ellen, join us," cried Aaron.

You can see how nice he is to Ellen, Gene thought. And the way he brought Lucy back to life. Of course, he's a doctor and you expect it, but still, the sight of him breathing life into her . . . And Brenda, the way she pitched in, making all those beds, bringing coffee and blankets . . .

Lucy called, "Come on, Papa Gene, you dance too."

So Papa Gene joined the whirl and gallop until, at last, Aaron brought it to a stop.

"I'm out of breath. Besides, I'm tripping over my trousers. Gene's trousers, I should say."

"It's clear where my husband gets his sense of humor," Ellen remarked when they had all sat down again.

Mark shook his head. "Mine's not half as good as Dad's. The funny thing is that he's quite serious while he's being funny. And when he's really serious, angry about something—watch out! Right, Mom?"

"Oh, my. Men," said Brenda.

"Men," echoed Ellen.

"When men are angry, they're like babies," Daisy said.

It's like old times in this house, Annette was thinking, with a little normal jibing and a lot of hilarity. But what if we hadn't come so near to tragedy? It would be shameful if it had to take a tragedy to bring about peace.

No, she resolved. Stubborn as I am, I would have found a way. I know I would.

When the dessert, a fluffy white meringue with strawberries, had been sliced and passed around, Mark stood up with his wineglass in hand.

"I'm proposing a toast to you, Gran. Let's face it, this morning we were all pretty upset because of your little plan." He smiled. "And now instead we need to apologize, to thank you and wish you a hundred and twenty years."

"Thanks, but a hundred will do very well. Seriously, I really took a chance, didn't I? Last night I was so scared that I called my friend Marian to come to my aid. And now look. I look at you all . . . I'd better stop before I get teary."

Yes, she looks, but not very long at me, thought Cynthia, nor at Andrew. You destroyed everything that I felt for you, she told him silently.

She looked at him quickly and looked away. He was staring down at his plate. He doesn't even know what he did, she thought. And my parents, who love me, do not really know either. I saw them talking to him before. What a total about-face! How can they do that? They are hoping I will go back to him. Oh, I saw my mother leaning on him up the hill to the house. He brought hot towels for her and a blanket and coffee. Very nice, very kind, but what has that got to do with me? When I look at Mark and Ellen, I am so glad for them. They deserve each other. And Dad, with Uncle Gene—I'm so glad for them too. It was time and past time. But all that, too, has nothing to do with what has happened to me.

They were rising from the table, Annette proposing, "Let's have coffee by the fire, or what's left of it."

In the library the fire was barely high enough to cast a

pink glow on a wall of books that were themselves a mosaic of soft colors. The coffee service was on a table, along with an enormous heap of chocolate macaroons.

"My goodness!" exclaimed Annette. "Where did these come from?"

"From your old favorite bakery on the East Side," said Gene.

"Oh, you went there too?" That was Brenda.

"Ours are from there." That was Daisy.

"We each wanted to be different," said Ellen.

And then there was more laughter over the macaroons. Annette felt the warmth of all the silliness. Feeling the peace in the room, she watched and listened.

Brenda was examining the portraits. Ellen was showing an album of old photos to Lucy. Daisy was browsing through the book shelves, and the men, all except Andrew, were in one corner, talking.

"I'm saving," she heard Mark say, "to buy into an uptown gallery. If I ever get enough together, it will be my dream come true. And I'd still have time to work on my book. I've got a publisher somewhat interested."

Gene remarked that it all sounded very worthwhile.

"Well, it may come true and it may not. Either way, we're okay, Ellen and I."

"Can't you get a loan?" asked Aaron.

"It's very hard to get one without a good deal of collateral."

For a few moments the two fathers looked at each other. Then Gene said, "This sounds like something that should be talked over some more."

"Very definitely," Aaron agreed. "It's a pity when a person has a real commitment to something and has to wait forever."

Lewis, who had been listening, remarked that that was quite true. He himself had lately been missing his own commitment. He had been wanting to get back to it with someone, though on a much smaller scale.

"Not impossible, I should think," said Gene with a meaningful smile.

"It's time for bed," Ellen called. "Lucy's falling asleep."

"I think we all are," said Aaron. "We've had a strenuous day, to say the least."

Annette was the last to turn out the lights and go upstairs. "Look at Mother," she heard Lewis remark to Gene as she closed her door. "Look at the happiness on her face."

Oh, yes, she was happy. . . . Except for Cynthia . . . All evening she had tried to catch her glance, to convey a message and plea. But plainly, Cynthia wanted to hear no message or plea.

Oh, what is the matter with me? I want perfection, Annette thought as she lay down to sleep. That's what's the matter with me. As if this evening has not been enough, I want more. I want it all. And I get so impatient.

Up and down the hall, around the corner into the wing, which Cynthia could see from her window, all the bedroom doors had been closed for the night. This would be the first time in what seemed like years that she would be sleeping under the same roof as Andrew was. It came also to her mind that the first time they had both slept under this particular roof was the night of the party that Gran had given for them when they returned from their wedding trip.

It would be far better now to forget all that. Yet there were hours in every human being's life that refused to be obliterated: times of unspeakable horror like today's, or else times like the one in the photograph, so beautifully framed, that Gran, for some reason known only to her, had placed on the chest of drawers in this room. There they were, Andrew looking unfamiliar in the traditional black morning coat and striped trousers; she in clouds of white silk with ushers and bridesmaids ranked on either side, all smiling, and he and she so happy that the happiness had bubbled up and wet their eyes. She stood now in the light of the bedside lamp, staring at the picture.

What innocence—summer, flowers, and a bottle of champagne in the room, kisses and joy forever after. Thank God that we never know what will happen to us tomorrow, to say nothing of any farther future. We had all the smiles and approval, we had everything, while Ellen and Mark had to sneak away to flee the storms.

She went to the window. The sleet had ceased, so that the pond was clearly visible, gleaming out of the dimness like a coin found on a dusty street. And the whole evil scene reenacted itself: Ellen's anguish, her mother stripping her skirt off, Andrew on the brink, hauling the rope, the abandoned baby crying on the grass . . . The whole scene.

Afterward there beside the fire and then later at dinner, I should have been at one with them in relief and thankfulness. In my heart, of course, I was, yet in my heart there was also something that kept me apart like a stranger watching a drama. You hear a tragic story and tears come to your eyes because you are human, a decent human being who feels a deep compassion, but still you are alone.

Pushing the curtain aside, she saw that clouds were slowly breaking apart and receding. Tomorrow might even be sunny. They would leave here as early as possible. Then her parents should return to Washington as soon as possible. She was not angry at them; she was only, and undeniably, hurt. And she thought again that they need not have been so cordial to Andrew. I'm going back to work, she thought. That's all I need. Work.

It was early yet, too early to sleep, but she had brought two books and could read comfortably in bed. This house, although it had never been her actual home, had always had the feel of a second, or other, home. Gran had a talent for giving comfort. In this room with its wide bed that was probably a hundred years old, the reading lamp was perfect, the down quilt was light, and there was a tiny flowering plant in a pot on the windowsill.

Tired as Cynthia was, she took a quick shower, laid out her clothes for the morning, and put on a warm bed-jacket over her chiffon nightgown. These articles, she reflected as she put them on, came from a life, or rather parts of a life, that had been spent with a husband and a career. Now both of these had been left behind.

She had not been reading for very long when somebody, no doubt Gran, who often liked a short evening chat, tapped on the door. Most likely, too, Gran would be seeking reassurance of her forgiveness for today's "little trick." Poor Gran, who believed she could right everyone's wrongs. Smiling at the thought, Cynthia got up and opened the door.

"May I come in?" Andrew whispered.

"What are you thinking of?" she replied in a furious whisper. "No, you may not come in."

"Please, Cynthia. I already am halfway in."

She had opened the door wide, and indeed, he was so far into the room that she was unable to close it. Now Andrew closed it firmly and stood leaning against it.

"What are you doing? Taunting me because I can't make an outcry?"

"Make one if you want to. You have the right. I am, after all, invading your room. Only, it might seem rather odd, since technically I am still your husband and have my right to be in your room."

"Macho man. Very funny. Go on. Say what you want and get out."

He was looking her up and down. "I remember that nightgown. My favorite color, sky-blue."

She wanted to slap from his face its unreadable expression, a mix of sorrow and plea.

"You're disgusting. Go on, take full male advantage of the fact that you're seven inches taller and weigh sixty pounds more than I do. Go on, it's typical."

"Ah, Cindy, haven't we had enough of this? It's time to get over it. Long past time."

"Is this what you've come to tell me? You're wasting your energy and mine. I'm in the middle of a good book."

"Please, listen to me. I was as shocked as you were when we met here today. I'd given up trying to communicate with you after a policeman stopped me for loitering at your—and our—front door. Well, to be accurate, I had almost given up. So when Gran invited me today, I thought that maybe she had some news for me, some good news."

"It's too late for good news."

"Why is it too late? I should think that after what we've been seeing here today, you'd realize that it's never too late."

"For you and me, it is," she repeated.

"Don't include me, Cindy. When I saw you holding Freddie today, I remembered—"

"I know too well what you remembered. And I have that, too, and more than that, to remember." She wanted to hurt him, and in a strange, perverse way of which she was entirely aware and was unable to explain, she wanted to feel the hurt herself.

Andrew sat down. For a few minutes he bowed, holding his head in his hands, not speaking. He looks white, he looks thinner, she thought. He looks beaten, sitting there like that. Yet she still wanted to hurt.

"You're bringing it all back," she said, breaking the silence. "It's indecent to do this to me. Haven't you done enough?"

"That silly woman—do you think she meant anything, for God's sake? I don't even remember her name, if I ever knew it. I wouldn't recognize her if I were to fall over her now."

"You've told me that a few times before, I think. Are you going to leave this room, or are you going to sit here all night? I'm freezing, and I want to go back to bed."

"I'm not leaving, Cindy. I'll sit here all night if I have to. Go back to bed if you're cold."

"Back to bed with you in the room? You must be out of your mind!"

"Go. I'm not going to touch you. I don't attack women. That's not my thing."

"Really? That's interesting."

In the bed again, Cynthia drew up the quilt and propped the book against her raised knees.

"How could you have?" she burst out.

"Cindy . . . I make no excuse. I guess in that crazy moment I just needed to feel alive again. I'd been dead for so long."

"*You* had? And I? What had *I* been?"

"Dead too. But I believe, I hope, that if you had done what I did, I would forgive you."

Yes, dead, she thought. We had not made love for more than half a year. When your heart is broken, what's left of you breaks too.

"I make no excuse," he resumed. "I say again that I wronged you terribly, and I'm sorry. Yes, I was a little bit crazy."

"Dead and crazy at the same time? Very unusual."

He got up and stood by the bed. White and thin, she thought again, like me. This has wrecked us both.

"You saw what happened today, and what else could have happened," he said. "The world is a dangerous place. But we don't stop living because it is."

"A noble philosophy," she answered bitterly.

"What else can I say, then, except ask you to try again?"

"I can't." She was trembling. "I can't go back to what there was before. Now let me sleep. Will you go now?"

He shook his head.

"What are you going to do? Sit up all night?"

"No. I shall sleep on the floor."

"Damn you. I'm going to turn off the light."

For a long time she lay awake. The hurt in her chest grew with the suffocating weight of memories: the twins, the agony, the betrayal.

The clock on the stair landing chimed once. One o'clock. She had perhaps dozed for a little while; it was often impossible to distinguish between true dreams and waking dreams. There was no sound in the room, not even a rustle. He had probably crept away while she dozed. She reached to the lamp and turned it on.

There he lay, asleep on the floor at the foot of the bed. He had removed his jacket and, in his fastidious way, much like her own, had hung it over the back of a chair. The room was too cold to be lying there on the floor in his shirtsleeves. From the easy chair in the corner she took an afghan, most likely one of those that Gran's mother had knitted, and laid it over him.

He did not wake. She stood there looking at him. He lay perfectly straight, flat on his back, as people lie in their coffins. The wedding ring was gone from his left hand; it had been his idea to have a double-ring ceremony. He needed a shave. By the end of the day he always needed another shave.

It was odd to think that she was the only person in the whole world who knew everything about him, or as much as you can ever know about another human being. She knew that his eyes filled whenever there was a lost dog in a book or a movie. She knew that he carried a toothbrush in his attaché case, and that in private, at home, he often ate with his fingers.

An entirely illogical swell of pity moved in her throat.

I heard him get up, said Marian. *I heard him walk across the room and fall.* Then she said something like: *We wasted so much time.*

You have been too proud, Annette said.

And Aaron quoted, *"A man's pride shall bring him low."*

Shivering in the chill, she kept standing there.

Damn you. She was so angry. Damn you, she said without making a sound, while tears rolled down her cheeks.

In his sleep he must have become aware of her presence, for he opened his eyes, blinking into the lamplight. Startled then, he sat up.

"Is there anything wrong?"

"I covered you, that's all."

He was looking at her tears, while she looked at his hands. They were blistered and raw.

"Your hands," she said.

"Rope burns. It's nothing."

"Have they been like that all day? Why didn't you ask for something?"

"I don't know. It seemed unimportant with so much else happening."

"I have no Vaseline, but face cream should help for the time being."

He got up, sat on the bed, and stretched out his hands. Her tears were still brimming, while, with soft fingertips, she anointed them.

When she was finished, he gave her a long, steady look, and took her into his arms.

"Damn you," she said, and began to laugh.

"We'll begin again, Cindy. We can have everything again. Believe me. Everything. Do you understand?"

"Yes."

"Darling, turn out the light. We've waited so long."

A December sky, thought Annette, can be as deeply blue as any sky in May. So it was, in the morning as the house emptied out. In the front hall after breakfast they were gathering their coats and possessions.

"I was thinking," Gene whispered, "about your friend Marian. You may think this is foolish, but you know, in a certain way, she reminds me of Susan."

"Not foolish at all. A little tartness and a lot of sweetness. Yes, I see the resemblance."

"Perhaps I will give her a call sometime. Invite her to the theater or something."

Rather touched and a little amused by her son's apparent shyness, Annette replied quickly, "Of course. Why not?"

They were loading the cars. Lewis and Daisy were to drive back together, while Cynthia was to go with Andrew. You had only to look at those two to know that they had slept together. Nevertheless, Cynthia, wanting to make sure that she knew, had hugged her and whispered, "Thanks," in her ear.

Annette had winked. "Okay?"

"Yes, Gran, very okay."

And so they all departed. She stood watching them roll down the driveway and down the road until they were out of sight. Turning, then, to look back up at the house, she was reminded of Robert Frost's lines: *Home is where, when you have to go there, they have to take you in.* Well, none of my people *had* to come here; it's I who wanted to take them in. And she wondered whether it needed a tragedy to make people value the treasures of home and love. I hope not, she answered herself, but maybe, sometimes, it does.

Back in the library she paused before her husband's portrait.

"Well, Lewis," she said aloud, "we've had a few troubles since you left us. They're straightened out now, you'll be glad to know. Oh, I'm not naive enough to think, for instance, that Gene and Aaron will become close, dear friends; their ways and paths are too far apart for that. But at least they accept each other now, so when they meet it will seem natural, and the children will not suffer from the poison of anger. And our sons are together again, thank God. Thank Him for Ellen and Lucy, for Andrew and Cynthia. Thank Him for everything."

Outdoors, ice was dripping glitter from the trees, and the sun was brightening toward noon. The day was splendid.

"Come, Roscoe, let's take a walk," she said. "Come, boys. I'll get my coat. Let's go."